The Choosing Chronicles: Ryker and Brynleigh's Duet

ELAYNA R. GALLEA

Contents

A GAME OF LOVE AND BETRAYAL
ELAYNA R. GALLEA

A SONG OF BLOOD AND SHADOWS

ELAYNA R. GALLEA

A HEART OF DESIRE AND DECEIT

ELAYNA R. GALLEA

A Game of Love and Betrayal

ELAYNA R. GALLEA

Cover and map designed by Elayna R. Gallea

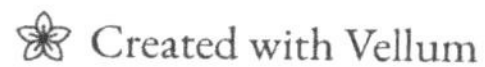

To my readers who have been with me since my very first book.

Thank you for sticking around.

Author's note

A Game of Love and Betrayal is a new adult fantasy romance set in a secondary world setting.

I never want my content to be harmful to any of my readers. This is a dystopian world and there are certain situations which may be triggering.

For a full list of content notes, please visit: https://www.elaynargal lea.com/contentnotes.

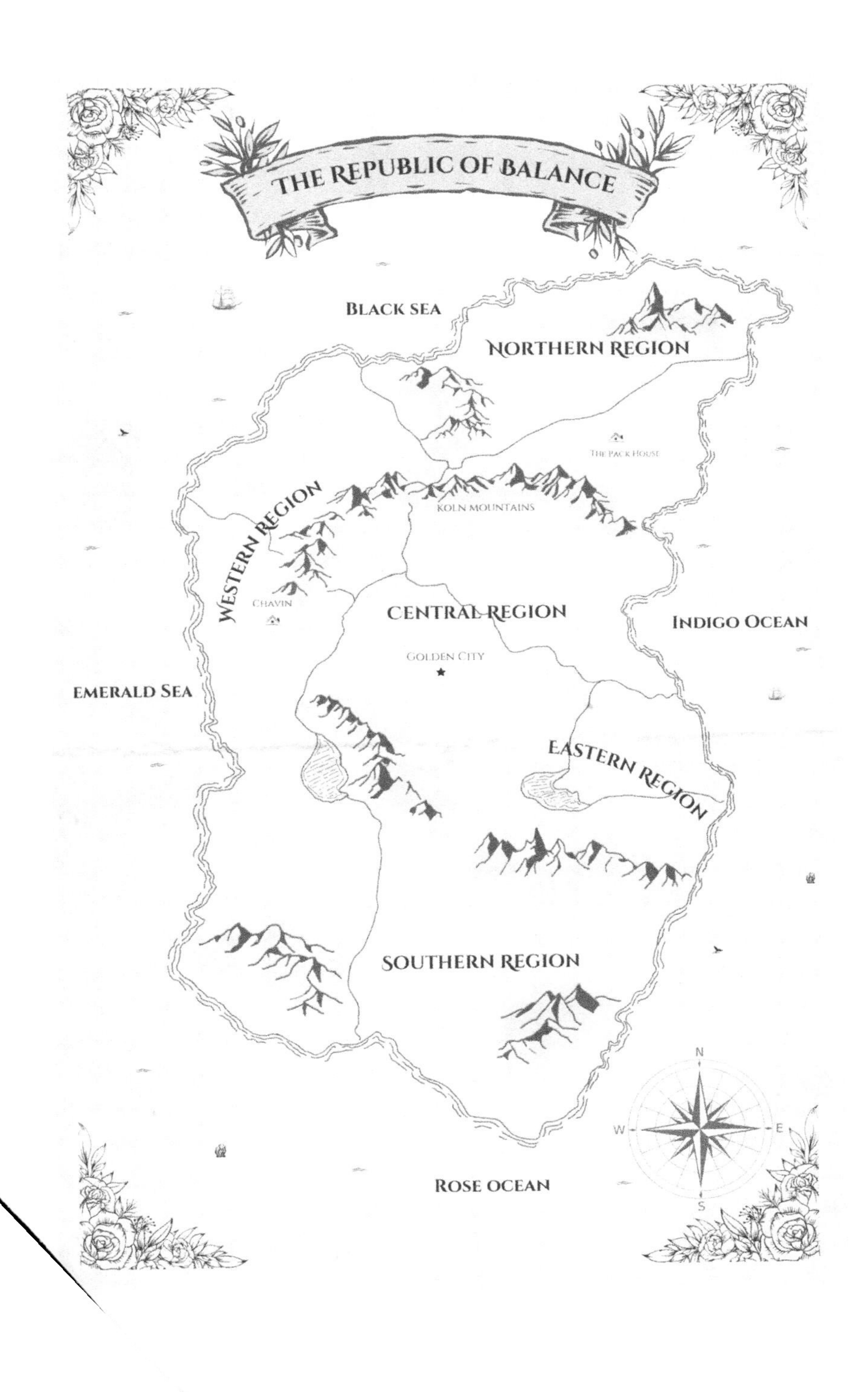
THE REPUBLIC OF BALANCE
BLACK SEA
NORTHERN REGION
THE PACK HOUSE
WESTERN REGION
KOLN MOUNTAINS
CHAVIN
CENTRAL REGION
INDIGO OCEAN
GOLDEN CITY
EMERALD SEA
EASTERN REGION
SOUTHERN REGION
N
W
E
S
ROSE OCEAN

Blurb

He requires a wife. She needs to kill him. All's fair in pursuit of love and revenge.

What's a vampire to do when the fae who made her an orphan is searching for a wife?

Make him choose her and end his life on their wedding night, of course.

Brynleigh has been carefully planning this for years. Her plan is simple: date Ryker Waterborn, the Fae Representative's son, make him fall in love with her, and kill him after they say, "I do."

Unfortunately, it will not be that easy. She won't be the only one going after Ryker's hand. Far from it. Two dozen men and women are competing in the Choosing, each searching for their perfect partner. The catch? It's a blind selection process, and contestants won't see each other until they have made their choice.

Nothing will stand between Brynleigh and her revenge, not even a competition for love.

Prologue

Long ago, many centuries in the past, an Empress ruled over this continent. The Rose Empire was vast, prosperous, and generally a good place to live.

Until it wasn't.

Internal wars tore the Rose Empire apart. Elves battled dragons, merfolk staked their claim in the Indigo Ocean, werewolf packs settled across the continent, and vampires moved to the frigid, frozen north. The citizens of the former empire formed kingdoms.

Four of them, to be exact.

Prosperity reigned in the Four Kingdoms as well... for a time. All too soon, however, the pull of power and money became too strong for some to resist. Once again, tensions rose. Wars were fought. Power ebbed and flowed.

Time went on.

Elves Matured and Faded. Vampires were Made and died. Werewolves lived beneath the power of the moon, growing their packs over the centuries.

And humans?

They simply... existed.

Life continued. The balance was broken and then reformed. For a time, peace reigned over the continent.

Several millennia later, the Four Kingdoms evolved again and united beneath a shared banner. The fae crossed the Indigo Ocean in the Great Migration, bringing their impressive magic. Technology soared in this new time, and all the species coexisted in the Republic of Balance.

It was during this time that our story took place.

CHAPTER 1
Fangs or Blade?

"I'm feeling benevolent this evening, so I'll allow you to decide how you want to die." Brynleigh de la Point pinned the sniveling, half-dressed man with a glare that she hoped said, *This is the last choice you'll ever get to make.* Out loud, she added, "Fangs or blade?"

The man blinked from his position on the bed, his sluggish mud-brown eyes struggling to follow the vampire's movements across the dimly lit, shoddy studio apartment. The faint glow of streetlights several stories below filtered through the grimy glass of the single window above his head, adding a yellow tint to the space.

His inability to focus could have been caused by his half-mortal blood, the prohiberis Brynleigh had liberally sprinkled in his drink earlier to block his magic, or merely a side-effect from the pints of alcohol he'd consumed throughout the evening. Judging by the smell wafting off him, it was probably a combination of all three.

The shadows binding the man's arms and legs likely weren't helping matters either. They operated on Brynleigh's command, and there wasn't anything he could do to break the dark bonds.

If the man hadn't already concluded exactly how dire his situation was, he would shortly.

Brynleigh tapped her booted foot on the dirty floor, avoiding a questionable stain a few inches from where she stood. The sooner she got out of this apartment, the better. "What's your choice?"

He slurred, his voice pitifully weak, "I... uh... neither?"

Brynleigh barely suppressed a sigh. Did he have no self-respect? The least he could do in the face of impending death was be strong and fight with everything he had.

"That's not an option." Brynleigh withdrew the sharp, thin dagger sheathed on her thigh. It was one of the many weapons she'd hidden all over her person before venturing out tonight. "Choose, or I will for you."

Providing an answer would have been the intelligent option.

Instead, this man proved that not only did he lack self-respect, but he was anything but intelligent. His lecherous gaze raked over Brynleigh, starting at her head and dipping past her black tank top to her dark blue jeans. He smirked, probably determining that her choice of outfit meant that she was ready for a night on the town, not to kill a scumbag such as himself.

The bound man proved her suspicions correct a moment later. "You're not going to kill me."

If his response hadn't been so predictable, Brynleigh probably would have been disappointed. It was just like a man to take one look at her golden hair and curvy body, and decide that she couldn't be a killer because she didn't look like one. He wasn't the first to make that erroneous observation, and much to Brynleigh's dismay, she was fairly certain he wouldn't be the last either.

"That's where you're wrong." Brynleigh willed her shadows to tighten, their constrictive embrace proving her deadly point. "Only one of us will be walking out of that door alive, and it will be me."

He scoffed, rolling his eyes. "Come on, baby. I just wanted to have a bit of fun."

Yeah, she wasn't interested in his type of fun. Especially not in a place like this. She guessed he'd be a two-pumps-and-done kind of guy. Not what she was looking for. Besides, the atmosphere in this small space left everything to be desired. Yellowed wallpaper hung off the walls in clumps, chipped tiles demarcated the kitchen from the dirty livi area, and the sheets on the bed looked like they had never seen the inside of a washing machine.

Not to mention the noise. The neighbors were far too loud. Tell-tale thumps came from the bedroom upstairs. The television next door blared, and a too-chipper voice filtered through the walls, announcing the arrival of a new, never-before-seen beauty serum. According to the saleswoman, it was designed to make even the most wrinkle-laden human young again.

Brynleigh barely stopped herself from rolling her eyes. That so-called miracle cure was probably made with vampire blood. Not that she had a problem with people doing whatever they needed to survive—obviously, considering her current predicament—but she wasn't a fan of hiding markers of age.

Getting old was a privilege many citizens of the Republic of Balance weren't afforded, including the halfling on the bed.

The man still hadn't decided, and Brynleigh's patience had run its course. Honestly, it was a miracle she'd made it this long. "Too late. Blade it is."

She spun the dagger in the air, catching the weapon by its engraved hilt before stepping towards the man. His eyes widened, and panic flashed through those brown orbs.

"No." His nostrils flared, and a hint of fear mingled with the apartment's musty aroma. "Please, don't do this."

The sigh that slipped from Brynleigh's mouth could probably be heard worldwide. Of course, this halfling bastard would beg. She should've known he was one of those.

Zanri, Brynleigh's handler, had probably laughed when he selected this mark for her. He knew how much she hated whiners. She would rather deal with someone who fought back any day. It felt... better when they fought back. Easier, somehow, to deal that killing blow. She liked when they tried to stop her, especially when she knew what they'd done.

Still, Brynleigh had to be certain. She didn't believe in killing innocents.

She crossed her arms, and even though it was the last thing she wanted to do, she leaned against the filthy counter. Her dagger dangled from her fingers as she eyed the man on the bed. "Your name is Geralt Warsh, correct?"

He stared at her.

Fine. Two could play at this game. With a flick of her wrist, Brynleigh silently commanded the shadows to tighten. "Halfling Death Elf, originally from the Northern District of the Republic?"

The man swallowed, his eyes darting back and forth. That scent of fear grew stronger until the bitter, cloying aroma was all Brynleigh could smell. During moments like this, she wished vampires didn't have such strong senses.

"N-n-no, you're wrong." He shook his head.

For Isvana's sake. This was getting ridiculous.

"Don't fucking lie to me, it's unbecoming." Brynleigh uncrossed her arms and moved across the room in a blur. She slashed her dagger across the halfling's hair in a movement too fast for anyone but a vampire to see.

A long copper lock fell onto the mattress that was three shades of brown too dark to be sanitary, revealing a pointed, pierced ear. A red swirling tattoo crawled down the side of Geralt's neck. It was a mark of his Maturation and served to confirm his identity. The three earrings hanging from his ear were additional proof that this was the man she sought.

"I know who you are," Brynleigh said, done with his games. Between the lecherous gaze, the lying, and the whining, she wanted to leave. She'd have to take a dozen showers to rid her skin of the disgusting feel of this place. "*What* you are."

Geralt Warsh, half-Death Elf, half-human, was not a good man. He was a hardened criminal, the likes of which Brynleigh rarely encountered. When Zanri had shown her Geralt's file, her fangs had burned in anger. The halfling had been convicted of several crimes against minors, which had led to him spending over three decades in Black Prison in the Western District of the Republic. Earlier this spring, Geralt had been released. Apparently, his time in prison hadn't taught him any lessons. He'd gone right back to his old ways.

The photos Brynleigh had seen were enough to turn anyone's stomach, including hers. She might have been a vampire, but she still had feelings, for the moon goddess's sake.

And Geralt? He was so fucking cocky he wouldn't get caught that he wasn't even covering his tracks. Finding him this afternoon had barely taken any effort. After studying the paperwork, Brynleigh had located the halfling at the Falling Star, a local dive bar. He'd been indulging in copious amounts of bottom-shelf liquor, happily telling anyone and everyone that he'd recently been released from prison.

As if that was a bragging point.

Being imprisoned meant he'd been caught, which by definition, was not something to boast about. Brynleigh, on the other hand, had never been caught. She'd never even come close to it. That was one of the many reasons she was confident she'd be the one walking out of here tonight.

Once she had arrived at the Falling Star, all Brynleigh had to do to procure an invitation up to the grungy apartment was slide next to the halfling and flirt a little. Honestly, it was child's play.

The criminal had been in the middle of removing his jeans—which, no, thank you, Brynleigh didn't have sex with pedophiles—when the vampire released her shadows and bound him to the bed.

Which brought them back to the present.

Geralt studied Brynleigh. At first, his eyes were dull and brown, like the stains on his mattress. He wailed and struggled against the shadows binding him, even going so far as to fabricate a story about a wife and two children he claimed waited for him in the suburbs.

It was all a lie.

Brynleigh had memorized his file. Like her, the halfling had no one. He was a lowlife criminal who preyed on those less powerful than him.

Eventually, Geralt seemed to realize his weeping would not get him anywhere. It was like a switch flipped inside the halfling. One moment, he was a sobbing, snotty mess. The next, his tears dried up as if they'd never been there at all. His back straightened, his chin rose, and an evil glint entered his eye. The facade of the weak, confused halfling vanished like a thief in the night.

A smile tugged at the corner of Brynleigh's mouth. *There he is*, she thought, almost gleefully. *Finally*.

Now, she'd see this man for who he truly was.

Geralt's eyes narrowed, and his mouth twisted into a sneer. "You fucking vampiric whore. You think you can do this to me?" He tugged on his bindings as if he could break free. "Don't you know who I am?"

Brynleigh raised a brow and calmly said, "I know exactly who you are."

Her response seemed to enrage him further. He wiggled and thrashed against her shadows.

It wouldn't work. Brynleigh was a doubly blessed vampire. The night of Brynleigh's Making, Isvana, the moon goddess, had gifted the new vampire with both wings and shadows. Most vampires had one or the other. A few had none. Some, like Brynleigh, had both. Even now, darkness pulsed a reassuring melody through her veins.

"Who is your Maker?" Geralt snapped, his face turning beet red. "I'm going to drive a stake through your shriveled black heart, and then—"

The end of his threat never came.

Tiring of the halfling's antics, Brynleigh slashed her silver blade across his throat from ear to ear. Arterial spray painted her and the walls. It would've been enough to kill a regular human, but Geralt Warsh was a Mature Halfling.

Elves, fae, merfolk, werewolves, shifters, and witches all Matured around twenty-five years of age. Maturation extended their lifespans and gave them increased access to their powers. It also made them harder to kill.

Brynleigh sighed. She hated this part of her job even more than the whining.

Maybe she should've picked fangs. It would've been cleaner, although she was certain that ripping out Geralt's neck wouldn't have been a pleasant experience. He probably had disgusting, sewer-flavored blood.

It was too late now, though. She'd made her choice.

Twisting the dagger in her grip, Brynleigh slammed the bloody weapon into Geralt's chest. It took significant force to drive a blade cleanly into a heart, but thanks to Isvana's blessings, Brynleigh had strength in droves.

When she was confident the halfling was the kind of dead there was no coming back from, even for a Mature being, she went to the sink and turned on the tap with her elbow. She washed her hands thoroughly and dried them on her jeans before slipping her phone out of her back pocket. She unlocked it, navigating to the camera before snapping a picture.

With a few taps of her finger, she sent the bloody image to Zanri.

B: He was a whiner. You owe me.

Two check marks showed up, and three dots swiftly followed. Her phone buzzed a moment later.

Z: You got it. Meet me at the usual spot.

No other instructions were necessary. Brynleigh was done.

For now.

"WAS IT A CLEAN DEATH?"

Brynleigh had barely stepped out of the Void—the dark, empty space that some vampires such as herself could use to travel from one point to another, as long as they'd been to the second location previously—when Zanri's deep tenor reached her ears.

The man in question stepped out of the shadows. His red hair fell to his waist, the lamp illuminating the streaks of brown running through it. Z was handsome in the way that most Mature beings were. His face was chiseled, his nose sharp, and his blue eyes dark as they swept over her.

Zanri was some kind of shifter, but Brynleigh had never seen his animal form. She assumed he probably shifted during the day when she couldn't go in the sun. If she had to guess, she'd think he was a cat shifter. His eyes had a predatory, feline glint. Tonight, he wore tight black leather pants that were probably a pain in the ass to take on and off. They were paired with a matching black T-shirt that looked painted on his muscled form.

Brynleigh blinked and rolled her shoulders as her vision cleared. The shadows had brought her to their safe house, the wards surrounding the building recognizing her blood and letting her enter without issue. She'd gone straight into the living room. Her plan for the remainder of the night was simple. She'd shower, grab a bottle of blood wine from the fridge, and relax in front of the TV for a few hours.

"What do you think?" was her response as she pulled her hair into a quick ponytail.

He pulled out his phone, tapping the screen and drawing the photo she'd sent him. She could see the crimson that coated Geralt's apartment from across the room. No one could ever clean that space now, not completely.

A dark chuckle slipped out of the shifter. "I think he got what he deserved."

"On that, we are agreed. He was disgusting." Brynleigh looked her handler over, noting the ruffled appearance of his red hair and his flushed cheeks for the first time since she arrived. She asked knowingly, "How's Owen?"

"He's good." Zanri's blush deepened, and the corner of his mouth tilted up, confirming everything she needed to know.

Owen Farnish lived in a desert city in the Southern Region but often worked with Brynleigh's Maker, Jelisette. He and Zanri had an on-again, off-again situation. When they were on, they would disappear for hours whenever Owen came to town.

"Tell him I said hello." Brynleigh liked Owen. He was one of the kinder people that Jelisette dealt with, and he always took the time to talk to Brynleigh, even back when she'd been newly Made.

"I will." Zanri smiled for a moment before his mouth flattened. "I left as soon as I got your message. Jelisette will want to debrief, and I need to wipe the security feeds."

There went Brynleigh's plans of lounging in front of trashy reality TV. Usually, Jelisette was out until dawn, but apparently not tonight. "How long until she arrives?"

"Less than an hour." In addition to being Brynleigh's handler, Zanri was in charge of technology and communication for their little operation. He had a gift for everything electronic in nature and ensured everything they did stayed under the radar. "She'll be proud, B."

Something sparked in the depths of Brynleigh's stomach. Even if she didn't exactly like her Maker—Jelisette was cold and icy, even for a vampire—Brynleigh was destined to want to please her. That was the nature of Maker bonds. Every vampire felt that way towards the sire who'd given them the gift of immortality.

Besides, Maker bonds were some of the strongest ones that existed. Even more than a mating bond, the link between Maker and progeny was incredibly powerful. There had only ever been one person who'd successfully broken their Maker bond, which happened thousands of years before.

Brynleigh owed Jelisette everything. The older vampire had found her after the worst night of her life and taken her under her wing. Before, Brynleigh had been nothing but a mediocre human, and now she was skilled in more ways than one.

She allowed a small smile to form. "Good."

Zanri pulled his hair into a bun and strode across the room. He gave her a gentle shove towards the bathroom. "Go shower. You have blood splattered across your skin. You should clean up. You know how she feels about looking good."

If anyone else dared touch Brynleigh like that, she would bite them —or worse. But she and Z had an understanding of sorts. They weren't really friends—she didn't do friends anymore—but they were colleagues who didn't mind each other.

"I know." Raising the pitch of her voice, she mimicked Jelisette's melodic, lyrical voice. "Rule number three: vampires are weapons. We must always look our best and be prepared to use every gods-given gift to our advantage."

Brynleigh's Maker had *a lot* of rules.

The shifter's mouth twitched, and he looked like he was holding in laughter. "That's the one. Now go."

She wouldn't argue with him. A shower did sound appealing. Especially after Brynleigh remembered the caked layers of dirt and grime in Geralt's apartment.

Brynleigh hurried into the bathroom, turning on the shower while she removed her weapons, stripped, and threw her clothes into the hamper. By the time she stepped under the water, steam billowed around her like a cloud. It was hot, and her skin quickly turned red, just as she liked it.

Twenty minutes later, Brynleigh felt like a new vampire. There was something about hot water and soap that was utterly life-changing. She toweled off, pulling on a fresh pair of black leggings and a white crop top as Jelisette's magic swept through the safe house. Seconds later, a lilac scent reached her.

Brynleigh tensed, and her heart beat faster. This always happened when her Maker came near. It was a remnant from that first night when Jelisette saved her. Flashes of lightning, booms of rolling thunder, and memories of waves taller than her head swept through Brynleigh's mind like an unwanted storm before she banished them. This wasn't the moment to remember the worst night of her life.

Curling her fists, she forced herself to take slow, deep breaths.

Inhale. Exhale. Repeat.

Again and again, Brynleigh continued the practice until her heart rate returned to its normal, measured rhythm.

She was a deadly vampire. A bringer of death. She needed to get a grip. She wasn't a child unable to control their emotions. She was twenty-three.

Well. Sort of.

She'd turned twenty-three six years ago, and then she'd been Made. Inside, she still felt twenty-three. She wasn't exactly sure when that would change. After a few decades? A century? Two? Eight, like Jelisette had seen?

Right now, Brynleigh couldn't imagine living for so long. The pains of her mortal life continued to haunt her, and she still experienced human emotions. Perhaps those would dull over time and lose their potency. Perhaps that was the key to living for centuries: letting herself get cold like Jelisette. Brynleigh had never even seen her Maker shed a tear, let alone laugh.

This wasn't the time for those kinds of thoughts, though. Jelisette did not take kindly to lateness.

Shadowing back to the living area, Brynleigh's stance was wide as she clasped her hands behind her back. Zanri leaned against the wall casually, studying the chess board that was a permanent fixture in the safe house.

Seconds later, shadows gathered on the mahogany hardwood floor near the entrance. Brynleigh's skin tingled. Her own darkness fluttered in recognition of the powerful magic entering the space.

Moments later, Jelisette's lithe form stepped out of the shadows. A shimmering crimson floor-length ballgown was draped over her tall body. The dress was sleeveless, sporting a V cut so low that it exposed the sides of her breasts and her navel. Long gloves ran to her elbows. Her chestnut hair was in an elaborate swooping bun, and a heavy black diamond necklace was her only adornment.

"Oh, good." The powerful vampire's midnight gaze swept over Brynleigh. "You're here."

Brynleigh nodded, keeping her shoulders straight. "Yes, ma'am. I finished the job."

"Good girl." Jelisette lifted a manicured brow. "It'll be the last one for a while."

The last one? Zanri usually had lots of work for Brynleigh. The Republic of Balance was extensive, spanning the entire continent. It used to be four kingdoms that had merged into one government long ago. There was no shortage of evil people who required their particular kind of deadly attention.

Although talking back to her Maker was never a good idea, Brynleigh questioned, "What do you mean?"

Something akin to a smile crept along Jelisette's face. "I did it. I got you in."

Brynleigh's brows creased as she tried to follow her Maker's words. Then, she gasped. "You mean..."

Jelisette crossed the room and gripped Brynleigh's shoulder. Her sharp nails dug into the younger vampire's flesh, but Brynleigh didn't care. Not if this meant what she thought it meant.

"Yes," Jelisette hissed, and her black eyes glimmered. "The gods have spoken, and the stars are aligned. Tomorrow, the Two Hundredth Choosing begins."

Brynleigh's heart, slow beating as it was, galloped in her chest like a wild stallion. Her mouth dried. Her fangs ached. She sucked in a too-shallow breath, taking in a sip of air instead of a gulp. "And I'm in?"

This felt too good to be true. She needed to hear it confirmed.

"Yes, my dear." Jelisette removed her hand and trailed a sharp nail down Brynleigh's face. The gesture was almost maternal. Almost. "This is the moment you've been waiting for."

It felt like Brynleigh's heart would explode out of her chest. She'd been training for this for six years, waiting for the moment she could finally exact her revenge.

Willing her heart to steady, Brynleigh stalked over to the chess board. Zanri silently watched as Brynleigh picked up the black king. She rolled the wooden carving around in her hand before trapping it in her fist.

This plan had so many moving parts, and this game had so many rules that Brynleigh hadn't been certain they would actually pull it off. She hadn't dared give too much thought to what this day would mean until now, for fear that if she did, the barriers she'd built around her heart would shatter.

If Brynleigh had spent too long thinking about her family's murderer and the free life he was living, she would have gone on a deadly, bloody rampage across the continent and fallen into bloodlust.

Then, who would avenge her family?

Instead, Brynleigh had become a master of compartmentalization. She shoved all her feelings into a box deep within her soul as she trained to become a killer.

That would end now.

Her fist tightened until a *crack* echoed through the room. Brynleigh unfurled her fingers, one by one, until the now-broken king lay in the middle of her pale palm. She placed the cracked piece on the board, looking first at Jelisette and then at Zanri.

"I'm going to enter the Hall of Choice, make Captain Ryker Waterborn, Head of the Fae Division in the Republic's Army, fall in love with me, and then I'll kill him on our wedding night," she declared.

Six years ago, the captain had vanished from the public eye. He hadn't been very visible before, but no one had seen him since. Living a quiet life wasn't abnormal for Representatives and their families. Some, like Chancellor Rose, were so secretive that even their children's magical affinities were unknown.

The captain's disappearance had been so complete that even in this technological day and age, finding him had been impossible. Jelisette had been able to confirm that the captain still lived, but even when he was at work, he was never alone.

Brynleigh had spent years hunting him, trying to get close enough to kill the captain, to no avail.

Until now.

The participants of the Choosing were supposed to be kept a secret, but Jelisette had a way of uncovering things that were meant to be hidden. *He* would be one of the twelve men taking part in the event.

"Revenge will be mine," Brynleigh said calmly.

Hearing the words out loud made them real in a way they hadn't been before. Her shadows twisted in her veins, and her dark magic pulsed at the thought.

Zanri's face was grave as he studied her, but Jelisette's black eyes twinkled. "Yes. No matter what, the captain will die before the year's end."

Jelisette's commitment to helping Brynleigh get her revenge was sweet. Brynleigh's Maker cared for her progeny. That was why Jelisette was willing to help Brynleigh avenge her family.

This had been Brynleigh's destiny since the night of her Making. Only one outcome was acceptable.

For the crimes he'd committed, Ryker Waterborn would die.

CHAPTER 2

I Won't Let You Down

The following day, before sundown, Brynleigh perched on the edge of her bed. She wore a black robe, her hair freshly dried from her afternoon shower.

Jelisette stood inside the walk-in closet wearing a sweater that seemed incongruous with the summer heat. Propping her hands on her hips, she tapped her foot on the floor. "Red or black?"

It may have been posed as a question, but Brynleigh knew Jelisette didn't want any answers.

Rule number seven: your Maker always knows best.

Instead, Brynleigh sipped her blood wine, relishing the dry taste as she swirled it around her mouth before swallowing. A non-committal hum slipped from her lips, and she twisted her pendant through the fingers of her free hand.

"Hmm. You're right." Jelisette walked around the space, shadows following her like dogs as she touched several dresses.

Brynleigh didn't particularly enjoy wearing formal attire, but she had several fancier pieces since she was often required to attend events with her Maker. Personally, Brynleigh would rather live in leggings. They were comfortable and convenient, and she always felt beautiful in them.

Jelisette pinched a scarlet sundress between her fingers. "You want something special. It needs to say, 'I could kill you with a single nip of my fangs, but I won't because I'm a good girl.'" She laughed cruelly, dropping the dress. "Though we both know that isn't true."

Another hum. Her Maker was right. Brynleigh wasn't a good girl. She'd never been one, even before her Making. As a child, scarcely a week went by that she didn't get in trouble for one thing or another. And now? Since her vampiric re-birth, Brynleigh no longer cared about trivial, mortal matters like "good" and "bad." Revenge was the driving force in her life, her reason for being, her first thought when she woke, and the fuel for her dreams.

It was those sweet thoughts of vengeance that propelled Brynleigh off the bed. Her bare feet padded on the plush cream carpet. She sipped her blood wine, entering the closet to stand beside her Maker. She pointed at a glimmering sequined garment tucked towards the back, half-buried by other clothes. "What about that one?"

Jelisette tilted her head, her brown hair falling over her shoulder as she pursed her lips. She pulled out the dress, studying it like a beast assessing its dinner.

"Hmm, good choice." She turned the garment around, taking it in from all angles. "Yes, this is the one. It will stand out from the others. No one will be able to resist you like this." Her brow rose. "The public's opinion is important, you know."

"I know," Brynleigh said.

The Choosing was televised and broadcast to the entire Republic. Couples who participated in the once-a-decade event were often considered semi-celebrities when it was over. Tonight was about more than just entering the Hall of Choice. This was Brynleigh's first chance to make an impression on the press.

Jelisette handed the dress to her progeny. Hundreds of black sequins sparkled like an entire galaxy was embedded in the fabric. "Get dressed; you're leaving in an hour."

There was no warmth in either Jelisette's voice or her countenance, and her assessing black gaze was equally cold as it ran over Brynleigh. That was fine.

Brynleigh didn't need warmth or comfort. Vampires didn't rely on emotions as humans did. It was one of her first lessons.

Jelisette glided out the door, her retreat silent thanks to her immortal grace, and as soon as she was alone, Brynleigh discarded her robe. The dress she'd selected was a tight onyx number that would hug her curves in all the right places. She'd never worn it before, and tonight seemed like the perfect opportunity.

Brynleigh slid the gown over her head, letting the fabric fall to the ground. Long sleeves tapered at her fingers. The hem trailed on the floor. Three strategically placed cut-outs highlighted her stomach and the curve of her breasts. The back scooped low, practically non-existent, and the material started right above the curve of her bottom.

If Brynleigh hadn't been a creature of the night, she probably would've been cold in a dress like this. Midsummer nights, even in the Central Region, got cold. The garment wasn't exactly built for warmth. Luckily for Brynleigh, being a child of the moon meant she could walk outside in the middle of a snowstorm and not be affected by the temperature.

Finishing her wine with one final gulp, Brynleigh placed the empty glass on her desk and grabbed her brush. She styled her hair into long flowing waves that tumbled over her left shoulder. For jewelry, she wore her pendant. Nothing else was required.

Rule number two: Doubly blessed vampires do not hide behind jewels or makeup. They let their gods-given gifts speak for themselves.

This was a rule Brynleigh was happy to follow. As a whole, vampires had an unnatural, too-beautiful-to-be-real quality about them, and Brynleigh was no different. She was the same as she'd been before her Making... but not. Her skin was smoother, lacking all blemishes; her eyes were sharper; her nose was slightly more delicate; and her hair was shinier.

Brynleigh drew in a deep breath and squared her shoulders. She reached within herself, pulling on the shadows that danced in her veins. They responded eagerly to her call, flooding out of her outstretched hands. Her wings were next. Those dark, bat-like appendages emerged and hung on her exposed back.

She rolled her shoulders, enjoying the added weight of her wings, before slipping her feet into three-inch black stilettos. Grabbing the matching clutch, she strode over to her dresser. It didn't take long to find what she was looking for. After all, very few of her personal mementos had survived the events of the night she'd been Made.

Gently picking up the yellowed piece of paper she sought, she studied it for a long moment before folding it on the creased lines. She worked carefully, not wanting it to rip, then slipped it in the clutch beside her phone and charger. Her packed duffle bag was on the floor by the front door. It would be sent to the Hall of Choice and arrive a few hours after her.

Brynleigh did not shed a tear as she left her room for the last time, nor did she worry about what she was leaving behind. Sentimentality was for the weak, and this was but a stop on her road to revenge.

Jelisette and Zanri were sitting at the chess board when Brynleigh entered the living room. Jelisette had changed and wore a long black sweater and a flowing skirt. Her sleeve slipped as she cupped her chin, revealing a thick black marking on her wrist.

Zanri, wearing his usual jeans and t-shirt, looked up. His eyes darkened as they swept over Brynleigh, and he whistled.

"I'll be damned, B," he said appreciatively. "If I didn't bat for the other team, I'd be all over you. No one will be able to resist you like that."

Brynleigh laughed, and her shoulders loosened as Zanri's comment diffused some of the tension running through her. "That's precisely the point."

Just because the Choosing was a blind love competition didn't mean Brynleigh couldn't let her competitors know she was willing to do anything to win. She was young and beautiful, confident in her body, and she didn't care who knew it.

Jelisette moved the knight before looking up. "Do you have everything?"

"Yes." Brynleigh's voice was cold and emotionless, like her Maker's.

"And you remember the plan?"

Another nod. "Of course."

They'd gone over it a hundred times. Brynleigh knew what she was doing. She would seek out Captain Waterborn and make him fall in love with her.

Zanri moved his bishop and folded his hands. "Your turn."

Picking up her rook, Jelisette slowly moved it across the board with predatory ease. "Very good. And remember, you can't—"

"Trust anyone." Brynleigh snapped her wings tight against her back and lifted her chin. "Yes, ma'am. Rule number one. I know."

She'd memorized the rules and knew them backward and forwards. This was her game to lose.

Jelisette released the rook, removing Zanri's knight from the board. The shifter cursed quietly under his breath, frowning as he studied the game.

Zanri would lose.

There were three paths to Jelisette's victory, all attainable within five moves.

"Then you're ready." Brynleigh's Maker stood and produced a golden envelope from her pocket. Handing it to her progeny, she waited until Brynleigh met her gaze. "Your ticket in."

The thick paper was cool to the touch, the embossed metallic filigree pressing into Brynleigh's fingers. "I won't let you down."

Brynleigh's shadows pooled at her feet, and she prepared to leave.

The last thing she heard was Jelisette's melodic murmur, "See that you don't."

BRYNLEIGH SAT in the back of the limo her Maker had procured, her fingers lying flat on her thighs as she stared out the window. The chauffeur wasn't talkative, which was fine with her. She was wholly focused on her task and happy to watch Golden City's sparkling skyline pass by.

The namesake triple arches rising above the city gleamed against the starless sky. Their gilded glow shone brighter than any other lights burning through the darkness of the night.

Golden City was the largest urban area in the Republic of Balance. It was the capital and housed the governing body that looked over the welfare of the entire Republic. The Council of Representatives met here, and millions of citizens called the sprawling urban area their home. It was one of the most prosperous regions on the continent, and the golden arches symbolized its wealth.

Some people said this was the most beautiful city in the Central Region. Others claimed there was nothing like it anywhere in the Republic, that its beauty was unmatched. Once, she'd even heard someone say that Golden City rivaled the ancient Emerald Palace in its resplendence.

Brynleigh did not see the beauty. She did not see the appeal of the golden arches or the glimmer of money found around every corner.

All she saw was a city fueled by bloodshed and deception.

No amount of gold could hide the broken aspects of this world. No money could stop the cracks in the gilded veneer from showing. The beautiful illusion of Golden City hid the inequality that reigned in this place. Death often visited those who were less fortunate.

When Brynleigh was a child, she'd learned about the formation of the Republic of Balance. They'd spent a year learning about the Unification of the Four Kingdoms. Many centuries after the Battle of Balance, the Founders of the Republic had dreamed of a country where everyone was equal and lived beneath a single banner.

It was all a fucking joke.

The limo turned a corner and passed a white marble government building. Two statues of the same material stood outside the building, facing each other. The ancient elves were the High Ladies, once responsible for resetting the balance. One was covered in green whorls and swirls, while the other's tattoos were red. Everyone in the Republic knew of these two and the lengths they and their mates had gone to restore the balance long ago.

The Republic's flag flapped above their heads, illuminated by solar lights. The white banner, nearly as large as a car, had four roses encircling a scale.

Brynleigh scowled. The citizens of the Republic of Balance lived under one government, but the equality the Founders had desired was nowhere to be seen.

The Representatives and their families held a disproportionate amount of wealth and power. They were the government, the law, the army. They were in charge, and those who had the misfortune of being born outside their glorious ranks—which happened to be the majority of the Republic's citizens—suffered greatly.

Brynleigh's fingers curled around her gilded invitation, and anger coursed through her veins.

She wouldn't let the emotion rule her, though. Grabbing that anger, she bottled it up and shoved it deep inside.

The limo slowed as it turned another corner, and the driver lowered the barrier between them.

His hazel eyes met hers through the mirror. "We're fourth in line, Miss de la Point," he said, his gravelly voice breaking Brynleigh from her thoughts.

"Understood." Unfurling her fingers, she smoothed out the invitation.

"It shouldn't be long now. I'll let you prepare." He rolled the divider back up.

Brynleigh ran her tongue over the tip of her fangs, letting the slight prick of pain ground her.

She was about to enter the Choosing. A flurry of excitement spun in her stomach despite her best efforts to remain cool-headed about the entire affair. It was fair, she reasoned, to be a little excited because this was the biggest event of the decade. Each participant would arrive at the Hall of Choice in a limo. Once they exited their vehicles, they would walk through an arch of shadows designed to hide them from view from the other participants. This was a blind love competition, after all.

Efforts would be made to keep the men and women separate before the official Unmasking on the night of the proposals. The Masked Ball was one of the most important moments during the Choosing when the participants finally saw their Chosen partners face to face for the first time.

That didn't mean they'd be invisible until then, however. Press events were a very real part of the Choosing. After all, the Representatives wanted to ensure their offspring had time in the limelight.

Even though the Republic prided itself on the technological advancements that had occurred ever since the fae migrated across the Indigo Ocean, the Choosing itself was an antiquated process. It was a relic of times past, a remnant of efforts aimed at ensuring that everyone felt unified. Watching people fall in love was supposed to help the Republic connect and find common ground. That was no longer the case. Now, the upper class used the Choosing as another way to hold their superiority over the rest of the world.

As much as Brynleigh was disgusted by the show of wealth in Golden City, she had no choice but to play along with it. She needed to get close to Ryker. This was her only chance. She'd searched for the fae all over, but finding him had been impossible after he'd gone underground six years ago. She'd never even seen a picture of him. Someone had gone to great lengths to wipe all evidence of the captain from any publicly available sources of information.

The limo moved closer, and the thick, black fog fell over the windows. Even Brynleigh's vampiric eyes couldn't see through the opaque mist. If she were mortal, she would've been afraid. She'd never much enjoyed the dark when she was human. But she was no longer mortal, and that kind of thing no longer bothered her.

She'd been reborn into a creature of the night, and the darkness was her home. Her safe place. It called to her.

She straightened her dress and smoothed out wrinkles. She kept her wings on display, wanting to show the press precisely who she was.

It wasn't long before the engine turned off. Hundreds of heartbeats were the melodic backdrop to the city's symphony. Most were the rapid, steady heartbeats of humans and elves, but a few other slow, rhythmic thrums told her other vampires were nearby.

The driver walked around and opened Brynleigh's door. Darkness rose above them, an arch of swirling night. Inside the shadows were dozens of people with cameras waiting to catch a glimpse of her.

She inched towards the open door, careful not to snag her dress. The moment Brynleigh's heeled foot touched the pavement, cameras flashed. The press' lights lit up the night like bursts of lightning in a spring storm. In one hand, Brynleigh held her clutch. In the other, she gripped her invitation. Her shoulders were back, and a pristine smile graced her face.

An elaborate, long, scarlet carpet led up the massive steps of the Hall of Choice. The path they wanted her to take was obvious, but Brynleigh wasn't an obvious vampire.

She took a few steps down the red carpet, smiled, and waved.

If they wanted a show, she'd give them one. Fanning out her wings, Brynleigh allowed them to stretch to their full length. They were heavy, capable of supporting her weight, and her favorite part of being a vampire.

A few murmurs rippled through the crowd, assuring her she had everyone's attention.

Only then, once she was certain they were watching, did she release her shadows. The dark wisps pooled at her feet, eager to do her bidding.

"A doubly blessed vampire," one of the reporters murmured.

Several more cameras flashed.

"A creature of the night," was another remark.

"Beautiful."

The comments swirled around Brynleigh as she flapped her wings. She rose in the air, remaining within the black arch, enjoying how the wind caressed her like a lover.

Someone else noted, "This one will be a favorite."

Brynleigh didn't hide her expanding grin as she flew towards the guarded entrance of the Hall of Choice, bypassing the steps entirely. She wasn't here for fame, fortune, or any other perks.

She was here for revenge, and finally, it would be hers.

CHAPTER 3
May the Gods Bless Your Choice

Brynleigh landed on the top steps, waved at the press, and grinned as she retracted her wings. She kept a strand of shadows wrapped around her wrist like a bracelet as a reminder of her power.

"Good evening, Miss de la Point." A guard dipped his head. "Right this way, please. The women are gathering in the Crimson Lounge."

Brynleigh handed her invitation and clutch to the man. Looking over her shoulder, she waved at the cameras one last time. Thanking the guard, she smiled demurely. She would be kind, but not too kind. Happy to be here, but not exuberant. Present, but not overly talkative. There were many things Brynleigh had to remember. Her plan hinged on walking a fine line of truth and lies, falseness mixed with the barest amount of reality.

The guard entered the Hall of Choice, and Brynleigh followed behind. Keeping her head down, she discreetly took in her surroundings. Several flashing red lights blinked at her from within vases and above doors, hiding cameras that were probably displaying her procession through the hall to the members of the Republic.

In preparation for this moment, Brynleigh had spent hours studying the blueprints for the Hall of Choice. The building was practically palatial, and not only did it house the participants of the Choosing, but it boasted an expansive ballroom, several staterooms, two prodigious libraries, and an industrial kitchen equipped to feed everyone needed to keep the building running. The residential area of the Hall of Choice was mirrored, with one section for men and another for women.

Hushed whispers filtered beneath closed doors as the guard led Brynleigh towards the Crimson Lounge. Most people wouldn't be able to make out their words, but the moon goddess had blessed vampires with the best hearing of everyone in the Republic. Even dragon shifters, with their extensive senses, couldn't hear as well as children of the night.

Tuning out the clicking of her heels on the marble tile, Brynleigh picked up snippets of conversations.

"My mother loves the Choosing..."

"... Another riot last night in the Eastern Region..."

"There are several elves..."

"... did you see..."

"He's so handsome..."

"... unrest in the Southern..."

Brynleigh's ears perked up at the final comment. News of riots and general unrest wasn't exactly new to her. One would have to be blind not to notice the inequality between the upper and lower classes in the Republic of Balance. Sure, the government said they were all for "equality," but it was all talk. Their actions showed how much they didn't value the lower classes.

In the real world—the one veiled behind a golden sheen—the Representatives and their families were the elite, and the rest of the population was considered less than. The upper class hid behind their rank and used the power of their names as shields from the laws that governed the rest of the continent.

Captain Ryker Waterborn was the perfect fucking example. If he hadn't hidden behind his mother's title, he would've been arrested and tried for the numerous deaths he'd caused.

But that never happened.

Brynleigh's family and their entire human village died, and no one paid the price for their lives.

One day, they were living happily. The next, they were gone. Dead, as if they'd never existed.

Brynleigh was finally taking matters into her own hands. For once, the archaic laws of the Republic were working in her favor. Captain Waterborn was duty-bound to participate in the Choosing, and sometime tonight, he'd be walking into the same building. He could hide from many things and become a recluse; he could wipe any trace of himself away, but even he had to obey the laws requiring the offspring of Representatives to join the Choosing.

"Here we are." The guard stopped in front of a golden door. He bowed. "Good luck, and may the gods bless your Choice."

"My name is Yvette Videntis," the redheaded Death Elf standing before Brynleigh exclaimed. Her voice was rather loud, and the vampire winced.

Yvette's hair was a loose, strawberry waterfall down her back, and she drank from a ruby goblet. While Brynleigh's dress was long and fit her like a glove, Yvette's dress was short and strapless. It did little to support Yvette's cleavage, and the material stopped mid-thigh. It was white, the traditional color most people wore to the Choosing.

The custom hearkened back to the Rose Empire when the Empresses would wear white on the day they met their potential husband during the opening ceremony of the Marriage Games.

Remembering her manners, Brynleigh forced herself to smile. "Nice to meet you."

When Brynleigh had initially entered the Crimson Lounge a few minutes ago, she'd been taken aback by all the red. The entire room was awash in it. The couches, the rugs, and even the paintings were all shades of the same color. Scarlet, crimson, maroon, and cerise were splashed throughout the space.

Their theme was probably love, but Brynleigh would rather interpret it as blood. Each Choosing had its own theme. Once, it had been a jungle. Another time, it had been fire and ice.

This one was good. Perfect, actually. The color reminded Brynleigh of her deadly purpose.

Yvette smiled kindly. "What's your name?"

Brynleigh didn't exactly want to share her life story with the Death Elf, but they were the only two here. After a moment, she said, "Brynleigh de la Point."

Her fingers went to her neck, twisting her necklace as a pang of agony ran through her. She shoved *that* emotion deep inside.

Once, she'd had another name. It was stolen by a rush of water in the middle of the night. Drowned, that name was forever gone. She'd given it up the same night her family had been taken from her. Now, following vampiric tradition, she used the name of her Maker.

The warmth in Yvette's voice was genuine as she said, "Nice to meet you. I like your necklace."

Brynleigh's hand fell, and she grimaced. "Thank you. It's an heirloom."

She really didn't want to get into it further.

"You're a vampire, right?" Yvette asked sweetly, her gaze sweeping over Brynleigh's. "I noticed your black eyes when you first walked in."

Obsidian eyes, sharp fangs, and a predisposed hatred of silver and wooden stakes were things all vampires in the Republic of Balance shared.

"Yes." Brynleigh nodded, hoping the questions would end soon.

Thank all the gods, a resounding gong sounded at the door, saving her from further interrogation. The exuberant Yvette went to greet the newcomer, and after exhaling and shaking out her shoulders, Brynleigh followed.

A beautiful elf with russet skin and silky midnight hair twisted in an intricate braid walked into the lounge. Gold earrings dangled from her pointed ears. Layers of gossamer white fabric hung over her shoulders, artfully covering the important bits of her body before pooling on the floor. She looked like a goddess brought to life.

The elf's gaze swept over the crimson room before landing on the pair. She smiled. "Hello, my name's Esmeralda Larousse, but most people call me Esme. It's nice to meet you."

Yvette handed Esme a ruby glass filled with wine of the same color.

She seemed a natural hostess as she ushered Esme over to the couches. Brynleigh trailed behind, hoping that her lack of speed would save her from being the target of any more questions.

Luckily, it seemed Yvette was happy to learn about Esme. "What kind of elf are you?"

Esme sipped the wine. "A Light Elf, though my grandfather on my mother's side is a dragon shifter."

Yvette gasped and leaned closer, intrigue scrawled across her face. "Are you a descendant of the Carinoc dragons?"

"Mhmm." Esme nodded, taking another sip.

Yvette looked impressed, and honestly, Brynleigh felt the same way. As a child, she'd often heard the story behind the Carinoc dragons. Their miraculous survival and subsequent contribution to the Battle of Balance were the stuff of legend.

"Can you shift?" Brynleigh asked, unable to help herself. She'd never met a dragon before.

Esme looked over the back of the couch and shook her head. "Unfortunately not. My elven side is much stronger, but my brother can."

"Really?" Yvette's eyes gleamed.

"Yep." Esme took an enthusiastic swallow of her wine. "His dragon is emerald. It's stunning."

"Fascinating!" the Death Elf exclaimed. She asked Esme a slew of questions, making Brynleigh eternally thankful that she was no longer the target of Yvette's interrogation.

Esme didn't seem to mind the questions one bit. She told them where she grew up (the plains of the Western Region), her favorite food (chocolate cake, and honestly? That was also Brynleigh's favorite before she was Made), what she did for a living (unsurprisingly, her father was an Elven Representative, so she was training to take his place when he retired).

Thank all the gods, neither of the women seemed to notice Brynleigh's silence. The vampire procured a glass of blood wine from the bartender, a quiet human with black hair and kind eyes.

By the time Yvette had run out of questions, more women had joined them.

Armed with her beverage and a desire not to answer any more questions, Brynleigh stationed herself against the back wall. She studied the participants as they filtered in, taking slow sips of her drink. Blood wine, like all alcohol except for Faerie Wine, didn't really affect vampires, but Brynleigh didn't want to risk being anything but alert.

Soon, the room was packed. Some women were as tall as her, while others were shorter. A werewolf with glowing orange eyes entered, followed by four more elves, two fae, and a shifter of some kind. So far, Brynleigh was the only vampire. Eleven women were present, and they were just missing one.

Excitement filled the air as the women milled around and introduced themselves. No one seemed to notice that Brynleigh was standing off by herself, which was exactly how she liked it.

An elf with long silver hair twisted in an elaborate knot sauntered up to Yvette.

"So, who do you think the last one is?" She twisted a lock of her hair through her fingers. "A child of a Representative or a commoner?"

Standing a few feet away, Brynleigh scowled. How dare the elf draw such a blatant line between the upper and lower classes?

Yvette didn't miss a beat before she shrugged. "I don't know, but regardless, they'll probably be a wonderful person. You shouldn't be so quick to judge others."

Just like that, Yvette rose much higher in Brynleigh's books.

The elf sneered. "It's not judging if it's true. My mother always says—"

The gong sounded one final time, cutting off the classist elf. The door didn't open immediately, though, and something felt different. Narrowing her eyes, Brynleigh pushed off the back wall and stood beside Yvette. The vampire's shadows swirled in her veins, urging her to pay attention. Some people followed their gut, but Brynleigh followed the call of her darkness. It hadn't steered her wrong yet.

The next contestant to walk through the door would be dangerous. As someone who claimed that title herself, Brynleigh felt confident assigning it to another.

Rule number five: always trust your instincts.

When the door finally opened, a tall beauty strode into the room as though she owned it. Danger emanated from her every pore. Blue-black hair was piled on her head, highlighting her pointed, pierced ears. Sharp cheekbones and a long nose looked down on the room. Bright, ruby-red lips were pressed together. Violet eyes glimmered with the promise of violence. Unlike most of the other women, this one wore a scarlet gown. When the light hit it, it sparkled like a thousand rubies were sewn into it.

Next to Brynleigh, Yvette gasped. "The Chancellor's daughter."

Shock rippled through the room.

One of the fae murmured, "I had no idea she was participating in the Choosing."

Brynleigh's heart, which usually mimicked a turtle, sped up. Now, *this* was interesting.

Dangerous but interesting.

There wasn't a single person in the Republic of Balance who didn't know about Valentina Rose. After all, her mother was Chancellor Ignatia Rose, the head of the entire government. The fae had kept her daughter sequestered and guarded for decades, only parading her out for select functions with the Representatives. She was so well hidden that no one knew which element her magic favored.

But now, Valentina was out in public. Here. At the Choosing.

Brynleigh studied the fae. Something about the other woman made her feel on edge.

Valentina's sharp gaze swung around the room. She silently assessed each participant until her violet eyes locked onto Brynleigh's black ones.

Those red lips twisted into an ugly sneer. "I thought this was a classy competition. Who let the bloodsucker in?"

Inhaling sharply, Brynleigh tightened her grip around her glass of wine. This wasn't the first time she'd heard that particular insult, or even the hundredth, but she hated it all the same.

Most people in the Republic of Balance didn't harbor much love for vampire kind. Growing up as a human, Brynleigh had seen some of the side glances directed towards children of the night. She'd heard the stories of vampires who ripped through the throats of others for fun. She'd learned about the Firsts who'd terrorized the previous Kingdom of Eleyta before being entombed in Hoarfrost Hollow, the evil Queen

Marguerite and her Favorites, and the Last King and Queen who ruled Eleyta.

None of that knowledge could have prepared Brynleigh for the hatred she'd encountered since her Making.

No one seemed to like vampires, probably because they were Made, not born. Unlike the other species who would Fade after centuries of life, Isvana's children were truly immortal.

Those violet eyes drilled into Brynleigh as if daring her to respond. With every passing second, the vampire's anger grew. Was Valentina purposefully baiting her? Wanting her to lash out?

Brynleigh's spine straightened, and she drew a few dark wisps from her veins. They gathered around her palms, and she slowly placed her wineglass on the nearest surface.

The other ten women glanced between Brynleigh and Valentina before taking a collective step back. The tension in the room ratcheted up as the seconds passed.

Valentina raised a manicured brow and snorted. "Do you have nothing to say, leech? No way to defend yourself? How very *typical*."

Brynleigh snarled, and she clamped her mouth shut. A sharp burst came from her mouth, and she tasted blood as her tongue came too close to her fangs.

Get a fucking grip, she chided. *You're not a Fledgling anymore.*

Although technically, that wasn't exactly true. Jelisette had worked closely with Brynleigh to help her overcome the initial urges of being a new vampire, but she was still less than a decade old. The danger with Fledglings was that since they were newly Made, they were less in control than other, older vampires.

Historically, hundreds of Fledgling vampires had succumbed to bloodlust, embarking on murderous rampages that ended with stakes shoved through their hearts.

Definitely not the outcome Brynleigh desired.

With help from Zanri and Jelisette, along with a significant amount of meditation, Brynleigh had successfully kept her murderous impulses under control. That was one of Z's main jobs as her handler: ensuring she *only* killed the right people at the right time.

Too bad he wasn't here right now. At this moment, there was

nothing Brynleigh would love more than to dig her fangs into Valentina's pale neck and teach the fae a lesson about respect. Unfortunately, that would have to wait. Brynleigh had a bigger kill in mind than some fae with definite mean-girl vibes.

Still, Brynleigh would keep an eye on Valentina. One day, when they weren't in the middle of a competition for love, she would destroy her.

"I have nothing to say to you." Brynleigh finally broke her silence.

Her mother, the gods be with her soul, had always taught Brynleigh and her sister that remaining silent was the best course of action if they didn't have anything kind to say. It had never been more difficult than it was at this very moment.

Valentina scowled. "Whatever. I'm going to keep an eye on you, bitch."

Brynleigh's nails dug into her palms, cutting open the flesh as she forced herself to remain still.

Thank Isvana, the gong above the door rang once more. This time, an older woman entered. She had silvery hair, her face was worn with age, and her cerise pantsuit matched the red theme of the room. The look would've been garish on anyone else, but somehow, this woman made it seem normal.

She strolled into the middle of the room, either oblivious to or ignorant of the crackling tension that had been building.

"Welcome to the Two Hundredth Choosing." The woman—a human—smiled at each participant in turn. "I'm Lilith, your Matron."

Brynleigh murmured a greeting along with the others.

"I see the gods have selected well for this year's Choosing," Lilith said. "The men will be blessed, no matter who they pick."

Yvette giggled into her wineglass, the drink clearly having gone to her head.

The Matron smiled kindly at the Death Elf before continuing, "Now that you're all here, tonight's itinerary is simple. Eat, drink, and get to know each other." A white brow rose to her forehead. "You're all adults, so I won't be enforcing a curfew. I trust you can behave?"

It was Valentina who smoothly replied, "We certainly can."

There was no trace of the earlier cruelty in the fae's voice, but Brynleigh wouldn't be fooled that easily. She would keep an eye on Valentina.

In Brynleigh's experience, the worst types of people were the ones who waited in the shadows for the perfect moment to strike.

"Wonderful." Matron Lilith strode to the bar, picking up the last unclaimed glass of sparkling wine. "You'll be expected to hand over your cellular devices tonight, and your clothes will be delivered by breakfast tomorrow."

"We won't be able to contact anyone at all?" the werewolf asked from her position on the couch. Her orange eyes glowed.

"No." Lilith shook her head. "Outside interference in the Choosing is strictly prohibited. Is that clear, ladies?"

"Yes, ma'am," Brynleigh said, along with the rest of the group.

"Good. Tomorrow, the twelve of you will be split into three groups of four. You'll participate in a series of interviews with select press members." She smiled. "It'll help you ease into things before the Opening Ceremony the day after."

Excited whispers flowed through the room as the women speculated about what they might encounter during the Opening Ceremony. It changed every time, but one thing remained the same—the men and women would not meet.

Brynleigh didn't engage in the chatter. She sipped her wine, her mind already jumping to when she would finally meet the captain.

If the Matron noticed Brynleigh's silence, she didn't say anything. "It would be wise to rest while you still can."

The whispers ceased.

"The gods only know you'll need it in the days ahead." Lilith raised her glass and waited for the women to follow suit. "Congratulations on being selected, and may the gods bless your Choice."

Soon after that, the Matron departed. Brynleigh maintained her position against the wall. Like a hunter eyeing her prize, she assessed each of the women.

After all, they were her competition for Ryker's hand in marriage. She would never forget her reason for being here.

THE NEXT DAY, the interviews went without a hitch. At least, they did for Brynleigh. Others didn't fare so well.

After breakfast, the women were given directions and split into groups. They would each meet with six reporters in interview rooms that were miniature versions of the Crimson Lounge, right down to the red goblets and ruby couches. The first member of the press had been waiting for them upon arrival.

Once the questions began, they went on for hours.

Brynleigh was well-prepared for every single question that came her way. Her answers rolled off her tongue smoothly, sounding practiced but not overly rehearsed. Most of the inquiries directed at her were related to her Maker. Jelisette de la Point was a well-known vampire in the Republic of Balance, and the press was naturally curious about her newest progeny.

Some of the other members of Brynleigh's quad didn't fare so well. Hallie, one of the elves, stumbled over many of her responses. Like Brynleigh, she was not related to any of the Representatives and was instead Selected from the general population to participate in the Choosing. This was a way to keep the main populace happy while ensuring bloodlines within the Representatives remained fresh.

Hallie was a pale, white-haired Fortune Elf with emerald eyes that sparkled as she spoke. She was kind and had greeted Brynleigh as soon as they'd sat down. She was notably nicer than the other women, and there was a softness about her that Brynleigh hadn't seen in a long time.

The reporters were vultures. They picked on Hallie relentlessly when they realized she wasn't as prepared as the others. When the last reporter, a witch from the Eastern Region, closed the door behind her, Hallie was wiping away tears from her green eyes. Her nearly translucent white wings fluttered behind her, betraying her nerves. They'd been doing that since the first reporter started asking them questions hours ago.

"I don't understand why they kept pushing me," Hallie whispered, twisting a tissue through her fingers. "Why wouldn't they leave me alone?"

Brynleigh handed the Fortune Elf a fresh tissue. "Because they're predators." Just like her. "They saw your nerves and fed on them."

Watching the reporters tear into Hallie had been terrible. This only affirmed Brynleigh's belief that the Choosing, like everything else in the Republic, was unfairly skewed towards the Representatives.

Esme sighed from where she sat on Hallie's other side. "You should ignore them." She brushed a lock of white hair from the Fortune Elf's cheek. "They're curious about us. The Choosing only happens once every ten years, and people want to know about the participants."

"It's easier for you." Hallie blew her nose. "How long have you known you'd be participating?"

"Since I was old enough to understand what the Choosing was," Esme admitted. "It's my birthright."

Like Brynleigh, Esme's answers had been practiced and perfect.

The fourth member of their quad was Trinity, the werewolf. She was soft-spoken. Her great-uncle was the new Alpha of the Northern Werewolves. An extremely rude reporter had dared ask about Trinity's older sister Malika, who'd died last year. Malika had initially been the one destined for the Choosing.

Trinity had barely made it through her answers before bursting into tears. She, too, clung to a tissue.

"Maybe tomorrow will be better," Trinity said hopefully.

Hallie sniffled. "Maybe."

Probably not. Beneath the facade of caring about equality, the Representatives were cold, hard people who only looked out for themselves. That's what made them so dangerous and why infiltrating their ranks was so difficult. They were powerful, wealthy, and commanded the entire world.

If Hallie and Trinity were lucky, they would find strength within themselves before the others tore them to shreds.

If not, Brynleigh would add their names to the growing list of people she was avenging.

CHAPTER 4

It Would Behoove You Not to Act Like Animals

Captain Ryker Elias Waterborn, Head of the Army's Fae Division, wrapped a black silk tie around his neck with the smooth precision of someone who had attended dozens of lavish parties where younglings were to be seen and not heard.

His light brown hair, streaked with red, was still damp from the shower. The ends tickled his pointed ears. He raked a hand through his locks, letting them settle where they wanted before he pulled on the black suit jacket slung over the back of the only chair in his room. The space was much smaller than his apartment, but he hadn't come into the Choosing expecting the accommodations to be luxurious.

Striding over to the desk, he picked up the red rose that had been delivered this morning and pinned it to his lapel. Even though they wouldn't see the women today at the Opening Ceremony, they had to look their best. After all, the cameras were always watching.

That would be... odd. Difficult to get used to.

Many Representatives, including Ryker's parents, kept their families shielded from the public eye. He had been raised in private, and after the Incident six years ago, he'd allowed that same privacy to wrap around him like a shroud, hiding him from the world. Now, he was stepping out of isolation and letting the world watch him find a bride.

All because of a promise.

Once he was happy with the placement of the rose, he slid his feet into the black shoes matching his silk shirt. He meticulously tied the laces, taking care to work with precision.

When other children played tag and chased each other through parks, Ryker was learning how to tie a tie, ride a horse, and never speak to an adult if they weren't directly addressing him. By his tenth birthday, he already had a decent amount of control over his birthright water magic. By his eleventh, he accompanied his mother to the monthly meetings of the Representatives in Golden City. Always under guard and hidden from the press, of course. By his fifteenth, he was already training to join the army.

When he Matured and came into his full fae strength, Ryker was the youngest captain the army had ever seen. One did not rise in the ranks as quickly as he had without having an innate understanding that laws were the reason order existed in the world. Rules and regulations were the backbone of his life.

Through all that, Ryker had always known that one day, he would participate in this event.

Two thousand years ago, when the Founders of the Republic of Balance first established the Choosing, they decreed that each Representative's oldest eligible offspring would participate in the Choosing when they came of age. It was a way to keep the peace among the many people who made up the Republic.

It wasn't a completely choice-less process, though. Children of Representatives decided when they would participate in the once-a-decade event. Ryker had planned to wait another two or three decades before seeking a wife, content to live in his bachelorhood for a little while longer, but when his father fell ill...

Cyrus Waterborn had begged Ryker to enter the Choosing now and find a wife. He wanted to see his son married before it was too late. Ryker's father was many things, including a provider, and he loved his children deeply. He refused to Fade without knowing that his son was settled. It was an old-fashioned idea, but Ryker didn't have it in him to fight with his father. Not after everything else that had happened.

Reluctantly, Ryker had agreed. He hated that this meant he'd have to come out of hiding, but he would do anything for his family, including this.

With that thought in mind, Ryker rose and gave himself a once-over in the mirror. He adjusted his suit jacket one last time before slipping out the door to join the other eleven men in the Ruby Lounge.

Their group was a good mix, or so he thought. It was symbolic of the current mosaic of citizens that called the Republic of Balance their home. The merfolk were the only ones who didn't participate in the Choosing. They preferred to remain in the sea and govern themselves as they always had.

Ryker was the last to enter the Ruby Lounge. The men stood in clusters of two and three, murmuring amongst themselves as they glanced at the door. Nervous energy thickened the air as they waited for the Matron to arrive with instructions on how today would go.

Ryker went to the bar, where a Light Elf with spiked hair was serving drinks. "Coffee, sir?"

"Yes, thank you." Caffeine was part of Ryker's everyday routine. He needed it to function. His younger sister River teased him about his addiction to the drink, but she was only twenty-one and didn't yet understand how much he needed it. One day, she would.

The Light Elf passed Ryker a red mug filled with steaming brown liquid. Ryker's nose twitched at the decadent smell of freshly ground beans, and a smile spread across his face.

"Thank you." Ryker ceded his place at the bar as a blond shifter approached him and asked for the same drink.

When Ryker had first arrived at the Hall of Choice, the shifter had introduced himself as Therian Firebreath. If his name hadn't been enough of a tell, his size was proof of the dragon living beneath his skin. Even in this form, Therian made Ryker look lean.

Coffee in hand, the shifter turned. "Morning, Captain."

"Morning." Ryker shook Therian's hand.

Both men were in the military, although they were in different divisions. Ryker had heard of Therian before, but he'd never met him. The shifter was a skilled fighter, known for the size of his black dragon. Therian had a reputation for never starting fights but always finishing them. He could either be a good friend or a formidable foe.

Ryker had a rule that it was always better to befriend those who could possibly cause him problems in the future. That was how he acquired his two best friends, Atlas and Nikhail.

"Those interviews yesterday were something else, weren't they?" Therian asked as Philippe, an Earth Elf, came over to join them.

"They were long," Ryker confirmed.

Philippe asked, "How did your quad do?"

"Good. The questions were run of the mill," Ryker said.

He'd known all the answers. Ryker always knew the answers. It was his job. He'd long since memorized the right things to say, knowing that something as simple as a slip of the tongue could endanger him and his family. No matter what, Ryker would never let anything happen to them.

Especially River.

It was rare for fae to have children so close in age—Ryker was only seventeen years older than his sister. As such, he and River had an affectionate sibling relationship that many fae lacked. The day his little sister was born, Ryker had sworn he would do anything and everything to protect her.

He'd never broken that promise.

Sipping his coffee, Ryker took quick stock of the room. Besides Therian and Philippe, there was another fae, two werewolves, three elves, a witch, and a duo of vampires. All the men wore black suits and red roses on their lapels, like Ryker.

The clock struck the hour, and the door opened. Matron Cassandra entered, her scarlet ballgown swishing around her. Her white hair was elaborately braided away from her face, and she held herself with authority. Each Choosing, the Matrons were selected from the population to help the participants navigate the Choosing. It was an honor to serve the Republic in such a manner.

Cassandra smiled warmly, reminding Ryker of his grandmother, Fannie. She'd Faded when Ryker was six, but before then, she'd always showered him with love.

"Good morning, gentlemen. It's time for the Opening Ceremony." She raised a brow, meeting each of their gazes in turn. "Remember, your future wife will be attending as well. Even though you won't be able to see the women, it would behoove you not to act like animals."

STARING ACROSS THE GRAND BALLROOM, Ryker gripped the railing of the elevated box where he and the other men waited for the ceremony to begin. Two elevated opera-style boxes spanned the length of the ballroom, one on each side. The men were in one, and the women were in the other. An unnatural wall of shadows that must have been created by a vampire stretched across the ballroom. Even with his elevated senses, Ryker couldn't see through it.

He tried. No one could blame him for that. After all, one of the women veiled in darkness would be his bride. Ryker *would* find a match in the Choosing. He'd accept no other outcome.

Shuffling came from the floor below as a crowd filled the seats. There were at least a hundred people, judging by their shadowy forms. Hushed murmurs and quiet conversations rose from the crowd beneath them Several bright lights illuminated the stage, and camera crews stood by, waiting for the Chancellor to take her place.

Minutes ticked by, and anticipation thickened the air. The hairs on Ryker's neck prickled, and his magic thrummed in his veins. This was unusual, and unusual things were never good.

"Do you think something is wrong?" Therian strode next to Ryker, his large hands gripping the railing. "It should've begun by now."

"I don't know," Ryker said honestly.

He reached for his back pocket, where he usually kept his phone, before recalling that it had been confiscated upon arrival two days ago. Damn.

"It's strange." The dragon shifter crossed his arms and frowned.

Ryker agreed. All his military training had taught him to be suspicious of anything that didn't go exactly as planned. He had a bad feeling about this, and his stomach was in tight knots. The last time he felt like this, he had to deal with a family crisis six years ago.

Peeling his gaze away from the empty platform, Ryker methodically searched for trouble. Even though he couldn't see anything wrong, that sense of unease remained within him.

Another ten minutes passed.

Ryker's fists were furled at his sides. He gnawed on the inside of his lip. This was a public event, and the tardiness was most unbecoming. Like most aspects of the Choosing, it was broadcast to the citizens of the Republic. People all over the continent would be waiting for the live stream to begin.

Eventually, he could wait no longer. He released the railing. "I'm going to find someone in charge and demand some answers."

"Alright," Therian grunted from his position at the railing.

Ryker was halfway to the door when the *click-click-click* of heels on wood came from below. His shoulders incrementally relaxed as he returned to his position at the railing.

Chancellor Ignatia Rose strode into view. Her blue-black hair was pulled back from her face, silver earrings dangled from her pointed fae ears, and she wore a tailored white pantsuit that looked like it cost thousands of dollars. A small microphone was clipped to her lapel, and she looked directly at the cameras, exuding confidence.

It wasn't the Chancellor herself that caught Ryker's attention, but the four soldiers, dressed head-to-toe in black, fanned out behind her. The Republic's sigil—a scale surrounded by four red roses—was on their chests, and each guard held a massive black gun. Their stern expressions gave nothing away as they coolly looked over the attendees.

Tension thickened, and the air practically crackled. The chatter from earlier was gone, and no one dared speak.

The door behind them clicked, and two guards entered the men's box.

Ryker walked over, his brows furrowed. "What's going on?"

The guards exchanged a look that set warning bells off in Ryker's mind.

The taller one said, "Nothing, sir. This is standard protocol."

Standard protocol, his ass. Ryker knew something was wrong. He could feel it.

Probing for answers would have to wait because the Chancellor cleared her throat. The microphone screeched. Ryker winced.

"Ladies and gentlemen of the Republic, I apologize for the delay." The Chancellor's smooth, melodic voice rang through the space. Like Ryker, Ignatia Rose was a fae, but her element was fire. "There was a slight incident."

That would explain the guards.

"Fortunately, the situation has been dealt with, and we can now begin." The Chancellor smiled, but nothing but ice came from the fire fae.

Ryker didn't believe the Chancellor. If everything was resolved, why were there so many guards present? The problem, whatever it was, still existed. He'd bet on it.

He remained alert as Ignatia continued speaking. As was tradition, she regaled the attendees about the history of the Choosing, and of the Founders' desire that the Choosing would bring strength to all and unite the continent. The Chancellor reminded them that the Choosing wasn't just for the Representatives and their families. Six participants were Selected from the general population to join the competition. It was an honor that would elevate their status and lift them into the echelons of high society in the Republic of Balance.

The Chancellor was in the middle of explaining the timeline of the next three months when suddenly, a scream ripped through the air from the back of the ballroom. It was so sudden, so unexpected, that for a moment, no one moved.

Then, that sense of dread exploded in Ryker. He released the railing and spun around as all hell broke loose.

CHAPTER 5

A Curse and a Blessing

Brynleigh was in the middle of an internal debate about how bad it would look if she slipped into the Void to escape this wearisome ceremony when a high-pitched scream cut through the Chancellor's monotonous speech. Was it bad that, for a moment, she'd been happy because it meant she could focus on something other than the history of the Choosing?

As soon as the ceremony had started, Brynleigh was looking forward to its end. Not only was the speech ridiculously tedious, but all the women wore floor-length black strapless gowns and four-inch stilettos. The shoes seemed designed to inflict agony upon the wearer's feet, and Brynleigh wanted to take them off as soon as possible.

Another scream came seconds after the first.

Brynleigh's head snapped back, her eyes narrowing as she searched for the source of the cry. Her shadows pulsed within her, and she let a few slip as her fingers curled into fists. The damned shadows cloaking the middle of the ballroom, designed to keep them from seeing the men, made seeing anything at all nearly impossible.

There.

At the back of the ballroom, by the exit, a guest was on the ground. Even through the shadows, Brynleigh made out their prone form.

Her nostrils flared, and her heart raced.

Blood.

She'd recognize the scent anywhere. It was her life, after all. The source of her immortality. Her *everything*.

A snarl rumbled through the elevated box, and it took a moment for Brynleigh to realize the sound came from her chest. She stared at the floor, warring with herself.

Half of her—the monstrous, deadly, violent creature built for death itself—wanted to vault over the railing. She'd summon her wings and make it onto the floor in one piece. The other half—the rational, logical one—remembered that she wasn't there to feed. It urged her to leave before she did something stupid and endangered her entire mission.

The other women were yelling, and Brynleigh could've sworn someone was crying, but their voices were muffled.

Brynleigh battled the dueling desires within her. Like all vampires, blood was her weakness and her strength. A curse and a blessing. The giver of her life and the pulsing, never-ending need in her veins.

Her fangs sliced into her tongue as she stared at the growing pool of red on the ground below. It wasn't that far. Two, maybe three stories. She could be down there in a flash. Her shadows would protect her while she fed. She could—

"Ladies!" a guard shouted, his commanding voice snapping Brynleigh from her thoughts.

She jerked her attention away from the body, turning to face the soldier.

"Follow me," he ordered. "I have orders to return you to the Crimson Lounge immediately."

A sigh of relief slipped past Brynleigh's lips as she moved towards the guard. Each step took her further away from the crimson pool of temptation.

Three more guards waited in the hallway. Two took the front, and the other pair flanked them from behind.

The predator within Brynleigh had awoken at the scent of blood; now, it was on high alert. It prowled within her, writhing like the shadows in her veins.

She jumped when something brushed against her arm.

"What's going on?" Hallie's voice shook as she hugged her arms around herself. Her pale wings twitched behind her.

Brynleigh's stomach twisted at the sound of the Fortune Elf's voice. Hallie sounded so much like...

No.

Brynleigh refused to think about that. She couldn't risk letting those memories take hold. Not right now. She needed to stay alert and present.

Still, she could take pity on Hallie and try to protect her. The Fortune Elf seemed too frail for this world, as if all the inequality and violence surrounding them would break her.

Brynleigh leaned in. "I'm not sure," she whispered. "I think someone was shot."

That was the most plausible explanation for the amount of blood. Even though they'd moved far enough away that the scent was gone, Brynleigh's fangs still burned. She needed to feed, and soon.

In the old days, when the Kingdom of Eleyta was ruled by vampires, Isvana's children used to have Sources. They were able to drink from the vein whenever they wanted. Now, that kind of behavior was frowned upon. Blood banks were the intermediary between vampires and the vital liquid they needed to survive.

For a fee, of course.

Paying for blood was considered more "humane" than biting. In fact, Brynleigh had never actually bitten and fed from anyone before. She was fairly certain that the blood banks were another way for the Representatives to keep vampires in check.

When creatures of the moon drank blood that didn't come directly from the vein, their powers were significantly reduced. Oh, their blessings of wings and shadows remained intact, but as Jelisette so often told her progeny, vampires had other gifts in the past. One of their blood ancestors had even been able to read minds. Brynleigh had never met Estrella de la Point, but she'd heard of her impressive skills.

Estrella, along with many of the vampires who'd lived in the Four Kingdoms, had voluntarily entered a deep sleep when the Republic was founded. Tales were told of the older vampires, who'd grown weary of life and required a rest. Their location was a well-kept secret, known only by a select few.

Hallie gasped, and several of the other women glanced her in direction. "Shot?" Panic flared in the Fortune Elf's eyes, and she stumbled.

Brynleigh caught Hallie's arm and righted the elf before she fell. "Don't draw attention," she cautioned.

Brynleigh knew better than most that flying under the radar was the best way to get through life. She didn't need anyone looking too closely at her.

"Oh gods," the Fortune Elf moaned. "This was supposed to be a safe place." Hallie wrung her hands in front of her, and worry leaked into her voice. "I never thought someone would get shot!"

So much for keeping her voice down. By the time Hallie spoke the last words, she was yelling.

Valentina appeared out of nowhere. "Aren't you a Fortune Elf?" she sneered. "You should've Seen this coming."

Hallie seemed to shrink in on herself. "That's not... it doesn't work..." Her wings flapped, and she was as white as a sheet of paper. "I can't... the paths of the future don't reveal themselves like that."

"Leave her alone," Brynleigh snapped. "She's in shock."

Not everyone was used to death like Brynleigh. Hallie obviously didn't know how horrible life could be, which was a blessing, in a way.

Brynleigh's innocence had drowned along with her family.

The mean fae wrinkled her nose. "Oh, I see how it is. The Fortune Elf has acquired a fangy bodyguard. Two misfits finding solace in each other. The bloodsucker and the commoner."

"Fuck off," Brynleigh snarled as she reached out and drew Hallie towards her. The elf trembled as she drew in massive gulps of air. "Go find someone else to harass."

Valentina's violet eyes widened, and she bared her elongated canines. "You vile blood-drinking bitch. Do you know who I am?"

Brynleigh raised a brow and haughtily replied, "You look like dinner to me."

A very nasty dinner whose blood probably tasted like putrid garbage. But Brynleigh didn't care. She didn't know what kind of fae Valentina was, whether she took after her mother's elemental abilities or her father's, whoever he was, but right now, she didn't care. Her control was already hanging on by a thread.

Valentina should know better than to pick a fight with a vampire already inflamed by the scent of blood.

Brynleigh released Hallie. The Fortune Elf stumbled back as a growl rumbled through the vampire. Somewhere outside of herself, Brynleigh was aware of the other women stepping back.

The guards were nowhere to be seen.

The Chancellor's daughter didn't move. She smirked as if she knew a secret no one else did. "You really have no idea who I am, do you?"

Valentina's eyes glimmered with violence, and Brynleigh knew she should drop this, but she couldn't seem to stop herself from saying, "Other than a bitch?" Brynleigh snarled and drew shadows around her. "No."

Valentina opened her palm. A flame flickered above her hand.

Instinctively, Brynleigh stumbled back.

Of course, Valentina was a fucking fire fae. Why not? That was the worst possible scenario. Just once, Brynleigh would like for things to go her way. Being in the Choosing with someone who could kill her with a flick of her wrist was a sick, twisted joke.

Vampires were essentially immortal, but three things could cause them significant harm and even death: silver, wooden stakes, and flames. Long ago, before electricity, vampires lit their homes with Light Elf magic to avoid fire entirely.

Despite her desire to remain strong, Brynleigh trembled at the sight of the small yellow flame. She hated that her stomach curled in on itself at the sight, and she despised the icy fear running through her veins.

She was a vampire, a true immortal that would never Fade, but *this* instilled fear deep within her.

And Valentina? Her horrible, red mouth twisted as an awful, mocking laugh left her lips. The sound was like nails running down a chalkboard.

Right then and there, the fire fae secured a spot at the top of Brynleigh's "to-kill" list.

"Not so brave now, are you?" Valentina sneered and took a step towards Brynleigh.

The deadly flame was now a foot tall.

Brynleigh staggered back and slammed into a wall. She didn't look away from the fire. Her fingers flexed, and she released even more shadows.

She prepared to fight.

If it came down to it, Brynleigh would do whatever it took to survive, including killing the Chancellor's daughter. She was aware that wouldn't go over well—honestly, she'd be lucky if she spent the rest of her immortal life in a prohiberis-lined prison—but she was being threatened. Rational thought had no place here.

"Ladies!" Matron Lilith screeched, appearing in the corner of Brynleigh's vision. "Enough!"

A long moment passed before Valentina smirked. She extinguished the flame and rolled her shoulders. "Don't worry, Matron," she said in a sickly-sweet voice. "I was just showing my new friend what I can do."

Boiling lava replaced the ice running through Brynleigh's veins. "We're not friends," she snarled. "I'll never be your friend."

The fire fae simply shrugged and sauntered into the lounge as if she hadn't been threatening to kill Brynleigh moments before.

Matron Lilith looked at Brynleigh and shook her head. She frowned. "You shouldn't let her get beneath your skin, dear. It will only make things worse."

Brynleigh knew she should answer—she'd been raised to understand the importance of manners, especially when dealing with one's elders—but her control was rapidly deteriorating. She dipped her head, following Valentina into the Crimson Lounge.

The other women were discussing the shooting, but Brynleigh ignored them and headed straight for the bar.

The Death Elf who was wiping down the counter looked up as Brynleigh approached. "Miss?"

"Blood, please," Brynleigh rasped, gripping the ruby countertop.

Thank Isvana, the elf took one look at her face and gulped. He ducked beneath the bar, pulling out two red bags. "Warm or cold?"

At that moment, Brynleigh didn't have any time to wait for the blood to heat up. "Cold," she replied. "Please hurry."

The bartender nodded and ran a knife along the top of the bags. He poured the crimson liquid into a goblet and slid it over. "Here you go, miss."

Brynleigh snatched the cup and took a long swallow. The blood settled in her stomach, taking the most brittle edge off her hunger. "Thank you," she breathed.

The bartender nodded as Brynleigh drained the contents of her cup. The anger subsided as she downed the blood. The burning in her fangs cooled, and although she still desired to teach Valentina a lesson, rationality ruled her thoughts again.

"Can I have some more?" she asked.

The elf nodded, grabbing another bag as the door opened. Brynleigh watched over her shoulder as Matron Lilith entered, flanked by two guards. Both tall guards were broad of shoulder, muscular, and had scary-looking guns holstered at their hips. Their matching brown eyes swept through the room, and Brynleigh would've bet good money that they were brothers.

"Here you go." The bartender handed the goblet to Brynleigh.

Matron Lilith sat on one of the crimson couches, folding her hands in her lap. "As I'm sure you're all aware, the Opening Ceremony didn't exactly go as planned."

"No shit," someone snarkily replied.

Brynleigh didn't see who it was.

"What happened?" This question came from Esme, who had her arm wrapped around Hallie.

The Matron sighed and signaled for one of the guards to step forward. "Harper will explain."

The soldier cleared his throat. "This morning, we received a tip that there may be a threat on the Chancellor's life."

A flurry of horrified gasps ran through the room.

"What?" someone exclaimed.

"Who would do such a thing?"

Valentina paled, and for a moment, Brynleigh felt bad for her. She imagined hearing that someone wanted your mother dead wasn't pleasant. Then she remembered the way the fire fae had threatened to kill her, and the pity was dissipated like a morning mist.

If Chancellor Rose was half as much of a bitch as her daughter, it was surprising that it had taken someone this long to threaten her life.

Brynleigh knew better than most that there was no safe place in the Republic of Balance. Not really.

"There's no reason to fear." Harper's voice was matter-of-fact.

"No reason to fear?" Hallie questioned. "Someone was shot!"

Brynleigh was surprised by the force in the Fortune Elf's voice, considering that Hallie had seemed close to fainting a few minutes ago. She was happy to see her new friend fighting back, though. Maybe Hallie did have enough mettle to survive in this cold, harsh world.

"I assure you; we are equipped to deal with any threats," Harper replied. "The woman who was shot was a rebel. She will no longer be a problem."

The undercurrents of his words were evident: the rebel was dead, and dead women couldn't cause problems.

Cold-hearted. To the point. Jelisette would approve.

"Due to the unusual circumstances, the Opening Ceremony is over." Matron Lilith gestured to the guards. "From now on, there will be added security around the Hall of Choice."

"There's no need to be worried," Harper added. "This is a precautionary measure, nothing more."

A hand raised in the corner.

"Yes, Calliope?" Matron Lilith nodded.

"What about the Choosing?" Calliope perched on the edge of a red sofa, twisting green threads of magic through her fingers. The Earth Elf's black hair had slipped from its bun on the hurried walk back to the lounge, and several strands dangled around her face.

Brynleigh stiffened. She hadn't even considered that such an act of violence could make the Chancellor halt the Choosing. She hadn't even met Ryker yet. She couldn't wait another decade to avenge her family.

For some vampires, ten years wasn't a long time, but Brynleigh was young enough that time still had meaning for her. Ten years might as well have been a lifetime. If the Choosing ended now, the captain would return to hiding, and then what would Brynleigh do?

Twisting her necklace through her fingers, Brynleigh forced herself to breathe. Not for the oxygen, since vampires didn't precisely require air to live, but for normalcy.

The Choosing couldn't end prematurely. It just couldn't.

A memory flickered across Brynleigh's mind. Her heart raced. Her stomach knotted. Flashes of too-sudden lightning and a deluge of rain forced their way out of the compartment where she kept them. She shoved them back down.

After what felt like hours but was probably a few seconds, Lilith smiled. "The Choosing will continue as planned. Chancellor Rose believes stopping it would give the rebels what they want."

Brynleigh's legs trembled in relief.

"And we're safe?" Hallie asked.

"Extremely," replied the Matron. "There has never been a single participant injury or death in the history of the Choosing. This one won't be any different."

Calliope asked a follow-up question, but Brynleigh didn't hear her. Relief liquefied the vampire's limbs, and she barely reached the empty seat on the couch next to Esme.

The Light Elf glanced at her, lifting a manicured brow in question, but Brynleigh shook her head. "I'm fine," she murmured.

And she would be. Rebels be damned, Brynleigh de la Point wouldn't be leaving the Hall of Choice without a ring on her finger.

CHAPTER 6
Today Would Change Everything

Ryker's alarm blared, the obnoxious tone pulling him out of sleep. He rolled over, blinking as his eyes adjusted to the darkness. His heart thundered, and he stared at the ceiling.

This was the day he'd been waiting for.

Today, he would meet twelve women. One of them would be his bride.

His stomach, which was usually rock-solid, was a churning mess. It took him a moment to realize what it was—nerves. That was strange. Ryker couldn't remember the last time he'd been nervous. He was a decorated soldier, for the gods' sake. He'd faced down entire armies without a trace of fear.

And yet, he was anxious. Even his magic roiled in his veins. Deep within him, he knew today would change everything.

That thought had Ryker rolling out of bed, quickly showering, and getting dressed in jeans and a black t-shirt. He raked a hand through his hair and headed to the Ruby Lounge.

He wasn't the only nervous one, it seemed. Breakfast was a rapid, loud affair as the men speculated about the women they'd meet. When the Matron entered a few minutes later, Ryker was polishing off a bagel with cream cheese.

Matron Cassandra's eyes sparkled. "Good morning, gentlemen. Are you ready for today?"

A chorus of "yes" rang through the room. Ryker joined them. Breakfast had eased his nerves, and now excitement flourished within him. He was eager for this day to get underway.

Smiling, the Matron instructed them to head to the ballroom when ready. There, they would check in with a woman named Lacey to receive their headphones, a necessary component for the Choosing. After confirming that no one had any questions, she departed.

Less than a minute after the Matron left, the first man followed suit. Ryker stood as well and was in the middle of the group as they made their way through the Hall of Choice.

The walk to the ballroom took a lifetime and a few seconds. Maybe Ryker was still nervous, after all. An armed guard stood at the ballroom entrance, his expression grim. Ryker counted at least three weapons on the man.

His fingers itched for his own gun, or even a knife, but he wasn't a captain here. He was a participant in the Choosing. Unarmed. Defenseless, but for the water magic that was his birthright.

He nodded at the soldier. "Good morning."

"Morning, sir." The guard opened the door. "Good luck, and may the gods bless your Choice."

"Thank you." Ryker had heard the blessing many times, but for the first time, it meant something more. He entered with a spring in his step, automatically scanning the dimly lit room for threats. He marked the exits, tucking the knowledge away in his mind.

The faint lilt of classical string music streamed out of hidden speakers, a backdrop to the quiet hum of conversation already filling the space.

A woman Ryker presumed was Lacey stood at a table nearby. Half a dozen white headphones were spread on the surface before her, and she held a clipboard as she spoke with Therian.

Two guards stood behind Lacey, and a dozen others were scattered through the room. They had their backs against the walls and were attempting to be inconspicuous. It was a nearly impossible task. The soldiers were dressed in black and had large guns holstered on their belts.

They were a stark contrast against the ruby theme that surrounded them.

The rebel threat must have been more significant than Chancellor Rose was letting on. Ryker was aware of an undercurrent of unrest in the Republic. In the past, he'd even been part of quelling riots. However, this was his first time being on the other end of things. He didn't like it.

Therian and Lacey were still speaking, so Ryker took in the space.

The ballroom had undergone a complete transformation. The stage and microphones were gone, and in their place was a giant wall that stretched from floor to ceiling. It stretched down the middle of the ballroom, splitting it in two.

Instead of a typical partition that might be found in an office, this one featured a slow-moving walk-through of a garden at night. Vines dangled from trees. Night-blooming roses blossomed amid dark bushes. Fruit trees dotted the garden. The moon glowed above it all.

The visual wall wasn't the only change. Several people had gone to great lengths to make the ballroom as comfortable as possible. Ruby couches and crimson armchairs were spread across the expansive room. A long black bar stretched across the back wall. There was even a temporary kitchen set up, where a pair of chefs were busy plating some delicious-smelling snacks. Dim lights dotted the ballroom, the dark ambiance reminding Ryker of the high-end restaurants in the Western Region that his sister loved to visit. She would've called this lighting romantic.

A pang of longing went through Ryker at the thought of his sister. For as long as he could remember, even in hiding, he'd seen River multiple times a week. They met for training, and for the weekly family dinner their mother insisted on holding.

This separation would be the longest Ryker had ever gone without seeing his family. He'd known participating in the Choosing would mean he couldn't speak to them, but it was different now that he was in the middle of it. Ryker had instructed Atlas and Nikhail to watch over his sister while he was gone, but he'd rather be there in person. Between his father's illness and the Incident six years ago, Ryker's family responsibilities were heavier than ever.

Clenching his fists, he forced thoughts of deadly storms out of his mind. He couldn't focus on that right now.

Thank all the gods, it was his turn to approach the table.

"Name?" Lacey picked up a clipboard.

He cleared his throat. "Captain Ryker Waterborn."

She dipped her head, checking something off on the paper in front of her before grabbing a labeled pair of headphones.

"Here you go, sir." She handed him the headset along with a red notebook and pen. "These are noise-canceling, and they're matched with that of your first partner. The system will automatically connect you with your date in five minutes. We suggest grabbing a drink and getting comfortable before that happens."

"Thank you, I'll do that." Making his way to the bar, Ryker fit the headphones over his pointed ears, appreciating how the custom set molded around them perfectly.

As soon as the headphones were on, a chime sounded within them.

"Greetings and salutations, Captain Waterborn," a disembodied, robotic feminine voice said. "It is my pleasure to welcome you to the Two Hundredth Choosing."

Ryker jolted, stopping in his tracks. "Uh... thank you?"

"You are welcome, sir."

He blinked. "Who am I speaking with?"

"I am a Computer Engineered Logarithmic Support Technology Expert. You may call me Celeste. I am here to assist you through the Choosing."

An AI. Like the moving visual partition, this was technology that the army had access to, but Ryker had never seen it used by civilians. This must have cost a small fortune to set up, especially since he'd noted a multitude of blinking lights embedded in various surfaces. The hidden cameras were small but certainly powerful as they recorded and broadcast the Choosing to the world.

Not for the first time since Ryker's arrival at the Hall of Choice, he wondered how much money was being poured into this event. As the son of a Representative, he was somewhat aware of the Republic's financial situation. Even though he wasn't privy to the finer details, he knew the government had fallen on harder times of late.

Where were the funds coming from?

"Captain Waterborn, you have three minutes before your first date," Celeste said.

"Thank you." Arriving at the bar, he ordered a coffee and grabbed a plate. Several different pastries were laid out before him, and he perused them.

As he did, Celeste spoke quietly in his ear. "This is your moment, Captain. Remember, the purpose of the Choosing is to find a wife without worrying about societal pressures. While you are in the Hall of Choice, nothing else matters. Over the next twelve weeks, you will narrow your choices until you are left with your perfect match."

Adding a lemon pastry, two apple turnovers, and a hand-held berry pie on his plate, Ryker moved towards a couch stationed halfway between the entrance and the door marked with a glowing "EXIT" sign. "What if people don't find love?"

He was fairly certain he knew the answer but wanted to hear the AI's opinion.

Celeste paused, then sighed. The reaction was strangely mortal for what was essentially a robot. "The Choosing is focused on unity and love, sir. All participants are encouraged to Choose a partner."

"I see. Thank you for explaining that to me."

That evasive answer was essentially what he had expected. A Choice couldn't be forced, but it was strongly recommended. Marriage was the only option for Ryker, though. He couldn't let his father down. He sat on the crimson couch, placing his notebook, coffee, and snacks on the table before him. A blanket hung over the back of the couch, and he pulled it onto his lap, getting comfortable.

"Of course, sir. That is my sole—" A high-pitched bell chimed in his headphones. "Your first date is incoming, Captain." Celeste's voice returned to the same sickly-sweet robotic tone from before. "Please stand by. If you require my assistance, say my name. If not, I will give you privacy."

The AI's voice switched off, leaving Ryker staring at the garden wall. Waiting-room music began playing in his ears, the slow pop song one he'd heard hundreds of times before.

It was him and his thoughts. He was actually here, in the ballroom, about to meet his first date. He'd known he would participate in the Choosing his entire life, but knowing something and experiencing it were two very different things.

He tightened his hold on his pen. "Get a grip, Waterborn," he muttered under his breath. He counted back from five in his head. "You're a gods-damned soldier. This won't be difficult. You'll ask some questions, meet the women, and find your wife."

Failure was not an option, especially when it came to those he loved.

The music came to an abrupt halt. The silence was so loud that Ryker's heartbeat was a drum in his ears. He straightened his back and stared at the virtual garden as he waited.

Three long seconds went by before a sharp inhale echoed through the headphones.

"Hello?" a soft, feminine voice whispered.

That one word was all it took to make Ryker feel like a youngling again. He palmed the back of his neck. "Hi."

By the Obsidian Sands, that was an awkward response. Internally, Ryker chided himself for not being more suave. One would think he wasn't a Mature fae nearing his fourth decade of life with monosyllabic responses like that.

The woman on the other side of the wall chuckled, apparently unconcerned by Ryker's lack of linguistic prowess. "This is... weird, right?"

"I'm staring at a wall and talking to a woman I've never seen." He leaned forward and grabbed his coffee. "Yeah, it's fucking weird."

She huffed a quiet laugh, and instantly, Ryker felt more at ease.

He'd been on his fair share of dates, but knowing he would end up participating in the Choosing, he'd never sought anything serious.

Sensing his partner was shy, he asked, "What's your name?"

After a moment, she said, "Hallie. You?"

He jotted her name down in his notebook, underlining it twice. "Ryker. It's a pleasure to meet you."

She exhaled, and he could almost feel her nerves as she spoke. "Same. This is... a lot, you know?"

Hallie sounded sweet, and Ryker smiled. She must not have been expecting to be here. Filing that tidbit of information away, Ryker stretched his legs before him and settled in comfortably. A glance to his left and right confirmed the other men were doing the same.

Therian was on the next couch over, the dragon shifter's large form taking up the entire piece of furniture. Beside him, Philippe drew green threads of magic absentmindedly through his fingers as he spoke to his date.

"Yes, it is," Ryker agreed. The attack yesterday hadn't helped matters, either. "Tell me about yourself, Hallie. Where do you live?"

A rustling sound came through the headphones, and Ryker imagined that whoever this faceless woman was, she was rearranging herself. Was she on a couch like him? Or perhaps she was pacing back and forth in front of the wall like Luca? The werewolf didn't seem agitated, but clearly, he couldn't sit still. He sipped from his red goblet, his mouth moving as he spoke to his date.

"I grew up on the tip of the Southern Region, near the Sandy Flats," Hallie replied after a minute.

"It must be hot," was Ryker's reply.

He mentally slapped himself for such an awkward response. He needed to shake that, and soon.

She giggled. "Very."

"How are you finding the more moderate climate of Golden City?" Summer was nearly half over, and the nights were rapidly getting colder. While it didn't get as cold in the Central Region as it did in the north past the Koln Mountains, the four seasons were pronounced. "It must be a shock after the desert heat."

Nikhail was from the Southern Region. The fae often complained about the changing weather in Golden City and lamented the lack of his homeland's prolonged, dry heat. Personally, Ryker found the idea of living in a desert unappealing on several fronts, but he could understand why some people enjoyed the warmth it provided.

Hallie paused. "It's... alright, I suppose. I don't think I could live here all year round. How about you?"

"I was born and raised here, in Central Region."

"Oh."

Ryker blinked at the wall. Were all the conversations going to be this stilted? He hoped it was just first-date jitters. Otherwise, this would be a very long day.

"My mother is a Representative of the Fae," he told her. "She took over the position from her mother before she Faded."

"Did your parents meet during the Choosing?" Hallie asked.

"They did." Ryker sipped his coffee. "They took part in the One Hundred and Eighty-Ninth Choosing."

Fae were long-lived, thanks to their Maturation, and of all the different species that made up the Republic, they had fewer children than most.

Hallie laughed. "Wow. That must be strange, although maybe comforting in a way. My parents met through old-fashioned dating. All this is new to me. I mean, I watched the last Choosing, but I never imagined I would take part in this one. My sister applied for me. Imagine my surprise when I was Selected."

"That must have come as a shock."

"It was. I fainted, which my sister found supremely funny." She giggled. "Do you have any siblings?"

"One." Ryker smiled. "River is the light of my life."

"That's wonderful." Hallie seemed more relaxed now that the initial jitters were wearing off. "I have two sisters and a brother at home. All younger than me."

"Tell me about them?"

"I'd love to. First, there's Harlowe. She's three years younger than me, and she's the one who thought it would be funny to apply for the Choosing. She's..."

The more Hallie spoke about her family, the more she relaxed. The pair eased into a conversation, and time started slipping by.

Eventually, another chime sounded in his headphones. "This is your one-minute warning, Captain Waterborn," Celeste said pleasantly. "Please say your goodbyes. You will have a five-minute break before your next date begins."

Another chime.

"Well, Hallie, it was a pleasure to meet you." Ryker meant it. The Fortune Elf was shy, but she was kind, and he'd enjoyed getting to know her.

"Likewise," was her soft response. "I hope the rest of your day goes well."

The rest of their date passed quickly.

When the gods-awful waiting room music returned, Ryker stood and stretched. He made his way to the bar, intent on refilling his coffee.

Philippe, the brown-haired Earth Elf, met him there. He tugged his headphones off one ear and raised a brow. "How did it go?"

Ryker leaned against the counter as the server filled his mug. "Good. She was a little shy but very nice. I'd talk to her again."

The Earth Elf grinned. "Yours was shy? Mine was anything but that. She was loud and spoke her mind." Philippe leaned in close. "She was a fae, like you. I want to speak with her again."

He kept talking as Ryker added some cream to his coffee.

"Thirty seconds, Captain Waterborn," Celeste warned.

Ryker wished the Earth Elf good luck before he grabbed his coffee and returned to his couch.

He'd just settled into his seat when the music cut off again. This time, he was the first to speak. "Hello, my name's Ryker. It's a pleasure to meet you."

Full, proper syllables. This date was already starting better than the last.

A smooth inhalation of breath was followed by, "Hi, Ryker, I'm Esme. I'm glad we're getting a chance to chat."

He smiled. "Likewise. Your name is beautiful, by the way."

She huffed a laugh, and he leaned forward, intrigued. Their date flew by far faster than his date with Hallie. Soon, Celeste was back in his ear, warning him their time was almost over.

After Esme, he met several more women in quick succession. His notebook soon filled up. By the time Celeste informed him they would have an extended break for lunch, he'd already met more than half of the twelve women.

There were a few he already knew wouldn't be a match for him.

The energetic Yvette was kind, but they wouldn't be properly balanced. Their date had been less of a romantic first meeting and more of an interrogation. She'd had a lot of questions for him. He'd been exhausted by the time the music returned.

The soft-voiced shifter named Isabella seemed to lack all confidence. That wouldn't do for his wife. He needed someone strong and capable of standing up for herself. He was certain she would make someone a good partner—she was kind and smart—but it wouldn't be him.

A third, Demetra, was another fae. He hadn't met her before but had heard of her through the grapevine. She was powerful, which his mother would certainly approve of, but early on in their date, Demetra made an off-hand comment about one of the other women's weight.

Right then and there, Ryker had stopped taking notes. They wouldn't be working out. He didn't need a partner who made snide comments about other women. He'd been polite until their date ended, but that was it.

Of all the women he'd met so far, one stood out above the rest. Valentina Rose. Ryker knew who she was, of course. It wasn't as if hundreds of eligible fae were running through the Republic with that unique name. Her position of power wasn't what drew him to her, but her sharpness as they spoke. From his first impression, she seemed like a worthy companion. He'd enjoy spending evenings verbally sparring with her. Their date had been the most enjoyable so far.

Lunch was in the Ruby Lounge, and it was a light, airy affair as the men gathered and shared tidbits about their dates. Most seemed to have made at least preliminary connections, and a few men were already talking about setting up second dates.

Tonight, they would submit lists to the Matrons about which women they'd like to speak with again.

Ryker didn't contribute much to the conversation. He was focused on the two guards stationed at the entrance of the Ruby Lounge. They spoke quietly, shifting from one foot to the other. Their jaws were hard, their eyes like steel as they searched the room for threats.

Discretely angling his body towards the soldiers so he could hear better, Ryker listened intently.

"... another threat," said the guard with a sharp nose.

"Did they catch them?"

"Yes, but... there are more..." Sharp Nose scrubbed his face. "There was a protest in the Western Region yesterday, and today, there was another riot in the North."

"Fuck. Do you think they'll cancel—"

The doors opened, and Matron Cassandra entered. Instantly, the chatty soldiers split apart, their backs straightening as they returned to their stations.

Turning back to the table, Ryker shoveled mediocre pasta into his mouth. He barely tasted it, his mind working overtime to process the information he'd heard. There was always unrest in the Republic. After all, it was an enormous continent that housed millions of people.

But between the shooting yesterday and now this...

Ryker would remain on his guard.

Thank the holy Obsidian Sands, he still had his magic. Even weaponless, he was still a force to be reckoned with. Finishing his lunch, Ryker pushed back his plate and summoned a sphere of water to his palm. It gathered in a translucent orb, waiting for his next command.

He didn't have time to play with his magic. Matron Cassandra announced the end of lunch, and they returned to the ballroom for an afternoon of dates.

Ryker replaced his headphones and headed for a red hammock closer to the entrance. When the music turned off, he was studying the night-blooming roses on the virtual wall.

Having undergone this process several times already, he knew what to expect. He crossed his arms behind his head and closed his eyes. "Hello, my name's Ryker. What's yours?"

A sharp inhale was the only response.

CHAPTER 7
A Meeting to Remember

This was it. The moment Brynleigh had been waiting for ever since she learned who was responsible for her family's murder. The man she'd been searching for was on the other side of the wall.

It had been a long day. Every time the AI connected her with a man who wasn't Ryker, Brynleigh felt a little more deflated. She had taken cursory notes in case anyone was watching, but she hadn't paid too much attention to the other men. She wasn't here for them, after all.

At lunch, Brynleigh had enjoyed a double serving of blood—warm this time, which was how she preferred it—and listened as the other women shared about their dates. Brynleigh hadn't joined in on the conversations. She'd spent the time in contemplative silence, wondering how she would react when she finally met the captain.

Brynleigh had run dozens of scenarios through her head, but she had never anticipated this. The moment she heard his voice, she froze. Her heart thundered at the mere sound. Her shadows writhed. She gripped her pen so tightly that it snapped in her hand. Eyes wide, she let the broken writing implement fall before the ink could stain her fingers.

For all her preparations, all her plans, all her meticulous calculations, Brynleigh hadn't anticipated this.

Ryker's voice sounded *good*. His gravelly, almost smoky tone sent a bolt of desire running through her.

She would be going to hell for this. What kind of person was attracted to the man who killed their family? Her fangs pulsed and burned in her gums. A completely irrational desire to break the wall between them and look upon the fae nearly overwhelmed her.

He was so close, and yet, so far.

"Hello?" Ryker said again. "Is anyone there?"

Brynleigh jolted, realizing she had to act quickly if she was going to save this relationship. How ridiculous would it be if this entire endeavor ended before it started because she couldn't get her head on straight? She rubbed her temples and forced herself to get a grip.

"Hi. Sorry about that; I heard your voice, and I... forgot how to form words for a moment." There was nothing like a sprinkle of truth in a relationship built on deception, right?

She was here for one reason, and one reason only: to make her enemy fall in love with her so she could get close to him. To do that, to make him Choose her, she had to be perfect. Not too hard, but not too soft. Desirable and easy to love, but not such an easy catch that he felt she was too simple.

Whatever Ryker Waterborn needed in a wife, she would be that person.

There was a pause, and Brynleigh imagined this man—this powerful fae—considering her words.

Please, believe me, she silently begged him.

Her nails dug into the flesh of her palms as she waited. She prayed to Isvana and Ithiar that she hadn't ruined everything.

Jelisette would never forgive Brynleigh if she destroyed years of planning because of something as pedantic as *attraction*.

Rule number eight: emotions are for mortals, not vampires.

A frisson of icy fear ran through Brynleigh at the thought of her Maker's displeasure.

The last time Brynleigh had forgotten one of Jelisette's rules, she'd barely been a year past her Making. The incident was so minor that Brynleigh couldn't even remember what happened.

It didn't matter if she'd forgotten her transgression because she would never forget the punishment she'd endured.

Jelisette had locked Brynleigh in the cellar for a week and strictly forbidden Zanri from helping the Fledgling. Brynleigh had nearly gone mad from lack of blood so soon after her Making. She'd begged until her voice went hoarse. Screamed until her cries were nothing but air. Sobbed until she had no more tears. No one had come, no matter what she did or said.

Seven long days. Alone. Cold. Starving.

When Jelisette had freed her progeny, she'd simply said, "Remember, Brynleigh, rules are rules. We must always follow them."

Brynleigh hadn't replied. There was no point. Her Maker had proven her point. Follow the rules, and nothing bad would happen. Break them, and... well, the next time, she wouldn't be so kind.

A baritone chuckle rumbled through the headphones, snapping Brynleigh out of her thoughts.

"I like you," Ryker said. "You're funny."

Brynleigh sighed in relief, her eyes momentarily fluttering closed. Thank all the gods, she hadn't completely ruined everything. Now, all she had to do was make sure he remained interested.

"Honestly, that's the first time anyone has called me funny," Brynleigh admitted, the words slipping from her mouth before she could stop them. "I'm not usually one to make others laugh."

Scream? Yes. Run away? Also, yes. Laugh? Nope.

"Fascinating. I think you're quite humorous."

She wasn't sure whether to be delighted or insulted by that comment. Was he laughing with her or at her? She supposed it didn't matter. He sounded intrigued, which was good.

"I shall endeavor to make you laugh again." If Brynleigh had to become a fucking comedian to make the captain fall in love with her, then she'd do it. She would be whatever he needed.

He chuckled. "Tell me, Oh Humorous One, what's your name?"

Had she forgotten to give it to him? Brynleigh blinked. Isvana help her, she must have been more affected by his voice than she'd originally thought.

She ran her hands over her braid, which hung over her shoulder. "Brynleigh de la Point."

He repeated her name slowly, like each syllable was a delicacy, and he was savoring each taste.

The vampire ground her teeth at the sound. Her name had no right sounding so good in his mouth.

He added, "It's a pleasure to meet you."

Why did it sound like he was being earnest? And why did she like the sound of his voice so much? A low, pulsing headache formed as Brynleigh puzzled through these new, troublesome developments.

"Agreed." Hoping to get back on track and regain control, Brynleigh took a large swallow of the blood wine she'd grabbed after lunch. Crossing her leggings-clad legs, she leaned back on the couch. "So, Ryker, how's the process agreeing with you so far?"

If any of his dates had been like hers, he'd already endured a hundred "get-to-know-you" questions. Brynleigh wanted to stand out and be remembered. What better way was there than to take a different approach than everyone else?

Several seconds went by in silence. Brynleigh imagined this faceless man with the intriguing, attractive voice mulling over his words. Was he on a couch like her or on a chair with his legs slung over the side like Yvette? Or maybe he was strolling up and down the length of the ballroom. The options were endless.

"It's been... more than I ever expected. This morning, I was nervous. I'm never nervous. It's not something I usually do. In my job, I need to be in control. But this is different." A choked sound came from him, and he groaned, "Gods. Why am I telling you this? We just met. It's strange, but I feel—"

"Comfortable," she provided before she could stop herself. The word slipped out of her mouth, and she cursed herself for speaking.

Stupid, stupid, stupid. Even though something innately easy came from speaking with this fae, she never should have admitted to it.

She was definitely going to hell.

"Exactly," he said on an exhale.

The problem was that Brynleigh felt it, too. It was like they'd known each other for years, not minutes. The vampire had felt varying degrees of awkwardness with all the other men. Aside from the first moment, where the sound of Ryker's voice made her forget how to speak, she didn't feel anything like that with the fae.

But maybe it was because she knew him. Not personally, but she'd been aware of Captain Ryker Waterborn's existence for years. She'd met him, not in person, but in the form of the magic he wielded.

That horrible night, with its sky-high waves, burning lungs, and floating bodies, was forever imprinted on her mind. Jelisette found her that same night, half-drowned and soaking wet.

After her Making, Brynleigh learned all there was to know about the captain. She had studied him like he was a difficult equation, and she was the mathematician determined to solve it. Even after he'd become a virtual ghost, she'd searched for him across the continent. She spent every waking hour trying to find morsels of information about him. Jelisette, Isvana bless her soul, helped Brynleigh as best she could.

Every detail they unearthed, no matter how big or small, was like a nugget of gold as Brynleigh sought to familiarize herself with the captain she planned to kill.

Brynleigh knew Ryker was under constant guard, both because of his position as the son of a Representative and as a captain in the army, and he was extremely private. He had a sister—River—who was almost two decades younger than him. She wasn't even Mature yet. His mother was a Fae Representative and worked closely with Chancellor Ignatia Rose. Brynleigh even knew that Ryker's father was ill. He'd come down with the Stillness over a decade ago and hadn't been the same ever since.

Maybe that was why when he spoke, she felt drawn to him.

Yes. That had to be it. There was no other reason he made her feel this way. None at all. Certainly, it had nothing to do with the way her fangs burned with the need to bite, nor did it have anything to do with the curling ball of want in her core.

It was just because Brynleigh knew who the captain was.

He's a killer.

Jelisette's voice echoed through Brynleigh's mind. Yes. That was a good, solid reminder of who she was speaking with. Brynleigh could never, ever forget why she was here.

It was time to get the conversation back on track.

Twisting her pendant through her fingers, Brynleigh asked, "What do you do when you're not seeking a wife in the Choosing, Ryker?"

"I'm a captain in the army."

"Oh?" She feigned surprise. "Have you done that for a long time?"

She imagined him nodding. "Since before I Matured. It's my calling."

And there it was. He was a bringer of death. It was his fault her family had died, his fault she'd been Made, and his fault she was alone.

"Do you enjoy your work?" Brynleigh asked.

He didn't even pause before saying, "I do. I'm good at my job and like what I do."

Fae couldn't lie. Everyone knew that. Whatever warmth had been flourishing in Brynleigh was doused as if someone had dumped a bucket of ice water on her.

"I bet you're very good at your job," she said flatly, unable to even infuse a bit of warmth into her voice.

"Most of the time," was Ryker's response.

"Oh? When was the last time you made a mistake?"

Part of her felt like she was making one right now, but she needed to know what he would say. If he answered her instead of staying silent, if he *told* her something, it would be the reminder she needed that he wasn't a good man. That he made mistakes. That he was a murderer.

"A few years ago," he said.

Fuck. Was that remorse in his voice?

"What happened?" She didn't want to know, but the question slipped out of her mouth. It was like her body had a mind of its own.

He sighed. "People... died." He spoke slowly, and there was a hint of something that sounded awfully similar to regret in his tone. "I still think about it to this day."

A collection of curses that would make even the most hardened Death Elves blush ran through her mind. The question wasn't supposed to make her feel bad for him. That emotion had no business here. Brynleigh grabbed it and threw it away.

"Oh," was all she could manage to say.

Ryker shifted gears. "Enough about me. I'd love to know more about you, Brynleigh. You said your last name is de la Point, right?"

"Yes."

"Are you, by any chance, related to Jelisette?"

She nodded before remembering that he couldn't see her. She had anticipated this question—it inevitably always came after she revealed her last name, but right now, her tongue stuck to the roof of her mouth.

Most people were biased against vampires. Was he one of them? Part of her hoped he was because it would be easier to hate him. But the other part, the remnant of her humanity, wanted someone to see her for who she was, not what she was.

There was only one way to find out.

"Yes. She's my Maker. Following vampiric tradition, I took her last name after my Making."

A long moment stretched between them. Brynleigh dropped her necklace, twisting her hands together.

From the next couch over, Hallie glanced over at the vampire. The Fortune Elf's brows creased, and concern radiated from her. *Are you alright?* her eyes seemed to say.

I'm fine, Brynleigh mouthed.

There was no point in worrying her new friend, especially since it seemed like Hallie was fully engrossed in her date.

Luckily, Ryker didn't keep Brynleigh waiting for long.

"I bet you have a very sharp bite," the water fae said, a hint of humor in his voice.

Brynleigh *laughed*. The mirth burst out of her so loudly that she drew stares from several women around her. Sheepishly, she mouthed, *Sorry*.

She hadn't been expecting that at all. She couldn't even remember the last time she'd chuckled, let alone laughed. Not really.

She didn't have much to laugh about these days.

"You don't mind that I'm a vampire?" she confirmed. "It doesn't bother you?"

"Not at all," was his immediate response. "I'm a fae. Does that bother you?"

It fucking *should* bother her. Other things about him bothered her. But somehow, that wasn't one of them.

Brynleigh didn't care what someone was. Human or vampire, fae or mer, shifter or elf, witch or werewolf, it didn't matter. True, world-ending, soul-crushing evil could exist beneath anyone's skin. Darkness could find a home anywhere if the right circumstances presented themselves.

"No." She twisted her braid through her fingers. "What kind of fae are you?"

Obviously, she already knew the answer. However, since it was imperative Ryker never found out exactly who Brynleigh was, she had to keep up appearances.

"A water fae," he said.

"What does that mean exactly? Can you summon a few drops of water? A sprinkle?"

This time, it was his turn to laugh. The sound was as deep as his voice, and it washed over Brynleigh like the first drops of rain after a long summer's day. It woke parts of her that had no business being awake right now.

She yearned to hear that sound again and again...

And she wanted him to never, ever do that again in her presence.

"Not at all, sweetheart. More like storms."

The nickname registered in Brynleigh's mind, and she stared at the wall. Part of her rebelled against it, but the other couldn't help but preen. She liked it—a lot. That could possibly be problematic, but just like the issue of her burning fangs and twisting core, she gathered up that emotion and shoved it down, down, down until she couldn't feel it anymore.

Thank Isvana, a chime sounded in her headphones, and the AI interrupted them. The date would soon be over. They said farewell, and Ryker was kind as he wished Brynleigh a good rest of her day.

It was horrible.

Brynleigh chugged the remainder of her blood wine as soon as the connection broke. She closed her eyes and rested her head on the back of the couch. That did *not* go as planned.

The remainder of the afternoon went by in a blur. No matter how many other men she spoke to, she couldn't get a certain water fae and his deep voice out of her head.

In all her planning, Brynleigh had never anticipated that she might actually be interested in Ryker Waterborn. That she might actually... like him. He was nothing like what she expected. He wasn't hard or ruthless or cold.

That was frustrating, to say the least.

There wasn't a rule for this.

CHAPTER 8
Butterflies and Silence

"What's your favorite childhood memory?" Ryker reclined in the hammock as he waited for Valentina to answer.

A few days had passed since their initial introduction, and he liked the fae. Not only was Valentina sharp-witted, but she had a fire in her. Ryker had a gut feeling his mother would love Valentina if he brought her home. They'd already been chatting for a half-hour, and Ryker smiled frequently during their conversation. He liked that.

Valentina chuckled. "I don't know if you'll believe me."

Curious, he raised a brow. "Try me."

She paused, and for a moment, he wasn't sure she'd answer. He ran this thumb down the side of his mug and waited.

"Are you familiar with the goldback butterfly?" she asked. Her voice was different than it had been earlier. Softer, like a harsh edge had been scrubbed away.

Ryker's brows furrowed. "No, I can't say that I am."

A sigh. "They're rare." Valentina paused. "When I was younger, I was rather... isolated."

Ryker understood that. For the past six years, he'd gone to great lengths to stay away from others. It was the best way to protect his family. "That must have been difficult."

Even as an adult, loneliness had often courted Ryker. He'd only kept it away during his prolonged isolation because of his dog Marlowe, his friends, and trips to his cabin.

"It was." Valentina drew in a breath through her teeth. "Anyway, I was alone a lot. Mother was often at work, and I spent time in the library when I wasn't at school. One day, I was reading an encyclopedia and found a picture of a goldback butterfly. It was beautiful. The wings shimmered in the afternoon sun like they were made of gold. The butterfly called to me."

"It sounds lovely."

"It was. The goldbacks were all I could talk about for months. I became obsessed with them, talking about them for hours. One day, Mother came home early. I'll never forget it because she'd abandoned her formal business wear for jeans and a yellow sweater. 'I have a surprise for you,' she told me." Valentina's voice took on a wistful tone, and he could've sworn her breath caught. "It was my first and only surprise ever."

A pang of sadness went through Ryker's heart, and he dropped his pen. He'd never had a great relationship with his mother—Tertia Waterborn was a fierce, sometimes cold woman—but she'd taken great care to spend time with her children. Enough that he never felt ignored by her.

Evidently, that wasn't the case for Valentina.

"I'm sorry," he breathed.

"Don't be. It was a beautiful surprise. She arranged an entire trip for me. I had her to myself for twenty-four whole hours. We went to a botanical garden in the Southern Region, where goldback butterflies were abundant. They flew around us in a flurry of shimmering gilded wings, landing on our heads and shoulders. It was amazing."

Ryker could picture the swarm of yellow wings caught in the afternoon sun. "It sounds incredible."

"It was," said Valentina. "I—"

"This date will end in sixty seconds," Celeste interrupted, her robotic voice jarring Ryker from the calm he'd settled into. "Please prepare to say goodbye."

The headphones clicked, and Ryker sighed. "I'm sorry, Valentina," he said. "But—"

"I heard." That harsh, polished edge was back. "It's fine. It was nice to speak with you, Ryker."

And as they wished each other well, he agreed. There was far more to this fae than he'd ever guessed.

AFTER HIS DATE WITH VALENTINA, Ryker's next few were... not as wonderful. That wasn't to say he didn't enjoy talking to the other women, but there was no connection between them. His mind wandered. When Calliope, an Earth Elf, was telling him about her job, his eyes grew heavy, and he almost drifted off to sleep.

By the gods, he had to pay attention. He needed to find a wife. His father didn't have long. The Stillness...

"Good afternoon, Ryker," said Brynleigh.

He hadn't even realized the music had stopped. Nevertheless, Ryker smiled, eager to spend time with the vampire today. He'd already come to recognize her voice. A spark came to life within him every time they spoke. Whatever tiredness vanished as he settled in. "How are you today, Brynleigh?"

"I'm... alright." Her tone made it sound like she was anything but.

An alarm blared in Ryker's mind. Finding out what was wrong was the only thing on his mind. "What's the matter?"

A long, heavy silence stretched between them. Ryker rose from the hammock, needing to stand. To do something. He wasn't one to let the people he cared about be hurt, and even though the Choosing was barely underway, he already felt something for the vampire.

"You can tell me," he murmured after a few minutes of silence.

"This... today... it's a difficult day," she whispered, her voice cracking.

Were those... tears he heard? Ryker's chest seized at the thought. He balled his fists at his sides. His water magic, which was usually calm, thrummed within his veins. It wanted him to climb over this wall and find the woman hurting on the other side.

But he couldn't. One glance at the guards, the blinking lights, and the other participants conversing quietly with their dates reminded him of that.

"Do you want to talk about it?" he asked instead.

Another pause. Each one was longer than the last. Heavier. Was she sitting? Walking like him? Was she crying quietly in a corner?

By the Sands, he wished he knew.

"I lost someone," she whispered. "And this is... it's the..."

Her voice trailed off, but he had heard enough. Ryker recognized the grief in her voice, the depth of hurt, the old wounds. He was deeply familiar with the kind of pain that rooted itself so deeply within oneself that there was nothing one could do except live with it.

"The anniversary?" he guessed, wishing he was wrong. Hoping he was wrong.

More silence.

He returned to his hammock, letting his head fall into his hands.

Eventually, she sighed, "Yes."

He rubbed his temples. "Fuck. I'm sorry."

She drew in a shuddering breath. "Me too. I'm so fucking sorry. I wish... they should still be here."

"I'm here if you want to talk about it," he offered.

Sometimes, when the Stillness got worse, talking about his dad helped. Reliving old memories or sharing something simple. On other days, words were impossible. Grief stole them from him, and he could barely get out of bed, let alone talk.

He would do whatever Brynleigh needed.

Another long moment passed before she said, "Can we be quiet?"

Her request was soft, and it went straight to his heart. He wished he could see her. Hold her. Embrace her until her grief passed. But he couldn't.

This, though, he could do. "Of course."

The rest of the date went by in contemplative, heavy silence.

That night, when Ryker went to bed, he realized there had been a comfort he'd never experienced before, even in that quiet. He hated that Brynleigh was hurting, hated that she'd gone through an entire day of dates with grief in her heart, but she'd opened up to him. Shared it with him.

And that made him feel... good.

CHAPTER 9
More Than She'd Bargained For

Red, puffy eyes stared back at Brynleigh in the mirror. She hadn't slept last night. She hadn't done anything after her dates except go to her room and cry. Once they had started, the tears had flowed and flowed and flowed.

She'd never cried on this day before. Never shed a single fucking tear.

It was him. The captain. His presence here. He was doing things to her. Twisting her up. She could feel it—even her shadows were responding to him.

When she woke up yesterday, she knew it would be a bad day. Her heart had been heavy, and she'd wanted to do nothing more than stay in bed all day and grieve.

Six years had passed since that fateful midsummer storm. Six years of being utterly and completely alone. Seventy-two months. Two thousand, one hundred and ninety days since she'd said goodbye to her family.

He'd stolen them from her.

After their date, where she'd revealed something she *never* wanted to reveal—not to him or anyone—she ran back to her room and wept. She hadn't known it was possible to have so many tears, hadn't known grief could slam into her like an unmovable wall and crush her.

She'd skipped dinner, forgoing nutrition in favor of sitting on the floor of her shower fully clothed.

Hours had passed, and even with her vampire blood, Brynleigh had been a freezing, frigid mess by the time her door creaked open. Hallie had cautiously poked her head into the bathroom and frowned.

"I Saw that you might want this," the Fortune Elf had murmured, holding out a bag of blood in Brynleigh's direction. "Let me know if you need anything."

Brynleigh had thanked the Fortune Elf through a veil of tears. She'd turned off the shower and shed her sopping-wet clothes as soon as Hallie had left. Naked and bone-tired with a grief that wouldn't leave, Brynleigh had climbed into bed. She'd inhaled the bag of blood, the food doing little to ease the emptiness within her.

She hadn't slept a wink.

Today, Brynleigh would do better. She needed to get a grip. Yesterday, grief had been a deep ocean of despair, but this was a new day. Things could only go up from here.

It was with that thought that Brynleigh showered again—this time with scalding, hot water, just the way she liked it. After, she dressed in black leggings and a comfy sweater. She brushed out her hair, letting the waves fall around her, before applying makeup. Arguably, vampires didn't need makeup because they were unnaturally beautiful, but sometimes Brynleigh liked how it made her feel. Strong. Powerful.

Today, she needed that.

Each brush of eye shadow and each swipe of lipstick was armor against the world.

Finally, she was ready.

Breakfast went by without a hitch. Brynleigh sat with Hallie and Esme, listening as they shared about the men they were seeing.

Everything was going alright until she put on her headphones, and Celeste connected her with her first date.

"Hello?" Brynleigh fiddled with her pen.

"Morning, Brynleigh." Ryker's concerned voice came through the headphones. "How are you feeling today?"

She barely bit back the bitter laugh threatening to burst out of her. Of course, the captain was her first date. It was just like the fates to play with her like that.

His concern would've been humorous if she were in a better mood. He was the reason she was upset. If it weren't for him, her family would still be here, she'd be human, and she would never have participated in the Choosing.

But there was no point in thinking about what might have been. She needed today to go better than yesterday, even if it killed her.

Casting aside gloomy thoughts of a life that could have been, Brynleigh forced a smile on her face as she settled into her seat. "Better, thank you."

It wasn't a lie, per se. She *was* better than yesterday.

His baritone voice rumbled, "Good. I was worried about you."

"Thank you." Brynleigh didn't want to dwell on yesterday. She wanted to set that overwhelming grief and aching heart aside. She rubbed a fist over her chest, trying to ease the ache. It helped… a bit.

Shutting her eyes and letting her head fall back against the couch, she asked the first question that popped into her head. Anything to keep the conversation moving and off her. "What's your dream travel destination?"

She didn't know why it mattered since they would never go anywhere after the Choosing—he'd be a rotting corpse before they could shadow anywhere or get on a plane—but it seemed like a safe question to ask. On a day like today, good and safe were all she could ask for.

"Are we talking about anywhere in the Republic of Balance?" he asked.

"Sure, why not." Whatever he wanted. Hopefully, he'd talk for a long time so she could compose herself. She didn't trust herself not to open up again and share something else she didn't mean to. "Where would you want to go?"

He hummed, and she focused on rebuilding the box where she kept her emotions. It had cracked yesterday, and she couldn't let that happen again.

"I'd love to visit the Black Sea," he said after a minute. "See the inky waters, skate on the ice, maybe even spend a few nights hiking the frozen mountains."

"Do you like to hike?" As a human, she'd enjoyed the activity, but she hadn't done anything like that since her Making.

"I love it." She could hear the grin in Ryker's voice. "I have a cabin in the mountains that I visit as much as possible. It's beautiful all year round, but especially at night. The bedroom overlooks the lake."

She smiled despite herself. "It sounds nice."

"It is. If we were in the north, we could go exploring. There are beautiful ruins in the Northern Region. Castle Sanguis, for one. Some of the old abbeys as well."

Warmth coursed through Brynleigh. Damn it all. She wasn't supposed to care about what he said, wasn't supposed to want to go on the trip he described. She'd never been to the Black Sea, even though the Northern Region was the ancestral home of the vampires. His trip sounded like fun, and Brynleigh hated that she wanted to join him on it.

So much for her simple question.

"That sounds nice," she said after a moment, realizing she needed to speak. "Does that mean you enjoy the snow? Is that a water fae trait?"

He snorted. "I mean, I like snow as much as the next person. I can turn my water to ice, but I feel the cold like any other fae."

"Hmm. Vampires don't feel cold," she told him, a touch of smugness in her tone. "We're made for the snow. I could dance in it, I suppose."

She'd never tried. Jelisette wouldn't approve.

"I'd love to see that," he said. "Tell me, Brynleigh, would you keep me warm if we were trapped in an icy cave?"

A grin stretched across her face despite herself. She relaxed in her seat. "Maybe. If you're nice to me."

He laughed, the bass sound resonating through the headphones. It was beautiful, like a crisp winter's night after a stormy day. Once again, her fangs reacted to his voice, and a fire burned in her gums. This reaction was quickly getting tiring.

"Oh, Brynleigh. I could be *very* nice."

Damn it all, but she laughed, too. She didn't want to, but she couldn't stop the sound from bubbling inside her.

They chatted about the Black Sea, discussing various things they'd do on their trip until Celeste informed them their date was over. When the music started playing, Brynleigh leaned back and rubbed her temples.

"Fuck me," she groaned.

This would be far more difficult than she'd ever bargained for.

CHAPTER 10
Game On

A few days later, Ryker was back in the crimson hammock. He was settling into a routine. After breakfast, he would spend most of the day in the ballroom, getting to know the women. Eventually, when the Choosing was past the halfway point, they'd move onto actual dates, but for now, they focused on creating that connection.

Surprisingly, at least to Ryker, he was enjoying this process far more than he thought he would. Who knew talking could be so agreeable?

He crossed his arms behind his head and closed his eyes. "What do you do when you're not hunting for a husband, Brynleigh?"

The vampire was his first date today, and he'd be lying if he said an enormous grin hadn't stretched across his face when her voice came through the headphones.

He still didn't know what she looked like, but it didn't matter. They were building a connection that wasn't based on how the other looked. He wanted to know more about this humorous vampire that made him laugh. Of all the women here, Brynleigh and Valentina intrigued him the most.

Brynleigh chuckled, and the sound was tinged with a touch of darkness and the night. "I work for my Maker."

That wasn't inherently surprising. Most vampires in the Republic of Balance preferred to remain with others like them. In fact, outside of the Choosing, Ryker hadn't met many vampires. They had a division in the army, but the Night Corps tended to keep to themselves. It probably had something to do with their aversion to sunlight... or maybe their general dispositions made them better suited to working alone.

"What do you do for her?" he asked.

"Odd jobs, mostly. A little bit of this, a little bit of that. Whatever she asks of me."

That, he understood. Life in the army was regimented, and whatever his superiors said, he did. It was the way of military life.

The hammock swayed beneath Ryker as he glanced at the garden wall. "Do you like it? Your work?"

She paused. "Mostly."

"I understand," he murmured. "There are moments when I wish I were anywhere else."

Like that stormy night six years ago.

He frowned. That was... not something he liked to think about. He shoved the thought from his mind and focused on the vampire speaking with him.

Brynleigh sucked in a breath. "That makes sense. Sometimes the things I do for Jelisette... I wish things were different. That's all."

A comfortable silence stretched between them, an understanding that each saw the other and knew where they were coming from. Ryker had never considered that he might meet someone who would understand him so profoundly in such a short period of time.

"How about you?" Brynleigh asked after a few minutes passed. "What does Captain Ryker do when he's not searching for a wife?"

Ryker's lips twitched at the obvious change in the topic of conversation. "Would you believe me if I told you I enjoyed playing games?"

A light, harmonious laugh rang through the headphones. It was like wind chimes tinkling in a night breeze. The sound of the vampire's pleasure seeped into his bones and stirred something deep within him. He would cherish her laugh and replay the memory repeatedly when he was alone.

"I have to admit, I wasn't expecting that," she said when her laughter died.

He chuckled and palmed the back of his neck. "No? What did you think I would say?"

"Honestly, anything else." There was a smile in Brynleigh's voice. "I, too, enjoy games. Especially chess."

Ryker's eyes widened, and he grinned. "That's my favorite."

There was no hiding the enthusiasm in his voice.

He'd been playing the game since he was a child. When he hadn't been at school, he studied strategies, memorized moves, and played against any willing opponent. Even now, he gravitated towards a chess board after a long workday.

Most people only played chess against Ryker once. Not because he was bad at it, but because Ryker played to win.

Every. Single. Time.

He firmly believed there was no point in playing a game if he wasn't trying to win. He was competitive, not just with others but with himself as well. He constantly strove to be the best at everything. He enjoyed games, liked the structure of rules, and he always aimed to defeat his opponent.

"You're joking," was Brynleigh's response.

"Not at all." Ryker sat up and placed his feet flat on the floor. Resting his elbows on his legs, he stared at the visual wall. Today, blue and pink flowers stretched as far as the eye could see. "I have a chess board from one of the ancient Eleytan abbeys. It dates to the time of the Vampire Queen who fought during the Battle of Balance."

Many artifacts from that age had been lost to time, having disappeared when the ancient vampires chose to sleep. Ryker's father gifted him the chess board on his eighteenth birthday. Ryker cherished it, and it remained in his apartment to this day. He rarely played with the ancient set but often admired the hand-carved black and white marble pieces.

"Truly?" A hint of suspicion entered her voice. "Are you pulling my leg?"

"Not at all," Ryker smirked. "Fae can't lie, after all."

"Hmm. I suppose that's true."

He chuckled. "It is. I swear to you that I can't, even if my life depends on it."

But he was skilled at twisting his words. All fae were. It was a skill passed down from generation to generation, a way to remain powerful while still telling a version of the truth.

"I'll give you that," Brynleigh conceded.

Ryker sipped his coffee. "I'll have to show you the board. Maybe challenge you to a match?"

Was it presumptuous of him to make plans outside the Choosing already? Maybe. But he didn't want to ignore the connection between them. And this, her playing chess, felt like a sign from the gods.

"At your home?"

"Yes."

She sucked in a breath, then murmured, "I'd like that more than you know."

Ryker's smile widened. So would he.

Their conversation shifted to different chess strategies, which occupied them until the chime rang.

"Apologies for the interruption, Captain Waterborn, but your next date will begin in five minutes." Celeste's voice was crisp and to the point. "This date will be over in sixty seconds."

"Damn," Ryker growled. He didn't want to say goodbye. Not now.

"Our time's up already?" Brynleigh sounded as surprised as he felt. "It feels like we just started talking."

"Doesn't it?" He capped his pen. "I really enjoyed this, Brynleigh. I hope we'll get to talk again soon."

A pause, and then she breathed, "Me too. You know, Ryker, you're nothing like what I expected. This was... nice."

"It was." He raked a hand through his brown hair. "Have a good day."

"You too."

Later that night, as Ryker replayed their conversation, he tried to picture the vampire. Was her hair dark like his or light like his mother's? She must have had the same black eyes that all vampires did, but what did her face look like? Was it round or heart-shaped? Was she tall or short? Curvy or slim or somewhere in between?

Even as he considered the possibilities, he rolled over and buried his face in the pillow. It didn't matter what she looked like. Not really.

All that mattered was that the vampire was occupying more and more of his thoughts.

THE NEXT DAY, after lunch, Celeste connected Ryker with Valentina. "Good afternoon, Ryker. I'm so glad we get to chat again."

"Likewise." He opened his notebook and turned to the page where he'd been keeping notes about the fae. "I find it interesting that we've never crossed paths before."

There weren't millions of fae in the Republic of Balance, and even fewer ran in the upper echelons of society. Unlike the other species that called this continent their home, the fae hadn't always existed here. Their ancestors had made the Great Migration from the Obsidian Coast after a series of natural disasters had destroyed much of their land. They'd brought technology with them and shared it willingly. Their technological advancements had shaped the Republic into the country it was and earned the fae seats on the Council of Representatives.

The Republic of Balance was divided into five regions. Each had a Representative from each species. These formed a council, which was ruled over by the Chancellor. The position used to be elected, but that hadn't been the case for several hundred years.

"It is strange, isn't it?" Valentina hummed pensively. "I must admit, Mother was a little... strict with my upbringing."

"I can relate to that." Ryker's mother wouldn't be considered warm by any stretch of the definition.

"It's ironic, considering Mother's position, but she doesn't like the press," Valentina said. "She wouldn't let anyone take pictures of me, and I spent most of my youth in private schools."

Ryker palmed his neck as memories of running from the press flashed through his mind. After dealing with the fallout of the storm, he learned the value of privacy. He probably would've started living at work if it weren't for his dog.

The last thing he had wanted was to run into one of the so-called journalists from the Daily Dragon or any other news outlet in the Republic of Balance. They fed off salacious information like starving sharks. He was certain that if given the chance, they would drag his family through the mud.

He sighed. "That, I understand. The press is—"

"Awful," Valentina interjected, at the same time that Ryker said, "Terrible."

Ryker didn't trust the press. They always asked questions about his family, always wanting information, and they never took "no" for an answer. He'd always been worried they would pierce through his shroud of privacy and destroy everything he'd carefully built.

Valentina snorted. "Yes. The press is a… necessary evil."

He wasn't sure they were necessary, but they were a part of life. Every Representative and their family dealt with them.

Settling back in his seat, Ryker twisted the top of his pen. "I'm glad we finally had the opportunity to meet." He liked Valentina's frankness. "Where did you go to school?"

"Mother wouldn't settle for anything less than the best. When I was six, she enrolled me in prep school," Valentina continued, telling Ryker all about how she attended Highmountain's School for Young Fae, a renowned preparatory school for girls in Golden City.

The Chancellor's daughter was everything a Representative's wife should be—well-educated, polite, and of a good pedigree. Ryker knew his mother would be overjoyed if he brought someone like her home.

But even though he tried to focus on Valentina and learn more about her, every so often, Ryker's mind slipped back to Brynleigh. He wanted to know more about the vampire, too.

Two weeks had passed since the Choosing started. Ryker stepped out of the shower, rubbing a towel over his hair as he mentally prepared for the day ahead.

Who knew dating was so exhausting? They weren't even leaving the Hall of Choice yet, for the gods' sake. But apparently, being emotionally and mentally available for days on end took a toll on one's body that was similar to the most stringent military training.

Whenever his parents talked about their Choosing, they never mentioned being this tired. Ryker felt as though he'd scaled the Koln Mountains with his bare hands, not spent the past fourteen days talking to women.

To call the experience abnormal would have been an understatement. Ryker did not ask the women about their appearances—he wanted to maintain the integrity of the Choosing and was enjoying getting to know them without thinking about how they looked—but that didn't stop them from invading his dreams.

Especially one particular vampire.

Brynleigh de la Point was a frequent guest in Ryker's mind during all hours of the day and night. He couldn't stop thinking about her.

He learned more about her each time they interacted, but it was never enough.

The vampire captivated him and made him comfortable. He always desired more time with her. Their conversations were easy, and their dates always passed quickly. When they weren't together, Ryker thought about her.

A lot.

He thought about the way she'd feel beneath his hands. About her body beneath his, pressed against a mattress. About the way she'd taste. About the sounds she'd make as he made her his in every way.

Ryker was becoming a master of listening. He'd learned that Brynleigh often sucked in a breath when she was surprised by something, that she laughed rarely, but when she did, it was a beautiful sound, and that in the morning, her voice was rougher than when they met in the afternoons.

He yearned to hear that voice after a night in his bed, hoarse from calling out his name as he spent himself inside her.

Ryker tugged on jeans and a navy sweater, turning to face himself in the mirror.

"You have it bad," he told his reflection.

Ryker hadn't officially made a Choice, but his decision was

becoming clearer every day. It wouldn't be long before he knew which woman he wanted.

Pleased with his appearance, Ryker headed to the ballroom.

Matron Cassandra was waiting for him, standing next to the guards who had become commonplace around the Hall of Choice. The rebels hadn't attacked again, but Ryker had repeatedly overheard the soldiers discuss unrest throughout the Republic.

The Matron bounced on the balls of her feet, and the corners of her eyes crinkled as she smiled up at him. "It's ready," Cassandra whispered, her head barely coming up halfway on Ryker's chest. "She's going to love it."

Last night, he'd asked the Matron if he could send a gift to one of his dates. Evidently, Cassandra was a romantic because she'd eagerly agreed.

"Do you think so?" Ryker was surprisingly nervous about this, which was strange. He'd given hundreds of gifts throughout his lifetime, but none had meant as much as this.

"Absolutely." The Matron nodded enthusiastically. She clasped Ryker's larger hand between her wrinkled ones and squeezed. "Young man, if that beautiful vampire doesn't already feel something for you, this will certainly push her in the right direction."

He hoped she was right. "Thank you, Matron."

Grinning up at him, Matron Cassandra released Ryker's hand and tapped him affectionately on the arm. "Go get your girl."

He couldn't help but smile as he entered the ballroom and grabbed his headphones. As had become his routine, Ryker ordered a coffee while Celeste informed him his date was incoming. He picked up a breakfast sandwich and went to what had become *his* hammock.

The item he'd asked Matron Cassandra to procure was waiting for him on the table. His grin widened. It was perfect.

He slid into the hammock, getting comfortable while balancing his coffee.

Today, the visual wall was taking them on a tour of a desert garden in the Southern Region. It was filled with vibrant flowers that ranged from the darkest of blues to the lightest of yellows. He was certain each shade had a name, but he didn't know what they were. Still, the garden was relaxing, and tension left Ryker's body as he waited for his date to begin.

He'd finished chewing by the time the classical music clicked off. He sat forward, almost falling out of the hammock in his haste to talk to Brynleigh. He felt like a schoolboy who had sent his crush a note, except... not. This was far bigger than that.

Reminding himself that he was a fully grown, Mature fae who was more than capable of conversing with the woman he had feelings for, Ryker cleared his throat. "Good morning, Brynleigh."

"Morning, Ryker." The smile in her voice was evident. "How did you sleep?"

"Well, thank you." Wondering where all his confidence had gone, he quickly added, "I sent you a gift. It should be on the table next to you."

"Really?" She hummed, and he pictured her searching for it. It didn't matter that he didn't know the shape of her body or the color of her hair because he was getting to know *her*.

He knew the moment she saw it because she inhaled sharply. "Oh, Ryker. A chess board."

His lips twitched as he reached over and picked up the matching one. "Not just any board. It's part of a set. The pieces are holographic, and I thought we might..."

"Play together?" She finished the sentence for him.

Gods, how was it possible that they were already in sync? It felt like they'd spent a lifetime together. "Exactly."

"I don't know, Captain," she teased. "What will you do when you lose?"

A chuckle started deep in Ryker's chest and rumbled through him. "Sweetheart, you don't know this about me yet, but I don't lose." He slid his finger down the side of the board and pressed the hidden button. It lit up, and he added, "Ever."

She snorted as black and white pieces appeared, flickering before stabilizing. "Maybe that used to be true, but now you've met me. You should get used to losing, Ryker. You'll be doing it a lot in the future."

"Cocky much?" Smirking, he settled the board on his lap.

"Only when I know I can win."

Ryker grinned, watching the board carefully as Brynleigh made the first move. “Game on.”

CHAPTER 11

My Programming Does Not Allow Me to Discuss That

Two weeks later, the Choosing was at the one-third mark. Ryker stretched out his legs before him as he got comfortable on the couch.

It was late morning, and he'd been chatting with Valentina for over an hour. This was their fourth encounter that week. She'd spent most of that time talking about her favorite stores in the Red Plaza, an upper-class district in Golden City.

"Enough about me," Valentina eventually said. "What do you do when you're not hard at work, Captain?"

Thank the gods, they were done with fashion. It wasn't that Ryker didn't appreciate good clothes—he admired the female body as much as the next man and recognized how certain garments highlighted curves and beauty—but he didn't care about fashion.

Leaning back, he closed his eyes. "Depends," he said after a minute.

"Oh?" Valentina purred. "On what?"

"On whom I'm with."

The fae laughed, but there was something strange about the sound. It was nothing like Brynleigh's and didn't make him feel anything inside.

Valentina was nothing like Brynleigh.

Over the past month, Ryker had slowly whittled his way through the other women, landing on these two as his best potential matches.

If he were smart, he would Choose Valentina. He knew that. On paper, she was the right wife for him. She was everything a proper partner should be. Well-educated, mannered, and already familiar with the way Representatives lived. He could hear his mother's voice in the back of his head, urging him to pick the Chancellor's daughter.

Valentina would produce heirs, which Brynleigh couldn't do since vampires didn't procreate. If he chose her, the Waterborn line would continue, mingling with the prestigious Rose line. Their children would be powerful, prominent members of society.

Theoretically, Valentina Rose was perfect.

Except every time Ryker spoke with the fire fae, he couldn't help but compare her to Brynleigh. They had nothing in common. Brynleigh was real in a way that Valentina wasn't. The vampire pulled on a part of his heart that no one else had ever touched.

Some of the other men had already chosen favorites. Therian and the shy Hallie spent every waking minute talking. Phillipe had taken an interest in Trinity, the werewolf. A few others were still dating several women, while it seemed some men weren't making the connections they desired.

"On a perfect day without work, one where the sun was shining, what would you do with me?" Valentina asked.

He knew what an ideal day would look like if he were alone. His days were regimented down to the minute when he was at work. Everything, from when he stepped onto the army base to when the gates closed behind him, was accounted for. When he was off, he preferred not to do anything strenuous. He liked to play games, relax with his dog, and watch sports with his friends.

Ryker knew Valentina well enough at this point to know she'd never be okay with that. If he Chose her, his life would be filled with endless parties, enormous credit-card bills, shopping, stuffy dinners, and high-society events. He'd never have a night off or a chance to play chess or relax.

He was exhausted thinking about it.

Taking a long drag of his liquor-laced coffee, Ryker rubbed his temples. "If I were with you, I'd probably wake up early and make you breakfast with all your favorite foods."

"Mhmm, I like the sound of that," Valentina hummed.

He figured she would. "After that, I'd take you shopping and let you buy whatever you wanted."

Ryker's mother, Tertia, and his sister, River, had expensive tastes and often went shopping together. It was one of the only times they weren't fighting. Although he hadn't joined them since the storm, Ryker often heard about their expensive escapades during family dinners.

He was certain Valentina would get along with them. She seemed like the type of woman with expensive taste who spoke eloquently and would enjoy the finer things in life. If Ryker picked Valentina, she would fit into the life his mother wanted him to live.

But was it the life he wanted?

A sigh of delight filled his ears. "Ryker, baby, you know the way to my heart."

It wasn't that difficult. The more Ryker talked to the fae, the more he realized the only two things she cared about were herself and money. Not that there was anything inherently wrong with either of those, but evidently, incompatibilities were rising between them.

Before Ryker could delve into his plans for dinner—he would take Valentina to an upscale restaurant with a chef's table, where they could watch their food being made in person—his headset dinged.

"Your date will be over in sixty seconds, Captain Waterborn," Celeste said.

A rush of something that could only be described as relief ran through Ryker. It caught him off-guard. He'd never felt this way after a date with Valentina before.

Raking a hand through his hair, Ryker groaned. This process was far more arduous than he'd ever expected. He never thought that the Choosing would leave him with such complicated feelings.

"Ryker?" Valentina's voice held an edge of sharpness, and he jolted. She must have been calling him. Irritated, she asked, "Did you hear me?"

By the Black Sands, he hadn't been paying attention at all. However, thanks to his mother and sister, he knew enough about the feminine condition to know that admitting to *that* particular flaw wouldn't go over well.

Instead, he said, "This conversation was enlightening, Valentina."

She paused, then sighed, "I hope we can talk again soon."

Ryker didn't answer. He couldn't lie to her and say the conversation had been nice. It had begun that way, but now, his stomach was in knots. Would Valentina be a good partner for him? He was having some serious doubts. If he Chose her, he'd always be doing something. Always be on display. With Valentina as his wife, Ryker would have no hope of privacy and quiet.

He wasn't certain he could live with that.

He could practically hear her frowning through the headphones. "Ryker—"

Strands of violin music swallowed the remainder of her words, freeing him from having to deal with the rest of that conversation.

Thanking all the gods for their perfect timing, Ryker rose from the couch and strode to the bar. On his way there, he counted the number of guards. They'd doubled during his date. Not only that but their faces were pinched with worry.

Ryker ordered another coffee, frowning as he scanned the room. Something was off. He could feel it in his gut.

Taking his drink, he made his way over to the red hammock.

"Celeste?" He summoned the AI.

"Yes, Captain?"

"There are more guards here than normal." He placed the coffee on a red coaster.

The AI said, "If you say so, sir."

"I can count, so yes, I know there are double. Why are there more guards here?"

A strange clicking sound came through the headphones, but there was no response. Ryker's lips slanted down. Had she misheard him?

He repeated the question.

After a moment, Celeste replied, "I am not at liberty to discuss the outside world with participants of the Choosing."

"I'm aware." His fingers twitched, and he wished for his phone.

Damn the technological blackout forced on Choosing participants. "Still, can you give me an update on the riots?"

This morning, he'd overheard several guards discussing the ongoing unrest.

"My programming doesn't allow me to discuss that," Celeste said curtly.

He scrubbed his face. "What about the unrest in the region?"

"My programming doesn't allow me to discuss that."

Ryker groaned. He fought the urge to rip off the headphones and fling them against the wall. "What's happening with the lower classes?"

"My programming doesn't allow me to discuss that."

Again and again, no matter how he worded his questions, she gave him the same response. It was infuriating. He got nothing out of the AI. That knot within him twisted tighter and tighter, sending sharp shooting pains through him.

What was happening outside these walls? He knew his family was safe—they were well-guarded, as were all Representatives and their loved ones—but what about the rest of the Republic?

When it became apparent Celeste wouldn't answer his questions, Ryker abandoned this course of action. This line of questioning wasn't getting him anywhere, and his tolerance for hearing the same answer had rapidly become non-existent.

By the time Celeste's too-chipper voice informed Ryker that his date was incoming, he'd devised a plan. After this, he'd speak with one of the guards and see if he could use his position in the army to gain information. The plan was solid, and he felt confident in it.

The music faded, and a sense of peace instantly washed over Ryker. He closed his eyes and settled into the hammock. Unlike the early days, when his date was a mystery, he knew Brynleigh was waiting for him on the other end of his headphones.

He greeted her, his voice filled with happiness that hadn't been present during his conversation with Valentina.

"Hey," she breathed. "I missed you."

Any remaining tension Ryker had felt from Celeste's non-responses melted away. It was always like this with Brynleigh. Everything flowed between them. They'd played several chess games and were tied with three wins each. Ryker learned more about the vampire every time they faced each other. Not only was she funny, but she was thoughtful, strategic, and surprisingly fierce.

"I did as well," he murmured. "How was your day so far?"

She sighed but didn't answer. That wasn't like her. She was quick-witted and often made him laugh. Today, though, something was different.

"Brynleigh?" He opened his eyes and stared at the winter garden separating them.

"I... didn't sleep well last night," she admitted after a moment.

A growl rumbled through his chest, and he clenched his fists. "What happened? Did someone say something to you?"

If they hurt her, he'd find them and make them pay.

Once again, she paused.

Ryker hated that he couldn't see Brynleigh right now. Was there indecision or fear in her eyes? Or worse, hurt? Was she curled in a ball on the couch, or was she pacing?

His brain had constructed an image of her, faceless and shapeless, and he wanted to fill in the blanks. He wanted to know more about her...

He wanted to know everything.

Big things and little ones, he valued everything Brynleigh shared. Each tidbit of information was a jewel he would cherish forever. No matter how much time they spent together, it was never enough for him. He always wanted more.

At that moment, Ryker realized he couldn't see Valentina again. His feelings for Brynleigh were far more potent than anything he had with the fae.

"No one hurt me," Brynleigh assured him. "I had a nightmare. It's... I get them a lot."

His chest tightened as visions of this vampire waking up screaming in the middle of the night ran through his head.

He'd had his fair share of nightmares, both due to his job and his father's illness. Waking up alone, tangled in sheets, was horrible.

"I'm sorry." His voice was rough, and his arms ached with the desire to hold her. "Do you want to tell me about them?"

A bitter laugh came through the headphones. "Why would you want to hear about my bad dreams?"

His brows tented, and he leaned forward. "Because they bothered you, sweetheart, and I care a great deal about you."

If he was honest, he could see himself more than liking Brynleigh. She made it easy for him to care about her.

This was the first time he had admitted to having feelings for the vampire out loud. He thought it would scare him to say something like that, especially after spending so many years without participating in the outside world, but it didn't.

His heart sped up as he waited for her response.

Their match was unorthodox. Ryker was the first to admit that fae and vampires didn't traditionally get along. But something about Brynleigh made him feel as if he could relax about the rules he so often followed, and the world wouldn't fall apart around him.

She hitched a breath, and when she spoke, her voice was quieter than before. "Ryker—"

"You know if I said it, it's true." He inhaled. "I—"

The ground beneath him trembled. A massive *boom* echoed. The walls rattled. Someone screamed, the sound audible despite the supposedly noise-cancelling headphones.

Jumping off the hammock, Ryker smoothly fell into a fighting stance. He called out, "Brynleigh?"

Harsh, abrupt static was the only thing he heard.

Time seemed to slow as the air in the ballroom shifted. Gone was the lightheartedness from earlier, and in its place was tense anticipation and worry.

Another tremor shook the ground. This one was worse than the last. A crack appeared on the floor in front of him.

"Earthquake!" someone yelled.

Again, Ryker shouted for Brynleigh, but there was no response. He tried Celeste next, but nothing happened.

"Fuck." He clenched his fists.

This was bad.

Philippe, the Earth Elf, dropped to the ground a few feet away. He ripped off his headphones. Tendrils of emerald magic slipped from his hands, and he placed his palms flat on the marble. The ribbons sank into the ground and disappeared.

Less than a minute later, Philippe raised glowing green eyes and shook his head. "No, this isn't an earthquake. The land has nothing to do with this."

A third tremor ripped through the building. This one was different from the first two. Closer. It stretched on and on.

Ryker's heart thundered as he fell back on his military training. He hurried towards the guards. The soldiers were already shouting orders at each other. Therian was picking up shards of glass where they'd shattered near the bar.

An ear-piercingly loud siren blared.

The image on the dividing wall shuttered, pixelating before transforming into a flashing red screen.

"Code Orange, Code Orange." Celeste's amplified voice came through a dozen hidden speakers. "Everyone within ten miles from the Hall of Choice must take cover immediately."

Ryker's blood was ice in his veins. He'd memorized these codes early on and knew them backward and forwards. Golden City was under attack.

His fingers twitched, and his magic pulsed in his veins. He needed to be out there fighting, not standing in some grand ballroom.

Ryker ran to the nearest guard. "I'm Captain Waterborn of the Fae Division." He rattled off his identification number. "What's happening?"

The guard's name tag read Orion. "I know who you are, Captain." Orion's voice was as harsh and unforgiving as his eyes. He was a military man through and through. "We're under strict orders to move all participants to the bunkers until the attack has passed."

Frustration was a churning storm within Ryker. They wanted him to sit this out like a civilian. That went against everything he believed in. "No. I can fight."

"Me, too," Therian growled, coming up behind Ryker. Black scales rippled on the shifter's skin, and his eyes flashed. His dragon was close to the surface."Let me out; I can shift."

Orion said, "No. Today, you are nothing but men going through the Choosing."

Therian swore. "You can't do that."

"We can," said Orion smoothly. "You agreed to it when you entered.

"These are obviously extenuating circumstances," Ryker said through clenched teeth.

The guard's face was as firm as stone. "I have my orders."

Clearly, Orion wouldn't budge. On one hand, Ryker respected that. On the other, worry coursed through him. Static still crackled through the headphones.

Another guard walked up, holding black strips of cloth. "I have them, sir," he said to Orion.

"What the hell?" Therian growled, exchanging a look with Ryker. "What's going on?"

The new guard, whose tag read Johnson, said, "We must take you to safety."

"We—" Ryker started, but Orion cut him off. "You cannot help," the guard said, his voice leaving no room for discussion. "The details of the attack are not for you to know. Outside these walls, you may be members of the military, but here, you are one of the twenty-four we are meant to protect."

Ryker snarled. His water magic bubbled up, demanding he fight.

A woman screamed somewhere on the other side of the wall.

Another yelled, "I'm not putting that on."

"Yes, you are," was a soldier's harsh, curt response.

The remainder of his words were muffled by distance, but another shriek echoed through the ballroom.

Ryker didn't think Brynleigh was the one yelling. She wouldn't do that. She'd probably bite someone who touched her without permission. And fuck if he didn't like that thought.

Not the time.

The siren continued to blare.

"We need to go." Orion turned to the participants, who were gathering around him. "You can't see the women. The integrity of the Choosing must be maintained."

Suddenly, the black strips of cloth and the woman's screams made sense.

"You're blindfolding us," Ryker said.

It was a statement, not a question.

"We are," Orion confirmed.

Another tremor shook the ground.

"No more talking. We need to go." Johnson clenched his jaw. "If anyone fights us, we'll tranquilize you. There's no time for chitchat."

Allowing someone to blindfold him and lead him into a bunker went against every single grain of Ryker's being. Control was part of the very fabric of who he was. It was the reason he was so good at his job, and giving it up was not easy.

But when another woman screamed, he stepped forward.

"Do me first." He took off his headphones and placed them on the table. "I won't fight you."

Relief flashed through Orion's eyes as he lifted the black cloth and secured it around Ryker's face. The thick material was manufactured specifically so that even beings with strong senses, like fae, vampires, and shifters, couldn't see out of it.

Once Ryker was blindfolded, the others quickly followed suit. Blaring sirens and faint screams accompanied the group as they entered the basement.

Another tremor hit as they descended below the Hall of Choice.

Death was in the air today.

CHAPTER 12
Unexpected Complications Arise

The bunker was freezing. Even though Brynleigh's blood ran cold, and the dropping temperature wouldn't kill her, she was uncomfortable. She could only imagine how bad it was for the others. She wore a thin violet t-shirt and workout leggings, not having dressed to spend the day underground.

A musty scent tickled her nostrils every time she inhaled, and a suspicious dripping sound came from nearby. At least there wasn't any tell-tale scurrying from mice or other rodents.

After the guards had blindfolded them—many of the women had cried and screamed during the process—they had led them down several flights of stairs. From what Brynleigh could tell from her limited information, they were deep underground in a cement room. If there were any lights, she couldn't make them out through the material they'd forced over her eyes.

Hours had passed since they descended into the bellies of the Hall of Choice. At first, a few women had cried. Some, like Esme, were stoic. In a display that confirmed how horrible Valentina was, the fire fae had verbally berated the guards, assuring them they would hear from her mother if the threat was fake.

Hallie had nearly passed out from shock. Now, the Fortune Elf rested her head against Brynleigh's shoulder. A shuddering sob occasionally ran through the smaller woman, but she seemed to have run out of tears.

The men were somewhere down here, too. Brynleigh could sense their presence, along with even more guards.

Another vampire must have been working with the soldiers. Their shadow magic crawled over Brynleigh's skin, and she sensed the presence of their darkness. They must have filled the bunker with shadows, adding another layer of security to keep the participants from seeing each other.

The guards had handed out protein bars and bottles of water, but they hadn't had anything for Brynleigh. She needed blood, and soon. Her stomach twinged, warning that hunger wasn't far off.

Instead of focusing on her need to feed because she couldn't do anything about it, she turned to Hallie. Keeping her voice low so no one else could overhear, Brynleigh asked, "How are you feeling?"

"I didn't See this," the Fortune Elf whispered hoarsely. "Mama told me I shouldn't Look ahead much while I was here in case I accidentally Saw my future husband. I shouldn't have listened to her. I should've walked the silver planes more often. If I'd known—"

Brynleigh reached out blindly and put her hand on what she thought was Hallie's knee. "You couldn't have changed anything. You heard the guards. The rebels attacked Golden City."

Brynleigh was surprised that it had taken them this long to attack a Choosing. It didn't take a genius to correlate the rebel attacks and the class disparity in the Republic of Balance. Issues were bound to arise, seeing as how the majority of the Republic suffered under the rule of the Council.

Even now, Brynleigh knew she and the other "commoners" were only Selected to take part in the Choosing to appease the citizens of the Republic. Valentina and the others whispered behind their backs, taking little care to hide how they felt about the women they deemed beneath them.

Still, it was frustrating that the rebels were causing problems during Brynleigh's Choosing. She'd spent years meticulously crafting her plan, and now everything was falling apart. This was an unexpected complication she'd rather not deal with... and wasn't the only one that had arisen.

Brynleigh and Ryker were forging a connection, which was her plan. What she hadn't seen coming was the way she couldn't stop thinking about him. He haunted her every minute of every day. Even while she slept, she thought about him.

The deep rasp of the fae's voice and the smoky quality that edged his words intrigued her. Her heart sped up while they talked, no matter how much she tried to stop it. Even though she imbibed blood daily, she couldn't get her fangs to stop aching.

Her body's reaction to Ryker was a problem, and she needed to fix it. He was supposed to want her, not the other way around.

Rule number six: let nothing distract you from your goal.

Today, Brynleigh had almost slipped up and told him about her nightmares. The words had been on the tip of her tongue. She'd been seconds away from admitting that when she slept, she dreamed of deadly waves and burning lungs.

The rebel attack stopped her just in time.

She needed to remember who Ryker was. What he'd done. Over the past month, he'd put on a good front of being a kind, caring man, but she knew the fae hiding beneath the surface was a cold-blooded killer. Her entire town was dead because of him.

Brynleigh was so caught up in remembering exactly why she hated Ryker that she didn't hear the guards moving at first.

"Can I have your attention?" a commanding voice came from the front of the room.

Silence fell. The bunker was so quiet that a pin dropping would have been as loud as a clap of thunder.

Brynleigh turned her head towards the voice. Hallie's fingers nudged hers, and she let the Fortune Elf lace their fingers together. Usually, Brynleigh refused to let anyone touch her like this, but between her friend's soft demeanor and earlier tears, she couldn't find it in her cold heart to refuse the elf.

The voice continued, "The situation has been contained, and it is safe to re-enter the Hall of Choice. The women will go first. Once you reach the residential sectors, head directly for your Lounges. The Matrons will be by shortly to deliver further instructions."

Hallie sagged against Brynleigh, her relief palpable. "Thank Kydona."

Brynleigh wasn't sure the mother goddess cared about the rebels or the Choosing, but she didn't say that. If Kydona brought Hallie peace, then that was all that mattered.

The soldiers gave a few more instructions before helping the women to their feet. They were herded out of the bunker.

A door clicked behind them, and the same guard said, "You may remove your blindfolds."

Brynleigh ripped hers off, her vision adjusting quickly to the faint fluorescent glow from the lights ribbing the ceiling. There were no windows, but several doors lined the concrete, gray hallway.

The soldiers split in two, half traveling at the front of the group and the other half at the back as they led the women upstairs. No one spoke as they climbed five stories. Pinched lips, furrowed brows, and tired eyes were all around Brynleigh.

"Remember, straight to the Crimson Lounge," the guard at the front reminded them, his hand on the door to the main level of the Hall of Choice.

Once everyone had agreed, the guard turned the knob.

Then it happened.

One moment, Brynleigh was fine.

The next, her world shifted.

A coppery scent slammed into her.

She stumbled and crashed into the cement wall.

The delicious aroma of blood called to her. It took over her, pushing aside rational thought as if it had never existed.

Blood permeated the air. This wasn't a paper cut or some minor injury.

No.

Multiple people had bled out and died nearby. Not miles away, in some unknown location, but right outside the building. Death would forever mark this place.

Brynleigh's fangs burned. They were fire.

An animalistic, predatory growl rumbled through her, echoing in the stairwell.

It felt like sharp knives were stabbing into her stomach as she clawed at the cement wall.

Brynleigh wasn't hungry. She was *starving*. Had she ever known, truly known, the sensation of requiring sustenance before this point? She thought not.

This new need, this deep-set desire to feed, was so potent that Brynleigh was certain she would die if she did not drink blood. Right. Fucking. Now.

Somehow, her feet started moving. Shadows flooded out of her. Her heart sped. She snarled. Red tinged her vision.

She shoved her way past the guards in a blur and made it halfway down the main corridor before realizing where she was going.

An iron grip grabbed her arm and twisted.

"Someone get this vamp some blood!" the guard holding her yelled.

Brynleigh snarled, trying to shake him off. The sound of her anger was foreign and vicious, like a dog unwilling to give up its prized possession.

Somewhere deep inside her, the remnants of Brynleigh's humanity were being dragged away by the bloodthirsty monster living inside her. The need for blood was so intrinsically tied to her, such an essential part of her being, that she didn't know where the bloodlust stopped, and she began.

She was becoming a creature of the night, through and through.

Brynleigh struggled to hang onto the thin strands of her control. At war with herself, she barely paid attention to her surroundings.

Someone shoved a bag of blood in her direction. The guard loosened his grip just enough so she could drink. It wasn't enough.

Her hunger was a steep cliff, and she teetered on the edge. Dancing between sanity and forever losing herself to the monster within her, she panted and growled.

That smell remained.

Another red bag was thrust in her direction.

She drank that, too.

It still wasn't enough.

Closer and closer, she danced to the ledge.

"Get a fucking grip!" someone screamed in her face.

Maybe she could bite them? They seemed angry. She wouldn't kill them. She just needed a little blood.

Brynleigh moved towards them, but that iron grip returned, this time around her waist.

"She's too young," the guard holding her said. "Little more than a Fledgling."

Shaking her head, Brynleigh tried to clear the fire in her fangs. If only she could shove this need aside, she could tell them it was fine. She was here for a reason. She couldn't lose control. Not yet.

But she was slipping, slipping, slipping away.

"I knew this bloodsucker would be a problem from the first day I met her," Valentina snarled.

Even through the bloodlust, Brynleigh recognized the horrible fae's voice.

Brynleigh's nostrils flared. She spun, growling and gnashing her teeth at the fire fae. "I'll kill you, bitch."

She'd have no remorse about it, either.

A flame appeared in Valentina's hand. "I'd like to see you try."

A snarl.

Someone kicked the back of Brynleigh's legs. She fell to the ground. A knee pressed into her back, forcing her to the ground.

Heartbeats.

So many gods-damned heartbeats. They got louder and louder until they were drums pounding painfully in Brynleigh's ears.

All these people had blood in them. Forget the dying ones outside. She could get what she needed here. She'd kill them all, starting with the one glaring at her with malice.

Deep inside, Brynleigh recognized this was a monumentally bad idea, but she couldn't remember why.

Feed.

The word echoed through her mind. Her body. Her spirit.

Feed, feed, feed.

People kept talking, but their voices were hard to hear beneath the pounding of the life-giving organs surrounding her.

"I can... it'll knock..."

"Do it." The order came from the guard, forcing Brynleigh to remain down.

Valentina shouted, "Let her..."

Something sharp pierced Brynleigh's skin.

An agony-filled scream burst from the vampire's lips.

Flames ran through her from the point of injury, burning her from the inside out.

Someone shouted. A softer, friendly voice cried out. Brynleigh's mind swam as she fought for control.

Then she tumbled headfirst into blessed darkness.

SOMETHING soft and pillowy was beneath Brynleigh. Yawning, she stretched her arms and arched her back. The softness surrounded her, and she decided she was on a mattress. A very cloud-like mattress, one covered in silken sheets and pillows. That was strange. She wondered where she was, but the moment she tried to think, a low throb started at the back of her mind.

That was not a good sign.

Even though she was in an unknown location, Brynleigh didn't feel tense. If anything, she felt... at peace. That was strange. She hadn't known a moment of peace since her family's passing.

Leaving aside the problem of where she was for another moment, Brynleigh cracked open her eyes and looked around. As suspected, she was on a bed. It was large and could hold several people comfortably. Massive windows stretched across two of the four walls, a black tint blocking the sun's dangerous rays.

Fuck, she missed the sun and its warming embrace. The way its yellowed fingers touched her face. The light it cast on the world around her. She'd only been a vampire for six years, yet she already longingly remembered the natural light she would never see again.

Because creatures of the moon had no business being in the sun.

Turning from the windows, she took in the rest of the space. High ceilings, elaborate crown molding, and golden picture frames spoke to a level of grandeur to which she was unaccustomed.

Maybe she *should* worry about where she was because this was not her home or anywhere she'd ever been.

Something urgent pressed at the back of Brynleigh's mind, begging her to remember. She tried to unearth the memory, but it remained out of her reach.

Then the doorknob twisted.

Instantly, Brynleigh was on high alert. Her heart thundered in her chest. Shadows were a sheet of darkness as they poured out of her. She kneeled on the mattress, and her wings formed effortlessly on her back. Peeling back her lips, she exposed her fangs.

Who dared sneak up on her?

Something slid across her thigh, and she glanced down, her eyes widening. Why was she wearing a thin black slip? This was far from her usual nightwear of choice: a tank top and shorts.

The door creaked open.

Her attention snapped back up.

"Brynleigh, are you awake?" a deep smokey voice asked.

That voice. It spoke to the deepest parts of Brynleigh and echoed in her soul. Her core twisted, and she stared at the shadowy figure entering the room. He was cast in darkness, and though she tried, she couldn't make out his features.

For some reason, that didn't bother her.

When she didn't respond, he said, "Sweetheart?"

Safe.

That was the first thing she felt when he spoke. This man, whoever he was, was a haven. He wouldn't hurt her. She wasn't sure how she came to this conclusion, but she knew it in the marrow of her bones.

"I'm right here," she breathed. She retracted her wings and called her shadows back. They were always present, always ready, but she didn't need them here.

Peace radiated all around her.

But she was forgetting something. It was important, this piece of her mind that had slipped away. There was something about this man with the deep, smoky voice, and the two of them...

She searched and searched, trying to shove past the strange mist clouding her mind, but she couldn't remember why she shouldn't trust him. She fought against her mind and sought the missing memories, but they remained out of her reach.

His hand trailed down her back. "What's wrong?"

The bed dipped as he kneeled behind her. She could see their reflection in the blacked-out windows but couldn't make out his face. He was bigger than her, taller by almost a head and bulkier. His ears were pointed, but she couldn't seem to focus on his individual features.

"I... I don't know," she admitted quietly. "I'm missing something, and my brain hurts."

What had begun as a low throb was now a rhythmic ache. Her fangs bothered her, and there was a need present within her that she had trouble identifying.

"Let me help you," the mysterious man murmured.

But was he mysterious? Not really.

His voice... she knew his voice. It had haunted her dreams. The inflections, the way he hummed, the hitch in his breath when he spoke of something personal.

She knew *him*. Of that, she was certain.

They'd been... together? That mist formed a firm wall, slamming down on her memories before she could remember much of their relationship.

Before she could think through the ramifications, Brynleigh nodded. "Alright. You can help me."

The moment the words left her lips, the world around her swirled. She blinked, and everything had changed. The grand room was gone, and in its place, floor-to-ceiling windows looked out over a moonlit bay. Pine trees hugged the bay, their green branches swaying in the night breeze. Stars shone brightly, day having suddenly given way to night, and the full moon cast its silver glow on the water.

The gilded room was gone, and a cozy log cabin was in its place. The bed was sturdy, a lush carpet covered the floor, and she peeked a claw-foot tub in the bathroom through an open door.

"What?" Her brows creased. "How is this happening?"

This wasn't real... right? It couldn't be real. And yet... It felt real. She'd never felt anything more real than this.

That same hand trailed up her spine, each touch blazing a fiery path as he ran his fingers over the thin silk of her slip.

"You needed me, so I came," he said as if it was that simple. As if she knew exactly who he was, and they had something deep between them. "I'll always come for you, sweetheart."

Did Brynleigh need him?

She rarely needed anyone, but if he said she did, maybe he was right. Maybe he knew her and could tell her what she was missing. It certainly sounded like they had something between them.

And the way his fingers caressed her back...

His touch, though foreign, was comfortable. Protective. It was like he cared about her.

She leaned into him, needing more.

"Do you like that?" His breath warmed her ear and sent tingles running down her spine.

She hummed her approval, and his lips ghosted over her bare shoulder.

"Fuck, you taste divine," he murmured, a baritone rasp edging his voice. "Like the night and shadows and everything I've been missing in my life."

He kissed her other shoulder.

She shivered beneath his touch.

"I've been dreaming about this," he whispered. "The way you feel, your smell, your taste. All of it."

She exhaled a shaky breath, and her heart raced. Her fingers gripped the sheets. "And what do you think now?"

His lips skimmed her back, settling in that spot where her shoulder blades came together. "I think my dreams didn't do you justice."

His hand landed on her hip, grounding her and holding her still as his mouth trailed down her back. Everywhere he touched felt like it was on fire.

Brynleigh had had her fair share of sexual partners before, but none of them had ever made her feel like this. Flames licked her insides, warming her always-cold veins. Her fangs throbbed. Unbidden, a deep-set need rose within her. To bite. To feed. Not to inflict pain but to share pleasure.

Fuck, she wanted more.

She needed it.

Moaning, Brynleigh's head landed on his shoulder, and her eyes fell shut.

"That's it, sweetheart," he said encouragingly, nibbling on her ear. "Let me take care of you."

Brynleigh probably should've fought him more. She should've tried to push past the fog and remember his name. Maybe if she'd wondered why she knew his voice but didn't know what he looked like, she would've realized this was a bad idea.

Except, she didn't care. If this man, whoever he was, made her feel safe, she would revel in that feeling for as long as it lasted.

Brynleigh nodded. Keeping her eyes closed, she inhaled deeply. He smelled of thunderstorms and bergamot, and the scent only made her fangs hurt even more.

She wanted to bite and taste him like he'd tasted her, but something told her doing that would bring this all to a sudden end.

She really didn't want to do that.

His hand tightened on her hip, his grip firm but not bruising. He kissed her ear gently as his other hand slid down her side. His touch was gentle but firm as he reached the hem of her slip and slowly dragged the material up. He exposed the swell of her ass, brushing his knuckles over her bottom.

She shivered, the action having nothing to do with the cold.

He froze, his voice a rasping caress as he breathed, "Is this alright?"

"Yes," she half-pleaded, half moaned. "Please touch me."

They'd already started. Why stop now?

A familiar low chuckle rumbled through him as his hand slipped beneath her, reaching for her core. His fingers grazed her inner thighs, brushing the lace of her undergarments.

His touch was all too brief as he teased her.

His fingers danced close—so gods-damned close—to her intimate flesh, but not quite there. Tracing the edges of her underwear, he explored her slowly as though mapping out every part of her.

She rubbed against him, trying to get him where she needed him the most. If she knew his name, it would be on her lips.

"More," she whispered, not caring that she was close to begging this unknown man for everything.

His lips found her throat, and he nipped her. Heat coursed through her, and she moaned.

"More, what? I need to hear you say it, sweetheart."

Isvana have mercy on her, but her heart raced at his demand. She loved the way he was taking control.

Swallowing, she forced her mind to focus. "Touch me," she requested. "I need to feel your hands on me. In me."

"Thank fuck," he groaned.

He didn't make her wait. Pushing aside the lace, he exhaled gruffly as he touched her. "Gods, you're so wet. Is this for me?"

"Yes." She didn't know how she came to this conclusion. His name was a mystery, as was his face, but the ache in her core was for him as much as his presence was her haven.

Finally—*finally*—his thumb found her sensitive flesh.

At the first touch against her clit, Brynleigh panted.

He pressed harder.

She moaned.

The sound spurred him on, and he slipped a finger into her wet heat. She moved against him, his hand firm on her hip as he held her in place.

He was hard behind her, his impressive length pressing against her lower back, and he slowly pumped his finger in and out of her.

"You're so fucking perfect," he growled.

She needed more. As if he sensed it, he added another finger. They drove into her, giving her more and more. She writhed against him.

Pleasure built. The fog in her mind remained, but she no longer cared.

There was just this moment, her and the man whose voice made her feel safe, and nothing else.

She was so close. So coiled. So ready.

It had been far too long since she'd been with anyone, and she needed this man in a way she'd never needed anyone.

"Fuck yes, that's it," he said encouragingly. He kissed the corner of her lips, her jaw, her neck. "Let go, sweetheart."

He added a third finger, stretching her as his movements sped up.

Moaning, her fingers curled in the sheets as she chased her release. It was so close.

He kept speaking as he touched her. Telling her how much he dreamed of this. How much he wanted this. How good she felt pressed against him. He told her how he'd take her next, lay her beneath him, and let her feel his full weight. He would take care of her, giving her everything she needed.

There was a forcefulness in his voice, a dominance that Brynleigh usually didn't enjoy from partners.

But here? Now?

She would let him do whatever he wanted to her.

His thumb found her clit once more, and she screamed.

"I'm so close," she whimpered.

He released her hip. She didn't have time to mourn the lack of his touch because he tugged down the straps of her slip, exposing her breasts to the night air.

"Fucking beautiful," he breathed.

His fingers grazed her hardened nipples. Every touch, every twist of his skilled fingers against her pebbled flesh, brought her closer and closer to that cliff. She kept her head on his shoulder, her eyes closed, with her mouth opened in a soundless scream.

His lips grazed hers. It was feather-light, a winter breeze against her mouth, not a kiss. It was airy, and she wanted more.

"Let go, Brynleigh," he murmured. "I've got you."

And she did.

He held her, never stopping his sensual touch, as she finally careened off that precipice. Waves of pleasure coursed through her until she was limp in his arms.

He kissed her and laid her down on the bed. "Sleep, sweetheart. I've got you."

He wrapped his arms around her and held her tight.

She drifted off to sleep instantly, the land of dreams welcoming her with open arms.

CHAPTER 13
It Won't Happen Again

Brynleigh's brain pounded against the confines of her skull, making a valiant effort to escape. She groaned, and her eyes opened. That only made things worse. The pounding increased as she took in her surroundings. Her brows knit together.

Wooden rafters stretched high above her head, and the bed was decidedly less cloud-like than before. The scratchy mud-brown blanket covering her wasn't delightful either. She wiggled her toes, the material itchy on her bare feet. White cabinets stretched along one wall, and the air was frigid. Several shiny medical instruments were displayed, and a doctor's coat was on a rack nearby.

She was in an… infirmary. How did she get here? And perhaps more importantly, why was she here?

"Hello?" Her mouth struggled to form the words, her tongue heavy like she'd eaten sandpaper.

A woman in pale pink scrubs with raven hair appeared in Brynleigh's field of vision. Kind blue eyes, much like Brynleigh's had been before she was Made, peered at the vampire through a set of wide-rimmed glasses.

"Oh, good. You're awake." The woman unceremoniously grabbed

Brynleigh's chin and shone a thin, bright light into each of her eyes before nodding to herself. "Your vitals are strong."

"I'm sorry, but who are you?" Brynleigh would usually be more polite, but between the headache and the strange surroundings, gathering information seemed more important than manners.

The woman didn't seem to mind as she smiled. "You can call me Carin, dear. I'm the doctor who's been looking after you."

Doctor Carin crossed the room to a desk Brynleigh hadn't noticed before. She picked up a black phone that looked like it belonged several decades in the past and quickly dialed.

Whoever was on the other line must have answered right away.

"She's awake," the doctor murmured. "What do you want me to do?"

Narrowing her eyes, Brynleigh tried to focus her hearing on the voice coming through the phone line. It was faint, but she picked up a few words.

"... keep... until it's passed... the Chancellor says..."

Carin dipped her head. "Understood. Do you want me to knock her out again?"

Brynleigh's heart seized. She would *not* allow that to happen, even if it meant going against the doctor. She needed to remain alert and figure out what was happening.

The doctor glanced at Brynleigh. "No, she looks normal. Pale, but they all are."

Brynleigh's fingers grappled at the sheet as she struggled to find her last coherent memory. The doctor's words insinuated they'd already knocked her out once.

She didn't remember any of that. She didn't even remember putting on the black sweater that currently covered her arms.

Her mind swirled as she sought her missing memories. Evidently, she wasn't in the Hall of Choice. This room was too small and quaint to be part of the massive building in the middle of Golden City.

Brynleigh had been on a date with her mark when—

"Fuck," she groaned.

Everything came flooding back all at once. The rebels. The bunker. And then... the blood.

Squeezing her eyes shut, Brynleigh fought the urge to scream. She'd been so close to falling into bloodlust and ruining everything. And then after...

The dream.

Heat rushed through her core.

Bad.

This was monumentally bad. Terrible, even. Brynleigh couldn't wrap her mind around how awful this was.

She'd sought the man she planned to murder for comfort in her distress. And she'd let him touch her and bring her to immense pleasure.

No, terrible was too simple a word for this. Catastrophic. That was more fitting. Had she thought the way she reacted to his voice was problematic? That was nothing compared to this.

Brynleigh recalled what she'd called him: her safe haven.

Gods damn it all.

She wanted to bang her head against the wall but decided the doctor probably wouldn't receive the action well. Instead, she rubbed her temples and attempted to talk some sense into herself.

The captain was not her safe place. He was the pinnacle of everything dark and dangerous in her life.

Brynleigh needed to get her head checked because mentally sane people did not find the man who killed their family attractive, let alone dream about him bringing them to orgasm.

The doctor hung up the phone and met Brynleigh's gaze. "You've had quite an eventful few days." Carin's voice was soft, and there was a trace of kindness in her eyes. "They tranquilized you in Golden City and transported you here."

Brynleigh's heart tightened, and a cold sweat broke out on her forehead. "Am I..." She licked her lips. "Am I still in the Choosing?"

"You are." A gentle, practiced smile likely meant to help her patients feel at ease danced on the doctor's lips. It didn't quite work, but Brynleigh appreciated the effort.

"Where are we?"

"We're in a safe place, dear. Your Matron will explain more when you're better. We're on a warded compound, and no one will get to us here."

Brynleigh blinked, her mind whirling as it attempted to keep up with this new information.

"You should rest," continued the doctor. "Now that you're awake and I've checked your vitals, there are a few things I need to take care of."

Carin went to leave, but Brynleigh reached out and grabbed her hand.

"My things." Desperation coated the vampire's words as she remembered her folded picture. She'd left it in the Hall of Choice. "Are they gone?"

She almost didn't want to hear the answer. If she lost the picture...

Grief cut off her airways and stole her breath.

No.

Tears stung the back of her eyes.

Panic rose and rose within her. This couldn't be happening.

She grabbed her necklace, but it didn't help. The picture... she needed it. It was too important.

Oh gods.

Her heart raced.

A warm hand covered Brynleigh's, grounding the vampire. "Not to worry." A squeeze. "Everything was packed and brought with you."

It was here. Not lost.

Slowly, so slowly, Brynleigh's heart slowed. Her eyes shuttered, and she exhaled. "Thank you."

"Of course." Carin strode to the fridge and withdrew a few bags of blood. "You know, I've been watching the Choosing. For what it's worth, I'm rooting for you and Captain Waterborn. The two of you make a handsome couple."

With a wink, the doctor handed Brynleigh the blood and pulled on a coat. "I'll be back soon. You should sleep. The tranquilizer they gave you is still in your system. Rest will help."

Brynleigh didn't move as the door slammed shut behind Carin. It closed too quickly for Brynleigh to see anything except for the dark outline of a man's body. A guard, she assumed.

Brynleigh frowned. Her gaze darted between the blood and the phone on the doctor's desk. Judging by the ache in her fangs and the hollowness in her stomach, she needed to feed, but she had no idea how long the doctor would be gone. This was the first phone she'd seen in weeks, and after the dream she'd had...

She had a call to make. Her lips pursed, and she quickly ran a dozen scenarios through her mind. In the end, her decision wasn't difficult. She didn't have long and needed to act now.

Her mind made up, she slipped her legs out from beneath the scratchy blanket. Her bare toes curled as they pressed against the frigid wooden floor, and she wondered where her shoes had gone. She banished the thought. There were bigger problems at hand.

Participants of the Choosing technically weren't allowed contact with the outside world, but this was one rule she was willing to break. If someone came in, she'd think of an excuse.

Brynleigh perched on the edge of the desk, keeping an eye on the front door as she lifted the phone from its cradle. It was nothing like the sleek, rectangular cellphone she usually used. This one was larger than her hand and had a long, coiled black cord that hung off the side of the desk. It reminded her of the one on the kitchen wall growing up.

At the memory of her familial home, a surge of acerbic anger went through Brynleigh. That kitchen, with its bright sunshine yellow wallpaper with daisies and light blue cupboards, was gone.

Destroyed.

By *him*.

The same man whom she'd invited to touch her in her dreams.

Bitterness burned at the back of Brynleigh's throat, and her grip tightened around the phone. She'd been an idiot but wouldn't make that same mistake again.

This time, she'd follow the rules to a T.

The only good thing about the dream was that it hadn't been real. She was the only witness to her extreme lapse in judgment. No one else had seen her break the rules.

Never again, Brynleigh vowed.

That was the first and last time Ryker would ever touch her, in dreams or reality. She would never let her guard down around him.

He was her enemy.

Dialing the number she'd memorized years ago, Brynleigh brought the phone to her ear and waited for it to connect.

It rang twice before someone picked up.

"Hello?" Jelisette sounded angry.

Shit. Little was more dangerous than an angry vampire, especially one as powerful and old as Brynleigh's Maker.

Brynleigh shifted on the desk. Maybe this was a bad idea. Maybe her Maker didn't want her to check in.

It was too late now, though. She'd already called.

She kept her gaze locked on the door and whispered, "It's me."

Jelisette sucked in a breath. "Brynleigh?" Her voice was slightly less venomous, but the icy tone remained. "Where are you?"

"I don't know." Brynleigh shook her head before she realized her Maker couldn't see her. "There was an attack, and—"

"I know about that. It's all over the news," the older vampire snapped. "Rebels attacked the Chancellor's residence, triggering riots throughout Golden City. They're still being contained. Zanri and I evacuated to the Western Region."

Brynleigh's eyes widened. This was worse than she'd imagined. "Did a lot of people die?"

"They aren't reporting casualty numbers yet. What happened to you? The feeds to the Choosing went black when the first bomb went off, and they haven't come back online."

Brynleigh made a split-second decision not to tell Jelisette about almost falling into bloodlust. She'd never lied to her Maker before, but she didn't want a lecture about being more careful. Besides, guilt was already a blade jabbing her conscience. She didn't need Jelisette to tell her it was wrong, too.

"They moved us," Brynleigh whispered, cognizant of the guard outside. "I'm in a cabin, and the air is colder. If I had to guess, I'd say we're in the Northern Region."

"Find out," Jelisette ordered, her tone one Brynleigh had heard many times before.

"Hold on."

Holding the phone to her ear, Brynleigh hopped off the desk. The nearest window was behind her. The phone cord stretched as Brynleigh reached for the thick, black curtain. She inched back the fabric. If it was daytime, the tiniest touch of sunlight on her skin would be like burning alive.

Luckily, the moon glowed in the night sky.

Brynleigh exhaled and peeked out the window. Snow-covered pines were all around, and fresh snow fell from the starry sky.

"Yes, it seems we're in the north," she confirmed.

The Northern Region, previously known as the Kingdom of Eleyta, was the ancestral home of the vampires in the Republic of Balance. It struck Brynleigh as odd. How could a stunningly beautiful land be home to beings as deadly and cold as vampires?

The faint outlines of more buildings through the trees were cast in silver moonlight. Brynleigh described them as best she could until her Maker was satisfied.

"How is your relationship?" the older vampire asked next.

Brynleigh's stomach twisted, and despite her earlier vow, a pulse of pure want ran through her. She couldn't help it. The memory of Ryker's skilled fingers was so fresh.

"It's progressing well." She forced the words out of a dry mouth.

"Good girl," her Maker said. "You remember the rules?"

The ones that Brynleigh had obliterated? Yes. She remembered them far too well. If anything, she wished she could forget them. Anything so she could feel better about the dream she'd had.

How could something that felt so good be so bad?

"Brynleigh, answer me!" Cold steel edged Jelisette's voice. "Do you remember the rules, daughter of my blood?"

"Yes, ma'am," Brynleigh replied automatically. "I won't get attached, and I'll kill him on our wedding night the moment we're alone."

It didn't matter that the captain seemed like a good fae, or that he was kind to Brynleigh, or that he made her feel safe.

None of that mattered because he'd murdered her entire family in cold blood.

Brynleigh would do well to remember that. The captain had a nice exterior, but inside, he was still a bad man. She just... hadn't met that side of him yet. She was certain it was there, though. It had to be there. What other explanation could there be?

A branch snapped outside, and Brynleigh jolted.

"I have to go," she hissed.

Brynleigh hung up without waiting for a response. Drawing on her shadows, she sped across the room and climbed in bed. Ripping open the first bag of blood, she downed the crimson liquid. She was almost at the bottom of the bag when the door opened.

This time, the door remained ajar long enough to give Brynleigh a good look around.

A pair of guards dressed in black stood in front of the cabin. Their stances were wide, and guns hung off their belts. They meant business as they stared straight ahead into the wintery forest. Wherever they were, it must have been far in the north. Snow wouldn't hit Golden City until right before Winter Solstice, which was still several months away.

Doctor Carin strode inside, kicking the snow off her boots before shutting the door. She spoke quietly into a cell phone, barely glancing at Brynleigh as she grabbed a sheet of paper off the desk. The doctor dropped into the office chair with an audible sigh and spun it around so her back was to Brynleigh.

The doctor's murmurs filled the cabin as exhaustion slammed into Brynleigh. It was sudden and all-consuming. Keeping her eyes open was a struggle. She fought to remain alert long enough to finish the bag of blood before letting her head fall back on the lumpy pillow.

Sleep. That's what she needed. Quiet, peaceful, rule-following sleep. There would be no dreams of troublesome, dangerous captains this time. Brynleigh wouldn't allow it.

One day, she would be old enough for sleep to be part of her past. Some vampires were so ancient that they felt no aches and pains and no longer required rest like mortals. A few vampires who had lived several thousand years no longer needed blood.

Right now, Brynleigh felt so mortal that she couldn't imagine living for that long. She would take this one day at a time.

This time, nightmares of deadly storms and watery screams plagued her all night long.

CHAPTER 14

Breaking Rules and Guilty Consciences

"Where. Is. She?" Ryker bit out the words and crossed his arms. He channeled his mother and sent a withering glare at the soldier at the door, hoping it would loosen the man's tongue.

The guard shook his head. "I told you, Captain, I can't share that information with you. She's safe; that's all I'm authorized to say."

Safe, but not here in the library with the rest of them.

Ryker barely contained the growl rising in his throat. The past few days had been an absolute shit show, the likes of which he hadn't seen for several years.

After the rebels' attack, Matron Cassandra briefed the men. Her information had been minimal, at best. There was an attack. No, she didn't know if there were casualties. Yes, they were safe. No, she couldn't tell them anything else.

Frustrating.

After the meeting, they were given thirty minutes to gather their belongings. A dozen guards shuffled them onto an enormous blacked-out bus. The women were transported in another vehicle, and armed guards had made up the rest of their entourage. They'd driven through the night, crossing from the Central Region into the Northern one.

When the driver had pulled through looming stone gates and driven up a long circular driveway, red streaked the sky. They'd stopped in front of a brick three-story home that was nothing short of palatial. The estate was large, and at least one other building, barely visible through the pines, was tucked behind the main one.

When the bus had stopped, Matron Cassandra had explained that for security reasons, the Choosing would continue in this more secluded location. Representative Therald, one of the werewolf Alphas, had kindly donated his pack house for the remainder of the Choosing. A team had flown up a few hours earlier and prepared the house for them. They had installed the necessary technology to stream the remainder of the Choosing to the world and covered all the windows with blackout blinds to accommodate the vampires in their group.

"Chancellor Rose is adamant that the Choosing continue," Cassandra had said. "After all, it's more important than ever to remind the Republic that we are a united country."

After the Matron's speech had concluded, Ryker disembarked the bus with the others. He'd found his room, showered, and then collapsed on the bed. It had been an extremely long night. He had slept most of the day, emerging long enough to eat before returning to the comfort of his sheets.

That was yesterday, though.

This morning, he'd woken up with a strong desire to talk to Brynleigh. He needed to make sure she was alright.

Following the Matron's directions, he'd located the two-story library, where a hastily erected wall bisected the room.

Everything had been going as expected until he'd slipped on his headphones. The morning had rapidly deteriorated from there.

First, Celeste had connected him with Valentina. He'd explained, in no uncertain terms, that although he had enjoyed their conversations, he would pursue another option.

She hadn't taken it well.

At.

All.

Ryker endured Valentina's wrath for the better part of an hour. It was the longest sixty minutes of his life. She yelled, and he spoke to her calmly. She berated him, insisting he would regret this. He knew she was wrong. She swore. He sighed.

At least she confirmed he'd made the right decision.

When Celeste had informed him the meeting was over, relief had coursed through his veins. He couldn't wait to speak with Brynleigh and tell her he'd broken things off with Valentina.

However, after Celeste had disconnected him from Valentina, the AI informed him that Brynleigh was unavailable. Not talking to someone else.

Unavailable.

The word had echoed around in Ryker's mind, a battering ram against his senses. If Brynleigh wasn't there, where was she?

Worry had gnawed at his gut, which led him to this tense conversation with the guard at the entrance.

"Why can't I speak with her?" He waved the white headphones at the man. "What happened to her? Is she still in Golden City?"

"As I previously stated, all Choosing participants have journeyed to this new location," the guard said evasively.

Ryker's worry twisted and grew. What wasn't the guard telling him? Brynleigh was strong, but even vampires weren't infallible. He couldn't shake the idea that the guard was keeping something from him.

The other men's conversations were the quiet backdrop to the pounding of Ryker's heart.

"I have to see her," he insisted.

Ryker's muscles were rigid, and his jaw was tense from being clenched for so long. Some might say he was overreacting, but after the events of the past few days, a little overreaction might not be entirely out of place.

A vein feathered in the guard's jaw, and his eyes flashed. "Sir, you cannot see the women. It goes against the very structure of the Choosing. You must know we cannot allow it."

Ryker's fists curled. The urge to acquaint this soldier with his fist was close to overwhelming.

The only thing that stopped him was the red light on the bookshelf behind the guard's head. They were being recorded, and Ryker had no desire to deal with the aftermath of his actions if he punched the unhelpful soldier.

Footsteps clicked in the hall, and Ryker glanced over the soldier's shoulder. Wearing white from head to toe, Matron Cassandra approached the library. She touched the guard on the arm and whispered in his ear.

When they broke apart, the guard turned back to Ryker. "You're in luck. Miss de la Point is indisposed, but Matron Cassandra will deliver a note if you want to send her a message."

"What the fuck does that mean?" Ryker bit out.

"She's indisposed," the guard repeated unhelpfully.

Ryker growled. He had even more questions than before. He'd learned his lesson, though. There would be no getting information out of this soldier.

Instead, Ryker shifted and met the Matron's gaze. "You'll personally deliver the note?"

Cassandra pulled a black pen and a small notebook out of her pocket. "I will."

Ryker took them, rolling the pen between his fingers as a plan formed in his mind. It was risky, but he couldn't sit around and wait for someone to decide to update him on what was happening. He needed to take matters into his own hands.

"Very well. I'll write one up, and then I'd like to rest." Not a lie. He would like to rest. He just didn't plan on doing it right now. "If Brynleigh isn't here, I don't want to talk to anyone else."

Truth.

The Matron frowned. "There is no one else? It's highly irregular—"

"No." His voice was firm. "She's mine."

Even though Brynleigh didn't know it yet, it was true.

Both the Matron and the guard widened their eyes as if the claiming words caught them off guard. They didn't surprise Ryker, though. They'd slipped off his tongue as easily as his own name. Now that he'd parted ways with Valentina, he was ready to make it official with his vampire.

A smile tugged on the Matron's lips, and her eyes twinkled. "I see. Of course, Captain. You may return to your room."

"Thank you." He had no intention of doing such a thing, but he kept that to himself.

Instead, he took the offered pen and paper with a smile. He slipped into a wooden chair that creaked as he put his full weight on it. Hints of the ruby theme of the Choosing were scattered throughout the library—mugs, pillows, and a few red armchairs—but the room was a study in woodwork.

Everything from the bookshelves to the high ceiling and the polished planks on the floor were made of wood. It reminded him of the hunting cabin he kept outside Golden City. He'd bought it a decade ago, and after the Incident six years ago, it had become a refuge for him. He'd spent nearly as much time at the cabin as he did at his home in the city.

He hoped Brynleigh would enjoy it as much as he did.

Ryker penned the note with the speed of a man desperate for answers. He wasn't a youngling and was well aware that writing something in a letter didn't guarantee it would remain private. He purposefully kept his message vague. Folding it in half, he scrawled his vampire's name on the front before handing it to the Matron.

"I'll deliver this as soon as I'm done here," Cassandra promised.

"Thank you." Ryker dipped his head and made a show of departing. Nodding at the guard, Ryker slipped his hands in his pockets and nonchalantly strolled down the empty hall.

Instead of returning to his room, he ducked inside the first doorway and watched the library entrance.

He didn't have to wait long. The Matron exited a few minutes later, humming a tune as she walked away from Ryker. She clutched his note, her hips swaying as she made her way to the end of the hall and turned left.

Keeping his distance, Ryker trailed her. It wasn't difficult. She was a human, and he was a trained fae. Tracking her movements without being seen required minimal energy. They strolled past the guards stationed throughout the house, and none of them noticed him. He supposed he couldn't hold it against them. They were searching for external threats, not internal ones.

Still, if these were Ryker's men, he'd have a few words with them. Evidently, this "secure" location had more than a few security issues.

However, their lackluster guarding was playing into Ryker's favor at the moment.

He kept pace with the Matron through the house. She stopped at the kitchen and picked up a pear tart before descending two flights of stairs. She went down a plain, small corridor, lifting a knitted shawl off a hook on the wall. She wrapped it around herself and slipped out the door without a backward glance.

That was unexpected. Ryker had assumed the Matron would deliver his note somewhere within this house.

"What the hell?" he muttered, his eyes narrowing. "Where are you going?"

As the questions piled up and the lack of answers became even more glaring, Ryker took the stairs three at a time. He scanned the door, searching for an alarm, but he didn't see anything.

At this point, all plausible deniability on his part was gone. If he were caught, he'd have some serious explaining to do as to why he was sneaking about the pack house.

He couldn't be caught. It was that simple.

Ryker didn't want to go outside without any sort of weapon. He didn't know what was waiting for him on the other side of the door. Opening his palm, he reached within himself and summoned his magic. The water was always there, waiting for him. It came eagerly, and he pulled it from his veins, forming a dagger of ice.

Armed and ready to go, he gingerly touched the door handle. It was cool. He held his hand there, waiting to see if there was an alarm, but nothing happened.

He opened the door, and once he was certain the coast was clear, he stepped outside.

A bitter, icy gale slammed into him like a wall of bricks. The sun shone on a blanket of white that covered everything in sight. The snow was beautiful when observed from inside, but outside, it was unpleasant at best.

He swore, rubbing his arms. His black t-shirt, jeans, and sneakers were not weather-appropriate. The ice dagger in his hand was a part of him, and the cold emanating from it didn't bother him. It was his magic, and it sang to him. But although he could hold his dagger for hours without his hand hurting, he wasn't impervious to weather conditions.

Still, there was no time to wait. He would have to put up with the cold. Picking up a rock from the side of the house, he jammed it inside the lock. Hopefully, the Matron wouldn't notice that the door didn't fully close if she returned before him.

The Matron's shawl flapped as she hurried through the trees, a flag leading him in the right direction. Ignoring the goosebumps crawling over his arms, he was a shadow as he trailed her.

A voice in Ryker's head chided him for breaking the rules as he prowled through the trees. This kind of behavior was wholly unlike him. He couldn't remember the last time he'd disregarded a regulation.

But it wasn't for him. It was for Brynleigh. It didn't matter that he'd only known the vampire for a month or that he'd never seen her. Ryker cared about her and would do anything to keep her safe, including going where he wasn't supposed to. Technically, they had never *said* the participants of the Choosing had to remain within the confines of the mansion, but it felt like an unspoken rule.

Birds chirped, and a squirrel hopped across branches, but he kept his eyes on the human ahead of him.

Several minutes passed before a small log cabin appeared through the trees. It wasn't very big, and midnight curtains were drawn shut. This small building was guarded, unlike the mansion side door he'd slipped out of. Two armed soldiers stood on a wooden covered porch. The Republic's insignia was on their chests, and they each held large guns as they scanned the forest for threats.

Ryker swore and ducked behind a tree, flattening his palms on the rough bark. Of course, there were guards here who seemed to be doing their jobs. Were they here because of Brynleigh? Perhaps more importantly, were they keeping her safe or holding her against her will?

He wasn't sure, but he would find out.

He would have to be patient. Years of military service had drilled into him the benefit of forbearance. He would discover what happened to Brynleigh, but he had to be smart about it.

Ryker studied the cabin, ignoring how the icy wind burned the skin on his bare arms. Although they were armed and seemed to be paying attention, the guards' relaxed aura boded well for Ryker.

Using the trees for cover, he slowly circled the building on silent, trained feet. There were six windows and two doors, one at the front and one at the back.

The latter was unguarded. A spark of hope came to life within him. He circled the cabin twice more, taking in all the details through analytic eyes.

Adjusting his grip on his ice dagger, he snuck towards the back door. The knob was cold, and it didn't budge as he wiggled it. Locked.

He huffed, and his nostrils flared. That would've been too easy.

In case the guards were in the habit of walking the perimeter, Ryker hurried back to the trees and crept around to the front to keep watch.

A few minutes later, Matron Cassandra re-emerged. She stepped outside, nodding to the guards before returning to the mansion. Her hands were empty, and his note was nowhere to be seen.

Confident that his vampire was inside the building, Ryker exhaled and quickly formulated a plan. It was risky but the best way to get eyes inside.

Now, he had to wait. Leaning against a tree, he allowed the forest to conceal him until the right opportunity arose.

Minutes went by.

The temperature dropped. He rubbed his arms in an effort to conserve heat, although the action didn't do much good. His teeth chattered, and his skin prickled.

He refused to let the temperature bother him. He could warm up later. Something as trivial as being cold could not force him to abandon his post. He would wait as long as necessary.

Finally, after an hour, Ryker saw his chance.

"Mind if I grab a smoke and make a call?" The shorter guard stretched his arms above his head and cracked his back. "I should check on Marie. You know how pregnant women get when they don't hear from us."

The other man snorted. "Yes, I remember my sister's pregnancy. Thank all the gods, Justinian and I don't have to worry about that."

"Thanks, man. Be back soon." The first guard jumped off the porch and strode into the woods away from Ryker.

As soon as his companion was gone, the second guard relaxed and leaned against the wall.

This was Ryker's moment. He hurried to the back of the cabin and placed his dagger on the ground next to him. Though far more vigilant than the ones in the house, the guards hadn't bothered to check the back door in the time he'd been here.

Drawing another stream of water from his palms, Ryker froze it into a pick and angled it into the lock. If this were a regular icicle, it would have snapped as soon as he put pressure on it. Thank the gods; Ryker was one of the strongest water fae in the entire Republic of Balance. His powerful magic was malleable and would serve him well in this task.

Feeding strengthening magic into his improvised tool, Ryker jiggled the pick around in the lock. They didn't teach these kinds of tricks in the military academy, but he'd picked up a few things hanging around with Atlas.

The earth fae grew up in the streets and had several less-than-reputable, but helpful, skills. Ryker made a mental note to thank Atlas for teaching him how to pick locks when the Choosing ended.

Pressing his pointed ear against the frigid door, Ryker slowly moved his pick until the tell-tale *click* of locks tumbling filled his ears. "I owe you a beer, Atlas," he murmured.

Exhaling a sigh of relief, he allowed the pick to melt back into liquid form. He rose to his feet, keeping a small sphere of water in his palm in case something awaited him on the other side.

Ryker slid the door open.

It was...

A supply closet.

"Damn." He slipped inside, careful not to jostle the broom and mop that were haphazardly placed near the door. The confined space was dark except for the artificial yellow glow of fluorescent lighting running along the gap between the door and the floor.

Ryker dropped to his knees and ran his hands carefully down the walls. Then he felt it. A grate, roughly the size of his head, intended to allow air to flow through the cabin, was on the left side of the door. He felt his way to the edges and worked on the exposed screws with his fingers.

Thank the gods, whoever had installed the grate had done so in a lackadaisical manner. The screws were already loose, and it only took a few minutes to remove all four of them. Ryker held his breath as he pried the grate off the wall and placed it beside him.

Drawing in his shoulders, which was a feat in this small space, he contorted himself and peered through the opening.

His breath caught. Resting on a cot not far from him was a woman. She faced the door, her back to him. Like shards of sunlight, long, wavy blonde hair fell over her pillow. A brown blanket was tucked under her chin. He wasn't certain whether she was sleeping or glaring at the front door, but she wasn't moving.

On the other side of the room was a desk. A woman in a medical coat and pink scrubs typed on a laptop, her fingers flying over the keys. Ryker studied her briefly before determining she wasn't an immediate threat.

Ryker's gaze returned to the cot. Something about this woman drew him like a moth to a flame. An unexpected, pulsing need burned within him. He wanted to go to her, draw her into his arms, and never release her.

Beyond the shadow of a doubt, Ryker knew this was her.

Brynleigh de la Point.

His vampire.

They'd only known each other for a month, but it felt like a lifetime. They'd spent hours talking about everything and nothing, but this was the first time he was putting a body to her voice.

And gods, what a body it was. Ryker would be lying if he said he hadn't frequently dreamed of Brynleigh since their first date. He'd fantasized about being alone with her. He'd thought about how he'd make her his. He would taste her mouth, then have her writhing beneath him as he licked and suckled every sensitive part of her until she shattered. Then he would claim her.

Before, they'd been nothing but dreams. But now...

Now he *knew*.

In the same way that Ryker knew the sky was blue, the grass was green, and his magic was strong, he knew she was meant to be his. They would be partners in every single way. Not just in marriage but also in life. She was the other half that would complete him.

His soul recognized hers.

He'd heard of this happening—not between fae and vampires, but fae with other fae. Unbreakable bonds forged between two beings were blessed by the gods and extremely rare. Ryker didn't think that was happening to him—he didn't know if a fae could form a mating bond with a vampire—but he was sure she was meant to be his. He wanted to shout, to reach through the grate and pull her towards him, to pick her up and embrace her until the end of time.

But he wasn't supposed to be here.

Ryker's gut twisted. What the fuck was he doing? Participants of the Choosing weren't supposed to see each other until the Masked Ball. If Brynleigh knew he was here, would she report him for breaking the rules? Would she leave?

He gasped, his stomach contorting in on itself at the thought. Fucking hell. He couldn't let that happen. He couldn't risk it.

Brynleigh rolled onto her back, and he could see the steady rise and fall of her chest. Not only that, but the doctor didn't seem concerned with the vampire's health. Maybe they were keeping her here until the sun set, and it would be safe for her to join the others?

He hoped that was the case. If she weren't back tomorrow, then Ryker would return. He'd raise hell to see this woman again. For now, he would retreat to the mansion and act like everything was normal.

He slid the grate back and replaced the screws. Pressing his palm against the wall, he breathed in deeply. Beneath the clinical, bleach-like quality in the air were traces of the night, shadows, and... something that he couldn't quite put his finger on. Whatever it was, he wanted more.

Soon, he promised himself.

Ryker slipped out of the cabin and discreetly returned to the main house. This time, he didn't notice the cold at all. He returned to his room and cranked the shower as hot as possible. As the hot water rained down on him, he dreamed of that silky blonde hair and how she would feel in his arms.

He promised himself this wasn't the only time he would see her. He wouldn't allow it.

CHAPTER 15
Young Love

Thunderstorms and bergamot.

At first, the scent was faint. Barely there. Brynleigh had caught a whiff of the unique fragrance on the note when the Matron delivered it. After that, she'd fallen asleep, holding the paper to her chest.

And when she woke?

The smell was everywhere. It had infiltrated the air, seeping into the particles themselves.

It was him.

Ryker had been here. His scent lingered even now, growing fainter but still present. She wanted to bathe in it. It was the best thing she'd ever smelled.

She'd looked around for him, but nothing was out of place.

He'd left.

What had he been doing here? Had he somehow discovered her secret and come to kill her, too?

Brynleigh ran her fingers over her pendant, mulling over the possibility that she'd been found out. It was unlikely that he knew who she was. After all, she'd taken on Jelisette's surname after the storm. Not only that, but the destruction of Chavin hadn't exactly been plastered all over the news.

Like everything else related to Brynleigh's family's demise, the untimely flood and the resulting deaths had been buried by the Waterborn's political influence. A fluke of nature, the few people who reported on it had said. Others speculated it was an act of Nontia, the goddess of the sea. No one cared. Not really.

A week after the flood, another event stole the spotlight, and the media forgot about Chavin.

Not Brynleigh, though.

She was the sole survivor from that night. Although, technically, she hadn't survived either. Vampires, in the truest sense of the word, had to die to become their immortal selves. Had she not been Made, she would not be here.

No, there was no way he knew. If he did, he would kill her on the spot.

Why had he come?

She unfolded his note and read it again. It was simple and to the point.

I missed talking to you today, sweetheart. I hope we can chat tomorrow.

Ryker's writing was atrocious, like that of a child. But... he'd written her a note. Even though it wasn't a declaration of love or a proposal, it had to mean she was making headway. Right?

Yes.

The note, combined with the fact that he'd broken the rules to see her, was a good sign. A fucking fantastic one, actually.

A luminous grin spread across Brynleigh's face. She knew how much the captain cared about rules from their countless conversations. It was evident in the way he spoke and carried himself. For him to throw them aside for her was... everything. This was the confirmation she needed that her efforts hadn't been in vain.

A month in the real world wasn't that long, but in the Choosing, every day was like a week.

The more she thought about it, the more Brynleigh was convinced she was right. This was good. Better than good, in fact. The rebels had done her a favor because now she had tangible proof of her mark's affections. He'd been here. For so long, she had hunted the reclusive captain. Now, *he* sought *her*.

Everything was on track.

She could still accomplish her mission despite all the complications she'd encountered. Wedding bells chimed in her head, declaring their union to the world. They sounded awfully similar to the music she imagined would play at Ryker's funeral after she got her revenge.

He had no idea he was courting the instrument of his impending death.

Maybe she should've felt bad about that, but she didn't. The people of Chavin hadn't had any warning when he called a deadly hurricane upon them, drowning them while they slept.

Brynleigh would be a silent assassin. She would play the role of doting bride until the life drained from the captain's eyes. She couldn't wait to see his face when he realized it was all a charade, that he'd been betrayed by the one person he thought he could trust.

Revenge would be sweet, indeed.

She focused on vengeance and nothing else. Those were the rules; this was her game, and she would be the victor.

Hours passed.

Brynleigh remained in bed with her thoughts as her only company. She had many of them. They were all of the deadly variety... or at least, that's what she told herself.

When a smile came to her lips, she convinced herself it was because she was excited by the thought of avenging her family, not from Ryker's lingering scent tickling her nose.

When her mind wandered to the dream and her core tightened, she shoved those feelings deep down. She was only happy because Ryker would be dead soon, not because of the way he had touched her and brought her comfort.

And when she wondered what it would be like to plunge her fangs into Ryker's neck and taste his blood, it was purely for the purpose of killing him and not for other more... pleasant activities.

Yes, all she thought about was revenge.

Nothing else.

Around seven, Doctor Carin's phone rang. The crisp sound shattered the silence. Brynleigh jolted.

Carin picked up the phone. "Hello?"

The voice on the other end of the line was too quiet for Brynleigh to hear.

"Yes, she looks much better." Carin's eyes swept over the vampire. "Mhmm." She paused, listening. "Understood."

After another minute, the doctor hung up and faced Brynleigh. "Are you ready to rejoin the Choosing?"

A flutter of delight ran through Brynleigh, and she grinned, displaying her sharp fangs. "Absolutely."

Chuckling, the doctor reached behind her desk and pulled out a spare pair of boots and clean socks. She handed them to Brynleigh with a smile. Carin's eye had a distinctive twinkle as she asked, "Looking forward to talking to your captain?"

"Oh, yes." Brynleigh sat up, swung her legs off the cot, and pulled on the socks and footwear. "I certainly am."

The events of the past few days confirmed that Brynleigh needed to concentrate. The dream was the perfect example. She'd momentarily lost sight of her goals and wandered down a path of simple pleasure.

That wouldn't happen again.

Killing the captain on their wedding night would be poetic justice, sure to inflict maximal pain on his family.

It was fitting.

Once Ryker was dead, Brynleigh would escape to the Rose Ocean and watch everything unfold from afar.

Jelisette promised to get Brynleigh to safety as soon as she accomplished her mission. The older vampire would protect her progeny from the long arm of the law.

The door swung open, and Matron Lilith entered. She stomped her boots and shook off the snow. Complaining about the cold, she frowned as she clapped her mittens together before turning to Brynleigh. "Are you ready?"

"Yes," Brynleigh exclaimed, perhaps a bit too eagerly. "I mean... I am." She tried to tone down the excitement in her voice as she stood. "I missed talking to Ryker today."

That was it, right? She just wanted to talk to him to make sure he would fall in love with her so she could kill him. No other reason.

"Ah, young love," Matron Lilith chuckled as she led Brynleigh out the door. "It's a beautiful thing."

Brynleigh didn't bother correcting the older woman, but she knew the Matron was wrong. She didn't love Ryker. She hated him with every fiber of her being.

Right?

Thanking the doctor, Brynleigh nodded at the guards and went outside. Snowflakes fell leisurely from the night sky.

Matron Lilith led Brynleigh through the trees towards a beautiful, snow-covered mansion. As they walked, Lilith explained that the remainder of the Choosing would take place here until the Masked Ball, thanks to the rebel attack.

Brynleigh nodded her understanding. Relocating them made sense. So did their isolated northern location.

It wasn't until they'd climbed steps to enter through large double doors that looked like they belonged in an ancient castle that the Matron's words shocked the vampire.

"The timeline has been condensed."

"Condensed?" Brynleigh echoed. Her mind raced. What, exactly, did that mean? How would this affect her plans?

Matron Lilith placed her hand on Brynleigh's and squeezed. "The Masked Ball will take place two weeks from today."

Two weeks.

That was... not long. Not long at all.

Fuck.

All that earlier confidence fled.

Brynleigh was supposed to have two more months to make Ryker fall in love and propose. Two weeks?

That was... incredibly short.

Her heart boomed in her chest, and a headache started to form.

Isvana have mercy on her. Brynleigh couldn't catch a fucking break. First, the rebel attack, then her dream, and now this?

"I know it seems quick," Matron Lilith added compassionately. "But trust me, you'll be fine."

Fine? Brynleigh wasn't sure that was the case. She nibbled on her lip. "I—"

"Someone was very worried about you yesterday." The Matron waggled her brows suggestively. "I can't say much more, but suffice it to say, I would be willing to bet a large sum of money that a certain captain will happily be on one knee in two weeks."

Brynleigh hoped Lilith was correct. She'd have to be even more compelling to ensure she received Ryker's proposal.

Fourteen days to make Ryker fall completely, irrevocably, mindlessly in love with her.

And then she'd destroy him.

LILITH GAVE Brynleigh a tour of the mansion, showing her the room where she would be sleeping before bringing her to a home theater on the first floor. The other women were gathering for a movie.

"This is where I leave you," the Matron said. "You ladies enjoy your evening."

"Thank you, Matron." Brynleigh pushed open the doors, stepping into the darkened room. A white screen stretched across one wall, and three rows of comfortable seating were spread in front of the screen. The mansion's owner must have been wealthy beyond measure because Brynleigh had never seen a private cinema before.

"Brynleigh!"

At the sound of her name, the vampire looked up. Hallie came barreling towards her, her translucent wings fluttering.

"Thank Kydona, you're alright!" the Fortune Elf exclaimed as she hugged Brynleigh tightly. "They wouldn't tell us where you were, and when I walked the silver planes to See you, I couldn't find your future."

A pit yawned in Brynleigh's stomach at the dire prediction. What did that mean? Probably nothing good. However, the more rational part of Brynleigh's mind reminded her that Fortune Elves had a flair for both the cryptic and the dramatic. Maybe Hallie just misinterpreted the future.

Hoping that was the case—because, to be honest, Brynleigh couldn't deal with any other problems right now—she shoved her worry aside and smiled at the elf. "You searched for me? That was so kind of you."

Hallie grinned. "Of course I did. You're my friend. I was worried about you."

An unfamiliar emotion sprung to life inside Brynleigh. It was nice—and a little strange, if she was honest—to know someone had been worrying about her. The vampire had never expected to make a friend, yet it seemed she had.

"Thank you." Brynleigh smiled. "I'm here, and I'm safe."

A pointed cough came from behind them.

Brynleigh turned around.

"Well, if it isn't the vile bloodsucking creature that nearly killed us all." Valentina's horrible, grating voice was almost as unpleasant as the sneer carved onto her face.

The fire fae wore a skin-tight white sweater and jeans that looked like they cost thousands. Her blue-black hair was swept into a high ponytail, and a dusting of makeup decorated her features. Valentina looked perfectly put together, whereas Brynleigh knew the last few days had taken their toll on her appearance.

Still, she held her head up high. "I had it under control."

"Liar." A promise of violence flickered in Valentina's violet eyes, and she stepped towards the vampire. "You were going to tear everyone to shreds because of a bit of blood. You shouldn't be here. This competition isn't meant for people like you." She scowled. "Return to the cemetery where you came from."

"Fuck. You." Brynleigh balled her fists. Shadows flooded out of her, and her wings burst from her back. Her sweater shredded, leaving her in her violet t-shirt, which had slits for wings. She didn't care about the ruined clothes. It was time to teach this fae a lesson.

"Oh, the vampire bitch wants to play," Valentina snarled. A flame flickered to life above her outstretched hand. “Let’s see how well you do around a little fire.”

Despite the pounding of her heart, Brynleigh didn’t move. She refused to give in to this bully. “You want to fight? Fine. I’ll fucking fight you.”

She could use the outlet for all the emotions she’d been shoving deep within her.

Valentina lifted a manicured brow and looked down on Brynleigh. “There is nothing I’d love more than to teach you a lesson, little leech.”

The other women stepped back amid a flurry of gasps and rude remarks. The tension was so thick that the air practically crackled.

This wouldn’t be the first fight Brynleigh had gotten into. At ten years old, she had tackled Diana Laurent on the playground after school when she’d learned the older girl was bullying Brynleigh’s little sister Sarai.

Displeased with the situation, the principal had threatened to suspend both girls, but Brynleigh didn’t care. She’d made her point. That day, Diana went home with two black eyes and never bothered Sarai again.

It was time Valentina learned precisely who she was dealing with.

Brynleigh was a heartbeat away from throwing her shadows at the fire fae when Hallie screamed at the top of her lungs, “Stop!”

The sound was so sudden that for a moment, it felt like time halted.

Then, both Brynleigh and Valentina turned to the Fortune Elf. “What the hell?” they said at the same time.

“You can’t fight here.” Hallie took Brynleigh’s hand and yanked her towards the door. “They’ll kick you out. Is that what you want?”

Brynleigh’s eyes widened, and she glanced back at the fae.

Valentina stood there with fire flickering in her outstretched palm. “They could try to kick me out,” she said haughtily, “but Mother would never stand for it. I can do whatever I want.”

Lips curled, Brynleigh snarled. That was precisely why she was here. “You are a horrible, awful—”

With a strength Brynleigh didn’t know the other woman possessed, Hallie jerked her out of the room and slammed the door behind them.

Hallie’s eyes flashed with silver, and she looked fierce. “Ryker was looking for you today," she hissed. "Therian told me he refused to stop asking about you. Think about him, not that rich fae bitch."

Brynleigh drew in breath to too-tight lungs. Wisps of shadows slipped from her hands. Her nostrils flared. She tried to do what Hallie suggested but couldn't get Valentina's sneer out of her mind. "She's awful."

"She is," Hallie agreed. "But she's also right."

"What?" That was the last thing Brynleigh expected to hear, and it caught her off guard.

The Fortune Elf's wings flared. "Valentina probably won't get kicked out, but you definitely will. You were Selected, just like me. You know we're not the same as them."

When the words sank in, they were like cement around Brynleigh's feet, holding her in place. Her friend was right. Brynleigh had to get her head on straight. She had to focus on Ryker and nothing else. She couldn't fight Valentina, no matter how horrible the woman was. She couldn't afford to leave after all she'd been through to get here.

Closing her eyes, Brynleigh inhaled deeply. She focused on the rhythmic throb of her heart, letting it ground her. Once she was certain she wouldn't bolt back into the cinema and rip out Valentina's throat, she exhaled.

Retracting her shadows and wings, she opened her eyes. "Thank you, Hallie."

Without a backward glance, needing to put as much space between her and the fire fae as possible, Brynleigh stepped into the Void.

The complete and utter darkness of the space in between consumed her, and for a moment, she was utterly at peace.

In her room, Brynleigh showered away any lingering desire to fight Valentina. She wasn't here for her.

Her vengeance was so close; she could taste it.

CHAPTER 16

Pen Pals and Nicknames

"Greetings and salutations, Captain Waterborn." Celeste's voice seemed more chipper today than normal, or maybe it was Ryker who was different.

Last night, he'd slept better than he had in years. The memory of Brynleigh's wavy blonde hair and luscious scent kept him company through his dreams.

It surprised Ryker to realize that he did not regret visiting her yesterday. He'd broken the rules, but it was for a good reason.

He would do it again in a heartbeat.

"Morning," he replied. Adjusting the headphones with one hand, he accepted a coffee from the Light Elf manning the temporary bar near the door. Thanking the elf, he moved towards the wall.

The library was significantly smaller than the ballroom in the Hall of Choice, and even with the headphones, he could hear the faint murmurs of the other men speaking as he situated himself in a cozy armchair.

"Your date is incoming, Captain," Celeste said pleasantly. "Please, stand by."

A languid cello concerto trilled through the headset. Clearly, they were getting right to it. He probably had the condensed timeline to thank for that. Some of the other men were concerned about the new timeframe, but not Ryker. He didn't need the two weeks.

He was ready to propose now.

Some might have said he was moving too fast, but Ryker had already decided. He wanted Brynleigh de la Point. She might not be the kind of wife his mother desired for him, but she was the woman *he* wanted.

Ryker would cherish the next two weeks. He would use the time to familiarize himself with his future bride and learn everything about her. Besides, Brynleigh might still need the time to make her decision. He wasn't so full of himself that he thought Brynleigh would fall over herself in a rush to the altar to meet him.

Love took work on both sides, and he intended to prove to the vampire that he would be the best possible partner for her. Ryker would provide for Brynleigh in every way, keep her safe, and give her a home full of love. He could see it now—their life would be filled with laughter, games, intelligent comments, and hours of conversation.

He couldn't wait.

The music quieted until all Ryker could hear was his thundering heart.

A soft inhale came through the headphones, barely more than a breath.

"Brynleigh?" he murmured, his coffee cup frozen midway to his mouth. "Is that you?"

What a stupid question. Of course, it was. After his final, disastrous conversation with Valentina yesterday, he'd requested that Brynleigh be his only date from now on. Still, he had to know.

The silence seemed to stretch for an eternity as he waited and waited for a response.

Was she there?

When a lifetime—or a few seconds, it was hard to tell—passed, a serene, feminine exhale caressed his ears. It was like a refreshing breeze whispering on his skin on a hot day. That voice that was becoming as familiar as his own breathed, "Ryker."

At the sound of his name on Brynleigh's lips, Ryker groaned. His cock stirred, and he adjusted himself as he let his eyes fall shut.

No one else said his name like that. It was half-prayer, half-plea, and all... her. The lilt of her voice, the specific way she pulled out each syllable, was everything he ever needed. Tension left his shoulders, and he relaxed.

"Hey there, sweetheart. I missed you." Truth.

"I missed you, too."

He'd never heard better words. Leaning forward in his seat, he opened his eyes once more. "Did you get my note?"

A wooden wall was all that separated them. He stared at the striations in the wood and waited.

Ryker used to be patient—his mother often described him as imperturbable—but he was so eager to hear his vampire's words that every second she was silent was too long.

"Yes, the Matron delivered it." A breathy laugh filled the air. "You know, no one's ever written me a note before. It was very sweet."

A smile stretched from ear to ear as he settled into the chair. If everything went well, this would be a long, comforting conversation. "Does that make me your first pen pal?"

He *really* liked the sound of that. He was greedy and wanted as many of her firsts as she would give him.

First proposal, first time seeing each other, first dance, first kiss when they were alone...

His mind ran wild with everything they would do once they were away from the public's watchful eye.

She chuckled. "I suppose it does."

"And did you like the note?" By the Obsidian Sands, he sounded like a schoolboy. Still, he had to know.

"I did." Brynleigh laughed.

"Good," he breathed.

There was a pause, and he imagined her twirling those long golden strands through her fingers. "Although, I do have a few critiques I'd like to submit."

"Oh?" Ryker tilted his head. "I'm all ears."

He would welcome any topic of conversation as long as it meant they were talking.

"Well, first of all, your handwriting leaves something to be desired."

Ryker snorted. "Yes, that's true."

His mother and the headmasters at the academy had always encouraged him to work on his penmanship, but as far as he was concerned, it was a lost cause. Ryker was left-handed; no matter how hard he tried, he couldn't achieve the nice, neat loops his mother desired.

"Quite frankly, I'm surprised they let you in the army with chicken scratch like that, Captain," Brynleigh teased.

"Is that so? Is yours much better?"

"It is." She sounded smug. "I was always first in my class for handwriting, which qualifies me to make such a statement."

A low laugh bubbled out of Ryker. "It's a good thing my job doesn't require a lot of writing. You'll be happy to know most of my correspondence is electronic these days."

"Oh, good. We wouldn't want anyone to misunderstand your orders because they couldn't read them."

"No, we certainly wouldn't." Ryker rested his chin on his fist. "What were your other critiques? I'm dying to hear them."

She huffed a laugh, and the sound warmed Ryker from the inside out. He wanted to hear that sound a million times over. "My goodness, Captain. I had no idea you were so eager to be criticized."

"I'm eager to speak with you." The words slipped off his tongue before he could even think about them. "It doesn't matter what we're talking about because hearing your voice is like listening to my favorite music. I could do it all day long. Like an enchantress, you enthralled me with your voice."

A hitched breath came through the headphones, and for a prolonged moment, Brynleigh didn't say anything. Every beat of his heart was long and drawn out. Every pulse of his magic in his veins was louder than before. Had he spoken out of turn? Was this too fast? Too much?

Ryker was a statue, unable to blink or move as he waited. Had he scared her off? Gods, he hoped that wasn't the case. He didn't want anyone else, and he needed a bride.

Then, the most beautiful sound came through his headphones. Brynleigh *laughed*.

His soul drank in each drop of her delight. He didn't move or speak. He just... listened.

"I'm no enchantress and I can't Persuade anyone, but I like you, too," she murmured. "Although I will say, your note was a little short."

Ryker's lips twitched. He never thought he'd enjoy receiving criticism, yet she was proving him wrong. "Is that so?" He arched a brow. "Would you have preferred a novel? A poem? A song?"

Ryker wasn't much of a writer, but for her, he'd try. It turned out that breaking a rule was the first of many things he was willing to do for this vampire stealing his heart.

"Maybe one day. I'll let you know."

The conversation between them didn't require any thought. "You do that, sweetheart."

She chuckled, the sound warming him through. "That's not my last critique, though."

He canted his head. "No?"

"You didn't sign or initial it. How was I supposed to know it came from you?"

Ryker's eyes widened. He hadn't even considered that she might think it came from someone else. A low growl rumbled through him. "Brynleigh, *I* sent the note."

The mere thought of one of these other men sending *his* vampire anything made him want to roar his frustrations skyward. She was his and no one else's.

Fuck. This was a level of possessiveness that Ryker had never experienced. Part of him knew it was irrational, but he still wanted to rip off his headphones and yell at the other men to stay away from Brynleigh.

"Hmm. Maybe you don't know how to sign your name."

"I know how to write my name," he growled, still trying to get himself under control.

"So, it must be a problem of length," she postulated, a hint of mirth in her voice. "Is that it? Ryker has far fewer letters than Brynleigh, but still..."

She paused, and he imagined she was chewing on her lip. Was it full? Plump and kissable? Waiting for him to lay claim to it? Probably. His fingers itched with the urge to tear down the wall between them and see for himself.

Two weeks, he reminded himself. *That's all.*

He could wait two weeks, right? Fourteen days wasn't that long, especially for long-lived beings like the fae.

The thought, though rational, did not ease his frustrations.

"Ry," she said suddenly.

His brows creased, and his mind raced to catch up. "Excuse me?"

There was a definite smile in Brynleigh's voice as she said, "You could've signed it, 'Ry.' I get that you were busy and all, but—"

"Ry?" he repeated. The name sounded foreign on his tongue, but he didn't mind it at all.

And when Brynleigh said it, it felt… right.

"Yes, Ry. It's a nickname." She snorted, and gods help him, but that sound made him fall for her even more. "Typically, something people choose as a term of endearment for someone they spent a lot of time with."

"I know what a nickname is, sweetheart." He couldn't sit any longer. Abandoning his coffee, he stood, stretched his arms above his head, and cracked his back. He strode over to the bookshelves and studied the spines. "I *am* a Mature fae."

A soft, barely there chuckle filled his ears. "Ah. I see what the problem is. Captain, has no one ever given you one before?"

The playful intonation of her voice warmed him from the inside out. Who could have known such a simple interaction could bring someone so much joy?

"No one whose company I enjoy as much as yours," was his murmured response.

She sucked in a breath, and Ryker's fingers stilled on the leather binding of the *History of Coral City*. He wracked his brain, trying to pinpoint whether he'd said something wrong.

By the Black Sands, Ryker was never usually like this. He didn't question his words. He was self-assured and confident, a leader in his own right.

"Do you enjoy my company, Ry?" Her question was quiet, almost… hesitant.

Enjoy was too simple of a word for how he felt around her. He'd spend every minute of every day with her if he could. In fact, that was exactly what he planned to do.

When this was over, he would be with her when he woke and come home to her after a long day. He would find refuge in her arms after inevitable hardships. She would rest her head in his bed at night. He could see it all now. Even the most mundane tasks, like walking the dog, would be more pleasurable with her.

Ryker inhaled deeply. "I enjoy coffee. Pastries, also. There's nothing like the thrill of playing a game of chess and winning against a worthy opponent. Those are all things I *enjoy*."

Turning from the bookshelf, he strode toward the wall and placed his palm flat on the surface. His eyes fell shut. "To say that I enjoy your company, sweetheart, would be a vast underestimation of how much I look forward to hearing your voice and spending time with you. I do not enjoy it because that is too simple of a word. Rather, I am quickly finding that I am desperate for your company. For you. I thought I proved that yesterday."

Resting his forehead against the wall, he curled his fingers against the wood. His heart raced in his chest as he waited for her to say something. Anything.

Every moment that passed in silence was longer than the last.

Right then, as he waited for her response, Ryker realized he was falling in love with Brynleigh de la Point. They had only known each other for a month, but his heart beat for her.

He'd promised his father he would enter the Choosing to find a wife, but he'd never imagined he'd find this kind of soul-completing, mind-bending, world-altering love.

And she...

Was still silent.

Ryker's heart seized, and he whispered, "Brynleigh—"

"I'm here," she murmured. "I just... I'm here."

The wooden divider was rough against his fingers as he dug his hand into the wall. "Tell me what you're thinking."

He couldn't stand the silence anymore.

"Do you... what you said... is it..."

"It's true," he whispered.

She blew out a long breath. "Because you can't lie."

"That's right." He exhaled, his heart still thundering. "I'm standing at the wall." He needed to tell her.

A silken chuckle that would follow him into his dreams came from her. "Me too."

He slid down the barrier until he sat on the floor. Resting his head against it, he breathed in deeply. They were close, separated only by this wall. How thick was it? Two or three inches? That was nothing. It would be easy to rip it down and see his vampire for the first time.

He wouldn't. Not yet.

But soon.

"I wish I could see you right now," he admitted. "I want to know everything about you."

That glimpse of golden hair hadn't been nearly enough for him. He was beginning to realize nothing would ever be enough. Not until she was fully his in every way.

His headphones echoed with the rustling of fabric. "I'm not going anywhere, Ry." She sounded almost... sad about that. But he had to be mishearing her. "Not today, not tomorrow. I'll be here every day. There's no one else I'd rather speak with."

"I love speaking with you, too," Ryker said.

Another pause, then she whispered, "I'm not as eloquent as you, but it seems I've taken a liking to you, too. It's... I didn't... It took me by surprise."

"Just a liking?" His voice was teasing, but he couldn't hide the undercurrent in his words as he pushed deeper. "Is that all you feel for me?"

He hadn't planned to ask the question today, but suddenly, hearing her answer was the only thing that mattered.

Waiting with bated breath, he rubbed his hands down his jeans. He straightened an invisible crease in the denim as time slipped on. He was a powerful water fae, the son of a Representative, and yet he was riddled with anxiety. Did she know she could crush him? That her words meant the world to him?

Even so, he wouldn't push her. He never would. Sometimes, time was the best gift one person could give to another. He would give her as much as she needed, and he wouldn't go anywhere.

Brynleigh sucked in a deep breath. "Maybe... I think... Maybe it's more." Her voice shook as if she was afraid to admit it. "I think..."

"Yes?" Hope sparked in his stomach, and his fingernails dug into his palms. His arms were empty, waiting for her.

"It's really scary to admit this," she breathed. "I don't... I'm not suppo... but..." A shuddering breath escaped her. "I think I could fall in love with you, Ryker."

Those last words were barely more than a breath, but he heard them as if she'd screamed them in his ear. That spark of hope exploded into a burning flame. He would cherish it for the rest of his life.

A long moment passed as her words settled into his heart.

He pressed his forehead against the wall. "Me too, Brynleigh."

"You could fall in love with yourself?" The teasing tone in her voice was back. "I had no idea you thought so highly of yourself."

He chuckled. "You know what I mean."

Her voice was a soft caress in his ears. "Yes, I do." She sighed wistfully. "I wish I could see you."

He groaned. "I know. Soon."

Maybe if he kept reminding himself that it wouldn't be long, the next two weeks wouldn't feel like an eternity. At the moment, he doubted it.

"Soon," she echoed softly.

Ryker didn't want their date to end. He could stay here for hours, talking with his vampire. "Did I ever tell you about my dad?"

She hummed. "No, I don't think so."

That didn't surprise him. "I thought so. I don't talk about him much," he admitted.

"Oh," she murmured. "Is he..."

"Both my parents are alive," Ryker answered, sensing where she was going with the question. "My parents both love me, but my father..." He raked a hand through his hair. "He's everything to me."

Memories flashed through Ryker's mind.

Riding with his father, galloping through the fields of the family's country house in the Western Region. The plains stretched for miles, a sea of grain in all directions. Watching sports together. Learning to read. Listening to music. Hunting. Playing chess.

Everything Ryker enjoyed doing linked him to his father in one way or another.

"Tell me about him?" The request was soft, as if Brynleigh was afraid to pull him out of his memories.

"Dad and I were close," Ryker said. "He taught me to ride a horse and was always my biggest champion."

Another memory, a much more recent one, flashed through Ryker's mind.

"How is he?" Ryker asked the nurse quietly.

She shook her head, her soft smile tinged with pity. "I'm afraid it's not a good day, Captain."

Ryker's mouth pinched. "I was worried that might be the case."

Still, he would see his father. Tomorrow, he was entering the Hall of Choice. He needed his dad to know.

Thanking the nurse, Ryker entered the room quietly. Once, it had served as one of the three studies in Waterborn House. Now, it was his father's sick room. Machines beeped, disinfectant covered the underlying scent of illness, and a hospital bed with crisp white sheets sat in the middle of the room.

"Dad." Ryker strode towards the bed.

His heart nearly stopped in his chest as he took in his father's sickly state. His father's condition had deteriorated since Ryker's last visit.

Unseeing eyes stared at the ceiling, and even after Ryker picked up his father's hand, they didn't even blink.

Ryker's cheeks were damp as he squeezed his father's hand. "I'm going to find a wife in the Choosing, Dad," he promised. "Like I told you I would."

There was no response.

"I'm going tomorrow," he said. "I won't be able to visit while I'm gone, but Mom and River will take good care of you."

Cyrus' fingers tightened ever so slightly around Ryker's. It was more than Ryker expected, and it stole his breath.

"I love you," Ryker said gruffly.

There was no response.

A tear slipped from the corner of Ryker's eye, and he quickly wiped it away. No matter what, he would keep his promise.

"WAS?" Brynleigh's quiet question drew Ryker out of his thoughts.

He ran a finger under his eyes, surprised when it came away wet. He was crying again. "My father's been sick for a long time."

"Oh no."

Ryker's chest burned, and he rubbed his heart. "A few years after my sister was born, Dad was infected with the Stillness. He's alive, but..."

A lump rose in Ryker's throat, and his voice trailed off. His unspoken words hung in the air between them. *Not for long.*

The Stillness was a deadly, incurable sickness. It only affected fae, and no one knew where it came from. There was no surviving it. The Stillness ate away at the victim's body, slowly stealing their ability to move. The best medical care on the continent could not stop its deadly advance.

Ryker had been watching his father slowly die for the better part of two decades.

"I'm so sorry, Ryker." Brynleigh's voice cracked, and silence stretched between them for several minutes. "Losing your family is an indescribable kind of pain. Mine... They passed away."

His heart squeezed. They both knew grief intimately. It was a thread weaving them together, drawing them closer than before.

He hated that she understood where he was coming from. Hated that they had this in common. Hated that she, too, had probably had sleepless nights and exhausting days filled with tears. He remembered their date when they had remained silent, sitting in grief.

By the Sands, he wished he could remove that pain from Brynleigh. There were no words that could describe the absolute, soul-shattering agony that was grief. No real way to explain the emptiness that sometimes settled within him when he remembered his father's illness. He knew words were often empty, and platitudes didn't get people far.

Ryker understood all this about grief, so he didn't offer Brynleigh meaningless words. Instead, he shook his head. "I'm sorry for your loss, Brynleigh."

Truer words had never been spoken. He would never wish the kind of melancholy sorrow that grief cultivated on anyone, let alone the woman he was falling in love with.

Minutes passed in heavy silence.

Ryker mourned. Not only for his father and the man he used to be but for the relationship they'd once shared. The ever-present pain throbbed in his chest, but today, something was different. Maybe it was because he'd shared with Brynleigh, or maybe it was something else, but it wasn't as acute as normal.

And so, when Brynleigh quietly asked him to tell her about his family, he did. He closed his eyes and shared stories he'd never spoken aloud.

He talked for hours, and Brynleigh listened. It meant more to him than he could ever put into words.

That day, they didn't play chess or laugh again, but when Celeste announced their date was ending, Ryker had made up his mind.

Brynleigh de la Point would be his bride because there was no way he was letting this vampire go.

She was his, even if she didn't know it yet.

CHAPTER 17

Rule Number Eight

Three days later, Brynleigh stepped out of the shower and wrapped a towel around herself before applying a fresh face of makeup. She was getting ready for a date, and she felt...

Nothing.

Brynleigh felt nothing because she refused to let herself experience emotions right now.

Rule number eight: emotions are for mortals, not vampires.

The day she'd returned from the library when Ryker had shared about his father, she had shoved all her feelings deep in her soul and locked them tightly away. She would never let them out.

It was easier this way.

If she were emotionless, then Ryker's words wouldn't affect her. His kindness wouldn't affect her. His grief over his father's illness wouldn't touch her heart. It couldn't. After all, the Choosing was almost over.

She was so close. Today, they weren't meeting in the library. Following an old tradition, the men had planned blind one-on-one dates with a partner of their choice.

If Brynleigh had allowed herself to feel emotions, her stomach would have been in knots. But it wasn't because she was numb. A blank slate. A weapon of death, nothing more.

Brynleigh was confident Ryker would invite her on his date. After all, he was enamored with her.

And Brynleigh?

She was definitely not falling in love with Ryker. That would be impossible because there was no way she would ever love the man who'd killed her family.

Anytime Brynleigh felt any emotions around Ryker, she shoved them down. Ignorance was bliss, after all.

When her fangs ached in his presence, she refused to acknowledge the desire blooming within her. Whenever his laugh made her feel a certain way, she bundled up those feelings and stuffed them deep inside. Every time he haunted her dreams, she woke up and refused to fall back asleep lest she think of him again.

She was the master of her emotions, not the other way around.

Fishing out cherry red lipstick from her makeup bag, Brynleigh applied it carefully to her lips. She needed the armor her makeup provided today more than ever before.

"You fucking hate him," she told her reflection sternly. "You hate him, you hate him, you hate him."

Why did the word hate sound suspiciously like another four-letter word? Something banned that she absolutely could not be feeling.

No.

This was not alright.

She hated Ryker Waterborn because that was the only acceptable response. Her mother, the gods be with her soul, had always said that love and hate were two sides to the same coin.

Brynleigh couldn't love Ryker. Her hate was just... different now that she knew him.

That was it.

She would keep reminding herself of that fact, over and over and over again until it was true.

A knock came on the door, pulling her out of her thoughts.

"One minute." Brynleigh placed the lid on her lipstick and wrapped her hair in a second towel before heading over and opening the door. "Yes?"

Matron Lilith stood in the hallway and grinned up at Brynleigh.

"Mail delivery." Giggling like a schoolgirl, she handed the vampire an envelope. "You're in for a treat, my dear. Of all the dates planned for today, yours is the most intriguing."

Brynleigh's stomach fucking *flipped*. It somersaulted within her as though she was a teenager, not a fully grown woman, and a deadly vampire.

She grabbed that nervous excitement and forced it deep inside herself. There was no reason for her to be excited about going on a date with Ryker. No reason to wonder what they were doing or whether she'd enjoy it.

This was nothing but a means to a bloody end.

Closing her eyes, Brynleigh inhaled and forced herself to pull up memories she rarely thought of. She remembered the screaming, the burning of her lungs, the deluge of water pouring from the sky. Her heart raced at the recollection of seeing a tall man cloaked in shadows standing next to a smaller form at the edge of the forest.

That memory had haunted Brynleigh for months after her Making.

Jelisette had filled in the blanks for her progeny. The man wasn't a man at all but a water fae. A captain in the army. He wouldn't be prosecuted for the deaths he'd caused. Nothing would happen to him at all because his mother was a Representative.

That was why Jelisette was helping Brynleigh. As a new vampire, no one would see her coming, making her the perfect weapon to teach the Representatives a lesson.

A hand landed on Brynleigh's arm, pulling her out of her thoughts. The Matron must have mistaken the vampire's pause for excitement because her smile was kind. "I'm sure you'll have a wonderful time with the captain. Go ahead and finish getting ready. I'll return to escort you in an hour."

Brynleigh thanked her and slipped the door shut. Letting the towel fall, she strode to the chair where her duffle bag sat. Tossing the envelope on the bed, she fished through her bag until she found the folded-up picture she sought.

Silver lined Brynleigh's eyes as she gently unfolded the paper and ran a finger down the creases.

A beautiful, smiling face with dirty blonde hair stared up at Brynleigh. A moment captured in time, a memory lost in a torrent of water.

Brynleigh wiped away a tear and sniffled. "I miss you," she whispered. "I'm getting closer, and I promise you, he's going to pay for what he did."

There was no answer. Of course not. Sarai's voice had been stolen that night, along with her life. This picture had been taken days before the hurricane. Sarai's blue eyes sparkled with joy, and her mouth was wide open, caught in a candid moment as she laughed at someone off-camera. She wore denim shorts and a red crop top. It had been her favorite outfit that summer.

Brynleigh had taken this picture, along with several others, but this was the only one that survived the tempest. It had been in her pocket when the storm struck.

The longer Brynleigh looked at the image, the angrier she got. Her shadows vibrated in her veins, red seeped into her vision, and she clenched her fists.

This emotion, this bone-deep anger, she kept. It was safe. Good, even. It wouldn't hurt her or break her heart.

Brynleigh let the anger grow until it was all she felt. She would not fail. She hated Ryker Waterborn for what he did, and he deserved what was coming to him.

Eventually, Brynleigh glanced at the clock. Over half an hour had passed, and she needed to finish getting dressed. She carefully refolded the picture and slipped it into her bag.

Rummaging through her things, she found the perfect dress. It was tight and hugged her curves in all the right ways. The sleeves were long, and the scoop neckline allowed her pendant to settle freely between her breasts. The hem fell midway down her thighs. She slipped on black heels and stepped into the bathroom to admire her handiwork.

Brynleigh tilted her head, her gaze assessing. A beautiful, deadly vampire smiled back at her. Her hair tumbled over her left shoulder. Black eyes stared back at her. Red lips highlighted her fangs.

All vampires were almost painfully beautiful—it was one of their gifts from the goddess of the moon—but the spark in Brynleigh's eyes had nothing to do with her beauty and everything to do with her impending revenge.

CROSSING HER LEGS, Brynleigh tapped the air with her foot. When it was time for Brynleigh's date, Matron Lilith had been waiting for her with Harper, one of the guards. He'd blindfolded Brynleigh before leading her to this room.

That was ten minutes ago.

Most vampires were patient, but that wasn't a skill Brynleigh excelled at. As a human, she'd never been good at waiting. That trait had carried over into her vampiric life.

Matron Lilith had handed Brynleigh a glass of blood wine before she left. Brynleigh sipped it now, letting the stillness of the room settle around her. She wasn't sure what their date would be, but she was certain Ryker had put a lot of thought into it.

If there was one thing Brynleigh knew for certain after a month of nearly daily conversations with the captain, the fae didn't do anything halfway.

Neither did she.

It was fitting. He truly was a worthy opponent in the game she was playing. Too bad he would have to lose.

Two heavy sets of footsteps came from the hallway.

Brynleigh tilted her head in the direction of the sound. The blindfold amplified her other already strong senses. Their heartbeats were steady, rhythmic drums in their chests as they approached, beating nearly twice as fast as hers.

The door creaked open, the hinges proclaiming their need for oil to the world.

Brynleigh moved gingerly, feeling for a space on the table for her wine before letting go. When it didn't spill, she exhaled and turned her head towards the entrance.

"Right this way, Captain." She recognized Harper's voice.

Her spine tingled, and her shadows flared within her. Ryker was here.

If his scent had been a mighty river on the day he sneaked into the infirmary, tonight, it was an Isvana-damned tsunami. There was no barrier between them. No wall to protect her from him. No AI to filter his voice.

The flimsy black blindfold was the only thing keeping her from experiencing all of him. It was hardly anything at all.

Her heart pounded in her chest, and she flushed.

An adverse reaction to his presence. That's what that was.

More emotions had the gall to rise within Brynleigh. She struggled to rein them in. She didn't give herself time to think about what they were or what they meant before she pushed them down. It was far more difficult than before. Nearly impossible.

Ryker smelled so fucking good. So right. So *delicious.*

There wasn't a single part of Brynleigh that didn't light up at the familiar aroma. Her skin prickled. Her shadows sang. Her eyes widened beneath the blindfold. And her fangs.

Her goddess-damned *fangs.*

Had she thought they ached when she first heard his voice? This was a hundred times worse than that. Now they were twin flames, burning in her gums. An overwhelming urge to leap from her seat and sink her fangs into his neck coursed through her. She gripped the table, the wood cracking beneath her touch.

Under no circumstances could Brynleigh ever taste Ryker.

Fuck, this was bad.

She shoved those illicit emotions and that awful desire she had no business feeling deep, deep, deep within her soul.

Brynleigh could do this. She'd once called herself a master of compartmentalization. She could keep everything separate and make it to their wedding night.

This was all an act. Like a masterful fisherwoman, Brynleigh was luring Ryker in. She was the predator and the bait. That must be why she felt like this. She was just very good fucking bait. Too good, if the twisting in her core and the dampness between her thighs were any sign.

Brynleigh's body was just... reacting to Ryker's. That was to be expected, right? She was a vampire, and he was a fae with a delectable scent, so naturally, she wanted to devour him.

It didn't mean anything.

Saying the words was one thing. Convincing herself they were true was another matter entirely.

Brynleigh pictured her sister in her mind and held her there as she drew a series of deep breaths. By the third exhale, she felt more normal. Or at least, less... drawn to Ryker.

She could do this.

For her family.

For her revenge.

For herself.

The guard was still in the room. Brynleigh sensed the man behind her, but his masculine scent did nothing for her. Unlike Ryker's.

You can end this now, a voice niggled at the back of Brynleigh's mind. *Get it over with.*

She could do it. She was certainly strong enough to overpower two men. But that wasn't the plan. If she acted now, she'd have no chance of escaping. No shot at freedom. Brynleigh was certain Jelisette would be displeased if she acted out of line.

Patience was key. She couldn't throw away years of planning because the captain smelled good.

That would be completely and utterly ridiculous.

Killing Ryker on their wedding night would send a message to his family and all Representatives: the way they flaunted the Republic's laws and acted without consequence had gone on long enough.

She had to stick to the plan, meaning she had to get out of her head and focus on the fae in front of her. Her mark.

Brynleigh reached out, intent on grabbing her glass of blood wine when her index finger grazed something warm.

She froze. Her heart stopped beating. Her lungs seized. Her shadows became ice in her veins.

They were touching.

And it...

Gods damn it all, but it did not feel bad. It did not feel like she was touching the man who murdered her family.

It felt like...

Home.

Brynleigh's head swam as lightheadedness threatened to pull her under.

This was...

It was...

Too much.

It wasn't enough.

Fuck.

She could barely think.

Then, instead of pulling away and giving her the space she desperately needed, Ryker's fingers traced up her hand. He clasped her wrist, wrapping his much larger fingers around her.

Brynleigh's heart chose that moment to remember it was supposed to be beating. Now, it tried to escape her chest.

How was it possible that in all her planning, she'd never accounted for the fact that he might touch her? Here she was, playing the game of her lifetime, and somehow, she had completely overlooked this possibility.

Butterflies fluttered in her stomach, having exploded within her at the point of contact. She scrambled to gather them all, shoving each one deep inside. How many could it hold? How many emotions could she suppress before they ruined her?

She wasn't certain.

All Brynleigh knew was that Ryker was touching her, and it felt like they were stepping onto a new game board. One where she didn't know the rules.

She was more frightened than she'd been since the night her family died.

CHAPTER 18

Universes Collide

One single touch was all it took to shift Ryker's world on its axis.

He hadn't even done it on purpose.

As soon as he'd entered the room, Brynleigh's scent had nearly bowled him over. Other aromas had diluted her fragrance in the infirmary, but that was no longer true.

Fae might not have the senses of vampires, but he could pick her out of a crowd, regardless. She smelled like a crisp evening and night-blooming roses. He'd never been one for flowers before, but now, he wanted to be surrounded by them daily for the rest of his life.

Her scent was as intoxicating as the strongest glass of Faerie Wine.

Ryker barely noticed the guard leading him to the table, barely heard him say the server would be around with dinner in a few minutes.

The entirety of his focus was on *her*.

Finally, the barriers between them were gone. Nothing was keeping him from her but a flimsy table and a pair of blindfolds.

Even sightless, he'd sensed her. His magic had bubbled within him, his water eager to play with her darkness. This had never happened before. Usually, his magic was calm, waiting for him to draw upon it, but not today.

He'd been reaching across the table for a glass of wine, careful not to knock it over, when it happened.

He *touched* her.

Her skin, soft and cool, had intercepted his. It was just a graze, barely more than a feather's brush against his hand, but it was *everything*. The moment they touched, his magic leaped in his veins. He sucked in a breath. His heart pounded.

Universes collided.

He'd dreamed of this moment, but the reality of their touch was far more than he'd ever imagined. Ryker wasn't a youngling, and he'd had his fair share of partners, but none of those moments had ever felt like this.

And it was a *touch*.

Brynleigh was soft, whereas he was hard and calloused. Her skin was smooth and unblemished. That, at least, he'd expected. All vampires were like that—polished versions of their previous mortal selves.

Fascinatingly, she was cold. Not freezing, but not warm. It should have worried him or made him want to pull back. Instead, all he wanted to do was cover her with his warmth.

She sucked in a breath, and her hand froze beneath his. Pulling away would be the right, gentlemanly thing to do, but he didn't. At that moment, Ryker wasn't feeling like much of a gentleman. Removing this one point of contact would be like taking a knife to his gut.

He'd rather die.

Instead of releasing Brynleigh, his fingers crawled up her wrist. He encircled her, noting the hitch of her breath as his fingers wrapped around her.

He was a starving man, and every touch she allowed gave him life.

Seconds ticked by. Minutes? Hours? He couldn't be sure. His entire existence was focused on this one gentle caress.

It was at once too much and not at all enough.

"Ry." The nickname was a whispered supplication as it slipped from her lips.

It sent a bolt of desire through him. He shifted in his seat, subtly adjusting himself. Had he wanted her before? Now, he needed her.

Ryker's dreams had not done her justice. He'd never been one for hand-holding, but he never wanted to let her go. His thumb brushed gentle circles over the slow beating pulse on the inside of her wrist.

"Hi," was all he could manage. It wasn't eloquent, but there was no room for that right now.

Several long seconds went by in silence. Was this simple touch shaking the core of her foundation as much as it was his? He'd never imagined something so small could be so life-changing.

She breathed, "I—"

The door opened with a bang, shattering the moment between them.

Brynleigh jerked her hand away from Ryker as though she'd been burned.

Barely holding in a groan, Ryker turned his head towards whoever had interrupted them. "Yes?" His voice was curt. He couldn't help it. He was finally in the same room as Brynleigh. He didn't want to waste a single moment of their time together.

Wheels creaked as something moved along the floor.

"I've brought your dinner, sir," said a small, meek voice. He hadn't heard it before and assumed it belonged to one of the many humans employed to keep the mansion running.

Their food. Of course. He'd forgotten all about it.

Ryker sighed and raked his hand through his hair. "Thank you."

Porcelain chinked as the server placed several items on the table, working silently.

"Chef has prepared several dishes for you this evening," the server said. "He recommends eating with your hands and discovering the food as you go."

"Oh, no," Brynleigh whispered. The words, though short, were filled with horror.

Ryker's eyes widened beneath his blindfold. What was wrong?

"Miss?" the server asked.

She cleared her throat, and her chair creaked. "I just... I don't exactly eat... food."

Blood rushed to Ryker's cheeks. By the Black Sands, how could he have made such a monumental mistake? He'd somehow forgotten this crucial fact about vampires.

He was a fucking idiot.

Thank the gods, it seemed the chef wasn't as obtuse as Ryker.

"Not to worry," said the server. "Chef has whipped up several vampire-friendly dishes. He took the liberty of lacing them with blood for you, and they're the ones I placed closest to you."

At least someone had their head on straight around here.

"That's so thoughtful," Brynleigh replied after a moment. "Honestly, I didn't expect this. Thank you."

"Of course, miss." The server explained that the chef believed the meal was best explored without further directions. According to him, it would increase their ability to taste individual, unique flavors. The server would be in the hall if they had any questions.

Kydona, the mother goddess the fae had adopted when they crossed the Indigo Ocean, must have been watching over Ryker because the server took his leave after that.

They were alone once again.

The moment the door slipped shut, Ryker turned back to Brynleigh. His fingers clenched and unclenched, and he wished he could see her. "I'm sorry," he blurted. "About the food... I wasn't thinking when I planned this."

That was a mistake he wouldn't be making again. Right after this date, he would find Jacques and Horatio, the two male vampires in the Choosing, and ask them what he could do to make Brynleigh's life more comfortable with him.

No more guesses, no more mistakes.

"No need to apologize," Brynleigh said.

"On the contrary, there is a need." He cleared his throat. "I made a mistake, and I will endeavor to do better by you."

"That's very sweet." The vampire hummed. "You know, we *can* eat. It's just that when we put food in our mouths, it tastes like ash. Not coffee, though. Thank Isvana, because I love it."

"I love coffee, too." He palmed the back of his neck. "So you're not angry with me? It's alright if you are. I should've thought ahead, and I didn't."

"No, I'm not. No one has ever prepared me food laced with blood before. Honestly, I'm intrigued."

"By me or the food?" he asked, unable to help himself.

Brynleigh chuckled, "Both."

Somehow, that was exactly what he needed to hear.

They dug in, trying a little bit of everything.

Once in a while, they touched. Each time was as explosive as the first, leaving Ryker wanting more.

Time slipped by. The meal was delicious, and they spoke about nothing in particular as they ate.

Ryker loved every single minute of it.

"Gods, that was good." Brynleigh sighed.

"Yeah?" Ryker chuckled. "You enjoyed it?" He'd quickly adapted to the blindfold, and it wasn't impeding his experience at all.

"It was amazing. I never would've guessed chocolate and blood paired so well together." She smacked her lips and sighed in delight. "I'm going to have to find this chef and get the recipe."

Ryker leaned back in his seat, his stomach full. The chef was undeniably skilled. The plates had varied from a spiced, roasted venison to a shaved, raw salad. Everything he'd tasted had been delicious. "The cake was that good?"

"The best," she gushed. "Thank you, Ryker. Truly. I didn't even realize I missed food until tonight."

The happiness in Brynleigh's voice sent a rush of heat through Ryker. Talking to her was always enjoyable, but tonight felt even better than normal. He wasn't sure whether it was the small, stolen touches or something else. Either way, his heart soared.

Ryker slowly navigated his way around the obstacles of empty dishes and cups strewn across the table until his hand found Brynleigh's once again. This time, nothing was unintentional about how his fingers laced through hers.

She inhaled deeply but didn't pull away. If anything, her grip tightened around his. "Ryker, I don't know if we should—"

"Dance with me?" he asked before she could finish that thought.

He was all too aware that their time together in the Choosing was slowly slipping away. He didn't want to waste a single second of their remaining time.

A tinkling laugh tinged with darkness slipped from Brynleigh's lips. "What? There's no music."

"We can make our own." Ryker rose to his feet, grateful he'd chosen to wear comfortable shoes tonight. "I want to feel your body against mine."

This date was probably being streamed to the Republic, but Ryker didn't care. He would do almost anything to have this fantastic, intriguing woman in his arms.

He stood beside the table, but she still hadn't responded. He squeezed her fingers. "Please?"

Brynleigh hitched a breath, and he sensed she was still unsure. "I have two left feet," she warned him. "I know most vampires are graceful, but not me. I'm likely to step on your feet."

"Sweetheart, if you think a little clumsiness is going to turn me away from you, you're wrong." He gently tugged on her hand and drew her to her feet. She was taller than most women in his life, and her head rested under his chin. She didn't fight as he brought her closer to him. "I'm all in."

She froze. "You mean—"

"I want you, Brynleigh." His hand slipped around her hip, settling on the small of her back. "Only you."

"What about the other women?" she asked breathlessly.

"They don't haunt my dreams the way you do." He only wanted her.

"There's still a week and a half," she reminded him.

He held Brynleigh to him as he navigated them away from the table. "I don't need it. I've already made up my mind."

The moment he'd followed Matron Cassandra into the snow, he'd decided. His conversation with Brynleigh about his dad proved he made the right decision.

Brynleigh sucked in a breath. "Does that mean—"

He bent his head, finding the curve of her ear and brushing his lips over it in the gentlest of kisses. "I want you to marry me, Brynleigh de la Point," he breathed. "I'll ask you formally on the night of the Masked

Ball, but there's no point pretending I haven't decided. If you'll have me, I'm yours."

Her heart thundered between them, and he held her close as they danced. Several minutes passed, but he didn't push her for an answer.

"Yes, I will." She rested her head on his shoulder and relaxed against him. "After all, you're what I came here for."

Ryker's heart soared at her words. They were exactly what he wanted to hear.

His body was airy, his feet light, his heart worry-free as he held Brynleigh close. Ryker led them around the room in dance after dance, humming tunes he'd heard hundreds of times before.

Ryker didn't kiss her. Not yet.

It wasn't that he didn't want to—on the contrary, his mouth yearned to be on hers and taste how—but he wanted to save their first kiss for the moment they saw each other face to face.

He was certain she was worth waiting for.

CHAPTER 19
Losing Was Not an Option

Frigid water poured from the shower head, pelting Brynleigh from above like tiny needles made of ice. She hadn't even stripped off her tank top and pyjama shorts before getting under the water, having sought refuge in the bathroom after several hours of sleepless tossing and turning.

She had hoped the cold would instill some sense into her, but it didn't seem to be working. She was freezing, which was a feat in and of itself for a vampire, but her mind was a wiring hub of activity.

This entire situation had become a gods-damned mess. Her date with Ryker had been a week ago, and she had been unable to get the fae out of her mind since then. She kept replaying his touch, the memory driving her mad with want. She had so many suppressed emotions. No matter how many she shoved down, there were still more.

Brynleigh needed to talk to Zanri. None of their contingency plans accounted for something like this.

"Fuck." She banged her head against the soaked wall.

Regrettably, other than making her head ring, the action was pointless. She couldn't hide from the truth anymore—she was in a world of trouble.

Brynleigh had feelings for Ryker. Actual, tangible, heart-twisting feelings. She swore again, the curses slipping from her mouth and being swallowed by the water.

The emotions grew stronger every single day. It was getting harder and harder to separate herself from them, and she didn't know how long she could last.

Every day, Ryker did something new to endear himself to her. She hadn't glimpsed the monster once, nor had she seen or heard anything that would lead her to believe an evil man resided in his skin. That was a problem.

An enormous, horrifying problem.

Brynleigh released her shadows. They darkened the bathroom but did nothing to ease the anger and doubt running through her.

The Masked Ball was in two days. Tomorrow, they were returning to Golden City. Apparently, the Hall of Choice had been repaired after the attack. Brynleigh wasn't worried about the journey or the rebels. The participants would be well-guarded, and she was strong enough to care for herself.

No, the problem lay entirely with Ryker. The more time she spent with the water fae, the more she learned about him and the more conflicted she became about her purpose.

He had killed her family in cold blood. By definition, that made him a monster. As someone with blood on her hands—blood of criminals, but still blood—she recognized when someone was evil.

But Ryker hadn't shown her the monster. She hadn't even glimpsed him. Where the fuck was he?

The captain was a sore loser—which secretly delighted Brynleigh, because one would think that a military man would be able to lose gracefully—but he was also kind, caring, and had a slight hint of possessiveness that Brynleigh enjoyed more than she dared admit.

Brynleigh groaned and shut off the water. She stepped out of the shower, toweling off. This would be so much easier if Ryker were evil.

Hanging up her towel, she strode back into the small bedroom. Sarai's picture was on the nightstand, but even that didn't spark the usual fire of revenge. She needed answers, and if she weren't going to sleep, she'd focus on finding out what was going on.

Stepping into a pair of black leggings, Brynleigh pulled them up before drawing on a matching sweater. She threw her hair in a messy bun and drew the hood over her golden locks before sliding her sister's picture into her pocket.

This was risky. The participants weren't supposed to leave their rooms at night. The men and women were staying in different wings of the mansion, and the Matrons had made it very clear that although they were not currently in the Hall of Choice, the structure of the Choosing was still to be respected. These included following archaic laws such as remaining apart during the dating process and abstaining from sexual relations until the wedding night.

Brynleigh wasn't sure what the recourse would be if she were caught, and she didn't plan to find out. She had something the other women didn't: shadows.

Darkness was a deep, powerful song in Brynleigh's veins. Her shadows were always there, waiting to be used. Her wings were an equally powerful form of magic, but unlike the shadows that were her birthright, they didn't itch to be set free if she didn't use them enough. On the other hand, her shadows were an intrinsic part of Brynleigh, an extension of her limbs, and needed to be used.

The vampire exhaled, opened her palms, and released the wisps of night. They flowed from her until the darkness swallowed everything, even the glowing light of the clock. She didn't have time to appreciate her dark magic's effectiveness because she had places to be.

Pulling on her shadows, Brynleigh stepped into the Void. The black, empty place allowed vampires to move from one location to another. Uncertain of whether there were wards that would keep her from journeying far from the mansion, Brynleigh decided the easiest and safest course of action would be to return to the small infirmary.

Traveling to the moonlit woods was a matter of seconds. She stepped out of the Void and wrapped her darkness around her like a cloak. The arctic wind bit at her exposed flesh, but she ignored it to study the cabin.

A burly guard dressed in black gear, gloves, and boots was stationed out front. The curtains were pulled back, and the light of a single desk lamp sliced through the night.

Damn. Brynleigh hoped Doctor Carin would be asleep, but apparently, she was a night owl.

Still, the vampire had made it this far. Giving up on her plan was not an option. Brynleigh was far too aware that she may not have another chance. She surveyed the door. She would knock out the guard if she had to, but she'd rather not leave any trace of her presence.

A quarter of an hour passed before the light flickered off. Isvana must have been smiling down on Brynleigh, because moments later, the doctor stepped out of the cabin. Wrapped in a thick fur coat, Carin carried a stack of files.

Brynleigh smiled at the sudden stroke of luck.

"Done for the night, Doctor?" the guard asked.

"I am, Lucas." She locked the cabin door. "Thank you. You didn't have to stay. I would've been fine."

Lucas shook his head and offered the doctor his arm. "I couldn't leave you alone. There are reports of increased rebel activity all through the Republic. Besides, I've met your wife. No one wants to piss her off."

"True, she's fierce." Carin chuckled and placed her hand on Luca's extended limb. "Thank you for waiting."

Brynleigh added more shadows around herself as the pair walked past, careful not to let her cloak slip. She waited until they had disappeared through the trees before running to the cabin door in a blur. She pressed her ear against the wall and listened intently.

When she was confident the cabin was empty, Brynleigh stepped into the Void again. The lock on the door might prevent most people from entering, but it wouldn't stop her.

Brynleigh's shadows dropped her into the middle of the cabin. She moved with stealth towards the desk and picked up the phone. She couldn't waste any time—what if Lucas planned on returning?

Her fingers dialed Zanri's number from memory.

Her handler picked up on the first ring. "Hello?" He sounded groggy, and for a moment, Brynleigh felt bad. She probably woke him up.

"It's me, Z," she whispered.

"Brynleigh, what the hell?" Someone grumbled in the background, and it sounded like Zanri stumbled into another room. A door closed. "You shouldn't be calling me. The risk—"

"Fuck the risk," she bit out. It didn't matter that she interrupted him. She didn't have time for his rambling. The guard could come back at any moment. "I had to call. It's important."

A sigh that could level cities slipped from Zanri's mouth. Leather creaked, and she imagined him dropping into his favorite red, worn armchair. "Jelisette isn't here."

"I figured," said Brynleigh.

As long as Brynleigh had known Jelisette, the older vampire had kept a standing appointment once a week. She'd never missed it.

"What's going on?"

"I called to talk to you, Z. I need your advice, not Jelisette's."

Brynleigh already knew what her Maker would say. Jelisette would remind her of all ten rules and reassure her she was on the right track. The problem was that Brynleigh wasn't so sure about that anymore.

"What do you need, B?"

She palmed her neck. "You've been watching the Choosing?"

"Of course. We all have."

Her eyes fell shut, and she groaned. "I'm having trouble."

That was an understatement.

"What kind of trouble?" Zanri sounded like he didn't want to know.

That made two of them. These feelings were wrong. These questions were wrong. And yet, she couldn't stop the next words from pouring from her lips. "Ryker is nothing like what I expected."

"Brynleigh," the shifter growled in warning. "The fae is your mark."

As if she needed the reminder. The truth of what happened to Chavin haunted her every waking moment.

"I know what he is," she hissed into the receiver, clutching the phone. "You think I've somehow forgotten that? Every day, I remember."

"Then what's the problem?"

She pressed the phone against her ear and picked at her pendant with her free hand. "I know what he did. I was there. But maybe..." She chewed on her lip. "Maybe he's changed? Maybe the reason he was in hiding, the reason we couldn't find him, was because he was turning his life around."

Six years was a long time. People changed, learned, and became better all the time. Or worse. Brynleigh was the perfect example. In six years, she'd become a cold-hearted killer. It was plausible that Ryker was no longer the same man as before. Right?

A long silence came through the line. A thousand-pound weight bore down on her shoulders. The sound of Zanri's breath was heavy in her ears.

Several minutes went by. Brynleigh's heart rapped an unsteady beat. Her hands slickened, and she passed the receiver from one hand to the other.

"Captain Ryker Waterborn is your mark." Zanri's voice was ice, altogether void of emotion.

"I know," Brynleigh replied.

"You entered the Choosing with one goal in mind. What was it?"

"Make him fall in love with me, marry him, and kill him on our wedding night," Brynleigh automatically whispered the words that had been drilled into her over years of practice.

A rumble of approval. "That's correct. And what is rule number ten?"

The hand gripping the phone trembled, and a cold sweat broke out on Brynleigh's forehead. *This* was why she had risked breaking the rules to call Zanri. This was the reminder she needed. She'd expected the words, but the pain...

She hadn't expected it to feel like a wooden stake piercing her heart.

"Focus, Brynleigh!" Zanri barked. "Rule number ten?"

Brynleigh closed her eyes and ran her tongue over her fangs. She took a deep breath and forced the words out of her dry mouth. "Once the game has begun, losing is not an option. The only alternative to winning is death."

Her voice trembled. Brynleigh knew the rules. She had agreed to them, having never even considered the consequences of losing. Her victory had been assumed... until she met her mark.

But now?

Now, doubt was an ember in her belly. It was warm and glowing, growing brighter by the day.

"Again," her handler demanded. "What is rule ten?"

Brynleigh briefly wondered why Jelisette and Zanri insisted on this course of action. Why were they pushing her so hard to kill Ryker?

But then Zanri barked her name, and she forgot those doubts. "Once the game has begun, losing is not an option," she repeated. Her voice was harder this time, and the doubt was further away. "The only alternative to losing is death."

Each word was crisp as it settled in her soul.

"Again," Zanri ordered for the third time.

She complied. Ten times, she repeated the rule. Soon, her voice was bolder. Firmer. That ember of doubt flickered and dimmed until it was nearly extinguished altogether.

Zanri was right. Losing wasn't an option. Ryker killed her family. He was responsible for their deaths. It didn't matter that the man wasn't what she expected. He was still a murderer.

Finishing the game was Brynleigh's only option.

"One more time," Zanri demanded coldly. The harshness in his voice was good. It reminded her of the realities she would face outside of the Choosing.

The box holding Brynleigh's emotions was fortified. She drew in a deep breath. "Losing is not an option. The only alternative to winning is death."

The ominous tenth rule rang through her head long after she'd hung up the phone and returned to her room.

Zanri was right, and rule ten was clear: Ryker Waterborn had to die.

CHAPTER 20

Retribution Would Be Hers

Ever since her phone call with Zanri two days ago, Brynleigh had replayed rule number ten through her mind until it was the only thing she heard. He was right. Losing was not an option.

Last night, under the cover of darkness, the participants of the Choosing had returned to Golden City. During the journey, Matron Lilith had explained that while they'd been in the north, the unrest in the Central Region had continued. As a result, the guard around the participants would be doubled. Other measures were being put in place, precautions to ensure everyone's safety.

Even now, a soldier was stationed outside Brynleigh's room. The vampire sat on her bed, brushing her hair and wondering what would happen if she dismissed him. It wasn't that she didn't appreciate his effort—she did. She'd be lying if she said the rebel activities weren't worrisome.

It was just that Brynleigh was antsy. Between everything going on with Ryker and the soldiers' presence, she couldn't find peace. Her fangs ached, and despite having imbibed in multiple pints of blood since returning to Golden City, she was starving.

Something was missing from her life, and she couldn't figure out what it was.

She wanted the guard to leave because she was itching for a fight. She would find Valentina, except getting kicked out of the Choosing hours before the Masked Ball seemed ridiculous. She'd done all the work to get here. Fighting that fiery bitch wasn't in the cards, but if a rebel showed up, Brynleigh would gladly take them on.

Someone knocked on the door.

Brynleigh's brow arched. What were the chances a rebel stood on the other side, serving themselves up on a silver platter? Slim, probably, but a vampire could hope.

Placing the hairbrush on the bed, she strode to the door and cracked it open. "Yes?"

Unless the rebels were in the habit of recruiting young elves with bright red hair and luminescent smiles, this wasn't one of them. The girl looked like she was in her late teens, not yet Mature, and she extended a long black garment bag in Brynleigh's direction. In her other hand, she held a smaller gift bag. "I've brought your gown, Miss de la Point."

Traditionally, in the Choosing, a woman's parents picked out her gown for the Masked Ball. Since Brynleigh's family was dead, she assumed her Maker had filled the role for her.

Thanking the elf, Brynleigh took both bags and let the door slip shut behind her. She returned to the bed and began unpacking her Maker's gift.

When Brynleigh saw the dress, she let out a low whistle of appreciation. This was, without a doubt, the finest gown Brynleigh had ever worn. This was the kind of dress most women admired from afar, and very few had the chance to wear.

It was stunning, perfect for a proposal, and...

Her family wasn't here tonight.

A tear lined the bottom of Brynleigh's eye. Her sister would have loved this dress. Sarai had always been interested in clothes and sewing in particular. A few months before the storm, Sarai had been accepted to the Western School of Design and Fashion to study fashion history. She would have attended in the fall.

Even without Sarai's sense of style, Brynleigh recognized a masterpiece when she saw one. Changing out of her leggings and t-shirt, she drew the gown over her head. Several well-placed zippers allowed her to get the garment on without help.

It fit her like a glove.

Once the zippers were closed, Brynleigh made her way to the floor-length mirror in the bathroom. After all, what was the point of wearing a beautiful gown if one didn't spend at least a few minutes admiring it? And this dress was meant to be admired.

It *screamed* vampire.

The scarlet garment was perfectly tailored to her body. It matched the theme of the Choosing beautifully. The ruby fabric shimmered and sparkled, making Brynleigh feel like she was wearing a jewel. The neckline was a low V that dipped almost to her navel. Long, slim sleeves ran to her wrists, and the dress pooled at her feet. A slit ran dangerously high up her leg, cutting off mid-thigh. She turned around and looked over her shoulder.

The back scooped low, barely covering her bottom. Perfect for wings. There was no doubt in Brynleigh's mind that her Maker had selected this dress for that very reason.

In the second bag was a pair of ruby heels, a crimson rose for her hair, a mask, and a piece of paper. Leaning against the dresser, Brynleigh carefully unfolded the note. Her Maker's handwriting looped across the page, and a splotch of ink on the top confirmed that Jelisette had used a quilled fountain pen to write the missive.

My youngest progeny,

May the goddess of the moon and the god of blood bless your Choice tonight. I know you will Choose correctly.

Remember what you've been taught.

- Jelisette

Brynleigh read the note twice before sighing and dropping the paper on the bed. A wave of disappointment washed over her, which was rather unexpected.

After six years, she thought Jelisette would have something a little more sentimental. Though her Maker wasn't exactly kind, Jelisette had filled a motherly role for Brynleigh over the past few years. This note lacked all sense of kindness though. There were only cold, regimented words meant to remind Brynleigh of her purpose.

If Brynleigh's parents were still alive, they would have words of wisdom for her. They would probably be excited for her—she was getting engaged, after all.

But her parents were dead. Sarai was dead. And Brynleigh? She was a vampire, and now, she was alone. Tonight, she would get engaged, but just like all the feelings she was ignoring, it was a lie. An act. A series of falsehoods.

Brynleigh's heart burned as dark fury ran through her veins. Maybe Jelisette knew exactly what she was doing when she penned that note. There was no room for emotions. No room for sentimentality. No room for anything at all except cold-blooded revenge.

Brynleigh was playing to win, and no one would deter her from her goal.

Not even the man who smelled like thunderstorms and bergamot.

The rules started playing through her head as she put in her earrings.

Rule number one: you cannot trust anyone.

Rule number two: doubly blessed vampires do not hide behind jewels or makeup. They let their gifts speak for themselves.

Her ears glistened, and she bent, sliding her feet into heels.

Rule number three: vampires are weapons. They must always look their best, ready to use their every gods-given gift to their deadly advantage.

Rule number four: vampires must always remain calm, even in the face of difficulty.

Rule number five: always trust your instincts.

She applied her makeup, the crimson lipstick reminding her of blood as she swiped it across her lips.

Rule number six: let nothing distract you from your goal.

Rule number seven: your Maker always knows best.

Rule number eight: emotions are for mortals, not vampires.

Gathering her hair, Brynleigh allowed some curls to fall halfway down her back before tying the rest in elaborate knots on top of her head.

Rule number nine: never turn your back on your enemy.

Rule number ten: once the game has begun, losing is not an option. The only alternative to winning is death.

Brynleigh stuck one last hairpin in her locks, then grabbed the rose. It was heavy, weighted like a tiara, and she pinned it behind her right ear. Other than that, the only jewelry she wore was the golden necklace. Last of all was the mask. It was crimson, like the gown and rose, and she tied it behind her head.

She stepped back, taking herself in critically before nodding approvingly. There was a certain lethal edge to her appearance that she enjoyed immensely.

Two things were missing.

Brynleigh reached within, drawing on her shadows and wings. The first pooled around her feet, the dark wisps giving her strength. The second hung on her back, the wings symbolizing her vampiric strength and power.

Now, she was ready.

Armed guards were stationed in front of the closed ballroom doors. Their faces were tight, and their eyes dark as they surveyed the hallway.

Brynleigh's gown swished as she strode towards them. She kept her wings tight against her back and held her head high.

"Miss de la Point," the guard on the left said. "Welcome."

Brynleigh smiled demurely, keeping her gaze locked on the closed double doors. Faint musical overtures trickled from the ballroom. "Is it my turn?"

Earlier, the Matron had explained how the Masked Ball would work. Each participant would enter separately so they could be announced. There would be drinks and small bites during the cocktail hour, but the real party would start after the proposals.

"Soon," he replied.

Heels clicked behind Brynleigh. An aura of wrongness settled around her. It was a warning, a pause before a storm, a moment of peace before danger. The vampire stiffened and turned around as a tall woman drew near.

Even in a mask, Brynleigh recognized Valentina. The fire fae's floor-length ballgown was so wide that it would barely make it through the door. Pale pink, almost white roses covered the dress from the top of the bodice down to her feet. Valentina's blue-black hair was in a tight bun, and tendrils floated around her face. Cruel violet eyes peered out from behind a cream mask and narrowed when they landed on the vampire. Red lips twisted into a wicked sneer.

"Well, if it isn't the fucking leech who stole my fae." Valentina stalked towards Brynleigh, her eyes flickering with an undisguised threat of violence. "If it weren't for you, he'd be Choosing *me* tonight."

Shadows frothed in Brynleigh's veins, and her fangs tightened in her gums. Her fists wanted nothing more than to connect with Valentina's ugly face, but she couldn't give in to her desire.

The fourth rule played in Brynleigh's mind. She amended it, adding a clause for awful fire fae with hateful vendettas. Gods, why couldn't Hallie have been here instead?

Brynleigh had the worst luck.

"Your fae?" Brynleigh tilted her head, forcing her face into a mask of calmness she did not feel inside. "I'm certain I don't know who you're talking about."

Valentina snarled, baring her elongated canines. They were nothing like the fangs within Brynleigh's mouth, but they were sharp... for a fae. "You undead, whoreish, night-walking grave dweller. You know exactly who I'm talking about."

Was Valentina so unintelligent that she could not come up with insults unrelated to Brynleigh's species? How incredibly unoriginal.

"Do I?" Brynleigh picked at non-existent dirt beneath her nails. "Hmm. I'm not sure."

An unladylike growl rumbled through Valentina. "Captain Ryker Waterborn, that's who. He was supposed to be mine."

Brynleigh's wings fanned out behind her, and her head snapped up.

She dropped her hands and curled into fists. "What the fuck did you say?"

She knew he and Valentina had been seeing each other early on during the Choosing—they were a small group, after all—but she'd never heard the fire fae lay a claim on Ryker.

And Brynleigh did not like it. Not one bit.

"You heard me." Valentina had the gods-damned audacity to take another step closer to her. "The captain is the most prestigious fae here. He would've made the best husband for me. And you had to come in with your dirty blonde hair and sharp fangs and ruin everything."

Anger was burning lava as it ran through Brynleigh's cold veins. Shadows flooded out of her, and she snarled.

"Fuck you." Brynleigh's fangs burned. Her nails sliced through her palms and drew blood. Stepping closer to Valentina, she met those violet orbs and hissed, "He's *mine*."

Her claiming words rang through the hall. Somewhere deep within Brynleigh, something shifted.

Valentina's eyes widened, and her mouth opened and closed. Was she in shock that Brynleigh would claim her man so openly? She wasn't the only one.

Brynleigh hadn't meant to speak the claiming words. At least, not with so much passion and truth. Of course, Ryker was hers... to kill. She refused to acknowledge that there might be any other reason she had claimed him.

The guard cleared his throat. "Miss de la Point, it's time."

Thank all the gods. Shooting Valentina one last glare for good measure, Brynleigh moved towards the doors. She ran her fingers down her gown and straightened an invisible wrinkle before drawing in a deep breath.

Once again, rule ten ran through her mind.

"I'm ready," she said confidently.

The guard nodded and opened the door. The music slowly died as hundreds of eyes turned towards Brynleigh at once.

She refused to feel nervous beneath the weight of their attention. Instead, she held her chin up high and kept her wings tight behind her as she stood in the doorway, taking in the ballroom.

It had undergone yet another transformation. There were no signs of the rebels' attack. Now, the ballroom was a grand space meant to house the party of the decade. Six diamond chandeliers glistened. Ruby tapestries adorned the walls, bearing the Republic's crest. Servers wearing black milled about handing out flutes of sparkling wine and small finger foods.

And the people.

Gods, there were so many of them. There had to be close to five hundred, if not more. The scent of their blood was enticing, but Brynleigh had already drunk plenty tonight in preparation for being in front of so many people.

Horned and winged elves stood among fae. Werewolves chatted with witches. Shifters interacted with vampires. There were even a few humans among the crowd. The clothes were a testament to the beauty and expansiveness of the rainbow, each outfit slightly different from the last. Everyone was masked, like her.

Despite the face coverings, Brynleigh noted many familiar faces in the crowd. Guards she'd come to recognize over the past few weeks intermingled with guests. They wore suits and gowns, attempting to blend in, but nothing could hide the glint of awareness in their eyes. Weapons bulged under black jackets, and she pitied anyone who tried to attack tonight.

A ten-piece orchestra sat on the stage, their stringed instruments poised mid-air.

A herald dressed in crimson-edged black stepped out from the shadows on her right. "Ladies and gentlemen." His voice boomed through the now-silent hall. "It is my honor to present the ninth participant in this year's Choosing, Miss Brynleigh de la Point."

Her heart pounded in her chest as she waited for someone to move. It felt like every second stretched longer than the last until finally, someone in the crowd clapped. They triggered the others, and a roar of applause soon filled the ballroom.

Blood rushed to Brynleigh's cheeks, and she fought the urge to look down at the floor. It wasn't that she minded the attention, per se, but simply that she wanted to get this evening started.

The sooner she got in there, the sooner they could get to the proposals and the sooner the evening would be over. She'd be engaged and one step closer to her goal.

And yet... those claiming words echoed in her mind. What was she thinking, saying them out loud?

He's mine.

Her heart thrashed in her chest, a wild animal. Emotions threatened to rise. Her lungs burned. She closed her eyes, inhaling deeply. Those watching her probably mistook her actions for nerves.

They were wrong.

Brynleigh was grounding herself in the one thing she knew—pain. Pulling forth memories of the past, the vampire did something she rarely allowed herself to do.

She remembered the night her family died.

"I SAW Mrs. Caldwell at the store yesterday." Isolde Larkspur, Brynleigh's mother, scrubbed at a pot in the sink while Brynleigh dried the dishes by hand.

"Oh?" Brynleigh's fingers tightened around the pale blue dinner plate.

Her mother didn't notice. "Yes. She mentioned Jonah will be returning home next month. He'll be staying with his parents until the new year." She smiled at her daughter, a twinkle in her blue eyes. "He's going to be here for the Winter Solstice."

Isolde was not subtle.

Brynleigh stared out the window. The cloudless sky was tinged with orange as the evening slowly gave way to night. "That's nice, Mama."

Please drop this, she silently added. Brynleigh knew where this was going. She and Jonah had known each other since they were children. He was a few years older than her, but she hadn't seen him since her return from university last year.

"And he's single." Isolde bumped her hip against Brynleigh's. "Maybe you should see if he's interested in being your date to the family holiday party?"

There was no way Brynleigh could miss the note of hopefulness in her mother's voice. She groaned. "We're just friends, Mama."

"But you could be more!"

That was unlikely. When Brynleigh was six and Jonah was nine, she'd witnessed the unfortunate event of Jonah eating a worm. There wasn't enough time to make her forget that. "I don't think so."

The neighbors probably heard Isolde's responding sigh. In the beginning, Brynleigh had found Isolde's not-so-subtle approaches to matchmaking amusing, but now they were becoming dreary. She wasn't even sure she wanted a relationship. She'd enjoyed her time at the University of Balance, experimenting with men and women as one did, but for now, she was happy to focus on her life.

She'd returned home to work in her parents' general store, unsure of what she wanted to do with her life. Chavin was a small town filled with hardworking humans. It wasn't a big city, but it was home, and Brynleigh liked it here. If her parents could make a life here, she could, too.

Isolde handed the pot to Brynleigh, and her gaze swept over her daughter as she leaned on the counter. "I want you to be happy, Brynny. That's all."

"I know." And she did. She'd never doubted her parents' love.

"We love you," her mother added. "It's important that we see you settled."

Isolde meant well. Her actions, though overbearing, were filled with love. Brynleigh knew her parents meant well. They had a good family life, and she couldn't complain about her childhood.

Setting the pot on the drying rack, Brynleigh sat at the round kitchen table and picked up the navy skein of yarn she was working on. Wrapping it around the knitting needle, she purled three stitches. "I am happy."

Her mother sat across from her and picked up her own project. "But you could be happier."

Brynleigh chuckled and shook her head. "Let it go, Mama, please."

Soon, the steady clicking of knitting needles filled the kitchen as the two women silently worked. This was the fourth time she and Isolde had this conversation this summer. Brynleigh was starting to understand why many of her friends hadn't moved back home after school.

"What the hell?" Isolde swore.

Brynleigh dropped a stitch, her mother's harsh language so out of place from her usual calm demeanor. She jerked up her head and turned around. The moment Brynleigh looked out the window, a slew of curses slipped from her own tongue.

The sky was an ominous dark gray edged with green. Lightning bolts shot above the endless plains of the Western Region. The wind swirled, and shouts came from outside.

Isolde didn't scold Brynleigh for using foul language. Instead, she ran as quickly as she could out of the kitchen. "Gavin! Sarai!" Her voice was frantic. "Come quickly!"

Abandoning her knitting, Brynleigh raced after her mother.

Footsteps pounded down the stairs of the modest two-story home as Gavin raced towards them. "What's wrong, love?"

"Look!" Isolde raised a shaking finger to the bay window in the living room.

Seconds later, Gavin was barking into his phone, calling the police.

The air crackled, and the scent of ozone surrounded them.

Isolde turned to Brynleigh, her eyes darting frantically between the staircase and the storm outside. "Where's your sister?"

Brynleigh frowned, and her stomach twisted. "I thought she was upstairs."

Sarai should have come down with all the yelling, though. She was nothing if not attentive.

"Get her," Isolde commanded.

"Of course." Brynleigh took the stairs two at a time. She shoved open her little sister's door, not bothering to knock. "Sarai, what's going on? There's a random storm—"

The room was empty. Where was she? A quick search of the closet and upstairs bathroom revealed Sarai wasn't there.

Thunder boomed, and Brynleigh hurried back into her sister's room. A calendar hung above Sarai's desk.

Today's date was circled, and scrawled underneath was "Fairgrounds."

"Fuck." Brynleigh whipped out her phone and speed-dialed her sister as she ran downstairs.

There was no answer.

Brynleigh pulled on her raincoat, tucked the necklace her parents had given her for her eighteenth birthday beneath her collar, and shot her sister a series of texts.

She stared at the screen, waiting for the telltale checkmarks to show them as read. The notifications never came.

Of all the days for Sarai to be unreachable, why did she pick today?

Rain pelted the windows, each drop sounding like a gunshot. The wind wailed like a screaming woman. Thunder roared its fury through the heavens.

Brynleigh had never seen a storm of this magnitude in her twenty-three years.

She shoved her feet in indigo rain boots.

"Where are you going?" Isolde ran up behind Brynleigh and grabbed her arm.

"To get Sarai." Brynleigh pulled her hood over her hair. "Stay inside. I'll be back as soon as I can."

Wide, horror-filled eyes met hers. "You're going out in this? You can't! It's dangerous."

"I'll be fine, Mama," Brynleigh said placatingly. It was a rainstorm. What was the worst thing that could happen? "Someone needs to get Sarai. She's not answering her phone, and I want to ensure she gets home safely."

It was Brynleigh's job as the older sister to look after Sarai. She'd always felt that way, even when Sarai was a baby. This was no different. Besides, the fairgrounds weren't far from their house. The massive clearing was a frequent gathering spot for young adults. Brynleigh had spent many a late night there in the past.

Gavin thrust an umbrella at his eldest daughter. "Be safe. This storm came out of nowhere. Get your sister and come home as quickly as you can. I'll check on Mrs. Cooper. She must be scared."

As if emphasizing his point, the power flickered and went out. Darkness surrounded them. A faint scream came from next door. Mrs. Cooper was an elderly widow, almost ninety years old, and as long as Brynleigh could remember, she'd lived alone.

"Good idea, Gavin," Isolde said. "I'll stay here in case Sarai comes back."

"Call me if she does." Brynleigh kissed Isolde on the cheek before hugging her father. She tucked her phone into her pocket and opened the door. "I love you both," she said over her shoulder. "Be back soon."

Streams of water fell from the heavens.

Brynleigh pressed the button on the side of the umbrella, and the waterproof fabric fanned out over her head. It did little to stop the deluge of water pouring over her. The storm was escalating. Where had it come from? She could ponder the origins of the storm after she found Sarai.

Brynleigh ran down the street, her feet pounding against the cement. She moved swiftly, barely seeing the other people running in the opposite direction. Everyone was soaked and confused, staring skyward as water pelted them from above.

She turned towards the fairground.

The sky was a swirling, furious mass of black and gray. There were no stars. No moon. The only light came from the flashes of lightning crashing through the midsummer night at regular intervals.

The closer she came to the field, the more worried Brynleigh became. She had expected to see Sarai on her way here, but there was no sign of her sister. Where was she? Sarai was smart. She would've started running home as soon as the storm hit.

The water rose far too quickly to be normal. First, it reached her ankles. Then, her knees.

Thunder bellowed its anger.

In the distance, someone screamed.

Dropping the useless umbrella, Brynleigh cupped her hands around her mouth and yelled, "Sarai! Where are you?"

The wind swallowed her words.

She ran to the fairgrounds, calling for her sister.

The water rose and rose. She half-waded, half-sprinted through the torrential storm. Soon, it was up to her thighs.

The fairgrounds were in sight.

"Sarai!"

Nothing.

Trees bowed in her direction, the wind pulling them nearly in half. Debris floated on top of the water. Branches the size of her arm flew through the air.

She swore, her stomach dropped as she scanned the area. No one was here. Even the stands, usually occupied by at least two or three couples enjoying each other's company, stood empty.

A chasmic, numbing panic settled in Brynleigh's stomach. She couldn't go home without Sarai. Her imagination ran wild as she imagined the look of horror on her parents' faces if she returned alone. She couldn't do that to them. Sarai was the youngest member of their family. She was kind and good and never caused any trouble.

Brynleigh had to find her.

The water was up to Brynleigh's hips when she turned and started back home. She swiped her hands over her eyes, trying to clear her vision. She waded, shivering and rubbing her arms as she searched left and right for Sarai.

The storm still raged. Chavin descended into watery chaos. Trees split. Glass shattered. People screamed. Wood creaked. The rain kept coming.

Brynleigh's heart pounded as she headed in the direction she thought Sarai would take to go home. Maybe she'd see her on the way. They could laugh about how silly this was as they found refuge inside. They would sit and watch the lightning from the living room, like when they were little girls. Isolde would—

There!

Sarai was down half a block, standing in hip-deep water at the street corner with her back to Brynleigh.

Hope surged in Brynleigh's chest, and she pumped her arms and legs as she hurried towards her sister. "Sarai! We need to go!"

Sarai wasn't moving. She was just... staring off into the distance.

What was she looking at?

"Hey!" Brynleigh screamed. "Turn around! We have to go home. This isn't safe!"

A boom of thunder that was like a stack of bricks being thrown crashed through the sky.

It felt like it took an eternity of pushing through water to reach

Sarai. Brynleigh fought against the current, the water from below nearly as powerful as the storm rushing from above, but she kept moving.

She'd never give up.

Her lungs burned, and her muscles ached as she grabbed Sarai's arm. "Let's go!"

Sarai lifted a trembling finger at the horizon. "L-l-look."

Brynleigh turned, her eyes widening as a scream ripped from her throat.

A wave taller than all the houses in their village crested over the roofs. It was a harbinger of doom, a bringer of death, and it was coming straight for them.

"Fucking run!" Brynleigh shouted, yanking Sarai behind her.

The unnatural storm chased them through the streets. No matter how fast they ran, they couldn't escape the screaming, the crashing of water against wood, and the destruction of one house after another.

And in the end, they weren't fast enough.

The water was a hungry, ruthless beast as it devoured them whole.

Brynleigh opened her eyes.

Time seemed to slow as she grounded herself in the present once more. She was in the ballroom, not in the midst of a deadly storm. Her heart thudded from a memory, not from being chased by an enormous wave.

Her shadows throbbed in her veins.

Death had reigned in Chavin that midsummer's evening. The entire town had flooded and been destroyed. Their prairie homes weren't built to withstand the force of nature that had been Ryker's storm.

It had raged for hours, killing everyone and destroying everything within ten miles of the town before abruptly ending. By then, Brynleigh was an orphan, and Jelisette had Made her.

Brynleigh took a deep breath and scanned the crowd. She wasn't certain what she was looking for, but she kept searching until she met a pair of chocolate-brown eyes across the room.

The moment their eyes locked, her heart ceased beating in her chest. Shadows spun around her feet.

Time froze.

They stared at each other, the crowd between them meaningless. It didn't matter that she'd never seen him before. It didn't matter that he wore a mask. She knew it was him. Ryker Waterborn. Holding his gaze, she stepped towards him.

It was time.

CHAPTER 21
A Meeting for the Ages

Ryker was standing at the far end of the ballroom discussing military maneuvers with Therian when the doors opened.

"Ladies and gentlemen," the herald announced, the microphone pinned to his lapel projecting his voice, "it is my honor to present the ninth participant in this year's Choosing, Miss Brynleigh de la Point."

Ryker's eyes flew to the ballroom doors. His height afforded him the ability to see over the heads of most of those gathered, giving him the perfect view of his intended bride. Like most of the men here, he was dressed to the nines. His suit and shoes were black, but he'd picked his tie for Brynleigh.

The moment she stepped into the ballroom, he knew he'd made a good choice. The crimson tie matched her stunning gown perfectly.

By the Sands, she was gorgeous.

Brynleigh paused on the threshold. Ryker's lungs tightened as he drank in the sight of his intended. The crimson mask hid her features, but the beautiful black bat wings and the shadows curling around her legs marked her as a creature of the night.

His creature of the night.

Ryker unabashedly studied his vampire. Immortal grace and poise emanated from her, and she was impeccably put together. Silken gold hair framed her face. A crimson gown hugged her body.

And her curves. His imagination hadn't done her justice. She was a dark goddess. The low V of her dress highlighted full breasts that were begging to be held and loved and admired. Her hips were rounded. A muscular thigh peeked through the slit in her dress.

Fucking perfection.

Ryker's entire body tightened as pure, hot, primal need ran through him. He couldn't wait to get her alone, to run his hands over her and claim her as his.

She stepped forward, poised and graceful. Her mouth tilted into a small smile, and her black eyes swept over the assembled group. Searching.

Kydona help him, but he'd waited so long for this moment. Tracing the outline of the box in his pocket, he turned to Therian.

"I've got to go." He clapped his friend on the back.

If the dragon shifter replied, Ryker didn't hear it. He was already moving across the ballroom, pushing past curious onlookers drawn towards her. The closer he got, the stronger her scent became.

Soon, night-blooming roses were all he could smell.

Nothing could keep him from going to her. Why were there so many people here?

Ryker was halfway across the ballroom when those beautiful obsidian orbs met his gaze. Though they were masked, it was like she stared directly into his soul.

He froze mid-step as if something had slammed into him. His heart was a drum in his ears. Shivers ran down his spine. The world stopped spinning, his magic thrummed in his veins, and deep within him, something he hadn't known he was missing settled into place.

A sea of people separated them, but it didn't matter. It turned out nothing mattered but her.

Time unfroze.

They both moved as if pulled by the same cord. He kept his eyes on her, pushing through the crowd until nothing but a few feet separated them.

Finally. Together at last. No barriers. Nothing keeping them apart. Not anymore.

Her lips parted, and he glimpsed two fangs nestled in her gums.

Hi, she mouthed.

He returned the silent greeting, vaguely aware that other things were happening around them.

The remaining participants of the Choosing were announced, and they entered the ballroom in turn.

He held Brynleigh's gaze.

Chancellor Rose took the stage, speaking into the microphone.

Brynleigh raised a brow as if saying, *Can you believe we have to listen to another speech?*

He smirked.

Ignatia Rose applauded the members of this year's Choosing for their "flexibility." A fucking understatement, but Ryker didn't even care. His vampire was here.

Ryker took another step towards Brynleigh. He committed her to memory.

Mine.

Soon, the entire world would know this gorgeous vampire was his, and his alone.

Earlier, Ryker had volunteered to propose first. Stepping up wasn't difficult—he was already certain of his decision and couldn't wait to see Brynleigh. His fingers twitched at his sides. He itched to rip the mask off her face.

He wanted to see her, touch her, kiss her.

It felt like the Chancellor's speech stretched on for hours, although it was likely mere minutes.

The entire time, Ryker's gaze didn't slip from his vampire's. Not when Chancellor Rose announced it was time for the first proposal. Not when the crowd moved back, lining the walls, until only the couples remained in the middle of the ballroom. Not when a spotlight shone down on them, illuminating them for the cameras that were certainly watching.

He was ready for this.

Ryker stepped forward, finally closing the distance between him and his vampire. Silence fell upon the ballroom as hundreds of eyes landed on them. They didn't bother him. As far as he was concerned, it was just him and Brynleigh.

No one else, not even the Chancellor, mattered.

Holding Brynleigh's gaze, Ryker reached out and took his vampire's hand in his. She hitched a breath at the contact, this touch as powerful as their first. Sparks coursed through him, and her fingers curled against his.

Once again, he marveled at the softness of her flesh. Her long, slender fingers fit perfectly within his hand. His thumb rubbed slow circles against her as he drew her closer.

When there was a mere foot between them, the corner of his lips twitched upwards. "You're beautiful." His hushed words were meant for her ears only.

Her red lips slanted up, giving him another peek of fang. She blushed, her cheeks turning a dusty rose that accented her beauty.

He would endeavor to make her blush every day.

"Thank you, Ry," she murmured. "You don't look so bad yourself."

The way her lips formed his name would forever be seared on his heart. He yearned to hear her say it a thousand times over, and he would cherish each instance.

His thumb swept across the back of her hand. "Ready, sweetheart?"

She drew in a deep breath and dipped her head. "It feels like I've been waiting for years for this moment."

In a way, so had he. When he'd agreed to enter the Choosing, Ryker had never imagined it would feel like this. So perfect. So right.

His entire body was on edge as Brynleigh stepped back and withdrew her hand from his. He let her go, his gaze glued to her willowy movements as she reached for the black silk strands securing the mask to her face.

His breath caught in his throat, and his eyes focused solely on the pull of her fingers. She tugged, and the silk knot behind her head came loose. The mask tumbled to the floor like an autumnal leaf.

Brynleigh was *stunning*. Beautiful in an unusual way that spoke to the deepest parts of him. Wide black eyes met his. Her cheekbones were strong. Her red lips were plump and kissable. She was everything he'd ever dreamed of, and yet, nothing like he'd ever imagined.

It took everything he had not to surge forward and wrap her in his arms.

Holding her gaze, his fingers rose and found the ribbons of his mask. He undid the knot and let the mask go.

His hands dropped, and his heart hammered as her gaze swept over his face. He would give anything for the ability to read minds right now. He wanted to know each of her thoughts.

After what felt like an eternity, Brynleigh stepped towards him. She reached up, her fingers grazing his cheek. "You're real," she murmured as if she couldn't believe it. "I'm touching you."

He felt the same way. This was like a dream.

Over the past six weeks, he'd learned to interpret every influx of Brynleigh's voice, every hitch of her breath, and every laugh. They'd shared some of their deepest secrets, talked about everything and nothing, and played chess for hours, and he was finally putting a face to the person behind it all.

And this was more than he'd ever imagined.

Seeing Brynleigh for the first time was like having lived his life in darkness and then stepping into the sunshine. Their connection was deep, powerful, overwhelming, and *right*.

"I'm real." Capturing her hand in his, he brought it to his mouth and grazed a feather-light kiss over her knuckles. "So are you."

Brynleigh sucked in a breath, and her wings flared out behind her. Someone in the crowd murmured, but he couldn't make out their words over the slamming of his heart against his ribs.

Threading their fingers together, Ryker held Brynleigh's hand as he dropped to one knee. The floor was cold beneath him, but the temperature didn't bother him.

Her mouth opened, and her tongue flicked against her bottom lip, wetting it.

Ryker reached into his suit pocket and closed his fingers around the black velvet box he'd tucked in there earlier. He drew it out slowly, prolonging the moment.

Silence enveloped the ballroom. It was so quiet that every sound, every hitched breath, was amplified a hundred times over. Nerves were tiny butterflies dancing in his stomach, and beads of sweat broke out on his forehead.

Ryker had practiced what he would say, but now the words didn't seem like enough. What if she said no? What if he was about to make a fool of himself?

His lungs squeezed, and for a moment, he thought he would pass out. Black spots appeared before his eyes, and he struggled to breathe. Right now, he wasn't a military captain or a powerful fae. He was a man hoping the woman he loved would accept his proposal.

Brynleigh gripped his hand, and her mouth curved up. *It's okay,* she seemed to be telling him. *We're in this together.*

Just like that, the nerves were banished. The butterflies found a new home, far, far away from him.

Ryker held Brynleigh's hand and stared deeply into those black eyes. "Sweetheart, getting to know you over the past six weeks has been the greatest honor of my life." His voice was steady and as unwavering as his grip as he spoke. "The day I walked through the doors of the Hall of Choice, I hoped to find a bride. I wanted someone smart, fierce, and loyal who could love someone like me."

He kissed the back of her hand. "I was hoping for you, even if I didn't know it yet."

Someone in the crowd gasped.

Another murmured, "This is so romantic."

Ryker tuned them out, focusing solely on the vampire before him. "Brynleigh Elise de la Point, I love you."

This was the first time the water fae had said those words aloud, but it wouldn't be the last. He would proclaim them every single day from now until he Faded.

"You are the moon, shining your brilliant light into my life," Ryker murmured, his voice deepening. "I lived in darkness before I met you and didn't even know it. You complete me. I wake daily thinking of you, and you've already taught me so much."

Brynleigh's gaze softened, and she whispered his name. "You've taught me a lot, too."

"I can't wait to see where the rest of our life goes." Ryker's grip tightened on her hand. Though his next words were quieter, their impact reverberated throughout his entire being. "Will you marry me?"

Brynleigh inhaled deeply, and her fingers twitched in his.

He silently begged her, *Please say yes.*

The entirety of Ryker's world revolved around the beautiful vampire before him. Every breath, every heartbeat, every second felt like an eternity as he waited for her response.

She opened her mouth and whispered, "Yes."

Ryker rose to his feet in one smooth movement. "Yes?"

His vampire—his fiancée—laughed. The beautiful, familiar sound washed over him like springtime rain. "Of course, I'll marry you." Her smile could have lit up the darkest room. "I've been waiting for this day since we first met."

Elation, unlike anything he'd ever felt, washed through Ryker. He grinned and picked Brynleigh up, twirling her in a circle. Her crimson gown trailed behind her, and she giggled.

"She said yes!" he shouted. He wanted everyone to hear their good news.

Cheers and claps filled the ballroom as Ryker returned Brynleigh to her feet. Remembering the box he held, he popped open the lid. Smaller onyx jewels encircled the sole diamond, and the ring sparkled in the light.

Brynleigh gasped. She reached for the ring, only to pull back at the last moment. "Ryker, this... it's too much."

She was wrong. Nothing was too much for her. She was his, and she would soon learn what it meant to be loved by him. Ryker always looked after those closest to him.

He shook his head. "No. It's perfect, like you."

She opened her mouth, but nothing came out.

Ryker was delighted that he'd rendered her speechless. He'd chosen this ring with her in mind. Lifting her left hand, he asked, "May I?"

She nodded slowly. "Of course."

Sliding the ring onto the appropriate finger with care, Ryker admired the fit. "Do you like it?"

Glistening black eyes met his, making him feel like the most important man in the world. "I love it."

The look on Brynleigh's face made Ryker forget they had an audience. She looked at him like he was the reason the world turned; she was there for him and only for him.

He felt the same way.

Threading their fingers together, he drew Brynleigh closer to him. He bent his head, his arm wrapping around her waist and settling beneath her wings.

She hitched a breath as his lips brushed the shell of her ear, and he whispered, "I love you."

She shivered beneath his touch, and he kissed her cheek before he could stop himself. The responding frisson that ran through her delighted him. He wanted to kiss her more thoroughly, but he would wait until they were alone.

While he was willing to share the beginning of their relationship with the world, their first kiss and everything that came after would be just for them.

He couldn't wait.

CHAPTER 22
Death is the Only Alternative

Brynleigh's container of emotions was dangerously close to overflowing. Everything had been going well until she locked eyes with Ryker and tumbled headfirst into a spiral of feelings. No matter how much she shoved them down, they insisted on making a reappearance.

After Ryker's proposal, seven more couples got engaged. That was a record number for the Choosing, and the air in the ballroom was one of absolute delight. Chancellor Rose took the stage and spoke for a few minutes about how pleased she was with the outcome of the Two-Hundredth Choosing. According to her, it was a sign of prosperity and good things to come for the Republic of Balance.

Brynleigh wasn't so sure. She noticed the guards lining the walls behind the Chancellor, their presence a reminder of the unrest outside these walls. No one else seemed to mind them, though. Maybe Brynleigh was wrong, and the worst had passed.

The stringed orchestra picked up their instruments before Brynleigh could delve too far into those thoughts. They began to play, their lyrical music stunningly beautiful.

Ryker turned to Brynleigh. A radiant smile shone on the water fae's face.

Guilt stabbed Brynleigh in the gut.

Ryker was so happy, and she was a terrible person for stringing him along. He had no idea about her true intentions. How could he? She was supposed to be marrying him for love, or at least the potential for love.

Instead, she was playing him.

"Dance with me?" Ryker dipped into a low, old-fashioned, courtly bow and held out his hand. A lock of his hair—a brown several shades darker than his chocolate eyes—fell forward, but he made no effort to brush it away.

Brynleigh stared at his hand, the inviting gesture drawing her towards him. She shouldn't dance with the handsome water fae. It was a very bad idea. The offer alone made yet another pesky feeling that she refused to acknowledge sprout up within her, and she shoved it deep down.

But it would be rude if she ignored him... right?

All around them, other couples danced. The muscular dragon shifter, Therian, spun Hallie in a circle. Her wings fluttered behind her, and they both laughed as he lifted her off the ground. They were a cute couple, especially with the way the dragon shifter towered over the smaller woman.

Less delightful was the couple dancing beside them. The second-to-last proposal had been from Edward, a fae, to Valentina. Brynleigh didn't know his affinity, but seeing as the fire fae had accepted his hand, she assumed he was powerful. Brynleigh would be watching them both carefully. Whoever put up with Valentina was either a saint or as horrible as she was.

Ryker was still waiting patiently for Brynleigh to accept his offer to dance.

For a long moment, she stared at his hand while her internal debate raged. She was moments away from declining when she felt a heavy gaze bore into her. She glanced up, and a familiar pair of black eyes met hers.

Brynleigh swallowed at the sight of her Maker.

Jelisette's gown matched her progeny's, except hers was a blue so dark it was almost black. She wore a matching mask that covered the top half of her face, but Brynleigh recognized her Maker on sight.

Standing next to Jelisette, wearing a crisp black suit, was Zanri. The shifter wore a tiger mask, his eyes sharp as he gazed through it. His red hair hung loosely around him, giving him a wild edge in this room full of polished people.

Jelisette's black eyes narrowed and locked onto Brynleigh's. The message hidden within them was clear: *don't mess this up*.

Brynleigh didn't intend to. Calling Zanri for a helpful reminder of why she was doing this was one thing, but being faced with her Maker was another. If Brynleigh admitted she was struggling with emotions, Jelisette wouldn't hesitate to punish her. She'd made that abundantly clear several months ago.

"Never forget, Brynleigh, death is the only alternative to winning." Jelisette's piercing gaze met Brynleigh's from across the chess board. Like Brynleigh, she wore a thick sweater as snow fell lazily outside.

Bobbing her head, Brynleigh picked up the black queen and twisted it in her hands before placing it across the board. "Of course."

Her Maker smiled, but there wasn't a drop of warmth in the gesture. Instead, the sight of Jelisette's sharp fangs sent a shiver down Brynleigh's back. Had Brynleigh been mortal, she would've screamed at the sight. This was a woman who killed without compunction, and she had no problem handing out punishments as she saw fit.

"Wonderful." Jelisette picked up her knight and took Brynleigh's rook.

Fuck. How had she missed that?

Brynleigh stared at the board, trying to think of a way out of the inevitable checkmate as Jelisette added, "Never forget, you must always be planning several steps ahead."

"I won't fail you."

Those words echoed in Brynleigh's head as she broke eye contact with Jelisette. Hoping her Maker couldn't sense the turmoil churning beneath her skin, Brynleigh dipped her head and forced a smile on her face as she retracted her wings. "I'd be delighted to dance, Ry."

She would just make sure there were no emotions involved.

Ryker smiled and took Brynleigh's hand in his. She ignored the way it felt good to be touched by him, ignored those sparks running up her arm as he led her onto the dance floor.

The first song wasn't too bad. The orchestra played a slow waltz, and she mostly succeeded in hiding her two left feet *and* keeping emotions out of this.

That wasn't the end of it, though.

The songs kept coming. She thought that after the first, they'd be done, but no. They danced and danced.

Damn it all, but this activity with Ryker was far more enjoyable than Brynleigh would ever admit. He moved with grace and ease, unencumbered by his tailored black suit.

Each wave of music, each dance, each moment Brynleigh spent in Ryker's arms chipped away at her resolve to keep emotions out of this situation.

It wasn't her fault. Not really. From a purely physical standpoint, Captain Ryker Waterborn was a well-built, muscular, tall fae. His jaw was chiseled, his ears were pointed, and a fire in his eyes burned brighter every time he looked at her.

"Do you trust me?" Ryker whispered into her ear, his hand splayed across her lower back as they danced their fifth song in a row.

There was a multitude of reasons why she shouldn't. And yet, as Brynleigh stared into Ryker's eyes, she nodded. "Yes."

Her eyes widened at the admission and the truth behind it. What did that mean? She couldn't trust him. She knew what he'd done.

And yet...

She didn't take back her statement.

Ryker's grip tightened on Brynleigh's hand. His eyes sparkled, and he spun her away from him before twirling her back. Brynleigh couldn't help it. She giggled like a love-sick schoolgirl. Ryker brought something out in her that she couldn't label.

It had to be his handsomeness. That was the only logical reason for this kind of reaction.

After all, Brynleigh wasn't the only one who noticed how good-looking her fiancé was. As they spun across the dance floor, she caught sight of several other women and even a few men eyeing Ryker with unmasked lust.

Brynleigh wanted to snarl at each of them to keep their eyes to themselves. This man, with his sharp jaw and lips made for kissing, was hers.

At least for now.

Was jealousy a bad emotion? Should she shove it down like the others? She wasn't sure if it was dangerous or not. It certainly wasn't as awful as the feeling that had welled up within her when he proposed.

That one, she refused to name. If she didn't label it, it wasn't real.

Except it felt far too fucking real. All of this did.

Ryker's gaze never wavered from Brynleigh's. His hand was a brand against her back. Even as he led them across the dance floor, he made her feel seen in a way that no one else ever had. It was like he peeled away all the layers of her identity and peered into her soul beneath.

It was extremely unnerving and made it difficult to remember this was all an act. He made her feel like...

No.

She wouldn't even acknowledge that feeling. Whatever it was, she would ignore it until after the life drained from those chocolate brown eyes.

Two more songs went by, and Brynleigh... enjoyed them. Each chord, each note, affected her more than the last.

Thank Isvana, eventually, a hand landed on Brynleigh's arm when they were near the edge of the dance floor.

"Excuse me, mind if I cut in?" Zanri smiled, his eyes twinkling behind his mask.

Ryker turned to the shifter, his face hardening. "Who are you?"

There was a gruffness in Ryker's voice that caused Brynleigh's core to tighten in wholly inappropriate ways. She squeezed her thighs together and turned to the masked shifter. "This is Zanri. I... work with him."

In as much as working meant that Zanri found criminals for Brynleigh to kill. Semantics.

"Ah." Tension slipped from Ryker's shoulders. "Would you like to dance with him?"

Honestly, the only thing Brynleigh wanted was for this entire evening to end. However, since that didn't seem possible, this was a close second. If she danced with Zanri, she could keep those frustrating emotions in check.

"I do," said Brynleigh.

Ryker reluctantly released her before leaning over and kissing her cheek. "I'll be right over there," he whispered. His voice was much firmer when he told Zanri, "One song."

The shifter nodded and led Brynleigh silently onto the dance floor. He drew her close—but not too close—and started swaying. "I hear congratulations are in order."

Brynleigh smiled. "They are."

Zanri spun her. It was nice but didn't compare to Ryker's impressive dance skills.

"And how are you doing?" he asked when he drew her back in.

That was a loaded question. There were many ways she could answer. Confused. Antsy. Emotional. Torn up inside. In the end, she asked for clarification. "You mean with rule number ten?" Her voice was low, meant only for Zanri.

He nodded. "Yes."

"I'm... alright." Lie. Her box was filled to the brim with illicit emotions. But what else could she say?

Twice now, Ryker had declared his love for her. Both times, she hadn't said anything. Lying to him was one thing, but proclaiming false love was another. It was a step too far, even for her.

Brynleigh had never said those words to anyone, and she wouldn't start now.

"You must stay strong, B." Zanri's soft voice was firm and grounding, as if he knew the inner turmoil she was experiencing.

"I will." Brynleigh nodded, trying to convince herself of the fact.

Somehow, her voice was unwavering despite the storm churning within her.

The shifter squeezed her hands. "You must."

Again, Brynleigh wondered at the forcefulness in Zanri's voice. Maybe it was just her time away from the safe house, but he seemed so... insistent. It struck Brynleigh as odd. Why was he pushing this? He didn't have anything at stake.

But then the song ended. Zanri stepped aside, and Ryker took his place.

The fae's hand settled on the small of her back again, and he pulled her close. His eyes searched hers. "Are you okay?"

No. She was so far from okay that she couldn't even remember what that felt like.

She couldn't say that, so instead, she said, "Yes."

His gaze searched hers, and his thumb rubbed circles on her exposed back. All night, he'd been touching her. It was gods-damned distracting and made it hard for her to think.

"You can tell me the truth, Brynleigh," he murmured, just loud enough to be heard over the music.

That was the last thing she could do.

If Ryker knew the truth of who she was and what she was doing there, this would all be for naught. He would either throw her in prison or finish the job he started six years ago. She imagined he'd be pissed if he learned about her true intentions.

Remaining silent didn't seem like it would work, though, so she looked out to the crowd. Several people were still watching her fae. Their gazes followed him, the lust evident as they blatantly checked him out. It was as good of an excuse as any. "People are looking at you."

Ryker's brown eyes twinkled at the tone of Brynleigh's voice. His lips twisted up into a devilish smirk, revealing...

Fucking great. Of course, the incredibly handsome water fae she was supposed to kill had dimples.

Why not?

He sported a pair of them, one on each cheek, and they only added to his attractiveness. It wasn't fair for one person to be blessed with such good looks. Couldn't the gods have thrown a wart on his face, or perhaps given him a crooked nose? *Something* to make him be not so... so... beautiful.

And fuck, he was perfect. Brynleigh felt like she had done a pretty good job of ignoring that fact until now, but it was becoming impossible.

"Why, sweetheart, are you jealous?" Ryker's deep, smoky voice was low as he spun her across the dance floor in a move she could never have done on her own.

Her cheeks heated. "No, I'm not."

Ryker whirled her through the air, the crimson fabric swirling around her. He settled her back on her feet, his gaze darkening as he looked her over.

"You lie so beautifully, little vampire." He held her so close that she could feel his heart beating in his chest.

Brynleigh had no words. She *was* lying... just not about what he thought. Her entire persona was nothing more than a facade. At least, that's what she kept telling herself. The problem was that the longer she remained in close contact with Ryker, the more difficult it was to remember what, exactly, she was lying about.

Thank Isvana, Ryker didn't seem to mind her silence. A baritone chuckle rumbled through him, and they continued dancing as the music picked up.

Several songs later, Brynleigh's throat was dry. She slowed, lifting her hand off Ryker's arm and rubbing the base of her throat absent-mindedly.

Instantly, Ryker's gaze darkened and locked on her hand. "Thirsty?"

Was she? Many desires pulsed through her, most of them illicit. There was only one she could give into right now.

She nodded, and he led her towards the bar.

A masked Death Elf with red markings crawling up his right hand put down the glass he was polishing as they approached. "Good evening, and congratulations on your engagement."

"Thank you." Brynleigh smiled at the bartender.

Ryker's hand never left Brynleigh's as he ordered a glass of blood wine for her and a beer for himself. Brynleigh usually took offense to men ordering for her. It was demeaning since she was more than capable of placing her own requests. But something was endearing about the way Ryker seamlessly took charge. To her eternal chagrin, Brynleigh liked it.

The bartender returned with their drinks in short order. Ryker thanked the man and took the glasses before tilting his head towards a shadowy alcove near the back of the ballroom.

"Come with me?" he asked in that rough voice of his.

A shiver ran down Brynleigh's spine, and her breath caught in her throat. She shouldn't be alone with Ryker. That could only lead to bad things. She knew that, and yet, she didn't say no. Not yet.

The prudent choice—the right choice, the rule-following choice—would be to stay with the crowd. She shouldn't be alone with him, couldn't afford for more emotions to try and get the better of her.

Rules six and eight popped into Brynleigh's head, reminding her of all the reasons this was a terrible idea. But just one time, she didn't want to follow the rules. She wanted to go with Ryker. Besides, they weren't *truly* alone. Others were here. They would be secluded but not isolated.

What harm could come from bending the rules this one time? Probably nothing.

"I'd love to," she said before she could stop herself.

Those damned dimples decorated Ryker's cheeks once again. Handing her the goblet of wine, he laced their fingers together and led her away from the crowd. They garnered a few curious glances, but no one stopped them.

The alcove was dark, hidden behind some large speakers, and it was quieter. Tension left Brynleigh's shoulders, and she exhaled. This was nice. Maybe it wasn't such a bad idea.

For a single moment, she relaxed.

And then she looked up.

Ryker stood right in front of her. Barely a foot separated the two of them. He was all fae, his gaze dark and hungry as it swept over her.

Brynleigh could barely think. Breathing was practically impossible, and speaking was definitely out of the question. He was close. Far too close.

Fuck, this was a bad idea. Maybe the worst one Brynleigh had ever had. That said a lot, because once she'd challenged Zanri to a drinking game involving Faerie Wine and a trashy reality dating show that followed merfolk and sailors as they tried to bridge the divide between their lives and make love work. The next morning, the two of them had been in so much pain that they'd both sworn off the beverage for eternity.

This was worse than that.

Ryker came even closer. His knuckles brushed her cheek, and she practically melted right then and there.

Brynleigh tried to remember the rules, to ground herself in them, but it wasn't working. Her mind was blank, empty of everything except for an awareness of the fae before her.

She closed her eyes, which amplified Ryker's scent until it was all she could smell. Her fangs ached. She wanted to draw nearer. She wanted to leave. Isvana help her, but she had no idea what to do.

She froze.

A finger landed under her chin, and Ryker rumbled, "Look at me, Brynleigh."

The commanding tone of his voice was entirely too pleasing. Brynleigh wasn't ready to dissect that, though. She'd never be ready. She grabbed those feelings and shoved them down, down, down.

When she was certain she wouldn't spontaneously combust, she opened her eyes. "Yes?"

"You were jealous earlier." Not a question. "I liked that."

Her breath caught. Fuck, she had no business enjoying the deep rumble of his words so much. Before she could reply, Ryker bent, slanting his lips over hers. It couldn't be called a kiss because it was barely more than a graze of their mouths. Still, it reverberated in the depth of Brynleigh's soul.

Her heart fluttered, which was a strange experience. A feeling rose. She snatched it, forcing it into away. Whatever it was, if she didn't acknowledge it, she couldn't let it affect her.

"I don't like them looking at us," she said honestly, though she didn't quite know why she was telling Ryker this. "I've never enjoyed being the center of attention. When I was young, I did almost everything to stay out of the spotlight. I never answered questions in school, nor did I speak up. It was easier to blend into the shadows, even then."

Sarai had been loud enough for both of them. She had been vibrant and full of life. Watching her sister bloom like a flower in spring had been a highlight of Brynleigh's life. It was a cruel joke that now, Brynleigh was still alive and in front of the cameras.

"Let them look. I'm drawn to you and no one else." Ryker's voice deepened. "My attentions are firmly where I desire them to be."

He lowered his head, his eyes never leaving hers. Brynleigh's heart pounded in her chest. She stared at his lips, her stomach twisting in what she told herself was dread.

She was a gods-damned liar.

Would he kiss her now? Really, truly kiss her? Would she let him? She had no idea.

Brynleigh watched Ryker's mouth descend upon hers like it was the most interesting thing she'd ever seen. Half of her wanted to dart back into the crowd, but the other half held her still, eagerly waiting for that first touch of his mouth against hers.

Anticipation thickened the air between them.

At the last moment, Ryker turned his head and skimmed her lips, kissing the corner of her mouth. She exhaled a breathy moan as his mouth landed on the side of her neck. Against her better judgment—which, to be honest, was hanging on by an Ithiar-damned threat—her eyes fluttered shut.

A thousand curses flew through her head, but not a single one made it to her lips. No was a simple, two-letter word. She should say it. She should stop him. This was wrong on so many levels.

Brynleigh knew all these things, but none of them stopped her from inching towards Ryker. She tilted her head, giving him better access to her neck.

His large, warm hand landed on her hip, pulling her closer. His sharp canines grazed her skin, not biting but sending enough pressure that the space between her thighs dampened. Her heart raced as he kissed a trail down her neck.

Control was careening out of Brynleigh's fingers. Some part of her still possessed enough common sense to realize she needed to maintain some power in their relationship.

Recalling their previous conversation was difficult with his mouth on her, but Brynleigh murmured, "And what if I don't want them looking?"

Truth. She didn't want anyone watching her with Ryker. Not anymore. They'd shared so much with the world already. She wanted to be alone with him and let him kiss her all over. She would let him remove all the barriers between them and take her however he wanted.

Wait.

What?

No.

That was wrong. *This* was wrong.

She wanted...

Ryker's fingers curled around her hip, and he *nipped* her. Oh gods. One simple action had no business feeling so good. A tremor ran through Brynleigh, starting at her toes and making its way up her legs and to her core. Her head fell back on a groan. Her glass of wine dangled from her fingers. She forgot everything else. This fae could do whatever he wanted to her.

"Then I'll get rid of them," he growled. "I'll do anything for you."

Darkness was laced in his words, an unveiled threat directed towards anyone that might come between them that Brynleigh liked far too much. She'd never been one to enjoy overt acts of possessiveness, especially not from fae males, but that seemed to be rapidly changing.

Brynleigh could get used to having someone willing to fight for her. She'd been alone for so long.

Except...

No.

What the fuck was she doing? This was incredibly wrong. She couldn't get used to this or let the captain talk to her in this fashion. She wasn't just bending the rules but breaking them all together.

Gods-damn it, what was she thinking? This was a game. She wasn't supposed to let him touch her like this. She wasn't allowed to have any emotions. They were far too dangerous.

Brynleigh's blood chilled, and her fingers spasmed.

The crystal glass tumbled from her hand in slow motion, the liquid spilling out in a red arc and staining the ground in a pool of blood moments before the glass shattered.

Her head ached. A buzzing filled her ears. She needed to get out of here right now. Shadows bubbled in her veins. Control was a foreign concept as her head spun.

There was no losing. Not in this game.

Ryker shouted her name, but she could barely hear him over the roaring. She blinked, trying to clear her head.

His hands landed on her forearms, and his grip was firm but gentle. "What's wrong?"

Mistake, mistake, mistake.

She needed to leave, but the panic...

Tighter and tighter, a fist squeezed her lungs. Air. She sipped it, but it didn't help. She gasped, "I—"

The power flickered, and then the overhead lights went out.

Someone screamed.

A man yelled, "Take cover!"

Another shouted, "Get the Chancellor!"

"For freedom!" a woman cried out.

Brynleigh's brows furrowed. The hairs on her neck stood on end. Her shadows pulsed in warning. "What—"

Her next words never came. The ground shook like the gods were throwing furniture around. An explosion.

Something slammed into Brynleigh's neck. Pain bloomed, drawing her into its agonizing embrace.

Someone roared. Arms wrapped around her.

Cold. So fucking cold.

She moaned.

Someone yelled her name.

Everything went black.

CHAPTER 23

Protective Measures and Perfect Control

"Sit down, son. If you keep that up, you'll wear a hole in the floor." Tertia Waterborn, Representative of the Fae, raised a chestnut brown manicured brow from where she sat at the dining room table and frowned.

Somehow, Ryker's mother looked put together despite the hell they'd endured over the past twenty-four hours. Her hair was perfectly coiffed in her traditional chignon, pulled away from her face.

Ryker didn't look so good. He raked a hand through his hair for the twentieth time that hour and groaned. Last night, he'd been kissing Brynleigh—a thoroughly enjoyable activity that he planned on resuming as soon as possible—when chaos had erupted.

"I can't do that, Mother," Ryker growled. How could his mother sit there having a coffee as if they hadn't left the Hall of Choice covered in blood?

"And why not?" Again, with the pleasant tone. It was driving Ryker up the walls. He loved his mother, but sometimes, she did not seem connected to reality.

Although Tertia Waterborn appeared like a human in their third decade of life, she was almost three centuries old. Fae aged slowly, and of all the species that lived on the Continent, they Faded the slowest... when they weren't hit with the Stillness. There was a chance Ryker's mother could live for another thousand years or more.

Ryker pointed to the closed door, his finger shaking with pent-up frustration. "I should be out there right now."

Tertia shook her head and slid her attention to the tablet before her. "Let the army handle the rebel situation," she said calmly, tapping the screen. "That's why we're here."

After the bomb had gone off last night, the Chancellor had ordered that all the Choosing Participants, the attending Representatives, and their families be brought to The Lily to be guarded. It was the most expensive hotel in the entire Central Region, and as such, it already boasted strong security measures. Chancellor Rose had pulled some strings and ensured there were enough rooms for everyone. Once they'd been transported here, soldiers were stationed at every hotel entrance and in front of every room.

Ryker hated places like this. Everything, from the floor to the ceiling, was gilded, expensive, and lacking in life. He'd much rather be at home or his cabin curled up with Brynleigh on the couch.

That wasn't possible right now, though. He was locked in this room, separated from his vampire. Fuck, he hated this.

He balled his fists. "I'm in the fucking army, Mother," he snapped. "It's my job."

One he wasn't allowed to do because he was trapped inside this gilded room like a prisoner.

"Excuse me?" Tertia's brown eyes, a mirror of his own, widened. She placed a hand flat on the table and power rippled through the room. A reminder. A warning. Tread lightly.

Ryker had seen what his mother could do. Witnessed her power. There was a reason her children were such strong fae.

He dipped his head ever so slightly, the message clear: *I understand.*

It wasn't enough for Tertia, apparently, because she said, "You may be going through a lot right now, son, but that doesn't give you the right to speak to me in such a vulgar manner."

Ryker's nostrils flared as he breathed heavily through his nose.

Damn it all. His mother was right, but he had nothing left. Manners were something civilized people used, and at the moment, he felt anything but that. How had everything turned out so badly?

The Masked Ball had been going without a hitch right up until the moment Brynleigh dropped her glass. She'd seemed shaken, but before he could find out what was wrong, the bomb went off.

"I shouldn't be here right now, Mother." Ryker tried to keep his voice flat, even though every single part of him shook with the urge to roar. "I need to be with her."

The Chancellor had decreed that all the participants needed to be kept apart while the soldiers contained the threat.

This separation was driving Ryker mad.

"The vampire?" Tertia sipped her coffee. "She'll be fine. They got to her in time."

He shook, his vision clouding, as his control slipped. His own magic thrummed, eager to help him feel better. But nothing would help. Not right now. Not after last night.

"Barely!" Ryker shouted. "Her blood covered me from head to toe!"

Last night, when he'd finally stumbled into the shower, the water had run red. When the bomb exploded, a piece of silver shrapnel grazed the side of Brynleigh's neck. If she'd been human, she would have died. As it was, she'd lost copious amounts of blood.

One moment, his vampire had been staring at him. The next, a crimson river spurted from her neck like a fountain.

Ryker would have nightmares about how Brynleigh's face went from pale to snow white for the rest of his life. Her blood had poured out of her so fast that he'd barely had time to comprehend what was happening. Vampires were immune to many things, but silver was one of the few that could kill them.

Thank the Blessed Obsidian Sands, Jelisette de la Point had been present at the Masked Ball. She'd swooped in, bitten her own wrist, and fed her progeny her blood. It was only because of her quick thinking that Brynleigh was still alive and in a different suite, receiving intravenous blood transfusions.

"I know you're worried, son," Tertia said in a business-like voice.

"But your vampire has the best medical care in the entire Republic. She'll be fine. Calm you."

Calm was not a word in Ryker's vocabulary. He wasn't meant to sit around and do nothing. He should be out there, searching for the bastards that built the fucking bomb. If they knew what was good for them, they'd fall to their knees and beg whatever deities they believed in that Ryker would not be the one to find them. When he did, he would tear them limb from limb for what they'd done.

Brynleigh wasn't the only one injured in the blast. Countless people were hurt, and several lives were lost altogether, including Luca, one of the Choosing participants. The young werewolf had been a good man and hadn't deserved to die so young.

"I need to see Brynleigh." Ryker had already tried to leave the suite, but a guard had stopped him at the door.

He pulled his hair, hating the helplessness churning in his gut.

Ryker understood the purpose of rules and knew they were in place for a reason, but right now, he didn't care. All he cared about was his vampire. Nothing else. Not right now. Once he saw Brynleigh with his own two eyes and confirmed she was healing, he would feel better.

Gods-damn it all. A growl rumbled through him, and he palmed the back of his neck. What were the chances he could sneak out of this suite and find the one where they were keeping her? He didn't know the guards stationed at his door, which was likely a conscious choice on the Chancellor's behalf, so he couldn't talk his way out of the suite.

But maybe...

A plan started forming in his head as he mulled over the possibility of getting hold of either Atlas or Nikhail. They might be working, but if they weren't, he was certain either would do as he asked.

Except Atlas was watching Marlowe. As much as Ryker loved Marlie, his dog wouldn't be much help in an operation like this. That left Nikhail as the more logical choice. Ryker nodded to himself, feeling incrementally better now that he had the semblance of a plan.

He turned on his heel, intent on heading back to his room and calling the air fae.

"I hope you're not planning on doing anything foolish, my son."

Tertia didn't even lift her eyes from the tablet where she was typing a message. "Remember—"

"Everything I do reflects on you," he finished for her, biting back the urge to roll his eyes. He stopped in his tracks, though. "Yes, I know."

He'd heard the refrain a thousand times over.

That was the burden of being a Representative's son. His mother lived in the spotlight, and even though Ryker had spent the past six years living as a recluse, sometimes he still got caught in those bright rays.

"Are you certain?" This time, Tertia looked up. Her piercing gaze met his. "Need I remind you—"

Thank all the gods, a door slammed shut on the other side of the suite. It saved Ryker from his mother's impending lecture.

A slender fae jogged into the main room, her brown hair pulled into a high ponytail. Diamond studs glittered in her pierced, delicate, pointed ears, and a black ring sat in the middle of her bottom lip. She wore a neon pink t-shirt that was cropped high enough to show off her pierced navel and ripped jean shorts. The outfit was a bright contrast to Tertia's refined apparel.

"Ryker! I'm so glad you're safe." River slammed into him, and he hugged her. "I wish I could have seen you last night before everything went down. It was so horrible."

"Perhaps if you hadn't been tardy, you could've seen your brother before he proposed," Tertia remarked from the table, her voice icy.

Both Ryker and River sighed at the same time.

River's inability to arrive anywhere on time had been a topic of countless conversations in the past. It wasn't that his sister liked being late. She just never seemed to get anywhere when she was supposed to. Ryker had thought she would grow out of it, but that didn't seem to be the case.

"I'm sorry, Mother." River rubbed her temples. "I got stuck at the university studying and lost track of time. But I made it! That's the most important thing, right?"

Tertia's face made it clear that it was, in fact, not the most important thing.

Ryker wasn't in the mood to referee a fight between his mother and sister. Instead, he put his hands on River's shoulders and angled her away from their mother. "How's school going, Shortie?"

River was in her fourth year of pre-med at the University of Balance. The oldest of the five universities on the continent, the school had been founded by the High Ladies of Life and Death soon after the Battle of Balance. It was the most prestigious academic institution on this side of the Obsidian Coast.

"Good." River smiled tightly. "I'm acing all my classes."

"Your sister is on track to graduate at the top of her class, as she should be," their mother added. "She wouldn't be a Waterborn if she didn't perform to the best of her abilities."

They'd heard the same refrain their entire lives. Waterborns did not fail. Waterborns did not cause scenes. Waterborns were chosen by the gods to lead the fae, and as such, they had to keep their heads on their shoulders at all times.

Being a Waterborn was fucking exhausting.

"Of course, Mother," Ryker and River said simultaneously.

Tertia studied them both for another moment before dipping her head. She returned to her work, but the air remained tense.

"I've been watching you, Ryker." His sister returned her attention to him. "Every day, whenever I'm not in class or studying. You're a star."

He chuckled. "I'm still your brother, River."

"I know you are." She punched his arm, and he faked being hurt.

River laughed and called him a baby.

"Well, children, I think that's my cue to leave." Tertia stood, tucking her tablet under her arm. "I have to call the Council." She glared at them both. "Behave, young ones. I'll return soon."

"Of course, Mother," the siblings said in unison.

Tertia was a good parent, and she wanted the best for her children, but the only person Ryker had ever seen his mother be affectionate with was his father. She wasn't built like the rest of them. Luckily, their father had enough love for them all.

Tertia smiled at them, the expression verging on cold, before gliding into the third bedroom in the suite. She moved with a grace that spoke of her age and power.

Once the door closed behind her, Ryker turned to his sister.

"How are you doing?" he asked seriously. He hadn't wanted to bring this up in front of their mother, but now that they were alone, the question pressed on his mind. "Have there been any more incidents while I was gone?"

River's face paled, making her piercings stand out even more. "No, none."

"You've been doing your exercises? Is it under control?"

"I haven't missed a single day, like I promised." River's brows rose and nearly touched her forehead. "You know, Ryker, I am twenty-one. Just because I haven't hit my Maturation doesn't mean I can't manage it."

All fae Matured around twenty-five years old. Maturation brought them to their full power and slowed their aging until they were practically immortal. Having undergone his own Maturation thirteen years ago, Ryker knew this, but he still worried about his sister. She was the most important person in his world. Well. Now, she was the second most important person.

He needed to make sure she was alright. "If it starts to get too bad—"

"I'll go to Isolation Lake and let the magic out," River finished his sentence, repeating the words he'd said to her each time they spoke over the past six years. "I know. Under no circumstances am I to go near any inhabited towns or villages, especially if I haven't released my magic recently."

Ryker exhaled. "Good. And if something does happen—"

"It won't," she said firmly. "Not again."

Ryker placed a hand on River's shoulder and waited until her gaze met his. "If it does, you tell me."

"So, you can fix it again?"

"Yes," he said gravely.

"I can take care of myself," she protested. "I won't lose control again, I promise. Gabriel and Carson have been teaching me, just like you asked them."

The pair of water fae were some of the best, but they weren't Ryker. He'd asked them to step in and take over his sister's magical education while he was in the Choosing. If Ryker could have been in two places at once, he would've done it. But the rules had been clear.

He couldn't allow River's training to lapse, though. The last thing they needed was another incident. The last one had been bad enough and with their father's health failing...

Ryker would do whatever it took to keep his sister safe.

"Show me," he said.

Instead of doing as he asked, River crossed her arms and glowered. "You know, sometimes you can be an overbearing ass."

The hairs on Ryker's neck bristled. Was it overbearing to want to ensure his sister's safety? All he wanted to do was make sure she didn't accidentally harm herself or anyone else ever again. That wasn't overbearing in his books. It was his job as her older brother.

Ryker did what he always did in challenging moments like these. He fell back on his training. His back straightened, and he looked down at River. Right now, she wasn't his little sister. She was simply a fae who had previously lost control of her magic.

"Do it," he requested again, his voice hard.

She scowled. "Seriously?"

He held her gaze. "Yes. Show me what those two fae taught you while I was gone."

With a groan that spoke to exactly how deep her frustration ran, River held out her hand in the space between them. Her lips pinched together, and she frowned, focusing on her outstretched limb. Her brows furrowed, and water pooled in her palm. It started as a few drops but quickly grew.

The air hummed as River pulled on her extensive power. The clear liquid surrounded her hand, crawling up her wrist and forearm like a glove. The water twisted, and tiny currents ran through the translucent liquid.

Ryker had to admit that he was impressed with his sister's control. Her magic completely contained the water, and not a single drop fell on the floor.

River spread her fingers and twisted them in the air. The water spun and danced above her hand, coiling into a tube several feet long.

She murmured an ancient fae prayer beneath her breath and stared at the tube. Her eyes flashed, the color momentarily shifting from brown to stark blue, and the temperature in the room plummeted.

Goosebumps pebbled on Ryker's arms as the water turned into solid, opaque ice.

River grabbed the new creation out of the air. Her lips twitched into a smirk, and she sketched a bow. "See?" She handed the ice to her brother. "Perfect control."

Reluctantly, Ryker had to admit that Gabriel and Carson had done a good job with her training. He'd chosen well—and thank all the gods for that. Ryker constantly worried about River. Her power exceeded both his and their mother's. It was both extraordinary and deadly.

"Good job, Shortie," Ryker said proudly. Rather than putting the ice in the sink—the suite was equipped with a fully stocked kitchen—he twisted his fingers.

Channeling his water magic had always been as easy as breathing.

The ice melted in a heartbeat, returning to liquid form. Before it could splash the absurdly expensive carpet, Ryker ordered the liquid to make a sphere. He sent it sailing through the air and out the open window before releasing it.

"Show off," River muttered, frowning.

He laughed, ruffling her hair. "I'm your big brother. I have to show off. It's in the handbook."

"Sure, it is." River turned and strolled towards the kitchen. "Want a coffee?"

Ryker's gaze darted between his sister and the door. A large part of him wanted to leave right now and call Nikhail, but the rest of him wanted to spend time with River. Their schedules were both so full, and he would be married soon. Who knew when they'd get to see each other except to train?

He could wait a little while longer.

"Sure," he called out. "Pour me a cup."

Reaching into his back pocket, Ryker drew out his phone. Thank all the gods, the guards had returned the contestants' technology on the way to the hotel. Typing up a quick message to Nikhail asking him to investigate the security at The Lily, Ryker followed his sister into the kitchen.

"How's school really going?" he asked, knowing his mother wasn't within earshot.

River groaned. "The classes are fine. The people? Not so great. Last week, I was at..."

Sipping his coffee, Ryker listened to his sister share the woes of life as a twenty-one-year-old in her fourth year of college. Apparently, there were many of them. It was nice to be with his family, but Ryker's mind kept returning to Brynleigh.

After this, he promised himself, he'd see her.

No matter what.

CHAPTER 24

Nothing But a Physical Reaction

Brynleigh was living in a cloud. Her head was light, her eyes were exceedingly heavy, and something soft and cushiony was beneath her. The air smelled strangely crisp, almost void of scents entirely. That would have struck her as odd, except her mind was having trouble focusing. Everything was foggy.

She frowned and tried to shove past the dark mist. She was missing something vital, but she couldn't remember what it was. That wouldn't do. She pushed and shoved against the fog. It hurt, but she didn't give up.

It was an unmovable wall. That wouldn't do.

She slammed against the fog. Harder and harder, until she was certain that if she were hitting a real wall, she would have dislocated her shoulder.

Eventually, her perseverance paid off.

A crack broke through the darkness, a sliver that soon let light flood in.

Events flashed through her mind, slowly at first but picking up speed like a snowball rolling down a hill. She'd entered the Hall of Choice and met Ryker. They dated. Then, he'd proposed.

The next thing Brynleigh remembered was the feeling of Ryker's lips on her neck, and then...

Oh gods.

Something had hit her. *Hard.* Pain, that strange mortal sensation that she'd rarely felt since her Making, had swallowed her. Demolished her.

And then she'd tumbled into blackness.

She'd been hurt. Maybe even killed? Brynleigh wasn't certain. She didn't feel dead, but then again, it was hard to tell. Vampires weren't truly alive in the first place, so perhaps true death was simply... peace? But that didn't make sense because when vampires touched silver or were staked, they screamed.

That was the mystery at hand.

Brynleigh was certain of one thing: when Ryker touched her, she felt alive. They had taken a leisurely stroll down a dangerous, forbidden path the night of the Masked Ball. Would she have let him go further if they hadn't been interrupted?

Before, Brynleigh would have said no. But now...

Maybe.

There was no denying the fact that her body desired Ryker's. She'd practically melted against him when they danced. But that was nothing but a physical reaction to his physique, right?

Good, old-fashioned lust. That's all it was. Lust was a completely normal, absolutely valid response when presented with someone as handsome as Ryker. There was nothing wrong with that.

Yes, there is, a small voice in the back of her mind reminded her. *He murdered your family. How could you forget that?*

The voice was right. Ryker wasn't hers to lust after. How could Brynleigh have forgotten who Ryker was, even for a moment?

She was definitely going to hell for this. Then again, it wasn't like she was perfect.

Brynleigh had done many bad things in her life, especially after Jelisette Made her. Why not add one more sin on top of it? Especially when the other person looked like Ryker Waterborn.

Maybe it wouldn't be so bad. Maybe she could—

"It's time to wake up, B," a familiar masculine voice said near her ear.

Zanri. She would recognize the shifter's voice anywhere. That had to mean she wasn't dead, right? They were friends, but she'd never dreamed about the shifter.

A hand gripped her shoulder, the touch just on this side of pain. "Wake up. We don't have long."

Brynleigh hitched a breath. It felt like fiery needles were being jabbed into her.

Well, at least now she knew this was real.

"Fuck, that hurts." Brynleigh opened her eyes, wincing at the bright light right above her. Her vision was blurry, which was an unusual event that hadn't occurred since her Making, and she blinked several times to clear it. "What happened?"

The shifter canted his head. Auburn scruff covered his face, and shadows hung beneath his eyes. "A bomb went off, and you were hit with a shard of prohiberis-lined silver. You don't remember?"

Another curse slipped from Brynleigh's lips. If her mother were still alive, she'd be shocked at how her daughter spoke. But she wasn't, so it didn't matter.

"Yeah, that was the same way Jelisette reacted." Zanri crossed his arms and looked down at Brynleigh. "You know, B, you're supposed to be getting ready to kill him, not get yourself killed."

"I know," she said through gritted teeth. "You think I planned to get blown up?" These gods-damned rebels were throwing a wrench in everything.

"Of course not." Zanri met her eyes, and a disapproving frown marred his features. "But I saw you with him, B. In the shadows."

When Ryker was kissing her neck...

Brynleigh's blood ran cold, and she gripped the sheets. The look in Zanri's eyes, the warning in his voice...

She whispered, "Did she see?"

Neither of them needed to clarify who Brynleigh was talking about.

Zanri held Brynleigh's gaze for a long moment before he sighed and shook his head. "No, she was talking with Representative DuBois at the time."

"Thank Isvana." Brynleigh blew out a sigh of relief and pushed herself up onto her elbows to take in the room. Even with the beeping equipment and screens surrounding the bed, this place was far fancier than the safe house. "Where are we?"

She should probably spend more time reassuring Zanri that she felt nothing for Ryker, but she was too tired to talk much right now. Words were hard to come by.

The longer Brynleigh was awake, the more she realized everything was muted. Dimmer than normal. Even her shadows were a gentle hum in her veins instead of the typical thrum they usually sang. If she hadn't just spent far too long battling against the fog to access her memories, she'd be concerned about that.

"The Lily." Zanri perched on the side of the bed. "Chancellor's orders. She moved everyone here after the bomb went off."

Brynleigh was surprised by that. "Even Jelisette?" The old vampire had an unusual attachment to the safe house. Brynleigh had never seen her stay anywhere else.

Whatever drew Jelisette there, she never spoke of it. Just like she never spoke of the reason she always wore long sleeves or she sometimes had a far-away, dead look in her eyes.

"No," Zanri chuckled. "Not even Ignatia Rose could make Jelisette do something she didn't want to. She and I are staying at the safe house."

That made sense.

Brynleigh took another look around. "It's... shiny."

She'd heard of this hotel, but she'd never been here before. It was far too expensive, and besides, vampires were rarely invited to establishments like this. To say the room was gilded would be a vast understatement. It was like someone had taken all the makings of a regular hotel room, dumped them in a pot of liquid money, and called it a day.

The bed frames were gold. The television stand was gold. The doorknobs? Gold. The entire space was luxury personified, and it was extremely obnoxious. The windowsills, the picture frames, even the gods-damned comforter shimmered when the light hit them.

This show of wealth was made even more disgusting by the fact that people were literally starving in the streets of Golden City. Little wonder she'd felt like she was in a cloud. It was a rich, golden one.

She understood why the rebels were attacking.

"Yes, it is. But focus, B." Zanri shook her shoulders roughly. "The medicine they're giving you makes you sleepy. The doctor said you'd only be awake for a few minutes."

Medicine? What medicine? She lifted her hand to grab his arm when she noticed the needle sticking out of her.

Brynleigh's gaze followed the tubing to a bag hanging beside the bed. There was no label on it, but the clear liquid was going into her body. All she knew was it wasn't blood. What were they giving her?

Ice filled her veins at the thought of something foreign being injected into her. She wanted to yank out the needle, but she was unsure of what would happen if she did.

"The rebels are getting bolder." Brynleigh's head felt like it weighed a thousand pounds. Her tongue was heavy.

Zanri nodded. "They are. They've been gaining traction over the past year or so, but this is..."

"More." She shifted to look at him, and her neck ached. She lifted a hand, feeling for an injury. Although her skin was sore, there weren't any wounds.

"Yes. Focus, Brynleigh."

"It's hard."

"I know. Jelisette gave you her blood at the party," Zanri explained. "After that, they brought you here to transfuse more. Even with all that, you almost died."

That black mist was returning. Paying attention was a monumental feat.

Brynleigh blinked, and now there were two Zanri's sitting beside her.

"I met him." She yawned, unable to hold it in.

Zanri's red brows furrowed. "The captain? I know you did. You're going to marry him in two weeks."

Her eyes shuttered. She fought to keep them open, but they weren't listening to her. "He seems so... nice."

"Fuck, Brynleigh. You can't talk like that. You don't know... you haven't seen the worst."

She wasn't listening to Zanri. Her cloud was so comfortable, and she was going to return to its fluffy embrace. "I think... I think I like him."

She might even more than like him.

Was this the medicine talking or something else? Brynleigh wasn't sure. But either way, it seemed like Zanri should know. Maybe he was her friend. He was here while she was sick, after all. That's what friends did, right?

Zanri grabbed Brynleigh's hand, and he gripped it so hard that she was certain it would bruise. "Listen to me. You can say that kind of stuff to me but don't ever let Jelisette hear you. Since you've been gone, she's been even more volatile than ever. You don't want to end up like me, B. Owing her..." His voice grew even more distant as Brynleigh fought to stay awake. "She's setting something up. Even if you..."

Darkness was a beast drawing Brynleigh into its black embrace once more.

THE NEXT TIME SHE WOKE, golden curtains were pulled back. The shimmering silver moon cast its light into the gilded room. Opening her eyes was easier this time, and the mist was gone from her head. Thank Isvana, the song of her shadows had returned and was as loud as ever. Their dark tune was a welcome symphony.

Brynleigh felt like herself.

Reaching over, she yanked the needle out of her arm. Whatever the medicine was, she no longer needed it. No, what she needed was to center herself. To do that, she needed more specifics about The Lily. What was the layout? Who was here? And perhaps most importantly, where was Ryker?

An urgent need pulsed within her, pushing her to find him. Because he was her mark. After all, it was good business practice for vampires to keep track of the people they intended to kill.

She glanced at the nightstand, searching for her phone, before remembering that she still didn't have it. She'd have to ask someone about that.

Step one: get a layout of the land.

Step two: find Ryker.

Step three: make a new, better plan. Probably something along the lines of adapting to her environment and grounding herself.

Zanri had said the weddings were in two weeks. That didn't give her long.

Step one would involve getting out of bed. That seemed like a good place to start.

Brynleigh glanced down and frowned as she took in her outfit. Her ballgown from earlier was gone—not surprising, based on how much blood she must've lost—and in its place was a black spaghetti-strap tank top and a pair of gray sleep shorts.

Comfortable, yes. Great for clandestine activities? Not so much. That didn't matter. While she preferred to wear leggings and hoodies when sneaking about, they weren't prerequisites for the endeavor.

A hairbrush sat on the gilded nightstand. She grabbed it and ran it through her knotted hair, trying to remove as many tangles as possible. When it became apparent that a shower would be required to return her hair to its prior silky state, she gave up and threw her hair into a messy bun on top of her head.

Then Brynleigh stood. She wobbled, her feet displeased with the task of bearing her weight once again, but she quickly righted herself. She released her shadows, letting them pour out of her. They were eager to play, crawling over her like a second skin until she was covered in darkness.

Brynleigh briefly considered the merits of shadowing to the safe house to talk with Jelisette before deciding that her initial plan was better. Besides, if The Lily was warded, there was a chance she would set off alarms by shadowing in and out. The last thing she wanted to do was bring attention to herself. Not only that, but there wasn't a guarantee that Jelisette would be at the safe house. The older vampire had a lively social life, and she had many contacts that even Brynleigh wasn't privy to.

Having decided, Brynleigh walked to the door on bare feet. The shadows absorbed the sound of her movements. She was as silent as the night itself.

The doorknob was cold in her hand as she curled her fingers around it and peered through the peephole.

Three figures cast in shadows stood in front of her door. This was a potential problem. She needed to leave the room the old-fashioned, mortal way: on foot. She couldn't shadow to another part of The Lily because she had never been here before. Traveling through the Void was a valuable skill, but it only allowed vampires to return to locations they'd previously been.

Silently cursing, Brynleigh assessed the obstacle in front of her. Two of them were clearly guards. They wore the same black uniforms as the soldiers who'd guarded them during the Choosing. The Republic's insignia was on their chests. Black guns were at their sides.

But the third...

Brynleigh inhaled deeply. Thunderstorms and bergamot flooded her nostrils.

At the same time, the last man took a step closer to the other two.

Ryker.

Her stomach somersaulted. That was a problem. So was the way her heart sped up at the sight of him. Inwardly, she groaned. To say that these bodily reactions were quickly getting frustrating would be an understatement of epic proportions.

Brynleigh had never experienced anything like this before. Why was it happening now, around the captain? It was utterly inconvenient and had to come to a quick end.

Forcing those ridiculous, out-of-place emotions aside—desire had no place here, only revenge—Brynleigh focused on the scene unfolding outside her room. Usually, she was able to hear through doors without any issue, but there must have been some protective barriers over this one to muffle sound.

Still, she picked out her fae's voice. Wait. No. Not her fae. *The* fae. Despite what Brynleigh had said to Valentina, she had no real claim to the captain except that she wanted to kill him.

"Let me in. I need to see her," Ryker said.

The guard with auburn scruff shook his head. "... orders... needs to rest... her Maker."

Ryker crossed his arms, his muscles bulging under his black t-shirt. Fuck, that shouldn't look so attractive. "I'm... superior officer..."

The guards glanced at each other and whispered.

Isvana must have been smiling on Brynleigh tonight. This obstacle wouldn't be difficult to overcome, after all.

Tuning out the guards, she dropped her cloak of shadows and retracted the darkness. She reached over and unlocked the door.

"Good evening, gentlemen," she said primly, as though she weren't dressed in nightclothes.

The guards straightened and turned towards her. Their hands fell to their sides, and they dipped their heads, murmuring greetings beneath their breath.

"I didn't realize you were awake, miss," Auburn Scruff said.

"I just woke up," Brynleigh replied. Then, there were no more words because her gaze drifted over the guards and landed on Ryker's.

The moment their eyes met, it was like worlds smashed together. Intensity and longing filled his chocolate orbs and stole her breath. Her core twisted as he devoured her with a single look. His eyes shone brightly as if he were a dying man, and looking at her was the only cure to his ailment.

Brynleigh's heart slammed violently against her chest. For several long seconds, she forgot to breathe. She moved to step towards him before she realized what she was doing. *Who* she was moving toward.

Gods-damn it.

She swallowed and grabbed the doorframe, forcing her eyes away from his. Breaking his stare was physically painful, but it had to be done.

It's just a physical reaction, she reminded herself. *That's all.*

Brynleigh would keep telling herself that until she believed it... or until he was dead beneath her, his lifeless eyes staring into hers one last time.

She refused to allow this to be anything but a physical response.

Those urges she felt? The desire to move towards him and let him hold her? The deepest need to seek refuge in his embrace? Just impulses that she wouldn't act on.

How hard could it be? Brynleigh would erect a few barriers and set some boundaries, and she'd be good to go.

Yes. Boundaries were a good, solid amendment to her plan.

Hand holding? Fine, she'd have to allow it. Ryker would probably be suspicious of her if she didn't.

Touching, though? Nope.

Kissing? Not a fucking chance.

This was a game, and these boundaries would help her get her act together. She desperately needed them to work.

Brynleigh forced a smile on her face. "Hi."

In her mind, she chanted, *Boundaries,* repeatedly, until it was all she could hear.

Ryker's lips tilted up, and the stern expression he'd been wearing moments ago melted away. He pushed past the guards and took Brynleigh's hands in his.

She leaned into his warm touch before she remembered that it went against her newly created boundaries. She straightened her back so fast; she was surprised it didn't crack.

"Hello, sweetheart." Ryker's gaze searched hers, those swirling depths of emotions still present. His fingers swept over the back of her knuckles, and he drew her towards him. "How are you feeling?"

Honestly?

She was fucked.

That was the first thing that came to mind. All the boundaries, all the rules, and all the reinforcements she'd rebuilt dissipated the moment his hand touched hers.

How could something so simple be so incredibly powerful? What was it about this fae that made her entire world turn upside down? She wasn't sure, but it was dangerous.

If Brynleigh were being honest with Ryker, she'd confess that he confused her. She didn't understand him at all. He was a powerful fae—proven not only by his rank in the army and the storms he commanded but also by the deference these guards showed him—but he was kind to her. A vampire.

Even though she knew better, what had begun as a kernel of doubt grew each time she interacted with Ryker.

Was there a bigger picture she wasn't seeing?

There were the facts: a storm hit Chavin. That was indisputable. Brynleigh had been there, seen the water and death and destruction. She'd also seen two shadowy figures, one tall and dark, the other slender and much shorter, standing on the edge of the forest as she floated, dying as her lungs drank in more and more water.

But what if...

Actually, no.

Brynleigh couldn't do this right now. She stomped on that kernel of doubt, smashing it to smithereens. It was Ryker. Who else could it be? It wasn't as if the Republic of Balance was overrun by water fae. Very few of them were powerful enough to summon a hurricane like that, especially so far inland.

It. Was. Him.

There was no other option.

Seeing as how she couldn't confess all that to Ryker, she tilted her head and smiled softly at him. "I'm a little worn out."

It was true. It must've been the emotions. They plagued her, draining her unlike anything else she'd ever experienced. She gathered them up and shoved them down. Like all the others, these would have to wait their turn.

She could unpack them after he was dead.

Maybe it was normal to feel some level of doubt. Maybe it was good. A sign she hadn't lost all traces of her humanity. She could not forget that this was an act. None of this was real, except for the fact that he'd killed her family.

Yes. That was a good, boundary-strengthening thought. Brynleigh latched onto it.

Ryker reached up and cupped her cheek. It took everything she had to remain rigid.

Boundaries. See? They worked.

"Do you need more blood? Sleep? What can I do for you?" he asked.

Her fangs ached at the suggestion. She didn't think he was offering to let her bite him—and even if he was, it was definitely off the table because biting was an inherently sexual act reserved only for lovers in this modern age—but it was sweet that he recognized her hunger.

Brynleigh paused. What? She never thought anything was sweet. Maybe she wasn't feeling so great after all. Maybe the medicine from earlier was addling her senses.

Actually, now that she thought about it, that seemed plausible. Could drugs make vampires doubt everything and forget their murderous purposes? Probably.

She latched onto the thought like it was a lifeline, and she was drowing. That's all this was. Just the drugs. She needed to sleep them off.

"More sleep." Abandoning her plan to explore The Lily, because now it seemed monumentally stupid, Brynleigh moved backward until she felt the reassuring curved doorknob behind the small of her back. She grabbed it, thankful the door hadn't slipped shut. "You're right, I'm... tired."

Ryker leaned forward, and despite their audience, he brushed his lips over hers.

It wasn't a kiss, she reasoned. Not really. It was a peck. It didn't count.

Her boundaries were still in place.

No kissing, starting *now*.

"Maybe tomorrow, we can find Hallie and Therian?" Brynleigh asked.

Group settings were good. They should avoid being alone as much as possible. She could respect her boundaries and see her friend. It was a win-win situation.

"I'd like that," Ryker said. "I'll see what I can do."

They finished making plans, and he scribbled his phone number down on a piece of paper for her to program into her phone when she found it before they said goodbye. Thank the gods, her boundaries remained intact.

Brynleigh slipped back into the room and turned all the locks. She leaned against the door, breathing heavily. Damn her body. Damn the pull she felt towards Ryker. Damn it all.

Several minutes went by before her heart rate returned to normal, and her lips stopped tingling from Ryker's non-kiss.

Two weeks.

She could do this.

First step: sleep.

Drawing the curtains closed, because the last thing she needed was to be burned by the sun when it rose, she stumbled back to bed and collapsed on the cloud-like mattress.

Even as her eyes fluttered shut, the unwelcome memory of Ryker's lips on hers haunted her.

CHAPTER 25
Welcome Home

"You'll be at the big house for dinner tonight, right?" River gripped Ryker's hand with surprising force, and her painted black nails dug into his skin.

A week had passed since the bombing. Today, Ryker's sister wore an all-black ensemble with as many cut-outs as fabric. It was... a choice, to be certain. One that Ryker didn't necessarily approve of.

"We'll be there." He squeezed his sister's hand reassuringly. "Is being alone with Mom and Dad so bad?"

River frowned. "Yes, it is. If you're not there, Mom will yell at me about my piercings. Again."

Ryker's sister and mother had a tumultuous relationship, at best. He'd seen more than a few of their fights, which usually lasted for hours.

This morning, things had been quiet. Not because the women had worked out their differences but because the Chancellor had finally given them the go-ahead to leave The Lily.

"You know, if you stopped provoking her, things would be easier." It wasn't a secret that Tertia hated the way her daughter marked up her body. Ryker was fairly certain River did it to anger their mother. "Can't you get through a single dinner without fighting?"

"No." River shook her head. "We cannot. We clash at every turn. You know this."

River's aptitude for lateness was only overshadowed by her desire to argue with their mother. Her first word had been no, and she hadn't stopped since then. Cyrus had been the buffer, and now, the duty fell to Ryker.

"I do. I promise we will be there on time." He embraced his sister. "Have I ever let you down?"

River shook her head. "Never, not once."

"Exactly." Ryker kissed her forehead. "I'm taking Brynleigh to the apartment to meet Marlowe, and then we'll head over for dinner."

Ryker was completely done with hotel life. During the past seven days, the participants had been under constant guard—for their own safety, according to Chancellor Rose—so he and Brynleigh hadn't even had a moment alone together.

She had gotten her phone back from the guards, though, and they'd been texting daily. The messages had been short, but they were the highlights of his day... other than when they were together.

Being near his vampire and keeping his hands to himself was slowly killing Ryker. When he signed up for the Choosing, he knew about the laws that kept couples out of the bedroom until their wedding night—some archaic purity bullshit that had no real ramifications in this modern time—but he hadn't considered the effects it would have on him.

Delayed gratification was one thing, but this was pure torture. The sooner Brynleigh was his, the better.

"Good," River said sternly. "Don't be late."

Ryker bellowed a laugh. "That's rich, coming from you."

His sister's reputation for lateness was renowned. She'd have to figure out a way around that before she graduated and started working as a doctor. He couldn't imagine hospitals were very forgiving of tardiness, especially from their staff.

"I live with Mom and Dad," she said primly. "I can't be late to my own house."

"Debatable." If anyone could do it, it was River.

She wisely ignored his comment. "When I video-called Dad yesterday, I told him you were coming. He's going to be so happy to see you."

Ryker hoped so. He had held off introducing Brynleigh to his mother and sister because he wanted his fiancée to meet his entire family at once. He hoped they would love her as much as he did. She was his perfect match in every way.

"How is Dad? Are the new meds working?" Gods, he wanted that more than anything. The Stillness had been around for so long that it was practically the fifth member of the Waterborn family while it slowly stole their father's life. He fucking despised it.

River nodded slowly. "It seems that way." Her voice shifted, taking on an academic quality he was familiar with. For all her rebellious streaks, River excelled at science and medicine. "This new study is groundbreaking, and the treatment combines several drugs."

"Gods, if this works—"

"It would be incredible," River finished, a small smile creeping on her face. "I agree."

Ryker took his sister's hand and drew her close. "Did you release some magic this morning?"

The last thing he wanted to do was bring Brynleigh into a potentially dangerous situation.

River sighed. "Yes, Ryker." She drew out his name, just like she had when she was younger. "I did it today like I have every single morning since... you know."

He knew exactly what she was talking about. "Good. Don't let it build up."

"I won't." A flash of pain went through her eyes before they shuttered. "I'll never forget, Ryker. Even if you don't remind me, I'll always remember. I live with it every day. All those people..."

She looked up at him with wide brown eyes, her unspoken words echoing in the air. *It won't happen again*.

Watching his sister wrestle with the burden of her magic pained Ryker. He helped as much as he could, but he knew River struggled with the weight of her gods-given gifts. Her piercings, her fashion choices, and even her attitude towards their mother were all ways of coping with the hand she'd been dealt.

River's phone rang, the upbeat, boisterous pop tune shattering the silence. Ryker didn't recognize the song. Moments like these reminded him that nearly two decades separated the two of them.

River glanced at the screen before shoving her phone in her pocket. The heaviness from a few moments ago dissolved as River stood on her tiptoes and kissed Ryker's cheek. "Got to go; my ride's here. See you at dinner."

She bent to pick up her suitcases, but Ryker grabbed them before she could. What kind of man would he be if he let his little sister carry her own bags out of the hotel? "Go on, I've got them."

River grinned and grabbed her purse—black, like the rest of her outfit—before holding the door for him. She chattered as they rode the elevator to the main floor, explaining more about the new drug their father was on.

The captain helped his sister into the taxi and loaded the suitcases in the back. She smiled as she closed the door, opening the window to shout one final reminder to come to dinner tonight.

Slipping his hands into his pockets, Ryker strolled into The Lily. He felt lighter than he had in years. His sister was happy and safe; her magic wasn't causing any problems, and tonight, he would introduce Brynleigh to the family.

What could go wrong?

One of the first lessons Ryker had learned as a youngling was that staring was rude, but he couldn't seem to stop. Brynleigh sat beside him in the car, silently gazing out the window, and his eyes were locked on her.

His bride-to-be was stunning. Like him, she was dressed casually. Unlike him, she looked like she'd walked off the pages of a magazine.

She wore an oversized maroon sweater that fell to mid-thigh and black leggings that hugged her legs. There were two slits in her sweater, which he assumed was an accommodation for her wings, although they weren't visible. Her chin rested on her hand as she looked out the blackened car window. Her blonde hair hung over her shoulders, and she wore a minimal amount of makeup.

He couldn't believe she was marrying him. She was a goddess of the night, and he was... himself. Barely worthy of being in her presence. Gods, he loved this woman. Now that he had said the words, he couldn't seem to stop.

Ryker held Brynleigh's other hand, and he rubbed his thumb over the back of her palm. She hadn't spoken much since he'd helped her into the darkened vehicle half an hour ago. The silence didn't bother him. He was at ease in Brynleigh's presence, and the quiet lacked all traces of awkwardness. It was companionable, peaceful, and everything he had hoped for.

Davis, the driver Ryker's mother insisted on paying for, had picked the couple up in The Lily's underground parking garage to avoid the sun. Admittedly, it would take time for Ryker to get used to staying out of the sun, but he was willing to do whatever it took to keep Brynleigh in his life. If she asked him to become fully nocturnal, he would do it. He certainly wouldn't be the first person in history to alter his lifestyle for vampires.

Besides, what was a bit of change when the person you were changing for was your whole world?

And Brynleigh was Ryker's entire world. In the six weeks since they met, she'd catapulted into the first-place position in his life. He couldn't imagine living without her. Watching her bleeding out on the ballroom floor had solidified how important she was to him.

Brynleigh was meant to be Ryker's. There was something so profoundly *right* about the two of them. Their connection was deep and wasn't built on superficial things like appearances. He had the Choosing to thank for that.

He felt like he knew everything about Brynleigh. Her likes and dislikes. Things she missed (the sun, no surprise there) and things she enjoyed doing (playing chess.) He knew her birth family was dead, although she never spoke of what happened to them, and her Maker was her only real connection to the world.

He hoped she would come to see his family as her own.

Ryker had many dreams for the future, and they all revolved around the blonde vampire beside him.

The car slowed, and the familiar sights of Ryker's neighbourhood came into view. He tugged Brynleigh's hand. "We're here, sweetheart."

The car stopped in front of a ten-story apartment building complex surrounded by flourishing gardens.

Brynleigh looked out the window, then back at Ryker. "This is your home?"

"Our home," he corrected softly, squeezing her hand. "Or at least, it can be if you like it. If not, I'm sure we can find something else. It's just... this is a good location. We're halfway to the base and halfway to my family home. But if you want to move, we'll move. We can do whatever you want after we're married."

Something dark flickered in Brynleigh's eyes. It was too quick for Ryker to be certain, but he could have sworn he glimpsed intense longing and regret in her black gaze. But that couldn't be right. It was gone before he could decipher it.

"How long have you lived here?" She looked back at the apartment complex, but her grip tightened on his hand.

"Just over a decade."

He'd moved here after his Maturation, eager to have his own place. Tertia had protested, of course. She wasn't delighted by the idea of her son, a future Representative of the Fae, living in such "downtrodden" conditions. He hadn't given in. He needed his privacy.

Besides, it wasn't like Ryker lived in a shack. His one-bedroom apartment was nice and clean, and he could afford it on his military salary without dipping into the family coffers. It was in a good part of Golden City but not in the luxurious neighborhood where his parents lived.

Even though Tertia was born with a silver spoon in her mouth and believed everyone in her family should live in a mansion filled with servants, Ryker disagreed. He didn't hate how he grew up—on the contrary, he'd had a good childhood—but he loved his apartment. This, and his hunting cabin, were his safe spaces.

This apartment was his. Maybe, with some work, it could be *theirs.*

That idea made Ryker smile. Raising his fist, he rapped on the roof.

Davis would understand his signal. The car started moving again, and they rolled into the underground parking lot, where the sun's deadly rays couldn't touch Brynleigh.

The vehicle stopped, and the door slammed, signifying Davis's departure. Ryker reached over and unbuckled Brynleigh's seatbelt. Earlier, he'd told Davis they would be here for several hours. The driver was meeting a friend nearby for lunch and would return to take them to Waterborn House.

But for now, they were alone.

Ryker tugged Brynleigh across the seat and over to him. She didn't protest as he cupped her cheeks, his gaze searching hers.

"I love you," he murmured. "And I'm so glad you agreed to marry me."

Brynleigh seemed to wrestle over her words for a minute before her fingers tightened around his. "Me too," she breathed, licking her lips. "I... I'm looking forward to our wedding."

Her voice cracked on the last word, but he assumed she was as anxious for their marriage as him. He just wanted to get it over with, to finally claim her as his in every way.

"So am I," he whispered.

Her fingers gripped his as if she never wanted to let him go.

Ryker would gladly remain with her. He laid a hand over hers and inched closer. "I want to kiss you, Brynleigh."

This was the moment he'd been waiting for. The cameras were gone, and for the first time, they were truly alone.

She hitched a breath, and her mouth opened, giving him a peek at her fangs. Gods, the sight of those sharp teeth sent a bolt of want through him. He had always noticed the unnatural beauty of vampires, but none of them had ever affected him the way Brynleigh did.

"You do?" Brynleigh's cheeks heated, which only added to her beauty.

He loved that she was flustered because of him.

"Yes," he breathed. He moved closer but still gave her room. "Is that okay?"

Her eyes searched his for the longest moment until she dipped her head in the briefest of nods.

Ryker had dreamed of this moment. Some nights, he had barely slept because his desire to taste her was so strong. And now, he finally could. Holding her gaze, his hand slipped behind her neck as he drew her close. His heart sped up and his entire being focused on Brynleigh.

He slanted his mouth over hers. Their lips met in an embrace that was at once gentle but powerful.

But it was... one-sided.

This wasn't the kiss he'd dreamed about. Brynleigh was a frozen statue next to him. She didn't move, let alone breathe.

His heart stalled in his chest. Had he done something wrong? Had he misread her consent?

Those beautiful eyes stared at him, unblinking. There was something in the depth of her gaze that he didn't understand. Dark. Strange. A flicker of... fear? Was she scared of him? Gods, he hoped that wasn't the case. He would never do anything to hurt her.

She was his.

Again, Ryker moved his lips tentatively over hers.

She still didn't react.

This was not how he thought this would go.

Ryker was about to pull away, to apologize and ask what was wrong, when Brynleigh muttered something that sounded awfully similar to "Fuck it" under her breath.

He had no time to be confused because whatever decision she reached meant she was no longer frozen beneath him. She transformed in the blink of an eye. No longer a stone sculpture, now she was a living flame, destined to burn him from the inside out. She returned his kiss with an urgent, fiery passion they had yet to explore.

By the fucking Sands, yes. *This* was the kiss he'd dreamed of. Brynleigh slid onto Ryker's lap, straddling him. She threaded her fingers through his hair and moaned his name against his lips.

Fuck, that sound went straight to Ryker's cock. He abandoned his confusion and held her close. He needed her now more than ever.

Evidently, Brynleigh felt the same. Their mouths fused in an ardent embrace. She kissed him like he was the air she needed to breathe; like she was dying and he was the only way she'd survive; like he was a bad decision that she couldn't keep herself from making.

He couldn't tell where his mouth ended and hers began. Their kiss deepened. She embraced him in a way that no one else ever had, and by the Obsidian Sands, he loved each and every moment.

Ryker would never get enough of this—of her.

His hand slipped from her neck to her hip, and he wrapped his other arm around her and held her close. She moaned, rubbing herself against his hardening length.

"Gods, Brynleigh," he groaned against her lips.

Their clothes were an unwanted barrier between them. He wanted to rip off each offending piece of fabric and lay her bare before him.

"I want you," she breathed against his mouth. "I know we shouldn't, but..."

"I want you, too." He could barely remember how to form words; her scent was so intoxicating. "Fucking archaic laws."

Whose damned idiotic idea was it to keep couples apart until their wedding night? It was completely moronic.

And Ryker *liked* rules. A lot. It pained him to acknowledge how ridiculous this one was.

Still, even without the law, Ryker knew their first time together wouldn't be in the back of a car. He had far bigger plans for them than that.

"It's horrible." She embraced him again, and they both lost themselves to the passion burning between them.

They kissed and kissed. Hands wandered. Their bodies rubbed against each other. Lust was a blazing fire between them.

Ryker gave Brynleigh control for a few minutes, even though letting someone else lead wasn't in his nature. Eventually, though, he needed more. He swept his tongue over the seam of her lips, and a groan ran through him as she parted them, granting him access.

At his first taste of her, his hand on her hip tightened. The rightness of the moment flooded him. Brynleigh tasted like shadows, the night, and the subtlest hint of oranges.

She tasted like she was always meant to be his.

His tongue swept through her mouth and grazed her fangs. The sound that left her lips was utterly delectable, and she ground herself against him wantonly.

At that moment, Ryker knew he would never kiss another woman again. How could he?

This was it for him—*she* was it for him.

Any control he might have had snapped when she nipped his bottom lip. It wasn't strong enough to draw blood, but it didn't matter.

His fingers slipped beneath the waistband of her leggings, seeking the warmth hidden between her legs. She moaned, her head arching and exposing the column of her neck as he ran the back of his knuckles against her sensitive flesh.

"Ry, don't tease me." She shifted in his lap.

He kissed her. "What do you want?"

He knew what he wanted but wouldn't do anything without her consent.

Her eyes darkened as they met his. "Touch me."

Those words. He'd fantasized about hearing her say them since their very first date. How could he deny her?

Capturing her lips with his once more, Ryker swept aside her underwear and ran his fingers over her. Touching. Teasing. He went everywhere except that warm heat that beckoned to him.

Brynleigh bucked. "Please, Ryker."

It was all the encouragement he needed. He slid one finger into her inviting warmth, letting the heat from her core envelope him. He groaned against her lips. She was so tight and wet and fucking perfect.

Gods, she would feel so good against his cock. It was that thought that had him adding another finger. He crooked them in a beckoning motion, and she gasped.

He kissed her mouth, her jaw, and her neck as his fingers thrust in and out of her heat. She writhed against him, begging him for more.

Each time his name fell from her lips, each moment she asked for more, his love for her deepened. The sounds Brynleigh made would forever be imprinted on his mind.

His thumb found her clit, and he rubbed it. She screamed.

He captured the sound with his mouth, swallowing her cries as he brought her closer and closer to the edge. Her fingers dug into his hair as if she was afraid that he would disappear on her and leave her wanting.

Never. He wouldn't leave her.

He added another finger, and she moaned. Her walls fluttered against him.

"I'm so close," she gasped, her words little more than air.

"Let go," he told her. "I've got you."

He held her, his fingers bringing her closer and closer to the precipice of oblivion until she shattered with a final scream. Still, he didn't move, letting her ride out of the waves of pleasure on his hand.

Brynleigh gripped his shoulders, panting as she came down from the high of what they'd just done. Only then did he remove his fingers from her warmth, sliding her leggings back into place.

Brynleigh's beautiful black gaze watched him as he lifted his hand. He opened his mouth and licked his fingers.

"By the Sands, you taste so good," he groaned, nearly losing the last strands of his restraint.

He licked every last bit of her off him. This was but an appetizer, he reminded himself. She was his, and this was their first moment of many to come.

Ryker couldn't wait to have Brynleigh spread out on the bed in front of him, naked and glistening. He would spend an eternity between her legs, feasting on her. She would be all he needed.

The only thing stopping Ryker from carrying Brynleigh upstairs to have his way with her, rules be damned, was that Atlas and Marlowe were waiting for them.

With a groan that reverberated through his entire body, Ryker lifted Brynleigh off him. Their chests heaved, and the air was thick with the scent of desire as they stared at each other.

Long, endless seconds went by.

"We should go inside." He didn't want to.

She studied him, running her tongue over her bottom lip, before nodding slowly. "Alright."

There was a rasp to her voice that made him feel alive. *He* did that to her. No one else. This moment was theirs and theirs alone.

It took every ounce of strength Ryker had to get out of the car. He held the door for Brynleigh and extended his hand. She adjusted her leggings and took his hand, their fingers sliding together as he helped her out of the vehicle.

"Who knew you were such a gentleman, Ry?" she teased, letting go of his hand to straighten her sweater.

He grinned, closing the car door behind her. Davis would bring up his suitcases later. "Perhaps I'm a man of many secrets."

Not a lie. Between his job and looking after his family, Ryker was the caretaker of more secrets than he'd like. Hopefully, in the future, he could share those with Brynleigh. He wanted his wife to be his partner in every way, someone who could help carry his burdens and share every aspect of his life.

"Is that so?"

"It is."

"It so happens I like secrets." She brushed her hair over her shoulder and slid her hand into his. "Take me home, Captain Waterborn."

Gods, he loved the sound of that. "With pleasure, sweetheart."

CHAPTER 26
Tendrils of Doubt

What the hell was wrong with Brynleigh? She'd worked so hard to build up her boundaries, only to let Ryker completely demolish them in a single moment. A very good, pleasurable moment, but still a moment.

Many things could happen in a moment. People were born. Others died. Lovers declared their affection. Killers took their final blows.

And Brynleigh?

She gave Ryker control over her body. She let him bring her to immense pleasure.

A thousand curses ran through her mind. She barely paid attention as Ryker led her into the elevator, barely noticed that he still held her hand. All she could do was think about what they'd done in the car. She needed to rebuild the wall between them, and this time, she would respect them.

It didn't matter that Ryker made her feel better than anyone else or that she'd come harder on his fingers than she'd ever been able to do alone.

It didn't matter that when they'd kissed—really, truly kissed for the first time—it was like the world exploded behind her eyes.

And it really didn't matter that his touch sparked things within her that she had absolutely no business feeling.

This was a game. She had one purpose. One reason for being here.

Brynleigh was just having a gods-damned difficult time remembering what that was.

Get through today. The thought churned through her mind. She could do this. In less than twelve hours, after dinner with Ryker's family tonight, Brynleigh would return to the safe house.

That was good. Once she was on familiar ground, she would have an easier time remembering her purpose. It would ground her. And after spending the past week in The Lily and what they'd done in the car, she needed that more than ever.

By the time the elevator dinged, Brynleigh was ready.

In an action that was becoming as familiar as tying her shoes, she collected all her emotions—there were more every gods-damned time she was around the captain—and got rid of them.

Just in time, too.

Ryker's thumb brushed against the back of her hand as they stepped out of the elevator. He led her down the hallway, pointing at several doors and naming the neighbors who lived in each space.

It looked like a clean, comfortable building, although the designer didn't seem to realize there were other colors besides brown and beige. Everything, from the carpet beneath their feet to the ceiling above their heads, was a dull, muted shade. It wasn't Brynleigh's favorite, but since she had no actual plans to reside here—Ryker would be dead before she officially moved in—it didn't matter.

They were halfway down the hall when a loud bark came from further down. Brynleigh tensed, but Ryker didn't seem concerned. In fact, he seemed... happier. They rounded the corner as a door opened at the end of the corridor.

An enormous inky lump of fur the size of a bear cub barreled towards them. It woofed, and then, two massive paws landed on Brynleigh's chest. She stumbled back at the impact, her back slamming into the wall. A slobbery tongue ran up her face, and the black furry monster nuzzled her cheek.

"Down, Marlowe." Ryker's stern voice left no room for discussion. "Let your new mom say hello."

Brynleigh's eyes widened as the bear—no, the dog—listened immediately. Marlowe sat in front of her, his tail thumping against the ground in obvious delight. His pink tongue lolled out of his mouth, and he looked up at Brynleigh with big, brown eyes.

"This is Marlowe?" She peeled herself off the wall. "You said he was a dog, not a bear."

Fae couldn't lie, but this animal was... enormous. Far bigger than she had expected.

A booming laugh left Ryker's lips and echoed around the hallway. "Marlie is an Eleytan Mountain Dog. They're..."

"Gigantic," Brynleigh finished for him. She hadn't known they made canines this huge.

A tall, red-headed fae with tattoos on his neck and arms jogged out of the open doorway, holding an empty blue leash in his hands. "Sorry, Ryker. I tried to keep him in, but you know how he is."

"No worries, Atlas, no harm done," said Ryker.

Pieces clicked into place. Ryker had spoken about the earth fae several times, and now she could put a face to the name.

Ryker slung an arm over Brynleigh's shoulder and kissed her cheek. "Atlas, this is my beautiful fiancée."

She waved awkwardly. "Hi."

"Atlas is a pain in the ass, dog-watcher extraordinaire, and he's also one of my oldest friends." Ryker nodded in the earth fae's direction.

"Nice to meet you." Atlas put out his hand, and Brynleigh shook it.

Even though Atlas was objectively handsome, with his tattoos and muscles for days, Brynleigh didn't feel a single twinge of attraction toward him. Not like she did for Ryker. When the water fae touched her, it was like she was burning up from the inside out.

Damn it all to hell. That probably meant something, but like everything else lately, Brynleigh shoved all those emotions down, down, down until she was somewhat numb.

No matter what, Ryker was still her family's murderer, and she would still kill him.

"Here, Marlowe," Atlas called.

The dog trotted after to the fae, his tail wagging. Smiling, Ryker put his hand on Brynleigh's back and led her into a small mudroom. Shoes sat on racks, and several jackets hung on hooks. A picture of Ryker and Marlowe was on the wall. The two of them were posing together, surrounded by pine trees. A shining blue lake was behind them. It seemed impossible, but between the relaxed posture and the grin on Ryker's face, he looked even more handsome than before.

More emotions went away. The box threatened to burst open right then and there.

That wouldn't do.

Desperate and in need of a new solution so she could survive this, Brynleigh decided she would try being numb. If she didn't acknowledge the emotions, they couldn't bother her.

That was good.

Numbness was the answer. She needed it to work.

If Brynleigh weren't numb, watching Ryker love on Marlowe and shower him with hugs and slobbery kisses would've tugged on her heart-strings. If she weren't numb, her smile and laugh would've been genuine when Ryker and Atlas shared stories about how they met in high school. And if she weren't numb, her insides would've warmed when Atlas pulled out his phone and showed her a picture of the two gangly fae as teenagers with big glasses and stacks of books in their arms. Ryker had certainly grown up since then.

But since she was numb, they didn't affect her. Nope. Not at all.

She was numb. Empty. A void. That's what she told herself.

Her heart certainly didn't grow three sizes when Ryker crouched down and hugged Marlowe, letting the dog give him a series of wet embraces before Atlas took him out.

That didn't happen.

She was ice. Emotionless. She focused on rebuilding her boundaries, brick by fucking brick.

A crack appeared in the cold, numb veneer when the door closed, and Ryker's hand landed on the small of her back. "Ready for your tour of the apartment?"

They were still in the mudroom.

"Yes." A blatant lie. Brynleigh was not ready for this. She should turn and run.

Was it too much to pray for a sudden illness? Something to stop this from happening. If she were mortal, she could claim food poisoning. Alas, she hadn't eaten anything.

Brynleigh supposed she could kill Ryker now, but there were witnesses. They'd seen her come up, and it was unlikely she'd get out of the apartment complex before being caught. It was daytime, which severely limited her escape routes.

And then there was the added complication that Brynleigh didn't want to kill Ryker. *Yet*. Following the plan was the best course of action. No need to act irrationally.

There was definitely no other reason she was hesitating.

"Welcome home, sweetheart." Ryker opened the door to the main apartment and held it for her.

One step was all it took for the ice around Brynleigh's heart to melt. Her boundaries? Smashed into smithereens. Her resolve to stay numb? Gone.

She stood in the doorway, unable to move. Her heart slammed against her chest, and she stared at the windows.

Ryker had assured Brynleigh that she would be safe in his apartment. She had believed him, expecting to see blackout curtains stretched across the windows to block the sun's deadly rays. That's what most people did.

This, though? This was far more than that.

Every single windowpane had been replaced with high-quality black glass. Specialty material that she'd heard of but never seen. And it wasn't like there was only one window. No. The corner apartment had an entire wall that looked out onto the balcony, and another large set of windows was over the sink in the kitchen.

Having this done on short notice must have cost Ryker an Isvana-damned fortune.

Brynleigh's feet were approaching the windows before she realized what was happening. She navigated around the leather couch and placed her palm on the tinted glass. Her breath caught in her throat, and she looked outside. She couldn't have torn away her gaze, even if she tried.

For the first time in six years, she saw the sun. It was muted and had grayish tones, but there was no doubting what it was. She fixated on that yellow orb. Gods help her, but she'd missed it so damn much. Her vision blurred.

"Fuck," she muttered, wiping a finger under her eyes.

She wasn't supposed to feel anything. This wasn't supposed to be real.

Except... Ryker had given her the sun. The one thing she missed most since her Making. How was she supposed to ignore that?

This unexpected gift was the single most thoughtful thing anyone had ever done for her.

Several minutes passed in silence. Ryker walked up behind her, his footsteps quiet as if they were in a temple. Neither of them spoke.

Brynleigh drank in the view. The sun. From this vantage point, the golden arches that gave Golden City its name were visible in the distance.

Eventually, Ryker moved. His chest pressed against her back, and his hands landed on her hips as he rested his chin on her shoulder. He didn't disturb her, didn't try to talk. He let her look at the sun for as long as she needed.

Minutes passed.

Heat bloomed in Brynleigh, and a feeling that she had absolutely no business experiencing came to life within her. She didn't even bother identifying it. She bundled it up along with everything else and shoved it down, down, down.

At this rate, Brynleigh would be a cold, numb, emotionless vampire when she married Ryker. Maybe that was for the best. Her emotions and her body were both clearly confused, having forgotten why this was the best course—the only course—for her vengeance.

Even now, Jelisette's voice echoed in Brynleigh's head.

Not only will killing the reclusive captain on your wedding night be poetic vengeance for the death of your family, but it will teach all the Representatives a lesson. From that moment until the end of time, they will always be watching, always waiting for the next hit. Because of you.

Brynleigh had heard the rhetoric a hundred times. She knew it by heart. It used to sound so good, so right. She used almost to feel giddy when she thought of her plan. But now?

Tendrils of doubt were weaving their way through her soul, taking root, and growing like hungry weeds. Every time she ripped one up, two more grew in its place.

"Let's take a look at the apartment." Ryker's hand landed on the small of her back.

Gods help her but she didn't pull away. She couldn't.

He added, "We can change whatever you want, sweetheart. Say the word, and it's done."

Great. Now he was being fucking considerate, too? How in the hell was she supposed to deal with this?

Cold-blooded killers weren't supposed to act like Ryker. They weren't supposed to give you the sun or be amenable to making alterations for your comfort. They were supposed to be horrible, awful people who didn't give a damn about you.

Turning around—and pointedly ignoring the fact that Ryker was touching her—Brynleigh took in the space. It was a nice apartment, a little masculine for her taste if she were being honest, but well-built. The large kitchen was clean, and it opened into the living area. There was a sturdy dining table with four matching chairs. A chess set sat on the coffee table in front of the TV. Down the hall were two doors that led to what she assumed were the bedroom and bathroom.

"Maybe a few coats of paint?" After all, she was supposed to be playing the part of the excited bride. Besides, she'd always been partial to springtime colors. "Or we could get a few throw pillows to liven it up."

"We can buy as many as you want." He wrapped his arms around her from behind and rested his chin on her head. "Anything you can think of, it's yours. I barely have any expenses, and I've been saving money since I started working."

See? Considerate. Why couldn't Ryker have been an alpha fae asshole who bossed her around and didn't have a trace of kindness in him? It would've made her life a hell of a lot easier. But no, she had to get stuck with the one fae who seemed to care about her thoughts and feelings.

This was... a lot. The longer they looked around the living room, the worse she felt. Her lungs squeezed, and old sweat broke out on her neck.

"Is there a bathroom?" Brynleigh extricated herself from Ryker's grip and stepped back, trying to put some room between them.

Space. That's what she needed. Space to breathe. To recover. To just... be away from all *this*.

"Of course." He smiled and pointed down the hall. "First door on the right."

Brynleigh thanked him and hurried down the corridor. She didn't slow down to look at the pictures on the walls. She slipped into the bathroom and shut the door behind her.

Gods, there was even a blacked-out window in here, right above the tub. Was there no escaping Ryker's kindness?

Closing her eyes, Brynleigh leaned against the bathroom door and released her shadows. They'd been thrumming incessantly in her veins since the incident in the car. As soon as she permitted them to slip from her hands, they whipped out of her violently, darkening the room until the night surrounded her.

Breathe. She forced her lungs to take in air.

Inhale. Exhale.

So, Ryker had a huge, cuddly dog that he seemed to love. That didn't inherently mean he wasn't evil. Even bad men could care about dogs. She'd probably be more concerned if he *didn't* like animals. What kind of psychopath didn't care about pets?

And the windows. Admittedly, the unexpected gesture was nice, but Ryker was still the same man who'd called down a tempest and drowned everyone she knew. He was still a cold-blooded killer.

Brynleigh twisted the necklace her parents had given her on her eighteenth birthday. It was a constant reminder of their loss. Right now, she desperately needed that reminder.

Opening her eyes, she met her reflection's gaze in the mirror. "They're gone because of him," she hissed, careful to keep her voice low. "Pull yourself together."

Captain Ryker Waterborn put on a good show, but he was still the cause of all her heartbreak. He still deserved to die.

The front door clicked open, and two male voices murmured. Claws scratched on the floor. A bark.

Atlas was back with Marlowe.

Turning on the tap, Brynleigh splashed her face with cold water. The frigid temperature was good for her. It helped snap her back to reality.

She was a doubly blessed vampire, for Isvana's sake. She thrived on blood and darkness and shadows. She wouldn't let something as trivial as a few considerate, kind gestures deter her from her goal. Gripping the countertop, Brynleigh hardened her eyes and glared at herself.

"You are strong and will not crack," she told herself sternly. "Remember why you're here. Respect your boundaries, and you'll be fine."

Confident in her renewed ability to keep emotions out of this, Brynleigh rejoined the others.

She could do this.

FUCK.

She couldn't do this.

By the time the clock struck four in the afternoon, and they were set to leave Marlowe behind in Atlas's capable hands, Brynleigh was a ball of nerves.

At least *those* emotions, she could keep. There was nothing wrong with nerves. Thank the gods they were safe because she had many of them. Apprehension gnawed at her stomach, eating her up from the inside out. It was those damned tendrils of doubt. They had exploded within her and were now a tangle of knots.

Brynleigh had always assumed that the Ryker she got to know during the Choosing was an act. A show he put on to attract a wife.

No one could actually be that good of a guy, right?

Except it didn't seem to be an act. Atlas shared story after story about his friend, even after Ryker asked him to stop, and though the words varied, the theme was the same. Ryker had saved Atlas from a life on the streets, giving him a home when he had none. Ryker had backed Atlas up when someone from his past came calling for blood.

Ryker did this. Ryker did that. Story after story painted the captain in the same light: he didn't seem to have a bad bone in his body.

And that was just... not fair.

Not fair at all.

And Marlowe? The big dog had leaped on Brynleigh the moment she'd left the bathroom, and he'd been glued to her side ever since. He was the sweetest animal, cuddling beside her on the couch and placing his head in her lap as she absentmindedly petted him.

Even worse than all that, Ryker kept checking in on Brynleigh. He brought her a mug of warmed blood from the stash he'd had shipped to the apartment, and he stayed beside her the entire afternoon.

And they weren't just sitting together. No. The water fae was always touching her. A hand on her shoulder. A thigh pressed against hers. His thumb on her hip, rubbing circles.

If their date had ended here and she'd been returning to the safe house right away, Brynleigh would have been fine. She could have handled that.

But no.

That had just been the beginning. Now, the real test was underway. Ryker's hand was a brand on Brynleigh's back as he led her to the underground parking garage. The same man who'd driven them there stood outside the car.

"Captain, Miss." The driver dipped his head. "I hope you had a pleasant afternoon."

Unfortunately, yes, Brynleigh thought to herself. She had the common sense not to say that, though. It would open a can of worms she had no intention of dealing with.

"We did, thank you, Davis," Ryker said.

Davis moved towards the door as though to open it, but Ryker got there first. In yet another considerate gesture—really, this was becoming overwhelming—he held it open for Brynleigh and waited for her to enter the vehicle.

Once Brynleigh was inside, Ryker slid in after her. The air still smelled of sex, and Brynleigh blushed as she buckled in. Gods, this day couldn't be over fast enough.

"How far is your parents' house?" Brynleigh tapped her pocket to make sure she hadn't forgotten her phone. She needed to be available in case her Maker called.

"Thirty minutes without traffic." Ryker slung his arm over her shoulder and drew her flush against him. "How do you feel?"

"I'm... nervous." And for good reason. She had no idea what she'd say to his parents.

Hi, it's nice to meet you. My name's Brynleigh de la Point. I'm twenty-nine, and six years ago, your son killed my entire family and almost killed me. I'm going to marry and then murder him to get my revenge in the most dramatic and emotionally damaging way possible.

She hadn't participated in many family gatherings in the past six years, but she was fairly certain that wouldn't go over well.

"They're going to love you as much as I do." Ryker kissed her forehead, and his lips lingered on her skin for several seconds before he added, "You're amazing, and they'll see that."

"I hope so," she murmured.

"They'd be stupid not to." He rapped on the roof, and then, they were off.

As Golden City passed them by, Brynleigh stared out the darkened window. Everything she'd learned about Ryker's mother scrolled through Brynleigh's mind. Although Ryker himself had become somewhat of a recluse since the flood, plenty of information was available about Representative Waterborn.

Born almost three centuries ago, Tertia was a direct descendant of the very first fae who'd crossed the Indigo Ocean and settled into what used to be known as the Four Kingdoms. Her great-grandfather, seven times over, was part of the initial council that had abolished the kingdoms' borders and created the Republic of Balance after the High Ladies of Life and Death and their mates Faded.

None of that research had told Brynleigh what Tertia was like as a mother, though. Was she kind, as Isolde had been? Or perhaps Tertia was distant, cruel, and preoccupied. Brynleigh wasn't sure. All she knew for certain was that the Waterborns were made of money.

That begged the question of why Ryker lived in a one-bedroom apartment in the middle of Golden City. Surely, he could afford to reside wherever he chose.

It was a question for another time. Or not. Ryker would be dead in a week. He could bring the answer with him to the grave. Brynleigh should be focusing on asking less questions, not more. She was already confused, and feeding that doubt was unwise.

The view slowly changed as they left the central city behind. Tall, looming glass buildings gave way to short, sprawling homes made of red brick. Shining offices became long one-story malls and individual shops. Packed neighborhoods became rambling estates with pristine gardens and emerald-green lawns.

Ryker sat beside Brynleigh, his quiet presence grounding her as they drew nearer to his childhood home. He didn't try to engage her in conversation, seeming to realize she needed the silence.

Because, of course, he did.

The car slowed as they entered a gated community. Brynleigh's palms slickened.

They drove up a long, paved driveway. Her heart slammed violently against her ribs. It hadn't beat this quickly since before she was Made.

No one had ever brought Brynleigh to meet their parents before. She wasn't a nice girl—even before she'd taken up vigilante killing and revenge plots, she hadn't been sweet. That was her sister's role in life.

This isn't real, she reminded herself for the hundredth time. *Remember your boundaries.*

But the problem was, it felt real. Far too fucking real.

It felt as if she'd fallen madly in love with Ryker during the Choosing, and now, she was preparing to meet her future in-laws.

Her feelings were wrong, though. She wasn't in love with Ryker. She hated him. After this, she should take up acting. She would excel at it.

A voice crackled over the in-car speaker. "We're pulling up to Waterborn House, sir," said the driver.

"Thank you, Davis. Please proceed into the garage." Ryker lifted his arm, ran his hands down his jeans, and rolled his shoulders. His face hardened almost imperceptibly, and his jaw feathered.

Within seconds, Ryker transformed from a relaxed fae into one who looked ready for a fight.

There he is.

For the first time, Brynleigh saw the warrior fae.

Other people might have been frightened by how quickly he changed, but her? Fear had no place here. Relief ran through her, coating her insides. She'd been beginning to think this part of him didn't exist.

This was the fae who'd murdered her family. It had just taken him longer than expected to rip off the mask.

This was good.

Davis drove into a luxurious garage that resembled an airplane hangar before cutting off the engine. The door closed as the driver exited, leaving them alone.

Ryker turned to Brynleigh, his countenance pinched as he palmed the back of his neck. "Before we go in, there's something I should warn you about."

CHAPTER 27

I Made My Choice

"Warn me?" Brynleigh echoed Ryker's words. "What do you want to warn me about?"

Ryker had spent the car ride debating whether or not he should have this conversation, but in the end, he decided he wanted Brynleigh to be prepared. Still, he picked his words carefully.

"My mother can be... difficult, at times." Most of the time, if he was being honest.

Ryker loved his mother, but she'd never exactly been soft. She wanted her children to be perfect in every way. After the Incident, she'd been colder and harder than before.

Usually, Tertia directed her ire at River, but this week, she had turned her sights off her rebellious daughter and onto her son. She'd made frequent passive-aggressive comments about Brynleigh whenever they spoke. She never expressed her displeasure directly, but it wasn't necessary.

Ryker understood his mother far better than most, and he knew she was disappointed he hadn't picked a more "appropriate" bride like Valentina Rose.

No matter how plainly Ryker put it, Tertia refused to understand that he wasn't interested in the fire fae. He didn't want someone who enjoyed throwing lavish parties and attending all the social events. He'd done these things for years, fulfilling the duties that came along with being the son of a Representative, and he hated them. He didn't want a party planner. He wanted someone who made him laugh, challenged him, and was gods-damned amazing in every way.

That someone was Brynleigh.

Ryker had explained as much to his mother multiple times during their stay at The Lily, but he still had a niggling fear that she might try something tonight. He needed to prepare Brynleigh for the fact that his mother might be... abrasive.

All fae knew how to watch their words—it was one of the first things they learned because lying wasn't an option—but they could also speak cutting jabs like no one else. Just because Tertia might not outright insult Brynleigh—he hoped his mother would exhibit more class than that—didn't mean she would be kind. She was the only one he was worried about. River and Cyrus would fall in love with Brynleigh as soon as they met her, just like Ryker had.

Two lines creased Brynleigh's forehead, temporarily marring her unblemished skin. "What do you mean?"

Ryker took her hand in his and kissed the back of her palm. "I love you."

She frowned, and he felt he was messing up all of this. "I know you do."

It hadn't escaped Ryker's notice that Brynleigh had yet to return those three words. He'd be lying if he said he didn't want to hear them, but he wouldn't pry them out of her lips before she was ready. Waiting would make hearing them all the sweeter.

Ryker forced his lips to form a smile. "My sister's going to love you, too. Dad will, too. Of that, I'm certain."

"Oh." Brynleigh ran the tip of her tongue over one of her fangs. That minuscule movement had no business being so attractive. "But your mother..."

"By the Obsidian Sands, I hope I'm wrong." If Ryker thought it would help, he'd travel to the nearest fae temple and pray upon the vials of sand themselves, begging the deities to hear his pleas. Unfortunately, he was a realist. He didn't think that anything, even the black grains that had been brought across the Indigo Ocean with the fae, could change Tertia's opinion about her son's bride.

Brynleigh was attentive, and she picked up what he wasn't outright saying. "Your mother won't like me, will she?"

His heart twisted at the doubt in her voice.

Ryker cupped Brynleigh's cheek, and she leaned into his touch. He loved that she relaxed around him and trusted him enough to let him touch her like this. "I hope she does," he said. "You are incredible. She'd be a fool not to see that."

"I understand." Disappointment flashed through Brynleigh's eyes.

The sight was a knife to Ryker's gut.

"Listen to me, sweetheart," he said gruffly. "No matter what she says in there, I picked you. I *Chose* you. I will continue to do so until the end of time."

Nothing would ever tear them apart. No person could destroy the relationship they'd built. It was steadfast, built on a stronger foundation than simply physical attraction. Their souls were linked.

Ryker's heart boomed as he waited for Brynleigh's response. Each moment stretched on and on until she finally nodded. "Alright, I understand."

He prayed to the gods that she did. Or that his gut was wrong, and he was worried for no reason. He hoped this dinner wouldn't be a disaster.

Only time would tell.

Ryker had been to his family home hundreds of times since he moved out, but this was the first time he felt strange about it. Almost like he didn't fully belong here.

It was because of the vampire at his side. He'd given Brynleigh his heart, and now, his life belonged with her. Where she went, he would always follow.

TWO HOURS LATER, Ryker knew he'd been right to worry. His mother had been kind enough to Brynleigh when she greeted them in the garage, but he'd caught the clench in Tertia's jaw and the hardness in her eyes.

Tertia was incredibly overdressed for the occasion. She wore a floor-length cerulean ballgown with three-inch heels as if she was about to attend a formal engagement and not have dinner with her two children and soon-to-be daughter-in-law. That was Tertia, though. She was the definition of dramatic.

Unlike Ryker, who'd had arranged for contractors to swap out the windows in his apartment to accommodate Brynleigh's inability to be in the sun, his parents hadn't changed their windows. However, they had installed blackout blinds since he had made it a condition of their visit. He wouldn't take Brynleigh anywhere that might endanger her.

It wasn't Tertia's words that had Ryker on edge. For the most part, his mother was kind enough as she played tour guide and showed Brynleigh through the mansion. It was what she wasn't saying that had Ryker ready to bolt far earlier than he had planned.

Whenever Tertia thought Brynleigh wasn't looking, she shot Ryker searing looks. When she spoke, she used the sickly-sweet tone she reserved for people she considered beneath her. Disapproval radiated from her pores.

Anger frothed and bubbled in Ryker's veins, worsening by the minute. Brynleigh was to be his bride, and he wouldn't allow his mother to continue treating her in such a fashion.

"This is Cyrus's study." Tertia pointed at the closed door, which hid the space that had sat empty for the past decade and a half. "It doesn't get much use anymore."

"Oh, I'm sorry," Brynleigh said softly.

So was Ryker. He waited for his mother to say something kind. To acknowledge Brynleigh's comment.

Instead, Tertia said, "Hmm," turned, and walked away. Her heels clicked on the marble flooring, and Ryker stared at her retreating back.

"I'm sorry," he whispered, squeezing Brynleigh's hand. "She's not usually... I'll talk to her."

"Thank you," Brynleigh murmured. "It's okay, though. She doesn't like me. I understand."

No, it wasn't okay. Not with Ryker. The sooner this tour was over, the better. He would be talking to his mother *tonight* about her attitude. This was inappropriate, and he would not stand for it.

They followed his mother.

As a child, Ryker used to love running down these halls. Waterborn House had over forty rooms and three floors. When his mother wasn't home, he had free rein. Ryker had many memories of racing through the house, roaring with laughter, and sliding down the floors in his socks as his father chased him, imitating a dragon.

Those shrieks of joy were long gone. Now, Waterborn House was simply a ghost of times long gone. A holder of memories. A keeper of the past.

Ryker tried to see his childhood home through Brynleigh's eyes. It was massive. Paintings of his ancestors adorned the walls. Centuries-old statues perched on tables. Gold trimmed the baseboards. A hundred other little touches screamed "old money." It was less of a home and more of a museum.

They finally reached the engraved library doors. Tertia stopped in front of them and turned. The Representative was nearly a foot shorter than Ryker, but there was no denying the authority with which she carried herself.

Tertia looked past Ryker to the vampire at his side.

"Tell me, Miss de la Point." His mother had yet to call Brynleigh by her first name, which was grating on Ryker's last nerve. He would be addressing that issue with his mother tonight as well. "Have you ever read the *Ballad of the Light Elves?*"

Ryker stared at Tertia. What the hell was going through her mind? The ballad predated the Battle of Balance, a pivotal turning point in their country's history, and it was written in an ancient dialect of the Common Tongue that very few people still spoke. He had only read the ballad because it was compulsory for his twelfth-grade literature class. The epic tale of good and evil took place during the Fall of the Rose Empire and had no ramifications on their current lives.

"Unfortunately, I haven't had the privilege," Brynleigh said sweetly. She hadn't stooped to Tertia's level, speaking kindly despite his mother's uncouth behavior.

"Hmm." Tertia lifted her shoulder and frowned. "Such a pity. All the girls attending Highmountain's School for Young Fae study the ballad during their fourth year."

Ryker slid Brynleigh behind him. It was a subtle movement, but he knew Tertia noticed. "Enough, Mother," he growled in warning, clenching his fists at his sides.

The Representative's eyes widened in mock shock, and her hand flew to her heart. Did his mother think him a fool? He knew she was doing this purposefully, and he understood precisely what kind of game she was playing.

"What?" Tertia had the gall to sound innocent. "I'm just curious about what kind of education my son's girlfriend received. What's wrong with that?"

"She's not my girlfriend; she's my fiancée," Ryker corrected, not bothering to mask the ire in his voice. "We're getting married in a week." He growled. "You know that."

As far as Ryker was concerned, the week couldn't go fast enough. He never thought he'd be one to look forward to a wedding, but he was eager to marry his vampire. The weddings promised to be extravagant affairs. When one had as much money as the organizers of the Choosing had at their disposal, lavish events could be thrown together in less than a month.

Tertia sighed. "You know I'm concerned for your well-being, Ryker. If the vampire doesn't even know the *Ballad of the Light Elves*, who knows what else is lacking from her education?"

"I—" Brynleigh started to say.

Apparently, Ryker's mother had lost her mind because she spoke right over Brynleigh. "I'm just saying that you need to be careful, my son. That's all."

Ryker growled, "Mother—"

"It's not too late, you know. I talked to Ignatia, and the Rose girl would be willing to break her engagement to Edward. I watched the Choosing with the rest of the world and saw you two together. Valentina would be a marvelous wife for you, Ryker, dear. She's powerful, strong, and well-educated."

Had Ryker been angry before? That was nothing compared to the fury churning in him now.

The air in the hallway practically crackled. His water magic thrummed steadily in his veins, itching to be released. There was a storm within him, needing to protect what was his. His nostrils flared. Red tinged his vision.

He stepped towards his mother, looming over her, and yelled, "Enough!"

Tertia gasped, pressing a hand against her heart once more. "Ryker Elias Waterborn, do not raise your voice to me!"

Power rippled from her.

Goosebumps broke out on Ryker's arms. So much for waiting until after dinner. Their conversation would be happening right fucking now.

"I will do whatever it takes to protect my fiancée, Mother." He held Brynleigh at his side. "I will not allow you to disrespect my Chosen bride in such a manner. Do not speak to me of Valentina Rose or any other woman again. I will not stand for it. I have made my Choice, and I will not go back on my word. I *love* Brynleigh."

His chest heaved as his words echoed around them. He had meant every single one and wouldn't take them back.

His mother's bottom lip wobbled. For a single moment, Ryker wondered if he'd been too harsh. But then Tertia opened her mouth. Her voice lacked all traces of maternal warmth, and she stared daggers at her firstborn.

"You dare speak to me about your Choice?" Her eyes narrowed, and the temperature in the hallway dropped as she moved closer to Ryker. "You've Chosen an undead bloodsucker who has no lineage, proper education, or finances to speak of. You don't want my advice? Fine. Don't come crying to Mommy when it all falls apart. I won't give a damn."

Ryker snarled, the sound feral as it ripped through him.

How fucking dare she? In all his years, he'd heard his mother be cold but never cruel in this fashion. He'd brought Brynleigh for a nice, civilized family dinner, but his mother was destroying it before it even began with her poisonous, barbed words.

"This won't fall apart. I love her," Ryker seethed. His fingers curled around Brynleigh's, and he stepped back from his mother. "This was a bad idea. We should—"

Footsteps came from behind them, and River hurried down the hall. She'd changed and now wore a knee-length black pencil skirt and a flowing purple blouse. It softened her look but did nothing to temper the rebellious spark in her eyes.

"Ah, my daughter. Late as usual," Tertia remarked caustically. Yeah, this wasn't going well at all.

"Am I late? It looks like I'm right on time for the fight." River crossed her arms.

Mother and daughter glared at each other, and the tension rose and rose. Gods damn it all.

Ryker clenched his jaw and inhaled deeply. If this evening could be saved, he would have to do it now. He pinned Tertia with a glare that would have sent soldiers scurrying to do his bidding. His mother glared right back.

"We're not fighting," Ryker ground out. "I was telling Mother how much I love Brynleigh and would do anything for her."

Ryker held his mother's gaze. He let her see everything on his face. His anger, his willingness to turn and walk out of this house with his bride, and his resolve to put Brynleigh first, always.

Tertia might have given birth to him, but it didn't give her the right to treat his Chosen partner with anything less than the utmost respect. Of all the things Ryker held dear, his family was at the top of his list. He respected his mother, but in a week, Brynleigh would be his wife. That put her above everyone else. He would not hesitate to remove them from this situation if it became toxic.

"That's so sweet, Ryker." River walked up behind her brother. She wrapped one arm around his waist and the other around Brynleigh's. Resting her head between them, River grinned first at him and then at his vampire. "Hi. I'm River. It seems my brother has forgotten to introduce us."

He hadn't forgotten. He'd been preoccupied with other things, like making sure his mother knew he wouldn't tolerate disrespect toward his bride.

Brynleigh disentangled herself from his arms and turned around. "It's nice to meet you, River. You know, I've heard quite a bit about you. Your brother is rather proud of you."

Proud was an understatement. River was the most powerful water fae of their generation, and with some training, she would be unstoppable. Not only that, but she was kindhearted and caring. Ryker would do anything for his sister. He'd proven that six years ago.

Memories that he usually kept under wraps pulsed through his mind. Water, pouring from the sky. His hands, outstretched. His well of magic, rapidly draining as he reeled it all in. Utter exhaustion that had kept him down for days.

"I'm proud of him, too." River smiled up at Ryker and touched his arm. "I came to let you all know dinner's ready. Dad's waiting for us." She bit her lip, making the ring in the middle stand. "He was... tired today."

Ryker heard the unspoken words as though she'd shouted them at him. *We don't have long.*

He turned and hurried to the dining room.

DINNER WAS a formal affair in more ways than one.

Instead of eating in the smaller dining room near the family's living quarters like they usually did for their family dinners, they sat in the massive one that could hold fifty people. The table was enormous, and the five of them looked comical sitting at it. A classical concerto dating back to the time of the High Ladies of Life and Death streamed from hidden speakers, adding to the ceremonious air of tonight's dinner.

Tertia sat at the head of the table, glaring icy daggers at Brynleigh. The Representative hadn't said anything to the vampire since the library, which was good. If she did, Ryker would either lash out with his magic, words, or both. He wasn't sure which he would choose if push came to shove, but he would defend Brynleigh to his last breath.

Either way, he knew his mother would not appreciate his actions.

He and Brynleigh sat together in the middle of the table. The pristine white tablecloth was long and hid their joined hands. River was across from them, and Cyrus sat beside his daughter.

No one spoke, as was the norm. For as long as Ryker could remember, Tertia always had one rule at family dinner: no one was allowed to talk until the food was served. Even though her children were grown, the rule still stood.

Ryker picked up his glass of red wine, curling his fingers around the stem. Beside him, Brynleigh had a similar beverage, although hers was spiked with blood. River stared at her empty plate, twisting a lock of hair through her fingers, but Ryker studied his father.

Cyrus's gaze was clear as he looked around the room from his wheelchair. Though the bags beneath his eyes spoke to the tiredness River had mentioned, it seemed like today was a good day.

Those were rare. The Stillness was a silent thief, stealing their father day by day. Soon, Cyrus would Fade to nothing but dust, his body returning to the black sands where the fae first came from. When the illness first hit, Ryker's father lost feeling in his toes. Less than a year after that, he'd woken unable to move his feet. Then, his legs.

Every year, it got worse and worse.

The Stillness varied from fae to fae. It struck some like a lightning bolt, stealing their ability to live in one day, while it drained others of life over several years or decades. There was no cure, only methods to make the end of life more manageable.

One day, Cyrus's heart would stop beating, and his lungs would no longer be able to draw air.

Ryker dreaded that day. All children were meant to see their parents Fade—it was a natural part of life. But this was different. Cyrus hadn't lived the thousand years his father had before him. He was young for a fae, only four centuries old.

Cyrus Waterborn was everything Tertia was not. Where she was cold, he was warm. Where she was focused on her work, he made sure their children knew they were cared for and loved. Ryker had never doubted his parents loved him because his father showed him affection daily.

And now, he was dying.

Everyone had their ways of dealing with the Stillness. Tertia threw herself into work. Ryker took over the patriarchal role in their family, ensuring everyone's well-being. And River? She spent hours praying to Dyna, the fae goddess of life and healing. When she wasn't at the temples, River was at school learning to be a doctor. She hoped to try and find a cure before it was too late.

Ryker wasn't sure his sister's prayers would do any good. It wasn't that he didn't believe in the gods and goddesses worshiped throughout the Republic of Balance. They were as real to him as the Obsidian Sands the fae revered.

He just didn't believe the deities were watching their every move. If the gods cared as much as River or the priests would have them believe, how could they let the world fall apart around them? How could they let people starve in the streets? How could they let his father die of the Stillness?

No, Ryker was reasonably certain the gods didn't care about what was happening in the Republic of Balance.

The dining room door slid open, and three servants entered the room. They were all Light Elves employed by his mother to keep the house and serve meals. There had been help around the house for as long as Ryker could remember.

Mr. Cobalt, the oldest of the three servants, cleared his throat. "The first course is served, Representative Waterborn."

"Wonderful, thank you." Tertia smiled, but the gesture was frigid. Evidently, she hadn't gotten over the incident at the library earlier, either.

The servants stepped forward, serving a chilled tomato gazpacho to the four fae. Another glass was brought for Brynleigh. This one was filled to the brim with dark, crimson blood.

"Thank you." She took a sip and hummed. "It's perfect."

The servants slipped out of the dining room as quickly as they'd appeared, closing the door behind them.

For a moment, no one spoke. The silence stretched on and on.

Then, Tertia picked up her spoon. "Well, let's eat." She sent a withering glare in Brynleigh's direction. "Or drink, I suppose, since you can't do anything else."

Ryker bristled, the spoon curling in his fist as he glared at his mother. This was going down in history as their worst family dinner, which was a feat.

Every part of Ryker's body was tense like he was moments away from shattering.

Seconds went by, long and endless and painful.

Then, the strangest thing happened.

A cough came from across the table. It was weak but so unexpected that it sounded like a gong.

"Be... kind, Tertia." The admonition was a murmur slipping from Cyrus's mouth.

The entire room seemed to take a breath.

Ryker's heart stopped beating momentarily as he lifted his gaze to his father's.

What he saw there stunned him. Cyrus's eyes were alert and lacked the glassiness that often ran through them. There was *life* in his eyes, a vividness that had been missing for many years.

At that moment, nothing outside this room mattered. Even if the rebels attacked, Ryker wouldn't notice.

His dad was *alert*.

"Daddy?" River's lip quivered, and tears lined her eyes.

The hope in River's voice made Ryker's heart lurch in his chest. This was real, right? It had to be real.

Cyrus turned his head slowly—so gods-damned slowly that it felt like an eternity passed—towards his daughter. His trembling, nearly translucent hand rose in the air, and he placed his fingers on her healthy, sun-kissed skin.

"Yes, Princess." His chapped lips formed the words with the utmost care. "I'm... here."

Ryker's heart remembered that it had stopped beating. It picked up, the rhythm a staccato in his chest. The spoon was a twisted piece of metal as he dropped it to the table, forgotten.

Everyone stared at Cyrus, whose gaze crawled from River to Ryker to Tertia.

The moment the patriarch looked at his wife, the Representative's composure shattered. She cried out, and her chair tumbled to the ground. She practically flew around the table.

"Dyna, have mercy on us," Tertia sobbed as she kissed her husband. "You're here."

CHAPTER 28

Complications Abound

What had begun as a formal dinner quickly evolved into something that made Brynleigh uncomfortable in more ways than one.

Earlier, Tertia's abhorrent, bitchy behavior had been one thing. It was fine. More than fine, if Brynleigh was being honest. If that was how his mother acted, maybe Brynleigh was doing the right thing by killing Ryker. Maybe that mask she'd seen in the car, the one he'd worn when they first entered the house, was really who he was, and he was just like his mother.

Brynleigh had been feeling more confident in her plan and boundaries right up until Ryker's father coughed. When Tertia's chair crashed to the ground, Brynleigh saw an entirely new side of the family.

It was wholly unwelcome.

Now, she felt like an intruder in the most intimate of moments. Brynleigh was a spectator, sitting back and trying to shrink against the wall as the family hugged their patriarch and cried.

The cold Representative had transformed into a warm, loving wife as she peppered her husband with kisses. She took his hand gently and spoke to him in soft tones.

The way River looked at her father—like he had personally hung the moon and stars in the sky—reminded Brynleigh of the love she'd had for her parents.

And Ryker.

Captain Ryker Waterborn of the Army's Fae Division fucking *cried*. Not just a tear or two. He openly wept, tears rolling down his cheeks as he kneeled at his father's side.

Gods damn it all, witnessing Ryker cry made Brynleigh feel all sorts of things that she had no business feeling.

She couldn't ignore the truth any longer: she was in trouble. Things were getting far too complicated for her liking. She had come to this dinner hoping to find more reasons to kill Ryker.

And now? This wasn't what Brynleigh had signed up for. This game was about death, brutality, and heartless revenge. She knew that, yet her heart insisted on breaking at the joy and sadness in this room. Damned tears lined her eyes.

This was too much. There were too many emotions. Too much going on in this room.

She must have made a sound because Ryker glanced at her as though asking if she was alright. She wasn't, but she still nodded. Ryker returned to his father, murmuring.

At some point, the servants brought in more food. There was a veritable feast on the table, which Brynleigh could not eat.

Avoiding the emotional scene still unfolding before her, Brynleigh studied the paintings on the wall. Some were landscapes, a few were portraits, and all looked expensive. Usually, displays of wealth like this turned her stomach, but she had bigger things to worry about right now. Tertia slowly spooned her husband some gazpacho while River and Ryker spoke to him through watery smiles.

The four of them seemed happy, and it was...

Horrible.

She needed to get out of here.

Brynleigh refilled her blood wine from the nearest decanter and pushed her chair back from the table. "Where's the ladies' room?"

Ryker met her gaze from across the table. "Down the hall and three doors to the left. Do you need me to come with you?"

So gods-damned considerate.

Another emotion arose. Brynleigh didn't analyze it before grabbing it and pushing it down. It barely fit. She shook her head. "No, I'm fine, thank you."

"She's nice," Cyrus whispered. "You Chose well, Ryker."

No, he didn't. He Chose a woman intent on killing him.

Panic was churning mass, threatening to spill the contents of Brynleigh's stomach. Fuck, she had to get out of here.

Ryker's attention returned to his father. "Brynleigh's wonderful. You're going to love..."

Brynleigh hurried from the room, and Ryker's words faded. She clutched her wine like it was a lifeboat and counted the doors. Thank the gods, the bathroom was precisely where Ryker said it would be.

It was luxurious, reminiscent of what she expected to see in The Lily's lobby, not a home. A long marble counter with three sunken sinks spanned one wall. A mirror ran above it. Soft lighting was embedded in the ceiling, casting a warm glow on the interior. Three stalls were behind her. The navy blue doors matched the striations running through the counter.

Opening each door to ensure she was alone—although really, who would be here?—she leaned against the counter and gulped the rest of her wine. Her head tingled and felt lightheaded, but it wouldn't last long.

Alcohol never had a lasting effect on vampires. Only Faerie Wine had any real influences on children of the moon, and this was not that.

Slowly, the panic dwindled, and she could draw deep breaths once more.

Her phone buzzed, and she pulled it out of her pocket.

Z: See you tonight. Safe house.

Short and to the point, exactly what she expected from the shifter. Brynleigh tapped back a brief reply confirming she understood, hitting "send" before sliding her phone away and staring at herself in the mirror.

Black, shining eyes. Silky blonde hair. Fangs. She was a vampire through and through. There wasn't a hint of the human she'd once been.

Why couldn't she follow the rules? Why was she so overcome with emotion tonight?

Quite frankly, Brynleigh's behavior was unbecoming of a vampire who'd killed more people than she could count.

"Get a grip," she told herself firmly. "His dad is alert and spoke for the first time in a while. So what? It doesn't mean anything."

Her harsh, callous tone didn't help her feel better. If anything, it made her feel worse. Odd.

She tried another tactic. Fingers digging into the counter, she glared at herself. "Remember the game. Rule number one: you cannot trust anyone." Okay, that was working. Her spine straightened. "Rule number two: doubly blessed vampires do not hide behind—"

The door swung open.

Brynleigh clamped her mouth shut and spun on her heels as River entered the washroom. Even red-eyed and puffy-cheeked, the slender water fae was beautiful. Her long brown hair hung to her waist, and there was an elegance about her that probably came from years in the same type of school that Valentina had attended.

River was leaner than Ryker and less battle-worn. However, she had enough piercings for both of them. Brynleigh counted three in each ear, one on River's lip and another in her nose. Beyond the piercings, though, there was a depth in River's brown eyes that Brynleigh recognized.

Grief called to grief.

And behind that, strength hid in River's gaze. It was the kind that could only come from surviving something difficult. Whatever the young water fae had been through, it hadn't been easy.

"Sorry about that scene in the dining room." River moved towards the sink closest to the door and turned on the tap. She splashed water on her face and rubbed her cheeks before drying her hands on a nearby towel. Her eyes were still red, and her cheeks still puffy as she smiled softly. "It's just, Dad isn't often..."

"You don't need to explain." In fact, Brynleigh would strongly prefer if River didn't. "Ryker told me about the Stillness."

A tear ran down River's cheek. "Yes. Dad's been sick for so long. Practically my whole life."

Apparently, they were going to talk about this. Great. What was it with people confiding in Brynleigh? First Hallie, now River. Brynleigh thought she did an excellent job of giving off a "leave me alone" vibe. Clearly, she was wrong. She'd have to work on that when all this was done.

"I'm sorry." Brynleigh truly was. No matter what she thought about Ryker, she couldn't deny that Cyrus Waterborn appeared to be a beloved member of his family.

"Thank you." River chewed on her lip, drawing her piercing into her mouth before popping it back out.

An awkward silence stretched between them. Brynleigh was reaching for her empty wineglass, intent on leaving when River's hand landed on hers.

"My brother is a good fae," River murmured.

Brynleigh blinked. Where did that come from? Had River deduced Brynleigh's true intentions?

A thousand curses ran through her mind, each worse than the last. She searched River's face, trying to see what the fae meant. That panic was back, a fist constricting her heart. "I—"

River shook her head and squeezed Brynleigh's fingers. "Ryker doesn't know I'm here. I mean, he knows that I came to the bathroom, but..."

He didn't know she'd come to talk to Brynleigh.

Against Brynleigh's good sense, intrigue unfurled within her. She canted her head and studied the fae. "Oh?"

River chewed on her lip, which seemed to be a habit. Probably not a great one, considering the placement of her piercing. "Ryker is... protective."

Brynleigh snorted. "I've gathered as much."

That was one of the first things she had noticed about the captain. She'd expected him to have some protective tendencies—most fae did—but Ryker exceeded her expectations.

He was protective and considerate. And kind. And...

Nope. She wasn't going down that road. She shoved those feelings down and concentrated on the conversation at hand.

"Anyways," River continued, "I wanted to talk to you alone. I know Mom can be... a lot."

That was an understatement.

"She's kind of... mean." Her meanness wasn't like Jelisette's, whose version of cruelty was deadly, but Tertia was unpleasant.

River's mouth twitched. "Yeah, she can be cold. When I was young, and Dad was healthy, she was different. But now..." She shrugged. "Grief changes people, you know?"

Yes, Brynleigh knew exactly what the water fae was talking about. She was far too familiar with the depth of grief. It was a blanket that shrouded one's life, coloring everything in shades of gray. Brynleigh and grief were old friends, whether she liked it or not.

"I do," Brynleigh whispered.

River's gaze searched hers for several long moments. "Yes, I see that. Come with me."

That intrigue remained as the water fae took Brynleigh's hand and tugged her into a small study next door.

They sat on a red couch. River folded her hands in her lap. "You're good for my brother, Brynleigh."

The vampire reared back. That was the last thing she needed or wanted to hear. She wasn't good for Ryker. She wasn't good for anyone, because she wasn't *good*. She was a vampire. A killer. A creature of the night. Created for darkness and destruction.

"I'm... No, I'm not..." She stumbled on her words and shook her head.

"Yes, you are. And that's why I'm going to tell you something I don't think Ryker will share with you."

Brynleigh's heart flung itself around her chest. What was River talking about?

The water fae smiled kindly. "You're about to be family, and if you're going to tie yourself to him... to us... you need to know everything."

Brynleigh's stomach was a tangle of knots. What was River talking about? Was she pulling back her brother's mask for her? Brynleigh would be eternally grateful to the pierced water fae if so.

She waited for River's next words with bated breath. Little did she know, no amount of time could have prepared her for what the fae was about to reveal.

CHAPTER 29

Mistakes Were Made

"Fuck!" Brynleigh screamed, her voice echoing across the night. Droves of shadows poured out of her, hiding the moon and stars as her powerful wings beat against the darkness. The wind swallowed her screams, stealing them away before anyone else could hear them.

It didn't matter. *She* heard them. Over and over again, she cried out into the darkness. Every second, every moment felt longer than the last. Anger, bitterness, and confusion were a twisted, acerbic trio pounding through her veins.

Hours had passed since she'd spoken to River in the study, yet it felt like mere moments ago.

The water fae's words would forever be seared in Brynleigh's mind. She had never seen this coming.

After River had finished turning Brynleigh's world upside down, Brynleigh walked back to the dining hall in a daze. She told Ryker she wasn't feeling well and needed to go home.

It was the truth.

She couldn't breathe. Couldn't think. Couldn't fucking do anything at all.

The moment the sun set, Brynleigh left the Waterborns in their mansion and launched into the sky. Shadows streamed from her, covering her as she flew aimlessly through the night.

She couldn't get River's words out of her head.

"Six years ago, I made a mistake."

A rushing, roaring sound had started in Brynleigh's ears, and it hadn't let up since.

"My magic was too powerful. I didn't know... it slammed into me. I was out with some friends, and it just... poured from me. I... tried to stop it, but I couldn't. I lost control." She shuddered. "It's my curse. My burden."

Lost. Control.

How could such small words be used to describe the death and destruction of that night?

River had looked at Brynleigh with tears in her eyes.

Gods-damned, fucking tears.

As if she cared. As if she was pained by it. As if she was the one who had lost everything that night.

"The storm was too big. I tried to reel it in, to make the rain cease, but I couldn't. It wouldn't listen to me."

Shadows had slipped from Brynleigh's fingers. She hadn't even noticed they left her until the light was nearly gone from the study.

No.

Brynleigh had wanted to stand, scream, and tell River to stop, but her mouth had been incapable of forming words. She was a statue, rendered immobile by the confession she'd never expected to hear.

"It poured out of me like water from a broken dam."

"No!" Brynleigh yelled again, her wings carrying her across the darkened sky.

How could this be happening? Brynleigh had done the math quickly, sitting on that blood-red couch. River had been fifteen at the time. Not even Mature. Not even an adult.

How could someone so young be responsible for such devastation?

Brynleigh had so many questions, so much to say, but in the end, she'd stared at River.

"Ryker came. He saved me and stopped the storm before even more people could be hurt, but the destruction..." More tears had slipped down

River's cheek, and she buried her face in her hands. "He's so good, and I'm so fucking dangerous."

How could Brynleigh have missed this? Moreover, how could *Jelisette* have missed this?

Brynleigh yelled into the night, letting the shadows devour the sound of her anguish. It didn't help. No matter how often she cried out, it didn't alter the reality of what she'd learned.

Wrong. It was all fucking *wrong*. Nothing made sense anymore. Not a single thing.

Brynleigh had left without hurting a hair on River's head. She'd been frozen by disbelief but couldn't have done anything even if she hadn't been.

Not really.

Killing Ryker was one thing. He was a decorated officer in the army and a fully grown, Mature fae.

River was twenty-one. Barely a legal adult. Even by her own admission, she'd lost control of her magic and made a mistake. One that had cost Brynleigh everything... but it was a *mistake*.

All these years, Brynleigh had operated under the assumption that Ryker had a reason—a twisted, wicked one, but still a reason—for what he'd done.

But no.

This was infinitely worse than that.

It was a gods-damned accident.

She flew and flew and flew.

Brynleigh's phone buzzed in her pocket, but she ignored it. She knew who was calling. She should have been at the safe house hours ago. She hadn't even texted Zanri or Jelisette before flying off. She should have responded, but she just... wasn't ready yet.

Maybe she never would be ready.

There were no rules for this. This wasn't a change in the game. Fuck, this wasn't even a game. Not anymore.

This was a new situation, and Brynleigh had no idea what to do. The ring on her finger was a thousand-pound weight, reminding her that she'd almost killed an innocent man.

The worst part of this entire thing was that it all made sense.

The moment River had started talking, pieces fell into place. It was little wonder that Brynleigh had been so confused by Ryker's behavior.

Everything she thought she knew was a lie.

Now, when Brynleigh thought back to that night when her world changed, she knew the much smaller person she'd seen standing next to Ryker had been River.

It was all River.

At some point during her flight, the box holding Brynleigh's emotions shattered. It didn't just break—it exploded into a million pieces.

All the feelings she'd shoved deep down inside came rushing out at once.

Tears flooded her eyes, pouring down her cheeks as she yelled her frustrations to the world.

No wonder Ryker seemed like a good man. No wonder she couldn't see the evil in him. She wasn't insane. She hadn't given her heart to the fae who had killed her family.

She'd been given the wrong information.

Did Jelisette *know*? Had she planned this whole thing? Did she have an ulterior motive, or was it like River had said?

"Ryker and my mother helped cover it up. I... I didn't mean to do it. I'm so sorry. I carry the weight of what I did every day."

Brynleigh could've had her revenge right then. She could've ripped out River's throat on that crimson couch and been done with it.

Something had stopped her. She didn't want River's blood on her hands.

Brynleigh killed people who deserved it. Bad people.

But River? Despite the water fae's confession, Brynleigh didn't sense any evil in her. She was hurting, like Brynleigh.

And now, Brynleigh had no idea what to do.

Hours passed.

She flew until the first rays of sunlight stretched through the darkness. The impending day clawed back the night. Her heart galloped as the dawn approached, the sun's deadly fingers drawing nearer.

One touch from them, and she'd be burned from the inside out. Dead. Forever. There was no surviving sunlight. Not for vampires.

She waited and waited and waited until she had mere seconds left.

It was only when the sun made its final stretch across the sky, its golden claws reaching for her, that Brynleigh called on her shadows and allowed them to draw her into their safe embrace. The dark magic enveloped her. She grabbed onto it and allowed it to pull her into the Void.

Keeping her wings out, Brynleigh moved through the shadows until she reached her destination. The safe house wards rippled as she passed through them. She landed in the living room.

As soon as Brynleigh stepped out of the Void, her Maker's eyes landed on her. Jelisette's gaze was as cold as ice, sending skitters running down Brynleigh's spine. "You're late, daughter of my blood."

Brynleigh had suspected this would be the reception upon her arrival. "I know."

There was no point in denying it. Besides, Jelisette disapproved of lying. A fact that Brynleigh was now realizing was rather laughable. But she wouldn't laugh. She had to tread carefully.

Over the past few hours, Brynleigh arrived at three conclusions. The first was that she absolutely would not kill Captain Ryker Waterborn. She had already been having doubts. This was the nail in the coffin. He was innocent, and Brynleigh did not murder people who didn't deserve it.

The moment she'd reached that conclusion, a powerful wave of relief had washed over her. Brynleigh's wings had faltered for a moment before she continued flying.

If her first realization had brought her immense relief, the second had brought worry. The rules had changed. In Brynleigh's mind, they no longer applied. But there was no way in hell that her Maker would understand or care about her sudden change of heart. The old vampire did not see things like most people did. Telling Jelisette of her change of plans would result in a swift execution for Brynleigh.

Instead, she'd come up with a new plan.

Brynleigh would marry Ryker in a week, and then, she'd strive to become exactly what River had called her: good.

She wasn't exactly sure how forgiveness worked—it wasn't something she'd engaged in particularly often—but it seemed like the better course of action. She couldn't kill River. The water fae had been little more than a child when she lost control of her magic. Brynleigh might be a vampire, but she wasn't heartless.

Brynleigh would protect Ryker and his family, including his icy bitch of a mother, for as long as she could.

If she survived this.

"I was with Ryker and his family," Brynleigh said calmly, careful not to let any emotion show in her eyes. "Things ran a little long."

"So long that you couldn't send me a message?" Jelisette snapped as shadows slithered from her palms. "I've been waiting for you."

"My apologies." Brynleigh bowed her head in deference, lowering her gaze to the floor. Her wings were snapped tight against her back, and her shadows were within reach, just in case.

Brynleigh may have looked the picture of the perfect, apologetic progeny, but inside, she was anything but.

Thankful that Jelisette hadn't inherited their bloodline's gift of reading minds, Brynleigh focused on keeping her face blank despite the barrage of questions swirling through her.

Did Jelisette know it was River, not Ryker, who'd destroyed Chavin? Did she care? What other lies and half-truths had she fed Brynleigh?

Fae couldn't lie, but vampires had no such trouble. Brynleigh had proven that time and again. Doubt caused her to reconsider everything she'd been told from the moment of her Making.

The clock ticked, echoing the hammering of Brynleigh's heart, as Jelisette glared at her. Brynleigh studied the striations in the wooden planks beneath her feet, waiting for her Maker's next words.

Survival was the only thing on her mind.

Eventually, Jelisette exhaled. "Alright. I believe you. Tell me what you learned."

Brynleigh lifted her head and met her Maker's gaze. Anything less than perfection would be viewed as an act of weakness. Brynleigh couldn't afford to be weak, especially if she was going to lie her way through this. She assumed Jelisette would have questions for her when Ryker was still alive the day after her wedding.

She had already thought about that. She would tell her Maker the water fae fought back, and she'd have to try again. Hopefully, after a few variations on the lie, Jelisette would back down. The plan was shaky at best, but it was the only one Brynleigh had.

She needed it to work because she had no other options.

The third and final conclusion Brynleigh had reached was one that she'd never expected.

After the box containing her emotions exploded, she'd had to deal with everything she'd ignored for weeks.

Of all the feelings, only one had slammed into her like a freight train, leaving her breathless.

She *liked* Ryker more than anyone else she'd ever met. Maybe even more than that if she was being completely honest with herself. She wanted him, not because he was her mark, but because he was hers.

And that frightened her more than anything else.

CHAPTER 30

A Visit to the Obsidian Palace

The ground shook beneath Ryker's feet as the pulsing, low base beat echoed through The Obsidian Palace. A renowned fae club in Golden City, this was *the* place to gather in the capital. White flashing lights burst from the ceiling like erupting stars. Music blared from massive speakers that stretched from floor to ceiling. Everything was black, from the thick columns supporting the roof to the tables and chairs.

The club mimicked a fae temple in the most debauched fashion possible. The men who worked at this establishment wore cropped black priestly robes that cut off at mid-thigh, while the women wore priestess garments that covered their breasts, asses, and little else.

This was a place where bad decisions were made, and Ryker was already on edge. Frowning, he glanced between his watch and the front door for the fifth time in as many minutes.

"Relax, Ryker, she'll be here," River shouted over the booming pop music pulsing through the club.

That was ironic, coming from his sister. He'd purposefully given River the wrong time, knowing her tendency to ignore all social parameters when it came to being on time, and she'd still been ten minutes late when he drove over to pick her up from Waterborn House.

River wore a tight pink dress that was far too short, with a cut-out along the midriff highlighting her new belly-button ring. When Ryker had pointed out the lack of material on his sister's dress when he'd picked her up, she reminded him that she was an adult and could do what she wanted.

This night out was River's suggestion. She wanted to get to know Brynleigh better since they'd be sisters-in-law in three days.

"I hope so." He pulled out his phone, hoping there was a message from Brynleigh.

Still nothing. The blank screen taunted him.

Brynleigh wasn't late yet, but it was getting close.

Two long days had passed since Ryker last saw his fiancée, and he was getting antsy. He wanted to have Brynleigh in his arms again, and this time, he wouldn't let her go.

The bartender, a tall fae with half her black hair shaved and the other half in a high pony, walked over. "Can I get you a drink?"

"That would be great." Ryker opened a tab and ordered a beer while his sister asked for a fruity cocktail that sounded sugary and disgusting.

The bartender went to work, and Ryker's gaze returned to the door. Still no sign of his vampire.

River jabbed him in the side. "Come on, Ryker. Don't you know how to relax?" she teased.

His frown deepened. "No."

Relaxing wasn't high on Ryker's priority list. He had too many things to worry about, too many different obligations pulling at him.

His sister chuckled as the bartender returned with their drinks. Thanking the fae, River took a sip of the drink that was the same color as her dress. "It's not good for you to be so uptight."

"I'll relax when Brynleigh's here," Ryker grumbled.

He wished he had insisted he pick her up.

Unfortunately, Brynleigh's Maker had kept her busy all week. Apparently, Jelisette de la Point cared little that her progeny was getting married in a few days. Even though Ryker had asked about the project occupying Brynleigh's time. She hadn't been able to tell him much about it.

"You worry too much," River said.

"Debatable." As far as Ryker was concerned, not worrying about the important people in his life was an impossible request. It was his job. He'd done it for years, ever since his father fell ill. Right now, when reports of rebel activities were at an all-time high, he had more reasons to be worried than usual.

River snorted and shook her head. Finishing her drink, she placed the empty glass on the counter and grabbed her brother's hand.

"You need to be patient." She tilted her head at the dark dance floor a few feet away, where fae were losing themselves to the music. "Come dance with me. Get your mind off everything else."

Ryker would rather jump off a cliff. It wasn't that he didn't occasionally enjoy dancing, but he had other things on his mind. Before he could decline, someone clapped him on the shoulder.

He stiffened and turned around, ready to yell at whoever touched him, but all tension left his body as he caught sight of his two friends behind him.

"Hey, man." Nikhail grinned. "Thanks for the invitation."

Even though this was a casual club, the air fae was dressed like he was attending a business meeting with high-ranking Representatives. That was normal for him. Ryker had never seen this friend in anything less than slacks and a dress shirt, even when they got together to watch a game of laser. Nikhail worked in intelligence for the government, and his position was so classified that even Ryker didn't know what he did.

"Of course." Ryker gave a one-armed hug to Nikhil, then Atlas. He was glad they came since he wanted them to get to know Brynleigh. After all, they'd be spending a lot of time together in the future.

Like Ryker, Atlas wore jeans and a black sweater. The earth fae waved his hand, getting the bartender's attention. "Two beers, please."

"Sure thing. One minute," she replied.

Atlas leaned against the bar top, and Nikhail moved to Ryker's other side. "You're looking beautiful tonight, River."

River's cheeks reddened, and she sucked on her lip ring before smiling. "Thank you, Nik." Her gaze crawled over the air fae's suit appreciatively. "You look good, too."

Ryker's mouth pinched in a line, and his gaze darkened as it darted between them. What the hell was going on here? He didn't like it at all.

The last thing Ryker needed was for his little sister to get involved with one of his best friends.

Especially Nikhail.

The man was like Ryker's brother, but he was known for his dalliances and one-night stands. That was not the kind of fae River should be interested in, especially not so close to graduation.

Before Ryker could do something stupid, like punch a certain air fae in the face, the club doors opened once more. His gaze slipped to the entrance, and he exhaled as a blonde with black wings entered.

"I'll talk to you guys later." Ryker walked away from the bar, shooting Nikhail a look that he hoped conveyed, *Stay the fuck away from my sister, or else.*

To Ryker's relief, the air fae nodded and stepped back from River, taking a swig of his beer. The problem, at least for now, was solved. Still, Ryker would be keeping a closer eye on Nikhail. He was a good man, but he wasn't right for River.

No one was.

Ryker pushed his way through the crowded club, moving past hordes of fae grinding against each other to the sensual beat of the music. Most of the dancers' clothes were severely lacking in the fabric department, but he barely noticed. He only had eyes for the vampire making her way towards him.

Brynleigh was a vision of death in her figure-hugging knee-length crimson halter dress and black wings. Her blonde hair flowed around her. As always, her only jewelry was her necklace and the engagement ring he'd given her.

The moment she was within arm's reach, Ryker took her hand and pulled her towards him.

"I missed you, beautiful," he breathed, his eyes sweeping over her before he claimed a kiss.

Their mouths fused, and Brynleigh melted against him. Instantly, none of his other worries existed. Not his sister and the looks she was exchanging with Nikhail, who was definitely off limits. Not the rebel activities or the report he'd received this morning about yet another riot that had resulted in three deaths in the Southern Region.

The only thing that mattered was Brynleigh and how she felt in his arms. It was like they'd been made for each other.

Eventually, he broke off their kiss and slid their fingers together.

She smiled up at him, her fangs peeking out. "I missed you too. Three more days."

"Three days," he echoed. Somehow, it felt like the longest and shortest seventy-two hours of his life. Pecking her cheek, he asked, "Are you thirsty?"

"I am." She leaned against him. "I'm glad we get to spend time together tonight, Ryker."

"Me too." Already, he felt better than he had in two days. Her presence was a balm to his soul.

Ryker led Brynleigh to the bar, never letting go of her hand. The trio he'd left behind was engaged in a heated discussion, which grew more animated as they approached.

Atlas crossed his arms and frowned. "I'm telling you both, the Vlarone Raiders will wipe the floor with the Drahanian Dragons. No one can beat them. They're the best laser team on the continent."

"You're wrong." River glared up at the earth fae, who was more than a foot taller than her. "The Dragons have won every single game this year."

"Only because the Southern Region hasn't come against the Western one yet this season," Atlas argued.

"Ugh!" River threw up her hands and huffed, "You'll see. They'll win, and you'll eat your words."

This scene was familiar. Comfortable, even. Ryker had mediated more than a few disagreements between River and Atlas. Both were enthusiastic about sports and willing to talk to anyone who would listen.

Ryker chuckled, pulling Brynleigh up next to him. "Atlas, did you make the mistake of asking River about sports?"

"Apparently," he grumbled, raking a hand through his hair.

"You know how seriously she takes them," Ryker said. "Dad and River have watched laser games together ever since she was a toddler, right, Shortie?"

"Right." River crossed her arms. "That's what makes me qualified to speak on the expertise of the Drahanian Dragons."

Tension simmered between Atlas and River.

Nikhail, in an apparent effort to relieve it, swigged his beer and walked between them. "Personally, I don't understand what you're fighting about. There's little appeal to the game."

River's eyes widened, and she sputtered as she turned on her heels and faced the well-dressed fae. "What? Inconceivable. Everyone loves sports." She looked at Brynleigh. "Right, Bryn? Which team is your favorite? It's the Dragons, isn't it?"

The hand Ryker held stiffened. "I... uh, don't know." Brynleigh pressed herself against Ryker's side, her wing brushing against his other arm. "I've never watched a game of laser."

In a dramatic move that proved River was Tertia Waterborn's daughter, she gasped and pressed her hand against her heart. "What? We'll have to rectify that immediately. This is an absolute travesty."

Ryker could think of other things that were actual travesties: the poverty crisis in the Republic of Balance, the rebels, the stack of papers piling up on his desk waiting for him to return after his honeymoon. This didn't exactly fit the bill. Still, his sister meant well.

"If Brynleigh agrees, sure." Ryker would never force his bride to do something she didn't want to.

River turned her eager gaze back to the vampire. "Will you come over and watch a game with me after the wedding?"

Brynleigh drew her bottom lip through her teeth before nodding slowly. "Sure, I guess."

That seemed to be the correct answer.

"You will *love* it." River bounced on the balls of her feet. "I promise. It's the best."

"It's—" Ryker's phone buzzed in his back pocket. He pulled it out, wincing. "Shit."

The number flashing across the screen was reserved for emergencies.

"What's wrong?" Brynleigh asked.

"It's work. I have to take this." He kissed his vampire's forehead. "Do you mind?"

Brynleigh shook her head and retracted her wings. "No, go ahead. I'll order a drink."

Promising that he'd be back as soon as possible, Ryker slid his credit card to the bartender before accepting the call. Pressing the phone against his ear, he yelled, "Hello?"

"Captain Waterborn, this is Major Ulysses. There's been a situation, and..."

CHAPTER 31
No More Rules

A low, steady beat hammered Brynleigh's ears. The Obsidian Palace was an assault on her senses. The lights were low, the music was loud, and the air pulsed with the heady scents of desire and lowered inhibitions.

Ryker's call had come in nearly half an hour ago. River had chatted with Brynleigh for a few minutes, but now she danced in the crowd. She had invited Brynleigh to join her, but the vampire had declined, wanting to finish her drink.

"Here you go, miss." The bartender handed Brynleigh another glass of blood wine. "Enjoy."

"Thank you, I will." Accepting the beverage, the vampire studied the throng of dancers.

River was easy to spot on the edge of the crowd, her bright dress standing out among all the black. Her partner was an elf with long, curling horns that reached for the sky. She seemed to be enjoying herself.

Nikhail, Ryker's black-haired friend, danced a few feet away with a redheaded fae. River and Nikhail hadn't spoken much, but Brynleigh had noticed them glancing at each other throughout the evening. That was interesting.

The Obsidian Palace wasn't Brynleigh's scene, a fact which became more apparent the longer she was here. She'd much rather be curled up in front of a movie right now, but she didn't want to pass up an opportunity to be with Ryker, especially after the day she'd had.

This morning, Jelisette had sent Brynleigh to an underground club in the Western Region to deal with a problem. Complications had risen, her mark had fought back, and the bloody task had taken her far longer than normal.

Brynleigh had showered for nearly an hour to scrub all the blood from her body before getting ready for tonight. Not only had her job been a lot, but Zanri had been hanging out at the safe house all day. Brynleigh itched to tell him the truth about River. Not so her handler could hurt the young fae but so someone else would know the truth.

Ultimately, she had decided it wasn't safe to share the information. Holding her tongue had been painful.

After the wedding, things would be easier. Surely, Brynleigh could make Jelisette understand why she couldn't kill Ryker. Besides, by then, they would be married.

Brynleigh planned to move out of the safe house and into Ryker's apartment when they returned from their honeymoon. With a few coats of paint and a couple of throw pillows, it would feel like home. Marlowe seemed to like her, giving her confidence that she'd fit right in.

As for work, Brynleigh would tackle that issue later. She assumed the law-abiding captain would probably take an issue with his wife killing criminals in her spare time, so she'd have to find something to do that was above the law.

But they would be happy, and that was all Brynleigh wanted.

Losing herself in daydreams about what their married life would look like, Brynleigh didn't notice Ryker's return until he stood in front of her.

"All done. Thank you for waiting, sweetheart." Ryker slanted his lips over hers, his kiss claiming and possessive.

Heat went straight to Brynleigh's core, and she clenched her legs together. Isvana help her, but she wanted him so badly. Waiting until the wedding night was torture. She replayed their stolen moments in the car over and over again. She reminded herself of the way his fingers felt deep within her and wondered what it would feel like when it was his cock.

"No problem," she murmured when their kiss broke apart. "Is everything alright?"

A shadow flickered across Ryker's face before he nodded. "Yes, just some trouble in the Northern Region. The rebels are being… difficult."

And the heat was gone.

Brynleigh frowned. "Are the rebels always this bad?"

She didn't remember them causing as many problems as they had over the past two months. Not that they weren't justified in their actions because the inequality in the Republic of Balance was impossible to hide, but their timing felt strange.

"No, usually…" Ryker sighed and palmed the back of his neck. "I'm sorry, love. I can't really talk about it. It's classified."

"I understand." And she did.

After all, Brynleigh had a world of secrets that she couldn't share with Ryker. She didn't even want to think of his reaction if he ever learned her true intentions in joining the Choosing. She'd be taking that truth to her grave.

Ryker smiled, and his eyes twinkled. "Thank you." His thumb brushed her chin. "Did I tell you how beautiful you look tonight?"

She chuckled. "You might have mentioned it."

Brynleigh didn't always enjoy wearing dresses, but this one was a favorite. It was comfortable, had pockets, and highlighted all her best assets. She had chosen it tonight specifically with Ryker in mind.

"You're absolutely fucking stunning." His hands landed on her hips, and he drew her against him for a kiss.

His hard length pressed into her, and she gasped against his mouth.

Ryker groaned, and he kissed the shell of her rounded ear. "If we weren't in a room full of other people," he whispered, "I'd show you exactly what this dress does to me."

Gods, the mouth on this man.

Brynleigh blinked at him, trying to think of a clever response, but a hand wrapped around her wrist and tugged before she could.

"Come dance with me, Bryn!" River's cheeks were flushed, her hair mussed, and she wore a grin that spoke to her having enjoyed several alcoholic beverages in quick succession. "Just because Ryker has a stick up his ass doesn't mean we can't have fun."

River didn't give Brynleigh a chance to refuse her offer. The younger water fae pulled her towards the crowd of moving bodies.

"I'm not a great dancer," Brynleigh admitted, shouting to be heard over the blaring music.

"You don't have to be!" River threw back her head and laughed. "Let the music speak to you."

Brynleigh was pretty certain that wasn't how it worked. However, she didn't want to say no to River. Not when the water fae reminded Brynleigh of her sister. Sarai would've spent all night on the dance floor, shaking her hips and letting the music move her.

For her sister, Brynleigh would dance. "Alright, I'll give it a try."

And she did.

The music blared, the beats were low, and the lights dim as they danced. Neither Brynleigh nor River spoke, letting the music guide their movements.

It surprised Brynleigh to realize she started enjoying herself sometime around the third song. Dancing to the pop music was a far cry from when she and Ryker had spun around the ballroom. It was easy. No one was looking at her.

For the first time in years, Brynleigh felt free. She was clumsy, but that didn't seem prohibitive with this style of music. Soon, she swayed her hips, her eyes hooded as she let the rhythm run through her. Her shadows danced in her veins, echoing the song.

This was... nice.

Several songs later, River looked behind Brynleigh and smiled. She nodded, then slipped away into the crowd of bodies.

Confused, Brynleigh went to turn around. Before she could, a pair of large, warm hands settled on her hips. The vampire tilted up her head, and a grin stretched across her features.

Ryker stood behind her, all broody and beautiful in his fae way.

"River said you didn't want to dance," Brynleigh murmured.

Ryker drew her against him, her back lining up with his front. He held her hips, and they swayed to the music as it slowed.

The captain's breath ghosted over Brynleigh's ear. "Sweetheart, it seems I'm breaking all my rules for you."

The shiver running through Brynleigh had nothing to do with the chill in the air and everything to do with the hardness pressed against the swell of her ass.

"Oh?" She twisted in his arms and gazed up at him.

Strobing lights cast Ryker in alternating blue and white, giving him an ethereal aura. His hands slipped around her and pressed against her bottom. "Yes." His head dipped, and he kissed the corner of her mouth. "I would do anything for you, Brynleigh de la Point."

Her heart pounded at his concession. Gods, how was it possible to care so much about someone in such a short period of time? Now that she knew the truth, Brynleigh could admit her true feelings to herself. She *really* liked Ryker, and there was nothing wrong with that.

Maybe she more than liked him. She would explore that thought when she was on her own. Either way, emboldened by her feelings, Brynleigh didn't wait for Ryker to kiss her properly. She threaded her hands behind his neck and pulled him towards her.

Their mouths slammed together in a passionate embrace. They remained like that for several minutes. Kissing. Swaying. Touching. Being together.

This was a moment Brynleigh would never forget. Right now, there were no more rules or games. No one watching or judging them. They were alone, and she allowed all the emotions rising within her to remain. She was... happy, and she loved it.

Eventually, the music shifted. The beat picked up, and the new song demanded they move their bodies.

So, they did.

Ryker's grip tightened around her hips.

Brynleigh ground herself against him, wishing there were no more barriers between them.

They kissed again and again and again. Hands explored. Her fangs ached. Her shadows throbbed.

They moved as one, dancing the night away until the sun was about to rise.

There were no rules, and it was good.

CHAPTER 32
Wedding Bells and Blessings

"Ready for this?" Nikhail clapped Ryker on the back.

Ryker straightened his black suit jacket, adjusted his crimson tie, and nodded. "More than ready."

After a short deliberation, Ryker and Brynleigh decided to hold their ceremony in Isvana's temple. It was packed to the brim. Black curtains covered the windows, but the darkness did not detract from the beauty of the space. Glittering lights hung from the columns. Through a trick of technology, stars danced on the ceiling. Rows upon rows of chairs were laid out before them, filled with an eager crowd.

Cameras were already in place. One pointed at Ryker on the dais and another at the back of the temple where Brynleigh would arrive.

Although the timeline to assemble the weddings had been quick, no expenses were spared. Everything, from the decorations to the clothes to the following reception, was expertly put together.

Cyrus and Tertia sat in the front row, and although Ryker's father wasn't as alert as he had been the other night, he smiled at his son. Their presence meant the world to Ryker. Along with his parents, several other familiar faces were at the wedding, including other Choosing participants. Numerous armed guards were hidden among the wedding guests, and more were stationed throughout the temple.

Although Ryker hadn't heard of any new threats, Chancellor Rose wasn't taking any chances. After all, the weddings were the most anticipated portion of the blind love competition.

Ryker straightened an invisible wrinkle on his black suit. He'd barely slept last night, thanks to the excitement of the day. Yesterday, they'd gone to a winery with Hallie and Therian, the evening a nice, quiet lead-up to today's wedding.

He would be lying if he said he wasn't eager to get this over with. He couldn't wait to get Brynleigh alone tonight. Her unique scent of a crisp evening and night-blooming roses had followed him into his sleep, and she'd starred in his dreams all week.

The doors opened, and a tall vampire with stark white hair entered the space. The priestess, who'd introduced herself as Plyana during their rehearsal yesterday, wore a long white robe edged in crimson thread. It trailed behind her as she strode into the temple. The crowd hushed, sensing that the ceremony was about to begin.

Ascending the steps to the stage, the priestess smiled at Ryker. "Are you nervous?"

"No." He stood tall, his shoulders back and head held high "Not at all."

Ryker was destined to marry Brynleigh de la Point. He wouldn't have been surprised if the gods had written their union in the stars.

"Good." Plyana made a religious gesture in front of her chest. "I pray that Isvana and Ithiar will bless your union."

"Thank you. That's my hope as well." They would journey to the fae temple during their journey north to receive a blessing from the priests and make an offering to the Black Sands.

Then, the time for nerves was over. The classical violin concerto, which had been playing quietly through speakers, switched to a traditional wedding march.

That was the signal. The ceremony was about to begin.

Keeping his hands flat at his sides, Ryker turned his attention to the large double doors across the temple. His heart, which had been doing an excellent job of keeping him alive since he was born, thundered. His hands grew clammy. His water magic pulsed a steady beat.

Anticipation was thick in the air, a sweet and slightly bitter taste at the back of his mouth. His back straightened, and he inhaled deeply as the doors swung open with a resounding bang.

River entered first, resplendent in a blue gown. After their night at the Obsidian Palace, Brynleigh had asked Ryker's sister to be her maid of honor. River had been shocked, but she had readily agreed. River's long brown hair was styled in delicate waves, and she'd exchanged all her flashy piercings for diamond studs. She looked like a star walking down the aisle.

It thrilled Ryker that his sister and his partner got along so well. This was a glimpse into their future, and he loved what he saw. This past week proved he had Chosen well. Brynleigh was a strong woman who could hold her own, and she made Ryker a better man.

River confidently strode towards her brother.

"Happy wedding day," she whispered as she stood across him.

A corner of Ryker's mouth twitched upward. "Thank you, River."

She smirked. "Before you ask, I already released my magic today, so you don't need to worry about it."

She might joke about it, but Ryker would always worry about River. Even after she Matured, he would watch over her. He didn't say that, though. He didn't say anything because there was a flurry of movement at the temple entrance.

Time crashed to a stop as Ryker's gaze landed on his vampire. The sight of her stole the breath from his lungs. He couldn't pull his eyes away from her, even if he tried.

His bride was exquisite.

In the place of a veil, she wore a white lace fascinator that fell over her eyes. Her gown was strapless and hugged all her curves. It glistened like fresh snow as the light fell upon it, as though thousands of snowflakes were embedded in it. Onyx earrings hung from her lobes. Her arms were bare, and she wore no jewelry except for her necklace and the ring he'd given her. Her blonde hair was elegantly styled in a complicated, twisted knot.

By the Black Sands, Brynleigh was the most beautiful being he'd ever seen in his entire life. Two large, jet-black bat wings extended from her back. They hung on either side of her, a symbol of her power. The shadows pooling at her feet were a direct contrast to the bridal ensemble she wore.

Then her gaze rose and met his.

The breath returned to his lungs in a whoosh. They stared at each other, the rest of the room disappearing into nothingness. Everything that had ever gone wrong in Ryker's world righted itself at that moment. She was his other half, his partner in all things, the woman he was destined to love forever.

There was a subtle movement as the cameras panned to the doors. He knew the world was staring at his bride. It didn't matter, though. They could look because Brynleigh wasn't looking at the cameras, the crowd, or the priestess.

Her eyes were locked on him. The distance didn't matter. Her searing gaze made him feel like he was the only man in the world.

"Please stand," Plyana commanded.

The crowd shuffled as they all stood, save for Ryker's father.

Music crescendoed. Brynleigh glided across the marble floor towards Ryker, holding his gaze.

Following vampiric tradition, Jelisette met her progeny at the end of the aisle. The older vampire wore a black ball gown that seemed better suited for a funeral than a wedding. Long black gloves went to her elbows, and glistening black diamonds sparkled in her ears. Strange.

Brynleigh never moved her eyes from Ryker's, even as she slipped her hand onto Jelisette's outstretched arm.

Priestess Plyana began speaking, regaling the crowd and cameras alike with the history of the Choosing like Chancellor Rose had done during the Opening Ceremony. The priestess reiterated the importance of the practice that unified the Republic of Balance, her voice echoing through the large temple.

Ryker barely heard any of her words. To be fair, he wasn't attempting to pay attention.

Brynleigh smiled at him, and he smiled back.

Hi, he mouthed.

His vampire's lips twitched. She mouthed back, *Hey.* Her eyes widened as if saying, *Can you believe this?*

He knew instantly what she meant. The grandeur, the temple, the crowd, the cameras, everything. They were all here to watch them get married. It was overwhelming, even for someone like him who'd grown up around wealth and the press.

He'd done everything he could to remain out of sight for the past six years, but the reporters didn't bother him today.

This was not about him—it was about *them*.

Plyana turned to Jelisette. Her voice boomed across the now-silent temple. "Do you give your progeny over to this fae to be married?"

Brynleigh visibly bristled at the priestess's words. Ryker could almost hear his vampire's voice in his head, railing against the injustice of being spoken about as though she was not a person but a belonging to be bought and sold. She didn't say anything, though, probably because she was as eager as Ryker to get this ceremony over with.

Jelisette's ancient obsidian gaze swung to Ryker's. It took everything the water fae had not to shudder. Something about this woman put him on edge.

She didn't break his stare, even as she said, "I do. After all, this is the moment we've been waiting for."

Had the words come from anyone else, they would've sounded kind. Coming from Jelisette, they made Ryker's skin pebble. No, he did not like Brynleigh's Maker. Hopefully, they wouldn't have to deal with her much in the future.

Ryker descended the steps and stood before the vampires, extending his right hand. Brynleigh held his gaze as she lifted her hand from Jelisette's and took his.

The moment they touched, fiery sparks ran through him. He raised her hand to his lips and held her gaze as he pressed his mouth against her pale flesh.

"You look beautiful," he murmured.

His vampire blushed, and the crowd made sounds of delight as he led her onto the stage.

Brynleigh retracted her wings into her back as they took their place before Plyana, but she kept her shadows around her feet.

Such a stunning vision of power.

Ryker was utterly enamored by the woman he was marrying. His fingers ran over the back of her hands, rubbing gentle circles, as the ceremony passed in a blur.

They exchanged rings—Ryker's was a thicker version of the delicate onyx band he slid onto Brynleigh's finger—and they signed the legal documents officially binding them as husband and wife.

Then came the moment Ryker had been waiting for.

The pair stood before Plyana; their hands joined in the space between them.

"You may kiss the bride," the priestess declared.

She may have said more after that, but Ryker stopped paying attention. He was utterly focused on his gorgeous vampire.

Ryker stepped towards Brynleigh, closing the space between them as he tightened his grip on her fingers. Their eyes met once again, and the crowd faded away.

Brynleigh breathed his name as he lowered his head. His lips descended on hers, anxious and eager to taste what was his.

The moment their mouths met, Ryker groaned. Slipping one hand behind Brynleigh's neck, he gently cupped the back of her head. With the other hand, he held her close.

Every single inch that separated them was far too much.

Ryker had gone six weeks without seeing, touching, or holding Brynleigh.

Never again.

She was his, and he was hers.

Brynleigh's lips were soft beneath his as they kissed. He'd intended for this to be a peck, a promise of what would come, but now that they were in the moment, he couldn't stop.

A soft moan slipped from her, and he tightened his grip on her neck. He held her close, angling her head as they embraced. His tongue swept the seam of her lips, intent on tasting her.

She was his everything.

His other half.

His Chosen partner.

His wife.

CHAPTER 33
Chocolate Cake, Happiness, and Suspicions

Brynleigh should've known that her new husband's kiss would blow her mind. After all, everything else about the fae had thrown her world off its axis, so why not this, too?

And this was far more than she'd ever expected.

Ryker's mouth fused to hers. It wasn't just a kiss. It was a claiming. A declaration to the entire world that he had Chosen her, and now, she belonged to him.

Brynleigh always thought something like that would bother her. After all, she wasn't a possession but a person. It turned out it didn't bother her at all. There was something about Ryker that had made her feel safe and loved, even as he asserted that she was his.

She let him kiss her like he owned her because maybe he did.

Her heart was his.

Tomorrow, she would finally tell Ryker she loved him. The time was right.

Gods, it felt good to be married to this man. He was intelligent, kindhearted, and protective in a way that she hadn't known she wanted in a partner. Yesterday at the winery, Ryker was attentive but not overbearing while she and Hallie chatted like schoolgirls about their upcoming nuptials. It was sweet, the way he kept checking on her, and Brynleigh couldn't believe she'd gotten so lucky.

Ryker's tongue probed her lips, and she opened her mouth. He tasted her. With each powerful sweep of his tongue against hers, she melted more into him. She gripped his suit jacket, holding on as they passionately embraced. Heat flooded her core, and she lost herself in him.

This was the only thing that mattered.

Over the past week, Brynleigh had perfected her acting skills. In front of Jelisette and Zanri, she'd worn a mask of indifference as they finalized their plans to murder Ryker. She hadn't revealed River's confession, even though it pained her to hide things from Zanri. He was her handler, and she'd come to realize over the last week, her friend. But Brynleigh couldn't risk him telling Jelisette that she'd changed her mind. She'd gone through all the actions, pretending that tonight, after the reception, she still planned on killing the captain.

But that's all it was.

An act.

This kiss, though? Isvana help her, Brynleigh was not acting now. This embrace was real. The emotions coursing through her were real. The vows she'd spoken were real. Their relationship was real.

Well... as real as something could be when it was built on a foundation of lies.

But she and Ryker could get past their rocky beginnings. They had to. Brynleigh wouldn't accept any other alternative.

Brynleigh would fight for this relationship because she was meant to be with Ryker. She knew it in the depths of her soul. Even though she'd entered the Choosing with dishonorable intentions, she still wanted Ryker to be hers.

His tongue flicked against her fangs, and she moaned his name. His hardness pressed against her, sending a surge of want through her.

Brynleigh couldn't wait until Ryker saw the surprise she had waiting for him under her dress.

Someone coughed in the audience, and Brynleigh's eyes snapped open.

Oh, gods.

She had completely forgotten they weren't alone. Judging by the sheepish look in Ryker's eyes, so had he. They split apart, their mouths plump and cheeks flushed, but he kept hold of her hand.

Priestess Plyana looked amused as she studied the newly married couple. Her cheeks were flushed, and her fangs were fully displayed and she smiled warmly. "Well, I suppose we have additional proof the Choosing works."

A smattering of laughter rolled through the crowd, and even Ryker chuckled. Brynleigh's chest warmed, but before she could crack a smile, the hairs on her neck stood on end. She turned her head ever so slightly, and sure enough, Jelisette's black eyes drilled into her.

Worry churned in Brynleigh's stomach. Had she gone too far? Did her Maker know she felt more for Ryker than she'd been letting on? What if—

Actually, fuck that. It didn't matter.

When the sun crested the horizon tomorrow and Ryker still breathed, Jelisette would know Brynleigh had broken all the rules. She would have to deal with it.

Brynleigh was an adult, not a puppet that her Maker could boss around and make do whatever she wanted. She had married this fae, and he was hers. They'd vowed to be with each other, for better or for worse. They were bound together beneath the eyes of the law. They'd Chosen each other, and no one, not even Jelisette, could break them apart.

Plyana rested a black cloth across Brynleigh and Ryker's joined hands. The ceremony was almost over. "In the name of Isvana, the goddess of the moon, it is my greatest honor to declare you husband and wife. May your union be Blessed from this day until your last."

She lifted the cloth, and the crowd roared their approval.

It was done. They were married.

Brynleigh thought she'd be nervous or frightened, but instead, a warm, fuzzy feeling filled her stomach. When she entered the Choosing, she'd never expected to feel like this on her wedding day.

She was happy.

A PLEASANT LIGHTHEADEDNESS floated around in Brynleigh's head as she nursed her glass of Faerie Wine. She'd already had two servings of blood while Ryker and the other non-vampiric guests had their appetizers, and she'd moved on to the pink wine while the guests enjoyed their dinner.

The grand reception hall reminded her of an elegant, five-star restaurant. Low-hanging chandeliers cast a light over the space. Off-white tablecloths covered round tables. Classical music trilled from hidden speakers. Servers dressed in black delivered copious amounts of food and beverages. The windows were bare, and the moonlight provided a romantic ambiance for their joyous occasion.

Brynleigh and Ryker sat together at a high table, just the two of them. Their family and friends, along with guests and several undercover guards, were scattered throughout the hall.

Jelisette stood at the back of the reception space, talking to a man cast in shadows, but Brynleigh had yet to see Zanri. It was strange since she'd ensured her friend was issued an invitation. After all, it wasn't like she had any family to invite to the wedding. It stung that he wasn't here.

What could be more important than this?

A warm hand landed on Brynleigh's thigh, drawing her attention to Ryker. His eyes crinkled at the corners, and he brushed a lock of hair behind her ear. "Are you alright, sweetheart?"

Gods, this man was so considerate. She loved that he was checking in on her.

"Yes," she replied honestly as she sipped her wine.

It bothered her that Zanri wasn't here, but she wouldn't let his absence ruin her night. This wonderful man beside her was her husband, and she would enjoy every second of their wedding.

"More than alright." Brynleigh *giggled,* which was wholly unlike her. It was, quite frankly, disconcerting. "I'm very happy. Delighted, even."

Clamping her mouth shut, Brynleigh eyed the glass she clutched. Maybe she'd had enough to drink. Everyone knew Faerie Wine loosened the tongues of even the most tight-lipped vampires.

A deep, warming chuckle ran through her husband. "Me too."

A familiar pair of white wings caught Brynleigh's attention.

Hallie hurried towards their table. She wore a beautiful ruby cocktail dress, reminiscent of the Choosing's theme, and matching heels. Therian followed behind, his hands in his pockets as he trailed his fiancée. The much larger dragon shifter dwarfed his partner, but they fit together perfectly. Just like Brynleigh and Ryker. Matches made in the heavens.

Brynleigh stood, wobbling slightly thanks to the Faerie Wine, and hugged Hallie. "I'm so glad you could make it. It's nice to have a friend here."

The Fortune Elf smiled. "Your wedding was beautiful."

"Are you excited for yours?" It would take place three days from now. Brynleigh looked forward to attending before she and Ryker went on their honeymoon.

A brilliant grin lit up Hallie's face. "Yes, I am." She glanced behind her at Therian. "We can't wait to get married, right?"

Therian bent and kissed Hallie's cheek. "Right, love." He looked up and smiled. "The wedding was very well done."

"Thank you," said Brynleigh. Even though she and Ryker didn't have a lot to do with the actual planning, the wedding planner supplied by the Chancellor had listened to their suggestions. Brynleigh would forever remember this day.

"Of course." Therian glanced at Ryker. "Captain, can we talk?"

Ryker stood and glanced at Brynleigh, an unspoken question in his eyes. *Do you mind?*

"It's fine," she assured him.

He slanted his mouth over hers, stealing a kiss. "I'll be right back." He trailed a finger down her collarbone, sending sparks running through her. "Wait for me?"

A smile danced on her lips. "There's nowhere else I'd rather be."

Ryker returned her smile as he and Therian moved away from the table. He whispered, "What's going on?"

Therian rubbed his neck. "I got a message from my squad. There's news about the rebels. They've..."

His voice dipped into a low whisper, too quiet even for Brynleigh to hear. Not that she tried. She'd ask Ryker about the conversation later. She was certain he'd tell her what he could.

She turned back to her friend. "I'm so glad you were able to come, Hallie."

Unlike Zanri. She tried not to think about her friend's absence because it was making her angry.

"You make a beautiful bride." Hallie ran a hand down Brynleigh's gown appreciatively. "This is absolutely stunning."

It was. The moment Brynleigh had seen the dress on the rack, she'd known it was hers.

"Thank you." Brynleigh moved her hips, the gown swishing around her. Yes, the wine was definitely getting to her head. "Isvana Blessed my Choice. Sometimes, I feel like this is a dream, you know?"

She never would've predicted this outcome.

Hallie's head bobbed, and she shifted from one foot to the other. "I know exactly what you mean. Looking at Therian, I can't believe we're getting married. It's insane how well we work. Does that make sense?"

Absolutely. Brynleigh couldn't imagine her life without Ryker now.

"It's like you're two halves of the same whole."

"Yes," Hallie breathed. "Exactly. I tried to explain it to my parents, but they looked at me like I was crazy. But they weren't in the Choosing. They don't understand the connections that we made."

Brynleigh glanced over her shoulder to where her new husband clapped Therian on the back.

"I completely understand." She took Hallie's hand in hers and stepped towards her friend. "It's like you were missing something, but you didn't know what it was until they were right before you."

"Yes, that's it!" Hallie beamed, and her wings fluttered.

The pair chatted for a few more minutes, the air between them light, before a server stopped by and slid an enormous slice of chocolate cake on the table next to them.

Brynleigh stared at it. Of all the foods she missed from her human days—and there were many—cake was the biggest one. She loved cake in all forms, but chocolate was her favorite.

Maybe it had been a mistake to ask for it because this one looked delicious. The lush, dark chocolate sponge was covered in thick swirls of brown icing, and it was the most inviting food she'd seen in years.

Her mouth watered at the sight. Logically, she knew that if she took a bite, it would taste like ash, but it looked *so* good. If only she'd requested the recipe from the chef who'd made the scrumptious blood-laced food she'd enjoyed on her date with Ryker.

Ryker slid his hand around Brynleigh's waist and held her to his side. "I'm back," he murmured.

Immediately, she relaxed and leaned against him. It was insane that she felt so comfortable in his presence, considering that she had been planning to kill him for the majority of their relationship, but his soul called to hers.

"Is everything okay?" she asked.

"Yes." He kissed her forehead. "It's nothing to worry about. I promise, I'm yours for the rest of the night."

Those words delighted her in a way that nothing else ever did. *He* delighted her. How could she have ever thought he was a monster?

Therian took Hallie's hand. "Dance with me?"

The Fortune Elf grinned. "I'd love to." Hallie looked back at the newly married couple, a knowing twinkle in her eye. "Enjoy your evening."

Brynleigh winked at her friend. "Oh, we will."

To say that Brynleigh was eager to leave this reception and be alone with her husband would be a vast understatement.

Like a gentleman, Ryker pulled out Brynleigh's seat for her. She sat and picked up her glass of blood wine. "What was that about?" she whispered.

Drawing over the plate, Ryker speared a piece of cake. "The rebels are on the move again," he murmured. "I might get called into work early."

Brynleigh had suspected that might be the case. She hadn't anticipated the resulting pang of disappointment that twisted in her stomach. It was a strange emotion she hadn't felt since before her Making. "Oh. Okay. I understand. You'll be careful, right?"

Ryker's job was dangerous, but he was powerful. Surely nothing would happen to him.

His hand curled around hers. "Look at me, sweetheart." He waited until her eyes were on him. "I'll be safe. I always am. My soldiers are the best because my squad is a family. No one is ever unguarded. I have their backs, and they have mine."

Logically, she knew that. The reason she entered the Choosing in the first place was to catch Ryker alone. Illogically, she didn't want him to go because they wouldn't be together.

That was ridiculous.

What was wrong with her? Brynleigh didn't need to be by her husband's side every minute of every day. That was actually impossible. They weren't Tethered together, and besides, she enjoyed her privacy.

It must be the Faerie Wine. She pushed the glass away, determined not to have another sip. It was making her delusional.

A knife tapped against a glass in the reception hall. "Kiss!" a woman shouted.

A distraction from all these nonsensical emotions. Thank Isvana.

Brynleigh's lips twitched as more people picked up the chant, calling for them to embrace. She'd never enjoyed wedding traditions much in the past, but she had to admit this particular one was no hardship.

Ryker turned to Brynleigh, his eyes sparkling as he squeezed her hand. His gaze caught on her lips, and a heady scent of desire flooded from them both. Sometimes, being a vampire with heightened senses was nice since she knew without a doubt that he wanted her as much as she wanted him.

He asked, "Do you want to?"

She wanted to do so much more than that, but she'd settle for this... for now. "I mean, the crowd is demanding it, Ry. We don't want to let them down."

He smirked, "Then I suppose we must."

His mouth lowered to hers. Their kiss wasn't soft or gentle, but little about her new husband was. It was filled with lips and tongues and teeth. His mouth worked hers as if he'd spent years researching how to kiss her in the most effective and passionate manner possible.

It was the small moments like these that made it seem impossible that she and Ryker had only known each other for a couple of months. They fit together so well; it was like they were always meant to be this way.

When they finally broke apart, Ryker's mouth went to her ear. His warm breath brushed her skin, and he whispered, "Soon."

One word. A promise of what was coming. And gods, Brynleigh couldn't wait. Before she could reply—or yank her new husband with her through the Void in haste to get to their hotel room—a swarm of black shadows pooled on the ground beside her.

That was all the warning Brynleigh had before her Maker appeared beside her. Jelisette's black dress clung to her frame, a deathly dichotomy to Brynleigh's bridal gown.

Jelisette met her progeny's gaze and raised her brow in silent question.

Brynleigh dipped her head, the movement subtle enough that only the most perceptive vampire would notice it. She had anticipated this moment, and yet her stomach still tied itself up in knots.

Leaning over, Brynleigh brushed her lips over Ryker's cheek and whispered, "I'll be back soon."

She had to pretend one last time. For both their sakes.

Ryker's thumb brushed the back of her hand. "I'll miss you."

Bubbles rose in her stomach that had nothing to do with the Faerie Wine.

A week ago, Brynleigh would've shoved those emotions down, but no longer. Now, she simply let the truth in those words wash over her. He would miss her, and she would miss him.

Tomorrow, when the sun rose and she'd officially failed at her task, she would unpack this emotion and give it a name.

Taking one last fortifying sip of good, old-fashioned blood wine—it was more of a gulp, if she was being honest—Brynleigh stood.

She glided on steady legs away from the head table to a shadowy alcove near the back of the reception hall. Jelisette's heels clicked as she strode alongside her.

Neither woman spoke.

When they were alone, Jelisette twisted her hand. Shadows slipped from her palms, and the familiar crawl of her Maker's magic swept over Brynleigh as the older vampire erected a privacy ward around them. Others could see them, but they would be unable to hear their words.

Brynleigh had been inside countless wards with Jelisette, but for the first time, she felt a tingle of unease twisting in her stomach at being in such a confined space with her Maker. She always knew Jelisette was dangerous, but ever since she learned the truth about the storm, she wondered what else her Maker was hiding.

But this wasn't the time for questions. This was the final test before Brynleigh could leave with her husband and spend the night in peace.

She had to pass with flying colors. Jelisette was a dangerous, ancient vampire, and if she knew what her progeny was planning...

Well, she couldn't know.

Brynleigh had decided to keep her husband alive, and she would deal with the consequences tomorrow. Maybe Zanri could help her develop a good story as repayment for missing her wedding.

"Are you ready?" Jelisette's icy tone matched the frozen, dark expression on her face.

Inside, Brynleigh screamed that she would never be ready. She asked a dozen questions, wondering why Jelisette was insistent about this course of action. Why was she pushing for Brynleigh to kill Ryker when River had been the one to destroy Chavin? What did Jelisette know that Brynleigh didn't?

Outside, Brynleigh wore a blank mask. She nodded briskly. "Yes, ma'am. I am."

The cousin of a smile, although it was bereft of all kindness, spread across Jelisette's face. "Does he suspect anything?"

Brynleigh dared to glance back at Ryker. Atlas was in her seat, and the two men were chatting amicably. The water fae must have felt Brynleigh's gaze on him because he looked over his shoulder. He caught her eye and waved. She smiled back.

"Not a thing. I've played my role perfectly."

Jelisette studied Brynleigh like the younger vampire was an interesting insect, and she was deciding whether or not to squash her. Brynleigh held her breath and remained statue-still, unwilling to give her Maker any reason to suspect she was lying. Steadying her breath, she stared straight ahead and kept her face impassive as she waited.

It felt like hours passed as Jelisette's steely gaze ran over every inch of Brynleigh before the older vampire nodded curtly. "I see."

Brynleigh exhaled, and her shoulders relaxed. She'd done it. She'd fooled her Maker. "Everything is in order."

"Good." Jelisette's red lips curled, showing a glimpse of a fang. "Make it painful."

That was, apparently, her goodbye. Jelisette twisted her fingers again and drew the shadows back into herself. A heartbeat later, she disappeared into a plume of shadows. She left so fast that Brynleigh didn't have a chance to ask about Zanri. Maybe the shifter was ill.

Brynleigh had half a mind to find her phone and call her friend before she decided it could wait until tomorrow. After all, tonight was for her and her husband. She was certain they could find plenty of ways to occupy themselves until the morning.

And then, Brynleigh would deal with the aftermath of her actions... or lack thereof. But she wouldn't worry about that right now.

Why borrow tomorrow's problems today?

CHAPTER 34
They Were a Pair

The party was still underway when Ryker and his wife danced one last time. Hours had passed since the servers cleared the last plate, and many of the older fae and other party guests had already departed.

It amused Ryker to no end that his vampire had two left feet. He'd never danced with anyone as clumsy as his wife. She'd stepped on him multiple times, but he didn't care. The flush of her cheeks was adorable, and he'd stolen dozens of kisses throughout the night.

Now, it was over. Thank the Obsidian Sands, they could leave without causing a scene.

Ryker pulled his bride off the dance floor as the music switched to a more upbeat tune. A guard stood against a column nearby, failing at blending in with the party guests. He averted his eyes as Ryker led his wife away from the dance floor.

Brynleigh was always beautiful, but tonight, she was something else entirely. Ryker hadn't thought it was possible to fall even more in love with her, but he was certain he loved her more tonight than he had yesterday. Her pale cheeks were flushed, several golden locks of hair framed her face, and her black eyes created a stunning contrast to the white gown. She was exquisite, this wife of his.

Ryker bracketed his arms above Brynleigh's head, boxing her in against the wall. He leaned over, using his body to hide her from view, and brushed his lips over hers. "How are you feeling, Mrs. Waterborn?"

Gods, those words caused his stomach to jump and a grin to stretch across his face. She was finally his.

"I don't know." Brynleigh's black eyes twinkled, and he sensed she knew what he was saying. "Are you asking whether I'm tired?"

He chuckled, kissing her jaw, then nibbled on her earlobe. "Maybe."

She sighed dramatically. "Alas, I regret to inform you that I'm not the tiniest bit tired."

"Pity," he murmured before kissing her neck. She gasped, arching her head back to give him more room. He asked, "Could I convince you to be tired?"

She clutched at the front of his jacket, holding him there as he kissed her. "I'm fairly certain you could convince me to do anything, Ry."

That name. It snapped the last bit of his restraint—not that there was much of it left.

"Good, then we're leaving." With one final brush of Ryker's mouth against his wife's throat, he straightened and scooped her into his arms in a bridal hold. She laughed, her heels kicking in the air as she settled into his hold.

"I *can* walk," was her weak protest.

"I know." He slanted his lips over hers. "I want to carry you."

She didn't argue after that.

Leaving was a quick, painless affair. First, Ryker said goodbye to Nikhail and Atlas. The two men were flirting with a trio of brunette fae he didn't recognize. Then he searched for his sister. River sat alone at a table, nursing a glass of wine. She met his gaze and waved.

Ryker was grateful he'd had the foresight to book a room for him and Brynleigh in the hotel where the reception was taking place. Marlowe was staying in a kennel, so they didn't need to rush home. The five minutes it took for them to pass the giggling couples in the hallway and wait for the elevator felt like a lifetime.

The ride up wasn't much better since Brynleigh had taken it upon herself to start kissing his neck the moment he stepped into the steel box, much like he'd done to hers earlier. Every time her lips met his skin, his vision clouded, and his legs trembled.

Gods above, he needed her.

Finally, the elevator dinged, and the doors opened on the penthouse floor. The honeymoon suite, one of two on this floor, was a wedding gift from his parents, as was the month-long trip to the Northern Region he and his wife would depart on after attending Therian and Hallie's wedding.

"We're here," he said gruffly.

In response, Brynleigh ran her fangs over his neck. Good gods. Tremors ran through him. Shifting her in his arms, Ryker reached into his pocket and felt around for the small key card he'd been given earlier.

"Keep that up, and we won't make it inside the room," he warned her hoarsely.

"Is this... bothering you?" She nibbled on his neck again.

He groaned, stumbling down the hallway and fumbling with the card. "It's... not bad," he managed to force out the words in a somewhat respectable voice.

Laughing to herself, his vampire continued her pleasant torture until he finally got the key to work. The door beeped, and then it unlocked.

Ryker carried Brynleigh over the threshold and kicked the door shut behind them. He listened for the tell-tale click of the lock before he set her on her feet. "One moment, sweetheart. I need to look around."

Even now, his military training remained with him.

Brynleigh watched him with an amused look in her eyes as he inspected every inch of the hotel suite, guided by the light of the moon shining in through the open window. He looked under the king-sized bed with its mountain of pillows, red comforter, and scattered rose petals. Then, he checked the closets and the balcony. Once he'd ensured those were empty, he went through the bathroom. There was a massive tub and a shower big enough for two, which he fully planned on taking advantage of later. The room was empty.

He strode to the door and flipped the deadbolt. "All clear."

He was about to turn around when a delicate hand trailed down his back.

"You are aware that I'm a vampire, right?" Brynleigh kissed the other side of his neck, and he shivered as her fangs scraped his skin. What would it be like if she bit him? "I'm capable of taking care of myself if there's a threat."

Something primal inside him roared at the thought of her being in a dangerous situation.

Ryker captured her hand with his, turning her around to face him. "I know you're strong." He met her dark gaze, loving how she caught her bottom lip between her teeth as she studied him. "But I want to take care of you. It's part of my nature. Will you let me do that?"

Looking after those he loved wasn't burdensome for Ryker. It was how he showed affection. He'd done it for River her entire life and planned to do the same for Brynleigh.

A long moment passed as she studied him. His vampire was strong —he had Chosen her in part because of that—but it didn't mean he would stop needing to protect her.

"You can take care of me. It's not... I'm not great at letting other people in, let alone letting them help take care of me. But for you, I'll try." A shy smile crept on Brynleigh's face. "I'll do just about anything for you."

"Thank you, sweetheart." He kissed her softly. "How can I help you tonight?"

"There actually is something." Tugging his hand, she led him to the middle of the room before releasing him and turning around so her back was to him. Tiny pearl buttons, half the size of a fingernail, ran up her spine.

She looked over her shoulder. "Care to help me out of this?"

"With pleasure," Ryker practically growled.

He'd wanted to get this dress off her from the moment he first saw it. The garment was beautiful, but she could have been wearing a paper bag, and he would not have cared. It was not what she wore or the way she styled her hair that he loved, but the woman beneath it all.

"Thank you." Brynleigh crossed her arms in front of her. "It took River half an hour to do up the buttons. They're fiddly."

Ryker snorted, accepting the unspoken challenge. "I assure you I will get this dress for you in less time than that."

He'd rip it off if he had to. He wouldn't resort to such measures yet, though. Working steadfastly and swiftly, he undid the buttons one by one. Excitement bubbled in his veins, and he felt like a youngling on Winter Solstice morning, ripping open his presents.

The buttons slowly fell away, revealing Brynleigh's skin.

Flawless. Every inch, every freckle, every part of her was gods-damned perfection.

She chuckled, glancing at him over her shoulder. "Thank you, Ryker."

He hadn't realized he'd spoken out loud. Smiling sheepishly, he continued. When he was halfway down the row of pearls, he sat on the edge of the bed. Brynleigh shifted with him, remaining silent as he worked.

Anticipation thickened the air, growing stronger with each flick of a button. *Soon*, his every heartbeat seemed to say. *Soon, soon, soon.*

Eagerness made his fingers move even faster until, finally, the last button fell away. The dress yawned, exposing Brynleigh's back from her neck to the swell of her ass.

Ryker didn't have time to appreciate the beauty before him because Brynleigh lifted her arms. The dress fell to the floor like snow falling from a tree.

Ryker's jaw dropped open, and he breathed, "Fuck."

His wife was completely bare, her beautiful body on display for him to see.

Ryker had been with his fair share of women, and he appreciated beauty as much as the next person, but he'd never seen anyone as incredible as Brynleigh. Her figure was curvy, her body superbly proportioned as if it were made for him.

He groaned at the striking sight of her, unable to believe this was real.

His vampire wasn't shy. She barely gave him a minute to adjust to the sight of her before she glanced over her shoulder and raised a knowing brow. "Oh no," she said coyly. "Did I forget to mention that I wasn't wearing anything underneath my dress?"

Ryker scrubbed a hand over his face. No, he would've remembered if she told him that. He wouldn't have been able to concentrate on anything else.

"All day?" he asked, apparently incapable of uttering anything but the simplest words. His brain was short-circuiting.

"All day." She studied him for a moment longer over her shoulder. "Will you pass out if I turn around?"

Possibly. At this point, he wasn't entirely sure he could feel his fingers. All his blood was rushing to his center.

"I'll try not to." He didn't want to miss a single moment of their first night together.

Brynleigh stepped out of the dress. Shadows slipped from her hands, lifting the garment and placing it over the back of the armchair in the corner.

"Nice trick," he said, still struggling to find his words.

"It's not my only one." Even with her back to him, he heard the smile in her voice. She deftly pulled pins from her hair, one by one, until her golden locks tumbled down her back. She raked her fingers through them, shaking her hair out.

Then, Brynleigh slowly turned around.

Ryker couldn't help it—he stared at his wife. For one thing, her breasts were level with his face because he was sitting on the bed. It wasn't like he was actively *trying* to look at them. They were inviting his gaze. For another, he didn't want to stop.

His fingers curled around the comforter as he drank in the beautiful sight before him. She was captivatingly alluring in a way that was meant solely for him. He wouldn't change a single part of her.

After a few minutes passed in silence, Brynleigh whispered, "Say something."

He pushed himself to his feet, cutting the distance between them in half. Taking her hands in his, he lowered his mouth until it hovered above hers.

"You're utterly fucking perfect," Ryker growled.

Brynleigh hitched a breath, her gaze searching his. "Really?"

Maybe his vampire *was* a bit shy. Interesting. That wouldn't do at all. The woman Ryker had come to love over the past two months was anything but timid. He wanted to draw her out to play with him.

"Really." Ryker's breath skated over Brynleigh's mouth teasingly. "Can I kiss you?"

She murmured her assent, and then, his mouth was on hers. Like the earlier kiss in the temple, this one was claiming, powerful, and filled with intense longing. Unlike that kiss, Ryker had no intention of stopping.

He poured everything he'd felt since he first heard Brynleigh's voice into this embrace, letting her know precisely how much he wanted her. One of his hands tangled in her hair, and he pulled her close. The tips of her breasts brushed against his still-clothed chest and hardened.

Fuck, she was so responsive. Continuing to kiss her, he slipped his other hand between them and gently rolled her nipple through his fingers.

She gasped.

"Beautiful." He broke their kiss long enough to murmur the word over her mouth before claiming her lips again. The next time he took a breath, he added, "Fucking incredible."

She loosened in his arms, but he wasn't done with her yet. She moaned. He swept his tongue into her mouth.

Their mouths fused together.

Emboldened by the way Brynleigh melted against him, Ryker brushed his tongue against the sharp tip of a fang.

She shivered.

Oh, he wanted her to do that while he was inside her.

Brynleigh tugged on his shirt. She lifted her lips from his long enough to demand, "Take this off."

There she was.

"Gladly." Ryker stepped away, his body instantly mourning the distance between them, as he slipped off his suit jacket. "Anything else?"

Brynleigh took his place on the edge of the bed. "The pants, too."

He happily divested himself of those, as well. Within minutes, he wore nothing but black boxers.

His fingers were in the waistband when she said, "Wait."

Ryker stilled instantly, his gaze returning to hers. "Yes?"

She stood and reached for him. "May I?"

He swallowed, suddenly feeling like he was fifteen again. "Of course," he rasped. "You can touch me however you want."

It would be the sweetest torture, and he would willingly submit to her. For now.

Brynleigh smiled and hooked two fingers in the elastic. Her black eyes smoldered as she tugged down his undergarments.

He stood there, letting her see all of him.

"Oh, gods." She licked her lips and stared at his hardened length.

The sight of that alone was enough to bring Ryker close to the edge. He stepped out of the clothes, kicking them at the wall as he approached his vampire. "Brynleigh, I want you."

This wasn't the time for coyness. They had spent more than enough time waiting. His heart drummed, and need to be coursed through his veins.

She murmured, "I want you, too. More than I ever thought I would."

Warmth sparked in his chest as he kissed her. They became a tangle of tongues, teeth, and wandering hands as they explored what had so long been hidden.

She groaned.

He moaned.

She nibbled on his lips, her fangs grazing him teasingly but never biting.

He palmed her breast, rolling her nipple between his fingers.

Her hand slipped between them. Her fingers grazed his cock, and any blood that he had left in his brain officially departed.

Ryker broke away from the kiss as he stared at Brynleigh through hooded eyes.

"Do you like this?" she asked softly.

Did he require air to breathe? Did water run through his veins? Was he completely in love with this woman?

"Fucking yes," he groaned, both wanting her to continue forever and needing her to stop before he made an utter fool of himself.

She chuckled as if she knew where his mind had gone.

"Enough." Ryker couldn't take it anymore. He grabbed her hips and, with a swift maneuver, landed them both in the middle of the bed.

Brynleigh blinked innocently as if she hadn't just had his cock in her hands. "What's wrong?"

This vampire would be the death of him. He could feel it now. But he would gladly die a happy man if it meant he got to be with her.

She reached across the bed as if to touch him again, and he growled. Capturing both her wrists with one hand, he lifted them above her head and held them there. She looked positively beddable, stretched out before him.

He wanted to lick and suck and taste every single part of her.

"If you keep touching me like that, this will be over before it starts," he warned.

"Oh?" A brow rose, and Ryker could've sworn a glint of amusement entered Brynleigh's eyes. "Is that so?"

He nipped her lip for her impish reply. Settling his hips against hers, he pinned her to the mattress. "It is, and it's not how I intend this evening to go."

She wiggled, bringing her core dangerously close to him. "Oh? How did you think it would go?"

His wife was such a tease. Did she think she was in control here? That was not the case.

Keeping Brynleigh's wrists up high, Ryker slipped his hand between them, finding her clit and pressing gently. She gasped, arching her back into his touch.

"Something like this." There was no hiding the masculine pride in his voice.

She moaned beneath him, her words a mess of gibberish as he circled his thumb. Every soft moan, every gasp, sent a thrill through him. Yes, this was what he'd imagined. He'd dreamed about how she'd come on his fingers since their stolen moments in the car.

He wouldn't stop there tonight, though.

Ryker bent his head and kissed his bride as he slid a finger into her heat. She was so wet and tight. He groaned, moving his hand slowly. She gasped. He added another finger, loving how she cried out against his lips as he curled them just so.

Brynleigh moaned his name, and his cock became almost unbearably hard. Had his name ever sounded as perfect as it did at that very moment? He thought not.

He added more pressure on her clit and sucked her bottom lip.

She panted, "So close."

"That's it, love. Come for me. Scream. Let them all hear how I make you feel." He punctuated each word with a kiss as she writhed beneath him, desperately seeking her release.

Brynleigh's words were a steady stream of nearly incoherent babble as he drew her closer and closer to the edge.

More.

Please.

Don't stop.

Fuck me.

Ry.

That last one was his favorite. And when she yelled his name as she came, her tight walls clenching around his fingers, he knew there was nowhere else he'd rather be.

Lifting his fingers from her soaking core, he licked them clean as she watched with wide eyes. "You taste incredible," he told her smugly.

In response, she arched her hips and spread her legs. "I want you."

That was all she had to say. He released her wrists, settling between her like he belonged there because he did. His tip brushed her core, and he nearly lost himself there.

Her fingers found his shoulders, and she clung to him as he brought his hips forward. Dipping his head, he kissed her. "I love you," he murmured.

He lowered himself into her, one inch at a time, as she stretched to accommodate him. He moved as slowly as he could, letting her get used to him.

Gods, it took every ounce of patience Ryker possessed.

A vampiric purr rumbled through Brynleigh's chest as he filled her to the hilt. Shadows slipped from her hands, and she moaned beneath him, rolling her hips. "You feel so good, Ryker."

His forehead fell on hers, and he panted, "You feel better than all my dreams."

He allowed her to take the lead at first, to move slowly while she got used to him. To them.

That's what they were now. A pair. Partners in every way. Brought together by the Choosing and forever bound to each other in love.

Nothing could ever tear them apart. No one could break them. He wouldn't allow it.

Eventually, Brynleigh's nails raked down his back. "More, Ry," she demanded. "Harder."

She didn't need to ask him twice. Withdrawing almost all the way, he thrust into her with all his strength. He wasn't worried about breaking this vampire of his. She was even stronger than him and could take anything he gave her.

Brynleigh moaned, her legs wrapping around him. She met each of his movements with her own. Their sweat-slicked skin moved together as they each climbed towards their release. Her nails dug into his back. He slammed into her. She cried out. He groaned.

They drew closer, closer, closer to oblivion.

"I want you to come on my cock, Brynleigh." His hand slid between them and found her clit. "Now."

She obeyed beautifully, shattering with a scream that he would never forget. She broke apart beneath him, and his own release quickly followed. He came so hard that stars appeared behind his eyes.

Later, after they'd tested out the shower—it did indeed have enough room for the two of them, especially when he pinned Brynleigh against the wall and took her standing up—they cleaned up. He locked the balcony doors and shut the curtains before climbing into bed behind his wife. The only light came from the dim glow of the alarm clock on the nightstand.

Brynleigh's head rested on his chest, and her eyes were closed as she drew circles on his skin. "I'm glad I entered the Choosing," she murmured. "This is... far more than I could've ever imagined."

He kissed her. "Me too, Mrs. Waterborn. Me, too."

Ryker couldn't imagine having Chosen anyone else.

Brynleigh was his.

Forever.

CHAPTER 35
New Game, New Rules

Brynleigh's shadows slammed through her veins, urging her to wake up. They swam into her dreams, pulling her out of her fantasies.

What was happening?

She blinked, staring at the glowing red numbers on the clock. It was barely four in the morning. She should've slept for a few more hours after the way Ryker had tired her out. An arm pressed her into the mattress, and a heavy thigh was pinned between hers. She was naked, as was he, but that wasn't what had woken her.

Something was terribly wrong. Brynleigh's stomach twisted, and her shadows writhed, warning her to pay attention.

Her eyes swept through the room, searching for trouble. Their clothes were where they'd left them. Their suitcases, which had been delivered sometime during the reception, were in the open closet. Her eyes lifted to the curtains covering the windows.

Wait. The curtains.

She could've sworn that Ryker had locked the balcony door and closed the curtains before they went to sleep, but now the fabric was cracked open.

That was odd. Maybe the air conditioning blew them apart? They didn't appear to be secured by any fabric.

Frowning, Brynleigh extricated herself from her husband's grip. She slipped off the bed and moved towards the window. Grabbing the curtains, she shut them tight. She was about to turn around when the hairs on her neck prickled.

Releasing shadows from her palms, her spine stiffened as she spun on her heels.

A large tabby cat, nearly twice the size of a house cat, sat on the TV stand. A bag dangled from its front paw, and it stared at her. The animal was unfamiliar, except...

Those eyes. She knew them.

Brynleigh swallowed the scream rising in her throat as a flash of white light erupted from the cat. Her heart pounded violently against her ribs, and she stumbled back a step.

The feline disappeared, and Zanri took its place. He was naked, and the bag that had looked so big against the cat's paw appeared much smaller now.

"What the actual fuck?" Brynleigh whisper-yelled, her gaze darting between her handler and the bed where Ryker slept soundly. "Why are you here?"

Panic caused her thoughts to run at a million miles an hour. She was supposed to have until the morning. They'd all agreed on the plan. It was still early, and the sun hadn't yet risen. How did they know? What had she done to give herself away?

Zanri looked at Brynleigh with something akin to pity in his eyes. "The fae is still alive."

Not a question. Was there... sadness in his voice?

Maybe Brynleigh could lie her way out of this. Maybe it wasn't too late. "Yes, for now." Zanri opened his mouth, but she continued, "I'll still do it, Z. The timing just... wasn't right."

It would never be right.

"Because you were fucking him." The shifter's knowing gaze swept over her.

Now, Brynleigh wished she wasn't naked. The way Zanri looked at her made her feel dirty, like she'd done something to be ashamed of. But she hadn't.

"No. Well. Yes. I..."

I wasn't ready.

I think I might love him, which scares me.

I'm not going to kill him because his sister is really the one who caused the flood, and I can't bring myself to hurt her.

I want him.

He's mine.

The words were on the tip of her tongue, but she didn't say any of them in the end.

Instead, she stepped towards the bed, trying to get between Zanri and Ryker. She didn't think Zanri would hurt the fae, but she wanted to be sure.

The shifter watched her carefully. "Jelisette knows."

She furrowed her brows, and her confusion wasn't faked. "What?"

"Love makes us do stupid things." Zanri reached into the bag, and there was a snapping sound. "I should know."

Brynleigh's eyes widened, and she reached for the shifter. "What? Don't—"

"I'm sorry, B."

"No—"

He pulled something out of the bag. There was a flash of silver, then a pop.

Pain exploded in Brynleigh's chest. A mangled scream slipped from her lips. She called for her shadows, but they were gone.

As she fell to the floor, darkness edging her vision, she could've sworn she heard Zanri say, "Jelisette said to remind you that rules are rules."

Brynleigh went to cry out, but nothing worked anymore. Not her shadows or her wings or her magic or her voice.

And then she tumbled into blackness.

Drip, drip, drip.

The sound of something wet smacking rhythmically against the floor pulled Brynleigh out of the emptiness that had become her entire existence.

How long had she been unconscious? A minute? An hour? A day or longer? She wasn't certain. But Isvana help her, she hurt all over. From her head to her toes, her body felt like it had endured the beating of a lifetime. There was a mortality to her pain that didn't make sense.

Brynleigh frowned as she struggled to understand what was happening to her. Once again, a thick, heavy fog blanketed her mind. This was becoming an exhausting reoccurrence. She pushed through it, struggling to get back to herself. It was like she was swimming through the Black Sea, the inky waters clouding her vision.

What the fuck was going on?

Instinctively, she reached within herself and searched for her shadows. But they weren't there.

Gone.

Next, she searched for her magic.

Gone.

Her ability to summon her wings.

Gone.

Stripped away as though they'd never existed.

Had the past six years been a dream? Maybe she would open her eyes and see Sarai leaning over her bed, grinning. Maybe the storm had all been a nightmare. Maybe her family was still alive, and—

Her tongue brushed against a tooth. A very sharp, very pointed tooth.

A fang.

None of it was a dream. All of it had been real. Which meant...

Her family was dead. Sarai was dead. She was a vampire. And Ryker...

Oh, gods help her. Ryker.

Every single memory smashed through the fog and collided with Brynleigh at once. The Choosing, their wedding, the reception, the hotel room, and then...

Zanri.

Gods-damn him. Brynleigh had guessed he was a feline shifter. Something about the way he carried himself was a tell.

Zanri had shown up, and then... he shot her. He must have had a special gun in the bag his cat carried.

She remembered the bang and then the flash of pain.

Her hands flew to her abdomen, and she felt for a wound. Her stomach was tender to the touch, but there weren't any open injuries. She was wearing a shirt, though. The material was itchy and unfamiliar. She didn't have time to worry about that right now because she remembered what happened after

Zanri shot her, and then...

She fell to the ground. Shouts. A scuffle. Another gunshot. Ryker crying out.

"No," Brynleigh moaned. "No, no, no."

Her handler must've killed Ryker after he shot her.

Was that what he meant when he said rules are rules?

It was the only thing that made sense.

He shot Ryker, and then he... did something to Brynleigh.

Where was she? Part of her wished she could keep her eyes closed a little while longer and remain oblivious, but she couldn't. She needed to know. To understand.

Ice coated Brynleigh's veins as she opened her eyes despite the pain. A whimper rose in her throat. The shirt wasn't a shirt at all, but a black jumpsuit. That wasn't the worst of it, though.

Gray and black stones rose above her on three sides. Iron bars blocked the only entrance on the fourth wall. There were no windows. There was no light except a single violet Light Elf orb suspended from the ceiling. Condensation dripped down the stones, falling onto the ground in the rhythm she'd heard earlier. Something resembling a toilet and a sink sat in one corner. No bed. No blanket. Nothing else.

A fucking dungeon.

Brynleigh scrambled into a sitting position, moving to the corner of the cell so she could see if anyone walked by.

Her heart was a mallet shaking her entire body, but she didn't cry out to Isvana or Ithiar. There was no point in begging the goddess of the moon or the god of blood for help. She'd gotten herself into this mess, and there was no one to blame but herself.

Brynleigh didn't even realize they still had dungeons in the Republic of Balance. Their society was supposed to be evolved. They had technology now, for the gods' sake.

But this?

This place looked like it belonged in the stories of the fallen Rose Empire. Black manacles hung from the walls, the cell across from her looked like it housed a skeleton, and the breeze carried faint moans to her ears.

Yes, this was definitely a dungeon, and she was definitely a prisoner.

Because Ryker was...

He was...

He was...

Dead.

Brynleigh's breaths started coming in short gasps. Her head pounded. She drew her knees to her chest and hugged them close. Tears burned her eyes.

Captain Ryker Waterborn was dead.

Because of her.

This was all her fault.

Dead.

The word echoed in her mind, getting louder and louder and louder.

She wheezed, sipping air as a fist compressed her lungs.

Something strange happened in her chest. An ache grew in her heart. She tried to ignore it, to gather the emotion and shove it away, but she couldn't.

The box was broken.

She was broken.

Her lungs squeezed, squeezed, squeezed until they were on the brink of exploding. Her heart boomed. Tremors ran through her, and she rocked back and forth.

Then her gaze dropped, catching on the ring on her fourth finger.

A shuddering, broken gasp escaped her.

Her soul *cracked*. Fissures spider-webbed from that point, spreading through her.

Agony engulfed her.

Dead.

She shattered into a million pieces. It was like she'd been shot all over again. The pain of a thousand wooden stakes being shoved into her exploded inside Brynleigh's heart.

She screamed, but the cry soon contorted, becoming a twisted, mangled keening wail.

Anguish flooded her, stemming from her broken heart. It filled every crevice, every crack, every fragmented part of her soul. It wasn't a quiet trickle of grief or a blanket of despair like she'd felt when her family died.

No. This was different. Deeper. Darker. More complete.

This devastating, world-shattering pain would destroy her. There would be nothing left of Brynleigh after this.

Not that it mattered.

He was dead, and she was alone. Oh, gods.

Betrayal coursed a bitter path through her. Zanri did this to her. Jelisette abandoned her. Ryker died on her.

She was alone, and it was all her fault. She had no one to blame but herself.

Tears streamed down Brynleigh's face as she stared at the wedding ring. The jewelry mocked her as if it knew that she'd been married for less than a day before becoming a widow.

Alone.

She wept and screamed and cried until her throat was raw and her fangs ached. And then, when she had no more voice, she rocked back and forth.

A deluge of pain ran through Brynleigh, the grief a never-ending torment of betrayal and anguish and despair.

And she broke.

Minutes passed. Hours. Days. Time had no meaning.

No one came to see her.

At some point, she must've drifted off to sleep. Curse her young vampiric body for still needing rest.

She woke with a start, still living the same nightmare. Still betrayed. Still forsaken by her Maker.

There were more tears.

How could there be so many tears?

Ryker was dead because of her. He was a good man, a great one even, and she'd gotten him killed.

She never should've agreed to this stupid plan.

And to think she once thought this was nothing but a game.

She was a fucking fool.

Brynleigh should have told Jelisette the truth about River's involvement in the storm as soon as she learned about it. Maybe that could've saved Ryker's life. Maybe she could've stopped Zanri.

Maybe, maybe, maybe.

There were so many maybes, so many things she could have done, but none of them would save her from this fate.

Her mind ran in circles as she replayed the past few months repeatedly in her mind. She recalled the joy she'd felt when she first entered the Choosing. It was a terrible contrast to the pain coursing through her now.

She'd accomplished her goal. Captain Ryker Waterborn was dead. The Brynleigh from a few months ago would've been celebrating this news. But now?

She was wrecked.

For the first time in her entire life, Brynleigh had found someone who truly understood her.

And he was...

Gone.

She ran through every single scenario in her mind. Every interaction, every word, every moment they were together, searching for something she could've altered.

Time slipped on and on.

Her fangs ached, and her stomach hollowed.

Eventually, she realized she was hungry. How long had it been since she'd last had blood? She wasn't certain.

And then she felt it.

The air in the dungeon shifted. A cold breeze blew past her. Goosebumps pebbled on her arms.

Footsteps rang out, getting louder by the second.

And stupidly—so fucking stupidly that if she weren't broken, she'd have laughed at herself for being such an idiot—a spark of hope came to life in Brynleigh's stomach.

"Ryker?" she called out, her voice raspy from disuse. "Is that you?"

A bitter, malicious laugh that sounded like nightmares brought to life came from beyond her cell. It sent shivers down her spine.

"No." The voice was as melodic as it was deep and deadly. "He's gone."

It felt like she fell from the top of a high-rise as her stomach plummeted. She heard herself cry out and felt her heart shatter once more as a tall, black-haired fae approached her cell.

Two onyx manacles and a silver muzzle hung from his black-gloved fingertips. He wore fighting leathers, and though he had no visible weapon, she got the sense he could kill her in a heartbeat.

Swallowing at the sight of the fae, she pressed her back against the wall. Silver and vampires did not mix. Brynleigh wasn't entirely sure what the muzzle would do to her, but she didn't want to find out.

Violence glinted in the soldier's eyes as they swept over her. "You're in a lot of trouble."

"Please, I didn't do this." She shook her head, and more tears gathered in her eyes. This whole situation was her fault, but she didn't kill Ryker.

He laughed wickedly. "Oh, this will be fun."

Moving the muzzle to his left hand, he pulled a bag out of his pocket. Reaching in, he withdrew a shimmering black powder and blew it in her direction.

As soon as it hit Brynleigh's skin, fire erupted inside her.

He stepped into the cell, a malicious grin carved into his face.

And Brynleigh screamed.

CHAPTER 36
The Cost of Silence

Brynleigh would never leave this dungeon alive. Her immortal life would end here. She was certain of it.

The guard's powder was a mix of silver and prohiberis. She recognized it the moment it hit her skin. Like the black stones on the wall, it stole her magic. And the silver? It fucking burned. It ate her flesh. It was fire, and she was dying from its flames.

She tried to shake it off, but there was too much.

The fae stepped towards her, and she kicked at him weakly. Her leg hit his shin, and he cursed, "Vampire bitch. You won't escape what's coming for you. You're going to pay for what you did."

Brynleigh attempted to scramble away from him, but her body refused to respond to her commands.

A cruel, humorless laugh burst from the guard as he watched her struggle before seizing her roughly. He slammed the cuffs on her wrists before grabbing her head with both hands.

"Hold still," he snarled. "Or this will hurt even worse."

"Fuck. You." Even while she burned alive, Brynleigh wouldn't listen to him.

She raised her leg despite the pain running through her and aimed for the precious bits between his legs. She missed, her knee connecting with his thigh.

"That was a fucking mistake." He knocked her head into the stone wall behind her.

Once again, darkness claimed her.

"WAKE UP, LEECH." That same cruel voice taunted her, pulling her from her painful nightmares.

Brynleigh moaned, shaking her head as she tried to remain asleep. At least then, the evil guard couldn't bother her.

A woman laughed. "Try this."

A grunt of approval came from somewhere to the right, and someone thrust a wet rag against Brynleigh's nose. An astringent, slightly sweet scent infiltrated her nostrils, swiftly followed by a bitterness that had her choking. Her eyes flew open, and she coughed as though she were hacking up her insides.

The moment her lungs felt somewhat normal, she looked around.

Oh, gods.

This was bad.

Worse, if possible, than the cell she'd first been in.

They'd put her in an iron chair in the middle of an otherwise empty stone room. The air was frigid. Suspicious rust-colored stains painted the cracked stones. A putrid stench that made her want to gag came through the air vents. One wall featured a black mirror, which she assumed was a double-sided window.

"Good morning." The soldier from before crouched in front of her. "Did you sleep well?"

Brynleigh snarled and lurched forward. Or at least, she tried to.

In reality, the moment she opened her jaw wide, her skin connected with the silver muzzle. Flames exploded within her. Fire burned around her mouth. She screamed. And her hands? They clawed at the iron chair, manacles binding her to the seat.

"I'll take that as a no." The guard stood, watching her carefully as he stepped back. "That's alright. It'll only make this more fun."

It was not the kind of fun Brynleigh enjoyed; she was certain of that.

Then she noticed they weren't alone. Two people stood behind the first guard, and their gazes were also trained on her.

The man on the left was clearly an elf. His curling black ram-like horns rose above his head, making him nearly as tall as Ryker had been. He wore fighting leathers on the bottom and a black t-shirt, highlighting the red swirling tattoos running up his arms.

A Death Elf, then.

How very... predictable.

Beside the elf stood the source of the feminine voice Brynleigh had heard earlier. The woman had long strawberry-blonde hair and glowing blue eyes. She stared at Brynleigh with malice, and it was clear she would not be of any help.

This was fucking bad.

The first guard canted his head. "Do you know why you're here?"

Honestly? No. Jelisette would never bring Brynleigh to a place like this. She would've killed her—painfully and slowly—before leaving her to rot. This wasn't her. Brynleigh was confident about that. Her Maker wasn't behind this imprisonment, but she had betrayed her and left her to die.

Brynleigh didn't say that, though. She stared at the inquisitor, unblinking. She might not have known there were still dungeons in the Republic of Balance, but she'd been trained in dealing with interrogations. After all, there had always been a chance her plan for revenge might end up with her in jail.

She'd assumed—wrongly, obviously—that they would put her in a more civilized prison with tables and water and lawyers. She'd also assumed that Jelisette would promptly get her out of prison.

Evidently, she had been wrong on many fronts.

Betrayal was tart at the back of Brynleigh's mouth.

Her body surged with a primal need to destroy, yet she couldn't.

She was trapped. Vulnerable. Exposed.

And...

Alone.

The sting of loneliness had never been as strong as it was at that moment.

Even though nothing was civilized about this prison, Brynleigh knew what she had to do. She would have to unpack her betrayal later.

Right now, she needed to concentrate on surviving. She closed her mouth and glared at the menacing trio. She could do this.

Seconds stretched into minutes as they waited for her to say something.

She wouldn't be talking. She might have been betrayed and left alone, but she was strong. She'd survived her family's death, and she would survive this. Somehow. Or not. Without Ryker, it didn't seem to matter. Nothing seemed to matter.

Eventually, the woman snickered. "I don't think she wants to talk to you, Victor."

The guard who'd slapped the manacles on her—Victor—tilted his head. "No, it seems she doesn't." He tsked. "Shame. I thought we might be able to do this the easy way."

This was easy? Brynleigh didn't want to know what the hard way was.

"Did you?" the Death Elf drawled. "Because Emilia and I both know how much you love it when the prisoners aren't talkative."

Emilia snorted. "You mean he loves to torture them, Preston."

Brynleigh's heart stilled. Torture.

Oh gods.

Damn Jelisette and Zanri for abandoning her. Their betrayal had hurt before, but now it was like a knife to her heart. She could barely breathe, barely think. Fear caused her blood to run cold. Her nails curled into the armrest.

Brynleigh had done everything Jelisette ever asked—save for killing Ryker—and this was how her Maker repaid her. She abandoned her and left her alone to be fucking tortured. Brynleigh's eyes burned, and tears tried to force their way out of her.

This wasn't fair. None of it. Had she been such a lousy progeny that this was how she was repaid?

Ignorant of Brynleigh's mental turmoil, Preston laughed. "Yes, well, it's semantics, really. One person's torture is another's—"

"Enough!" Victor snapped.

The other two instantly fell silent.

The guard leaned close to Brynleigh, and her nose wrinkled at the horrible scent wafting from his mouth. Had this man never heard of personal hygiene? "Are they right, little one? Am I going to have to force the words out of you?"

"I'll never tell you anything," Brynleigh seethed.

Victor didn't seem worried about her declaration. If anything, he looked amused. He reached out and trailed his finger down Brynleigh's cheek.

It took everything she had not to shudder.

"She'll talk," the fae said confidently. "She's a vampire, and the prohiberis cuts off all her healing. All it will take is time."

"How much time?" Emilia questioned. "You know she's waiting for answers."

She? The Chancellor, probably. It didn't matter, though. Not really. Nothing would ever matter anymore.

"Not long." Victor flicked his wrist, pulling a silver blade from a hidden sheath on his thigh. "I'd give it a day. Two at the most."

Then, faster than Brynleigh could follow, he spun the weapon in the air, grabbed the hilt, and slammed the dagger into her leg.

Black stars filled her vision as she cried out.

FOUR FUCKING DAYS. Give or take. Keeping track of time was getting harder and harder as the hours passed. But at least four days had passed. Maybe five.

She was alone in the cell... for now.

They let her out of the chair when they left, and she would relieve herself before curling up on the stone floor and trying to sleep. It was a nearly impossible task in this place that reeked of death. Every sound, both real and imagined, woke her up as she waited for them to return.

They *always* came back.

Victor, Preston, and Emilia were a trio of torturers. They hit her, broke her bones, stabbed her, and made her wish she'd never been Made.

They never gave up, never stopped. Each time they returned, they brought more questions for Brynleigh. So many fucking questions.

Who sent you? Who do you work for? Why did you do it? Was this always your plan?

Those, at least, she understood.

But then others left her feeling more confused than ever.

Tell us about the rebellion. Who is your leader? What do you know about the Black Night? How many of you are there? Why are you targeting Representatives?

Brynleigh didn't understand those questions. Wasn't she here about Ryker's death? What did that have to do with the rebels? They'd almost killed her with their bomb at the Masked Ball. Of course, she wasn't one of them.

If she were talking to her torturers, she'd tell them they were way off track.

But she wasn't doing that.

It took everything Brynleigh had, but she kept her mouth shut. They'd come in and out, ask their questions again and again, but she was silent.

Broken—but silent.

Sometimes, she felt like someone else was watching her, but the only three people she ever saw were the torturers.

Her heart was bitter and icy and cold.

Her tears had dried up days ago. She was too tired, too sore, too hurt to cry.

Brynleigh stared at the closed door, wondering who would come through next. Would it be Victor with his knives? Preston with his deadly red magic? Or would it be the true devil of the trio, Emilia?

It hadn't taken Brynleigh long to realize the other woman was a powerful witch. Emilia's magic was blue, tinted with strands of black, and it felt *wrong* as it danced over Brynleigh's skin. It wasn't until the magic sank into her that the real torture began, though. One moment, Brynleigh was on fire. The next, she was ice.

It was more than physical discomfort. More than pain.

Emilia played with Brynleigh's mind, sending her image after image of death and destruction until it was the only thing she could see. The only thing she felt. There wasn't a single part of her that didn't feel broken.

Every day, they came and played and tortured her.

Every day, she bled and screamed.

Every day, she refused to speak.

And every day, without fail, she grew weaker and weaker. Brynleigh needed blood. She wasn't sure how much longer she would last without it.

She wasn't even sure she wanted to.

The trio had all but confirmed Ryker's death. Jelisette had abandoned her. Zanri, too. Brynleigh assumed there wasn't anyone else who even cared about her. Not really. Hallie was her friend, but what could the Fortune Elf do?

Upon reflection, Brynleigh realized she'd been the perfect pawn in Jelisette's game. She had no family, no friends, and no connection to anyone.

She'd been *played*.

Every time her heart throbbed, it sent pulses of anger, betrayal, and grief through her.

She grieved for Ryker, for their love, and for the life they could have led. She mourned what they had and wished there was something else she could have done. That grief would remain with her for the rest of what would likely be a very short life.

But the rest of it? The hurt at Zanri's betrayal? The shock that Jelisette wasn't coming to save her?

It was gone. It had vanished around the same moment Victor used her thighs as pincushions, stabbing several silver-tipped daggers into them and leaving them there while Brynleigh screamed.

Now she was fucking furious.

If she ever got out of here, she would destroy her Maker. Brynleigh considered herself to be a somewhat intelligent woman, but Jelisette had completely fooled her.

Brynleigh spent every moment she wasn't being tortured rethinking the past six years. She studied each interaction through a new lens. Jelisette had used Brynleigh and then discarded her like a piece of garbage.

Fuck her.

Brynleigh stared at the door, fists clenched, and waited for it to open.

She wouldn't talk. Not today. Not tomorrow.

Not ever.

CHAPTER 37

Questions and Answers

"I'll admit, I never expected you to last this long." Victor tapped the flat end of his blade on Brynleigh's bloody thigh, where another silver dagger was embedded in her flesh.

She breathed through her teeth, her nostrils flaring as a stab of pain ran through her. She was back in the chair, enduring another session of torture.

Don't cry out, she told herself.

Today was worse than yesterday. Every day was worse than the one before. She thought three weeks had passed, but she couldn't be sure.

Brynleigh was *so* hungry. Her stomach was a hollow void. She barely recalled what it felt like to feed. Her skin was shrinking in on itself. Her fangs were burning. It was getting harder and harder to remember why she wasn't talking.

Victor rocked back on his heels, his evil gaze studying her shrewdly. "Yes, I definitely underestimated you." He pursed his lips. "Or maybe we haven't given you the right incentive to speak."

Brynleigh stared at the fae. The artery in his neck pulsed so beautifully. She wondered what he would look like with his head removed from his shoulders.

Her stomach twisted.

Leaning forward as far as her restraints allowed, her lips pulled back to reveal her fangs.

Victor met her gaze and smirked. "Are you hungry?"

What kind of question was that? Of course, she was.

Victor didn't wait for an answer. He stood and wiped his hands on his black jeans, and walked to the door. He was gone for mere seconds before he returned with a bag of blood dangling from his fingers.

Brynleigh couldn't help it. She reacted instantly, snarling and fighting against the prohiberis manacles.

Hunger was a living, breathing monster within her.

She pulled against the cuffs locking her to this damned chair. She snarled through the muzzle, hating the silver they'd forced onto her.

A slow, pernicious smile crept along Victor's face. "Ah. I see. That's wonderful. Why don't we play a game?" He swung the blood, keeping it just out of her reach. "Every time you answer a question, I'll give you a sip."

Brynleigh's chest heaved as she stared at that crimson liquid. It called to her in a way that nothing else did. She needed it.

Every cell in her body strained towards his offering.

She just hurt so much, and she was so hungry.

It felt like years passed in the time it took for her to dip her head.

"Good." Victor pointed to the muzzle. "I'm going to take this off, and you won't bite me. Understood?"

Not fucking understood.

Brynleigh would kill Victor the moment she got the chance. But she was also a realist. She needed blood to survive, and right now, this was her best chance to get it.

Her gaze dropped to the silver knife sticking out of her leg.

He chuckled. "I won't be removing that, my dear. I need to keep some assurances you'll behave."

Brynleigh closed her eyes for the briefest moment. How had this become her life? Hating herself for it, she nodded again. She had no choice. Not really.

Victor rose to his feet and walked around her. His fingers worked quickly as he removed the muzzle. The moment the silver was off her face, Brynleigh felt like she could breathe for the first time in weeks.

A tear came to her eye, and she couldn't stop it from rolling down her cheek.

"There." Victor returned to where she could see him and leaned against the wall. The bag of blood hung from his fingers, taunting her. "The first question is easy, so you can get a taste of what you'll get if you behave."

He paused, and Brynleigh raised a brow as if to tell him to get on with it. She was hungry, but she wouldn't beg him for the blood. She wasn't that far gone yet.

"Where were you born?" Victor asked.

"Chavin." The word was raspy coming from Brynleigh's mouth, and she winced at the effort it took to force it out.

"Good." The fae stepped towards her slowly, uncapping the bag.

She stared at it, salivating as the precious drops she needed to live came nearer and nearer.

"Open," he said, as if she were an animal.

Gods help her, but she did. She opened her mouth like a bird, waiting for sustenance.

A solitary drop of blood landed on her tongue. It was the ambrosia of the gods, the first ray of sunlight after a long winter, a crisp drink of water after a dry, hot summer day. It was everything Brynleigh needed.

She swallowed and went for more, but he'd already pulled back out of her reach. "Now, now, you know the rules. One question, one drop."

A whimper slipped out of her.

"Where were you Made?"

"Chavin."

Another drop. Not enough.

"How old are you?"

"In human years? Twenty-three."

A drop.

"When were you Made?"

"Six years ago."

Another drop.

On and on they went, the questions getting incrementally harder. Each bead of blood was at once everything Brynleigh needed and not nearly enough. It took the hardest edge off the blade of starvation that had lodged itself in her stomach, but she was realizing that the blood in that bag wouldn't be enough. Not after what she'd endured.

She was just so gods-damned hungry.

The questions shifted gears.

"Why did you enter the Choosing?"

Brynleigh blinked. She could lie. She *should* lie. Every ounce of her training and every rule she'd ever learned told her that concealing the truth was the best way out of this. But was it really? She was in prison and had been tortured for the better part of a month. She was cold and dirty and hungry.

Lying hadn't gotten her anywhere. If she'd stopped doing it earlier, maybe Ryker would still be alive. Maybe she wouldn't have gotten him killed. Maybe they'd still be together.

Brynleigh had thought a lot about her husband over the past three weeks.

It was Ryker's face she pictured while Victor slammed endless silver blades into her. Ryker's voice that soothed her as the Death Elf wrapped red cords of magic around her neck, squeezing tightly. Ryker's fingers that grazed her flesh while Emilia sent deadly magic into her skin and twisted her mind.

She missed her husband more than she ever thought was possible.

"My goal was to kill Captain Ryker Waterborn," Brynleigh whispered, hating the words as they left her lips.

Shock flickered through Victor's eyes. "Come again?"

She repeated, "I entered the Choosing to kill Ryker."

He stepped forward and gave her several drops of blood.

"Why?" he asked.

Tears welled in Brynleigh's eyes, and despite her best effort to blink them away, she couldn't. "I thought..."

"What did you think?"

Those hot tears streamed down her cheeks. "I thought he was responsible for the death of my family. The flood that took out Chavin six years ago. His magic is powerful, and I just... I lost everyone."

She kept going. Now that she'd started stopping seemed impossible. She poured out her entire story to Victor. He didn't even give her blood for it. She started at the very beginning and explained it all. Her Making, the Choosing, even her confusion when she met Ryker. The way she didn't understand how someone so evil could be so good. River. All of it. She didn't hide anything. Why fucking bother?

When Brynleigh was done, she sagged in the chair. Her eyes closed, and tears fell down her face.

"I could have loved him," she admitted, mostly to herself. "I think maybe I did. And now, he's gone."

For the longest time, silence stretched in the room. She felt Victor's gaze on her, but he didn't say anything. Neither did she.

Her words echoed in the quiet. Her admission lodged itself in her broken heart. She hadn't thought it was possible to hurt even more than she already had, but she was wrong.

She was still hurting, still in pain, still broken.

And Ryker was still fucking dead.

What did it matter if Brynleigh regretted everything she'd done?

He was gone.

"Do whatever you want with me," Brynleigh muttered. "I have no one and nothing."

Victor didn't say anything.

Minutes stretched by. The weight of everything she'd confessed fell around her.

She wept and wept and wept.

Someone banged on the wall. Footsteps shuffled. The door closed.

She didn't bother moving or opening her eyes. Victor would be back, or maybe it would be Preston or Emilia. It didn't matter. They would bring more pain, more torture, and more questions about the rebels that Brynleigh didn't know how to answer.

This was her life now until they decided to put her out of her miserable existence.

When the door creaked open again, Brynleigh sighed and waited for the next burst of pain.

It never came.

There were two other people in the room. She could hear their breaths in this too-quiet place of agony, and she felt their gazes on her.

She didn't know who they were.

Once, without the prohiberis blocking her magic, she could've scented them. Right now, her nose worked like a mortal's. Those drops of blood hadn't been nearly enough to heal her, let alone restore her former strength.

Footsteps circled Brynleigh. A hand grazed the back of her shoulders. She stiffened. The touch was oddly familiar, but she couldn't place it.

Then, the pair left. She knew they were gone because the air in the room lightened. She exhaled, keeping her eyes shut. Why bother opening them?

When Victor came to release her from the chair, she'd look at her injuries long enough to catalog them before taking care of her personal needs and curling up in the corner to sleep.

The door opened again. That was strange. Usually, they didn't return so soon. Maybe they'd forgotten something?

"Open your eyes, Brynleigh."

That voice. She knew that voice. She'd been speaking with it for weeks. It haunted her dreams and, more recently, her nightmares.

Was she hallucinating? Was this the end? Maybe the blood had been drugged. Maybe they'd decided to kill her after all.

"Look at me," they commanded. There was a hint of apology in their voice, as if they felt bad for her. But that couldn't be true. Brynleigh was alone, and no one cared about her.

For a moment, she didn't reply. She couldn't. She sat frozen, shock running through her like ice. And yet, she had to know.

What if...

She didn't finish the thought. She couldn't let herself hope. That was dangerous. Deadly. This was another trick. It had to be.

Brynleigh knew that, and yet, she slowly peeled open her eyes. Because... What if?

The two words echoed through her head. *What if, what if, what if.*

She had to know.

Time crawled to a stop as her vision adjusted.

Disbelief coursed through her like a raging storm. Breathing was impossible.

A cry tore out of her chapped lips. Her heart slammed against her ribs. Her broken fingernails dug into the iron chair.

She rasped, “Ryker?”

The end... for now

Thank you for coming along with Ryker and Brynleigh for the first half of their journey.

Reviews mean the world to indie authors like me. If you enjoyed this story, it would mean the world to me if you could leave one.

Want to talk about this ending? Come hang out with me and my readers on Facebook! Join Elayna R. Gallea’s Reader Group

A Song of Blood and Shadows

JELISETTE AND EMERY'S SHORT STORY

ELAYNA R. GALLEA

To anyone who wants to see two vampires in their villain eras fall in love...
This one's for you

Blurb

One night can change everything.

At least, that's what Jelisette de la Point believes. After all, all it takes for her life to change is locking eyes with Emery Sylvain across the lake. The moment she looks upon the other vampire, she knows her immortal life will never be the same.

Emery Sylvain has been living beneath the light of the moon ever since he was Made against his will. A centuries-old vampire, he is growing tired of life. Or at least, he was. But when his path crosses with a beautiful vampire who isn't afraid of a little blood, nothing will ever be the same.

Fate brought them together, but can the two independent vampires find a place in their lives for each other?

CHAPTER 1
Immortal Life was Tedious

Jelisette de la Point's immortal life was irrevocably changed the moment she locked eyes with the handsome vampire across the lake.

She brushed a lock of her chestnut hair behind her ear, her pale skin glistening beneath the light of the moon as she held his gaze. Even with the expansive, frozen sheet of translucent white ice between them, it was like he looked into her very soul.

Well. What was left of it. Four hundred and forty-nine years had passed since her Making, and during that time, her soul had frayed.

At first, she'd lost bits and pieces of it, then larger swaths had fallen away as time went on. Some, when she watched her parents die from afar. More, when her brothers passed away. It was seeing her great-nieces and nephews die that took the biggest chunk of her soul out of her.

They all lived a mortal life and died a mortal death, but not her.

Jelisette looked the same as she had the day of her immortal rebirth. Average height, pale like all vampires, with a smattering of freckles across the bridge of her nose.

As a mortal, Jelisette had been plain, but as a vampire, all her hard edges had been smoothed away. It was only right, since Isvana, the goddess of the moon, blessed all her children with immortality, grace, and beauty.

At first, Jelisette had enjoyed the blessings of being a vampire. She derived a certain delight from being one of the most powerful creatures in the Republic of Balance. Although the continent was home to many, only vampires were truly immortal. Even the most powerful fae and elves Faded after many centuries of life.

But now, Jelisette found her immortal life tedious. She was tired of finding willing mortals to feed her hunger, tired of endless nights, tired of doing the same thing each and every time the moon rose.

She'd shadowed to this lake in the Northern Region, in the land previously known as the Kingdom of Eleyta, because she'd hoped to see the aurora. Hoped the brilliant lights would pull her out of this slump.

She stood, preternaturally still beneath the moonlight, with her hands in her pockets. Despite the snow falling leisurely from above, she wore a black sweater and jeans. Her phone, a new-ish invention that had been popularized two centuries ago, sat silently in her back pocket.

She wasn't looking at the aurora, though.

She was still gazing at the man across the water. He was staring at her, too.

The man—the vampire—was tall. Even from here, she could make out the golden hue of his hair. His eyes were sharp—black, like hers, another marking of Isvana's blessing—and his face was chiseled. A strong nose, chiseled jaw, and high cheekbones gave him an other-worldly, deadly beauty. He was clad in black, like her, although he wore jeans and a leather jacket.

But his eyes.

Ithiar help her, but they held a glimmer of wickedness that delighted her to no end. She was drawn to him, unlike anyone she'd ever been drawn to before.

The vampire tilted his head. The corner of his lips twitched, and he smirked. In a move she'd remember for the remainder of her immortal life, he winked.

Her jaw fell open. She had killed mortal men for lesser causes. But coming from him, it did nothing but send a flurry of warmth through her.

In the next heartbeat, enormous, jet-black bat wings made of shadows and darkness burst from his back. They filled out the night, drawing the darkness towards him. The nameless vampire nodded as if to say, *nice to meet you*, and then he launched into the sky like a dark angel.

Each flap of his wings was like a boom of thunder against the silent night.

The vampire rose in the air, and Jelisette broke into a run. Her arms pumped. Her legs ate up the distance as though it was nothing. She ran across the frozen ice as though it was a sheet of glass, her feet barely leaving prints as she moved with the speed and grace of her kind.

By the time she made it to the other side, he was gone.

"Damn it," she cursed.

With her hands on her hips, she turned in a circle. The mysterious vampire had vanished as if he'd never been there. No prints, no scent, nothing. She would've considered that it was all some strange dream had a glimmer in the snow not caught her eye.

Jelisette bent and dug through the white power with her bare fingers. The cold pricked at her, acknowledging her presence, but it didn't bother her. As a child of the moon, her blood ran as cold as ice.

There.

She plucked the smooth object out of the snow. Standing, she examined it beneath the light of the moon. It was a button, black like the starless night, except for the silver initials engraved into it. *ES.*

She ran her thumb over the carvings and brought the object to her nose. She inhaled deeply, calling on her vampiric senses to come to her rescue.

The faint scent of shadows, pine, and cinnamon lingered, wafting up to her. It beckoned to her, stirring at part of her soul that she'd thought was long since gone.

Jelisette's fingers closed around the button, and she gripped it tightly.

Right then, she vowed to find her mystery man again, no matter how long it took.

"HAPPY BIRTHDAY!" The cheer rose through the crowded pub, and the ground shook as the two dozen gathered vampires stomped their feet.

Jelisette did not do that because, quite frankly, it felt beneath her, but she did lift her glass of blood wine in the air.

"Happy birthday, Narie," she echoed before tipping back her cup and taking a long dredge of her wine.

Narie Bellant was newly Made, barely three decades out of her Fledgling years, and she still maintained many of her mortal qualities.

She stood at the front of the bar, her silky black hair in a high ponytail as she accepted kisses from Ilana and Justus, her partners. Dressed in a short silver dress that looked more like a napkin, she grinned. "Thank you, everyone. I appreciate you all coming out."

"How old are you?" someone in the crowd asked.

Narie grinned. "Now, it's not nice to ask a lady that question." She paused and snickered. "So it's a good thing I'm not a lady. I'm fifty-seven."

Justus kissed her cheek. "She doesn't look a day over twenty-five."

Jelisette barely stopped herself from rolling her eyes. The love between the three partners was sickening. She wished she hadn't accepted the invitation to this stupid party. Who celebrated birthdays when they were immortal? Jelisette hadn't done it in over three centuries.

Was she glad to be alive, at least in the loosest sense of the word? Yes. Would she celebrate the day she was given this life? No.

But Jelisette considered Narie and her partners to be friends... or at least, they weren't her enemies.

After one lived for as long as Jelisette and many of the other vampires in the Republic of Balance had, that was sometimes all that it took to constitute a friendship.

She nursed her glass of blood wine, leaning against the bar top as she listened to the conversations around her. They were all fake. All full of false flattery.

Half these people would stab a stake through Narie's heart at the first possible opportunity. They were all here for one reason: money and power.

Everyone knew that aligning themselves with Narie's triad was a good idea. They had old money, and Justus was powerful. He was one of the only vampires who hadn't gone into a deep sleep after the Four Kingdoms had reformed into the Republic of Balance.

The fakery continued around Jelisette. No one spoke to her, which was exactly how she preferred it.

Jelisette gave off a strong "leave me alone" vibe. She had for the past several centuries. One of her biggest pet peeves was when people were fake. She always preferred it when people spoke their minds, having lost her ability to endure pedantic, pointless conversations about two centuries ago.

Three and a half weeks had passed since she saw the mysterious *ES* at the lake. She'd returned twice, but both times, there was no sign of him. She didn't know why, but that disappointed her.

She had so many questions about him. Why had he been there in the first place, and why was she so intrigued by him? All vampires were dangerously beautiful, but there was something about this man that made Jelisette's core tighten.

She lost herself to the memory of ES's wicked smirk and dark wings until enough time had passed that it would be socially acceptable for her to slip into the night without anyone noticing. Finishing her third glass of blood wine, Jelisette paid her tab with the bartender and walked towards Narie's table.

"Congratulations on another birthday," Jelisette said, infusing as much warmth in her voice as she could muster.

It was just on this side of icy, so not much.

Narie either didn't notice or didn't care because she smiled. Gods, she really was still so innocent. "Thank you, Jelisette. It was so nice of you to come."

Justus stood behind Narie's shoulder. The vampire used to be a fierce fighter. He served under the Last Vampire King and Queen, for Ithiar's sake. He used to be known for his viciousness and brutality. He'd drained more than one Source of their lifeblood over his existence.

But now?

He smiled dotingly at his progeny. A century ago, he fell in love first with Ilana, and then with Narie. He Made them, and now they lived in a mansion on the outskirts of Golden City.

Justus had called it domestic bliss when Jelisette had made the mistake of asking about it a decade ago.

She thought it sounded more like a prison. How could he just turn from bloodletting and violence like he'd never found joy in it? Jelisette didn't understand. How could something as stupid as love and devotion ruin such a wicked vampire?

It turned out Justus was nothing but a weak, weak man.

"I appreciated the invitation," Jelisette said smoothly. "Unfortunately, the night is calling me." Despite the blood wine she'd enjoyed, she was still hungry. "I might go search for something... more filling."

Justus nuzzled Narie's neck, kissing her skin softly. "Perhaps you should find a Source, Jelisette. Someone to remain with you permanently."

Jelisette did not think that would happen. She wasn't inclined to keep Sources like some of her brethren. "Perhaps I will."

Justus's fangs glistened in the purple light. "Think about it."

"I shall." Jelisette dipped her head, her chestnut locks falling over one shoulder. "Have a wonderful evening."

With that, she took her leave. The bell above the door chimed as she pushed it open and slipped into the cold night. Her breath clouded in front of her, and icicles dangled from the lampposts.

Her apartment was on the other end of Golden City, but there were hours until sunrise, and besides, she'd always enjoyed walking.

Keeping to the shadows, she let the darkness running through her veins trickle from her fingers. She strolled down the streets of Golden City slowly, letting the symphony of the night caress her ears as she moved. It had snowed earlier, and the sidewalks were still dusted in the white substance.

Streetlights created pockets of illumination, but she didn't need them. The shadows were her home. Mortal women didn't walk the streets of Golden City alone. It was asking for trouble—not even the Representatives and their families were that stupid.

But Jelisette had no reason to fear. She practically wished for someone to try and attack her. She would relish the opportunity to destroy them in a physical match before draining them of their blood.

Unlike in the past, when vampires lived in the Northern Kingdom of Eleyta, and they ruled all the humans around, there were *laws* in the Republic. Rules and regulations meant to stifle and oppress vampires.

No longer could Isvana's children find blood from any Source—willing or not.

Now, they had to get consent. Not only that, but the Representatives had decreed that if a vampire lost control, they would be tried for murder.

Just last year, Dominica Leblanc had been tried and found guilty of killing a pair of teenage elves when she lost control of her feed. The Chancellor had personally laid down the ruling: she would spend the rest of her life in Black Prison in solitary confinement. Apparently, Dominica was supposed to be happy they decided not to stake her.

It was gods-damned ridiculous. After all, vampires were blessed by the gods. They required blood to survive. Regulating the source of their life was ridiculous.

Unfortunately, there were no vampire Representatives. It was a vast oversight, especially considering that every other species in the Republic of Balance was represented on the Council, including the fae. No one was looking out for the children of the night.

Maybe one day, Jelisette would do something about it. She'd like to knock the Representatives down a few pegs. They were always so high and mighty.

She turned right, walking down Main Street. She passed the statues of the High Ladies of Life and Death. Shrouded in green and red markings that ran over their entire bodies, the two elves were forever immortalized for their work in restoring the balance to the Four Kingdoms.

Jelisette had almost reached the end of the block before something tickled her nose. The scent was barely there, a mere hint beneath the city's perfume, but it called to her. The moment she smelled it, her shadows thrummed in her veins. She turned slowly, sniffing until the smell grew even stronger.

There.

Cinnamon, pine, and shadows. Her fingers slipped into her pocket, and she felt the button. She'd kept it on her ever since the meeting on the lake. It was silly since Jelisette wasn't an emotional vampire, but she couldn't bring herself to part with it.

Was *ES* here, in the Central Region?

She had to know. Tucking the button back in her pocket, she turned to follow the scent.

CHAPTER 2
That was Rather Impressive

Emery Sylvain had been minding his own business, strolling down the snowy streets of Golden City, when a whisper of magic tickled the back of his neck.

Instantly, he perked up. Not all vampires could sense when others used magic, but this was his particular gift from Ithiar, the god of blood.

Someone—two someones, actually, judging by the magical signatures wafting around them—was trailing him. A bold move on their part. Emery wasn't exactly inconspicuous. His wings were out, the black appendages heavy on his back as he strode through the street. Shadows curled at his feet. Power radiated from him, as it had from the moment of his Making nearly nine centuries ago.

It amused him that someone dared follow him. They didn't know who he was, of course, but they would find out soon enough.

Emery walked through Golden City, and his pursuers never left. They weren't very subtle, whoever they were. They stalked him down the main city streets, through the shopping districts, until he reached the edge of the governmental sector.

Emery skirted that part of town. He had no desire to go in there and deal with the Representative bastards who ran this country.

Though he moved normally, pretending not to hear the dual sets of footprints behind him, he paid careful attention to his surroundings.

In this part of the capital, there were no residential buildings. Industrial structures surrounded him on all sides, tall silver and glass buildings reaching for the sky. Unlike the endless sand dunes in the Southern Region, where Emery had grown up, the city structures screamed "manmade."

At first glance, Golden City was beautiful.

The silver and gold contrasted with the glass and aluminum, a testament to the industrial revolutions the continent had undergone since the fae had migrated from the Obsidian Coast to live on their continent. But when one looked closer, cracks appeared on the golden surface.

Refuse filled the alleys between buildings. Unhoused elves, fae, shifters, werewolves, and humans were on street corners and in parks. Lower classes struggled, and food banks often had lines going down the sidewalks. Poverty existed in Golden City, and no matter how much the Representatives tried to hide it, it showed.

Emery crossed the street, where the overhead lights were burned out.

His pursuers were still stalking him. They were getting bolder, drawing more magic around them.

Ahead, he spotted a dark alley shrouded in shadows. It was basically calling his name. Emery had come to Golden City for work, but he'd already taken care of his job. If someone else wanted his particular brand of work, who was he to deny them the pain they were asking for?

His fangs burned at the thought of more blood.

Maintaining an air of nonchalance, Emery slowly made his way over to the dark alley. He flexed his back, his wings taut, as he drew shadows from his palms. The darkness slithered around him like snakes, and he knew without turning around that his pursuers had followed him.

Perfect.

A lazy grin stretched across Emery's face as he slowly turned around.

"Good evening, gentlemen." He cocked a brow, his hands hanging loosely at his sides. "Can I help you?"

The two men who had stalked him across the city stared at him from across the alley. Delicately pointed ears, elongated canines, and a glimmer of violence marked them as fae. Both were tall, though not as tall as Emery. One was dark, whereas the other was light. Raven hair stood in stark contrast to the white, almost blue hair of the other fae.

Both fae extended their hands, and magic flickered above their palms. Not the colored magic of elves, but true, elemental power.

Water hung above the raven's hands while green vines sprouted from the other's fingers.

"That depends, bloodsucking scum." Raven stepped further into the darkness of the alley and flexed his fingers.

Emery scoffed. "On what?"

"On whether you come easily or not," said the other.

That wouldn't be happening. He had no intention of letting them bleed him. Vampire blood was sold on the black market, often used by other species to ward off the Fade.

The two fae lunged towards Emery, but no one was faster than a vampire. He stepped into the Void, shadowing behind the two fae. His wings were outstretched as he grabbed them by the back of their collars.

Pulling on the strength of his kind, he slammed them headfirst into the brick walls and let them drop to the snowy ground. The resounding boom was satisfying, but nothing kept a fae down for long.

"Fucker," growled the white-haired fae as he clambered to his feet. "You're going to pay for that."

No, Emery was quite confident that wouldn't be the case. He opened his palms, shadows swirled around his palms, and he made a, *come get me,* gesture.

The fae obliged him. They charged at him, their magic spinning around them.

Darkness and light collided in a thunderous boom. Water, earth, and night clashed, lighting up the night sky.

Emery shot a bolt of pure shadows at the raven fae, and the man cried out as he crashed into the brick wall. Mortar fell on him like snowflakes. The other fae yelled, throwing a curtain of vines at the vampire. He sidestepped them, his wings beating as he flew into the air.

Raven stood, an animalistic growl rumbling through him. "Fucking hell, we just wanted your blood, but now we're going to kill you slowly."

Emery didn't even bother answering him. Instead, he released the full power of his shadows.

Night flooded from the vampire, blanketing the entire city block in darkness. He was a flurry of death as he dealt with the fae, their screams of terror as he ripped them apart limb from limb, feeding his bloodlust.

This was his calling. Emery served Ithiar as he had since the day he was Made. He was a weapon, a creature of the night, a tool of Death itself. It didn't matter that the old times had passed. There was always a need for death, even in the Republic of Balance.

Emery let the sweet call of his purpose envelope him as he finished off the fae. It wasn't like they didn't deserve it—they'd stalked him halfway across the city with the intent to harvest his blood and sell it on the black market.

He knew what people did with vampire blood. They sold it to the highest bidder, letting them use it for everything from healing to buying near-immortality.

He didn't feel a single shred of remorse as he pulled back his shadows and took in the alley.

Blood coated the walls. The snow was crimson. The broken skids piled in the back were painted in scarlet. The fae were irrevocably broken. Their necks were snapped at horrible angles, and their throats were a mess of blood and gore.

He took in the scene and smiled. Licking his fangs, he savored the final drops of blood.

"Well, that was rather impressive," said a musical female voice at the front of the alley. "I don't know how you managed to do that without getting any blood on yourself."

Emery stiffened, his back straightening as he swung around. A snarl ripped through him, but he swallowed it when he saw who stood before him.

It was *her*. The vampire from Starlight Lake. He had no idea what she'd been doing there, nor did he know anything about her other than she was beautiful.

Long, chestnut hair hung in silky waves to her waist. Black hugged her curves. She was an average height, but her vampiric grace and the heeled boots she wore more than made up for that.

Emery wasn't in the habit of dreaming of other vampires. In fact, ever since his Making, he had lived a rather solitary life. Remaining on the outskirts of vampiric society suited him.

In his past mortal life, he'd been a librarian. Not anymore. He'd been Made against his will, in a time when such a thing wasn't punishable by law, and he'd lost control barely a year after that.

Fledglings were dangerous, and he'd just... slipped up.

A papercut. That was all it had taken. He'd been shelving ancient histories from the Rose Empire when the scent of blood had reached his nose.

One sniff, and he'd ripped through the necks of every patron and librarian unfortunate enough to be at the Ipothan Library that night. He'd bathed in their blood, and by the time the sun had risen, not a single person had been left alive in his wake.

After that, he'd left libraries behind for good. He'd never been able to pick up the *Ballad of the Light Elves* again, even though it was his favorite of the famous four Rosarian ballads that had survived the passage of time. He didn't deserve to be around books or those who loved them.

Instead, after he killed his Maker for what they did to him, he devoted his time to cleaning up the streets of the Republic of Balance. Evil was everywhere, and there was no shortage of people for him to kill.

"You," he said, surprised at the gravelly tone of his voice. He should've been upset that the woman found him, but he wasn't. Instead, he was... intrigued.

The vampire from the lake didn't look at him with fear or disgust, as most people did when they found Emery with bodies. Then came the screaming—he couldn't leave witnesses, after all. Chancellor Bellamy Rose would be less than pleased if he knew a vampire was cleaning up the streets for him.

But this woman was different. Emery felt it deep within his soul. His dark shadows sang at the sight of her, and he knew she'd leave this alley alive.

Her eyes widened, and she moved towards him with immortal grace. She carefully avoided the blood, a feat in and of itself, and came closer.

She drew her bottom lip through her teeth, exposing her fangs. "I... like your style."

There wasn't a trace of disgust or fear in her voice. No sign to indicate she was lying.

What were the chances she wasn't horrified by the sight behind him? Emery glanced over his shoulder at the two men, verifying that they were, in fact, very dead.

No one, not even a near-immortal fae, could rise from what he'd inflicted upon them. There was a beauty in their deaths, he supposed. An artistry to the way their blood painted the bricks. "Thank you."

"Were they causing you problems?" She sounded curious.

"They wanted to kill me." Emery lifted a shoulder. "I just returned the favor."

Killing was what he was good at. Everything else, the man he used to be, died when he was Made in that library.

"Good," she breathed. "They sound like real bastards."

There was barely a foot between them now. Emery's heart, which usually remained slow and steady in his chest, beat faster. "They were."

"I hate men like that," she said. "I would've done the same thing."

All the gods, that declaration sent a bolt of desire through Emery. He hadn't felt anything like that in years. Emery wasn't a monk by any means, but his feeding habits had remained purely platonic of late.

Life was growing tedious.

But now? Here? He was intrigued by the woman in front of him. It surprised him to realize he didn't want to leave. It would be so easy to flap his wings and escape to his hideaway, to shower and rid himself of the dirt of this night, but he wanted to learn more about this woman.

"How did you find me?" he asked.

She tilted her head and studied him. The movement shifted her hair, exposing the long, pale column of her neck. A breeze blew by, bringing her lilac scent to his nose.

His fangs ached. Vampires didn't typically drink from each other unless they were Bound Partners, a ceremony which rarely took place thanks to its eternal consequences, but he wanted to taste her. He bet she was delicious.

The woman moved slowly, as if she knew sudden movements were a bad idea, and reached into her pocket.

She pulled out a small black button. "You dropped this at the lake."

Emery had been wondering where he'd lost that. It hadn't overly concerned him—he wasn't a dragon, hoarding his possessions and snarling at anyone who came near—but he hadn't anticipated this particular turn of events.

"Ah." He nodded. "You scented me."

Not a question.

"Yes." She inched closer. "I'm Jelisette."

Her name hung between them, an offering. Of friendship. Of something more. He wasn't certain, but either way, he would play along.

It had been too long since anything had intrigued him.

"Emery," he supplied.

"Hello, Emery," she said, drawing out the vowels in his name as she tasted the sounds.

Gods, he loved the way his name sounded in her mouth.

Jelisette's black eyes rose slowly, locking onto his. The inches between them suddenly seemed like far too great a distance. Emery's breath caught in his throat. His shadows sang a resounding symphony in his veins. His heart stuttered, his lungs tightened, and everything else seemed to fade away.

He only knew her name—and that she didn't mind a little bloodletting—but suddenly, he wanted to know everything about her.

Shadows slipped from Emery's hands unbidden, swathing them in darkness. He stepped towards her, closing the gap. Lowering his head, he cupped her cheek with one hand. Smooth, unblemished, cold skin. She didn't pull away.

"Have a drink with me?" he breathed, unwilling to break whatever spell surrounded them by speaking too loudly.

All of a sudden, the only thing that mattered was staying with her a while longer.

Her lips tilted up. "I'd love to."

Ignoring the bloody scene behind him, Emery gave into the call of desire pulsing through him. He bent, brushing his lips over hers. This wasn't a kiss because it was barely more than a breath, but it left him wanting more.

Lacing their fingers together, he drew on his shadows and pulled them into the Void. The dark, empty space allowed vampires to traverse from one location to another in the blink of an eye. "Hold on. I know the perfect place."

CHAPTER 3
Her Dream Come True

Jelisette gripped Emery's hand as he pulled them through the Void. This was reckless and, quite possibly, stupid. It was so far out of character that she didn't even recognize herself. And yet, her shadows were quiet, and she felt... safe.

Strange.

If things changed, she could always just rip out his throat and divest him of his head. Vampires could survive many things, but even they couldn't live after that. One didn't become a four-hundred-year-old vampire without picking up a few self-preservation tricks along the way.

More than a few men with wandering hands had died when they tried to touch Jelisette without her consent. No one did that. Not since the events that had led to her Making.

The black shadows cleared as they stepped out of the Void. Jelisette's eyes widened, and she stared at their new location. When Emery had suggested they get a drink, she'd assumed he would shadow them to one of the many blood bars that catered to vampires. She'd never expected this.

Jelisette turned in a slow circle, her fingers still laced with Emery's, as she took in the space.

Glowing sky blue and emerald crystals hung from a cavernous

ceiling high above their heads. Clusters of luminescent mushrooms added their light to the space. A massive wooden bed covered in furs was pushed against one wall, and stacks of books were piled throughout the cave on top of every available surface.

How was it possible that Emery was both a skilled killer and a lover of literature?

He was Jelisette's dream come true.

Emery strode over to a wooden trunk pushed up against the base of the bed and lifted off a pile of books. He reverently placed them on the floor, opened the lid, and withdrew a glass bottle. Amber liquid sloshed as he poured two servings before extending a glass to Jelisette.

She took it with a smile. "Thank you." Cocking a brow, she glanced at the glowing crystals. "Is this your home?"

His lips twitched up into a smile. "If I said yes, what would you say?"

She made a show of looking around, first at the books, the crystals hanging from above, and the massive bed. If she didn't know any better, she'd think this was better suited for a dragon shifter than a vampire, but who was she to judge? She lived in a plain apartment in Golden City.

Like most vampires who'd lived for several centuries, Jelisette had accumulated a significant amount of wealth. However, she'd never truly found a use for most of it. She kept her money in Golden City Bank and lived in a modest one-bedroom apartment. Most of her money was spent on acquiring blood.

"I think it's beautiful," Jelisette admitted. It felt comfortable and safe, away from the world. She liked it. "Much better than my apartment. But I'm sure all the women you bring here say that."

Emery eyed her for a moment. "Would it surprise you to hear that I don't have many visitors?"

Jelisette stared at him. Was he lying to her? She studied him, searching for any signs that he was lying. There was an undeniable connection between them, but it didn't mean he couldn't deceive her.

She didn't see any signs of untruths on his face, though. Eventually, she nodded. "I... yes, it would."

Jelisette had assumed that Emery would be bringing a new woman back here every night. There certainly were enough willing elves, shifters, werewolves, even humans in the Republic of Balance. After all, Jelisette had never seen a vampire as stunningly beautiful as Emery. *She* had been dreaming about him every night since she first saw him across Starless Lake.

He smiled and lifted his glass in cheers. "To surprises."

She echoed his phrase, chinking her glass against his before sipping the amber liquid. It burned as it slid down her throat, the liquid gloriously smooth. Alcohol like this didn't affect vampires—she was as alert as ever—but it tasted delicious.

Jelisette drank, studying Emery carefully. Her shadows continued to sing, and that feeling of safeness had only grown since they'd come here.

Perhaps a younger vampire would've finished her drink and left Emery with her number, but Jelisette had lived far too long to let the opportunities of life pass her by.

If there was one thing she'd learned over her centuries, it was that most things in life could be bought, stolen, or found. But true connections? Relationship? *Love*?

They rarely happened. And when it did, when someone was lucky enough to find a person they connected with, they were to hold onto them with all their might.

Jelisette had never been in love, but she'd witnessed what it did to others. This wasn't love—she wasn't stupid; she knew one didn't fall in love in a night or even a few weeks—but there was something here that promised... more.

She wanted to explore it. She needed to explore it. How could she leave this cave and go back to her dreary life from a few weeks ago?

Since finding Emery in the alley, she felt more alive than ever before. More vibrant. More... real.

Whatever this was, she wasn't prepared to let it go.

With that thought in mind, she placed her now-empty cup on the ground and stepped towards Emery.

CHAPTER 4

Consider My Home Yours

Emery could not believe how this night was turning out. When he had followed the call of his shadows and invited Jelisette back to his home, he'd known there was something special about her.

He never brought other people here. It was his sanctuary and had been for years.

But she fit in perfectly.

There was something about Jelisette that made all of him pay attention. His shadows stirred, his heart raced, and his eyes followed her across the room.

He'd heard of vampires making connections like this, but he had never known it for himself. Never even thought it was possible.

He finished his drink as she stepped towards him.

"When I saw you across the lake, I felt... drawn to you." Jelisette's black eyes shone as she moved closer. "Do you... Did you feel it, too?"

It wasn't just him, then.

His lips twitched up, relief flooding through him. "Yes, I did." The gravel in his voice surprised him. Many things about tonight surprised him. He closed the distance between them with a few smooth glides, leaving his empty glass on a stack of books. "I meant what I said earlier. I never bring anyone here."

"Not even those that you intend to spend some... quality time with?" The insinuation was clear as Jelisette asked the question.

Smirking, Emery shook his head. "No. I haven't done anything like that in quite some time."

He hadn't wanted to. In fact, until this vampire showed up tonight, he hadn't wanted to do much of anything at all. Even killing evil people, which used to give him some sort of satisfaction, had been growing tiresome. None of that remained in his bones now, though.

"Oh." Her red lips parted, revealing beautiful fangs. Between her long chestnut hair, her vampire-pale skin, and those fangs, she was stunning.

Every part of Emery tightened, and a growing sense of possessiveness grew within him. He wanted Jelisette.

The following words slipped off Emery's tongue before he could stop them.

"Will you stay with me tonight?"

She stared at him, so he felt obliged to keep going.

"Not to... you know. Stay... as a friend. I like your company." Gods, was he a Fledgling? His typical eloquence was nowhere to be found right now. "Please."

He didn't know what had led him to ask the question, but now that the words had left his lips, they rang with truth. He wanted her to stay. For a night? A week? Eternity?

He didn't know.

Right now, all he knew was that he didn't want her to leave. The sunrise was coming, and for the first time in a long while, he didn't want to be alone.

Jelisette opened her mouth, then closed it again as her eyes swept over his.

Each second felt like an eternity as he waited for her response. His heart beat faster, and he clenched and unclenched his fists. Was this fast? Yes. Was it right? Also yes.

After what felt like several lifetimes, Jelisette smiled. Her fangs were on full display, and a glint of something dark entered her eyes as she held his gaze. "Yes, I will."

Something that felt awfully similar to relief fluttered through Emery's stomach.

"Wonderful."

THAT NIGHT, they stayed up well into the early hours of the morning. They talked, drank, and laughed—all things he hadn't done in many, many years.

When the time came to sleep, each took a side on the bed. Neither touched the other and yet, when Emery woke the next night, he realized he'd had the best sleep of his life.

"I need to go home," Jelisette said when they woke up.

And there went the happy feeling in Emery's stomach. "Oh," he said. "Alright."

He had no reason to be upset about this. For the gods' sake, they hadn't even done anything. But he felt like she was leaving him behind.

"Not to stay there," Jelisette said. "But I need to shower and gather some clothes. Unless you don't want me to stay, in which case..."

"No." Emery sat up so quickly that the mattress bounced a little. "I want you to stay for as long as you want."

Preferably forever. It was fucking insane, feeling like this after such a short period of time, but he did.

"Okay." Jelisette shook out her hair as she rolled out of the bed and drew shadows from her palms. "Come with me?"

He took her hand. "With pleasure."

JELISETTE'S APARTMENT was small but clean. Emery ran his fingers along the spines of the books in the living room. Two empty glasses were drying on the kitchen counter. The pair of vampires had enjoyed several bags of blood when they'd first arrived. Not nearly as delicious as drinking from the vein, but available and satisfying... enough.

Jelisette had gone into her bedroom to shower and pack, leaving

Emery to explore. The space was clean, and there weren't any traces of anyone else here except for Jelisette.

That knowledge lit a glowing ember within Emery. They'd known each other for such a short time, but that didn't really seem to matter. He was inexplicably drawn to Jelisette. He rarely felt comfortable with others and usually kept strict barriers erected between himself and others. He didn't feel the need for those at all when it came to Jelisette.

A few minutes later, she exited her bedroom with a black suitcase in hand. "I'm ready," she said. Her hair was still damp from her shower, and she looked positively sinful in a crimson sweater and black pants that hugged her curves. She wore heeled boots that he was certain weren't comfortable, but they looked hot as sin.

Emery strode over, his legs eating the small space in three lengths, and he took the suitcase from her. "Need anything else?"

Jelisette took a look around and shook her head. "No. This is just an apartment. Nothing more." She ducked her head, a shy look that he hadn't yet seen taking over her features. "And I think... I'm more comfortable with you. If you'll have me in your cave."

"You can stay as long as you want," he said. "Consider my home yours."

He'd never lived with anyone before, not even when he was mortal, and yet there was nothing but a thrill of pleasure that went through him at the thought of this vampire staying with him.

A dazzling grin danced across her face. "Thank you, Emery."

She slid her hand into his, and that ember grew into a tiny flame. Fire was deadly to vampires, but there was nothing wrong with this heat burning within him.

If anything, it made him... want her more.

That night, they stayed in the cave and talked about everything and nothing. Emery told Jelisette about his life as a librarian, and she shared stories from her mortal childhood with him.

On the third night, Emery woke up with a smile on his face. He glanced over at the vampire sleeping beside him and sighed contentedly. He was... happy.

Fuck. He hadn't been happy in a long, long time.

In what felt like the blink of an eye, a week had passed. The last seven days had been the most pleasurable ones of Emery's entire existence, and they'd yet to do anything physical. Not that he didn't want to —gods help him, but Jelisette was starring in his fantasies every time he slept—but they weren't there yet. It didn't seem to matter.

At dusk on the eighth day, Emery woke to a raven's caw. He propped himself up on his elbow as the black bird flew into the cave, a piece of parchment in its mouth.

He plucked the missive. "Thank you."

With a caw, the bird left.

Emery unfolded the message, read the contents, and frowned. He'd expected something like this to happen, but he'd hoped a few more weeks would pass before it did. He was just enjoying his time with Jelisette so much. Unfortunately, evil never took a vacation, and neither could he. A man had to work, even a centuries-old vampire such as himself. Emery sighed and slipped the note under his pillow.

An arm's length away from him, Jelisette slept peacefully. She wore silky blue pajamas, the outfit far more fashionable (and expensive) than the sweatpants that he currently wore. Her hair fanned out around her, her eyes were shut, and her lips were parted just enough to give him a peek of one of her fangs.

Ithiar-damned beautiful.

A heartbeat later, Jelisette cracked open an eye. A smile danced on her face. "Hey."

Her voice was raspy when she first woke, and Ithiar help him if it didn't make him feel all kinds of ways. "Hi," he returned.

"Were you looking at me?"

He reached out and tucked a lock of her hair behind her ear. They'd been doing this all week—small touches, stolen moments here and there. "I was."

He couldn't help it. She was a siren, and he was called to her side.

"Did you like what you saw?"

"Gods, yes." Emery reached out and trailed a hand down Jelisette's face. Her skin was soft against his calloused hands, and she leaned into his touch. "How would you feel about taking a trip with me tonight?"

She cocked a brow and sat up, the blanket bunching at her waist. "Where do you want to go?"

"I have a… job." He ran his tongue over his fangs and puzzled about how best to say this. He didn't want to scare her off now. "You could say that my particular… abilities are required."

They had yet to discuss the fae that Emery had killed in the alley, nor had they talked about what he did for a living.

Jelisette's brows furrowed. "What, exactly, does that mean?"

Hoping he was choosing the right words, Emery paused before saying, "People are evil."

She snorted. "Yes, and the sun is deadly to our kind. These are both things I am well aware of."

He loved her sharp tongue. There hadn't been a moment of dullness all week. "True," Emery said. "In this case, I've been summoned to… deal with someone."

Her black orbs searched his. Every second seemed to stretch on for a lifetime before she nodded slowly. "I see."

Did she really?

"I'm going to kill them." Emery threw subtlety aside for the sake of ensuring she understood what he was saying. He pulled the missive out from under his pillow and showed it to Jelisette.

While she read it, he explained that Yvan Thorn, a renowned werewolf criminal, had been spotted in the Eastern Region. Thorn's crimes ranged from bad—money laundering—to horrific—crimes against children that would have even the most hardened of vampires or Death Elves sick to their stomachs. Emery's contacts had been hunting Thorn for months, and they finally found him.

When he finished, he sat back and waited for Jelisette's reaction. He studied her eyes, her lips, her entire body for a sign of what she would say. His heart thundered in his chest as he waited and waited.

Eventually, a smile crept across Jelisette's face. "Can I help?"

He blinked. Of all the things he thought she would say, *that* wasn't one of them.

"You want to help me… kill him?" Stunned, Emery had to clarify.

"Yes." Jelisette canted her head, and a dark glimmer entered her eyes. "I've always found bloodshed... invigorating."

Gods damn it, his entire body warmed at the heat in her words. This was a wholly unexpected—and delightful—turn of events.

"Yeah?" Emery hopped off the bed and stretched. "Well then, let's go."

CHAPTER 5
A Warrior of Death

Jelisette crept through the shadows behind Emery, following as he led her through dark streets and twisted mazes deep within the underground city once known as Vlarone. Rumored to have been built by the gods—or giants, no one really knew—the city within the mountain was now an empty ruin.

The once-thriving cavernous metropolis with its spiral levels and glowing clusters of mushrooms lighting the walls was as empty as a graveyard. Houses were destroyed by the passage of time. Roads were cracked. Paths went nowhere. Life no longer resided within this place of old.

The deeper they went into the mountain, the colder the air became. More than once, Jelisette rubbed her arms as a sensation of death crawled over her.

It was no surprise that their prey had chosen this as his hiding place.

Neither she nor Emery spoke as they prowled through the darkness, going deeper and deeper into the mountain. As they moved, her shadows thrummed in her veins, her fangs burned, and every sense was on edge. In front of her, Emery wore black fighting leathers. His hair was slicked back, and shadows wreathed his hands.

He was a warrior of death, and she was drawn to him unlike anyone else. When he'd told her about this job, she got the sense he was worried this might scare her off. Nope. If anything, this was just confirmation for Jelisette that whatever was pulling her to Emery was right. Good.

Ever since her Making, Jelisette had never minded death. Maybe it was because of the brutal way she'd come into this immortal life, but it was a part of life. Normal. Good, even. And this werewolf they were hunting? He was evil incarnate. Watching the life drain from his eyes would be nothing but delightful.

Emery stalked in front of Jelisette, his movements smooth and calculated like a panther. She kept pace with him, her strides graceful and her footfalls silent.

Thorn wouldn't know what hit him.

Time slipped by.

They'd just passed a glowing cluster of blue mushrooms when Emery abruptly halted and held up a hand.

She obeyed, and moments later, she heard it. A feminine whimper. It was little more than a whisper on the wind coming from deep within the mountain, but it was like a wooden stake to her heart.

Not only was their prey here, but he had someone with him.

Anger was a living monster within Jelisette's veins. Flashes of memories she long kept buried forced their way to the forefront of her mind.

Large hands, holding her down. Begging for mercy. Heavy hips pinning her to the ground. Laughter when she cried. Pain. So much fucking pain.

Her heart raced in her chest. Each pulse was a drum, an echo of cries that had once slipped past her lips.

She'd been too weak to save herself that time long ago. Too weak to stop him.

Not fucking anymore. Now, Isvana's power ran through her veins. She was a creature of the night, meant for death and destruction. She would be damned if she allowed someone else to suffer in the same way she did.

Jelisette's shadows flooded out of her, darkening the space around her like a cloak of the night. Before her, Emery did the same. They were swathed in darkness, and they moved as one towards their prey. They did not have weapons because they didn't need them.

Each of their bodies was as lethal as a dozen mortal weapons. Knives and guns had nothing against their Ithiar-blessed bodies.

The cries grew louder.

Jelisette's anger throbbed in her veins. Her nails dug into her palms, leaving crescent moons behind.

"Faster," she hissed at Emery.

He took one look at her and nodded. They ran through the night, shadows streaming around them both as they moved with the speed of their kind. Jelisette would be damned if they were too late to save this woman, whoever she was.

Finally, after all these years, she had a purpose once more.

Seconds trickled by. Minutes? It didn't matter. Nothing did except the impending death of the horrible man they hunted.

Finally, they rounded the last corner.

Horror unfurled in Jelisette's stomach as she took in the scene before them. It was like reliving a nightmare.

Thorn was half-naked, wearing only a pair of jeans. His back muscles rippled, and his brown hair was pulled back as he towered over a rail-thin woman cowering in the corner.

The woman was frantically pulling her dress over her body and kicking weakly at the man. "Stop," she cried out. "Please."

Jelisette didn't wait to see anything else. She didn't look at Emery to ask if he had a plan, nor did she stop long enough to wonder whether the werewolf had any silver weapons that might harm her. She didn't do anything except snarl viciously at Thorn as she shed her cloak of darkness and launched herself at the werewolf.

Death was the only thing he deserved.

CHAPTER 6

Death was an Art Form

Emery had always considered himself a good killer. It wasn't exactly a title he enjoyed having, but he was an honest vampire, and he could admit the truth to himself.

But Jelisette?

She took death to another level. It was an art form. He watched her work, wholly impressed by the way she killed the werewolf.

She was violently gorgeous as she slammed her fangs into Thorn's throat. Beautiful as she clawed at him, pulling him away from the poor woman in the corner. Stunning as blood poured like a fountain from the werewolf's throat, coating her in red.

Right then, Emery knew he would do whatever it took to keep Jelisette de la Point by his side. How could he let such a magnificent creature go?

He was so enamored by the violent vampire in front of him that he didn't hear it. A whispered snarl behind him. A pebble skittering on shale. A warning.

Jelisette turned, a violent smile carved onto her face, as she let Thorn's mangled body fall.

"The bastard is—look out!"

Her eyes widened, and a mangled scream ripped through her as a bundle of fur leaped out of the darkness towards Emery. He stumbled back, lashing out with his shadows, but it wasn't enough to stop the clamp of teeth that locked onto his arm.

Searing, flaming pain ran through Emery's arm, and he roared. The wolf bit down harder, and black spots appeared in Emery's vision. He shook his arm and went to pull the beast off, but his movements were sluggish. Quiet.

The song of his shadows was... gone.

Alarm pulsed through Emery. Had the werewolf somehow injected him with prohiberis? The magic-blocking substance was a rare commodity in the Republic of Balance, known for its ability to incapacitate and halt all magic, even that of vampires. Shifters could still shift, their animals being a part of them, but vampires...

No.

The wolf tugged on Emery's arm, and he felt something break. He cried out.

Jelisette screamed.

Emery's eyes shut against his volition, and he fell to the ground.

More screams. Growling. The weight lifted from his arm, but the pain... it remained.

The last thing he heard before darkness claimed him was the snapping of a neck.

Then, there was nothing.

Sharp, deadly needles were being shoved into Emery's arm. Each was a fire, burning him alive from the inside out. He groaned.

"Hold still, Emery." Jelisette's voice was sharp and left no room for discussion.

As per her request, he didn't move, but he opened his eyes. That was a damned mistake. The movement sent pain lancing through him, and he groaned as he took in the familiar surroundings of his cave. He was on the middle of his mattress, and Jelisette crouched in front of him, wearing an oversized sweater and leggings.

"What happened?" he croaked. His shirt was gone, and blood covered his upper body.

"The wolf damn near tore your arm off," she mumbled, holding a threaded needle between her teeth. "Fucking pack animals. They're horrid. I shadowed the girl to the nearest hospital, then came back and brought you here."

Then, there were no more words as she took the needle and expertly wove it through his skin. She tugged and pulled, the skin drawing closed.

Emery couldn't help it. His fists clutched the sheet beneath him, and he *roared*. Every movement of the needle through his skin was like fire running through his flesh.

"Sorry." Her brows knit, and concern radiated from her black eyes. "This is the only way. I washed the wound with rubbing alcohol to get rid of any traces of prohiberis, but you aren't healing naturally."

Well, fuck. That wasn't good.

In all his years and all his encounters with venomous characters throughout the Republic of Balance, he'd never been injured like this. What if Jelisette hadn't been there? The wolf would've killed him. Although perhaps he wouldn't have minded.

But now? He didn't want to die. Not when he had finally found this vampire who had sparked a sense of life in him.

So Emery laid back, gritting his teeth and counting the crystals hanging from his cavern's roof as Jelisette sewed up his arm. She worked silently and swiftly, his grunts of pain the only sound for several long minutes.

When she finally sat back on her haunches, putting the bloody needle beside her, she pursed her lips. "It's probably going to scar." She frowned. "I'm sorry, I—"

"Don't." He reached out and took her hand. "Don't apologize. You saved my life."

He had been a fucking idiot, not checking the perimeter when they were searching for Thorn. Emery knew better. It wasn't like this had been his first hunt. He'd just been distracted by Jelisette's presence.

Next time, he'd do better. And there had to be a next time because he couldn't fathom letting her go. Not now.

Jelisette's black eyes searched his, and it was like she was staring into his soul. Emery had never felt like this before, never been so exposed and yet so... comfortable. He never wanted to put an end to this connection between them.

"It was a life worth saving," she said after a few minutes.

Emery smiled, and despite the pain running through him, he pushed himself up onto his elbows. "You were amazing," he said. "Watching you kill was... incredible."

Her cheeks reddened, and she lowered her lashes. "Thank you, that means a lot, coming from you."

Emery's hand was still on hers, and he squeezed. "I don't want you to leave, Jelisette."

"Well, obviously." She stared at the arm she'd just been stitching. "You'll need me to take those out."

He shook his head. "No. Not because of that." Perhaps a few hundred years ago, he would have waited longer before making a declaration like the one he was about to make, but Emery had nearly lived for a thousand years. He didn't want to waste any time. His heart was drawn to Jelisette, and he wanted her. All of her. "I want you to stay because I want you."

Her breath hitched. "You do?" There was a hint of shyness in her voice that drew him towards her like never before.

He nodded. "Yes." His voice was deep. "I think I've wanted you from the first moment we locked eyes across Starless Lake."

The pull between them had been present even then. It was why he'd left in such a rush—it had caught him off guard, and fleeing was the only thing he could think to do.

Another long moment passed before Jelisette's lips parted, and she dipped her head. "I'd like that very much."

"Thank the gods," Emery groaned.

Ignoring the pain running through him, he pushed himself up and drew her towards him. Their mouths crashed together in a kiss that was all tongues and teeth. It was not gentle, nor was it soft. Need radiated from them both as they kissed. Emery reached up with his good hand, weaving it through Jelisette's hair and holding her close as he devoured her.

He swept his tongue across the seam of her lips, and she opened for him with a moan. At the first taste of her, he groaned. She tasted like cinnamon, cloves, and the darkest night, and he couldn't get enough of it.

They kissed and kissed until Jelisette pulled away. Her chest heaved, and she rested her forehead against his. "As much as I enjoy this,"—she drew away just enough that he could see the twinkle in her eyes—"and I am enjoying this immensely, we haven't solved the problem as to why you aren't healing."

Emery's eyes widened, and he glanced down at his arm. He'd forgotten all about that. To be fair, he'd been rather preoccupied by something far more important.

"I think I need to feed," he admitted.

The blood in Jelisette's apartment a week ago had been enough to hold him over, but when vampires were injured, they often needed fresh blood to heal properly.

She studied him before nodding. "I think so, too." A long moment passed as she trailed her fingers up his arm. "We could find you a Source, or..." Her voice trailed off, and she shook her head. "No, that's crazy."

Emery's brows furrowed. "What's crazy? You can tell me."

He didn't think anything Jelisette could do or say anything that would ever put him off.

Jelisette frowned. Drawing her legs up onto the bed, she sat cross-legged and took his hand in hers. "I was thinking... but I don't know... it seems insane."

In all the time he'd known her—which, admittedly, wasn't that long—Emery hadn't heard her speak in circles like this. "Tell me, please."

She chewed on her lip for a long moment before blurting, "IwasthinkingmaybeyoumightwanttoBindyourselftomeandthenneitherofuswouldneedtogetanotherSource."

He blinked. "You want to Bind yourself to me?"

Emery knew what a Binding was, of course. Every vampire did. Bindings were rare, sacred events that brought two (or more) souls together beneath Isvana's sacred touch. They were eternal, unbreakable commitments. If done with a human, as it was long ago when the Last King and Queen were Bound, it extended the mortal's lifespan to match the vampire. When vampires were Bound, they didn't need any other Sources.

The only thing more permanent and life-changing than a Binding was a Tether.

"Well, I thought... but maybe... it was stupid. Never mind." Jelisette moved as if to dart off the bed.

Emery grabbed her arm and tugged her back. "Don't go," he said gruffly. "Please. I want to do it."

If someone had asked him a month ago if he would ever Bind himself to someone, he would've laughed in their face. What a ridiculous notion. But now? He was all in. Jelisette had seen him at his worst —twice now—and she was still here. What more could he ask for?

It felt like an entire year passed before Jelisette nodded. "Okay. Good. Let's do it." She rolled up her sleeve and moved towards him. "We should do it now so you can heal."

He wouldn't argue with that. The pain of the wolf's bite was radiating through him, and each moment was worse than the last. He wasn't sure if a werewolf could kill a vampire, but he was not interested in finding out.

Emery shifted on the bed, moving so his back was against the headboard, and he looked over at Jelisette. The crystals glowed all around her, giving her a radiant aura. She was absolutely gorgeous, and she was going to be his.

"Have you witnessed a Binding before?" he asked Jelisette.

She shook her head. "No, have you?"

"No, but I have a book around here somewhere that talks about it." His gaze swiveled around his home before he found the title he sought. "There. The third one from the bottom."

Usually, Isvana's Chosen priests and priestesses performed Bindings, but it wasn't a requirement.

Jelisette slid off the bed, her movements lithe as she crossed the cave and found the book. "*Isvana's Blessings: A Recounting of Bindings and Tetherings throughout The Three Eras.* Well, this reading material is... delightful."

It *was* delightful. Emery had a variety of books, both fiction and non-fiction, to suit all his literary needs. However, he recognized that perhaps not everyone enjoyed reading as much as him.

Jelisette brought the book over, and Emery flipped through it with his good hand until he found the passage he was looking for. He read it quickly, then nodded. At his direction, Jelisette found a cup before taking a seat beside him.

"This shouldn't hurt," he said.

She smiled. "I don't care if it hurts. I'm ready."

So was he.

Keeping the book open, Emery turned to Jelisette. "You're sure?"

It wasn't like they could go back after this.

"A thousand percent. Let's do this." Without waiting for him to respond, she brought her wrist to her mouth and bit. She pulled her mouth away, and crimson trickled into the cup she held underneath her arm. The skin healed quickly, and then Jelisette turned to Emery.

He already had his good wrist in his mouth. His fangs broke the skin with ease, and he quickly held his wrist over the cup, adding his scarlet contribution to the drink.

As his blood trickled into the cup, Jelisette held the book open on her lap. Her voice was melodic and smooth as she read the Binding spell. It had been translated into the Common Tongue, the words heavy and archaic as she read them. Magic thickened the air, and shadows slipped from her palms.

Then, she turned to Emery. "It's time," she murmured.

He took the cup wordlessly, his gaze locked on hers as he lifted it to his lips. The blood was warm as it slid down his throat, and he groaned at the delicious flavors flooding his mouth. Her blood was everything he'd tasted in her mouth but amplified a hundred times over. It was ambrosia, the most delicious thing he'd ever tasted, and he wanted more. He needed it.

Already, he was beginning to feel better. The pain in his arm was less pronounced, and it felt like he could breathe.

Jelisette took the goblet, swiftly drinking the rest of the blood. The moment the cup was empty, warmth spread through Emery. It started in his chest and quickly spread through all of him. The song of his shadows grew louder and louder until their thrumming beat was the only thing he could hear. Magic rushed through the air, and Emery's skin tingled as the Binding took effect.

He took over the reading, speaking the final words of the spell. "Two are becoming one. Bound together through eternity. Never to be undone."

The tang of magic thickened as he spoke the final words, and a flash of crimson light burst from both their palms. The magic twisted around their wrists, tightening as it sank into them.

Then, just as quickly as the crimson light had appeared, the magic vanished. In its place, an intricate black swirling tattoo formed a permanent bracelet on Emery's wrist. A glance up confirmed that Jelisette had a matching one on hers. Both were as thick as three fingers put together, a mark to all the world that they were Bound.

Jelisette closed the book with a resounding *thud* and turned towards Emery. Her black eyes gleamed, and she whispered, "Bite me, Emery. Take what you need."

This time, Emery didn't ask if she was sure. He wouldn't do her that disservice. Instead, he wound his hand behind her head and slowly pulled her towards him. His Bound Partner arched her neck, giving him clear access. He licked his fangs and, with a groan, surged forward.

CHAPTER 7
Forever

Emery's fangs sank into Jelisette's neck with ease. There wasn't even a pinprick of pain. His sharpened teeth slid into her like they'd always belonged there.

She moaned, her fingers curling on the comforter as she inched closer to him. There was no pain or discomfort. Just pure, endless bliss.

Maybe—just maybe—Jelisette could understand why Justus was always talking about his partners. If this was what it would feel like every time Emery drank from her...

Gods. Just the thought sent a thrill of pleasure through her. He drank, pulling deep draws of her blood, and she sank into the bliss he provided her. His arms wrapped around her, and she let him hold her as her body became boneless.

This was *everything*.

Jelisette let him take as much as he needed. Bound Partners could not take too much from the other—theirs was a relationship created by the goddess herself.

The Binding Mark on Jelisette's arm tingled, and she knew the Isvana-blessed magic that now tied them together would keep them both safe. Their bodies, their blood, and their souls were now Bound.

And she was... happy.

Gods, it felt good to say that. Jelisette hadn't made many rash decisions in her life, but deciding to come with Emery to his home had been the best one she'd ever made.

Eventually, he lifted his fangs from her neck. Red stained his mouth, and Jelisette watched as he licked them clean.

"You taste fucking amazing," Emery growled. The wound on his arm was healed, and his eyes shone a deeper black than before. He moved closer until there was barely an inch between them, and his breath warmed her lips. "Like the darkest night, and I can't get enough of it."

She licked her lips, studying him carefully. "What do you want, Emery?"

His eyes darkened until the night itself seemed to bleed around them. "You," he growled.

The meaning of his words was clear, and they sent a deep flurry of want through Jelisette.

"Do you feel—"

Before she could finish the question, Emery's mouth had crashed into hers. He kissed her like she was the only thing he needed to live; like he was starving, and kissing her would keep him alive. There was nothing gentle or kind or soft about this embrace, but Jelisette didn't need that.

"I'll take that as a yes," she murmured, lifting her lips off his long enough to talk. "I want you, too, Emery."

The words were an unleashing.

His mouth slammed into hers once more. Jelisette moaned. He groaned. Lips and tongues and teeth danced in a tale as old as time itself. Hands wandered. Clothes disappeared, ending up all over the cave.

It didn't matter.

The only thing that mattered was the man before Jelisette.

Emery's eyes darkened as he stretched her out before him. "You're gods-damned amazing, love," he growled.

He bent, kissing and licking and sucking his way down her body. He lavished her with attention, and her head fell back with a moan.

Love.

Was that what lay between them? She wasn't sure, but maybe... maybe it did.

Her heart certainly felt fuller than it had before they met, her life more complete, and her soul more right.

Maybe this was love.

One thing was certain: their Binding would keep them together forever. If one Bound partner died before the other, it would rip their souls in two.

So they wouldn't die.

Jelisette would protect Emery with everything she had, and vice versa. They would be everything for each other, partners in every way.

Then her thoughts were no more because Emery's marked wrist traveled down, dipping into her wet core.

She gasped, arching her back as he drew her closer and closer to pleasure. He was skilled with his touch, and soon, she was moaning his name.

"Close," she gasped. "So close."

His eyes darkened, and he dragged his fangs over her inner thigh. The pressure of his teeth, the promise of what would one day come, was enough to make her shatter.

Waves of pleasure ran through Jelisette as Emery moved, fitting himself between her thighs. He bent, his mouth claiming hers in a searing kiss as his hard length slid into her.

"You're mine," she murmured against his lips. "Forever."

"Forever," he agreed.

Words were no longer needed between them as they climbed and climbed towards their peak together. They were two, joined as one. Bound and Blessed by Isvana and Ithiar.

Nothing would ever tear them apart.

The End

A Heart of Desire and Deceit

ELAYNA R. GALLEA

To anyone whose heart has been stomped on and broken into pieces,
this one's for you.

Author's note

A Heart of Desire and Deceit is a new adult fantasy romance set in a secondary world setting.

I never want my content to be harmful to any of my readers. This is a dystopian world, and there are certain situations that may be triggering, including violence and death.

For a full list of content notes, please visit: https://www.elaynargal lea.com/contentnotes.

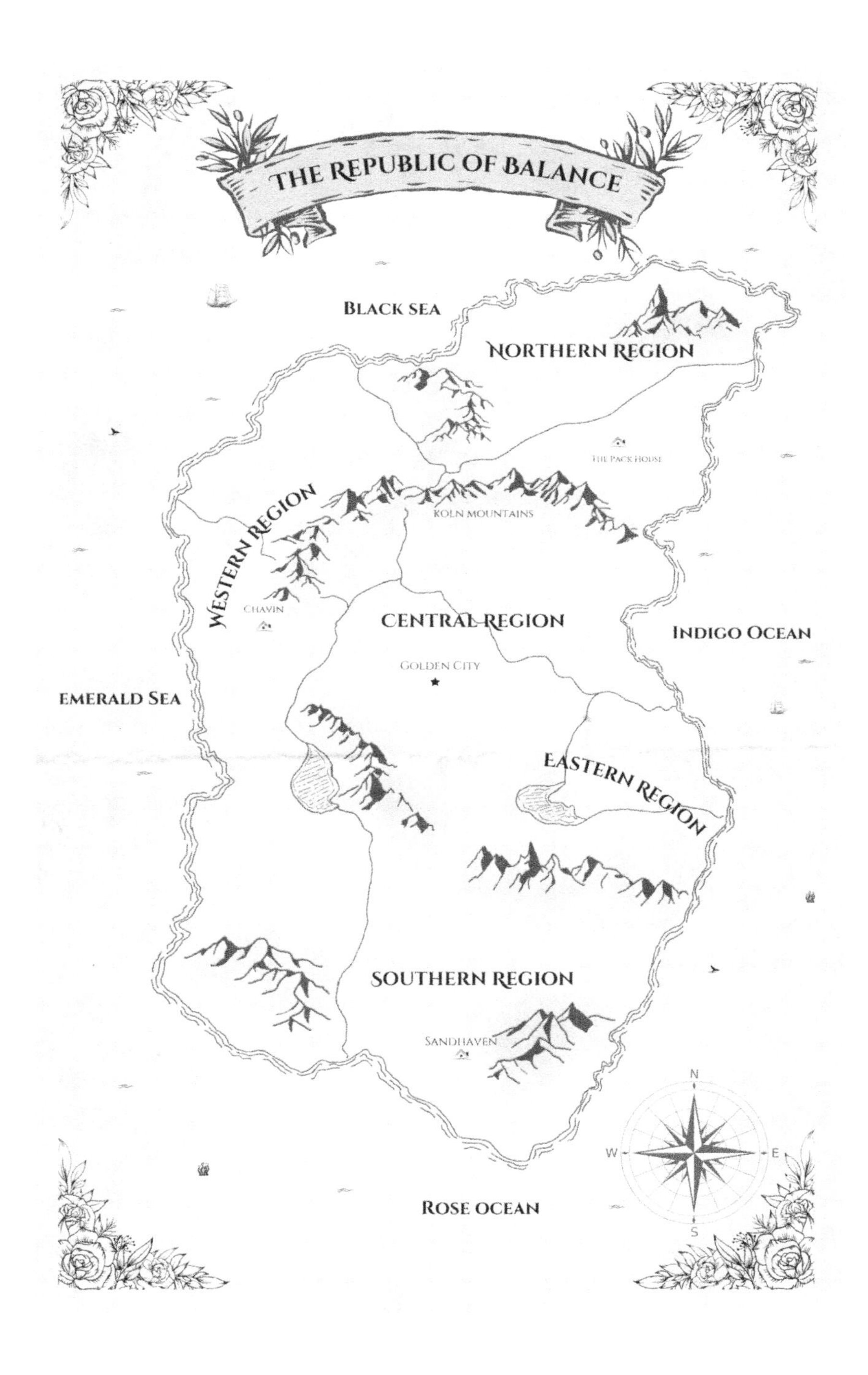
THE REPUBLIC OF BALANCE
BLACK SEA
NORTHERN REGION
THE PACK HOUSE
WESTERN REGION
KOLN MOUNTAINS
CHAVIN
CENTRAL REGION
INDIGO OCEAN
GOLDEN CITY
EMERALD SEA
EASTERN REGION
SOUTHERN REGION
SANDHAVEN
N
W
E
S
ROSE OCEAN

Blurb

How does one pick up the pieces of their life after it has been obliterated by the person they mistakingly trusted?

Ryker Waterborn's heart is broken, and his wife is a killer. Their marriage is a sham, built on a foundation of murder, lies, and deceit. They're broken. Destroyed. Yet, even after hearing her confession, Ryker cannot leave Brynleigh in the Pit.

In an act of foolish love, he makes a deal to set Brynleigh free. All she has to do is go back to her Maker and find evidence that Jelisette de la Point is a traitor.

That's easier said than done, but Brynleigh is left with no choice. She can either accept the deal or rot behind bars. Worse than all that is her relationship with Ryker.

Once, she thought they'd get a happy ending. Now, an ocean divides them.

She broke the rules and fell in love, but is love powerful enough to save them?

CHAPTER 1
An Aching Heart

Staring at his broken wife through what he hoped were dispassionate eyes, Ryker attempted to quell the racing of his aching, broken heart. For three weeks, the fae captain had existed in a state of anger and disbelief, unwilling and unable to accept the truth of what had occurred on his wedding night.

His beautiful, intelligent, intriguing vampire had lied to him.

She'd played him for a gods-damned fucking fool.

Ryker knew that was true. He understood it in the same way that someone understood that the sky was blue, flowers bloomed in the spring, and the sun rose in the east every morning.

That understanding did nothing to dispel the absolute agony coursing through him like a raging river during a thunderstorm. It did not heal his brokenness.

Every breath was like inhaling shards of shattered glass. Every pulse of his pulverized heart was like throwing salt in an open wound. Every single second was worse than the last.

Broken.

They were so fucking broken.

Once, they'd been whole. Better than that, they'd been *one*. But

Brynleigh had taken what they'd carefully formed during the Choosing and shattered it.

Ryker didn't know how to fix this. He didn't even know if it could be done. When he surveyed the shattered pieces of his heart, which had been a daily endeavor since their wedding night, all he felt was soul-deep pain and burning anger.

He had no idea how to put his heart back together. Was it even possible to pick up the remnants of his life after the one person he'd mistakenly trusted obliterated it?

Right now, that seemed impossible.

Brynleigh's black eyes were wide, and she was staring at him as though he were a ghost. Her face, pale on a good day, was as white as a fresh snowfall. Her hands trembled against the manacles binding her to the chair, and her chapped lips opened and closed repeatedly.

She rasped, her voice rough and scratchy like she'd been screaming for hours, "You... you're dead."

By the Obsidian Sands, Ryker wished that were the case. Death would have been easier than this.

Agony was a spear lancing through him, stealing his breath, as he truly looked upon the woman he'd married for the first time since entering this gods-forsaken place.

A galaxy of black and blue bruises mottled every exposed inch of Brynleigh's skin. Dried blood crusted her face and arms. One of her eyes was nearly swollen shut. Her hair was matted and greasy, and the once-blonde ends were rusty. Her black, ill-fitting jumpsuit was covered in dirt and other substances.

She looked... bad.

Ryker had been around enough prisoners to know this was normal, but to see the woman he loved like this—

No.

The prisoner before him wasn't the woman he'd fallen in love with. This wasn't the woman he'd Chosen. *That* woman, the one he'd spoken with for hours on end and broken rules for, was a different person. One who, apparently, had never existed.

Ryker gritted his teeth. Brynleigh had lied to him, yet no matter how many times he told himself she'd played him, he still couldn't believe this nightmare was real.

How had everything turned out so horribly?

"No, I'm not dead." His voice was a low growl as he answered her previous question. It seemed to echo in the windowless cell.

Ryker had to get a grip. He was a soldier, for the gods' sake. Emotions did not belong in a place like this.

Forcing a mask of composure on his face, he hardened his eyes and steadied his heart. Even though his hands twitched at his sides with the need to rip off the silver shackles, gather Brynleigh in his arms, and take her away, he was a statue.

If Ryker had known Victor Orpheus had been put in charge of the fucking interrogation, he would have stopped it earlier. The sadistic fae couldn't be trusted with anyone, let alone Ryker's... his... Brynleigh.

But Ryker hadn't known. He hadn't wanted to know.

Grief had been an ocean, and he'd been drowning in it for three weeks.

He'd barely breathed, barely slept, barely thought. All he'd done was work, work, work.

Ryker had allowed his soldierly duties to bury him. Better that than to feel his emotions. The anger. The frustration. The grief. They had all battered against him like endless waves until he'd ignored them entirely.

He hadn't even seen his wife until now. He hadn't asked about her, which, in hindsight, was a grave mistake.

Fuck, he hadn't even known she was being held in The Pit.

Like a gods-damned idiot, Ryker had assumed Brynleigh would be incarcerated in either Silver or Black Prison. If that had been the case, he would've come and dealt with her once his anger cooled off. If it had cooled off.

But The Pit?

Gods-damned awful, terrible, nightmarish things happened here. This place was reserved for the worst of the worst.

And his wife was here.

A prisoner who, if the bruises and prohiberis manacles were any indication, was being tortured daily.

His heart twisted into a painful knot as he studied his wife.

His lying, deceitful wife.

Conflicted was too simple of a word to describe how he felt about the hell where he currently resided.

Ryker hadn't known a heart could hurt like this. He hadn't known that in the blink of an eye, love could evolve into a monster hell-bent on destroying him from within.

Brynleigh inhaled sharply, the sound drawing Ryker from his thoughts. She blinked, a trail of crimson running down her leg from where a silver knife was lodged in her thigh.

"H-h-how?"

How indeed.

Stepping back, he forced that steel mask he'd donned earlier to remain in place. He had replayed those moments with horrifying clarity a hundred times since that fateful night.

Still, his next words tasted like ash as he forced them out of his dry mouth. "I wasn't asleep."

Time and again, he'd analyzed that night, but it still felt like the worst kind of nightmare.

THE DIPPING of the mattress drew Ryker out of his slumber. The fae captain cracked open an eye, watching his beautiful vampire strode towards the window with predatory, silent grace. Gods above, she was stunning. His cock hardened as he studied her. He'd had her twice before they fell asleep a few hours ago, but he still wanted her. He suspected he'd always want her.

She was his.

Brynleigh drew the curtain shut and turned towards the bed. Instead of coming back, she froze. Her back straightened, and she inhaled sharply.

The air in the room shifted; a too-quiet calm before a storm.

Ryker opened both eyes and followed Brynleigh's gaze. A frown tugged at his lips. A cat was in the room. Strange. He blinked, wondering if he was dreaming, but the feline was still there when he looked again.

His magic swirled in his veins. A warning. A harbinger. A premonition of what was to come.

It was too little, too late.

Before Ryker could act, a flash of white light erupted from the cat-that-wasn't-a-cat.

In a heartbeat, Ryker's world turned upside down once again.

This was the moment he couldn't stop thinking about, the one that had haunted his nightmares, the one that had him questioning every single thing Brynleigh had ever told him.

A redheaded man stood a few feet away from Brynleigh, and she... wasn't screaming. Why the fuck wasn't she screaming?

Ryker's heart thundered like a bear banging against the bars of its cage. He recognized the newcomer from the Masked Ball as the man who'd danced with Brynleigh.

Danger, danger, danger.

A roaring filled his ears.

Shocked, he listened as Brynleigh conversed with the shifter. As if she wasn't surprised by his arrival.

As if she had... expected him.

Icy horror coursed through Ryker's veins, freezing him in place and forcing him to watch as his new wife of less than twenty-four hours betrayed him. The one person he thought he could trust, the one person to whom he'd given his heart, took it and ripped it to shreds.

He couldn't move, couldn't think, couldn't do anything at all except listen.

"Love makes us do stupid things," the shifter said. "I should know."

What did that mean?

Brynleigh reached out a hand towards the shifter as if in protest. "What? Don't—"

"I'm sorry, B." The man's voice hardened, the promise of violence clear in his voice.

Danger, danger, danger.

The fae captain gave up pretending to be asleep and threw off the blanket.

He was too late.

Brynleigh shouted, "No—"

A flash of silver filled the space, and then something popped.

Brynleigh screamed, the high-pitched sound forever ingraining itself in Ryker's memory. She fell to the ground with a loud thud, her limp body covered in blood. The life-giving substance streamed endlessly from her chest. He'd always remember that, too.

How could he forget the worst moments of his life?

The next few minutes were a blur.

Ryker formed ice daggers, one in each hand. He leaped out of bed, and instincts took over his movements.

The shifter came at him, his murderous intent clear.

Ryker didn't even remember fighting the other man. All he knew, all he cared about, was that he won.

The shifter was still alive when Ryker was done with him, but he would probably wish for death soon enough.

After Ryker knocked the shifter out and tied him up, he called for backup. He managed to get the request out without his voice shaking, which was a gods-damned miracle.

And then he went to Brynleigh's side.

Crimson rivers flowed from her chest, staining everything in sight. There was so much fucking blood.

Ryker didn't stop to think about what he was doing as he fell to his knees. He didn't think about her betrayal because if he did, he might break.

His military training had him reaching inside her chest and pulling out the prohiberis bullet. He didn't think the magic-blocking metal could kill a vampire, but he didn't want to find out.

Even now, after everything, she was still... his.

Ryker chucked the bloody bullet across the room. It clinked, colliding with the wall. He didn't bother to see where it landed.

He gathered Brynleigh in his arms, her blood coating them both as the wound in her stomach slowly stitched itself together.

They had one, maybe two minutes before the others arrived.

Pressure built behind Ryker's eyes, and he finally allowed the full weight of what happened to hit him. The shifter came to kill him, and Brynleigh knew.

She *knew.*

He stared at his vampire through a watery curtain, brushing back her hair with a trembling finger. "How could you do this to us?"

He thought he knew her. He thought he loved her. He thought she was his.

Wrong. He'd been fucking wrong.

There was no response. She just lay in his arms, looking far too broken for someone who had caused him so much pain.

With every beat of Ryker's heart, an ache expanded in his chest. It started small but yawned until it was the size of a canyon.

A tear fell on Brynleigh's cheek, and Ryker whispered, "How could you break us?"

Thick, unnatural silence covered them.

She didn't answer him, and he didn't ask again. He just... held her close.

One last time. One last hug. And then, he would let her go. He had to. She'd betrayed him. He'd already deduced that much from her earlier conversation.

How much worse could things get? Her deception was already a bitter river flowing through his veins.

A minute passed, but it could have been a lifetime. The door swung open. Reinforcements were here.

A buzzing filled Ryker's mind. He was present, but not. When arms reached down to pull Brynleigh out of Ryker's embrace, he didn't fight them. He didn't even say goodbye.

Ryker watched as the Chancellor's military police took his vampire and the murderous shifter into custody. He didn't attempt to stop them as they assessed the scene, took pictures, and spoke among themselves.

He pulled on a pair of sweatpants, answered their questions—there were so many fucking questions—and promised to come down to the station later.

Eventually, the reinforcements left.

The door closed behind the last officer, and Ryker was alone. Yesterday had been the happiest day of his life, and now...

Crimson covered everything in sight. The floor. The bed. His hands.

Ryker lifted his fingers, staring at them until red was the only thing he could see.

Then he felt it.

Anguish wormed its way into the depth of his being. At first, it was just a crack, distant and barely there.

Then, he drew in a pained breath.

The crack exploded. Like ice breaking in the middle of a frozen lake, it rippled, fissured, and shattered.

He shattered.

Devastating, world-ending, soul-crushing heartbreak consumed him.

It was like he was made of sand, and his heartbreak was the water crashing into him again and again and again. The waves kept going until he was completely, utterly destroyed.

Falling to his knees on the bloody carpet, Ryker lifted his head to the heavens and *roared*.

"Oh," Brynleigh breathed, her voice pulling Ryker back to the present. "Then, you... saw." She swallowed, and her black eyes dimmed. "You heard?"

A lump formed in his throat, and the pain in her eyes caused his heart to twist. That was a gods-damned emotion that he had no business feeling.

Not here. Not now. Not with *her*.

Red tinged his vision, and his nostrils flared. Every beat of his heart sang the same horrible song.

Betrayed, betrayed, betrayed.

His heartbeat was a booming drum. Even his body refused to let him forget that he'd made a monumentally bad Choice.

Part of Ryker knew that Brynleigh belonged in The Pit. Although this place was horrible, she'd been planning on killing him.

Not only that, but ties had been uncovered linking Jelisette de la Point, Brynleigh's Maker, to the Black Night. The rebel group was responsible for the bombing at the Masked Ball, as well as several other incidents that had taken place over the decades.

Rules and laws existed for a reason. Prisons were designed to keep bad people inside, and all signs from the past three weeks pointed to the fact that Ryker's wife was not a good person.

But the other part of Ryker—the part that fucking loved Brynleigh—was dying at the sight of her in this place of death. That part was overriding his anger, screaming for him to take action and save her.

He thought he understood pain, but nothing could have prepared him for this.

By the Obsidian Sands, he had heard Brynleigh's confession. He had listened as she admitted to everything, from being a fucking vigilante to plotting to kill him.

Ryker should despise her. He should want her dead and out of his life for good. He should be happy she was so broken.

But he wasn't happy.

Not. At. All.

Gods damn it all, but he didn't even hate her. He was angry with her—so fucking angry that his magic was a barely contained storm in his veins—but hate? He didn't even know if he could, now that he'd given her his heart.

And didn't that just make him the biggest fucking fool of them all?

"Yes, I did," Ryker said calmly, falling back on years of military training.

He would not let her see the turmoil that existed beneath his skin, nor would he let her know the depth of his deep-seated pain or the currents of anger coursing through him.

Brynleigh's black eyes shuttered, and her shoulders slumped. Her head hung low, and matted hair curtained her face. As if she was sorry. As if she wasn't the one who had wanted to kill him.

Fuck, that anger was coming back.

He forced himself to breathe. He was so busy not screaming that he barely heard her next words.

"I understand," she said softly, her voice as broken as his heart. "I couldn't... After our wedding... I changed my..."

She drew in a shuddering breath but still didn't meet his eyes.

He didn't say anything. He couldn't.

After a few minutes, she continued, her words even softer. "In the end, I wasn't going to..."

Her voice trailed off, and she mumbled something too low for him to hear.

"What?" The word slipped out of him, harsh and booming.

Brynleigh jumped, her arms pulled against the restraints, and then a half-sob, half-sigh left her lips.

"Forget about it," she whispered. "It doesn't matter."

He stared at her, his heart racing as he tried to process her words.

Not matter? How could she say that?

Nothing mattered *more* than this. She had wanted to kill him, for the gods' sake.

Never, in all his years, had he been this hurt. This angry. This fucking destroyed.

By Brynleigh's own admission, she had spent years crafting a meticulous plan designed to end Ryker's life. She *was* a killer.

Not in the way that all vampires had blackness in their hearts. That would have been one thing.

But no.

She truly was a bringer of death. She'd sought to bring about his death.

And yet...

I wasn't going to...

Her words echoed in Ryker's head, and despite everything he knew, despite everything he'd learned, he couldn't stop thinking about them.

It took everything he had not to scream his frustrations to the heavens.

Over the past three hellish weeks, Ryker had steadily ignored thoughts about his treacherous wife and instead conducted a deep dive into her Maker. The things he'd discovered had painted a clear picture of exactly who the vampire was, and it wasn't pretty.

Ryker hadn't even had time to train his sister River—not that he wanted to face his family right now—but he was keeping up with the updates Gabriel, another water fae in the army, was sending him. Thank the gods, Gabriel had been willing to help train River. Ryker didn't want his sister to suffer because his personal life was imploding.

Earlier, Ryker had been stepping out of the shower, preparing to review the tapes of the shifter's interrogation for the tenth time that day, when his phone vibrated.

NIKHAIL

Get to The Pit, Ryker. She's going to talk.

A stone had lodged itself in the captain's stomach as he read his best friend's message. His fingers had curled around the phone, and the metal cracked before he realized how tightly he was holding it.

Ryker hadn't had time to consider why Brynleigh was in The Pit and not in a less dangerous prison. He threw on some clothes and raced over to the dungeon, breaking a dozen speeding laws to get there as quickly as possible.

He arrived just in time to hear his wife confess everything. He thought she'd admit her involvement with the rebels—after all, learning about her involvement with the Black Night was the reason she'd been subjected to this level of interrogation in the first place—but the words she'd spoken had been so much worse.

Brynleigh had wanted to kill him.

Her plan had been simple and terrifyingly dark. She'd make Ryker fall in love with her, and then she'd kill him on their wedding night.

Every word had curdled his stomach until he felt like he'd ingested a gallon of spoiled milk. He wanted to believe she was lying, but in his gut, he knew she was telling the truth. There were too many similarities between her story and the one Zanri Olyt, the shifter who'd attacked Ryker, had shared.

And that meant that Ryker's wife truly had plotted against him in the worst possible ways.

Instead of stopping her, he had served her his unguarded heart on a silver platter.

A smarter fae would have heard her confession and walked away, content to let her die for her crimes. Up until a few months ago, Ryker would have said he was a smart fae.

It turned out that he was the biggest gods-damned idiot of them all.

I wasn't going to...

Those four words echoed in his mind on a never-ending track.

He should leave. He should kill her for what she did. He should yell.

He should scream. He should punch the walls. He should turn around and never, ever come back.

Everything he had left—his family and his job—pulled at him to go out those doors without a second glance. A smarter fae would've done just that.

But he couldn't get his mind off those words. He couldn't ignore them and let his anger win.

If there was even the slightest chance that Ryker hadn't been wrong, that he hadn't married a cold-blooded, merciless killer, that the woman he loved somehow had existed, then he couldn't leave.

Seeing her here, broken and bleeding, hurt more than her betrayal. More than her deceit. More than watching her bleed out on the carpet in their hotel room. More than the anger burning a hole in his chest.

He couldn't turn and walk away, abandoning her to die.

A risky, stupid plan formed in Ryker's mind. It was foolish, could potentially cost him the job he loved, and was likely something he'd regret in the future, but it was the path he needed to take.

His stupid heart, with its stupid need to protect those he loved, wouldn't let him do anything else.

Consequences be damned. He'd deal with those later.

Making up his mind, Ryker took one last look at his broken wife, hardened his heart, and walked to the door.

Brynleigh's rattling breaths spurred him onwards. They must've done something to her to keep her in this state without succumbing to the bloodlust Fledglings often fell into. Victor liked to work with a witch. Ryker wouldn't be surprised if she'd used her magic to keep Brynleigh mentally sane so she could endure more torture.

The thought, like many others from the past few weeks, made him see red.

Palming his phone, Ryker unlocked it and navigated to his messages. His fingers slid over the screen as he texted a number he'd memorized years ago.

Representative Challard wasn't someone he interacted with often, but in this case, she might be the only person capable of helping him.

Once the message was ready, Ryker read it, adjusted a few words, and pressed send.

A moment later, his phone vibrated.

MYRRAH

Are you sure?

RYKER

Yes.

He was certain of very few things these days, but this was one of them. Brynleigh would not spend another night in this prison.

Okay. I'll arrange it.

That was all he needed to hear. Taking a deep breath, he opened the door.

Victor Orpheus leaned against the double-sided mirror, a sneer twisting his lips as he glared at Brynleigh through the glass.

Gods, Ryker hated the man. Orpheus was one of the worst soldiers in the entire army. He had climbed through the ranks thanks to his cunning duplicity, and his taste for blood and torture was well-known.

More than one prisoner had mysteriously died after spending time in Orpheus' interrogation chambers.

But Ryker couldn't touch Victor. Not right now. He had to focus on getting Brynleigh out of there.

Standing in the doorway, Ryker let authority ripple around him. Orpheus might be a powerful fae, but Ryker was the son of a Representative, and he was born to power. Right now, he let the other fae see exactly how displeased he was by the prisoner's mistreatment.

"I'm taking her." Ryker held up his phone, flashing the message from Representative Challard.

He wasn't asking for permission, nor did he require it.

Perhaps sensing that his interrogation had gone too far, Victor did not push the captain. Instead, he simply pulled something out of his pocket, put his hand between them, and said, "Good luck."

Ryker's eyes narrowed as he stared at Victor's extended hand. Disgust twisted his insides, and his primal instincts had him wanting to kill the other man for touching what was his. He buried those instincts, though.

This needed to be quick and simple.

Maintaining his emotionless mask, Ryker slid his hand into the other fae's. Victor's palm was cold, and it took everything Ryker had not to shiver.

"Thanks." Ryker closed his fist around the metal key Victor had slipped him.

Without sparing the other fae another glance, Ryker grabbed a small bag of blood from the cooler by the door and stepped back into the cell.

Black, pain-filled eyes rose and met his.

For a single moment, it was like he and Brynleigh were back at the Masked Ball.

Two souls, already connected, but seeing each other for the first time.

Everything else faded away. The dungeon, the silver blade, the blood, even the fae behind the glass.

For a moment, it was just the two of them.

For a moment, it was good.

Then, somewhere in the bowels of the dungeon, someone screamed.

The moment shattered like a broken window.

Brynleigh inhaled sharply, and a tear rolled down her cheek before she closed her eyes.

She dared cry after she planned to murder him? How fucking hypocritical. He was the one she'd wanted to kill, yet he wasn't crying.

Ryker was just... angry. With himself. With her. With the world.

Everything they'd shared was gone. Their moments were in the past. Now, they were just two broken people.

With that depressing thought in mind, he slowly approached the chair. Her eyes opened, and her lips parted, but she was silent. Maybe that was better.

Ryker's heart leaped as he drew near, but he pointedly ignored that feeling. It had no place here.

He uncapped the blood, and her eyes followed him greedily.

It wasn't a lot, and it certainly wouldn't be enough to fix everything that had been done to her, but he didn't want her to faint or worse before he got her out.

Ryker went to hand the blood to Brynleigh when he realized her hands were still bound. Wondering exactly how he'd ended up here, offering his tortured, murderous wife blood, he raised the drink to her mouth.

Her chapped lips closed around the top, and in under a minute, she'd sucked the bag dry. A slight touch of color returned to her cheeks.

Just enough to remind him she was still alive.

"I… thank you," she breathed.

He grunted in response. He didn't give her the blood to be kind. It was a precautionary measure. That was it.

Reaching over, he yanked the silver blade out of her leg. The situation was eerily similar to when he'd pulled the bullet out of her only weeks ago, and a shudder ran through him as he threw the knife away.

Brynleigh hitched a breath, but Ryker didn't dare meet her gaze. Not again.

He wasn't sure if he'd see a dream or a nightmare within the depth of her eyes, but either way, he wasn't ready.

Ryker crouched and focused on unlocking the prohiberis manacles binding her to the chair. They fell away, exposing reddened, bleeding flesh.

"Can you stand?" he asked, surprised that his voice was smooth and lacked any hint of all the emotions he was ignoring.

Maybe he could do this.

She sucked in a breath and shook her head. "I… don't know."

Gods damn it all, but her words were like knives to his gut.

It was harder than ever to keep that mask in place.

He held out a hand and briskly said, "Try."

The command echoed through the room, laced with the innate power of his position.

She didn't fight him. Her bloody hand trembled as she lifted it off the armrest. Her fingers shook as they landed in his, and like the first time they'd touched, sparks ran through him.

Forcing those sparks far, far away, he focused on her hand. He couldn't help but notice the dirt coating her fingers, the broken fingernails, and the dried blood caked on her exposed flesh.

Gods, he would kill Victor for this. Not today, and probably not tomorrow, but one day, he would destroy him.

Who had authorized letting this monster loose on Ryker's wife? Rebel or not, she didn't deserve this treatment.

No one deserved this.

Brynleigh whimpered, "That hurts."

Wide-eyed, Ryker looked down, realizing he had an iron grip on her frail fingers. A curse that would've made even the most battle-hardened soldier blush slipped from his lips, and he loosened his hold.

As if she were a hundred and not twenty-nine, Brynleigh slowly pushed herself to her feet. Whatever magic Victor's witch had been using to keep the Fledgling vampire at bay seemed to have drained Brynleigh's strength. She trembled, her legs barely straightening, before her knees buckled.

"Fuck." Ryker caught her before she could slam into the ground. "I've got you."

That was the last straw. She wouldn't be spending another hour in this prison. They should've brought her somewhere else. Somewhere civilized.

Maybe if he'd surfaced from his grief and anger long enough to wonder where she was, he could've prevented this.

But it was too late for maybes.

As Ryker wrapped his arms around Brynleigh and cradled her to his chest, he noted her skin's frigid temperature. The opposite of a fever, it was like she was made of ice. Her skin was so pale beneath the blood and bruises that it was almost translucent.

He carried her towards the door and clung to the only truth he knew for certain: he wouldn't let her die.

Even though she had planned to kill him, even though she'd ripped out his heart and stomped all over it, she was still his.

She'd always be his.

CHAPTER 2

Death Would Bring her Peace

A *few minutes ago*

Brynleigh had been a fool to think she would never break under her tormenters' hands.

It turned out that all it took was three weeks of continuous torture to reduce her from a functioning vampire to nothing but a physical embodiment of pain.

There wasn't a single part of her that didn't hurt. Her soul, her body, and her heart were all so broken and bruised that she couldn't remember what life had been like before everything ached.

When Ryker asked if she could stand, Brynleigh barely stopped herself from laughing. Standing was the least of her problems. Breathing through the pain was nearly impossible.

After being surrounded by prohiberis for so long, she was nothing but a mortal suffering from endless torture.

Emilia, the witch, had done something to Brynleigh. She must have used her magic to stop the adverse effects of being a Fledgling vampire and going without blood for so long.

Brynleigh had no idea witches could be so powerful, but Emilia had already proven herself not to be a normal witch. Usually, staving off bloodlust and not losing her mind would've been a positive thing, but in this case, it just meant the torture could keep going and going.

Even now that Ryker had removed the prohiberis and pulled out the knife, Brynleigh wasn't healing. That didn't surprise her. Nothing would surprise her anymore.

She had too many injuries, she was too broken, and she hadn't had nearly enough blood.

Her shadows were gone, and she couldn't call upon her wings.

The physical pain wasn't the worst of it, though. She could handle being in pain. She'd been injured countless times before.

No.

The worst was the hurt and betrayal Brynleigh had glimpsed in Ryker's eyes before he walled off his emotions. The pain she saw would have been enough to rip her heart to shreds if it hadn't already been broken.

Ryker was *alive*.

He was alive and here and...

Nothing was repaired between them. Nothing was better.

If anything, her heart hurt more now than it had before.

Brynleigh hadn't known it was possible to feel joy and endless agony simultaneously.

And then Ryker spoke.

When she heard his voice, she knew that whatever they'd had was irrevocably destroyed.

He'd built a wall between them, and there would be no climbing over it.

This was her fault. She'd done this to them.

Even after Ryker pulled the knife out of her leg, she remained in the chair. She had so many questions and no answers.

Had he known where she was this whole time? Was he aware she was being tortured daily?

Since Ryker was here, she assumed Zanri was dead. She'd seen the violence in the shifter's eyes, and there was little doubt in her mind that he would've done anything he could to carry out Jelisette's orders.

Rules are rules.

Tears gathered behind Brynleigh's eyes.

Fuck the rules. Fuck the game. Fuck it all. None of it mattered anymore.

She couldn't decide which answer would be worse—that Ryker had been aware that she was being tortured and that he'd ignored her or that he'd forgotten about her the moment he let them take her away.

And then he caught her when she almost fell, and none of her questions seemed to matter anymore.

Nothing mattered except for the searing heat of his flesh against hers. How had she not noticed that she was freezing until now?

He was a furnace, and she was made of ice. Bloody, bruised, broken ice.

Brynleigh stared at Ryker's black T-shirt as he carried her. Such a normal piece of clothing to wear to a place filled with so much pain.

His grip tightened as they neared the door, and Brynleigh bit back a whimper.

He must've heard something because he glanced down at her. That brown gaze that had once looked upon her with so much love was hard and emotionless.

"Where..." The word was a breathy rasp. She tried again. "Where are you taking me?"

Rocks were softer than his voice when he answered, "I'm taking you into my custody."

Custody.

The word clanged like a loud bell in Brynleigh's mind, reminding her she was a prisoner, not his wife.

Not anymore.

She looked at the hard pinch of his mouth before nodding and closing her eyes.

She understood the underlying meaning of his words.

Her death would come at his hands.

Brynleigh was grateful for that small mercy. It certainly wasn't one she deserved. They could've let her rot in this prison for an eternity.

Death would be a reprieve from such an awful existence.

It made sense, in a way.

She'd confessed everything and told them all she knew. There were no more secrets, no more lies.

Maybe this time, death would bring her peace.

"Okay," Brynleigh whispered.

Resigned to her fate, she kept her eyes closed and let her head loll back into the crook of Ryker's arm.

She would find refuge in his embrace one last time before he killed her. And then, she would cling to the memories of their wedding and those fleeting happy days as her life ended.

There was little doubt in Brynleigh's mind that Ryker would kill her slowly. She was deserving of such a death.

She had devoted her immortal life to learning the art of revenge and murder. Her heart was black, and her hands were stained crimson with the blood of others.

No amount of soap could remove the marks of death from her soul.

For six years, Brynleigh had allowed Jelisette to twist her into a person that her sister, Sarai, would never recognize.

And after all that hard work and planning, what did Brynleigh have to show for it?

A broken heart and a husband who hated her.

She'd been used, deceived, and betrayed. Now, she was done. She'd failed her task, and she would enter death's cold embrace willingly.

Heavy footsteps pounded down the hallway, but Brynleigh didn't open her eyes.

"This is a bad idea, Captain," a gruff man said. It was a new voice, one she hadn't heard before.

"I'm taking her," Ryker growled. "Get out of my way. This is my decision."

Before she'd learned the truth of who caused the storm in Chavin, Brynleigh would've been happy to hear the threat of violence in the captain's voice. It would have proved that Ryker deserved what she'd planned. She would've latched onto it, shoving away all the feelings she'd developed over the course of the Choosing.

But now it just fed her numbness.

Ryker was angry, and that was fine. He had every right to feel that way.

All that Brynleigh could do was hope that he wouldn't drag out her death too long.

She was tired. So, so tired.

There was a shuffling and then a feminine huff. "Chancellor Rose won't be happy about this. You think you can hide behind your mother's name?"

Brynleigh stiffened at that voice. Emilia was the worst of the three tormentors, and there was something wholly wrong about the witch.

Tension tightened Brynleigh's shoulders and stole her breath. She hated Emilia and the way her body reacted to her. Brynleigh's insides churned, expecting an influx of pain.

Before her imprisonment, Brynleigh would've fought back. She would've killed the witch without thinking twice about it.

But now?

She didn't even open her eyes.

Something had shattered within her during the seemingly neverending torture sessions. There was a hole deep within her soul. She would never be the same person again.

But Ryker was taking her into his custody to kill her, so it didn't matter.

"I'll deal with the Chancellor myself," the captain said, his tone brokering no room for arguments.

Emilia snorted. "Good luck with the bloodsucking bitch. She's fucking useless."

A snarl rumbled through Ryker's chest, and his grip tightened around her.

Brynleigh didn't say anything.

More footsteps. So many footsteps. They must've been keeping her deep underground.

Time slipped on.

Coldness enveloped Brynleigh despite Ryker's arms around her, and her sluggish brain finally caught up to the fact that her frigidness was caused by a lack of blood. She needed to drink, but she was so tired. How long would the witch's magic last, keeping the worst of her Fledgling status at bay?

Hopefully, it would be long enough for Brynleigh to be done with all this. The last thing she wanted was to fall into bloodlust before she died.

At some point, a vehicle door opened. Ryker placed her on a seat. His voice was cool and detached as he explained that the car was lined in prohiberis, so she couldn't shadow out of it.

Brynleigh didn't respond. She was far too tired and hurt to explain that his concern was a moot point. She couldn't shadow right now. Other than her fangs, she was basically a mortal, broken from all the torture and lack of blood.

At least she wouldn't die in the prison. It was a small mercy that she hadn't expected. Not after what she'd planned.

How had this become her life?

Betrayal, torture, and death.

She'd have never pictured this end for herself six years ago, yet here she was.

A single tear slid down her cheek, and she curled into a ball on the seat. The smooth leather was cool against her bare feet, but she didn't worry about shoes or bother buckling up.

What was vehicular safety when she was on the way to her death?

A throbbing pain started in the back of her skull, slowly migrating to the front. She assumed it was nighttime since she wasn't burning alive, but she didn't open her eyes to check.

The car was silent save for Ryker's steady breaths and the crunching of wheels on gravel.

Minutes passed. Hours? She wasn't certain.

Keeping track of the passage of time was something people did when their lives weren't in utter shambles.

Brynleigh had no use for time anymore. She had no use for anything at all. She and Ryker could've had something good, but she'd destroyed it all.

If only Zanri hadn't come to the hotel room. If only Brynleigh had told Ryker what was happening before their wedding. If only she'd confessed as soon as she'd realized the truth about the storm.

If only, if only, if only.

It was too late for thoughts like that, though. Too late for maybes and possiblies. There were no more options, no alternate paths.

Brynleigh's husband, the fae she'd Chosen and the man she loved, was going to kill her, and she would let him. She wouldn't fight back. She'd already done enough damage.

Brynleigh knew death intimately, and now, it was her turn to enter its cold, dark embrace.

She was ready.

EVENTUALLY, the vehicle slowed.

Brynleigh remained curled up on the seat as Ryker cut the engine. The silence was sudden, and her heartbeat roared in her ears.

Soon, she wouldn't have a heartbeat.

Maybe then, she would be at peace. Maybe then, she would be done.

A door opened, and a cold breeze rushed at her. Her arms broke out in goosebumps. Would death be cold?

"We're here," Ryker said briskly from outside the vehicle.

Brynleigh shouldn't have expected his voice to carry any trace of kindness, but the lack of warmth still sent tears to her eyes. She refused to let them fall, though.

She would be strong, even in this.

Unfurling from her ball, she pried open her eyes. Her brows creased.

This was... not where she'd expected to die.

Ryker had brought her into the woods.

Pine trees towered above them. Water lapped at a distant shore. Leaves rustled. Branches cracked. And the air was clean. There were no exhaust fumes, no factory emissions, and no scent of blood.

In fact, there was no sign of Golden City at all.

It was just the two of them.

And then she looked behind him.

Confusion was tart on Brynleigh's tongue. Had she hit her head during the car ride? This didn't seem like a good killing location. If anything, it seemed... almost serene.

She frowned. Wondering if she was hallucinating, she shut her eyes and drew in a deep breath before opening them again.

The scene remained the same.

A small blue bungalow was nestled in the moonlit pines, partly covered by the trees. A wooden porch wrapped around the home, a flourishing garden sat out front, and a birdhouse hung on a nearby tree.

It looked... nice.

Of all the places Brynleigh thought she would meet her final death, this wasn't one of them.

All her earlier bravado burned away like an early morning fog kissed by the afternoon sun. She was mistaken.

She wasn't ready to die.

Thinking that Ryker would kill her in the dungeon or in a cold, dark place where death reigned was one thing.

But this...

There was a cruelty to dying in a serene location like this, and she didn't want any part of it.

Ryker opened her door, and Brynleigh stared up at him. He seemed so much bigger, with her inside the car and him looming over her. It was like he was a giant, and she was an ant.

Squishable. Breakable. Easy to kill.

Frigid fear coursed through her, and she gripped the leather seat. Her newfound will to live froze her in place.

She met his gaze and blurted, "Please don't do this."

Begging for her life was fucking ironic, considering that she always hated when her marks whined when she came to kill them, but she couldn't stop the words from leaving her lips.

Ryker had been reaching into the car, but he froze. "What?"

She searched his gaze beseechingly. Her heart thundered, and though part of her knew this was useless, she had to try.

"Please don't kill me," she breathed.

She couldn't even believe the words were coming out of her mouth since she'd been ready to die minutes ago, but she'd been wrong.

The will to live lent her strength, and she repeated her request.

Ryker's brown eyes widened, and surprise flashed through them. He stumbled back, shaking his head.

Slowly, Brynleigh unfolded her limbs, the movements stiff and unnatural, and got out of the car. She only took one step towards the fae captain because his face hardened, and something harsh flickered through his eyes.

"I want to live," she said.

Brynleigh reached for Ryker but paused before she could touch him.

The moon cast a silver glow on her raw, red wrists. Her skin was torn and destroyed from the prohiberis, a reminder of what she'd suffered.

"I know I deserve to die, and you'd be well within your rights to take my life, but... please," she whispered. "Don't do it."

The last words were little more than air as they slipped past her lips. It took all her strength and willpower to say them. And now...

It was up to him.

Brynleigh's plea hung between them, growing heavier with each passing second.

Her legs knocked together, tears streamed down her cheeks, and her head felt far too light, but she didn't dare move.

His chest heaved. He didn't say anything.

Seconds became minutes.

"Please," she murmured. "If you cared about me at all—"

"Of course, I cared about you!" Ryker yelled, his eyes flashing as water streamed from his hands.

It was only for a moment, but the loss of control was telling.

The water vanished, but the tang of magic remained in the air. The temperature dropped, and power radiated from the fae captain.

And his face...

Storms passed through his eyes, and fury radiated from his features.

Brynleigh's legs decided they could no longer hold her weight. Her heart flipped, and the next thing she knew, she was on the ground.

All her aches, pains, and all-too-human woes returned ten times worse than before. She clawed at the cold dirt beneath her and heaved in a breath.

This was too much, too hard, and she was too fucking broken for this.

Tears blurred her vision, and her heart raced.

She had to get on her knees and plead her case. She couldn't give up. She knew that, yet her body refused to listen to her commands.

It was done, even if she wasn't.

Her fangs had gone past aching. They were throbbing entities residing in her gums.

Her soul, her body, and her heart were all *done*.

Nearby, autumnal leaves crinkled. An owl hooted. Life was in this place.

Brynleigh sucked in as deep of a breath as she could manage, but her lungs didn't want to fill.

Boots filled her vision as Ryker kneeled over her.

"I fucking *loved* you, Brynleigh," he snarled. Each word was clipped. "I Chose you. And you *broke* us. You destroyed us. I hope you're happy."

An undercurrent of pain and anger coursed through his words. He was just as hurt, just as broken as her.

"I'm not," she whispered.

This was about as far from happy as she'd ever been.

"Good. Neither am I," he growled, balling his fists at his sides. "Get up and come inside. Don't try to shadow. The house is warded."

Apparently, that was all he was willing to say.

Ryker straightened, wiped his hands on his jeans, and strode up the porch. He punched in a code to unlock the door and let himself into the house.

The door slammed behind him, the sound echoing through the now-silent forest.

Brynleigh stared at the place where Ryker had stood moments before.

Loved.

The word reverberated through her entire being. Her body. Her heart. Her soul.

It became all she knew. All she could feel. All she heard, again and again and again.

He *loved* her.

But not anymore.

Eventually, Brynleigh mustered up enough strength to rise to her feet. She stumbled after him, half-surprised that the door opened when she turned the handle.

The house was small but quaint. Ryker's back was to her when she entered. He was tense, gripping the back of a kitchen chair, and he didn't turn around.

"The bedroom is down the hallway on the left," he said gruffly. "You can use the bathroom, but don't go anywhere else. There should be clothes in the dresser. Take your pick."

As if she would leave. She was bruised, battered, and starving.

Brynleigh was too tired to fight. Too tired to do anything, really. If he wasn't going to kill her right now, then she would shower. Anything to get this grime and blood off her.

She didn't look around as she walked to the bedroom. If she was still alive in the morning, she'd think about exploring then.

She closed the curtains, stripped off her clothes, and stepped beneath the shower head. Turning the water on as hot as it could go, she let the steam burn away the remnants of the dungeon.

Tears flowed freely down her cheeks.

Brynleigh wept for herself, for Ryker, and for the utter fucking disaster that was their relationship.

She wept until she had nothing left. Only then did she stumble into the bedroom and collapse on the bed, pulling a blanket over herself. Her hair soaked the pillow, but she didn't care.

He had *loved* her.

And she had destroyed them.

CHAPTER 3
Broken Hearts and Lies

The old grandfather clock in the living room struck three in the morning as Ryker paced the length of the small one-bedroom bungalow's living room. The unfamiliar floor creaked beneath his feet, and he raked his hand through his hair for what felt like the millionth time that night.

He ground his teeth, trying to extinguish the storm rising within him.

What a fucking disaster.

Of all the things Ryker had expected to be doing less than a month after his wedding, bringing his wife to one of the many safe houses owned by the army wasn't one of them.

At least this home, though small, was equipped with all the necessities: a single bedroom, a three-piece bathroom, and a kitchen. There was a dresser filled with men's and women's clothing and a pantry full of staples.

More important than all that, though, were the wards. Vampires were unable to shadow inside of the magical perimeter.

The house wasn't exactly homey, but after what had happened, that was probably for the best.

Ryker didn't need to play house with the woman who'd planned on killing him.

Navy curtains covered the windows, and the location was isolated. Golden City was an hour away. Close enough that they could travel there if needed but far enough away that no one should bother them.

In freeing Brynleigh from The Pit and bringing her here, Ryker had added another title to his growing list.

Fae, son, brother, Captain, husband, and now... his wife's jailer.

By the Sands, his life was fucked up.

Ryker groaned and rubbed his bleary eyes. He hadn't even tried to sleep. Shutting down his mind, which was running a million miles an hour, would've been an impossible task.

It was Brynleigh.

Ryker couldn't stop thinking about her. He vacillated between rage at her confession and horror at her condition when he'd found her. He kept hearing her say those four words.

I wasn't going to...

Who knew a few words could make him throw away everything he'd worked for?

Stupid. He was so fucking stupid.

He'd berated himself the entire drive here for risking everything, but he was in too deep now. He'd put everything he had into this ridiculous plan, and soon, he'd find out whether it would all blow up in his face.

And yet, he'd do it again.

He was such an idiot. His heart beat for her, even after everything she'd done.

The drive to the woods had been awkward and silent, but it had been a walk in the park compared to what happened when they arrived.

Ryker would never be able to erase the visual of Brynleigh pleading for her life.

How could she ever think he would do something like that? The very thought of hurting her made his blood run as cold as ice from the Northern Region.

Ryker wasn't the murderer in their relationship. He wasn't the one who had harbored a secret plan of revenge. He hadn't hidden an entire part of his life in the Choosing.

No.

She was the one who had lied, deceived, and broken them.

He balled his fists. All he'd done was react.

What a pair they made.

The murderous vampire and the angry fae she'd betrayed.

Ryker didn't usually have problems keeping his cool, but then again, he'd never fallen head over heels in love and planned a life with someone only to be destroyed by them. She had her reasons, but he couldn't even begin to pretend he understood them.

And then, there was his magic.

It was unsettled. Angry. Swirling.

It had taken him an hour to get it to calm down after he'd stormed inside. Then he'd realized just how quiet it had become.

Once Ryker had been certain he wouldn't do anything stupid, he checked on Brynleigh. The moment he'd cracked open the bedroom door, any residual anger he'd felt had vanished.

She was curled in a ball on the bed, naked beneath a thin red quilt that barely covered her. The shower had washed away the blood, but like a child's finger painting gone eerily wrong, bruises covered her entire body.

He'd stared at her, aware that it was probably wrong, but he couldn't seem to stop. He gripped the doorframe, holding himself back from going to her.

Asleep, she looked so peaceful. Innocent, even.

It was all a fucking lie.

Last night, he had been alone in his apartment, and now, he was his murderous wife's jailer.

Ryker had shut the door and walked away. The never-ending sting of betrayal kept him awake.

Nothing good could come of pacing for hours, but he couldn't make himself stop. Not now, when a door was the only thing dividing them.

Instead, Ryker gave up on sleep entirely. Rest was for people whose lives weren't disastrous messes.

He pulled out his phone, sending various messages. He placed orders and set things in motion. When his phone was close to dying, he plugged it in and kept going.

There was a lot to do, after all.

Brynleigh's freedom hadn't been cheap. If she agreed to the plan, they might be here for a while. And if she didn't, he'd have to bring her back to prison.

Ryker didn't think either of them could survive that.

BANG, bang, bang.

The repeated sound of someone's fist slamming against the front door pulled Ryker out of a fitful sleep. He yanked open his eyes and blinked furiously to clear the fog of sleep before glancing at the clock.

It wasn't even ten.

"Damn," he grumbled.

Every part of him ached, protesting each small movement. He felt worse than before.

At some point around dawn, Ryker had collapsed on the lumpy couch that had seen better days in the living room, giving in to his body's need to rest. He'd fallen into nightmares the likes of which he hadn't experienced for many years.

Ignoring his body's protests, he flung himself off the couch and landed on his feet. Military training kicked in, and he forced himself to be alert as he approached the door.

Calling magic to the palm of his right hand, he pulled back the curtain covering the square window on the door with his left and peered outside.

One of Ryker's two best friends, Nikhail Galebringer, stood on the porch. The air fae's amber gaze met Ryker's, and Nikhail's crisp black business suit was discordant with their forested surroundings. A blue cooler sat at his feet, and a small box was on top.

Ryker wasn't surprised by Nikhail's formal attire. His friend only had one look: business.

Relieved to see a familiar, friendly face after the hell that had been yesterday, Ryker exhaled and released his hold on his magic. The water disappeared as though it had never been there, and he unlocked the door.

"Morning, Nik," he rasped, his voice rough from sleep.

The air fae's gaze crawled over Ryker's rumpled T-shirt and jeans, and he frowned. "Fuck, man, you look like shit."

Trust Nikhail to always point out the obvious. The man was many things, and subtle was not one of them.

"Thanks for pointing it out." Ryker scrubbed a hand over the scruff on his face and added shaving to the long list of things he should do today. He picked up the items off the porch and invited Nikhail into the small house.

The air fae's gaze flitted around the bungalow. To anyone else, his attention would've come across as simple curiosity, but Ryker knew Nikhail was cataloging every detail and storing them in case he needed them later.

"She's in the bedroom?" Nikhail asked, following Ryker on silent fae feet.

Sometimes, it seemed like Nik's feet didn't even touch the ground, as if he walked on the air itself.

That's what made him so good at his job.

Placing the cooler on the kitchen island, Ryker tucked the box in his back pocket. "Yeah. She's still asleep."

Knowing amber eyes roved over him for a long moment before Nikhail dipped his head.

"I'm sorry, Ryker." Truth. No fae could lie, whether they were water, earth, fire, or air fae. "That this is... that it happened this way."

Nikhail was the only person in Ryker's life who knew the complete, unedited truth of what had occurred on Ryker's wedding night. The rest of the world, including Ryker's family and the other Choosing participants, had been fed a carefully constructed web of half-truths. Not lies but crafted, palpable versions of the events that had taken place.

Some thought Brynleigh had fallen ill after their wedding. True. Others thought the newlyweds were on a trip. Also true, but instead of honeymooning in the Northern Region as they'd planned, Brynleigh had taken a trip to The Pit.

That familiar, angry fire burned through Ryker's veins. Punching the wall probably wouldn't solve any of his problems, but he had the urge to introduce his fist to the drywall, just to see if it helped.

Instead, he clutched the counter.

"Me too."

The words were short and clipped, but what else could he say? That he was sorry he'd been duped? Sorry he was living in his own personal hell, which seemed to be worsening by the day? Sorry his wife had wanted to kill him, and now he was stuck working with her because he'd made a deal to get her out of prison?

The problem was, he wasn't even sorry he'd Chosen her.

Angry, yes. Sorry? No.

What the fuck was wrong with him?

The world did not contain enough words to properly convey how incredibly awful this situation had become.

Thank the gods, Ryker was saved from further exploring his broken, angry, pain-filled heart because the floor creaked in the bedroom. He met Nikhail's eyes, and the pair turned their attention down the hall. The bungalow was compact; besides the solitary bedroom, everything was out in the open.

The sound could only mean one thing. Brynleigh was awake.

Seeming to arrive at the same conclusion, Nikhail raised a brow. "Want me to stay?"

On one hand, Ryker would appreciate that. His friend was an intelligent man, and Ryker could use his help with… everything if he were being honest. But on the other hand, things were already complicated enough.

Besides, Ryker was a trained soldier. He'd been to war across the Rose Ocean. He could carry on a conversation with one weakened vampire on his own.

"No, I've got this."

Nikhail studied him for another long moment, his gaze disturbingly perceptive, before he nodded.

"Alright. I'll leave your suitcases on the porch. I packed everything you asked for."

Late last night, Ryker had texted his friend, asking for help.

This morning, Nikhail swung by the apartment, packed a bag for Ryker, and grabbed Brynleigh's suitcase. Her things had been delivered the night after everything went to hell, and Ryker hadn't had the heart to deal with them yet.

And now...

Well, at least she would have some clothes.

He didn't have the mental energy to think about anything else at the moment.

"Thanks, man."

Nikhail clapped Ryker on the back in a one-armed hug. "Good luck."

Even if the oceans were filled with luck, there wouldn't be enough to help Ryker out of this situation.

But this was his problem and not Nikhail's, so he nodded. "I'll message you."

With that, Nikhail left. The door had just closed, the lock slipping into place, when another creak came from the bedroom.

Closing his eyes, Ryker cast out his anger, erected a brick wall around his heart, and slid his steel mask back over his features.

Emotionless, expressionless. He could do this.

The bedroom door opened, and Ryker opened his eyes. His heart, unaware of his resolve to keep his emotions out of this, thudded as he beheld Brynleigh.

She'd shed the prison jumpsuit, exchanging it for a borrowed oversized black sweater that fell to mid-thigh. She'd paired it with leggings that hugged her curves, ending just above her ankles. Golden hair tumbled over one shoulder, and tired lines were etched on her face. Bruises covered her skin, and several open cuts marred the beautiful canvas of her flesh.

Blank, obsidian eyes rose to meet Ryker's, and his heart thudded again.

Damn.

She tugged on the bottom of the sweater and rasped, "Morning."

Gods above, Ryker hated that his body responded to the sound of her voice.

He hated so many things lately. He hated that he was thankful she'd found something to wear, hated that he reacted to her, hated that her rough tone brought back fond memories of their wedding night.

More than all that, he hated that he wanted to reach out and touch her, to make sure she was real and not a figment of his imagination.

The hatred was even worse than the anger.

Ryker's fingers twitched, but instead of giving into his body's ridiculous urges, he dropped his gaze to the counter. Gripping the marble with all his strength, he ground his teeth, swallowing the greeting that tried to rise out of him.

She was an asset. That was all.

He would remind himself of that fact a thousand times a day if necessary. In planning on killing him, she had betrayed them. Their sham of a relationship was shattered, and all that remained between them was devastation and lies.

Footsteps whispered on the floor.

Ryker's chest tightened as her scent grew stronger. When he looked up, she stood just outside the kitchen. Pot lights cast a silver glow on her too-frail body.

She looked like he felt inside.

Broken. Shattered. Destroyed.

She wrung her hands in front of her, a dejected look on her face as she stared at the floor.

The confident vampire Ryker had fallen in love with was nowhere to be seen, and for some reason, that bothered him nearly as much as everything else.

Get a fucking grip.

The vampire he'd fallen in love with had been a lie. She'd been a murderer, a rebel sympathizer, an adversary.

What kind of idiot fell in love with and married their enemy?

A flash of watery rage coursed through Ryker's veins as he recalled exactly how stupid he'd been.

His mask cracked, and he snapped, "What?"

Brynleigh flinched, and for a moment, he felt bad for how he'd spoken.

This whole situation was a clusterfuck, and it was making him question everything.

A small voice niggled in the back of his brain that he should hear her out and listen to her reasons for why she acted like this, but he wasn't ready for that. He just needed to get through this. He could think about her reasons later. Maybe. He wasn't sure she even deserved that.

Brynleigh licked her lips, her face growing paler with each passing second. "I... I was wondering..."

She stumbled over her words, and his heart twisted before he realized he was supposed to hate her.

They were opposites in every way, and by the gods, she'd fooled him.

His wife was a *killer.*

Gritting his teeth, Ryker hardened the walls around his heart and waited for her to continue.

"I need to feed. If you're not going to ki... can you find me some blood?" Black eyes met his, and he was taken aback by the level of despair within them. "Please."

That last word was little more than a whisper as it left her lips, and she stumbled back a step. As if she wasn't sure how he would react. As if she thought he might lash out at her.

Despite the bricks surrounding Ryker's heart, his life-giving organ ached. Gods above, he was being an ass.

"I'm not going to hurt you, Brynleigh." He didn't think he could, even if he wanted to.

Hating her was hard enough. Being angry at her was killing him, too. Hurting her?

It would destroy him.

Releasing the counter, he moved to the cooler. Aware of his size and the fear leeching off the vampire, he slowly lifted the lid.

He pulled out a few bags of blood and slid them across the counter.

"Of course, you can feed. I'm not a monster."

Unlike Victor Orpheus.

Relief flickered through Brynleigh's eyes, and she darted forward.

"Thank you."

Grabbing the bag closest to her, she ripped the top off with her teeth. Like she had in the cell, she downed the crimson liquid within seconds.

She dropped the empty bag on the counter and moved on to the next. She drank that one, too, guzzling it like she'd been moments away from death, and it was a life-giving elixir.

He supposed it was.

Relief shone in her eyes, and soft sighs slipped from her mouth as she drank.

It was too much for Ryker. He couldn't bear to stand there in silence and watch her any longer.

The island between them might as well have been an entire world.

Turning away, he busied himself with the coffee maker. He grabbed a pod and shoved it in the contraption, fiddling with buttons until, finally, caffeine trickled into the mug he placed underneath.

Even after the coffee had finished brewing, Ryker didn't move. He stared at the steam rising above the black liquid and attempted to formulate words. His mind was a jumble, and every time he opened his mouth, no sounds came out.

Once, communication between them had been as easy as breathing. They'd been able to speak for hours about everything and nothing.

Not anymore.

Anger tied his tongue, and he couldn't think of anything to say. He wrapped his hands around the mug. The coffee was hot and just on this side of being too much, but he let the slight pain ground him.

He wasn't sure how long he stood there, staring at his drink.

Eventually, she whispered, "I wasn't going to do it, you know."

Those words again.

That storm in his veins became a barely contained tempest.

Ryker's spine stiffened, and he drew a sharp breath through his nostrils. Clinging to the mug as though it were a life raft in the midst of a storm, he slowly turned around.

She dragged her eyes up to his. They shone a little brighter than before, and her cuts were already healing. The bruises were more muted, and that fucking stupid side of him was relieved to see that she was looking better than when she'd walked in.

"I couldn't do it." She worried her bottom lip. "I wasn't going to kill you. Not in the end. I decided not to. River told me what happened, and I... I knew I couldn't."

Slowly, Ryker placed the mug on the counter and flattened his palms on the cold surface.

She stared at him expectantly as if he knew what to say to move them forward from this. As if her words didn't spark fury within him. As if he wasn't reeling inside from her admission yesterday.

The problem was he had no fucking idea what to do with any of this.

People usually went to him for help solving their problems, but most people's problems didn't involve a murderous wife.

Ryker's heart thundered, and he barely stifled a groan. There were no rules for this, no training that could have ever prepared him for this situation.

Gods-damn it all.

"But you planned to do it." His fingers curled against the marble, and anger leaked into his tone. "You entered the Choosing so you could kill me."

That, at least, he could understand from a soldier's perspective. She hadn't known him then, and she'd had her reasons. But even after they'd met and he'd fallen in love with her, she still intended to kill him.

Her intent was as sharp as any dagger she could've plunged into his heart.

"I—"

"Just admit that you tricked me," he snarled. "Even after I proposed, you were planning on killing me."

Not a question. He'd heard her confession.

Her eyes shuttered, and pain flashed across her countenance.

"Yes," she admitted.

Hearing her tell Victor everything had been painful enough, but this felt worse. Deeper. More fucking personal.

His nostrils flared, and he shook his head.

This entire situation was so fucked up.

"Thank you for not dancing around your answer," Ryker said, his voice as hard as the marble beneath his fingers. "It seems you can tell the truth... sometimes."

But not when it mattered. Not when it came to them.

Her gaze dropped, and she traced a line down one of the empty bags. "I didn't... Not everything was a lie, Ryker."

Hearing her speak his name used to bring him joy, but now it just caused twin cords of hurt and anger to twist through him.

"But you did lie." The words came out harsh and cold, like the ice he wished he could freeze in place around his broken heart.

Silver lined her eyes as she opened and closed her mouth.

The lack of denial was admission enough.

"I don't want to do this right now." He picked up his coffee, his movements so jerky that the liquid splashed over the side. He wiped the mess with a rag before throwing it in the sink. "Are you still hungry?"

A long moment passed before she said, "No, I'm fine."

"Okay."

"Thank you for the blood. You didn't... have to do that. You didn't have to do any of this." She fiddled with her sleeve. "You could've... but you didn't. So, thank you."

Ryker didn't want her gratitude. He didn't want to be her jailer. He didn't want to be risking his job for this ridiculous plan.

By the gods, he didn't want any of this.

He wanted a wife that he could love, a life partner, the woman he'd Chosen. For a few days, he'd had that, and it had been fucking good.

Now, it was gone. Destroyed. They were reduced to this. Whatever it was.

Grunting, Ryker strode past Brynleigh, making sure not to touch her. He couldn't deal with that right now.

The living room wasn't exactly filled with furniture. Other than the couch where he'd slept, there were two uncomfortable-looking armchairs and a circular blue rug that had seen better days.

Choosing an inevitable sore back rather than dealing with the awkwardness of sitting beside Brynleigh, Ryker settled into the armchair on the right. Keeping his feet flat on the ground, he pulled the small black box out of his back pocket as she approached him.

She sat in the other armchair, her hair covering her face as she stared at the floor.

Awkwardness settled over them both, and minutes dragged on in terrible silence.

Every beat of Ryker's heart was too loud, and every breath was too disruptive. The ring on his left hand was the heaviest of weights. He wasn't sure why he still wore it, but it felt like it was dragging him into the ground.

Maybe he should have asked Nikhail to stay. Maybe he should've let his anger out. Maybe he never should've made the deal.

Eventually, the silence grew unbearable. Ryker put his now-lukewarm coffee on the small table between them and lifted his gaze.

"You must be wondering why you're no longer in the Pit."

That got her attention.

Her head snapped up, and her eyes sharpened. "I suppose I have you to thank for that?"

"You do." He twisted his wedding ring. "But your freedom comes at a price."

CHAPTER 4
The Cost of Freedom

Brynleigh wasn't surprised that her freedom had a price tag. Nothing in this world was free, especially for someone who had the misfortune of not being a Representative.

It wouldn't surprise her if, one day, even the air they breathed was taxed. Nothing was sacred in this world where golden veneer hid the cracks of darkness, despair, and death.

She knew that, yet she still asked, "What is the price?"

Storms filled Ryker's dark gaze. He sat a few feet away, but an ocean might as well have been dividing them.

She'd done that to him. To them.

Brynleigh couldn't bear to look at Ryker for more than a few heartbeats. The air was cold, but it had nothing compared to the frigidness stretching between them.

Dropping her gaze, she studied Ryker's coffee mug. Focusing on that was a much better option than thinking about everything else.

The blood had helped take the edge off her hunger, and most of her external wounds were healing. That was good. There was still a hollowness in her stomach, though. Maybe it would always remain, a reminder that she'd spent weeks starving and being tortured.

Being full was a distant memory, but at least her fangs no longer burned, and her shadows were returning. They hummed gently in her veins, their song a muted version of their usual symphony.

She wasn't sure she could call on her wings if she needed them, not that it mattered. Ryker had made it clear she wasn't leaving this place.

She was still a prisoner; her cage had just been upgraded.

The fae captain inhaled deeply and twisted a box around in his hands, staring at it as though it contained the secrets of the universe.

His voice was gravelly as he asked, "Have you ever heard of Emery Sylvain?"

Brynleigh canted her head, repeating the name in her mind. It sounded vampiric in origin, but it didn't ring any bells.

She frowned. "No, I can't say that I have."

It was unique enough that she was certain she'd remember if she heard it.

Ryker's fingers tightened around the box. Brynleigh stared at the movement, fascinated. His fingers were bigger than hers—no surprise there, all of him was bigger than her—and callouses covered the pads of his fingers. His hands had a rough elegance that spoke to a life of hard work.

Sadness swept through her as she recalled the first time they'd touched.

Maybe looking at his hands had been a bad idea.

She dropped her gaze and swallowed. The uncomfortable air between them was painful, and her chest ached. Seconds ticked by. Each was longer than the last and filled with a horrible tension that never used to plague them.

"You're certain? Emery Sylvain." Ryker drew out the syllables as if she hadn't properly heard him the first time.

She looked up. Instantly, she regretted the action. He was staring at her, his gaze sharp, and his mouth pinched in a line.

She shook her head and shrugged. "I have no clue who that is."

His eyes narrowed as he studied her. There was nothing kind in his expression—he looked at her as if she was a puzzle he was trying to solve.

After a few painful minutes, he sighed. "Are you lying to me again?"

Again.

She hated that he even had to ask that. She squeezed her eyes shut so he wouldn't see the hurt flickering through them, and she curled her fists. Her nails cut crescent moons in her palms.

Did Ryker know his words were sharper than any of the silver instruments of torture she'd been subjected to over the past three weeks?

After what Brynleigh had done, she deserved the question, but it still stung. All of this stung.

She wouldn't cry, though. She wouldn't let him know how deeply he was hurting her.

Her pain was her penance.

"I'm not lying," she said when she could trust herself to speak without her voice breaking. "I swear on my family's graves, I will never lie to you again." What would be the point? She and Ryker were already shattered. "I have never heard the name."

His stormy gaze pinned her to her seat. She was no longer confined to that iron chair, yet she could not move beneath the weight of his attention.

This was the fae captain, she realized.

This was why he had risen in the ranks so quickly and gained so much power. It wasn't just because of his mother's position as a Representative—although that certainly must have helped—it was because everything he did, every movement he made, screamed that he was in control.

After an eternity, Ryker loosened his grip on the box and nodded. "Okay. I believe you."

As he should. She wasn't lying about this.

She breathed, "Thank you."

They stared at each other, neither speaking as that awkward ocean grew and grew between them.

After several uncomfortable, frigid minutes passed, Brynleigh asked, "So... who is he?"

Ryker palmed the back of his neck.

Damn it all, but she couldn't help but notice the way his muscles tensed beneath the fabric of his shirt. Even now, after everything that had happened, she still found him incredibly attractive.

What did that say about her? She was still healing from being tortured. She shouldn't be having these kinds of thoughts.

"I can't believe you don't know about him," Ryker muttered. It sounded like he was talking to himself.

"I have no idea who he is," she reiterated.

Ryker's brows furrowed, and he shook his head. "He's... Emery Sylvain is Jelisette de la Point's Bound Partner."

Bound Partner.

The words didn't register for a minute, but when they did...

Oh, gods.

Had Brynleigh been feeling better before? That was no longer the case. Her stomach bottomed out, and her head spun.

It felt like she'd just been thrown off a high-rise building, and now she was careening through the skies without her wings to save herself.

Bound Partner.

Her fingers grappled at the armrests, and she swayed from side to side. Her mouth dried, and black spots filled her vision.

"Excuse me?" The words tasted like ash.

She must have heard Ryker wrong. Fae couldn't lie, but this... it... that wasn't possible. It wasn't like a fucking Binding could be easily hidden, for the gods' sake.

"Jelisette doesn't have a Bound Partner." Her head reeled, and her words came faster and faster. "That's not... No. I would know if my Maker was Bound to someone."

Bile rose in her throat, and she held a hand over her mouth.

Ryker was a fae, and he couldn't lie, but this...

A Binding?

Brynleigh knew what they were, of course. Everyone did.

Binding Ceremonies, like Tetherings, were rarely done. Bindings were eternal commitments blessed by the gods themselves. They could never be broken. Vampires could be Bound to fellow vampires but also to humans, elves, and shifters.

The Binding was a blood ceremony that tied lifespans together. For mortals, it extended their lives to match their Bound Partner's. For vampires, it meant they would never again require a Source that wasn't their partner.

Bound Partners rarely separated from each other. Why would they? They provided life for each other. They were blessed by Isvana, the goddess of the moon, herself.

And if Jelisette had a Bound Partner, that meant Brynleigh had missed something significant. It meant her Maker had been lying since day fucking one.

Brynleigh's heart raced, and disbelief coursed through her. She drew in short breaths as she thought over every interaction she'd ever had with her Maker. Assuming it was true, there would be signs. Markings.

How could Brynleigh have worked so closely with someone for six years without noticing they were Bound to another being?

None of this made any sense.

Her head swirled. Her lungs squeezed. It was like someone had dropped a thousand-pound weight on her chest.

And Ryker was sitting there, studying her every movement.

"I... I don't understand." Perhaps she would've taken this news better before her imprisonment, but now... "Jelisette wouldn't have kept this from me."

Right? There had to be some level of trust between them. After all, Jelisette had Made Brynleigh. Some vampires saw their progeny as their children, and they shared everything.

While Brynleigh had never had that kind of relationship with her Maker, this was...

Impossible.

Right?

It seemed like a small omission from the outside, but the more Brynleigh thought about it, the worse it got. She had spent years with her Maker, and Jelisette had never mentioned anything like this. She'd never even hinted at having a Bound Partner. Brynleigh had never seen her with anyone; for Isvana's sake, she'd never even seen Jelisette's supposed Marking.

Ryker raised a brow.

"Really?" His tone made his position on the matter clear. "She wouldn't have?"

"No." Brynleigh shook her head adamantly. "I... She's my Maker."

She could still remember the feeling when Jelisette saved her from a watery grave, still remember the way her sire had first drained her of her blood and then given her the gift of immortality.

Brynleigh whispered, as if trying to convince herself, "There's a sacredness to our bond."

If this was true, it meant she couldn't trust anything that had happened to her since her Making.

Ryker leaned back, his relaxed posture almost laughable in the face of Brynleigh's inner turmoil.

"Your Maker hid this from you."

His voice was so calm. So certain. He might as well have been telling her that the sky was blue.

It was like this was just another workday for Ryker, and he wasn't delivering life-altering news that would forever change how Brynleigh saw the world.

Some of her light-headedness abated, giving way to anger instead. Why was he doing this? Was it a trick?

"How do you know?" She narrowed her eyes. "What proof do you have?"

She refused to accept that this was real. Somehow, he had to be lying.

He raised a brow. "You want proof?"

It wasn't a want. Brynleigh wanted many things—for this to be over, for them to return to the way they were, for her heart to stop aching—but this was different. She needed it.

"Yes."

"Alright." He pulled out his phone, tapped the screen a few times, and slid it across the coffee table. He inched back his fingers before she could touch him.

Trying not to show how much the action hurt, Brynleigh drew the phone towards her.

An old, grainy picture filled the screen. She put her fingers in the middle and pulled them apart, zooming in. The date stamp on the bottom right corner was from several centuries ago.

She scrolled up to the two people frozen in time. Her mind stalled, unwilling to accept what she saw.

This was... impossible.

And yet, she was staring at it. It was as real as the rug beneath her feet.

"Tell me what you see," Ryker requested, his voice softer than it had been all day.

It was as if he knew this was turning her world upside down. But how could he know? And why did he even care?

Questions for a later time, when her world wasn't imploding.

She swallowed. "I... it's a picture."

"Of what?" he probed.

Her gaze dropped back to the phone.

"I mean... at first glance, it's a snapshot of a couple enamored with each other." An aura of happiness surrounded the pair. Even through the screen, it seemed infectious. "Like they're living in their own little bubble."

He nodded, his expression gentle. That was almost worse than the earlier harshness.

"And when you look closer? What do you see?"

Brynleigh hated that he was forcing her to confront the truth.

Tapping the picture, she frowned.

"This is Jelisette." Her Maker looked nearly identical to the way she did now. "Except... she's smiling. I've never seen her do that."

Not only that, but Brynleigh had never seen Jelisette without long sleeves or gloves. In this picture, she wore a bright sundress, and her arms were bare. Her chestnut hair was in a high ponytail, and there seemed to be a bounce in her step.

Brynleigh couldn't be sure from this angle, but it looked like the couple was holding hands.

"What about the man?" Ryker's voice broke through her thoughts. "Do you recognize him?"

"No, I've never seen him before." She would have remembered a man like this.

He was unforgettable. Like all creatures of the moon, he was beautiful, but there was something distinct about him. His face ensured no one could cross his path without remembering him.

A prickle of discomfort twinged in Brynleigh's gut. None of this made any sense.

Ryker reached over, still not touching her, and swiped right. Another picture filled the screen, the time stamp marking it as having been taken a few minutes before the first one.

In this image, both their arms were visible.

Brynleigh's mind emptied of all thought. Words were impossible to come by.

Unblinking, she stared at the picture as if it might miraculously change if she looked at it long enough.

Midnight ink wrapped around the vampires' wrists. The unmistakable mark of a Binding stood out against their skin, proclaiming to all who saw it that these vampires belonged to each other.

Brynleigh couldn't breathe. This was proof that Jelisette had lied to her. Her mouth dried, and her hands trembled. She lifted her gaze to Ryker's.

"You were telling the truth."

He nodded slowly. "I can't lie."

She knew that, but...

"How?" The words barely made it past her heavy tongue.

She had so many questions she wasn't even sure which one she was asking.

How was this possible? How come she didn't know? How come she was just finding out about this now? How many times had Jelisette lied? How was Brynleigh so stupid?

Pity flickered through Ryker's eyes.

That was worse than everything else. Worse than the hurtful comments. Worse than his obvious hatred and anger. She didn't want his pity.

She wanted his love.

He cleared his throat and slid the phone back over to himself. "These photos came from a security camera in the Southern Region. They were pulled as part of an investigation into a murder that occurred around the same time."

Brynleigh stared at the empty table, trying to wrap her mind around this.

"I've never met that man before."

How could she not have met her Maker's Bound Partner? It seemed inconceivable.

"No, you wouldn't have." Ryker's voice hardened. "Emery Sylvain is dead."

CHAPTER 5
Living with Half a Soul

Brynleigh froze, her heart a booming drum as Ryker's last words echoed in her mind.

Dead, dead, dead.

For the longest moment, she couldn't breathe, let alone think. Dead? How could he be dead?

When her mouth started working again, she breathed, "Impossible."

It couldn't be true. Bound Partners didn't up and die on their other halves.

All vampires were immortal unless killed, but if a Bound Partner perished, the surviving partner would be living with half a soul.

A Binding was more than just a physical connection. It wove the tapestry of the partners' lives together until they were so interconnected that separation was impossible.

A frown tugged at Ryker's lips as he navigated through the phone.

"I assure you, it's possible. Look," he said gruffly, his voice far harsher than it had ever been in the Choosing.

Anger radiated off him like steam. Once again, he slid the phone over to her, careful not to touch her hand.

The moment she saw the screen, it was like someone threw her head-first into a lake of pure ice.

She shivered, goosebumps erupted on her flesh, and her stomach turned. She wanted to tear her eyes away and look elsewhere, but she couldn't make her body function.

The blood she'd consumed soured in her stomach, her heart pounded, and her shadows screamed. Their cry was haunting, loud, and unending as they throbbed in her veins.

She'd seen death many times before, but this...

Oh, gods. This wasn't just awful. This was gruesome.

Her hand trembled as she traced the screen.

The handsome man from the previous photo was nowhere to be seen. In his place was an ashy corpse. Emery Sylvain, or what was left of him, was on his back on a translucent sheet of ice.

A bloody wooden stake protruded from his chest. Black marks spiderwebbed across his gray, sunken skin. His flesh stuck to his skeleton like a dried piece of fruit. His black eyes were wide, and his face was contorted in a never-ending scream. His right arm was outstretched towards the heavens and frozen in death, his Binding Mark stark against his gray flesh.

This was the kind of death there was no coming back from, even for vampires.

Acidic bile rose in Brynleigh's throat, and she gagged.

Oh, gods.

Throwing her hand over her mouth, she dropped the phone and stumbled to her feet.

"I'm sorry," she mumbled through her hand. "I... I can't."

Staggering to the bathroom, she fell to her knees in front of the toilet. The porcelain was cold between her hands as she retched. All the blood she'd consumed earlier came up, but she didn't stop. She kept going until there was nothing left within her.

Every time she closed her eyes, that image flashed through her mind. Her stomach cramped, and her heart ached as she imagined Emery's pain as he died.

There was no doubt in her mind this was real. There was no faking that kind of image.

Eventually, when her stomach was empty and she had nothing left, she stood. Rinsing her mouth out with water, she washed her trembling hands.

A shadow stood in the open doorway, watching her.

"Emery Sylvain was staked," Ryker said calmly, as though they were discussing the weather and not a man's final death.

She stared down at the sink. Although she thought she knew the answer to her next question, she needed confirmation.

"A Representative killed him, didn't they?"

Long, horrible seconds passed before a grunt of acknowledgment came from Ryker.

Fuck, fuck, fuck.

Brynleigh's head spun with this new information. No wonder Jelisette was filled with so much hatred. No wonder she was out for Representative blood.

It was all starting to make some sick, twisted sense.

Clutching the counter because she wasn't certain she'd be able to remain upright on her own, she slowly turned around.

"They truly were Bound?" Horror laced her every word. "That man and Jelisette?"

His lips were set in a grim line. "Yes."

And now, Emery was dead.

She'd never seen a staked vampire and hadn't known it was so... so... horrifying. She would have nightmares about that man's death for years to come.

If she lived that long.

Every single experience Brynleigh had had with her Maker flashed before her eyes. Suddenly, Jelisette's temper, coldness, and inability to care about anything all made sense.

"When did this happen?" Brynleigh whispered.

"Right before the One Hundredth and Eighty-Third Choosing."

She quickly did the math in her head. Their Choosing had been the Two Hundredth. So a hundred and seventy years ago, Jelisette's Bound Partner had died.

Nearly two centuries had passed while Jelisette lived with half a soul. Brynleigh's heart ached as she imagined her Maker's daily, excruciating pain.

The immeasurable grief. The sorrow. The agony of being half a person.

Her legs trembled, and dizziness swept through her. She didn't even know vampires *could* be dizzy, but this was a day of nasty surprises.

"I need... I need to sit down."

Ryker nodded, his mouth pinched in a line as he moved aside.

Releasing the sink, Brynleigh stumbled to the living room and dropped back into her chair. Her head fell into her hands, and she forced her lungs to intake air.

Every breath hurt.

Was this what Jelisette felt like every minute of every day? Was she drowning in grief and sorrow and pain?

Eventually, Ryker reclaimed his seat across from her. She felt his gaze on her and looked up to meet brown, dispassionate eyes.

Gods.

The anger lining the hard edges of his face was a knife driving into her side. This was too much for right now. Too soon.

Her gaze plummeted. She picked at a stray piece of lint on her borrowed sweater and shook her head.

"Why tell me this?" she muttered. "Why not just leave me in that prison?"

Was his goal to hurt her? Was that why he hadn't killed her yet?

Instead of taking her life swiftly, he would kill her with a thousand empty looks that stung like stakes, cold stares as beautiful and deadly as blades of silver, and utter loneliness as harsh as a million lifetimes without blood.

That would be the more painful way to go.

Before him, Brynleigh hadn't known what a true partnership could feel like. She hadn't known it was possible to have another person complete you.

Perhaps the worst thing to come from all this was that she'd learned the value of having someone love her, only to have it stripped away.

For the longest time, silence was the only thing between them. She wasn't even sure Ryker had heard her question.

"I... I couldn't leave you there," he confessed.

Couldn't.

Such a strange word. It denoted a lack of ability, but that didn't make sense. Jelisette apparently had no problem lying to Brynleigh, hiding a Binding, and abandoning her in prison, so why was it so hard for Ryker to do the same?

Confusion roiled through her as she tried to parse what he was saying. "Why not?"

He inhaled sharply.

"I just... couldn't." There was that word again. "In order to get you out of the... interrogation—"

"Torture," she quietly interrupted, rubbing her wrists. The sweater hid the ruby marks, but they were still there. Even now, she felt the ghosts of those manacles on her wrists.

"What?"

Her voice was soft as she canted her head. "They were *torturing* me, Ryker."

Memories of her time in the prison flashed through her mind. Screams and pain and agony, all intermingled with grief because she thought Zanri had killed her husband. She'd been so lost in the hurt, and she thought it was her penance because she'd gotten him killed.

Except...

He was still alive. He'd been alive the whole time.

"They were inflicting never-ending pain on me. The least you can do is have the decency to call it what it fucking *was*." She paused as a tear ran down her cheek, and then she whispered, "Torture."

Brynleigh wasn't ready to dive into the specifics of what had been done to her—what he had *allowed* to happen—but she could do this. That simple word acknowledged her pain and suffering, and she needed him to say it.

Storms passed through his gaze again before he briskly nodded. "Understood."

So formal. So detached. Her heart ached once more. Maybe that would be her constant state of being now.

Ryker continued, his voice monotone and his eyes hard, "In order to get you out of the *torture*, I had to make a deal with Myrrah Challard."

A deal.

Her shadows twinged, and a pit formed in her stomach. Whatever was coming would be bad.

A large part of her wanted to shut this conversation down, but she wasn't sure where that would leave her with Ryker. Instead, she twisted her fingers together.

Brynleigh supposed she had Victor and his merry band of torturers to thank for *that* new development. She never used to get nervous, but then again, being used as a living pincushion for several weeks changed a woman.

She chewed on her lip. "What kind of deal?"

Ryker's eyes darkened, and the tang of his magic filled the air. Had he always had this much power so close at hand? She hadn't noticed it as much before.

"Ever since our... wedding,"—he seemed to choke on the word, and his nostrils flared—"the military has been conducting an in-depth investigation into Jelisette de la Point."

She swallowed. "An investigation?"

That didn't sound good. But then again, nothing these days sounded good.

Ryker stared directly at her, his eyes drilling into hers. "Your feline... friend was very talkative after a few days of encouragement."

"My friend... Zanri?" All the blood drained from her face, and she gripped the armrests. "He's alive?"

She thought that Ryker had killed him.

The captain's jaw clenched, and he gritted out, "Barely."

That one word spoke fucking volumes.

Brynleigh's heart pounded as she processed this latest development. On the one hand, fuck Zanri. He'd betrayed her and came to kill Ryker. He was the reason she was in this mess. On the other hand, she'd been through hell, and to think that Zanri had probably suffered worse...

Grateful her stomach was empty, she groaned and rubbed her temples. She couldn't process this right now. Not on top of everything else.

"I see." Her voice was monotone.

Ryker's fingers twitched as though he wanted to reach for her but decided against it. "It was during that time that we uncovered Jelisette's Binding to Emery Sylvain."

"The dead vampire."

"Yes." His jaw feathered, and he held her gaze. "That's not all we discovered. We also learned that Jelisette is connected to the Black Night."

Too much.

This was all too much.

Brynleigh's head pounded as she stared at Ryker. Her trio of torturers had asked her about the Black Night, but she didn't know what that was. That hadn't changed.

"I've never heard of the Black Night," she whispered.

Ryker assessed her for a long moment before he nodded.

"I believe you. But that doesn't negate that even if you don't know what it is, Jelisette certainly does. The Black Night is a rebel organization, and she's one of their members."

He said the words with as much certainty as one would when declaring the grass was green.

Brynleigh knew rebels existed within the Republic. But this. This was a joke. It had to be a joke, right? How could her Maker be a part of this? If the Black Night were who Ryker said they were, and Jelisette was working with them...

She stared at the fae captain, waiting for him to laugh and tell her this was a prank, but he didn't.

Her heart throbbed, and she couldn't wrap her mind around this. First, the Binding. Now, a rebel?

How could Jelisette be one of the people hell-bent on overthrowing the current structure of the Republic of Balance? She'd been at the Masked Ball when the rebels' bomb went off. She was the one who saved Brynleigh's life.

It didn't make sense.

It couldn't.

Except, deep in the back of Brynleigh's mind, a niggling sensation insisted this might make the tiniest bit of sense. Jelisette had hidden her Binding. Why was it impossible that she'd hidden this, too?

Maybe every single fucking thing Jelisette had ever said or done was a lie.

Maybe Brynleigh was just an Isvana-damned naive idiot who believed everything she was told.

She curled her fists. Had Jelisette and Zanri laughed at her expense? Had they played games with her, finding her gullibility amusing?

Brynleigh had trusted them. She thought they were looking out for her. Maybe the actual game had been to see how many lies she would believe before she found them out.

Minutes went by, and Brynleigh considered everything she'd learned today. The rebels, the Binding, the deception.

No matter which angle she took, she kept arriving at the same conclusion: she'd been played. If Jelisette was a rebel, then everything—*everything*—had been a lie.

The game, the rules, and Brynleigh's involvement in the Choosing had all been part of something far bigger than her.

And that meant...

Fuck it all.

Curling her fists, Brynleigh drew in a deep breath. She was done.

This would either be the biggest mistake of her life, or it would bring her to freedom.

Looking at Ryker, she asked, "What do you need me to do?"

CHAPTER 6
Two Options

Ryker was exhausted. He'd thought the Choosing had been draining, but the marriage competition had nothing on the past day.

He had taken no pleasure in telling Brynleigh about Emery Sylvain's death, nor did he enjoy watching her reaction. Seeing her be sick had twisted his stomach in the worst of ways.

"It's not going to be easy," he warned, meeting her gaze.

Whenever he looked at her, he imagined her in Emery's place. It was her broken body on the ice. Gray. Staked. Lifeless.

It made him want to burn the world.

"Nothing ever is," she said.

Ryker grabbed the small black box he'd placed on the coffee table earlier, forcing himself to remain calm and in control. He couldn't think about the fact that Brynleigh had wanted to kill him because he had to keep a level head.

He needed her to accept this deal he'd made Myrrah Challard, the Witch Representative of the Northern Region. He'd gambled on the fact that Myrrah's desire for information and actual leads into the Black Night would be strong enough to get Brynleigh out of the prison.

After all, the rebels had nearly wiped out Myrrah's coven two centuries ago. She'd been a witchling then, not even Mature, but after most of her coven died, she rose to power.

By the time Ryker was born, she was a Representative. Five years ago, she'd been appointed as Head Witch over the seven covens that called the Republic of Balance their home.

Myrrah had spent considerable time and resources tracking the rebels, but they were slippery and kept evading her.

Ryker drew in a deep breath.

"The Black Night is a rebel organization that has been terrorizing the Republic of Balance for centuries." He spoke calmly as if he was talking to an informant. "Until recently, their actions have remained out of the public eye."

Brynleigh rubbed her neck, and he stared at the column of her throat. He could still remember his horror as the silver shrapnel had torn through Brynleigh's neck during the Masked Ball.

Unbidden, a vision of her bleeding out flashed through Ryker's eyes, but he banished it. There was no room for thoughts like that right now. No room for emotions.

He was stone. Cold. Lifeless. Strong.

She said, "But not anymore."

"No, it seems they've abandoned their secretive agenda and have decided to work out in the open."

After the attack on the Two Hundredth Choosing, everyone knew there were rebels within the Republic. There was no more hiding their existence.

"What does this have to do with me?" she asked.

Straight to the point. That was something he'd always enjoyed about her. Now, it was just another reminder of the way things had changed.

He cleared his throat. "As I said before, Emery Sylvain had ties to the Black Night. So does his Bound Partner."

Brynleigh winced, but he ignored it. He had to get this over with. This was nothing but a fucking mission.

After all, that was only fair. She was the one who'd treated their relationship like a job first—one where he forfeited his life at the end—so this course of action seemed fitting.

"If Jelisette is a member of the Black Night—"

"She is," Ryker growled. "The intel is clear. We have an overwhelming amount of evidence confirming it."

They didn't know much about the rebels, but once they'd discovered her link to Emery Sylvain, it had been easy enough to connect the rest of the dots.

Brynleigh tilted her head and narrowed her eyes. "Then why not just arrest Jelisette?"

"It's not that simple." He gritted his teeth, and his voice was sharp when he continued, "There are laws in the Republic, although I'm not sure you fucking realize that."

The moment he spoke, the air thickened.

She balled her fists and snapped, "I know laws exist."

"Do you?" His chest heaved as some of the anger he'd been tamping down bubbled up. "Because I'm not so sure."

Glaring at him, she rubbed her wrists. "I'm not an idiot."

"No, just a killer." The last word ripped out of him in a vicious snarl.

She recoiled.

"Fine. Yes! I'm a fucking killer." Her eyes blazed with fury. "Is that what you want to hear?"

"No!" Of course, it wasn't what he wanted. "I want the wife I Chose."

But apparently, that wasn't going to happen, and now he was stuck in this deal of his own making.

Several minutes passed in terse silence, the walls seeming to fold in on them, as Ryker wrangled his anger back under control. It was more difficult than ever.

"Listen, Jelisette isn't in prison because she hasn't been caught breaking laws," he said. "There's nothing directly tying her to the attacks, and we can't just throw her behind bars for no reason."

If they could, it would make things a lot easier.

Ryker furled and unfurled his fists. His stomach growled, but he ignored it. This wasn't the time for hunger.

"We can argue about this for days, but it doesn't change the fucking facts."

Long moments passed.

When Brynleigh's eyes rose once again, they lacked some of the life that used to be in them.

He'd done that. Maybe not on purpose, but he'd let them take her. He hadn't fought for her, hadn't looked for her.

This situation was her fault… but it was also his.

By the Obsidian Sands, their situation was so gods-damned complicated.

"What do you need from me?"

She sounded resigned, as if she knew there was only one way this could go.

She was right. Either she agreed to these terms, or Ryker would have to return her to prison.

Not The Pit—never the fucking Pit again, not while he still drew breath into his lungs and his heart still beat, especially now that he realized she wasn't involved with the rebels—but his influence could only go so far.

He couldn't fathom the thought of her languishing in any cell, though. Even after everything that happened, he didn't want to see her in pain.

See? Gods-damned complicated.

Maybe one day, after Ryker's mother passed the mantle of Representative onto him, he'd have more power, but right now, he'd used every ounce of influence he had to accomplish this.

Doing his job had never been so difficult.

"You need to return to Jelisette and work for her while you uncover information about the rebels," he said simply. "We need tangible proof of her involvement in the Black Night, and you're in the perfect position to obtain it."

She didn't say anything. She just stared at him.

The weight of Brynleigh's gaze was heavy, and he swallowed before continuing, "The Black Night doesn't use regular technology to communicate. That's why it's been so gods-damned hard to get a read on them. But they must be using something. Coded letters, books, word of mouth, spies, *something*. You're our best shot."

Their only shot, really.

The grandfather clock ticked away, echoing the pounding of his heart as he waited for her response.

Each second felt longer than the last. He forced himself to maintain an impassive look, although, on the inside, he was begging her to accept the deal.

He couldn't take her back.

And then, after a lifetime that was probably only a few minutes went by, Brynleigh *laughed*.

It was just a chuckle at first, a raspy sound, as if her body had forgotten how to make that particular noise, but it kept going. It grew louder until her mirth boomed around the house. She bent in half, gripping the edges of the chair as she wheezed.

There was no humor in the sound. It was cold and lifeless, and the hairs on his arms rose.

Fuck, maybe her mind had broken. It wouldn't be the first time Victor Orpheus had shattered someone.

Something deep within Ryker twisted at the thought.

Before he could do something fucking idiotic, like reach out and touch her, Ryker tightened his grip on the black box. Thankful for something to hold, he forced his blank mask to remain in place.

"Care to fill me in on what's so amusing?" He kept his voice low and calm, the same one he'd use for a random informant and not his potentially broken wife.

A choked half-laugh, half-gasp came from Brynleigh and she slowly dragged her eyes to his.

"She'll kill me."

Another laugh. This one was encased in ice, and it sent chills crawling down his spine. Or maybe it was her words.

"You don't know that," he said carefully.

"Oh, I do." She chuckled darkly, and a few shadows slipped from her palms. "This is your grand scheme? You couldn't kill me, so you decided to get my Maker to do it?"

Now, it was Ryker's turn to wince. He hated hearing her talk about dying. "She won't kill you."

But the words sounded weak, even to his ears.

Brynleigh stared at him in utter disbelief. "Putting aside the ridiculous assumption that Jelisette wouldn't kill me—because she would—what's your plan?"

Shadows flickered through her eyes, and she laughed again.

"Am I supposed to waltz in there and say, 'Hey, Jelisette, long time, no see. Where have I been? Oh, I've just been in a fucking dungeon, getting tortured because you sent Zanri to kill my new husband, and he was understandably pissed, but I'm out now, and we're all good. Anyways, got any work for me?'" Brynleigh raised a brow. "How do you fucking think that will work out for me?"

Anger flashed through her eyes as if *she* was furious at *him*. As if he was the one ruining everything.

That was absolutely ridiculous. Ryker was trying to help Brynleigh, and she was the one who'd destroyed everything they'd built.

Another crack appeared in his mask, and his nostrils flared. He clenched his jaw, and his fists furled.

"You'll have to figure it out," he ground out. "There must be something you can say that will keep Jelisette from killing you."

Another long moment, another laugh.

He didn't respond.

What did she think would happen when she concocted her plan? Did she honestly think she could just murder the son of a Representative and get away with it?

Eventually, the laughter died off, and she blinked.

"Fuck me, you're serious." Brynleigh shook her head, her eyes wide in disbelief. "This is... you want me to double cross my Maker?"

She had to. There was no other way he could help her.

"Yes."

Brynleigh opened and closed her mouth repeatedly.

Worse. He felt worse than before. How was that possible?

"This is... You should've just killed me yesterday," she whispered. "That would've been kinder than this."

Kind.

As if she understood the meaning of the word.

He *was* being kind. He'd gotten her out of prison, for the gods' sake.

Had it only been a day since he first saw her? It felt like an entire lifetime had passed. Their wedding seemed like eons ago.

All of a sudden, Ryker was done with this.

He needed space. He had to put some room between him and Brynleigh, with her sad eyes, broken laugh, and golden hair that called to him even now.

She'd betrayed him and planned on killing him, but his body didn't seem to care. He wanted her as much as he had the first time he saw her.

His heart urged him to put aside his anger and consider her reasons, but that organ was a fool, and he wasn't ready to listen to it.

With a flick of his finger, Ryker opened the small box.

A topaz bracelet sat on a bed of inky velvet, and a single silver teardrop hung from it. He took the jewelry out carefully, undoing the clasp.

"Give me your wrist."

She didn't move. Of course not. Nothing would be easy between them anymore. He was beginning to see that.

She asked, "Why?"

Pinching the bridge of his nose, Ryker sighed loudly. His mask of calmness was well and truly gone.

"So, I can put this tracker on you." He held it up. "It's been a long twenty-four hours, and I need more coffee."

What he actually needed was to turn back time to before this happened, but since that wasn't possible, caffeine came in a close second.

"We can go over the logistics of the plan tonight. You need to sleep and have more blood before we leave," he said.

He could tell she wasn't back to full strength yet, and they wouldn't go anywhere until she was better. Because she was his asset. He had to ensure she was healthy enough to accomplish the task at hand.

That was it.

Brynleigh's eyes hardened. "Aren't you missing a step?"

His brows knit together. "No."

He'd thought it all through. This was the only way.

"Yes, you are." She glared daggers at him. If looks could kill, he'd be a dead man a hundred times over. "I haven't agreed to this asinine suicide mission."

"Do you want to go back to prison?" he snapped.

He hadn't intended for his voice to be so sharp, but he was just so gods-damned *done.* He used to have the patience of a saint, but that seemed to have vanished on their disastrous wedding night.

"Obviously fucking not." Her gaze was deadly. "They tortured me, Ryker." She rolled up her sleeves, showing him the still-pink flesh of her wrists. "I'd rather die than return to that hellhole."

"Then we are in agreement," he snarled.

His magic was a storm as he struggled to remain in control. He'd never been so close to losing his grip on his power as he was in that moment.

"There are only two options. Two paths you can take. That's it. This is *your* doing. It's called a fucking consequence. Deal with it."

Fire flashed through her eyes. "I'm not a child. I know what consequences are."

She snarled.

"Good. Then make up your mind. Will it be prison, or will you help find out what the fuck Jelisette is doing with the Black Night? This is it. I have nothing else. There isn't another option, nor do you have anyone else you can deceive and betray." Ryker knew he was all she had, and gods help him if that didn't make him feel horrible. "Decide."

Everything between them always came down to choices. It was a fucking cosmic joke.

After what felt like a lifetime, she held out her wrist, and snapped.

"Fine, I'll do it."

Thank all the gods. Neither choice was good, but this was the better path.

Exhaling a sigh of relief, Ryker slid the bracelet onto her wrist. He was careful not to touch her skin as he shut the clasp.

Blue sparks rose, the air crackled, and the bracelet fused together.

An accusatory glare that would've killed a lesser man crossed her face.

"What the fuck was that?"

"The bracelet is enchanted," he informed her. "You can't take it off. No matter where you go in the Republic of Balance, I'll be able to find you. This is not up for debate. It was part of the deal I made for you."

Myrrah had insisted upon it. To say that Brynleigh was a flight risk was a damned understatement.

"I see." Somehow, her voice was even harder than before. "Are we done here?"

She looked at him like she hated him, like she wasn't the one who had tried to kill him, and his insides twisted into knots.

Ryker still couldn't believe this was happening, still couldn't believe *this* was their life.

So much for fucking happily ever after. How could he have ever thought they'd get a fairy tale ending to their story? He'd been a fool.

Happy endings were for people whose relationships weren't built on a foundation of murder, lies, and deception.

Drained by this entire conversation, he raked his hands through his hair and sighed.

"Yes. We're done."

Everything else could wait.

"Thank Isvana." She rose to her feet, a tremor still present in her legs.

Ryker forced himself not to notice the shaking in her hands, the paleness of her skin, or the bruises that still bloomed on her flesh.

He remained seated as she made her way to the bedroom, waiting until he heard the shower running before rising to his feet.

This entire situation was a gods-damned disaster.

As luck would have it—and to be clear, he was not feeling lucky at all—things rapidly deteriorated from there.

While Brynleigh showered, he put a few bags of blood in the bedroom for her, along with her suitcase. He wasn't a monster, no matter what she believed. Then he grabbed some food, made another coffee, sat at the kitchen table, and pulled out his phone.

It had been vibrating nearly non-stop since early this morning.

Sighing, he unlocked the device and stared at the notifications. He had two dozen unread emails. He tapped on the first one, the subject line simply titled *Urgent*.

Captain Waterborn,

What is this I hear about Brynleigh Waterborn, formally Brynleigh de la Point, being removed from The Pit? The vampire has proven ties to the Black Night.
Under whose authority were you acting?
An immediate response is required.
- General Killian

Ryker typed out a quick reply reiterating that he was acting under orders from the Head Witch and to direct any concerns to her.

He closed the email, only to realize that each message in his inbox was a variation of the first. A low throb came to life in his temples, and he rubbed his forehead.

An hour later, he finished answering each message. He had started copying and pasting his replies halfway through, but by then, it was too late. The throb had turned into a pulsing ache.

Brynleigh had yet to emerge from the bedroom.

Needing to stretch his legs, he tucked his phone in his back pocket and strode over to her door.

A frown tugged at his lips, and he pressed his ear against the wood.

The room was completely silent.

His frown deepened as he knocked and called her name.

Still no response.

She wouldn't have been so stupid as to try and escape, right? Not after he'd just freed her from prison. Although maybe she did. After all, it wasn't like he truly knew her.

A thousand curses ran through his mind as he twisted the handle, opening the door. A growl rose in his throat, but he tamped it down as he took in the scene before him.

The room was washed in darkness. Curtains covered the window. The carpet was black. The wastebasket by the door was filled with empty bags that had once contained blood. Shadows snaked around Brynleigh's hands and feet.

She was naked and stretched out on the bed, her body covered by the same thin quilt. Her right arm reached above her head like she was trying to grab something. Hair flowed down the side of the mattress, and her eyes were shut as she slumbered.

A whimper escaped her, and she rolled onto her stomach.

Ryker clenched his fists, and though this felt like an extreme violation of her privacy, he couldn't make himself move. Anger held him in place.

Half of him wanted to throttle her, to kill her for wanting to kill him, and yet, the other half was drawn to her. He wanted to brush her hair away from her cheek, to check on her bruises and ensure they were disappearing. He wanted to be with her. Hold her and kiss her and love her like he had before their world imploded.

Right now, she didn't look like a monster. She didn't even look dangerous. If anything, she looked like she was his.

Except, she wasn't fucking his. She'd never been his.

He rubbed a fist over his aching heart. She'd lied and intended to kill him, and like a fucking fool, he'd fallen in love with her.

The headache worsened.

Space.

He needed more gods-damned space.

He slipped the door shut just as his phone started vibrating.

Groaning, Ryker fished the troublesome piece of technology from his pocket. His sister's name flashed across the screen. He quickly unlocked the phone, his stomach plummeting as he read the message.

RIVER

Heads up, Mom's on a rampage.

He had no time to react. Less than thirty seconds later, the phone buzzed continuously. *Representative Waterborn—Mom* appeared in flashing letters.

"Fucking hell," Ryker breathed.

Couldn't he get a moment's reprieve?

Palming the back of his neck, as if that could help him with the shit storm he was certain was about to be unleashed on him, he moved to the other end of the house. It wasn't like he could go far in this bungalow, but he would at least attempt to find some privacy.

He'd successfully dodged his mother's calls for the past three weeks, but now...

If he didn't answer, she might do something incredibly stupid and insane, like show up here. That was the last thing he needed.

As Ryker often had over the past month, he wished he was anywhere else in the world but here. Alas, wishes, just like fairy tale endings, were for other people.

Dropping into a chair at the kitchen table, he slid his thumb across the screen, accepting the video call. He propped the phone against an empty fruit bowl and waited for the call to connect. He couldn't even claim spotty signal issues—the Central Region had some of the best technology in the entire Republic, and the signal was perfect, even in the woods.

As soon as the call connected, Ryker winced. He looked even worse than he thought. His hair was disheveled, dark bags hung under his eyes, and his shirt was wrinkled from being slept in.

He wouldn't usually be concerned about his appearance, not after everything he'd endured since his wedding night, but he knew his mother. She would take personal offense to how he looked, as if his lack of care reflected on her.

It didn't matter that no one else was around. It would still bother her.

Sure enough, a scowl marred her features. Internally, Ryker sighed. Not externally. Nothing to set her off.

As usual, Tertia Waterborn was perfectly put together. She looked like she had stepped out of the page of a magazine.

The Representative of the Fae sat at the large mahogany desk in her home study. Brown hair was coiffed and styled away from her face. Diamond studs adorned her delicate, pointed ears. Her black silk blouse shimmered in the light, and her chin rested on a manicured hand as she stared into the camera.

Despite the distance between them, Ryker could have sworn the temperature dropped in the room at his mother's obvious disapproval.

"Ryker Elias Waterborn," Tertia said in a cold, quiet voice that he had to strain to hear. "You have Chosen poorly, and your actions have dishonored the illustrious Waterborn name. I am incredibly disappointed in you."

Apparently, they were skipping hellos and going straight to admonishment.

How delightful.

Ryker had known his mother would call sooner or later. There wasn't much one could keep from her, but why today? Why now?

The gods hated him. That was the only plausible explanation.

"Hello, Mother," he said calmly. "It's so nice to see you, too."

Perhaps if he was kind and well-mannered, she would leave him alone. He certainly had enough to deal with without bringing his mother into the mix.

Tertia's eyes glinted as she leaned forward. She tapped her manicured nails on the desk, the sound crystal clear.

Tap, tap, tap.

On and on the solo drumbeat went as her eyes drilled into him.

Ryker knew better than to speak before his mother. He'd learned manners when most children were learning their primary colors.

Long, drawn-out minutes passed before Tertia deigned to speak again. Every breath was an entire percussion section in Ryker's ears.

"This afternoon, I was at the Crystal Garden having lunch with Representative Havill." She raised a brow. "It was important, Ryker."

Everything Tertia did was important, at least from her perspective.

Ryker didn't respond. She hadn't given him leave yet.

"I had just ordered my salad when suddenly, I received the most disturbing phone call." Her words were clipped, and the drumming ceased. "Do you know what I was told?"

He wished he didn't, but he could guess. It seemed his time of avoiding his family and the press was coming to an end.

Sighing, he kneaded his temples. "Mother, I can explain—"

"You will not," she snapped. "Not over the phone."

Tertia's voice remained at the same decibel, but it felt like she was screaming at him. Each word was an ice pick in his ear.

He didn't have the energy to fight with her. Not now, after the day he'd had. His head throbbed, and he groaned, waiting for his mother to continue.

"I warned you, Ryker," she said icily.

As if Ryker could forget his mother's "warning." She'd gone after Brynleigh and decided that since the vampire had no lineage, proper education, or finances, Ryker had Chosen poorly. Ryker had defended his then-fiance, but now...

Now, it turned out the truth was so much worse than that.

"I know," he replied tersely.

His mother scoffed, and her voice chilled impossibly further. "I told you the bloodsucker wasn't the right match for you. I warned you this would happen. But you did not heed my warning and married her anyway."

The wedding band on Ryker's left hand was heavy, emphasizing his mother's point.

"You made a foolish Choice, and it will have far more repercussions than you know," Tertia admonished.

Ryker narrowed his eyes.

Was she threatening him?

Hot anger churned and bubbled like lava in his veins. He was a Mature fae, and his position should afford him at least a modicum of respect.

Unfortunately for him, his mother seemed hell-bent on making his day even worse.

"Do you know what I hate more than vampires who don't know their places?" Her searing gaze was one of intense displeasure, and he fought the urge to squirm. "*Surprises.*"

A stone lodged itself in his stomach. Never mind that he was well into his third decade of life. His mother was scolding him like he was a misbehaving child.

He knew exactly how this would go.

Tertia would go on and on and on about how Waterborns were supposed to be perfect. They weren't allowed to have problems. They weren't allowed to disrupt the natural way of life in the Republic of Balance.

Waterborns weren't allowed to fucking *live.*

Ryker balled his fist, careful to keep it out of sight of the camera. "Mother, I would have told you—"

"I do not recall granting you permission to speak," she snapped.

Cursing inwardly, he slammed his mouth shut. As much as he wanted to end the call, doing so abruptly would be worse.

The last thing he needed was to see Tertia face to face. Not now. Possibly not ever.

His head pounded, and he glanced longingly at the kitchen. A bottle of amber liquor sat above the cabinets, calling his name.

"I *do not* enjoy being kept out of the loop, my son," Tertia spoke quietly, each word calculated and as sharp as the icicles she wielded.

He understood where she was coming from, but keeping his mother up to date in the middle of all the craziness that had been the last three weeks of his life was very low on his list of priorities, so he didn't really have many other options.

Tertia wasn't finished.

"Nor do I enjoy being delivered news like a commoner in the middle of my lunch. I had to hear about this from Connie Evander, of all people." She scoffed. "Do you know how much joy that spineless Light Elf will take in knowing something before me? She was born Without, Ryker. *Without*!"

The way Tertia said the word, it was as though being born lacking magic was the worst thing in the entire world. It wasn't Connie's fault she was born that way.

Most beings—not humans, of course—in the Republic of Balance were born with magic coursing through their veins, but every so often, some people were born Without the blessings of the gods.

Tertia's voice raised a notch. "Connie has always been jealous that her husband isn't part of the Inner Council of Representatives, and now, she'll lord this over me for the next century. By the Black Sands, the woman will be more insufferable than she already is."

Ryker barely stopped himself from rolling his eyes. That's all life was to his mother. Social games, gossiping, and politics.

Meanwhile, Ryker had real problems, like a murderous wife.

The Representative was still scolding him.

Ryker listened with half an ear as Tertia told him he should have informed her of what happened earlier, how he was a disappointment, how he needed to shape up if he ever wanted to bear the mantle of Representative in the future.

These were all things he'd heard before.

A half-hour passed, during which Ryker said maybe three sentences. He was ready to throw his phone out of the window when a floorboard creaked. He looked up, and a pair of onyx eyes met his from across the room.

How long had Brynleigh been standing there?

"I have to go, Mother." He flicked his gaze back to the phone. "I'm sorry. I'll message you."

She screeched, "Ryker, don't you hang up—"

He ended the call, flung the phone face down on the table, and dropped his head into his hands.

CHAPTER 7

Wishes were for Fools

Several minutes ago

The sound of voices pulled Brynleigh out of a restless, nightmare-filled sleep.

She'd been back in that chair. Silver daggers pierced her arms and legs. Rivers of blood streamed down her limbs. Emilia, the witch, had been taunting her with her magic, burning her over and over again until she broke down in tears.

And then Brynleigh woke up. Naked. Alone. Safe... for now.

It took her several minutes to calm her heart rate and realize the voices weren't just in her head. She dressed in the same sweater and leggings as before and tied her hair in a messy bun before moving on silent feet to the door.

Her shadows had fully returned, and their song was a soothing lullaby. Her wounds were healed, and her skin was back to normal.

On the outside, she looked like herself again, but on the inside, she knew she'd never be the same person she'd been.

Her old normal was gone, never to be seen again.

Ryker hated her; Jelisette had betrayed and abandoned her; and she would probably die when she returned to her Maker's safe house.

Maybe things were always destined to turn out this way. Maybe she'd been a fool even to pretend that she and Ryker could have a happy life together.

It was obvious now that would never happen.

Ryker's anger was palpable. It had been the third member of their conversation earlier.

His feelings were justified and understandable.

The thing was, Brynleigh was angry, too.

At first, she thought she was just angry with Jelisette and Zanri. *That*, at least, was obvious.

But now that she was feeling better, she realized she was angry with Ryker, too.

This fresh fury had a rawness to it that burned her heart from the inside out. During the Choosing, Ryker had told her how much he loved his family. He swore he'd do anything for them.

Why couldn't he see that her actions had been rooted in the same kind of love?

He had a right to be angry, but she did, too.

She'd suffered for weeks because of him. Been tortured by his people.

Just because she was a bad person didn't mean she wasn't allowed to be angry about their treatment of her.

Fresh anger churned in her veins as she padded out of the bedroom. For the first time since their arrival, she took in her surroundings.

The only bathroom was accessible from both the bedroom and the main living space. All the walls were bare, save for a few generic scenic shots of farmland in the Western Region. The wooden floor was worn but well taken care of. Curtains covered the windows, blocking the sun's deadly rays. The living room where they'd been earlier had a small TV, and the fireplace was unlit.

Thank the gods for that small mercy. Vampires and fire did not mix.

Ryker sat at the small kitchen table, staring at his phone. He gnawed on the inside of his cheek, and beneath the table, his fist clenched and unclenched.

It didn't take a genius to realize his mother was on the other end of the call. Especially as the Representative went on and on about how disappointed she was in Ryker.

Some of Brynleigh's anger dissipated as she studied the fae captain.

He looked exhausted. Despite the rigidness of his shoulders, his eyes were heavy with sadness. He didn't talk back as his mother berated him.

Brynleigh's gut twisted. It had been doing that a lot since she'd been freed.

A defeated, fatigued look had settled onto Ryker's face. He looked so unlike the confident fae she'd married that her anger deflated until there was nothing but frustration and sadness left in its wake.

They were both broken, both hurting, both betrayed...

And it was her fault.

Brynleigh fiddled with the bracelet, waiting for him to notice her.

It didn't take long.

His eyes slid up to hers, and he held her gaze for a long moment before hanging up his call. She thought he would ask why she'd been eavesdropping, but instead, he groaned and dropped his head into his hands.

Tension filled the air, and Brynleigh hated it.

Like everything else, this felt wrong.

She moved towards him slowly, careful not to come too close. Even the air felt fragile, like the wrong move or word could destroy everything.

Several minutes passed in silence before she whispered, "Can I ask you something?"

The question had been weighing on her ever since she entered the hallway.

Ryker slowly lifted his head, sighing. "Yes?"

"Why do you let your mother talk to you like that? Why didn't you tell her to stop?"

He could stand up against Tertia—he'd done it for Brynleigh the first night she'd met his mother, for the gods' sake.

"I couldn't." He scrubbed a hand over his face. "If I did, she'd show up here."

Brynleigh swept her eyes over his, and her brows furrowed. "And you... don't want that."

"No."

Her mouth dried. "Because of me?"

A long moment passed before he pushed back from the table. "Yes."

She had expected that response, but the pang of hurt that lanced through her took her by surprise.

She sucked in a sharp breath and pressed a hand against her heart. "I'm sorry, Ryker."

More apologies rose to the tip of her tongue.

Sorry for breaking us.

Sorry for ruining what we had.

Sorry for taking you away from your family.

Sorry that your sister killed mine.

Sorry, sorry, sorry.

Brynleigh had so many apologies that they all jammed up in her mouth. Words weren't enough to fix this—to fix them—and she couldn't decide which ones took precedence over the others.

Ultimately, she shook her head and repeated, "I'm so sorry."

Ryker stared at her for a long moment before dipping his chin. "Me, too."

Her unspoken words were so heavy that she couldn't breathe or think. She just watched him.

He strode past her into the kitchen and grabbed a glass bottle above the fridge. He took out a cup, pouring himself a generous serving of dark amber liquid before tossing it back.

When the glass was empty, he looked up at her.

"We're leaving as soon as the sun sets in an hour." He placed the cup on the counter. "It would be best if you took this time to prepare yourself."

His voice left no room for discussion, let alone apologies.

Biting her lip, Brynleigh hung her head and retreated to the bedroom.

She had one hour to figure out what the hell she would say to Jelisette.

It turned out that an hour wasn't enough time. When the sun

dipped below the horizon, Brynleigh was no closer to knowing what to say. She had dozens of questions but not a single answer.

She'd spent the hour getting dressed and braiding her hair, hoping the repetitive movements would help calm her down.

They did not.

She'd finished a few minutes ago. Now she sat on the edge of the bed, fiddling with the hem of the maroon sweater she'd pulled from her suitcase.

A knock came on the door.

"Ready?" Ryker asked.

Brynleigh stared at the door. How could she be ready for this? She was almost certainly walking to her death.

However, Ryker had already made it clear this was their only path. Arguing would get her nowhere.

She had gotten out of prison. She'd slept in a real bed. She'd taken a hot shower. If this was her time to die, she would go to her death with dignity.

Brynleigh rose to her feet and walked to the door.

With this barrier between them, she could pretend everything was still okay. She could pretend they were still speaking through headphones in the Hall of Choice. She could pretend that everything wasn't destroyed.

For a single moment, she was happy.

Then Ryker turned the knob, opening the door. Her illusion shattered when she took in the hardness in his eyes.

Happiness was a distant memory, and all that remained between them was hurt.

That thought weighed heavily on her shoulders, and she dipped her head. "Yes, I'm ready."

There was no point in putting this off any longer.

He grunted a reply and spun on his heel, marching towards the front door. His posture was rigid, and he'd changed into black jeans and a T-shirt that hugged his muscles. He'd showered, his hair damp as it clung to the back of his neck, and his pointed ears were more pronounced with the haphazard way he'd styled his hair.

He moved with confidence, and power rippled off him.

If this was Brynleigh's last night alive—and that was highly likely, considering that her Maker was difficult to deal with on a good day—at least she would get to spend time with Ryker. Even though he hated her. Even though she was angry with him.

Even though they were broken, they still... were.

Brynleigh clung to that fact with all her might because the alternative was too much to consider. She was about to stroll into the lion's den, having broken all the rules, destroyed the game, and fallen in love with her mark.

She needed *something* to hold onto, something to give her a semblance of hope. Of life. Of love. There were worse ways to spend one's last night alive.

Ryker stopped a few feet from the front door and turned. His gaze dropped to the bracelet he'd given her and then rose to meet hers again.

"Don't try to run. I'll find you."

The words were a dark promise, echoed by the glint of violence in his eyes. The captain was a predator through and through, his natural darkness rippling off him in waves.

This was the fae male she had always expected to meet.

Too bad she'd gone and fallen in love with him.

"Where would I go?" She frowned. "I have nothing and no one. I'm alone."

She was a vampire with no family and no home. Her only friend was Hallie, and she couldn't go to her. Even if Brynleigh knew where the Fortune Elf lived—and she didn't—she assumed Therian, Hallie's husband, had told her about Brynleigh's betrayal.

Brynleigh's husband hated her, and her Maker...

Well, she would find out soon how Jelisette felt about her, wouldn't she?

That depressing thought spurned her forward. She wouldn't wait for an answer. Instead, she leaned around Ryker and opened the door, careful not to touch him.

The gentle pitter-patter of an autumnal rain greeted her as she stepped outside. The moon's silver light was barely visible through the clouds. A chill in the air spoke to the coming winter.

She inhaled deeply, breathing in the fresh forest air.

Not too bad for a final night alive.

She gripped the wooden railing, looking out over the forest from the wooden porch. Even though this rain was nothing like the raging storm River had called to destroy Chavin, Brynleigh's childhood home, it still drew forth memories of that fateful night.

Her lungs burned at the memory of nearly drowning. Her heart ached as she recalled the loss of her family.

Running her fingers over her necklace, Brynleigh traced the individual loops. Thankfully, it had survived her time in the dungeon—the one Ryker called The Pit.

Brynleigh didn't move until Ryker strode past her into the rain. He prowled through the trees like a predator, and she trailed him without a word.

They got in the car, buckled in, and Ryker asked for Jelisette's address. She gave it to him, and he punched it into the GPS.

Once the map came online, he navigated the vehicle out of the woods.

Silence fell upon them once more.

The crunch of gravel beneath the tires echoed the rain pelting the windshield, the strange symphony keeping Brynleigh company as she stared out the streaky window. Seemingly endless forests slowly gave way to fields. They passed a few cars, but for the most part, the road was empty.

And then she saw them.

The glowing triple arches that gave Golden City its name rose in the distance. They shone like beacons, their light cutting through the darkness of the cloudy night.

Cold fear settled deep within her, and she suddenly wished she'd had more blood. Her fangs ached. Her shadows sang a worrisome song of lament.

Shuddering, she drew her legs onto the seat, wrapped her arms around them, and rested her chin on her knees.

More than ever before, Brynleigh was convinced the gilded metropolis was a place of death.

No wonder the rebels took such great offense to the Representatives and their rule. Not having wanted to spiral into what threatened to be a never-ending circle of doubt and fear, Brynleigh hadn't permitted herself to think about the Black Night earlier. Now, her mind wandered in that direction.

On the surface, the rebels' cause was just.

The Representatives were a problem. They held an unfair amount of power, which allowed them to control everyone and everything. She even understood Jelisette's involvement in the movement.

If Ryker's sources were right and a Representative had killed the vampire's Bound Partner, then she had ample reason to hate the ruling class.

But Brynleigh still had so many questions.

Why had her Maker abandoned her? Why had Jelisette hidden her Binding? Why had the rebels attacked the Choosing? And perhaps most importantly, why had Jelisette kept so many secrets from Brynleigh?

These were all questions she would have to ponder... if she survived tonight.

The closer they got to the city, the less Brynleigh paid attention to what was happening outside. She focused everything she had on staying alive.

When the automated voice providing directions informed them they were a few minutes out, Ryker pulled the car into a dark, vacant lot and parked.

The silence, which had almost felt natural, took on an oppressive air. The car was suddenly too small, the rain too loud, Brynleigh's heartbeats too thunderous. Even the captain's steady breaths were like gusts of wind in her ears.

During moments like these, Brynleigh wished she was a much older vampire, one who was more detached from her mortal emotions. If she could shut down her frustration and the stress that these loud noises created, that would be fucking fantastic.

But wishes were for people who weren't broken, so she didn't even bother. Besides, if the past few weeks of her life were any indication, she wasn't certain Isvana would hear her pleas.

Brynleigh kept her arms wrapped around her legs as the fae captain reached into the center console. He withdrew a small black velvet box. Popping it open, he tilted it towards her.

Curiosity had Brynleigh canting her head just enough to peer into the box, a frown pulling at her lips. Two diamond earrings rested in a bed of ivory.

She glanced at them, then back at him. "What is this?"

She wasn't foolish enough to think she'd ever get another gift from him. Not after everything.

He confirmed her suspicions moments later when he handed her the box.

"They're earpieces. They aren't detectable by scanners, and the embedded microphones will allow me to hear everything that's happening inside."

His unspoken words were so loud that it was like he shouted them. *So don't try anything, because I'll be listening.*

Between the earrings and the tracking bracelet, it was almost too much. Too many reminders of her betrayal. Too many knives digging into her heart at the same time.

This was no way to live, yet what choice did she have?

Pressure built behind her eyes, but she refused to let the tears fall.

Once, Ryker had trusted her. He'd even loved her. And now, he was treating her like nothing more than a tool.

Something deep within Brynleigh fractured as she reached for the earrings and placed them in her lobes.

She hardened her soul, gathered the remnants of her aching heart, and stuffed them deep inside herself. She'd deal with these emotions... tomorrow.

If there was a tomorrow.

The cold steel in Ryker's gaze matched the metal's icy bite in her ears. Clasping the back of the second earring, she folded her hands in her lap.

"I understand." If he was going to treat her like an asset and nothing else, she would act like one. "Anything else, *Captain*?"

He stiffened, his shoulders going back, and he slowly turned to stare at her. Ice hardened his gaze, and the temperature dropped in the car.

For a moment, she thought he would say something. Anything. Would he fight? Would she want that?

Yes.

She wanted them to be... something. Fighting with him would be far better than this too-strange quiet that was a heavy blanket between them.

He didn't fight with her, though. He just clenched his jaw and shook his head.

"There's nothing else. Do you know what you're going to say?"

Brynleigh scoffed. "No."

She had no idea what kind of mood Jelisette would be in or what she was walking into, and there was no real way she could plan for that.

She'd come out alive... or she wouldn't.

If tonight was any sign, Brynleigh didn't think Ryker would care much either way. Not anymore. And damn it all, but that hurt more than anything else.

She didn't let her pain show, though. She was just an asset, and an ocean of silence divided them. If he rejected her once more, she might drown in the waves of their brokenness.

"No matter what she says, you can't reveal you're working with me." He gripped the steering wheel with white-knuckled hands.

She didn't know why he was afraid. He wasn't the one going to meet with a Maker who was dangerous on a good day.

He ground out, "Is that understood?"

"It's crystal fucking clear." Brynleigh stared out the windshield. The rain had let up. "I understand exactly what's happening here, Captain. No further clarification is needed."

She had destroyed his trust, and now, she was nothing but a tool for the army to use. Just a vampire with a connection to someone dangerous.

"Okay." He sighed, and for a moment, she thought she heard a trace of pain in his voice. "Let's get this over with."

THE MOMENT BRYNLEIGH stepped out of the car, she released her wings. They fanned out behind her, the black appendages heavy on her back as she strolled down the street.

The safe house was a block away, but she would make the remainder of the journey on foot.

Knowing that Ryker was listening on the other end, she was cognizant of every breath, every footfall, and every heartbeat.

He was still in the car, waiting where Jelisette couldn't see or scent him.

Once, this path had been familiar.

The safe house was mediocrity at its finest. Located in a nondescript residential neighborhood in Astera, a modest subdivision on the outskirts of Golden City, the house wasn't the largest on the block, nor was it the smallest.

The two-story home was well-kept but not extravagant. A white picket fence stood guard around it. A single-car garage housed Jelisette's vehicle, which she never drove. The coup de grace was the solitary light flickering in the living room. It topped off the entire facade, screaming, "Nothing to see here."

The only thing setting the safe house apart was the dark, shadowy mist constantly hovering around the base of the home. It had been there as long as Brynleigh could remember. Even now, shadows curled around the foundation. It was like they were drawn to the building, sentient beings wanting to protect its inhabitants.

For the first time, Brynleigh wondered about the shadows. Were they a remnant of her Maker's Binding? Had they always been there?

She added those questions to her seemingly never-ending list.

Brynleigh made it to the fence before she was ready—although truth be told, she would probably never be ready for this—and unlocked the gate. It creaked as she pushed it open. She stepped into the yard, her skin tingling as the wards washed over her.

There was no turning back now.

The wards were an alarm, alerting Jelisette to her progeny's presence.

Brynleigh strode up the walkway on vampire-silent feet, her movements graceful and smooth. The first time she'd come here, the homey quality had been comforting, enveloping her in a sense of peace.

That feeling was long gone.

Her shadows writhed in her veins, and although her skin was free of damage, the torture she'd endured had left chasmic gouges on her soul.

She was returning to face the woman who'd betrayed her, sent Zanri to kill her, and hadn't even had the decency to try and get her out of prison.

Jelisette was the closest approximation to a mother figure Brynleigh had left. Her sire should have looked after her, cared for her, and guided her as she learned how to be a vampire.

Instead, she had used her progeny as a fucking pawn and abandoned her when she needed her the most.

And now, Brynleigh was prey, walking into a predator's den.

Before she could change her mind or remember what a monumentally bad idea this was, Brynleigh raised a fist and knocked.

Her hand had barely connected with the wood when the door flung open.

Swathed in shadows and wearing a black sweater dress and tights, Jelisette was darkness personified. Piercing, ancient black eyes met Brynleigh's, and ruby lips peeled back in a snarl.

Danger, Brynleigh's shadows screamed. They throbbed and writhed in her veins, urging her to get away from here. But there was no backing out now.

"Inside," Jelisette snapped. "Now."

Brynleigh's heart was a thundering drum. On one hand, she didn't want to enter this house. An air of death surrounded it. On the other hand, she didn't really have a choice. Ryker had made it clear that if she didn't hold up her end of the deal, they would put her back in prison.

She would rather die a thousand deaths before letting that happen.

Swallowing the icy fear rising in her chest, Brynleigh shoved aside all her feelings and followed her Maker inside.

As soon as she stepped over the threshold, the door slammed shut.

Shadows streamed from Jelisette's hands as she turned the deadbolt. It fell into place with a terrifying *thunk*, like an executioner's axe hitting the chopping block.

"You broke the rules, daughter of my blood."

CHAPTER 8
Predators and Prey

Curses, each viler than the last, ran through Ryker's mind, frost crept down his spine, and his magic swirled in warning.

Zanri had mentioned the rules during his interrogation, too. Ryker wasn't entirely sure what they were, but he knew they were bad. Nothing that came out of Jelisette's vile mouth could be good.

A hitched breath that Ryker was intimately familiar with came through his custom headphones. His cock didn't get the message that this was a serious moment because it decided now was the time to come to life. He shoved those thoughts aside.

Forcing himself to stay on task, Ryker pressed his palm flat on his ear, as if that would help him hear better. If he closed his eyes, he could pretend they were still in the Choosing. Pretend their wedding night hadn't yet taken place. Pretend their love was still uncomplicated and unbroken and perfect.

Brynleigh whispered, "I know. I'm sorry."

A vicious, death-kissed snarl ripped through the air.

Instinct had Ryker drawing translucent orbs of water into his palms and readying to fight, even as he realized the snarl came through the headphones.

Then, a pained grunt filtered through the earpiece.

Ryker dissolved his magic, his own gut cramping as if he'd been punched.

It went against his natural predisposition to stay in the vehicle. Everything within him screamed to get up, to do something, to *help*.

He was a protector, through and through.

And Brynleigh needed him.

His heart broke all over again, and his anger was further away than it had been in weeks as he listened to the sounds coming from the safe house.

He flinched when skin slammed against skin.

He drew his own blood, his nails digging into his palms, when there came a muffled cry.

And when a heinous laugh filled his ears, the car handle bent in half from the force of his grip.

Ryker was intimately familiar with the sounds of a fair fight, and this wasn't one. Brynleigh wasn't defending herself against her Maker. She was just taking it.

Because of him.

He froze as a muffled cry filled his ears. This was his fault. He put Brynleigh up to this. He made this deal.

If she died, he would never forgive himself.

Suddenly, silence fell. Somehow, it was worse than the sounds of pain from moments before.

Too quick, too quiet.

Was it over? Had he waited too long?

Brynleigh's words resurfaced in his mind.

She'll kill me.

What in the name of all the gods had he done? Horror shoved all his earlier anger aside, and his heart pounded as he debated whether he should risk being seen.

Ryker was one second away from throwing caution aside when a whimper filled his ears.

A single noise had never sounded so good.

Alive.

Thank the blessed Obsidian Sands.

Brynleigh was still alive.

The fae captain closed his eyes for the briefest moment, resting his head against the seat.

He didn't want Brynleigh to die. Not at her Maker's hands. Not at Victor's hands. Not at anyone's hands.

Even though she'd wanted to kill him, even though he was still so furious with her that at times he could barely breathe, he needed her to live.

"What is rule number ten?" Jelisette asked.

Not even a heartbeat later, the sound of a hand connecting with flesh made Ryker flinch.

Brynleigh's resounding groan caused bile to rise in his throat.

What was the fucking point of asking a question if there wouldn't be a chance to answer?

Brynleigh was strong, though.

Heavy breathing came through the headphones, and Ryker imagined that she was holding herself up against a wall and staring at her Maker. Her eyes would be dark and her face grim as she gathered her strength.

"Once the game has begun, losing is not an option," she rasped, each word sounding weaker than the last. "The only alternative to winning is death."

At the mention of the so-called game, Ryker balled his fists. Games were good. They were fun. Chess was one that he immensely enjoyed—and he hadn't touched it since his wedding night.

But this?

Playing with life and death was not a game.

"And tell me, young one, did you win?" Jelisette's voice was a silky-smooth whisper laced with promises of endless pain.

Every part of Ryker was on edge as the predator made herself known. His magic had never let him down—except when it came to trusting Brynleigh, apparently—and he trusted the pulsing power in his veins when it warned him that Jelisette was one of the most dangerous enemies he'd ever come across.

Not only had the older vampire fed her progeny lies and forged her into a weapon of death, but she'd played her. Brynleigh was a victim in this, too.

Ryker knew that, but that knowledge left him with even more questions.

Where did that leave them? How could he forget everything else that had happened? He had to protect his family and the remnants of his heart.

"No." Brynleigh inhaled sharply. "I lost."

That was it? Did she have nothing else to say?

Ryker held his breath, waiting for her to continue and defend herself, but nothing else came. Why wasn't she begging for her life? Pleading for mercy? Doing fucking *something* to survive this encounter? Did she have no self-preservation instincts at all?

Iron mallets flung themselves against Ryker's skull, his headache returning in full force.

Time ticked by agonizingly slowly as the silence stretched on and on. Ryker's stomach twisted into knots, and a cold sweat coated his forehead.

By the Obsidian Sands, what was she thinking?

"Your... *husband* killed Zanri." Disdain and hatred dripped from Jelisette's words, and Ryker's insides curdled.

A pause, and then Brynleigh said, "Yes."

A lie. She knew the shifter was still alive. Ryker had told her as much.

More ominous, sickening silence. Each moment was worse than the last.

Ryker held his fist in front of his mouth, his head spinning. He was going to be sick, which was wholly unlike him. He was usually calm, reserved, and focused on the job at hand.

Not tonight.

"I should kill you for this failure," Jelisette said conversationally.

Ryker formed an ice dagger in his hand and gripped the car door.

"But I won't," continued the predatory, malicious vampire. "Not yet, anyway."

He paused.

"I... thank you."

"Mhmm. Now, explain *how* you are standing before me. The last I'd heard, you'd been dragged off to The Pit. Usually, that's a one-way ticket to death. How did you survive?"

"It wasn't easy," Brynleigh admitted. "They tortured me."

Several seconds passed in that horrible, too-quiet silence.

Groaning as he melted his dagger, Ryker wished he had eyes inside the house.

"Yes, well, that was always a possibility," Jelisette said dismissively. "You know how those Representatives are."

A deep breath, then Brynleigh murmured, "I do."

The older vampire hummed, the sound as melodic as it was deadly. "And I suppose your husband freed you out of the goodness of his heart?"

Brynleigh laughed bitterly. "No. He wants me to do something for him, but he hasn't told me what it is yet. He's still... upset about what happened."

Understatement of the gods-damned century.

"You will inform me the moment he asks something of you," Jelisette purred.

"Yes, ma'am," Brynleigh said in a cold, robotic tone that sent ice cascading down Ryker's spine. "I understand."

A sound that was like knuckles cracking filled his ears.

"Does the captain know you're here tonight?"

Ryker's heart stalled, and he didn't breathe, waiting for Brynleigh's response. If she wanted to, she could ruin all this with one word.

"No, he thinks I'm sleeping off the torture."

Another lie. The ease with which they rolled off Brynleigh's tongue frightened Ryker. Her tone didn't change, her breath didn't hitch, and each word carried the same inflection.

Ryker exhaled, pressing a hand against his chest as his heart beat once again.

Brynleigh continued, "I shadowed here as soon as I was healed enough to get away. I must return soon, or he'll grow suspicious."

The fae captain had to hand it to her, she was weaving a masterful web of deceit. If he didn't know the truth, he would have believed her.

He *had* believed her.

But did Jelisette?

Gods above, waiting had never been so painful.

"Alright," the older vampire eventually said. "I'm assuming you're still looking for work?"

Such a strange way to refer to murder.

"I am," Brynleigh said.

"Mhmm." Jelisette made a clicking sound with her tongue. "And if I told you to kill the captain?"

Ryker's chest seized.

"I'd do it," Brynleigh said. "Although I think I've lost the element of surprise, thanks to Zanri."

Another pause. "Yes, well. It had to be done. The rules and all that."

"I understand," Brynleigh repeated.

Ryker fucking didn't understand. How two women could discuss murder so casually was beyond him.

Jelisette hummed. "Yes, I believe you might." A drawer opened. "Take this. I'll call when I have something for you."

Fabric rustled, and Ryker assumed Brynleigh was putting whatever her Maker had given her in her pocket.

Sensing the meeting was almost done, Ryker turned on the car. The engine purred to life like a quiet kitten, and he shifted the vehicle into gear. The sooner they got out of here, the better.

"Oh, and Brynleigh?" The coldness of Jelisette's voice made Ryker's breath catch in his throat. "If I find out you're lying to me, I *will* kill you. Your death will be long and drawn out. It will make whatever you suffered in The Pit seem like child's play. I will delight in drawing every last drop of your treacherous blood from your veins before driving a stake through your heart."

Fucking hell.

Ryker's heart twisted in on itself as the dark words hung in the air. This was his fault. He never should've made this deal. He'd assumed that Brynleigh had been exaggerating, that Jelisette wouldn't actually kill her progeny, but now...

By the Holy Obsidian Sands, he had vastly underestimated the older vampire's cruelty.

His heart was a galloping horse, and seconds moved like hours.

"I understand," was Brynleigh's murmured reply. "I knew what I was getting myself into when I came here."

Another long moment passed during which Ryker clutched the steering wheel with white-knuckled hands before Jelisette said, "You may leave."

Ryker closed his eyes, releasing a long breath.

"Thank you," Brynleigh whispered.

A cold, tinkling laugh came from the older vampire. "Don't thank me, daughter of my blood. Just do what you're told, and this time, follow the rules to the letter."

The unspoken threat hung in the air. *Or else.*

"Yes, ma'am."

A door slammed moments later.

Ryker did not release the steering wheel, even as a hushed "I'm coming" came through the headphones.

Shadows pooled on the sidewalk beside the car a moment later, and then Brynleigh appeared. She stumbled as her feet landed on the concrete before righting herself.

Ryker took one look at her, and a growl rumbled through his chest.

He threw the car back into park and was on the sidewalk before he even registered that his feet were moving.

He didn't need to ask who did this to Brynleigh because he already knew.

Jelisette de la Point had just signed her death warrant.

Brynleigh's beautiful black wings dragged on the sidewalk. Bloody, they hung limply behind her.

A long laceration ran from below her left eye down her cheek. Her right eye was black and swollen. Her sweater was ripped, barely covering her skin. Crimson dripped from her split lip.

Fuck staying hidden.

Who did Jelisette think she was?

Ryker's feet pounded the sidewalk as he ran toward the safe house. Red tinged his vision. Ice daggers were clutched in his palms. His blood roared in his ears.

Bitter anger coated his tongue, and his magic was a throbbing mass within him.

Jelisette would pay for this. He would tear the vampire limb from fucking limb, deal be damned. He'd—

"Ryker, stop."

The words were barely a whisper, but it was as though she'd shouted them at him.

He was still wearing the headphones.

Turtles moved faster than Ryker as he turned and met Brynleigh's black gaze from down the street.

"She hurt you," he snarled, not recognizing his own voice.

Part of him recognized that he was being irrational. He shouldn't care if Brynleigh was hurt. Not if she was just an asset. Not since she was his would-be murderer.

But he did.

He cared too gods-damned much.

"Yes." Brynleigh looked resigned as she lifted a shoulder. "I told you this would happen."

She retracted her wings, wincing as the dark appendages slipped out of sight.

He growled, the need to kill someone surging through his blood.

She sighed, her sad, obsidian eyes pleading with him. "Please, let's just go."

In the end, that look had Ryker marching back to the car. He didn't want to cause her any more hurt.

By the time he'd returned, Brynleigh had buckled in and removed the earrings.

Her chin rested on her fist, and she stared out the window as blood dripped down her face. She was healing slowly, but it wasn't fast enough for Ryker.

He'd never felt the need to take a life as strongly as he did at that moment.

"What did she give you?" he asked, jerking the car into drive. He needed to get away from here.

"A phone and credit card," she whispered.

"Do you want to talk about it?"

"No."

And after that, no more words were exchanged between them.

CHAPTER 9
It wasn't a Lie

Six days had passed since Brynleigh's meeting with Jelisette.

Six very quiet, very tense days followed by silent, long nights. Brynleigh's nightmares were back, filled with lightning and storms and death.

So much death.

When Brynleigh and Ryker came back to the bungalow after the disastrous encounter with her Maker, she had retrieved blood from the fridge and fed under the weight of the fae captain's silent stare.

He had been upset about the way Jelisette treated her, but what the fuck had he expected?

Brynleigh had warned him that her Maker was likely to kill her, and she'd been right.

Isvana help her, but being right had never been so agonizing. It wasn't just Brynleigh's body that hurt. She was used to that. Physical pain came and went all the time.

It was her heart that burned with a never-ending ache, like an ember had lodged itself within her life-giving organ and was incinerating her from the inside out.

Between that and the mental exhaustion plaguing her, she'd been too sore to talk about what had happened that night. As soon as the blood had kicked in, healing her wounds, she had silently retreated to the bedroom. There, she'd slid the phone and credit card Jelisette gave her on the nightstand, stripped, and climbed into the shower.

Usually, hot water calmed Brynleigh, bringing her peace.

Not this time.

Between Jelisette's anger and Ryker's... well, everything, she'd still been tense when she'd turned off the water. In an exhausted haze, Brynleigh had toweled off, put on her coziest clothes, and climbed into bed.

Ryker hadn't come to talk to her, and she hadn't sought him out before falling into a fitful sleep.

The next day had gone similarly. Same with the one after that. And the next.

The house was too small for them to hide from each other completely, but they'd been engaged in a strange, silent dance. Brynleigh spent most of her time in the bedroom, and Ryker occupied the living space. Whenever he used the shared bathroom, she made sure the door to the bedroom was closed.

Neither of them talked about the divide between them. They didn't talk about anything, and that fucking sucked.

Even though they weren't speaking, she was constantly aware of his presence. It was like her body was attuned to his. Her ears picked up the sounds of his movements no matter what he was doing.

A quick investigation of the nightstand had unearthed a book, *The Shadow and the Sparrow*.

Even the historical enemies-to-lovers romance between a six-hundred-year-old vampire lord and a bird shifter couldn't distract Brynleigh from the fae on the other side of her door.

For every page she read, she spent twice as long listening to Ryker.

Who knew one person could make so many sounds?

She cataloged each one: his low, tense voice when he spoke on the phone; his grunts as he exercised in the living room every morning; the quiet clash of cutlery as he ate; and even his soft snores as he finally slept, tossing and turning on that too-small couch.

Twice, Ryker's friend Nikhail had stopped by, delivering food and blood.

Both times, Brynleigh stayed in the bedroom.

The men spoke in low tones, too quiet even for her to hear, but their voices were like gentle rivers rumbling through the house.

Much like it had during the Choosing, Ryker's voice haunted Brynleigh, waking and sleeping.

He haunted her.

She couldn't get him out of her head. Despite the anger she felt towards him for allowing them to torture her, her mind still sought him in her dreams.

Whenever she wasn't plagued by nightmares, it was just them and their feelings, and it was *good*. Anger, betrayal, and deceit did not exist in her dreamscape, and they were happy.

But dreams were nothing but figments of imagination, and they never lasted.

When she woke, they faded away, and reality tumbled back into her. She couldn't hide in the bedroom forever. Their silent little bubble would pop sooner or later, forcing them to deal with everything.

Chances were, when that happened, it wouldn't be pretty.

So, for now, Brynleigh was content to be quiet, listen to Ryker, and dream of a world where they weren't broken.

THE SILENCE SHATTERED at six p.m. that same day.

The Shadow had just declared his undying love for the Sparrow by providing her with the decapitated heads of her enemies as a wedding gift when a shrill ring sliced through the quiet.

Brynleigh jolted.

The book fell flat on the bed, and her eyes flew to the dresser. Sure enough, the phone Jelisette had given her was lighting up.

The door opened, banging against the wall.

Ryker loomed in the threshold.

Isvana help her, but Brynleigh's core heated at the sight of him. She wanted him, even now, and she wasn't sure what to do about that.

But this wasn't the moment for desire.

He raked his hand through his hair, and his wide eyes landed on the dresser.

Grabbing the phone, he tossed it to her. "Answer it."

As if she would do anything else. Keeping Jelisette waiting was a bad idea on any given day.

Brynleigh accepted the call, setting the phone to speaker. "Hello?"

"Tonight. The Rosewood." Jelisette skipped pleasantries and went right to business, naming an elite club in the Southern Region that Brynleigh had been to a few times before.

"What do you need me to do?" Brynleigh asked.

She could almost feel Jelisette's eyes roll.

"What I taught you, obviously," the older vampire snarled. "Or did participating in the Choosing rob you of your ability to spill blood?"

Such a kind, loving, and compassionate Maker.

"Of course not," Brynleigh said as calmly as possible. "I'll do it."

After all, she had no choice. Ryker's deal dictated as much.

"Good. Your target is someone I've had my eye on for a while. He shouldn't be a problem for you." Jelisette paused, and the phone vibrated. "I've sent you the files."

The call disconnected as quickly as it had begun.

Jelisette had never been a paragon of warmth, especially considering their line of work, but that was cold even for her.

Brynleigh turned the phone off as soon as the call disconnected, not yet prepared to look at the files. She usually did this part with Zanri, but now she'd have to do it alone.

A fresh sting of betrayal ran through her. How many more times would she have to feel the weight of what had happened? She couldn't help but wonder about Zanri, though.

Did Owen, his on-again, off-again partner, know about his betrayal? Had he played a part in it, too?

More questions to ponder at a later date. There were so many fucking questions.

Right now, she had a fae captain to deal with.

His gaze drilled into her head, and she knew without seeing him that he was watching her.

Her cheeks heated. She lifted her eyes slowly, a little frightened of what she might see in his expression.

"It's true." Ryker's eyes were wide with fascinated horror, a frown digging into his face and marring his handsome features. "You're going to kill someone. For *her*."

Brynleigh stared at him, trying to decipher the emotions she saw on his face. Was he... angry with her again? How fucking dare he? It wasn't like she asked for this. This was what he wanted. This was *his* deal.

"Yes, I am," she bit out.

This world was kill or be killed. That was how Jelisette worked. No matter what, someone would be dying tonight, and it wouldn't be Brynleigh. Not if she could help it.

Ryker took a step towards her before he stopped. His fist clenched and unclenched, a line creasing his forehead.

"Who... Who are you?"

He looked at her like she was a monster.

Maybe she was.

"I'm the same person you've always known."

She'd been this way since her Making. Her sire had made her into a creature of darkness, and her heart was black. She was the worst of the worst, and she'd always known it.

Now, he was learning that, too.

The answer didn't seem good enough for him. He shook his head as though he was disappointed in her.

The fucking gall.

It wasn't like Ryker was an innocent lamb, unused to the hard ways of this world.

Brynleigh bore the marks of his precious army's torture on her soul—torture he'd allowed to happen.

Even though he hadn't been responsible for Chavin's destruction, she knew he had blood on his hands. His military records proved he'd been present at several battles, and he hadn't flinched when he showed up in The Pit.

They were both predators, both deadly.

She stood and furled her fists. Her book was long forgotten in the face of the fae's hypocritical anger.

"What did you think would happen when you sent me back to my Maker? Did you think we'd have a tea party and reminisce about times past? That I could just waltz in and get your Isvana-damned information?"

He kept staring at her, which only fueled the blazing inferno in her soul.

"No," she snarled, pulling back her lips and showing her fangs. "I have to play the game, and this is how I fucking do it."

Like a statue, he stood in the doorway. Of course, he was reverting to his earlier silence.

Her heart would've ached, but it was too far gone for that.

Groaning, Brynleigh shook her head and grabbed the phone. She opened the first file and scanned it. The document lacked Zanri's finesse, which didn't surprise her. The feline shifter was a whiz with electronics, and Jelisette hated them. Still, the information was all there.

Target: Tathdel Crystalis, Earth Elf
Age: 241
Crimes: Convicted of three murders, suspected of a dozen more.

Brynleigh kept reading, her eyes growing incrementally wider as she scrolled through the pages.

Tathdel Crystalis was not a good Earth Elf. If anything, he might be one of the vilest creatures she had ever gone after.

A macabre slideshow filled the screen, but she didn't look away. These victims deserved to have someone witness what had been done to them.

Vines bound corpses to the ground. Thorns ripped through flesh. Trees grew out of cement, their limbs choking those trapped in their branches. Blood coated everything in sight.

Earth Elves, more than their Light, Death, and Fortune Elf counterparts, were meant to use their magic for good. For life. After all, long ago, the High Lady of Life had restored the balance using her earth magic.

But this?

It was wrong on so many levels. What would the High Lady of Life have done if she knew one of her descendants would become *this*?

Brynleigh shuddered. Maybe it was a good thing vampires couldn't physically bear children. At least she would never have to deal with an errant descendant many centuries down the line.

The proof was undeniable: Tathdel deserved the death coming to him.

By the time Brynleigh had read all thirty-two pages, cool relief ran through her. Part of her had wondered if Jelisette would test her by giving her a target who wasn't her usual type, but thank Isvana, she'd been wrong.

And then she looked up.

The fae captain was still watching her with that same expression on his face.

The relief vanished as though it had never existed.

"Before you judge me for what I'm about to do, take a look at this." Brynleigh thrust the phone at him, leaving the file pulled up, and went to the bathroom to get ready.

She shut the door behind her and turned on the tap. Shivering at the icy water, she scrubbed her face and hands.

A strange sense of peace filled her as she twisted her hair into a braid. For years, this had been her life. She'd get a name, read a file, and kill the criminal. It was what she did.

Some people were good at mathematics, others were skilled at the arts, but Brynleigh?

Death was her calling, her talent, and for many years, it had been her reason for being.

So why, when she gripped the counter and met her gaze in the mirror, didn't she recognize the woman looking back at her?

Her eyes seemed darker than usual, filled with shadows and secrets. Her lips weren't as red as they used to be. Tiredness was written into tiny lines on her face.

That Isvana-blessed otherworldliness that all vampires had was still present, but torment was a shroud over Brynleigh's features. Even her necklace, a gift from her parents before they died, seemed dimmer.

It was as though a light had been snuffed out inside her. For years, she'd been living for revenge, and now, that was gone.

Who was she without the driving force of her vengeance?

Swallowed by the darkness in her eyes, Brynleigh lost track of time. She stared into those endless depths until a knock came on the door, startling her from her thoughts.

"The sun is setting." Ryker's voice was gruff and low, not unlike the first time they'd spoken in the Hall of Choice.

Despite everything that had happened, something deep within her sparked at the sound of his voice.

Even now, he called to her like no one else.

"Oh." She released the counter and exhaled. "I didn't realize so much time had passed. Tonight—"

"I'm coming with you," he growled. "It's my job to protect the army's assets. Where you go, I go."

That vow would have caused butterflies to flutter in her stomach a few weeks ago. His promise would have been romantic, and it would have warmed her from the inside out.

But now...

If Brynleigh closed her eyes and forgot about the tracking bracelet, the torture she'd endured, and the fact that his sister had killed her family, it was almost as if none of their problems existed.

"Is that all I am to you? An asset?" She regretted the question the moment it slipped off her tongue, but she wanted to hear the answer.

It took far too long for him to respond with a whispered, "Maybe."

She wanted to be angry with him for that answer. She wanted to hate him for it. How dare he feel that way?

But instead of hatred, her idiotic heart fluttered because he didn't outright say no.

Stupid fucking emotions.

Brynleigh missed the box where she used to keep her feelings. Life had been much easier when she didn't have to deal with them.

"I'll have to shadow us both," she warned.

The Rosewood was too far to travel through regular, mortal options.

"I know."

She pressed her forehead against the door, feeling each grain of wood as her hand landed on the knob.

Memories of a different wall in a library during a time when they weren't yet broken flashed through her mind.

"Ryker?" She breathed his name, the word barely a whisper as it left her lips.

A human wouldn't have been able to hear her—but he wasn't a human.

"Yes?" He sounded close. Was he also pressed against the door?

She squeezed her eyes shut, gathering her courage. "I... I need to tell you something. In case tonight doesn't go as planned."

There was always a chance that things would go wrong on a job. It was a liability for what she did. Someone could fight back, or the police could show up, or she could be injured.

Risks were a part of her life. They had never really bothered her before the Choosing. Back then, she hadn't had anyone. No one would have cared if she'd died.

But now?

Even with everything dividing them, Brynleigh's heart still beat for her fae captain. The past six days of silence had confirmed that for her.

She still loved him—she would always love him.

But she didn't think love would be enough to fix them.

He growled, "Brynleigh, nothing is going to—"

"You don't know that," she breathed. "Please, let me say this."

A resigned sigh came from the other side of the barrier, and her heart broke a little more. She'd done this. Ruined them. None of this would've happened if she'd figured out a way to tell the truth before the wedding night.

"Go ahead," he said after a minute. "I'm listening."

Brynleigh drew in a deep breath. Nerves twisted her stomach. Her mouth dried, but she placed her palm flat on the door and forced her lips to form words.

"It wasn't all a lie," she whispered. "I need you to know that. The things I confided in you, the chess games we shared, the kisses, none of them were fake. They meant something to me."

Tears streaked down her cheeks, and she did nothing to stop them.

The silence was back, and this time, it was louder than ever. There were no cameras, no one watching or listening, and no guards.

It was just... them.

Seconds bled into minutes.

The silence grew until the racing of her anxious heart was the only thing she could hear.

Then, just when she thought he had left, there came a sound like knuckles drumming on the other side of the door.

"I loved you, Brynleigh." His baritone voice echoed with remnants of deep pain. "I gave you my heart in the Choosing. I bared my soul to you."

There it was again. Fucking past tense.

She'd never hated it more than she did at that moment. It was nothing but a reminder of the things they'd shared.

She sniffled, not bothering to wipe away the tears. Not now, when they were finally talking.

It was easier with the door between them.

Easier because she didn't have to see the hurt in his eyes. She didn't have to look at that painfully beautiful face. She didn't have to see that mouth that didn't smile for her anymore.

"I know," she murmured. "I love you."

Falling in love with Ryker had nearly killed her, but she'd done it. She'd given him her heart, and even after the torture and his cold treatment, it still belonged to him.

What did that say about her?

A pained chuckle came from the other side of the door. Something thumped, and then he groaned.

"Of course, *now* she fucking says it. Give her time, I told myself. She'll get there, just wait."

The door rattled like he dropped his head against it.

She should've told him on their wedding night. She knew that, but she thought they would have more time.

Of all the fucking times to be wrong.

"Ryker—"

He snarled, and she clamped her mouth shut.

"The fucking problem is that while *some* of what you told me was true, I *never* lied to you," he said. "From our very first meeting, I spoke the truth. I gave you my heart, and you..."

His voice trailed off, and he didn't finish the sentence. He didn't need to. His meaning was clear, and his unspoken words echoed as though he had screamed them.

You broke us.

You destroyed us.

You shattered everything we could have had.

You ended us.

More tears flowed down her cheeks, and she rested her head against the door. Who knew unspoken words could cause so much pain?

"I... I can't do this tonight." His voice cracked, and he groaned. "Just... come outside when you're ready."

Footsteps announced his departure, and moments later, the front door slammed shut.

He was gone.

The brokenness between them was a gaping ocean.

"Fuck." She'd meant for the word to come out strong, but it was a half-mangled sob.

Her heart had been twisted and stomped on, burned and frozen. It hurt so much, and she didn't know what to do about it.

So, she didn't do anything.

Brynleigh gave herself five minutes to cry. Five minutes to let all the pain pour down her cheeks. Five minutes to sit in the hurt washing through her.

And then she stood, wiping away her tears.

She had a job to do, and even if her heart was in pieces, she would do this. Because she'd made a deal, and she wouldn't go back on her word.

She dressed mechanically, barely noticing the black V-neck sweater and jeans she slipped on.

It took everything she had to put her confession aside and focus on what was to come.

Grabbing the phone her Maker had given her off the floor, Brynleigh shoved it in her back pocket with Jelisette's credit card. She put on black ankle boots and zipped them up, before striding out the front door.

With every step she took, Brynleigh fortified a wall around her heart. She couldn't let feelings hamper her mind during this mission. Emotions did not mix with killing.

Instead, she dove headfirst into her inner darkness. Her shadows sang a somber tune as she approached the door, and she found solace in their dark lullaby. She released them, letting the shadowy wisps curl protectively around her.

Brynleigh thought she had succeeded in erecting a wall around her heart until she opened the door. The moment she stepped outside beneath the golden glow of the porch lights, her breath caught in her throat, and she froze.

Charcoal clouds covered the night sky. Bright lightning bolts raced through the heavens. Mist hung heavy in the air, warning of an impending storm. But this wasn't a natural occurrence.

No.

This storm was contained. Controlled. Deadly.

And the source of it all stood with his back to her.

CHAPTER 10
The Rosewood

Brynleigh's heart raced as she stared at the powerful water fae in his element. Ryker's arms were extended, his fingers stretching skyward as magic flowed from his hands. Powerful. Strong. Dangerous.

The storm clouds churned.

Her fingers curled into fists, and her breath came in short bursts. Her legs trembled.

Flashes of another storm went through her mind. Screams. Cries. Water. So much fucking water. It was everywhere. Her sister, drowning.

Oh gods.

She'd somehow never considered what it would be like to witness Ryker unleash the power he kept beneath his skin.

A tremor ran through her, and she swayed.

This is not that night. You are not in danger.

Ryker wouldn't hurt her... right? He hadn't killed her when he had the chance, and he hadn't left her in the dungeon.

She wasn't entirely certain she was safe, but she couldn't stay here forever.

Drawing a deep breath, Brynleigh took a trembling step off the porch. The rain hadn't fallen yet, but the clouds were close to bursting.

When she didn't collapse into a ball of tears after the first step, she took another. And another. And another.

Soon, she was halfway to the water fae.

Magic trickled over Brynleigh's skin at some point, and she walked through the wards surrounding the property. She barely noticed them, her attention never straying from Ryker.

She would've thought he was a statue if not for the power rippling from his hands.

He funneled magic into the sky.

More, more, more, until it seemed practically impossible that he still had magic left within him.

And then he *roared*.

Like waves crashing against rocks, the sound went on and on and on.

Tinged with grief and despair and anguish, Ryker's cry wrapped around Brynleigh's heart and squeezed like a vise.

She had caused this. Once again, she'd brought him pain. How many more times would they hurt each other?

The ocean between them expanded until it seemed like it would swallow her whole. She would drown in her grief, forever lamenting the love they'd once shared.

She wasn't sure how much time had passed before he fell silent, but eventually, his voice cracked and then stopped.

The silence was louder than his roar.

Ryker's arms fell to his sides, and he drew his power towards him. The storm clouds receded, the lightning stopped, the mist disappeared, and the traces of magic vanished.

He straightened, throwing back his shoulders.

Brynleigh's heart raced as Ryker turned. Even though there were no visible weapons on his person, she was sure he was armed.

His face was blank as if he hadn't just been on the brink of losing control.

"Ready?" His voice was hoarse, and his eyes were dark with the same clouds that had been swirling overhead.

Apparently, they were going to ignore his storm. That worked for her—she had enough on her mind already.

Brynleigh checked the wall around her heart—it was still in one piece, thank Isvana—and nodded. "Yes. Let's get this over with."

Closing the distance between them, she stopped a few feet from the captain. The sooner she did this job, the better.

"Moving through shadows can make some people feel sick," she warned. "Don't let go."

She wasn't entirely certain what would happen to Ryker in the Void if she wasn't holding onto him, but instinct told her it would be bad.

"I won't."

Ryker didn't move, though.

Awkward. This was so gods-damned awkward.

Wishing for the ease that had existed between them during the Choosing, Brynleigh raised her hand.

"We... We have to be touching." She swallowed past the dryness that had suddenly appeared in her throat. "For this to work."

His gaze dropped to her outstretched hand, and he clenched his jaw.

Had he not known contact was required?

Brynleigh had realized it the moment he declared he was coming with her.

They hadn't touched yet. Not really.

She could still remember the world-altering impact of their first touch, and she was equally excited and petrified to see if that spark remained between them after... everything.

Ryker inhaled, and his face hardened as though he was preparing himself. After several long moments, he finally moved.

It seemed to take him ages to cross the divide between them and put his hand in hers, lacing their fingers together.

Brynleigh's heart seized at the familiarity of the gesture. Ryker was warm, whereas she was cold. Calloused where she was soft. His hand enveloped hers, and...

Oh gods, the sparks remained.

She almost hated them for still being present after everything they'd been through.

Was she the only one feeling this way?

She glanced up at him and frowned. His face was blank. The only sign that the touch affected him was the slight feathering of his jaw.

Maybe he didn't care anymore. And maybe... maybe she should try to do the same.

After all, she was just an asset.

With that depressing thought in mind, Brynleigh called on her shadows. They curled lovingly around her, cloaking them in darkness.

"Hold on," she reminded him again.

In response, Ryker's fingers pulsed around hers.

Her stupid heart fluttered at the action.

She didn't have time to focus on her feelings. Instead, she drew on her darkness and pulled them into the Void.

One moment, they were in the forest. The next, they were passing through the emptiness that belonged to vampire-kind.

Darker than the night itself, light never existed here. Stars were a foreign concept. Life did not have a place in the In Between. There was nothing but shadows and darkness and flickers of power.

Brynleigh had heard tales that the goddess of the moon inhabited the Void, but she'd never been to Isvana's moonlit palace. No one had, except the Sunwalking Queen, many millennia ago.

Ryker's breaths came in short bursts as Brynleigh pulled them through the Void. This method of travel wasn't kind to most non-vampires. True to his word, his grip was like iron around hers.

She glanced at him, the darkness not impeding her vision, and her lips slanted down. Sweat was beading on his forehead, his skin was paler than normal, and a pained grimace twisted his beautiful mouth.

"We're almost there," she murmured, wishing she could urge the shadows to move faster.

He grunted, squeezing her hand.

Several more seconds went by before the shadows delivered them to their destination. The darkness melted away, leaving them in an alley.

The moment they were on solid ground, Ryker disentangled their fingers and stepped away from Brynleigh.

Her heart twisted at his obvious rejection.

Ryker crossed his arms and studied the alley. "Where are we?"

He was looking better now that they were out of the Void.

"Can't you feel it in the air?" Brynleigh pulled the collar of her sweater away from her skin, the heat making her regret her clothing choices. "We're in Sandhaven."

The southernmost metropolis in the Republic of Balance, Sandhaven was the oldest still-standing city in the entire continent. Founded during the Rose Empire by the seventh Empress, it was still a thriving city.

And it was *hot*.

Even now, with the moon high in the sky, it felt like they were standing in an oven. The air smelled of sand, heat, and sweat. Pockets of light dotted the street beyond the alley, sirens wailed in the distance, and the wind carried faint streams of music from the Rosewood into the hot evening.

It looked and sounded the same as the last time Brynleigh had been here, but something was different.

Brynleigh was different. Or maybe it was the fae beside her. Either way, nothing was the same.

"Let's go." She wanted to get this over with. Usually, she didn't mind shedding a little blood, but tonight, the thought didn't thrill her as much as usual.

Yes, Ryker's presence definitely threw a wrench into things.

She was halfway down the alley, her boots clicking on the cobblestones, when the fae's hand landed on her arm.

Now, he touched her willingly.

Of course.

"What's your plan?" Ryker asked gruffly.

Wasn't it obvious?

"I'm going to do what I always do. I'll enter the Rosewood, find Tathdel Crystalis, and kill him."

Easy. Simple. Quick. It was her favorite way to work. In and out, without any complications.

Ryker stared at her. His mouth pinched in a line, his eyes darkened, and his grip tightened.

"You speak of death so easily." He shook his head. "Doesn't it bother you?"

Did he really care?

She could have shaken him off, but instead, she considered his question.

"I… it used to," Brynleigh admitted.

Her first kill had been a few weeks after her Making, and it had haunted her for months.

His gaze searched hers. "And now?"

What did he want her to say? That she laid awake at night, thinking about the people she killed? That was rarely true. Now, she lay awake thinking about him.

"Not anymore," she admitted.

Crimson stained her soul.

Besides, she only killed people deserving of her brand of justice. None of them were innocent, and she was doing the world a favor by getting rid of them.

Ryker looked like he wanted to say more, but in the end, he just nodded. "Okay. I'll follow your lead."

That was the end of their conversation. What else was there to say?

There was no time to be upset about this. She lifted her chin. The time for talking was over. Exuding confidence, she sauntered down the moonlit street. Her shoulders were back, she stood tall, and her face was blank.

True to his word, Ryker remained behind her, a silent shadow.

The familiarity of this moment was comforting in a strange way. Right now, Brynleigh wasn't a vampire who'd recently been tortured. She wasn't a broken-hearted woman.

She was a killer with a purpose, and she was damned good at her job.

From the outside, the Rosewood looked like every other building in this part of the city: three stories, red bricks, blackened windows. The only difference from the rest of the block was the burly werewolf in a suit guarding the entrance.

He raised a brow as they approached, his orange eyes glittering in the darkness. "Card?"

Names weren't done at The Rosewood.

It was one of the reasons Brynleigh hadn't been too worried about coming here—even if she and Ryker were recognized as participants of the Choosing, it wouldn't matter. If Jelisette asked why Brynleigh took

Ryker to The Rosewood, she would claim she was using him as a cover. It wasn't exactly a lie.

Everything that happened in The Rosewood remained within its four walls. It was a temple, and secrets were the god its parishioners worshipped.

Identities were never revealed, which made The Rosewood the perfect place for high-powered Representatives to conduct unsavory business away from prying eyes. It fronted as a high-end dining establishment, but its true purpose was an open secret.

Brynleigh pulled out the phone Jelisette had given her and navigated to the second file. She tapped on it, and a black card with golden filigree borders filled the phone screen.

On the right side was an unfurling rose, and on the left was the phrase, *When the night blooming roses wilt, the moon will never rise again.*

A bit morose if you asked Brynleigh, but she wasn't the one who had come up with the phrase.

She handed the phone to the werewolf. He studied the card carefully before flicking his eyes over to Ryker. "He's with you?"

"He is," she said.

Another minute passed before the guard returned the phone.

"Have a good evening, miss. The Rosewood welcomes you."

Stepping back, he opened the door.

Tucking the phone into her pocket, Brynleigh strode forward.

Warmth at her back told her Ryker was following. Together, they entered the darkened establishment.

It was time to do what she did best.

THE MAIN FLOOR of The Rosewood was everything one would expect from a fine-dining restaurant.

A beautiful Light Elf with raven hair and a lyrical voice sang onstage. Servers dressed in black delivered food and drinks. Fae, werewolves, elves, witches, shifters, and humans sat clustered around dimly lit tables and booths, speaking in hushed tones.

Brynleigh ignored them all. Navigating around tables, she headed straight for the thick black curtain at the other end of the room.

Tathdel's file had noted the man's penchant for flogging, and there was only one room in The Rosewood that catered to that specific kink.

No one so much as glanced their way.

If Ryker thought The Rosewood was strange, he didn't comment on it.

Brynleigh pushed back the velvet curtain, revealing a dark, spiral stone staircase.

If the main floor was a fine restaurant, this was more akin to the entrance of a dungeon from the Four Kingdoms. A cold breeze blew past, and she shivered as she descended the steps.

An unmarked door waited at the bottom.

An aura of danger surrounded this place, and her skin prickled. Her shadows writhed, warning her to be careful. She released a few of them, allowing them to wind protectively around her arms and legs.

Though they hadn't spoken to anyone, others were here.

Someone was always watching in The Rosewood. The guards wouldn't bat an eye or interfere with anything unless the right people called them at the right time.

The Rosewood valued secrets more than lives.

"Are you sure about this, Brynleigh?" Ryker's voice was gruff as he broke his silence. "There might be another way."

Of course, now his conscience decided to make an appearance.

Brynleigh should have known this would happen. The captain was too good for this kind of thing. There was a difference between killing in war and... *this*.

Still, his judgment rankled her.

Brynleigh's hand rested on the knob. "This is the only way. It's my life or his." When Ryker didn't reply, she added, "I have to do this. Remember the deal? It's not my fault that you decided to come with me."

Part of her was glad that he was here. He was about to see firsthand what he'd signed her up to do. If the killing bothered him, he could've stayed away and remained oblivious.

Without waiting for a response, Brynleigh opened the door and entered the dark corridor.

Violet Light Elf sconces on the walls gave off a faint lavender glow. Cold air prickled the skin on her arms. Inky carpet absorbed the sound of their footsteps.

Mentally preparing for the task ahead, Brynleigh ensured the wall around her heart was sturdy.

The long, winding hallway was home to several numbered doors. Each room housed different desires, kinks, and secrets. None of them bothered Brynleigh—as long as everyone was consenting.

Behind the first, moans and cries of pleasure could be heard. In the next room, a man was begging for someone to "give it to him," reiterating that he'd been a bad boy. The third was silent, save for the rhythmic slapping of flesh against flesh.

With each door they passed, each step they took, Ryker inched closer to Brynleigh. She wasn't sure he was aware he was doing it.

The fourth and fifth doors were ominously silent, and they stopped in front of the sixth. The cracking of a whip and the whimper that followed confirmed this was the right room.

Brynleigh exchanged a look with Ryker.

"Stand back and don't interfere, no matter what happens," she warned, taking in his tense form and clenched fists. "Jelisette doesn't accept failure."

Unease was carved into every part of Ryker's being, and he was tense, like a storm cloud moments away from bursting.

Brynleigh shuddered, recalling how his magic had lashed out of him earlier.

"I understand," Ryker said in his baritone voice.

She searched his gaze for a long moment before sighing. "You don't, but you will."

Despite Ryker's presence here, Brynleigh didn't think he was fine with any of this.

Ryker enjoyed rules and rarely broke them—except for covering up his sister's involvement in the destruction of Chavin, apparently—and Brynleigh doubted he would be okay with what she was about to do.

If they were in a better place, Brynleigh would assure him that she would kill Tathdel quickly and cleanly. She would remind him that this was a place of secrets, and their presence wasn't strange, even when they left a dead body in their wake.

She would remind him that she was strong and in control and that even with the presence of spilled blood, she wouldn't fall into bloodlust.

That trap that some Fledglings fell into felt further away than ever. She thought it might be because of what she'd endured in The Pit. It wasn't exactly a silver lining, but she'd take it.

Brynleigh didn't say any of that, though.

That ocean still divided them, and those words seemed too far away. Instead, she placed her hand flat on the knob and called on her shadows. They wormed inside the mechanism, and within a few minutes, a telltale *click* came from the lock.

This skill didn't work on all doors—Jelisette warded the locks in her house against shadows—but luckily, it worked here.

Brynleigh pulled back her hand, drew in a deep breath, and twisted the knob.

She was a creature of the night, and this was her calling.

Death had come to The Rosewood.

CHAPTER 11

Back When They Were Whole

Discovering that the vampire you'd Chosen to marry was a cold-blooded killer was one thing, but watching her in action was another entirely.

Ryker had known his wife was dangerous, but this…

He had never expected this.

He was equal parts afraid and strangely aroused by the way Brynleigh moved with swift, predatory grace. She swung the door open and entered the room like a deadly dancer.

A tall, broad-chested Earth Elf with cropped red hair and green markings running along his bare chest and sinking beneath the waistband of his pants stood before a bed. A naked werewolf kneeled on the middle of the mattress. The woman's long brown hair covered her breasts. Her back was red and cut in several places.

They turned as one.

"What the fuck?" the elf growled, dangling a whip made of vines from his fingers. "Who the hell are you?"

"Don't worry about that," Brynleigh replied in a low voice, shadows twining around her legs. "Are you Tathdel Crystalis?"

The Earth Elf narrowed his emerald eyes. "Who's asking?"

Black wings burst from Brynleigh's back through the slits in her sweater, and she smiled. The expression was nothing short of nightmarish.

She snarled, "Your gods-damned reckoning."

By the Black Sands, Ryker really liked the commanding tone of Brynleigh's voice. It stirred something deep within him. That fucking bothered him. He shouldn't like any of this. He shouldn't even be here.

The thing was, even though Ryker's presence in this place crossed a plethora of lines, he didn't regret it. He didn't regret any of this.

He'd make the same deal over and over again if it meant getting Brynleigh out of prison.

Hearing her admit that she loved him earlier had been like ingesting acid. His entire body had burned at her words. But he would endure far more than that to keep her out of The Pit.

Brynleigh turned to the woman and snarled, "Get out of here if you want to live."

The werewolf's eyes widened. To her credit, she didn't waste a second before wrapping a sheet around herself and bolting out the door.

That was probably the right move.

The door slammed behind the fleeing woman, and the Earth Elf tightened his grip on the whip. He looked between Ryker and Brynleigh, his gaze mistakenly settling on the captain's.

"I know you." A wry smile of recognition tugged on Tathdel's lips. "You were in the Choosing. Why are you here? Fuck right off."

The amused expression on the Earth Elf's face disgusted Ryker. He'd read the man's file. Only a monster wouldn't be repulsed by the things Tathdel had done. Apparently, Jelisette was not only part of the rebellion and a cold-hearted vampire, but she also had a knack for finding the world's worst criminals.

This elf did not deserve to be free.

If Ryker had his way and this was his operation, he'd arrest the elf and throw him into The Pit. *This* was a man Victor Orpheus could torture for weeks on end without issue.

But Orpheus wasn't here, this wasn't The Pit, and all the rules Ryker followed were nowhere in sight.

And then the man glanced at Brynleigh.

Ryker barely suppressed a snarl. He didn't like the way the evil elf was looking at his wife. Not one bit. If it were up to him, he'd claw Tathdel's eyes out so he could never look upon his vampire, or any other woman, again.

But Brynleigh had asked him not to interfere, so he wouldn't.

Ryker raised a shoulder and smirked. "I'm not the one you should be worried about."

By the time the Earth Elf's gaze snapped back to Brynleigh, it was too late.

She'd already wrapped the elf in shadows and advanced with the speed of her kind. Darkness swept out of her, coating the entire room in a blanket of pure night.

Even with his fae vision, Ryker couldn't see a thing. He pressed his back against the wall, his fingers finding the hilt of the knife sheathed on his thigh as he stared into the unnatural darkness.

Nothing impeded his hearing, though.

He had been around death many times. He'd delivered it, witnessed it, called it into being.

But this...

This was different.

The sounds Ryker heard in this room would forever be imprinted on his mind.

In the darkness, the Earth Elf pleaded for mercy. His cries fell upon deaf ears.

A vicious, animalistic snarl ripped out of Brynleigh. It should have frightened Ryker and reminded him that he'd married a killer, but he *liked* it. He'd always known Brynleigh could defend herself, but hearing it was an entirely different story.

Time seemed to have no real consequence in this room shrouded in shadows.

Seconds, or maybe minutes, passed as the sounds of death washed over him.

Try as he might, Ryker couldn't forget that he was the reason Brynleigh was in this situation. It was his plan that had brought them here, and it was his fault she'd returned to Jelisette.

On some level, this man's death was on his hands.

He'd forever remember the sound of teeth tearing into flesh and the elf's final, strangled cry before silence—blessed, much-needed silence—blanketed the room.

In the quiet, Ryker's heartbeat was a mallet pounding against his chest.

The air seemed to pulse as the shadows receded.

Ryker didn't move until the last dark wisp was gone. His vision adjusted quickly, and his mouth dried as he looked over the scene before him.

Suddenly, Ryker had a greater appreciation of the fact that he'd survived his wedding night. He thought he'd understood how deadly vampires could be, but this...

Brynleigh wasn't just a predator; she *was* Death.

She stood over the Earth Elf's body, a few stray vines still scattered through the room where he'd tried to fend her off.

The evil man had failed miserably.

His head was bent at an awkward angle, two puncture wounds were on his neck, and a thick, bloody vine protruded from his chest. It was a horrid rendition of spring's first blooms bursting through the snow.

"I had to make sure he was really dead." Brynleigh frowned, eyeing the vine. "He was Mature."

Her voice was strangely cold and detached, almost robotic. It was nothing like the one Ryker had come to know and love during the Choosing.

"I see. You did..." He swallowed past the dryness in his throat. "Well."

Was that what one said when complimenting a killing?

From a cleanliness perspective, Brynleigh remained surprisingly blood-free. A red streak swept across the back of her hands, but other than that, even her braid was still in place.

She fanned out her wings, which were also spotless. Sliding her phone out of her back pocket, she snapped a picture and sent a text.

"Now what?" Ryker stared at the dead man, his stomach churning. "The body..."

Black, unconcerned eyes met his. "We leave him. He's no longer our problem."

Ryker hated the frigidness in her voice. He balled his fists, but before he could speak, Brynleigh's phone buzzed.

She glanced at the screen. "Jelisette is sending a clean-up team. I'm to report to her tomorrow night to debrief."

She talked about this like it was a normal job with normal tasks and consequences.

But it wasn't.

Ryker Waterborn, son of the Representative of the Fae, was officially an accomplice to cold-blooded murder. He wasn't sure it would matter to the courts that the Earth Elf had been an evil man.

There was no going back now.

His only hope—their only hope—was that Brynleigh would uncover useful information about the Black Night.

Neither of them spoke as she extended her hand between them in a silent request. With one last glance at the body, he laced his fingers through her bloody ones, the red speckles a reminder that they were in this together.

Brynleigh drew on her shadows, and then, the Rosewood disappeared.

RYKER'S STOMACH spun as they traveled through the Void, making him eternally grateful that he hadn't eaten in several hours. He closed his eyes, hoping that blocking the blackness would help calm his stomach.

It didn't.

Every second dragged on, feeling endless, until his feet met solid ground once more. The porch light shone through the trees, and the moon glowed above them.

He swayed, legs trembling, and he removed his fingers from Brynleigh's. Bile rose in his throat, his body protesting their form of travel, but he forced himself to keep it down. Throwing up was a sign of weakness, and he hadn't done it in years. He had no intention of starting tonight.

Putting his hands on his knees, Ryker bent in half, dropped his head, and closed his eyes. He forced his lungs to draw breath and let the fresh forest air ground him.

Each inhalation helped, and soon, he felt more like himself.

Several minutes passed before the forest floor rustled in front of him.

Ryker opened his eyes to find that Brynleigh had moved.

She stood a few feet away with her hand outstretched as though she'd been about to touch him. The vampire chewed on her bottom lip, the action sending a bolt of want through Ryker.

Gods, he'd never wished he was a lip more than he did at that moment.

Concern filled her eyes. "Are you... Did I... Was it the body?"

The coldness in her voice had thawed, leaving behind traces of the vampire he'd once loved.

He shook his head, careful not to move too quickly as he straightened.

"No, the shadowing."

It had been years since he'd last traveled with a vampire, and the experience was as unpleasant as he remembered.

"Oh." Brynleigh sucked her lip through her teeth. "That's... good."

Her hand remained in the space between them. Her fingers twitched, the movement capturing his attention. Those hands had just killed a man.

Rationally, he should've been repulsed by that. He should've been horrified that she'd murdered someone while wearing his wedding band.

But he wasn't.

He was drawn to her like she was the moon, and he was a star lucky enough to shine in her presence. He couldn't pull his gaze from her, even if he tried.

So, he didn't try.

Ryker's heart thundered, and every part of him wanted to get closer to Brynleigh. To talk to her, kiss her, forgive her.

He needed her.

Exhaling, Ryker murmured, "There's blood."

"What?"

He reached out and captured Brynleigh's fingers. They were so soft, so much smaller than his. So right.

By the Obsidian Sands, how he'd missed this. Her. Them. Touching.

He could barely think, barely breathe. His entire world revolved around the sensation of her hand in his.

Gently, he tugged her closer.

Thank all the gods, she didn't pull away. He wasn't sure what he would've done if that had happened.

A groan rumbled through Ryker's chest, and his entire body warmed at their nearness.

Fuck, he'd missed this more than he could ever put into words. They hadn't had nearly enough time together. Before he could think too hard and convince himself this was a bad idea for numerous reasons, he brushed his thumb over the back of her knuckles.

Brynleigh breathed his name, and gods help him, those two syllables had never sounded so right.

Ryker was in this now, for better or for worse.

Holding her gaze, he inhaled deeply. Her unique scent of a crisp evening and night-blooming roses flooded him.

The touch wasn't enough.

He needed more. He needed all of her.

His feet carried him closer. He couldn't help it.

As bees were drawn to flowers and rivers were drawn to oceans, he was drawn to Brynleigh. She might destroy him, might ruin him, but at that moment when they were finally touching again, and neither of them was pulling away, he didn't fucking care.

Maybe being ruined wouldn't be so bad if she was by his side.

"See?" Ryker's thumb stilled on the back of Brynleigh's hand, pointing to the red streaking across her pale flesh. "Blood."

She sucked in a breath, and he dragged his eyes up to her mouth. Those lips that he'd dreamed about parted, and he glimpsed her fangs nestled in her gums.

"Oh," Brynleigh breathed, the sound drawing him straight back to their wedding night. "That... happens."

It did seem like a rather normal side-effect of killing someone.

Stillness overtook them both. Each moment, each breath, was longer than the last.

He noticed everything and nothing at once.

Birds sang melodies from within the woods. Wolves howled, a pack responding to their leader. Stars shone brightly, lanterns in the sky providing witness to this stolen moment.

Every second was somehow the longest and shortest moment of his life.

Still, neither of them moved.

He should let go. He should walk away and give himself a stern talking-to. He should, but he couldn't.

Somehow, Ryker knew that if he stepped away now, he might never get to touch her again. And damn it all, but he refused to allow that to happen.

Instead, his fingers curled around hers.

Not too tightly—they both knew she could break his hold in a heartbeat if she wanted to—and his gaze crawled up to hers.

Ryker slowly swept his thumb over her moonlit hand until he got to Brynleigh's fourth finger.

"Why did you keep the ring?"

It felt like their wedding had been years ago, not a mere month. How was it possible that so much had happened over such a short period of time?

Her obsidian orbs shimmered with an emotion Ryker wasn't ready to unpack.

"You gave it to me. Even when I thought you were dead..." A choked sob slipped out of Brynleigh, and she shuddered. "I kept it."

Ryker swallowed. It meant something that she was still wearing his ring, just as it meant something that she wasn't pulling away from him. His thumb traced the cool metal, turning it around her finger slowly. He'd spent hours mulling over engagement ring options until he found the perfect one.

Back when he thought she loved him.

Back when they were whole.

Back when he had no idea who she truly was.

So much had happened between them, and yet...

Ryker didn't know if they could fix this. The only thing he knew for certain was that being with Brynleigh felt right in a way that nothing else ever had. It was like they were two parts of the same whole, always meant to be together.

Everything else faded away. He didn't notice either of them moving, but eventually, barely a foot of space existed between them.

The air was so thick that he could hardly breathe. His magic pulsed, his heart thundered, and everything within him urged him to close the distance between them.

Nothing else mattered at that moment. Not the dead Earth Elf, not Brynleigh's betrayal, not his anger over her murderous plans.

It was just them and the feeling of rightness deep in his soul.

He breathed her name, and he tightened his grip on her fingers.

Just one kiss.

That's all he wanted. A taste, a reminder of what they had, and then they could go back to figuring everything else out.

Ryker bent his head, his breath dancing over her mouth as he drew closer. He moved slowly, giving her time to pull away, but she didn't. His heart boomed, and he felt like a youngling going in for his first kiss.

Wide-eyed, Brynleigh gripped his fingers. Something dangerously akin to hope shone within her eyes.

She breathed, "Ryker—"

A shrill ring sliced through the silence like a bolt of lightning cutting through a stormy night. Ryker's phone vibrated in his back pocket.

"Fuck," he exhaled, his heart sinking like a stone.

Brynleigh blinked, and a shadow flickered around her hand. She stepped back, eyes shuttering, but not before he saw the flash of pain and disappointment in her eyes.

It echoed the ache in his soul.

He reached into his pocket and withdrew the phone. Swiping to answer, Ryker didn't even look at the screen, keeping his gaze on Brynleigh.

"Yes?" he barked, unable to keep the frustration from his voice.

"Ryker?"

Oh gods.

"What's wrong, River?" He clutched the phone. "Have you been crying?"

She sniffled. "I..."

Ryker braced himself as he asked the question he'd feared every night for the past six years. "Did you lose control again?"

Dozens of worst-case scenarios paraded through his mind, each worse than the last. A canyon opened up in his stomach as he waited for his sister's response.

River half-choked, half-sobbed, "No, but... I need you."

CHAPTER 12
It's Not That Simple

Brynleigh stumbled back, her heart thundering in her chest. What the actual fuck was she doing?

Bringing Ryker on a kill with her was one thing, but almost kissing him? That was another matter entirely.

Isvana help her, but Brynleigh could not afford to lose her mind around Ryker. She had to keep her head on her shoulders.

The fae captain was making that maddeningly difficult.

One minute, he was staring at her like he didn't know her, and the next, his lips were hovering over hers.

The problem—and it was a problem—was that she wanted him to kiss her. She wanted him to give her everything, even though their problems weren't solved. All it had taken was a few moments of attention, and her body was ready to forget every one of their issues.

She wasn't sure how she felt about that.

Ryker pressed the phone against his ear, and a line creased his forehead. Brynleigh could sense his rising panic.

He asked, "What's the matter?"

A choked sob came through the phone, audible thanks to Brynleigh's vampiric hearing.

"You need to come home," River said. "Now."

Ryker inhaled sharply. "Is it—"

"Come home," River repeated. "Hurry."

Blood drained from the fae captain's face, and he assured his sister he would be there soon before hanging up. His face was far paler than it had been moments before.

The fear in his eyes made Brynleigh's stomach want to curl in on itself.

Ryker cleared his throat. "That was... My father..."

"I heard." Brynleigh shook her head. "You need to be with your family."

Her heart ached. She had no right to include herself in that group. Not after the lies she'd told and the game she'd played.

His distraction was evident on his face as he nodded and started moving towards the house.

"Yes, I have to..." Ryker halted, a groan escaping him that could have leveled cities. "Damn it. I can't leave you..."

Alone.

He didn't say the last word, but it echoed through the forest like he'd screamed it.

Because Brynleigh was untrustworthy.

Just like that, any warmth they'd cultivated earlier was gone.

Wrapping her arms around herself, Brynleigh shook her head and strode past Ryker up the steps.

"Don't worry, I'll come with you and won't cause any problems." Her voice was miraculously steady.

"You can't talk to my sister," Ryker said sharply.

Brynleigh turned and blinked.

"You and I are..." He gestured between them, as if that made any sense, and groaned again. "But River is young. I don't want you interacting with her." Because Brynleigh was dangerous. "Promise me that you'll stay away from her. I have to protect her."

Protect her.

His words echoed through Brynleigh's mind, and she flinched, unable to stop herself from reacting.

That was how he saw her—a threat.

Fucking ironic.

She wasn't the only dangerous one here.

Not only was Ryker a force to be reckoned with, but he conveniently seemed to be forgetting that his sister had killed Brynleigh's family.

Did he not realize that Brynleigh could've killed River the moment she learned the truth about Chavin? That she'd already been merciful and spared his sister even though she had admitted to murdering an entire village?

Brynleigh wished Ryker's words didn't hurt. She wished they could return to almost kissing. But she couldn't turn back the hands of time any more than she could heal their relationship.

"I understand." This time, her voice was ice. "After all, I'm just an asset, right?"

He sighed. "No, Brynleigh. It's not that simple."

Except it seemed it was. She was an asset, he didn't trust her, and they were both hurting.

Gods damn it, where was her box of emotions when she needed it?

Pulling on strength she didn't know she possessed, Brynleigh rebuilt those walls around her heart.

"Don't worry, I get it. I'll stay out of your way, and tomorrow night, I'll update Jelisette. While I'm there, I'll uphold my end of the deal and look for the information you need."

Keeping Ryker out was easier than letting him in to hurt her again. She'd rather throw away the warmth she'd been feeling earlier than admit that him choosing his family over her was painful.

Ryker's mouth pinched, and for a moment, it looked like he was going to argue, but he didn't. Instead, he unlocked the door.

Brynleigh inched past, careful not to touch him again.

"Pack a bag and get in the car," the captain instructed. "I don't know how long we'll be at Waterborn House."

Brynleigh didn't bother asking why they weren't shadowing. She was an asset, and assets didn't ask questions. They just did what they were told.

Nodding, she wordlessly made her way to the bedroom.

She did as he asked and packed her things, not that there were many to begin with. She washed up in the bathroom, making sure to rid herself of every spot of blood, and rebraided her hair before returning to the living room.

Ryker was waiting for her, a bag sitting at his feet as his thumbs flew over his phone. When he looked up, that haunted, worried look remained in his eyes.

"Let's go."

He grabbed their bags and left without another word.

Brynleigh trailed behind him. She was well aware that she'd betrayed Ryker. She knew she wasn't deserving of his trust, not after the way she'd lied to him since the beginning of their relationship.

But a disconnect existed between her head and her heart. Her mind knew there was a divide between them, but her heart...

That organ still beat for Ryker. Every pulse belonged to him, and it didn't understand that he wasn't hers anymore.

Rubbing the back of her hand, Brynleigh frowned. If she concentrated hard enough, she could still feel the ghost of the captain's hand on hers.

Cast in darkness, Ryker's childhood home was exactly as Brynleigh remembered it.

The drive had been silent, with Ryker deep in whatever pit of worry his sister's call had thrown him into and Brynleigh dealing with all the emotions that had been plaguing her ever since she found out Ryker was alive.

Wrought-iron gates guarded the winding driveway leading up to the mansion. Electric lanterns stood on both sides, illuminating the path. Two stone statues of dragons stood in front of the massive double doors at the front of the house. Curtains covered every window—there were over fifty that she could see. The lawn was immaculately manicured, the bushes trimmed to perfection, and the gardens didn't have a single flower out of place.

The Representative's mansion screamed of ostentatious wealth and privilege.

"We're here," Ryker announced, pulling the car to a stop in front of the home. "Someone will park for us. Come on."

The engine cut off and Ryker got out of the car. He was halfway up the steps by the time Brynleigh unbuckled and got out.

She wasn't insulted by the fact that he didn't open her door. After all, assets didn't require chivalry.

Brynleigh was reluctant to enter Waterborn House. Her last experience here had been less than delightful, and she was fairly certain Ryker's family hated her now. Whatever potential friendship had been blooming between her and River was long gone.

Fuck, even Ryker didn't want Brynleigh here. His rejection and the return of his anger were more painful than the torture she'd endured.

Death would've been easier than this.

Wordlessly, Brynleigh followed Ryker up the stairs and through the doors. She barely noticed the splendor of the foyer. This place was cold and lifeless, more of a museum than a home.

What had it been like growing up here?

They hurried up a grand staircase and down a long hall with closed doors lining both sides. Brynleigh remained two steps behind Ryker, hugging her arms around herself.

The Rosewood had been mere hours ago, but it felt like a week had passed.

Who knew broken hearts made telling time so difficult?

The steady beeping of machines and the scent of cleaning supplies grew stronger with every step. If the lower level of Ryker's family home reminded Brynleigh of a museum, this one reminded her of a hospital.

Death hid in the shadows. She could feel it watching. Waiting.

Life had not flourished in this place for some time.

She shivered and rubbed her arms.

"Thank the Blessed Black Sands, you're here." River jogged out of a room at the end of the hall.

The younger water fae looked like she'd been up for several days. Between her form-fitting black leggings, oversized gray sweater, and messy bun, she appeared far more frazzled than the rebellious fae Brynleigh had first met. Mascara streaked down her cheeks, her eyes were red and puffy, and she gnawed on her lip ring.

Ryker choked out his sister's name, and River broke into a run, jumping into his arms. He caught her, squeezing tightly.

Neither sibling looked back at Brynleigh as they embraced, and that was...

Fine.

Well. Not fine.

Not fine at all, actually.

A fresh wave of grief so powerful she could barely breathe slammed into Brynleigh. She stumbled back as though someone had shoved her. Her heart ached, and tears rushed to her eyes.

Brynleigh had underestimated how devastating it would be to see River again. She was just so similar to Sarai.

But River was here, and Brynleigh's sister was dead.

Because of River.

Brynleigh's chest burned as if someone had punched her in the heart.

The old grief of loss was still present, but a fresh ache burrowed its way into her heart.

She could've had this. A place in a new family. Hugs. Kisses. Love.

Maybe things would've been different if Brynleigh had stopped Zanri and explained everything. Maybe she wouldn't have ended up in the dungeon. Maybe Ryker could have forgiven her if she'd confessed everything sooner.

Maybe, maybe, maybe.

All the maybes were silver knives stabbing Brynleigh's heart.

Ryker still held River, who had buried her face in his shoulder. He murmured something too quiet even for Brynleigh to hear. This was a fucking private moment, and she was interrupting it.

This was wrong. She shouldn't be here. Shouldn't be witnessing this.

Not after everything.

Brynleigh staggered back, needing distance.

Alone. She was so gods-damned alone.

The pain of her loss had never been as poignant as it was right now. No matter how tightly she hugged herself, it wasn't enough. Her stomach cramped, and tears pricked behind her eyes.

She hadn't shed a single tear when she killed the Earth Elf, but now it felt like she was moments away from weeping.

Her gaze dropped to the floor. Baseboards had never been so intriguing.

After a few minutes, Ryker murmured, "What's wrong, River?"

The concern in his voice made Brynleigh feel even worse.

Ryker loved his sister so much. It was fucking selfish to even think about it, but Brynleigh wanted him to talk to *her* like that again. She wouldn't be nearly as lonely if she even had a fraction of the affection Ryker showed River.

The younger water fae hiccuped.

"Mom's still on her work trip in the Northern Region, so it's just me and the nurses watching Dad. I had an exam earlier, and I was up all night studying. When I came back... It's bad. He was lucid earlier, but now..."

"The Stillness is getting worse?" Ryker whispered.

Brynleigh looked up in time to see his hand curl into a fist.

"Yeah." River nodded.

"Fuck." Ryker exhaled and closed his eyes for a brief moment. "You did the right thing by calling me."

"I'm... I'm so worried about him," River admitted. "If he... If this... If it's..."

"Don't." Ryker's voice was firm, but tinges of grief edged his voice. "Don't say the words."

If there was ever a moment for the floor to open up and swallow Brynleigh whole, this was it. She wished she could call on her shadows and step into the Void, but the bracelet on her wrist meant Ryker would find her. Besides, making him chase her right now would be selfish. Finding reprieve from this situation wouldn't be worth it, not when it would tear him away from his family.

She didn't want to force Ryker to pick his *asset* over his dad and sister.

She didn't want to be here at all.

Brynleigh stumbled back another step and bumped into a vase. It rattled, and she grabbed it before it could hit the ground, but she wasn't fast enough.

The siblings turned to her.

"Oh, Brynleigh." River's eyes widened, and she shook her head. "I'm so sorry. I forgot you were here."

Brynleigh's lips pulled into a tight grimace. "It's okay."

Remembering Ryker's warning from earlier, Brynleigh took another step back and looked anywhere but at her sister-in-law. Ryker didn't want them interacting, but she didn't see how she could get out of this conversation smoothly.

"It's not okay," River said. "I know you guys were on your honeymoon. That's why I was hesitant about calling."

Brynleigh's brows furrowed, and her eyes swung over to her sister-in-law as she tried to process her words. "Hon—"

"You did the right thing," Ryker spoke over Brynleigh, turning River around and pulling her to the closed door. "You should always call me."

River sighed. "I know, but—"

"No 'buts,'" Ryker said firmly. "Let's go see Dad."

They disappeared into the room without a backward glance. The door shut behind them, leaving Brynleigh alone. The empty house loomed over her as she stared at the door blankly.

Did...

Did River not know?

Brynleigh had thought Ryker told his family about the betrayal, but this interaction did not go how she thought it would. It was almost as if he had lied to his sister. Or at least, he had omitted the truth and twisted his words.

But... why would he do that? Why wouldn't he tell everyone what she'd done? Why would he protect Brynleigh?

Confusion swirled through her, and her head grew light.

Between The Rosewood, the almost-kiss, and now this, it was all too much. She missed the days when she just shoved her troublesome emotions aside and ignored them. That was so much easier than *this*. Now, the damned things insisted she pay attention to them, listen to them, fucking *feel* them.

Brynleigh slid down the wall, stretched her legs in front of her, and closed her eyes. Eventually, she drifted off to sleep.

BRYNLEIGH WAS VAGUELY aware of a pair of hands beneath her. Someone lifted her and cradled her in their arms. Thunderstorms and bergamot washed over her, the scent achingly familiar.

"I don't know what the hell I'm going to do with you," the voice murmured.

Brynleigh tried to open her eyes and respond, but she was drifting between dreaming and waking. She stood with one foot in each land, and neither would release her. All she could do was sigh and burrow her head into the chest of whoever was carrying her.

"Fuck," they murmured. "Why do you look so innocent when you're sleeping?"

Did she? She didn't feel innocent. Blood coated her hands and her soul like a second skin. It was invisible, but she knew it was there.

The hands rolled her away, and she landed on something soft. Moments later, her shoes were tugged off her feet. A blanket was pulled over her, the sides tucked around her.

Lips brushed over her forehead in a feather-light kiss.

"I want to fix this, Brynleigh. To fix us. But I don't know how."

The words twisted deep within her.

She wanted to reach out and grab the other person, but sleep hooked its claws into her. It pulled her down, down, down, into its deep embrace.

Her last conscious thought was that she wanted to fix it, too.

CHAPTER 13

She was His, Even If They were Broken

Ryker had thought he'd already sustained the maximum amount of heartbreak one person could bear, but he was wrong. Sitting beside the hospital bed they'd brought into Waterborn House for his father, Ryker's heart broke all over again.

The aching hurt was different than the one he'd felt when Brynleigh betrayed him, but it was no less painful.

In the twelve hours since he first pulled up to his childhood home, Ryker had only left his father's side once. He'd ordered River to go to bed since she had another exam in the morning before moving Brynleigh from the hallway to his old room.

He told himself he didn't move her to be nice but to keep her out of the way when the servants came to clean in the morning. He was lying, but it didn't matter.

Nothing mattered right now except the broken, aging fae beside him.

How had Cyrus Jacob Waterborn been reduced to this shell of a man? Skin so pale it was nearly translucent clung to his skeletal frame. Blue, almost purple, veins stood out against his flesh. Brown, wispy hair remained on his head, far thinner than it used to be. An aura of illness permeated the room.

Tears pricked Ryker's eyes, and he scrubbed a hand over his face. Rough stubble scratched his palm. He needed to shower and shave, but he didn't want to leave his father's side.

Before the Stillness struck, Ryker's father was one of the most powerful water fae in the entire Republic of Balance. Life and vitality used to flow from him like water from a fountain. He'd always been the center of attention, and people were drawn to him. He'd been a torch in a room full of candles.

Now, Cyrus's light had faded to a mere flicker.

Ryker dreaded the day his father's flame would be snuffed entirely.

Reaching out, he picked up his father's hand. Fingers that had once taught him how to hold a softball properly were now brittle and covered in strange brown spots.

"Dad?" Ryker murmured. "Can you hear me?"

There was no response, just like the last dozen times he'd asked.

Cyrus's light brown eyes were open, staring blankly at the ceiling.

Ryker sighed, and his heart broke a little bit more. "I'm here, Dad. I came back."

He shouldn't have stayed away for so long. What if his father had died while he'd been dealing with Brynleigh? Ryker would have never forgiven himself.

A soft knock came from the door, pulling Ryker from his melancholy thoughts.

"Captain Waterborn?" asked a soft female voice.

Ryker didn't release his father's hand as he looked over his shoulder. "Yes?"

A human nurse stood in the doorway. She looked around River's age. Curly blonde hair was swept in a ponytail, and she wore cheerful blue scrubs that somehow made Ryker feel even worse.

"It's time to administer your father's medication."

Most fae afflicted by the Stillness required round-the-clock care, and Cyrus was no different. Tertia refused to put her husband in a residence and instead paid for in-home care. The last time someone had dared suggest that Cyrus might be better off in a medical facility, Tertia verbally eviscerated them. Often, she showed little emotion, but Ryker knew the love his parents had for each other was as vast as the Emerald Sea.

He dipped his chin in the nurse's direction. "Can I stay?"

The last thing he wanted to do was leave his father right now.

A small, understanding smile tugged at the nurse's lips. Her blue eyes were kind, and she nodded.

"Of course. I'm Megan, by the way." She glanced at Ryker's hand, which had tightened around his father's. "I'm sure he knows you're here."

Did he? Ryker wasn't so sure about that. He hadn't seen a flicker of life in Cyrus's eyes since his vigil had begun.

Guilt was a heavy ball of lead in Ryker's stomach. He should have checked on his father since the wedding, but he'd been a gods-damned coward. He hadn't wanted to answer the questions that would have been thrown his way if he had shown up without Brynleigh.

That his mother knew what happened was bad enough, but Ryker didn't want River to discover the truth. He didn't want his sister to look at him like he'd made a mistake. He was supposed to protect her and be there to fix her problems, and if she knew the truth...

Ryker couldn't bear to disappoint his sister or add another burden to her plate. Not when their father was slipping away more with each passing day.

Megan moved methodically through the room, opening drawers and gathering various implements. She withdrew several clear bottles and two empty syringes from a locked medicine cabinet, the key dangling from a cord around her wrist. She laid out her equipment, preparing the medication with steady, sure hands.

"What are you giving him?" Ryker asked after the nurse filled the first needle.

She flicked the top, a small bead of liquid forming over the tip, and moved to the other side of the bed.

"It's a cocktail of drugs." She rattled off their scientific names. The terms went over Ryker's head, but he was certain River would know what they were. That was the benefit of having a sister who was in medical school. He made a mental note to ask her about them later.

"And these should help?" he clarified.

"Yes. After yesterday, we're modifying them slightly. Hopefully, this will slow the Stillness, if not halt its progress altogether. Theoretically, he should be more alert in a day or two."

Hope.

What a fickle, fickle thing. Almost as fickle as the gods River prayed to each day. What good were prayers and hope when their father was still wasting away?

No, Cyrus didn't need hope. He needed medicine, healing, and science.

After a few minutes, Megan stepped back. She gathered her things and dipped her head in Ryker's direction. "I'm almost done."

She placed the used needles in a yellow bin and moved through the room, jotting down several numbers on a clipboard before returning it to the foot of the bed.

Ryker squeezed his father's hand and met the nurse's gaze. "How is he, really?"

Pity flickered across the nurse's face. "He's stable, for now."

Those last ominous words twisted his stomach.

"Have you ever seen someone return from the Stillness?"

Her mouth pinched in a line, and she shook her head before adding, "I'm sorry, no."

He had expected her answer. They had consulted dozens of experts when Cyrus first fell ill. But it still hurt to hear.

Megan gave him a polite smile and pointed to a red button on the wall near the door. "I'll leave you two alone. Just hit that if you need me, and I'll be right in."

"Thank you." Ryker's chest was tight. "Is there anything I can do?"

He hated sitting by helplessly, watching his father waste away. He was the one people went to when they had problems, and he wasn't used to feeling like there was nothing he could do.

"You should try to talk to him. Sometimes it makes a difference."

Ryker thanked the nurse, and she slipped out the door, closing it behind her.

Talk.

Such a simple action, but right now, it felt like all his words were lightyears away.

Death was inching closer to his father, ready to steal its prize.

Ryker's chest burned at the thought. His eyes stung, and he shut them, forcing the tears to remain in place. He would not cry. His father needed him to be strong, to hold everything together.

But Ryker didn't feel strong. He didn't feel like the protector he was supposed to be. He felt broken, hurt, and on the verge of tumbling into a pit of despair. Things with Brynleigh were so gods-damned complicated, and he wished more than anything that his father could give him advice.

Cyrus couldn't die. Ryker wasn't ready. None of them were ready. How did one navigate life without their beloved parent by their side?

A millstone pressed down on his chest. Every breath hurt, every second ached, and everything was wrong.

The Stillness was threatening to tear his family apart from the inside out.

Somehow, Ryker needed to hold the pieces together and help them survive this. Even if it broke him, he would do everything he could to keep his family intact. Tertia was difficult, but she was still his mother. And River was his only sister. He loved them both deeply, and he would do anything for them.

Anything and everything.

Just like Brynleigh had done everything for her family.

Fuck.

Ryker sucked in a sharp breath, and understanding crashed into him like an anvil dropping on his head.

He groaned, his stomach twisting painfully. His heart was a mallet, battering his ribs. His blood chilled, and his magic whirled as his control slipped for a single second.

"Oh, gods."

How could Ryker not have seen this before? How had he been so fucking ignorant?

It was like a veil had shrouded his sight, and now it had been burned away. He saw *everything* from a different perspective. By the Blessed Black Sands, it hurt more than anything he'd ever experienced.

He might not have summoned the storm, but those lives had been lost because of his family.

Pressing a fist against his heart, Ryker tried to ease the burn that felt like it would destroy him from the inside out.

For weeks, he had wondered how Brynleigh could do this to him. How could she betray him and make her love him for something as simple as revenge?

But now...

Gods above, it all made sense.

It wasn't that Ryker had ignored the devastating losses and deaths River had caused in Chavin. He'd grieved for those lives far more than any deaths he'd personally caused on the battlefield. But the people of Chavin had been far away and faceless, while River's pain was right in front of him.

Not anymore.

Now, every time Ryker thought of that night, Brynleigh's face flashed before his eyes. His imagination ran wild, filling his mind with her terrified screams as everyone around her died.

Ryker bent in half, feeling like a truck had run over him.

"I understand," he whispered, his voice as broken as his heart. "I fucking understand."

Those damned tears returned, and this time, he let them fall. Burning trails of hurt and pain, they tumbled down his cheeks, echoing the churning grief inside him.

If someone hurt River, Ryker would burn the world for her. Nothing would stand in his way. No one would stop him. His reaction would make the way they'd dealt with the Incident seem like child's play. There would be no boundaries, no rules.

Family above all else.

And Brynleigh had been doing the same thing.

What the fuck was Ryker supposed to do with this information? The situation with his wife wasn't black and white. Shades of gray coated their entire relationship.

Nothing was easy. Nothing was simple.

Ryker groaned, the mangled sound too loud in this small room. He rubbed his temples, his shoulders tight as he slumped forward.

He wasn't sure how long he stayed like that before a beeping drew him from his thoughts.

Pulling his head out of his hands, he gazed upon his father.

Megan's words echoed through Ryker's mind.

Talk to him.

Now, at least, he had something to say. Ryker scooted closer, his knees rubbing against the side of the mattress. He pressed his forehead against his father's cold, translucent palm.

"Dad, I... I don't know what to do," he whispered. His voice cracked on the last word.

Ryker hated admitting a weakness, even to his unconscious father, but this problem was larger than him. He didn't even know if it could be solved.

Cyrus didn't stir. The only sound was the slight whirring of the machine monitoring his heart rate.

"Things have been... difficult," Ryker admitted. "With the Choosing... and with my wife, Brynleigh."

Still no response.

He closed his eyes and blew out a long breath. In a low voice, he told his father about everything that had happened since the wedding.

Ryker skipped over certain details—he would rather die before sharing details of his sex life with his family—but he laid the rest out as plainly as he could. The shifter's arrival, Brynleigh's reaction to him, her pleas, the shooting, and the pain Ryker felt after, knowing she'd betrayed him.

He didn't stop there.

He shared about the agony, heartbreak, and pain that had been his only companion for days. The hurt he'd felt at Brynleigh's betrayal. How he'd found her in The Pit and heard her confession. And the more recent events. Jelisette de la Point. The deal. The Rosewood.

"The thing is, I... I *understand*." Ryker opened his eyes and stared at his father's immobile form. "Her motives make sense, in a dark way, but I don't know if understanding why she did this is enough. I loved her with all my heart, Dad." If the ache in his chest was any sign, maybe he still did. But he didn't know what to do with that information. "And now..."

What did people do with broken hearts? How could pain like this be mended?

Their problems weren't one-sided. Ryker was self-aware enough to acknowledge that he wasn't fucking perfect.

But...

The door creaked behind Ryker, and he jolted. Dropping his father's hand, he twisted around.

"Sorry, I didn't mean to startle you." Brynleigh stood in the doorway, her wide black eyes staring at him. "I knocked several times, but you didn't hear me."

She was still wearing the same sweater from yesterday. She twisted her hands, the black sleeves falling to her fingertips. The uncertainty in her voice made his heart hurt, and despite everything that lay between them, he wanted to gather her in his arms.

But he didn't.

The brokenness of their relationship was like a canyon stretching between them. He wasn't sure they could ever close the divide.

Ryker stood, and his fingers flexed at his sides. They itched to touch her.

"What do you need?" he asked softly.

A frown pulled at Brynleigh's lips, and a line marred her forehead. "It's almost dusk, and I have to go to Jelisette's tonight."

The debrief.

With everything that had happened with his father, Ryker had forgotten all about it. He hadn't even realized an entire day had passed.

"Oh."

Brynleigh worried her lip. She'd been doing that a lot since he rescued her.

"I'll need to leave soon. Jelisette doesn't like it when people are late." Pain flashed across Brynleigh's face, a whisper of hurt that had Ryker wanting to punch Jelisette.

"I understand." His gaze swept over Brynleigh, cataloging the paleness of her skin, the darkness in her eyes, and the way her fingers tapped nervously against her leg. "Are you hungry?"

Relief flashed through those black orbs.

"Yes," Brynleigh breathed. "I wasn't sure... Is there..."

"There should be blood in the kitchen." He'd made his mother promise to keep some stocked before he married Brynleigh.

Back when giving her the sun and providing blood were their biggest problems. Things had changed, but hopefully, the blood would still be there. If not, he'd figure something out. "I'll take you."

Walking on quiet fae feet, Ryker slipped the door shut behind him. He found the nurse in a room down the hall, letting her know they'd be downstairs.

Brynleigh trailed him through the corridors of Waterborn House. With every passing moment, that canyon between them yawned. By the time they arrived in the kitchen, crossing the divide felt almost insurmountable.

But Ryker had to try. He couldn't let things remain the way they were.

He flicked on the kitchen light.

This had always been his favorite room in the house. Despite the industrial appliances and enormous double fridge that belonged in a restaurant, the kitchen had a homey feel that most of Waterborn House lacked. An enormous island stretched across the length of the room, white cabinets covered the walls, and usually, open windows overlooked the garden. Now, they were covered in black drapes.

Ryker pulled out a stool for Brynleigh, waiting for her to slip onto it before he strode over to the fridge. Tucked behind a row of condiments, as if someone had tried to hide them, were several bags of blood.

He reached inside, gently maneuvering around the glass bottles and jars. "Warm or cold?"

"Warm," was her whispered reply.

Ryker nodded, shutting the fridge. Even though years had passed since he had last lived here, the kitchen layout was exactly the same. He located a mug and scissors with ease.

He worked silently, pouring the blood into a cup and heating it in the microwave. A coppery tang filled the air, mingling with the lemon-scented cleaner his mother preferred.

The whirring of the microwave was the backdrop to Ryker's spinning thoughts. He couldn't wait for the divide between him and Brynleigh to miraculously repair itself.

First of all, it didn't seem possible. Secondly, and more importantly, if he'd learned one thing from watching his father slowly Fade from the Stillness, it was that time was precious.

He refused to wait for the "right moment" because they were rare.

He would make his own moments happen.

The microwave beeped, and Ryker bent, pulling out the cup. Iron tickled his nostrils, and he slid the mug across the island.

He rested his forearms on the counter. "Let me know if it's warm enough."

Brynleigh flashed him a soft smile, raising the cup to her lips. She sipped it slowly before taking a larger swallow. "It's perfect. Thank you, Ryker."

He wasn't sure if it was the smile or the gentle way she spoke his name, but his chest warmed.

When he searched within himself for the anger that had been his companion for days, he didn't find it. Its absence confirmed he was taking the right course of action, emboldening him.

Still leaning against the island, Ryker reached across the counter and captured Brynleigh's fingers in his.

Sparks ran through him at the touch, and she didn't pull away.

That seemed like a good sign, so he repeated the words he'd whispered to her last night when he brought her to bed.

"I want to fix us, Brynleigh."

CHAPTER 14

A Walking Contradiction

Of all the things Brynleigh expected Ryker to say, that was not one of them. Her heart hammered in her chest, and for the longest moment, she stared at him.

Fix them.

Was that even possible?

Her eyes widened, and she pulled her hand from his. She needed a moment without his hypnotizing fingers on hers. When he touched her, it became the only thing she could think about, and she needed a clear head.

They weren't cleanly broken, like a twig snapped in half. A piece of tape wouldn't fix them. They were more like a picture that had been torn into several pieces. They had jagged edges stemming from the hurts caused by both of them.

But even with all that, part of Brynleigh wanted to try.

Most of her, if she was being honest.

When she looked at Ryker, she saw the fae she married. Wisps of brown hair tinged with red framed his face. Sharp, pointed ears adorned the sides of his head. The stark, strong bones of his face made him beautiful. Storms filled his eyes, and there was power in the way he moved.

Ryker was handsome and powerful, and *hers*...

And he was also the fae who'd played a part in her torture.

He was her husband but also her jailer.

Her lover, but his sister murdered her family.

Her Chosen partner and the one her heart desired, but he was intimately connected to the reason she was no longer truly alive.

They were a walking contradiction.

Forget opposites attract—they should never have been together in the first place.

How ironic was it that the Head of the Army's Fae Division fell for a vigilante vampire who killed evil people?

And yet.

And. Fucking. Yet.

Even though they were ripped apart with jagged edges and their relationship was paradoxical, Brynleigh's heart swelled with hope at his words.

"Who's asking? My... husband?" The word tasted strange after weeks of disuse. "Or the fae captain looking after his asset?"

Brynleigh held her breath, her fists clenched as she waited for him to reply. She didn't dare move lest the moment disappear. It was important. She could feel it in her bones. This could alter the course of their future.

If Ryker was asking as the fae captain, the answer would be 'fuck no.' Having already been used by Jelisette and Zanri, Brynleigh had no use for yet another person who saw her as a tool.

But if he was asking as her husband, as the man who'd invaded her dreams and broken rules for her and kissed her like she was his entire universe...

Then, by all the gods, her answer would be different.

"I'm asking as your husband," was his gravelly response. "My job has no influence over this conversation."

Brynleigh wasn't a fool, and she read between the lines. His job would influence other conversations, other parts of their life, but this...

She inhaled and ran her tongue over the tip of a fang. A single drop of blood remained in the mug, and she stared at it, tracking its crimson trail as it spread out across the bottom of the cup. Her meeting with

Jelisette was at the back of her mind, but not even an earthquake could move her from this seat.

"Do you really think it's possible?" she asked.

There was a whisper of movement, and Ryker's scent deepened. Without even looking, she knew he'd moved. She could feel his presence beside her.

Her chest tightened as memories of the time they'd had together before everything went to hell haunted her. The wedding and the days preceding it had been some of the happiest of her entire life. She wanted that back and was beginning to realize she'd do almost anything to make that happen.

"Honestly? I don't fucking know. But I want... I want to try. If you do." Ryker's voice, usually strong and confident, was so quiet she had to strain to hear him.

Standing on her right, he placed his hand on the island between them. His palm faced upwards, and his fingers twitched.

The invitation was clear.

Their first touch in the Choosing had been accidental during their blindfolded date, but there was nothing unintentional about the way Brynleigh slowly lifted her hand and inched it toward his. She slid her fingers through his until they were intertwined. The warmth of his hand seeped into her, and her eyes fluttered shut.

They were a walking contradiction, but in the end, her answer was easy.

"I want to fix us more than fucking anything."

If she were granted one wish in this world, she would ask to be his once again.

Ryker drew in a deep breath and curled his fingers around hers.

"Gods above," he breathed, moving closer to her. His chest brushed against her arm. "Where do we go from here?"

That was the real question. How did one repair a break such as theirs? It wasn't as though there were marriage counselors specializing in "What to do if your wife was planning on killing you and decided not to, but her evil Maker still tried to go through with the plan, and then your wife was tortured for three weeks before you made a deal to get her out."

There wasn't a guide for this. Even if the ocean was filled with glue, Brynleigh wasn't sure it would be enough to fix them... but she would fucking try. She'd give repairing their relationship everything she had.

She slid off the stool, still holding his hand. Barely a foot divided them.

Her gaze caught on his lips. Would Ryker taste the same as he had on their wedding night?

That familiar warmth sparked in her core, and she leaned closer. Would he let her kiss him? They'd had a physical connection from the first moment they were in the same room.

She breathed his name and added, "I think—"

A shrill ring sliced through the air, cutting her off.

Brynleigh sucked in a breath, her heart hammering.

Twice now, Ryker's phone had interrupted them. She was ready to smash that troublesome piece of technology to smithereens and get rid of it forever.

Who needed phones, anyway? Kissing was a much better use of their time.

Ryker jumped, his eyes widening as his hand slipped from hers. He pulled out his phone, glancing at the screen.

"Shit. I'm so sorry, Brynleigh. I need to take this." He grimaced, his gaze darting back to her mouth. "Hold that thought?"

She nodded mutely, unable to find words. Lifting her fingers, she rested her hand against her lips as he accepted the call.

"Hello?" He pressed the phone against his ear and strode out of the kitchen. "Yes, this is Captain Waterborn..."

His voice was a low murmur as he continued speaking.

Brynleigh could've tried to listen in, but her mind was still spinning from their conversation.

Ryker was her everything. Even with the current state of their relationship, she was drawn to him. She'd never felt safe or at home with anyone else.

Mulling over the recent developments, she helped herself to more blood. Before the wedding, Ryker had told her that his mother never hired vampires, so she assumed she'd be the only one drinking it. It would be wasteful to leave it in the fridge.

She had it cold while waiting for him to return.

For the first time in weeks, Brynleigh felt a glimmer of hope. Maybe, just maybe, this wouldn't be the end. Maybe they could still have that life they'd discussed in the Choosing. They could play chess late into the night, with Marlowe asleep on the rug by their feet, as they laughed and talked about everything and nothing.

A slow smile stretched across her face.

Maybe all was not lost.

Maybe—

"There's been another attack." Ryker's baritone rumble broke her from her thoughts.

She sucked in a breath and spun around. "Where?"

"Sandhaven," he growled.

Dark storm clouds roiled in Ryker's eyes, and a pit formed in Brynleigh's stomach. This was bad. She could already tell.

Even though she didn't want to know the answer, she asked, "What happened?"

The temperature dropped in the kitchen.

"There was another bomb." He dropped his phone on the counter and curled his fists. "The Black Night hit a fucking boarding school."

Brynleigh recoiled, her vision clouding. Attacking the Choosing was one thing, but this...

"You mean... they went after children?" she asked, her throat dry.

Some things in life were off-limits. There were unspoken rules that even killers like Brynleigh followed, and staying away from children was one of them. Children were the fucking future of the Republic. No one touched them. Except now, the rebels had done just that.

Ryker raked a hand through his hair. "Some were injured, but none of them died."

Relief rushed through Brynleigh, and her legs knocked together.

She gripped the counter. "Thank Isvana for small mercies. How old were they?"

"Teenagers, mostly." He looked as distraught as she felt. "The students of Jade Academy were putting on a concert for their parents."

"Oh, gods. So young." She swayed, the counter the only thing keeping her upright.

How could the rebels do that?

"They're insane, that's how," Ryker growled.

Brynleigh hadn't realized she had spoken the last part out loud. He was right, though.

The rebels had officially lost their minds. There was no other reason anyone would attack youth. The Representatives were terrible, but this...

This was no way to go about forcing change.

Fuck them all.

Fury replaced the horror running through Brynleigh's veins, and her grip tightened on the countertop. "You said it was a boarding school?"

He nodded grimly.

"Most of the Southern Representatives send their younglings to Jade Academy. It's the most prestigious finishing school in the Southern Region, and it's safe." Another growl rumbled through Ryker's chest. "Or it was before the Black Night showed up."

"You're certain it was them?" Although, how many rebel groups were there in the Republic anyway?

"Yes." The word was guttural, and it sent shivers down her spine. "Bomb makers leave signatures, just like artists on paintings. This one was identical to the one that blew up the Masked Ball."

"Oh."

Brynleigh rubbed a phantom pain on her neck where she'd been injured during the masquerade.

Back when she thought revenge was the extent of her problems. Back when things had been simple. Back when she hadn't known the depth of her Maker's lies.

"I have to go." Ryker's hand brushed against Brynleigh's wrist. "The vampires from the Night Corps are shadowing soldiers to Sandhaven to help with the investigation. I'll be there for a few days, at least. The timing is horrible."

Especially considering what they'd been about to do.

Brynleigh glanced at the clock and frowned. "Jelisette is expecting me."

"I know." Ryker stepped towards her, lifting a hand as though to touch her before dropping it back to his side. "After you meet with Jelisette, I want you to go to my apartment."

It took a few heartbeats for his words to register, and when they did, Brynleigh blinked. After everything she'd done, she'd never thought she would be welcome at his home.

"Are you sure?" she asked before she could stop herself.

"Yes. I'll meet you there as soon as I can." Ryker yanked open a drawer, grabbed a slip of paper, and scribbled a code on it. "The apartment is warded, but this will turn off the alarms. Make yourself at home. I'll have someone bring your suitcase over tomorrow."

A broken part of Brynleigh's soul repaired itself at his words.

"Thank you, Ryker." She couldn't express how much this meant to her. "I... thank you."

"You're welcome." He handed her the paper, and his fingers tightened around hers. "Shadow in as soon as you're done, and don't go anywhere else. The rebels might attack again, and I don't want you near them."

Because he cared about her.

Her heart soared at his declaration. It didn't care that they still had problems. All it cared about was that Ryker was holding her hand, and he wanted to keep her safe.

She glanced upstairs. "What about your dad and sister?"

"Dad's nurse Megan is here, and the house is guarded and warded. They'll be alright." Ryker released her hands, and Brynleigh instantly missed the warmth of his touch.

How had she ever survived the coldness of being a vampire before him?

The captain looked like he had more to say, but his phone started vibrating, the motion driving it off the island.

It was official. Brynleigh was ready to boycott phones forever.

"Fuck." Ryker grabbed the device, pressing a few buttons before shoving it into his pocket. "I'm out of time. The army doesn't wait for anyone."

Until that moment, Brynleigh hadn't fully understood Ryker's job.

Most people ran from danger, but he was heading straight towards it. He was a powerful fae, as were his team members, but still. She knew how quickly a situation could turn dangerous.

Worry gnawed at her heart, propelling her forward. She folded her fingers around his and gazed into his captivating eyes.

There were so many things she wanted to say, so many conversations they still needed to have, and yet, all she could manage was to softly say, "Be safe, Ryker."

Before Brynleigh could lose her nerve, she lifted her chin and closed the distance between them.

Resting one hand flat on Ryker's chest, right above his beating heart, she inhaled his stormy scent and brushed her lips over his cheek. It was barely a touch and didn't count as a kiss, but neither her body nor her heart received that message. His rough stubble tickled her lips, her mouth tingled, and her heart soared.

She murmured, "I'll miss you."

His head dipped, and he brushed his thumb over her bottom lip.

The air between them thickened, and his breath warmed her lips. "I—"

Bang, bang, bang.

"By the Sands," Ryker cursed, stepping back. He raised his voice. "I'm coming!" His chest heaved as he looked at her. "I'm sorry."

She flexed her fingers before placing them over her own racing heart. "I'm... I'll see you when you get back."

And then, they would fix things. That was the only acceptable option.

Ryker's gaze searched hers for a long moment before he nodded. He was halfway to the front door when he paused and glanced over his shoulder.

"When you get to the apartment, check the top drawer on the left nightstand in the bedroom."

"Left nightstand. Got it." Intrigued, Brynleigh followed Ryker to the front door.

He picked up a black bag from the floor, slinging it over his shoulder. She assumed it was the go-bag he told her he always kept here, just in case.

With one final longing glance, he murmured, "Goodbye, Brynleigh."

He opened the door and stepped into the dusky twilight that had overtaken the sky. A tall, pale-skinned man dressed in black and silver army fatigues and combat boots stood on the porch. The soldier's black gaze flicked to Brynleigh's, and he dipped his head, pulling shadows from his palms.

Ryker clasped the vampire's elbow, and then, they were gone.

Brynleigh's lips were still tingling, the lingering memory of the kiss-that-wasn't-a-kiss remaining as she pressed her fingers to her mouth. If she focused, she could still catch a hint of Ryker's scent.

She stood there for several minutes before she, too, vanished into the shadows.

CHAPTER 15

As Dark as Her Maker's Heart

"The Earth Elf died cleanly." Brynleigh's back was straight, her stance was wide, and her hands were clasped behind her. She was the perfect image of a dutiful progeny reporting to her Maker. "I dealt with him in The Rosewood, as requested."

Jelisette sat in front of the chess board in the safe house's living room, her hands clasped beneath her chin as she studied the game intently. Her silky maroon blouse covered her arms—and her Binding Mark, apparently.

Brynleigh still had trouble believing her Maker had hidden a Binding. She tried not to dwell on that because she feared that if she did, she might start asking questions that would land her in even more trouble.

Instead, she pinched her mouth shut and waited for Jelisette to look up.

She could be here for a while.

Once, Brynleigh's sire had made her wait all night before acknowledging her. She hoped that wouldn't be the case tonight. She was tired and wanted to leave as quickly as possible.

Jelisette didn't even look up as she moved her rook forward. She spun the board around, humming to herself as she studied the game from another angle.

Minutes went by. Ten. Twenty. Forty-five.

Brynleigh was a statue. Moving would only incite her Maker's ire.

Chess pieces slowly filtered off the board. Black was winning, but several paths to victory existed for both sides.

When nearly an hour had passed, Jelisette picked up a pawn and moved it forward two spaces.

"Very good." She spoke as though she hadn't just made Brynleigh wait an ungodly amount of time. "I sent the crew to clean up after you."

She spun the board again and went back to studying the game.

Gods damn it. At this rate, Brynleigh would be here all night.

Her lips tingled, but she refused to think about Ryker. She couldn't afford any distractions right now.

Forcing the handsome fae captain from her mind, her gaze moved studiously through the room. She drank in every detail, dedicating them to memory. She would sort through them later, searching for signs that Jelisette was working with the Black Night.

Eventually, the older vampire pushed back from the table. She stood, her movements fluid with immortal vampiric grace, and tilted her head.

"Come to my study."

Jelisette stepped into the Void without waiting to see if her command had been heard. She didn't need to. Brynleigh was her progeny, and she would obey her.

At least, that was how Maker bonds were meant to work.

Brynleigh wasn't sure if it was because of her time in the Choosing, her attachment to Ryker, or the fact that her heart twisted in knots when she thought about Jelisette's multiple betrayals and lies, but the Maker bond didn't seem as strong as it used to be.

In the past, when vampires were allowed to draw blood directly from Sources, Makers could summon their progeny through the bond. That was one of the many gifts vampires no longer had access to, thanks to the "humane" blood banks.

For once, Brynleigh was grateful that the Representatives had placed strict laws over vampires. The less control her Maker had over her, the better.

Less than a minute after Jelisette vanished into the darkness, Brynleigh released her shadows. Calling on the moon goddess's magic was as easy as drawing breath, and she moved through the Void with the ease of stepping from one place to the next.

Brynleigh landed in front of Jelisette's desk, where her Maker pressed a phone against her ear.

Jelisette was scribbling on a piece of paper. She didn't even look up as the younger vampire arrived, instead lifting a finger in the air.

Brynleigh barely bit back a sigh.

Back to waiting.

Shadows rippled around the desk, and a tingle of magic swept over the younger vampire's skin. Even though her Maker's lips moved, Brynleigh couldn't hear a thing. Many vampires used privacy wards to create walls of magic that blocked all sound from coming through.

Instead of expending her energy on the fruitless endeavor of trying to hear what her Maker was saying, Brynleigh assessed this space much like the last.

The only door was at her back. Floor-to-ceiling bookshelves took up space on two walls, crammed with leather-bound books. A famous painting, *The Weeping Widow,* covered the only window, blocking all light from the shadowy space.

The artist's dark depiction made Brynleigh's blood run cold. A naked, bloody human woman knelt in a crimson pool. Her hands were outstretched to the heavens. A silent scream contorted her features, and tears flowed down her face. The background was a swirl of scarlet and black, as if the sky was bleeding.

Brynleigh had always hated that painting and how the woman looked like her heart had been ripped from her chest.

She tore her gaze away from it, refocusing on the desk. A solitary green lamp illuminated the papers strewn over the wooden surface. A quill sat next to an ink pot; both remnants of times passed. The carpet was crimson beneath Brynleigh's feet.

It was dark, just like her Maker's heart.

Other than the phone still pressed against Jelisette's ear, the room was technology-free. The older vampire had often said that while she understood the value of computers, she didn't like them. She'd avoided using technology as much as possible, and she forced Zanri to keep all their electronics in his office in the safe house.

Several minutes later, Jelisette hung up the phone and closed the folder. Waving a hand, she dismantled the ward and looked at Brynleigh. The young vampire barely suppressed a shiver.

Jelisette interwove her hands together, rested her elbows on the wood, and cradled her chin on her intertwined fingers.

"Tell me, daughter of my blood, why did your husband release you from The Pit?" The words were silky-soft but laced with an unmasked threat of violence.

Brynleigh's skin pricked. Maybe she should've spent more time trying to hear through the ward. Who had been on the call?

She swallowed, twisting her fingers in front of her for half a second before realizing that was a nervous tell. She stopped and forced herself to remain calm.

Chances were, Jelisette didn't know about the deal.

Brynleigh would make sure it remained that way. The last thing she wanted to do was betray Ryker's trust just as she was regaining it.

But she had to tell her Maker something.

Brynleigh rapidly formed a plan. It wasn't great, and honestly, it could very well turn sideways on her, but it was still a plan. And that was... good.

Well.

Good might be an overstatement, but it was *a* plan.

She wouldn't betray Ryker. Instead, she would use her knowledge of her Maker's involvement in the Black Night, infiltrate the rebels' ranks, and use the information she received to win Ryker back.

Imagining how pleased he'd be when she provided him with detailed information about the rebels, Brynleigh decided this was the best course of action.

"The fae captain is a sentimental fool." She willed her face to be blank despite the pain the words caused her.

"Oh?" Jelisette raised a manicured brow.

Brynleigh's heart twisted, and she nodded. "Yes, and he believes in love, so he bargained to get me out of prison."

After your actions landed me there in the first place.

Brynleigh didn't say those words, but she wished she could.

Jelisette propped her chin on her hand and studied her progeny. She didn't look a day over thirty, except for her eyes. Her dark gaze was like looking at death itself. Brynleigh had seen killers with warmer expressions than the one currently surveying her.

Her Maker asked, "He loves you?"

He used to. Brynleigh wasn't sure if Ryker felt that way now, but she wouldn't say that, either.

"Yes."

"And how do you feel about him?"

This would be the hard part. Brynleigh wanted to shout her love for the captain from the rooftops, but she was under no false pretenses about where she stood with Jelisette. Doing that would get her killed.

"I have no feelings for Ryker Waterborn." The words burned like acid at the back of Brynleigh's throat. "He was, and still is, my mark."

Lies, lies, lies.

Her heart raced in her chest. She eyed her Maker, watching for any reaction at all.

"I see," was Jelisette's monotone response.

Did she? Brynleigh was walking a dangerous path, spinning a web of deceit. She couldn't find it in herself to feel bad about it, though. After all, Jelisette had lied to her for years. It was her turn to be on the other end of things.

Since Brynleigh's throat was still intact, she continued with the next step of her plan.

"I'm playing him." She approached the desk and placed her palms flat on the wooden surface. "I know I was supposed to kill him, but it turns out that one Representative isn't enough."

The smallest semblance of a smile crept onto Jelisette's face, and she made a noncommittal sound.

Brynleigh had to be careful. She had to leave enough breadcrumbs so that Jelisette would trust her but not enough so that her Maker would be suspicious that this change of heart came too fast.

"I want to hurt them all. Do something that would forever alter the Republic of Balance."

More lies.

She didn't like the way the Representatives ran the Republic, but it was apparent the rebels were no better than them.

Drawing in a deep breath, Brynleigh spoke the one sentence that would either be the cause of her death or the gateway to her freedom.

"I want to find the rebels and join their cause. They want to hurt the Representatives, and I want the same thing." Again, with the lies. If Brynleigh had a penny for every falsehood she uttered in Jelisette's presence tonight, she'd be rich. "I still want revenge for my family."

Her shadows throbbed in her veins, desiring to come out and protect her, but she held them in. She'd placed all her cards on the table, and now, she would wait.

This wasn't a moment for a show of force but of submission.

Eyes made of pure onyx ice drilled into Brynleigh's. Jelisette tapped her index finger on her chin. The movement caused her sleeve to inch down, revealing a sliver of the black band wrapped around her wrist.

The Binding Mark.

It took everything in Brynleigh's power not to react.

"And how does your fae captain feel about all this?" Jelisette eventually asked.

That was a good question.

If Ryker knew what Brynleigh was proposing, he'd be outraged. But he didn't know. Besides, she was doing this for him.

"He has no feelings about it because I'm keeping him in the dark." Truth. "It's not that difficult. Men are... easily swayed. Besides, he thinks since I was Made, I'm weak."

Another lie, although there were bits of truth nestled within those words. Even though Brynleigh knew Ryker thought she was strong, others in the Republic of Balance looked down on vampires because they were gifted with, not born into, their magic.

"Does he now?" The silky smoothness of Jelisette's voice deepened, and she canted her head.

One moment, the deadly vampire was behind the desk. The next, thick, unnatural darkness shrouded the room.

Brynleigh went to scream, but no sound came out. Sharp nails dug into her throat, compressing her airway.

With vampiric strength, Jelisette lifted her progeny off the ground and *squeezed*.

Oh gods, oh gods, oh gods.

Maybe Brynleigh had miscalculated. She stiffened, her heart a mallet pounding against her chest as she tried to remain calm.

It wasn't fucking working. Calmness was a distant dream.

Brynleigh's palms slickened.

Pressure built, built, built behind her eyes.

Her lungs squeezed as they tried—and failed—to draw air.

She flexed her fingers, wanting to reach up and pull those nails out of her throat, but she didn't dare do that.

Not yet.

Giving in now would only prove to Jelisette that she was weak and untrustworthy.

So, Brynleigh remained still, even as those sharpened nails sank deeper. At first, they were needles, but soon, each one was a knife digging into her tender skin.

Brynleigh didn't dare move. She wanted to keep her head, thank you very much.

The scent of copper grew stronger, wet rivulets trickling down her neck.

Her shadows throbbed in warning. Her head spun. Her fangs ached.

Death's cool eyes drilled into the back of Brynleigh's neck.

"Are you lying to me, daughter of my blood?" The question was soft, like a feather wrapped in velvet.

Brynleigh tried to talk, but the hand around her throat was too tight. Jelisette loosened her grip just a touch.

"No," Brynleigh gasped through the pain. "I'm not."

Those nails dug in deeper. "Tell me, child, why should I believe you when you already broke the rules once?"

"Because I want the same thing as you," Brynleigh rasped. "I want revenge."

Those claws sank in further.

Rivulets became rivers, blood coursing down her throat.

Black spots swam in Brynleigh's vision, and tears pricked behind her eyes. She hadn't said goodbye to Ryker. Not really.

If she died tonight, would he come looking for her? Would he mourn her just as she'd mourned him?

His face was all she could picture as she inched closer to the end.

Deeper, deeper, deeper, those claws dug.

Even vampires couldn't survive without a head.

Eventually, Brynleigh's survival instincts kicked in. She reached up, trying to pull her Maker's fingers from her neck.

An animalistic snarl ripped out of Jelisette's chest. She squeezed Brynleigh's neck so tightly that air was nothing but a dream.

This was it.

Brynleigh closed her eyes and prepared to die.

I love you, Ryker, she shouted into the darkness of her mind.

They weren't mates and didn't have a mental connection, but that didn't matter right now. As her immortal life drew to a close, Brynleigh hoped her fae captain could feel her thinking of him.

Death was cold as it came for Brynleigh with its dark, shadowy arms outstretched.

Her vision clouded, and she repeated the same phrase in her mind.

I love you; I love you; I love you.

If they'd had more time, she would have apologized and told him how sorry she was that she'd broken them in the first place. She would tell him that he had shown her that people could be kind, strong, and loving. She would make sure he knew he'd made her the happiest she'd ever been in her entire life.

Now, it was too late.

Hopefully, when Brynleigh was dead, Ryker would remember that she loved him.

Her eyes fluttered shut, her heart took one final beat, and then—

The nails were gone.

The shadows cleared.

Brynleigh collapsed in a heap on the crimson carpet, her blood staining the fibers, as Jelisette stepped back.

Holding a hand to her bloody, torn-up throat, Brynleigh greedily inhaled gulps of air. Her skin slowly stitched itself back together. Her fangs ached.

She wasn't out of harm's way yet, though. She would never forget the true predator standing in front of her.

Dragging herself to her knees, Brynleigh lifted her gaze.

Cold black eyes gazed mercilessly down at her.

There would be no blood for Brynleigh here, tonight. She wouldn't even bother asking.

"You want revenge against the Representatives?" Jelisette asked calmly as if she hadn't been about to tear her progeny's head from her shoulders.

Keeping her hand against her throat, Brynleigh nodded. The movement sent bolts of pain lancing through her, and she barely held in a whimper.

Long minutes passed.

Jelisette's punishing, judging stare was unwavering.

Brynleigh's knees hurt from kneeling on the ground—all of her hurt, to be honest—but she didn't dare move. She would endure this for hours if it would get her the information she sought.

"I must admit, you surprised me." Jelisette tilted her head, her eyes gleaming with interest. She was a predator, and her progeny was her prey. "Tell me, my daughter, what would you do for your revenge?"

"Anything," Brynleigh breathed without a second thought.

Jelisette pursed her lips.

"Alright." She turned and wrote something out on a slip of paper. "Be at this address two nights from now. If you dare."

She dangled the paper in front of Brynleigh as if taunting her.

Despite the blood on her fingers and the still-healing wound on her neck, Brynleigh grabbed the paper, careful not to smear her blood on the page.

"Thank you."

"Don't make a mess of my carpet." Jelisette gave her one final stern look before turning and striding from the office.

Brynleigh stared at the paper clutched between her bloody fingers.

Midnight
16 Upper Red Road
Back entrance
Ask for Dimitri

Brynleigh had so many questions and not nearly enough answers, but this was better than nothing.

When her Maker was halfway down the hallway, Brynleigh finally stood. Tremors ran through her, the shock of nearly dying still coursing through her veins.

She needed to get out of here.

Her palm was extended, and she was about to call on her shadows when something caught her eye. A thin black book was by the door, squished between two ancient leather tomes.

The Night Will Rise Again was scrawled on the spine.

The author was unknown.

Something about the book called to Brynleigh. It was out of place in the study, a far cry from the ancient tomes filling the rest of the shelves.

Before Brynleigh could stop and think about what she was doing, she grabbed the book. When no alarm blared, and Jelisette didn't immediately reappear in the office to finish removing Brynleigh's neck from her shoulders, she exhaled.

Tucking the address in the book for safekeeping, Brynleigh pulled shadows from within, stepping into the Void with blood dripping down her neck.

THE OBNOXIOUS, shrill shriek of Ryker's security alarm greeted Brynleigh when she stepped out of the Void. Of course, he would have the loudest alarm system she'd ever heard. It was like someone was clashing cymbals in her ears. She released her shadows and hurried to the front door.

Brynleigh dumped Jelisette's book and phone on the nearest surface. Extracting the slip of paper Ryker had given her from her back pocket, she squinted and tried to decipher his terrible handwriting.

Her fingers trembled as she punched in the security code. It took three attempts to shut off the horrid sound. In the wake of the blaring alarm, the silence was deafening. Every heartbeat was a drum; every breath was a shout.

The quiet was too much.

The weight of everything that had happened slammed into Brynleigh like a fucking freight train. Her head, her heart, and her body hurt. It was too much to bear.

She slumped against the wall, grabbing the doorframe to remain upright.

"Fuck."

Brynleigh had never been in shock, but that seemed to be precisely what was happening. Her head swam, her heart raced, and all her movements were sluggish. This wasn't bloodlust—she was fully in control. A quick check of her neck confirmed that the wounds had healed.

Sleep.

That's what she needed.

Brynleigh released the door and pushed herself off of the wall. She checked the locks, because she'd never be caught unaware again, and stumbled towards the bathroom.

Bloody handprints streaked on the wall where she held herself up, but she'd deal with them later. Exhaustion tugged at her, its relentless pull getting stronger with every passing moment.

Elbowing her way into the bathroom, she quickly washed her hands and ran a washcloth over her raw, pink skin.

Once she had removed most of the blood, she stripped and dumped her clothes in the hamper. Locating the laundry facilities would be a job for tomorrow.

Wearing nothing but her underwear, Brynleigh made her way to the last door in the hall. She remembered from her tour that this was Ryker's room.

She couldn't imagine how much worse she'd have felt if she'd been forced to return to Waterborn House or that bungalow where she and Ryker had gone after he'd freed her.

At least here, an air of familiarity calmed a part of her.

Brynleigh opened the bedroom door and immediately stopped as Ryker's scent slammed into her. Thunderstorms and bergamot permeated everything in this space.

She breathed deeply, filling her nose with his comforting, grounding scent. Her trembling slowed, and some of her exhaustion lifted. She knew she shouldn't snoop, but she couldn't help herself. Anything to get to know Ryker better.

The room was masculine, which was unsurprising. Navy drapes matched the comforter. A large, empty dog bed sat against the far wall. Two black dressers stood near the door. A king-sized, comfortable-looking bed took up the place of honor. The mattress called to Brynleigh, but she ignored its summons.

Looking at Ryker's room was one thing, but she couldn't sleep in his bed and invade his space.

There was a black T-shirt on the ground, though. Likely discarded from the last time Ryker was here, it looked comfortable and worn. She crept into the room and grabbed it.

Bringing the material to her nose, she sniffed.

His scent drowned everything else out. Her heart rate slowed to its normal, turtle-like rate. The trembling was almost non-existent. For a moment, it was as though he was standing right next to her.

Brynleigh didn't let herself think about what she was doing as she slid the shirt over her head. She didn't let herself wonder about whether Ryker would be upset she was wearing his things. She couldn't because she was afraid if she overthought it, she'd take off the shirt.

Right now, she couldn't imagine anything worse than that.

Content with how the garment fell to mid-thigh, Brynleigh grabbed a pillow and a blanket from the foot of the bed. She was about to leave when she remembered Ryker's instructions.

"Left nightstand," she murmured.

The drawer was unlocked and slid open easily.

Brynleigh's eyes widened and she inhaled sharply. Resting on top of several books was a folded-up photo, her phone, and a charger.

Tears rushed to her eyes as she swept all three items into her arms. She forgot about her exhaustion entirely as she hurried to the living room.

Dropping the pillow and blanket on the pull-out couch, Brynleigh plugged in her phone and waited for it to boot up. She sat, holding her breath as she gently unfolded the picture. Running her finger down the creases, she lay it flat on her lap.

A shuddering sob ripped through Brynleigh. The picture had been in her clutch with her phone on their wedding night, so it shouldn't have surprised her to see them together, but it did. She'd assumed the picture had been lost, but she was wrong.

Even when he hated her, Ryker had been looking out for her.

"Hey, Sarai, I miss you." Brynleigh traced her sister's infectious, beautiful smile with all the care in the world. "I wish you were here. I think... I think you'd like Ryker. I know you'd like his sister."

They would have gotten along so well.

Brynleigh lost track of time as she stared at the picture. She recommitted her sister's face to memory, soaking it in until her phone started vibrating uncontrollably next to her.

Messages were undoubtedly flooding in, but she wasn't ready to read them. She was fairly certain they would be negative. After all, she'd missed Hallie's wedding. Brynleigh didn't have many friends, but she was confident that friends didn't miss their friends' weddings.

It was cowardly of her, but Brynleigh didn't want to face the Fortune Elf yet. She didn't want to lose the one friend she'd made.

But there was one message she wanted to send before bed.

Navigating through her contacts, not that there were many, she clicked on Ryker's name. Opening their thread, she scrolled up to their wedding day.

Her last message had been sent an hour before she walked down the aisle.

BRYNLEIGH

Are you ready for today, Ry?

The response had come in seconds later.

RYKER

More than ready, sweetheart. I could barely sleep last night.

Who says you'll be getting a lot of sleep tonight?

...

winking emoji

The hairdresser's here. I have to go. See you soon!

There was so much hope in those few messages. So much to look forward to. And now everything had changed.

Ryker's words from earlier echoed in her mind.

I want to fix this.

So did she.

Brynleigh's eyes were heavy, but she wasn't ready to sleep yet. Her thumbs traveled over the keyboard.

I miss you.

No, that wasn't it. She pressed the backspace, clearing the screen.

Please be safe. We have a lot to talk about when you get back.

That felt wrong. Delete.

What if we can't fix this?

With a groan, she got rid of that one, too.

She typed three more messages, and she deleted them all. She had too many words and things she wanted to say, and she was far too tired for this.

In the end, she settled on something simple.

Thank you, Ryker.

She sent the message and turned the phone on silent before dropping it on the ground. Pulling the blanket over herself, she stretched out on the sofa and promptly fell asleep.

CHAPTER 16

Death and Sunny Dispositions

"Any signs of the rebels?" Ryker addressed the fae beside him as he crossed his arms and shifted his stance, rubble crunching beneath his feet.

Charred seats, tumbled columns, a burned stage, and snowflakes made of ash were all that remained of Jade Academy's concert hall.

Ryker had arrived in Sandhaven four hours ago. As soon as he'd stepped out of the Void, he'd started digging through the remnants of the building with dozens of other soldiers. The hours had gone by quickly. Ash and dirt clung to him like a second skin, but they were no closer to uncovering any answers.

"No, sir." First Lieutenant Felicity Cross, an earth fae who'd been on Ryker's squad for years, shook her head. The movement dislodged a few strands of dark brown hair from her braid, her olive skin dusted with as much ash as Ryker's. "We're still sweeping the area for them."

"Good," he grunted.

The rebels had vanished like a morning mist, but they couldn't hide forever.

Ryker had sent three of his best fae trackers to look for them on the ground, and several winged elves were searching the skies.

They would find them. It was just a matter of time.

Until then, Ryker would remain in Sandhaven. In many ways, he was grateful to be here. He wasn't one to sit back and let others get their hands dirty without participating. Not joining the investigation after the explosion at the Masked Ball had nearly killed him.

However, he'd be lying if he said his mind was entirely devoted to the task. Between his father's illness, River's training that he was woefully neglecting, and everything with Brynleigh, Ryker's mind was split and running in a thousand different directions.

The sooner they got a lead on the rebels, the better.

At least Brynleigh made it to his apartment. The tracking device in the bracelet had notified Ryker of her movements half an hour ago, and a short while after that, she'd messaged him. Relief had been a cool river coursing through his veins when he'd read the message. Thank all the gods, she was safe. That was one less thing to worry about.

"Have the injured been taken care of?"

"Yes, sir. They've been transported to the nearest hospital for treatment, and extra medical teams have been shadowed in," Felicity said.

Ryker ran the back of his hand over his sweaty brow. The desert heat wasn't his favorite, and his lack of sleep was catching up with him.

"Keep me updated." Hopefully, there wouldn't be any other casualties.

By the time he had arrived, the death toll had risen to twenty-five. Three Representatives, fifteen humans who worked at the school, five elves, and three shifters had all died at the hands of the Black Night.

The only consolation was that none of the youth had lost their lives. A few were injured, but the production had been running behind, so most of them hadn't been in the building when it blew up.

So many deaths, and to what end?

The rebels hadn't made any demands, and no one could figure out the game they were playing.

"Do you need anything else?" Ryker asked, hoping the answer would be no.

Between the dirt, ash, sweat, and the fact that he'd been awake for over twenty-four hours, he only wanted to shower and sleep.

Unfortunately, with a single nod, Felicity dashed his hopes. "Representative Challard asked to speak with you, sir. She's outside."

Ryker's stomach twisted in a knot. He wasn't sure what the Representative wanted, but considering he had her to thank for Brynleigh's limited freedom, he couldn't ask her to reschedule.

Knowing it was never wise to keep a powerful witch waiting, Ryker thanked Felicity and went in search of Myrrah Challard.

RYKER FOUND the witch Representative fifteen minutes later. It wasn't that difficult. Not only had the blast destroyed the concert hall, but it had wrecked much of the massive park outside as well. Charred trees were bent in half, benches were in shambles, and the once-green grass was black.

The night was fading, darkness giving way to dawn. Pastels streaked along the sky, the perfect backdrop to the sky-blue ribbons swirling in the air several hundred feet away.

A witch was here. The magical ribbons were as good as a calling card. All magic that didn't come from elemental fae was colored.

Green for Earth Elves, purple for Light Elves, red for Death Elves, silver for Fortune Elves, and blue for witches. Ryker had heard stories of golden, godly magic before, but it hadn't been seen since the time of the High Ladies of Life and Death.

Ryker strode past several groups of soldiers and Representatives, following the magic until he saw Myrrah.

The witch was crouched over something Ryker couldn't see, magic slipping from her palms. She looked like she'd just stepped off the pages of a history book from the Four Kingdoms. A long black robe flowed around her. Midnight hair swirled in an unseen wind, tendrils flying every which way. Bare feet stood on the ashy ground, toes digging into the soil. The wind carried her voice to Ryker's ears, the incantations murmured in a language he did not recognize.

His magic thrummed in his veins, power calling to power.

Keeping his distance because only a fool would dare interrupt a witch while they were working, Ryker slipped his hands into his pockets and leaned against a tree. He would wait for Representative Challard to notice him.

Soldiers milled around, gathering evidence, taking photos, and roping off the scene. They glanced in his direction, but no one approached him.

Several minutes passed before the blue ribbons disappeared into the early morning sky. Myrrah straightened, dusted off her hands, and turned.

Physically, the Representative looked around thirty years old, but she'd seen two centuries come and go. Myrrah's face was smooth, save for a few wrinkles at the corners of her dark brown eyes. Her mouth curved up, and those eyes flickered with recognition.

"Hello, Captain." She dipped her head in greeting. "You're right on time."

Ryker's brows furrowed. "On time for what?"

Myrrah extended an arm, her sleeve flowing like an inky river. "Tell me, youngling, what do you see here?"

It grated on Ryker's nerves when people answered questions with questions, but what was he supposed to do? A lifetime of dealing with his mother and her colleagues had taught him that one should not ignore Representatives and their questions.

Ryker stepped forward and eyed the item at Myrrah's feet.

His lips slanted down. "It's a rock."

More specifically, it was a charred stone the size of a large melon. Flat on one side, it was edged in black as if it had been plucked out of a fire.

"Not just a rock," she said cryptically. "Look more closely."

Ryker did as she asked, leaning over and studying the stone. Several lines were gouged into the surface, but he didn't recognize them.

He reached out, intent on touching the stone, when the witch hissed, "Careful, Captain."

His hand froze mid-air, and he glanced up. "What's wrong?"

"Don't touch it. Death has been woven into the fabric of this magic," she said ominously. "You may look, but you must keep your hands to yourself."

That warning would've been helpful before she asked him to take a closer look.

Gritting his teeth, Ryker drew back his hand and pulled a thread of water from his palm. The translucent ribbon swirled in the air, seeming out of place amid all the destruction. He twisted his fingers, directing the magic to curl around the stone.

The moment the liquid touched the rock, the shale glowed. The swirling lines rearranged themselves over the flat surface, forming an emblem he knew from his research. A dagger speared a crescent moon—the Black Night's symbol.

"This is how you knew who did it," he murmured.

"Mhmm," the witch said.

Ryker pulled back his magic, and the lines returned to their prior state.

"Fascinating." He stared at the rock. "The dark magic laced into the shale... what do you think it means, Representative?"

He had his suspicions, but he wanted to hear her thoughts.

Myrrah's robes rustled as she kneeled beside him.

"Nothing good. Black magic is dangerous no matter which form it takes. It always requires a sacrifice. Sometimes, it's blood. Other times, it takes part of a soul." She turned to him, her eyes piercing. "It's unnatural."

Ryker grimaced.

Gods damn it all. Of course, black magic was at play. Why not? With his luck, this meant he'd be away from home for even longer. In the past, he never cared when work pulled him out of Golden City for extended periods, but it wasn't just about him anymore.

Brynleigh was waiting for him.

That thought had Ryker turning to the witch and lowering his voice.

"Thank you for your help with my wi... vampire." He raked a hand through his hair. "I couldn't leave her there."

The Representative shifted, her gaze sweeping over him for a long moment. He didn't flinch beneath her scrutiny, letting her look her fill.

Eventually, Myrrah sighed. "I had a wife once."

Threads of ancient pain were woven through the Representative's words, forming a tapestry of grief Ryker was far too familiar with.

"I'm sorry, I didn't know." He prided himself on knowing each of the Representatives and their family members by name, but there were far too many for him to know their individual histories.

"It was a long time ago." Myrrah stared straight ahead, twisting a blue ribbon through her fingers. "Ven died a few months before the Black Night attacked my coven. We were so young, Ven and me, and we thought that together, we could conquer the world."

A small smile danced on Ryker's face. He was familiar with that feeling, too. When he first met and fell for Brynleigh in the Choosing, it felt like the entire world was at their fingertips. He thought they could do anything, be anything.

"You loved her," he murmured knowingly.

"With all my heart," Representative Challard agreed.

Myrrah wasn't known for being forthcoming with her words, often spending days considering even the smallest request before answering it. When she spoke, people listened. For that reason, Ryker fell silent once more, not wanting to pry into obviously painful memories.

"We fought the day she died," the witch whispered, her voice far off. "We were always fighting and making up, but this was one of our worst arguments ever. We both screamed and threw things at each other. We said things we didn't mean. And then, Ven..." Myrrah shuddered. "She was stolen from me before we could mend what was broken between us. She died that very night."

Ryker's chest ached. "I'm so sorry."

The words felt painfully inadequate.

"Me, too." Myrrah stared at the destruction, her jaw working as several more minutes passed in silence. When she spoke again, her voice was softer than before. "Ven would've wanted you to have the chance to fix things with your wife. She was such an optimist and always saw the best in people. That's why I agreed to your deal. Of course, more information about the Black Night will be helpful, especially considering all this, but..."

Ryker's heart twisted as he put himself in Myrrah's shoes. Living with that devastating kind of hurt for so long would break most people. He dipped his head as a newfound respect for the witch Representative filled him.

"Thank you. We're... it's hard, but we're working on things."

That was why he had asked Brynleigh to return to the apartment.

He was done running. He was under no pretenses that rebuilding what they had would be easy, but he wanted to give them a fair shot.

"If the love you share is true, never give up." Myrrah stood, and Ryker followed suit. The witch's eyes crinkled, lines creased her forehead, and suddenly, she looked much older. "Whatever you do, Captain, don't let her go. You never know when your last day might be upon you. Cherish every single one you've been given."

Were those prophetic words or ones stemming from a broken heart? Ryker wasn't sure. Either way, he stored the advice deep in his soul.

"I will."

Their conversation drifted back to the charred stone.

Myrrah would bring it back to her coven, where they would attempt to disentangle the threads of black magic woven through it. She left soon after that, and Ryker was called into a meeting. He listened with half an ear, Myrrah's words echoing through his mind.

Whatever you do, don't let her go.

He wouldn't let Brynleigh go. Not ever again. He would continue to fight for them because deep down, buried beneath the pain, hurt, and sorrow, he still loved her.

Even if it killed him, he'd love her until the day he Faded.

Buzz, buzz, buzzzzzzz

Ryker's phone vibrated on the nightstand, waking him from a nightmare. Around noon, he'd stumbled into the hotel room the army had procured for him. After taking the fastest shower of his life, he'd collapsed on the bed and fallen into a deep, dreamless sleep almost instantly.

He glanced at the clock, grimacing. It was just after five. He hadn't gotten much rest, but it would have to be enough.

Groaning, he reached over and pulled his phone off the charger. He held his finger over the sensor, unlocking the phone and swiping past work emails. He would deal with those later.

A missed text from his sister a few hours ago caught his eye.

RIVER

Dad's improving, thank Dyna. He's awake, and this morning, he raised his right hand. They're going to try him on solids tomorrow. The meds seem to be working.

Ryker exhaled and typed a brief message, reminding his sister to train and thanking her for the update. He didn't expect an immediate response. River was probably at Dyna's temple, praying to the fae goddess and making an offering.

He scrolled up to the message that had just come in and clicked on it.

BRYNLEIGH

Hi.

One word had never sounded so good.

A smile pulled at the corner of Ryker's lips as he sat up, the sheet falling to his waist. Myrrah's words echoed in his mind as his thumbs flew over the keyboard.

RYKER

Hi, back.

Two checkmarks confirmed the message was read, followed almost instantly by three dots. He leaned against the headboard, waiting for the phone to vibrate.

How are things?

That's a stupid question. Of course, they're bad.

I think I'm nervous.

Ryker huffed a quiet laugh, bringing the phone with him to brush his teeth and prepare for the evening. They'd be working around the clock until they uncovered a lead.

I'm nervous, too.

And things are... not great. I'll probably be here for a few more days.

Setting the phone on the counter, he ruffled through his duffel bag for some clothes. He'd just pulled on his pants when his phone vibrated again.

Okay. Yesterday, I... retrieved a book that belongs to Jelisette. I think it might be of interest to you.

Ryker frowned.

Retrieved?

Black dots appeared and disappeared as time ticked by. His stomach twisted into knots.

Stole.

Does that bother you?

It probably should bother him, but a few days ago, he'd watched her kill someone. A minor theft didn't seem like that big of a deal in comparison. Besides, it was for a good cause.

Honestly, not really. Did she see you?

That was the far more pressing question. He held his breath and waited for her reply. Every second dragged on until those black dots danced across the screen.

I wouldn't be alive if that were the case.

True.

An alert popped up on his phone, reminding him of a meeting in half an hour. He confirmed his attendance and finished getting dressed before letting Brynleigh know he had to go.

I'll update you if I find anything interesting in the book.

thumbs up emoji

The moment he pressed send, he berated himself. What kind of Mature fae sent emojis? She probably thought he was an idiot, which was not exactly the impression he was aiming for.

"Way to fucking go, Waterborn," he muttered, unwrapping a muffin from the hotel mini-fridge and devouring it in three bites. It was dry, and he grabbed a water bottle to wash it down.

His phone vibrated again.

Bat emoji *Sun emoji*

The corner of Ryker's lips curved up, and he chuckled.

What's that supposed to mean?

He was used to the normal face emojis, but these were more advanced. Maybe River could help him. She was more up-to-date on these types of things.

You don't know?

He shook his head before he realized she couldn't see him. His fingers flew over the screen.

Let me guess, it means you have a… sunny disposition?

There was a pause, and if he listened hard enough, it was like he could hear her laugh as those three dots appeared.

Only when I'm with you.

His smile transformed into a grin, and he slipped on his shoes.

I like that.

Is there enough blood in the apartment for you?

Let me check the fridge.

She must have sped over there because the following message came through almost instantly.

I have enough for a few days.

That wouldn't do. He didn't want her to run out.

Ryker navigated through his contacts. Tapping on Atlas's name, he quickly asked the fae to pick up their bags from Waterborn House and more blood before dropping them off at the apartment.

Atlas agreed, adding that he would also bring extra food to the kennel for Marlowe on his way to the university. The earth fae was a professor, his studious nature having helped Ryker pass several classes in university.

Gods, Ryker was lucky to have two best friends who would do anything for him.

Letting Atlas know he owed him one, Ryker switched back to his chat with Brynleigh.

Atlas will bring more tonight after class. I don't want you to go without.

Three dots appeared, disappeared, and then appeared again.

Thank you, Ryker. That's very kind of you.

Ryker glanced at the clock, realizing he would be late if he didn't get going. He slipped out of the hotel room and took the stairs two at a time. Gripping the railing with one hand, he balanced his phone in the other.

Have fun reading.

Have fun... captaining. Is that a word? If not, I'm making it one.

He snorted and pushed open the door with his hip. As he was slipping his phone into his pocket, it vibrated again.

This was nice. *Heart emoji*

Despite the morose reasons for his presence in the desert city, Ryker felt more relaxed than he had in weeks. Maybe talking through texts was easier because it reminded him of how their relationship had started, or maybe it was just because they were both trying to fix things, but things between them almost felt... normal.

And it was good.

CHAPTER 17
Danger Comes in Many Forms

Like all urban areas, Golden City had good areas and bad ones. Happy homes filled with loving parents and laughing, smiling children co-existed alongside places where darkness reigned.

Dressed in fitted black leggings and a tight sweater with slits in the back for her wings, Brynleigh stood across from one such dark spot now. Shadows wrapped around her like a cloak, and she studied the location where Jelisette had sent her.

From the outside, 16 Upper Red Road looked like every other warehouse in the northern district of Golden City. The building was a nondescript, enormous rectangle nestled among other factories and warehouses. White metal walls and a steel roof added to its industrial appearance.

It was quiet...

Too quiet.

Darkness surrounded this place. It was in the shadows swarming at the base of the building, in the cold midnight air, and in the starless night. Clouds hid the moon from view as if protecting it from whatever occurred within this building.

Danger, danger, danger, Brynleigh's shadows shouted. *Turn back now.*

She did not heed their warning. She couldn't. This was bigger than her.

Besides, danger came in many forms. Perhaps whatever was happening here wouldn't be so bad. Maybe instead of physical danger, it was more of the "we're scamming people out of money" danger. Still bad, but not nearly as terrible.

A vampire could hope.

Either way, it didn't matter. Brynleigh was here, and she would follow through with this meeting.

She'd spent the day texting on and off with Ryker. Their conversations had been less stilted with every message, and she'd had a smile on her face for hours.

Earlier, Brynleigh had told Ryker she had another job to do for her Maker. She'd considered not telling him she was going out, but then she remembered the tracking bracelet. Zanri probably could've helped with that, but obviously, that wasn't an option. Besides, she was in this mess because of the shifter.

To say that Ryker had been displeased would have been an understatement, but Brynleigh had stood her ground. This was important.

She pulled out her phone, rereading her last text.

BRYNLEIGH

Cooperating with Jelisette is how we get information about the Black Night. That's why I'm going.

Ryker's reply had been so *him* that she'd heard him say the words as if he'd growled them in her ear.

RYKER

If you get yourself killed, I'll never forgive you.

The words would have sounded harsh coming from anyone else, but Brynleigh knew better. She heard the care in his words and felt his worry wash over her.

Even now, after everything, he wanted her to be safe. That's precisely why she was in this dangerous place.

For him.

For them.

Brynleigh would risk her personal well-being a thousand times over if it meant they could repair their brokenness and return to the way things were before.

Giving herself exactly one minute to be sentimental about Ryker's messages—she'd enjoyed texting him far more than she ever thought she would, considering her recent hatred of cellular technology—Brynleigh put the phone away and drew in a series of deep breaths.

The time for happiness was gone. Now, she had to concentrate on the warehouse.

She'd been surveilling the area for the past two hours.

Every few minutes, a vehicle approached the warehouse and pulled around back. Someone got out, their faces covered by hoods or hats, and the car sped away. People entered the warehouse, but so far, no one left.

When midnight was a few minutes away, Brynleigh pushed off the alley wall. She slinked around to the back of the warehouse and quickly located the entrance. The door was nothing special, other than the image of a crescent moon stabbed with a dagger painted in silver, and the hulking shifter stationed in front of it.

He was enormous. Blond, almost white, cropped hair revealed his curved ears. A black suit hugged his body. Sunglasses were perched on his nose despite the late hour. He clutched a tablet in his right hand, the technology laughably small in his grip.

Brynleigh wondered about the man's animal counterpart. Was he a dragon? Perhaps a bear or a lion. Either way, he looked like he could devour someone whole, even in this form.

Sarai would've commented that the shifter looked like a bodyguard from the action movies she loved to watch... if she was alive to make comments.

Grief stabbed Brynleigh in the gut, the emotion wholly unwelcome at a time like this. She couldn't afford to think about her family right now.

Brynleigh was on a new mission: get information about the Black Night, fix things with Ryker, and get her damned happily ever after. She would do whatever it took to make that happen.

Forcing her grief aside, Brynleigh returned her assessing gaze to her surroundings.

A bulb flickered overhead, casting waning light over the shifter. A blinking security camera sat above the door. Cigarette butts littered the broken, cracked pavement. Disgusting.

She kicked at one with her booted toe. Why did people insist on sullying the land where they lived by throwing their trash on the ground? If Brynleigh were an Earth Elf, she'd be horrified by how some people treated this world.

But she wasn't an elf. She was a vampire, and she was here with a purpose.

A glance at her phone confirmed it was time. Drawing in a fortifying breath of crisp midnight air, she let her shadows fall away.

The shifter's attention snapped to her. He straightened, his muscles tensed, and he watched her like a hawk as she approached.

"Name?" the burly guard asked in a baritone voice.

"Brynleigh de la Point." She could have offered an alias, but something told her this entire evening was a test from Jelisette. She didn't want to risk messing it up.

The shifter grunted and tapped on his tablet. After a minute, he looked up.

"Welcome to Horizon, Miss de la Point. Your Maker has set everything up for you."

Brynleigh furrowed her brows. Set what up? She was supposed to meet with someone named Dimitri. Still, this didn't seem like the time for questions. A car was pulling up behind her, and she needed to get inside.

No matter what waited for her on the other side, she would handle it.

After all, nothing could be worse than The Pit.

STEPPING across Horizon's threshold was like walking into another world. Brynleigh had expected to walk into a meeting of rebels, not... this.

Whatever this was.

As she entered the warehouse, magic pressed against her skin. It was like walking into a bubble. Pressure built in her ears for a moment, and then it popped.

A ward.

As soon as she was within the magic's protective sphere, hundreds of sounds collided with her at once.

Even when she'd been human, Brynleigh would've found this place overwhelming. As a vampire, she could barely suppress the shiver that ran through her.

Noise assaulted her from all sides.

Loud conversations battled with booming music. A steady beat shook the floor. Feet stomped. People cheered and roared.

She stood still for several seconds, letting the sounds wash over her until she got used to them.

Only then did her other senses kick in. The scents of alcohol, sweat, and bodies tightly packed together wove through the space. Beneath them all was the cloying, coppery aroma of blood. Her fangs ached, and she curled her fists at her sides. She'd had several servings of blood earlier in the evening to ensure she'd be prepared for anything.

And the people.

The warehouse was packed to the brim. Horned and winged elves, shifters, werewolves, witches, fae, vampires, and humans milled about. A long black bar stretched along one wall. Dozens of bottles were shelved behind the three bartenders filling countless drink orders.

The lighting was dim, save for two blinding spotlights shining on an elevated platform in the middle of the warehouse. Though the stage was empty, people kept glancing at it.

Brynleigh grabbed the arm of a horned elf walking by. The woman was stunningly beautiful, with umber skin and long, silky black hair that reached her waist.

"Excuse me, would you know where I can find Dimitri?" asked Brynleigh.

The woman looked at her like she was asking whether the moon hung in the sky.

"Of course." Her tone made it clear that Brynleigh was an idiot for asking such a ridiculous question. "He'll be out later."

Before Brynleigh could ask a follow-up question—like what this place was or who this mysterious Dimitri was—the elf disappeared into the crowd.

Brynleigh asked about Dimitri three more times. Each time, she got the same looks and story. He would be out later.

Vague as hell.

Annoyed and wondering why Jelisette had sent her here, Brynleigh made her way to the bar. Thankful she'd brought money, she ordered and paid for a glass of blood wine. Once the beverage was in hand, she turned and leaned against the countertop.

A frown pulled at her lips. She'd told Jelisette she wanted to take down the Representatives, and her Maker had sent her here. This was one of the strangest things Jelisette had ever done.

What was Brynleigh doing here?

Sipping her blood wine, she meandered through the crowds. Luckily, she'd adapted to the noise, and though it was still loud, she could filter out the conversations from everything else. Some were everyday discussions she'd expect to hear anywhere: relationship woes, life troubles, job problems, and other pedantic issues.

Other conversations were far more interesting, though.

A pair of Death Elves a few tables over were sipping neon pink drinks that sported plastic umbrellas hanging over the edges. They leaned against a high table, their sparkly outfits barely more than strips of fabric covering their important bits.

The shorter of the two had strawberry blonde hair, pale pink butterfly wings, and red Maturation marks circling her neck like a collar. She leaned forward and sipped her drink before loudly whispering, "Did you hear what Chancellor Rose did last week?"

Her companion, another Death Elf with curling black horns, shook her head. "That bitch? What did she do now?"

Brynleigh's eyes widened as she glanced between the two women. She'd never heard anyone disparage the Chancellor so openly before.

"Well, I heard she was the one who backed the newest laws in the Eastern Region."

"The Registration Decree for those born Without?"

Brynleigh swallowed. She knew that many in the Republic looked down on those born Without almost as much as they did vampires, but she hadn't realized a law forcing them to register had passed in the Republic. Registration was a slippery slope leading nowhere good.

"Mhmm." Butterfly Wings sipped her drink. "The one and only."

"Fuck that. It's just another way to discriminate..."

Brynleigh moved away from the women, not wanting to be caught eavesdropping on their conversation. Her interest was piqued, though. She made a mental note to ask Ryker about the Registration Decree.

It wasn't long before she heard a similar conversation. Then, a third. Soon, Brynleigh started to understand why Jelisette had sent her here.

The conversations varied, but hatred of the Representatives was a common thread through them all. This was a place where being associated with the upper class could get someone killed.

And Brynleigh was married to a future Representative.

Talk about potential problems.

Then she noticed something else. People were complaining about the Chancellor, but no one said a word about Jade Academy.

How could no one be bringing it up? Didn't they care that people had died a few days ago?

Part of Brynleigh wanted to scream at them and ask why they weren't talking about it—after all, it had been all over the news—but the other, wiser part of her knew drawing that kind of attention to herself was dangerous.

Then, it was too late.

The air in the warehouse shifted. Hushed whispers ran over the crowd like a wave, starting in the far-right corner and rippling through the space.

"Dimitri's coming."

"He's here."

"He's early. I thought..."

"Hush."

The last word was a murmured command, repeated until silence blanketed the warehouse.

Brynleigh stood on her tiptoes, trying to glimpse the mysterious Dimitri. After all, he was the reason she was here.

The crowds parted, and then she saw him. Her breath caught in her throat.

Dimitri was incredibly beautiful in a violent way. Black hair streaked with red flowed to his waist. He was nearly a head taller than most of the crowd. A strong jaw and crooked nose lent him a fierce appearance. Like Brynleigh, he wore all black, although his outfit was somehow refined and casual at the same time. His orange eyes glowed.

A werewolf.

Not just any wolf, judging by the power radiating from him. If Brynleigh were in a betting mood, she'd say he was an Alpha. She hadn't met many other werewolves, save for Trinity, who had also participated in the Choosing.

Dimitri reached the empty stage. Instead of using the stairs, he leaped onto the platform with the grace of a predatory animal. He turned in a slow circle, a smile creeping over his lip.

Anticipation thickened the air.

"We have a good crowd this evening," Dimitri declared, his voice booming through the warehouse. "Welcome to Horizon."

The assembled group cheered.

"Who's ready for a fight?"

This time, the crowd's roar was deafening. Feet stomped. People yelled. Fists pumped.

A wicked smile graced the werewolf's lips. "Wonderful. Then, without further ado, may I introduce our first contestant?"

Another wave of cheers went through the warehouse. Each was more frenzied than the last, and Brynleigh's shadows swirled in her veins.

Then Dimitri caught her eye. He raised a brow, a devilish smirk dancing on his lips.

A sickening, horrible feeling unfurled in Brynleigh's stomach.

"It is my pleasure to welcome a newcomer to Horizon's stage." Dimitri paused, clearly a showman, and Brynleigh felt like she was going to throw up.

Fuck, fuck, fuck.

How had she not seen this coming?

Two realizations slammed into her at once.

First, Jelisette had sent her to a fight club. In hindsight, that seemed obvious, and she probably should've realized that the moment she walked through the doors.

Second, and probably more important, considering her current circumstances, she was absolutely fucked. Dimitri had just pointed to her and called her name.

CHAPTER 18
The Crimson Shade

Why did these types of things always happen to Brynleigh? Why couldn't she live a regular life where she wasn't constantly being thrown into dangerous situations?

Granted, she had put herself in this situation, but still. This didn't really seem fair. And Brynleigh knew all about unfairness. After all, that had landed her here in the first place.

Just because she was a vampire didn't mean she enjoyed fighting others. Especially not in an arena for other people's enjoyment.

She briefly considered slipping into the Void, but when she tried to pull on her shadows and step into the darkness, she realized she couldn't. The gods-damned wards surrounding the warehouse must have ensured that no one could shadow in and out.

Damn it all.

"Well, Miss de la Point?" Dimitri stood on the edge of the stage and stared at Brynleigh, his orange eyes twinkling with what she was sure was amusement. "Your Maker said you were eager to show off your talents."

Wishing she had a stake to shove into Jelisette's cold, black heart, Brynleigh clenched her fists. Unfortunately for her, there was only one clear path forward. Dread mixed with anger as she moved through the crowd towards the stage.

Even though she didn't want to participate in this, her inner vampire yearned for her to spill blood. Her fangs burned, and though bloodlust seemed worlds away, her shadows throbbed in her veins. A reminder of the darkness in her soul.

She would have to be careful not to give in to the bloodthirsty monster living within her.

Brynleigh still wasn't sure what the witch had done to her to stave it off in The Pit, but she knew that falling into her Fledgling need for blood in a packed place like this would only result in copious amounts of bloodshed and probable death.

Jelisette had undoubtedly already thought about that. Maybe that was the reason for this test. It was just like the older vampire to throw her progeny headfirst into a situation where she could only sink or swim.

As Brynleigh approached the platform, whispers rippled through the crowd.

"Is that…"

"Is she one of us?"

"Wasn't she in the Choosing?"

Brynleigh felt the weight of hundreds of eyes on her back. She hated being the center of attention, hated being in this place, hated being used as a pawn.

With every step she took, Brynleigh cursed her Maker.

The whispers continued as she drew closer to the stage.

"I know her."

"What the fuck is she doing here?"

"Her husband is a snack."

That last comment caused a snarl to rise in Brynleigh's throat. She wanted to dive into the crowd and punch the person who dared comment on Ryker's physique. True, he was handsome, but he was hers. Not theirs.

Unfortunately, she was already at the stairs leading up to the wooden platform.

Dimitri smiled down at her, but there was no warmth in his expression. This was a cold, violent man.

As a bringer of death, Brynleigh recognized darkness when she saw it. And darkness clung to the Alpha.

This is for me and Ryker.

If passing this test would bring Brynleigh one step closer to fixing things with her water fae, then she would do it. She would do anything for her husband.

"Welcome, Miss de la Point."

Dimitri extended a hand to Brynleigh to help her onto the stage, but she didn't take it. The last thing she needed was for someone to perceive her as weak. She climbed on the platform, wincing at the full force of the blinding lights.

From here, the crowd was barely more than a black blob. If the excitement in the air was any indication, they were bloodthirsty.

The Alpha turned to Brynleigh. "Would you like to know who your opponent is?"

Sensing that it didn't matter whether she said no or not, Brynleigh shrugged. "Sure, why not?"

After all, how bad could it be? She was a powerful, doubly blessed vampire. She could take someone on in a fight and win. Besides, the sooner she completed this test, the better. She was already over this.

The Alpha smirked and turned to the crowd. Someone turned off the music.

"What do you think?" Dimitri yelled. "Should she battle The Champion?"

Brynleigh's eyes widened, and she swallowed. She was all for bravado, but this didn't sound good. If she'd had time to prepare for this fight, it would be a different story. But she'd come here expecting a meeting, not... this.

A thousand curses ran to the tip of her tongue, and she wished she was anywhere but here.

The crowd screamed their approval.

Brynleigh's heart raced in her chest, and dread swirled in her gut.

"Wonderful." The werewolf grinned, and the sight would have

frightened most children. "Join me in welcoming our Champion, The Crimson Shade."

If the crowd's cheers had been loud before, now they were deafening. Screams of delight, catcalls, and roars of approval echoed off the steel warehouse walls.

Brynleigh's gaze swiveled around the crowd, but even with her vampire-blessed sight, she couldn't make out any faces. All she could see was the crowd parting as *someone* approached the stage. The people stepped aside, letting the man move through unencumbered.

Whoever this Champion was, he was taking his time. That was fine.

Brynleigh used the opportunity to harden her heart and prepare herself as best she could. She would win this fight, pass the test, and get one step closer to getting the information Ryker needed.

Her resolve was firm enough that even when her opponent finally came into view, she didn't shake. Much.

A slight tremor ran through her because, *come on*.

This man was barely a man. He was a mountainous elf who made the bulky guard from the back entrance look like a child. He had to be at least seven feet tall. Naked from the waist up, his muscular, sun-kissed chest was mottled with scars. Swirling crimson markings ran from his waistband to his neck. Between his red tattoos and pointed elf ears, his Death Elf heritage was apparent.

Gods damn it all.

Brynleigh's chest tightened as unbidden memories of Preston, the Death Elf who'd participated in her torture, rushed back to her. She recalled the way he had pulled red threads of magic from his palms, molding them into various instruments of torture.

Death Elf magic was malleable, painful, and a tool for ending lives.

Famously, the Crimson King had used his Death Elf magic to terrorize Ithenmyr during the time of the Four Kingdoms. He'd destroyed the balance and thrown the entire continent into darkness. It was only because the High Ladies of Life and Death had restored the balance that the Republic existed today.

Breathe. Fucking breathe.

This wasn't Preston, Brynleigh wasn't in The Pit, and she would win this fight because she had no other choice.

The Crimson Shade clambered onto the stage and stood on Dimitri's other side.

Brynleigh's heart thundered as she stared at the mountainous man. Isvana help her, this would fucking hurt. Even if she won, there was no way she'd be able to leave without experiencing at least a bit of pain.

Brynleigh was about to grab Dimitri's sleeve and tell him she'd changed her mind when a familiar head of chestnut hair caught her eye.

Jelisette stood at the foot of the stairs, a cruel smile painted on her face. She caught Brynleigh's eye and raised a brow as if to say, *I'm watching you.*

The warning was clear.

There was no backing out.

Dropping her arm, Brynleigh swallowed. This definitely hadn't been her brightest idea, but it was too late now.

Dimitri strolled to the edge of the stage and extended his arms.

"The rules are simple." The Alpha's voice boomed. "No fangs. No wings. No blades. The first one to knock out their opponent wins."

Oh, gods, this was even worse than Brynleigh had initially thought.

Dimitri stepped onto the first stair and yelled, "Begin."

Bile rose in Brynleigh's throat, but she forced it down. She could panic later. Right now, she had a fight to win.

The Crimson Shade turned to her. He held her gaze, cracking his neck to the right and then to the left. His movements were slow, almost lazy, as his eyes crawled over her.

"Ready, Little One?"

First of all, that name was horrible. Brynleigh was not little, nor did she appreciate the elf's tone. Second, and perhaps more importantly, she was not ready.

But she was out of options.

Reminding herself of the reasons she was doing this, Brynleigh made a beckoning motion with her fingers. "Bring it on."

THE CRIMSON SHADE was built like a mountain, but he fought like he was made of water. His movements were fluid, almost graceful. It was like he was one with the magic swirling from his fingers.

A quarter of an hour had passed since the fight had begun, and both fighters sported several cuts along their bodies.

Brynleigh's breaths were labored, pressure was building in her head, and her heart was beating so fast she was worried it might explode.

For every strike she'd achieved, the Champion hit her back twice as hard.

Despite her resolve to win, Brynleigh's limbs were dragging. Even lacking Isvana's blessings, the Death Elf was almost as fast as her.

He ran across the stage, a war cry echoing through the warehouse as he raised his fist.

Brynleigh leaped out of the way, barely avoiding his punch. Drawing shadows from her palms, she sent them slamming into the back of his legs.

He barely trembled at the impact.

The crowd *roared* as Brynleigh hurried to put space between her and her opponent. Every noise the audience made was tinged with violence. They were rooting for the Champion to take Brynleigh down.

In their defense, she was the clear underdog.

The Death Elf hadn't even broken a sweat. Even now, as he danced on the other end of the stage, he looked like he was taking a walk in the park. A bloody walk, but still, a walk.

Not Brynleigh.

Standing upright took far more effort than it should have as she gathered shadows in her palms. She had begun this fight on the defensive, and she'd been there ever since.

She couldn't win like this.

Every part of her hurt, and even though she was still firmly in control, this needed to end.

Brynleigh looked down, glimpsing Jelisette at the base of the stage. A reminder of her purpose.

The Crimson Shade moved to the right. Brynleigh took a few steps to the left, maintaining the space between them.

He lunged; she ducked. He kicked; she rolled away.

The crowd's bloodthirsty chants continued in the background.

"Finish her!"

"Champion! Champion! Champion!"

"Knock that vampire out!"

Darkness glinted in the Death Elf's eyes, and Brynleigh swallowed. She knew that look. He was done playing and meant to finish her off.

The Champion's fists curled again, but instead of lunging towards her, he drew red ribbons into his palms.

"Crimson Shade! Crimson Shade!" the crowd chanted frantically.

Brynleigh reached within herself and frowned. Her shadows were still present, but she was weakening. She was still a fairly young vampire, and it hadn't been that long since she'd been being tortured daily.

No fangs, no wings.

The rules seemed unfairly biased against her, especially as the Champion twisted his fingers and formed a long, barbed whip out of his crimson magic.

He snapped the whip in the air, and before Brynleigh could move, the tail end slashed across her cheek.

Sharp pain bloomed in her face, and she hissed.

Behind the Champion, Jelisette's black eyes gleamed in the darkness. *Put an end to this,* she seemed to say.

Closing her eyes briefly, Brynleigh drew in a deep breath. She could do this. Even tired, she was still a gods-damned powerful vampire.

She would defeat this man if it was the last thing she did.

Imagining Ryker's voice encouraging her forward, Brynleigh drew on strength buried deep within her. She ignored the Champion's whip, moving as quickly as possible. Her arms pumped, and her legs pounded as she raced across the stage.

She charged the Death Elf head-on. His eyes widened as she drew near, and he coiled his whip to attack her again.

He wasn't fast enough.

This time, Brynleigh avoided that painful slash of magic and leaped in the air.

A cry slipped from her lips as she landed on the Champion's back, clinging to him like a monkey. Sweat ran down his back in rivulets, and it took everything Brynleigh had not to cry out at the disgusting feeling of his slick skin against her hands.

The Champion roared and swung around, trying to buck Brynleigh off. She held on tight. Directing her shadows to wrap around his middle, they secured her to the Death Elf's back like a harness.

The rules banned fangs and wings but said nothing about vampiric strength.

She would have one shot at this.

She wrapped her arms around his throat, said a little prayer to Isvana, and *squeezed*.

Brynleigh didn't want to kill him. She just needed him unconscious.

Winning was the only thing on her mind.

Everything was too loud. The roaring crowd, the bellowing Death Elf, the thrumming of her shadows, and the pounding of her heart.

The Champion contorted his arm and yelled. The whip slashed across her back, and a flash of red filled her vision.

It burned, and yet, she held on. She squeezed tighter and tighter, calling on all her strength.

Everything blurred.

Finally, after what felt like far too long, the Champion stumbled to his knees. The wooden platform trembled beneath the weight of his gigantic frame, and he thrashed wildly in a final attempt to dislodge her.

Brynleigh didn't let go. She needed this victory.

"Come on," she gritted through clenched teeth. "Just pass out already."

In response, the Death Elf roared.

She constricted his throat harder.

He kept struggling, but she refused to let go. She couldn't.

And then she felt it.

The Death Elf slumped forward. His head slammed into the wooden platform. The crowd's cheers tapered off into an uneasy silence.

Brynleigh drew in heavy, gasping breaths. Each thundering heartbeat rang in her ears, echoing the call of her shadows.

That had been too fucking close for comfort.

The Crimson Shade stopped moving, and Brynleigh's shadows confirmed the man was unconscious.

She didn't move until a hand pried her arm away from the elf's throat and raised it in the air.

"Ladies and gentlemen, your new Champion!" Dimitri proclaimed.

Three silent seconds passed before the crowd roared. Their cheers seemed even louder than before.

It was over.

Relief coursed through Brynleigh, and she exhaled. She looked up, and sure enough, Jelisette was staring at her. Something akin to pride shimmered in her Maker's eyes, and Brynleigh knew she'd passed the test.

Later that night, Jelisette took Brynleigh to a back room. She introduced Dimitri as someone who could help her find vengeance against the Representatives.

Thank Isvana, it had all been worth it.

CHAPTER 19

Ash, Smoke, and Thundering Wingbeats

A storm was brewing on the horizon.

Ryker tasted the impending rain in the air, and he felt it in the marrow of his bones. His magic strummed a steady beat within him, his elemental fae side feeling even closer than normal.

He always got like this when it rained.

Fae derived their strength from the land around them. Whether they were fire fae like the Chancellor and her daughter, air fae like Nikhail, earth fae like Atlas, or water fae like Ryker and River, their power came from the world. Their magic was a gift from the gods, and it grew stronger the more time they spent in the elements.

Once, when his kind lived on the other side of the Obsidian Coast, their power had been even more potent. Back then, before natural disasters destroyed their home, the fae had lived in royal courts.

Those were gone, but their magic remained.

Ryker stood outside the destroyed auditorium at Jade Academy, and his gaze was trained on the sky.

Not much had changed in the four days since he'd first arrived. The land was still scorched, the school was still destroyed, and they were still searching for clues. The academy had been cordoned off. Students had been sent home, temporarily replaced by soldiers, investigators, and

Representatives. Some milled about aimlessly, many chatted in small groups, while a few barked orders into phones.

Everyone was tense.

It was like those rebel bastards had planted the bomb and disappeared into thin air. If they were still in the Southern Region—and right now, that seemed unlikely—they weren't anywhere near Sandhaven.

Chancellor Rose had even sent the Core. A tight-knit group of soldiers who worked solely for Ignatia Rose, the Core consisted of two Death Elves, an Earth Elf, a fire fae, and a witch.

The soldiers worked in the shadows and were known for their cruelty, abrasive attitudes, and overall sense of unpleasantness. They didn't have ranks because they didn't believe in them. They were a group of equals whose entire mission in life was to do the Chancellor's bidding.

And they did.

The Core got shit done.

When they arrived on the scene yesterday, Ryker had thought the investigation might finally get somewhere. Alas, they still hadn't uncovered anything new.

Even Myrrah had run into roadblocks with her coven as they sought to learn more about the charred stone.

Dead ends surrounded them, and it was fucking exhausting.

Ryker was at the end of his rope. He was tired of the desert heat, tired of not getting enough sleep, and tired of not being with Brynleigh. The only highlight from the past four days was their almost constant communication. He'd never valued his phone as much as he did right now. Every moment when he wasn't in a meeting or working, he was texting his wife.

It was almost like old times.

Almost.

They still hadn't talked about what happened on their wedding night, but each conversation was easier than the last.

A flash of dark brown hair appeared in the corner of Ryker's eye, and he turned as Felicity approached him.

"Captain." She dipped her chin in greeting. "Are you waiting for the Carinoc Division?"

He crossed his arms and glanced skywards. Still nothing but the impending storm. "I am."

"Hopefully, they were able to find something." Felicity hugged her clipboard to her chest and frowned.

Or this might all be a failure.

Ryker heard the undercurrent in the First Lieutenant's words even though she didn't say them out loud.

No one wanted to fail, especially now that Chancellor Rose had gotten involved.

Failure on a regular day in the Republic of Balance meant embarrassment or, potentially, a mark against your record. That was bad enough. But failure when the Chancellor was closely monitoring the situation? This was the type of thing that could irrevocably ruin careers.

Ryker needed his job not to be affected by this. It was the one thing that had kept him stable in the years after the Incident, and now, it was the reason he was able to keep Brynleigh out of prison.

They needed to find something about the rebels—anything to show that these days in the desert had been worth it.

Grunting, Ryker trained his eyes on the sky. Grey clouds swirled in the distance, darkening the horizon and promising sweet relief from the punishing heat in a few hours.

Extending his fae senses, Ryker listened to the wind. He might not have been a vampire, but his hearing was far better than that of a human.

Beneath the whisper of the breeze, the rustling of leaves, and murmurs of conversations came a steady *thump, thump, thump.*

Ryker couldn't help but smile.

The sound grew louder with each passing moment. The wind was the symphony, and the thumping was a drum announcing the impending arrival of the creatures of fire, ash, and death.

"They're coming," he breathed.

The words rippled around him. Variations of the same phrase rose over the field. Conversations dropped off. Gazes lifted. Anticipation swirled in the air.

Thump, thump, thump.

Ryker's magic whirled, and his heart thundered as true alpha predators drew near.

All creatures in the Republic of Balance, even powerful fae, recognized the strength of the dragon. The land itself seemed to tremble in eager expectation.

And then he saw them.

Breaking through the dark clouds, their wings outstretched, and fire ripping from their maws were ten dragons. They fanned out in a V formation, their wings flapping in perfect synchrony. They were so high that they were little more than specks against the sky, but they drew everyone's attention.

Thump, thump, thump.

As one, they beat their wings.

As one, they slowly descended.

Nothing in this world was more powerful than them.

Soon, they were close enough to the ground that Ryker could make out the beasts' individual features.

At the tip of the formation, in the position of leadership, was a black dragon twice the size of the others. Onyx horns rose above his head, spikes ran along his back, and his tail was barbed.

Flurries of excitement rose. Even the sternest soldiers couldn't help but get caught up in it. The Carinoc Division was well-known, and their existence was legendary throughout the entire Republic. After all, dragon shifters were a rare breed.

Long ago, the Crimson King had attempted to wipe all dragons from the continent. He'd failed, but they were still few and far between. Even rarer were dragon shifters willing to enter the Republic's army.

Ryker remembered the first time he saw the fire-breathing creatures.

The summer Ryker turned nine, his mother had been overwhelmed with work, so Cyrus took him to their country home in the Western Region. They were fishing at the lake when that same *thump, thump, thump* filled the air.

Ryker had dropped his pole, the fishing implement promptly sinking to the bottom of the lake. He gazed skyward in wonderment as a trio of dragons flew overhead.

Three decades had passed, but the wonderment remained.

Pulling out his phone, Ryker snapped a picture. He sent it to Brynleigh, along with the caption, *Look who showed up.*

Not even a minute later, his phone vibrated several times in a row.

BRYNLEIGH

Oh, my gods!

dragon emoji

They look even bigger in real life.

A grin pulled at Ryker's lips.

Other than their leader, who was as black as the night, the dragons were a lesson in the colors of the rainbow. Their scales ranged from the palest of yellows to the deepest of blues. They flew as one, and as a unit, they let out a deafening roar that could undoubtedly be heard for miles.

The dragons certainly were dramatic.

RYKER

I felt the same way the first time I saw a dragon.

fire emoji If you see Therian...

She didn't finish the sentence, but Ryker knew what she was asking. Therian Firebreath had also participated in the Choosing. He was married to Hallie, a Fortune Elf and one of Brynleigh's closest friends. Even though Brynleigh hadn't said anything about it, she had to be missing Hallie.

I promise, I'll try to talk to him.

The dragons were even closer now, and Ryker could make out the sharp points of their talons.

Slipping his phone into his pocket, he took several large steps back. The others did the same, pressing themselves against trees and buildings in an effort to clear the center of the field.

The massive creatures landed one by one, causing tiny tremors like small earthquakes to rumble across the field.

When the tenth dragon, a smaller navy one, landed at the back, the black dragon leader smacked a foot on the ground. The dragons echoed the signal, thumping their tails three times. Then, iridescent white light erupted from all ten at once.

One moment, fire-breathing creatures of death stood before Ryker. The next, naked men and women had taken their place. Several soldiers ran forward, each bearing a bundle of clothes. Within minutes, the dragon shifters were dressed.

Someone called Ryker's name. He turned as Therian Firebreath strode towards him. The shifter's long legs ate the distance between them in seconds.

Despite everything else that had happened recently, Ryker smiled. He'd grown close to the dragon shifter over the course of the Choosing.

"Good to see you, Waterborn," the dragon shifter said.

"Likewise." Ryker gave Therian a one-armed hug. "Although I wish we were meeting under better circumstances."

Very few people in the Republic truly understood what participating in the Choosing was like. Something about being put under the societal microscope changed a person.

"Same." Therian shook out his blond hair as someone called his name in the distance. He lifted a hand, signaling he'd be right over, before turning back to Ryker. "I'm glad I caught you. Hallie's been so worried about Brynleigh. We were sorry to hear she got sick so soon after the wedding."

Ryker's mouth dried. "Yes, she was... indisposed." Not exactly a lie, but the words still tasted like dirt. "But she's feeling better now. I'm looking after her."

He would never stop looking after her.

The other night, when Brynleigh had gone on a job from Jelisette after Ryker had specifically asked her to stay in the apartment, he worried about her all night long. He hadn't slept until she texted him that she was safe and back at the apartment.

Although Ryker's body was in Sandhaven, his heart was back in Golden City.

"Excellent." Therian clapped Ryker on the back, and the fae winced. That would definitely bruise. No wonder the Carinoc Division was so well respected. "My wife will be delighted to hear that. We'll see you at the Reunion, right?"

Ryker's eyes widened, and he inwardly cursed. By the Sands, he'd completely forgotten about that.

Roughly two months after the last wedding took place, Choosing participants gathered for one last celebration. It was the final send-off into the world for the new couples and the closing ceremony of the Choosing. Like the rest of the marriage competition, it would be broadcast to the entire Republic. With everything else going on, it had slipped Ryker's mind.

Forgetfulness wasn't sufficient cause for missing the Reunion, though. He could already hear his mother's sharp voice in his mind.

Waterborns do not fail. Waterborns do not cause scenes. Waterborns attend all social events required of them, even if they do not care to attend because they are the public face of the Central Region fae.

Tertia was already angry with him. He wouldn't dare risk incurring more of his mother's wrath.

"When is it?" he asked Therian.

"Three weeks from tomorrow," the dragon shifter said.

Ryker mentally cataloged that information and nodded. "We'll be there."

They had three weeks to fix everything... or at least enough that going to the Reunion wouldn't break them. It was a tight deadline, but he wasn't intimidated.

He and Brynleigh would repair their relationship, even if it was the last thing they did.

CHAPTER 20

Irrational Fears and Night-Blooming Roses

BRYNLEIGH

Tell me, Captain, what's your most irrational fear?

Stretched out on his hotel bed, Ryker smiled at his phone. He held it above his head, his fingers flying over the screen as he typed out his reply. He was tired, but it was a good kind of exhaustion. It had taken them far too fucking long, but finally, with the dragons' help, they'd uncovered some actionable intelligence.

Ryker had spent most of the day tracking leads with his team. It was after midnight, but he couldn't sleep. He'd texted Brynleigh an hour ago, and she'd replied immediately.

RYKER

Who says I have an irrational fear?

Three dots instantly appeared.

Everyone is afraid of something.

True.

The problem was that Ryker knew fear on an intimate level. He was afraid of many things, and none of his fears were irrational. At least, not to him.

There were so many, sometimes he was worried he would drown in them.

He was afraid that even with daily training, River's power would grow too strong, and she'd lose control again. He was afraid he and Brynleigh wouldn't be able to fix what was broken between them. He was afraid his father would die and leave them alone, with Tertia as their only parent.

But more than all those combined, Ryker was afraid that even if he followed all the rules and regulations, he would fail his family.

Those fears weren't irrational or ridiculous. They were real, and they kept him awake at night. When he did finally sleep, they fueled his nightmares.

That was too much to put into a single text, though. Too raw.

Why don't you go first?

He wasn't sure she'd answer. Gnawing on his bottom lip, a habit he'd picked up from River, he stared at the dim screen. Several minutes passed before those three dots appeared.

snake emoji

I fucking hate snakes. Big ones, small ones, they're all horrible, slippery little devils.

Ryker snorted and rolled onto his side. He was wearing loose gray sweatpants, and his chest was bare. The southern heat made all clothes nearly unbearable. Stretching out his arm above his head, he typed with one hand.

I never would've pegged you for having a fear of serpents, sweetheart. Is that your biggest fear?

He pressed send before he even realized what he'd done. He'd just been so caught up in the moment, so relaxed, that the nickname had slipped from his fingers.

And now...

Now, it was gone. Two blue checkmarks showed the message as read, but she didn't respond.

Ryker's heart pounded, and he stared at the phone. Dread pooled in his stomach. What was she thinking? Had he just ruined everything?

Minutes ticked on, each longer than the last.

Three dots appeared.

They disappeared.

They appeared again.

Gone.

The cycle continued, and a ball of nerves came to life in Ryker's stomach. He'd never been glued to his phone before, not understanding the way River and her friends seemed to be texting day and night, but now...

Now he got it.

Ryker would stare at this phone for hours if it meant he'd see the message the moment Brynleigh replied.

Finally, a new text popped up.

> My biggest fear—the one that haunts me far more than snakes, storms, and spiders—is that you'll never forgive me. I'm afraid that we'll never get back to what we had. I'm so sorry, Ryker. I should have come clean before the wedding. Maybe if I had, we could've figured something out together. I don't want us to be broken, and I'm afraid it's too late. I'm afraid that nothing can fix us, and I hate that more than anything else.

By the time Ryker got to the end of the message, he couldn't breathe. He pressed the green call button, and she picked up on the first ring.

"Hello?" she said breathlessly.

Fuck.

Hearing her voice after days apart was like the coolest drink of water on a hot, dry day. It soothed a hurt in him that he hadn't even known existed.

"I'm fucking sorry, too, sweetheart." Now that Ryker had called her that, he couldn't stop. "You never should've been in the Pit. I should've paid more attention to what they were doing. I should've stopped it. I'm so sorry that happened to you."

His grief over her betrayal had blinded him, but he saw things clearly now.

"It's not your fault," she replied. "Not really. You were just reacting. I don't blame you for being upset."

Gods, he hadn't realized how much he needed to hear that until now.

Ryker exhaled. His eyes slipped shut as his head fell against the wall. "I miss you. So gods-damn much."

She drew in a deep breath, and the sound made his heart stir. There was something incredibly familiar about talking like this, and for the first time since their wedding night, a deep sense of peace filled his heart.

"I miss you too, Ry." That name. It sent shivers down his spine. For so long, he thought he'd never hear it again. "When do you think you're coming home?"

Hearing Brynleigh call his apartment home warmed his heart. "Tomorrow, hopefully. We finally got a lead."

"I'm glad. Maybe when you get back..." Her voice trailed off.

"Yes?" he prodded.

No matter what she was about to ask him, he'd agree.

There was another pause, and then she blurted, "Maybe when you get back, we could play chess?"

A smile stretched across his face. "I'd love that more than you know."

"Me too," she whispered. "Do you have a few minutes to chat?"

"I have all the time in the world for you." What was sleep when they were finally talking and building a bridge over the divide separating them?

And so, they talked. Brynleigh described the sunrise she'd watched earlier, and he told her more about the dragons. She was fascinated and asked a dozen questions, which only stopped when a yawn slipped from Ryker's mouth despite his best efforts to hold it in.

"Go to sleep, Ry," she murmured. "I'll see you tomorrow."

"Goodnight, Brynleigh," he replied, wishing he could stay awake forever and continue talking to her. "Sweet dreams."

Night-blooming roses perfumed the air, the floral scent nearly overwhelming in its intensity. There was something else beyond the flowers. Something deep and crisp and entirely... *right*.

Ryker's soul sang at the fragment, and his magic hummed a quiet, honeyed melody in his veins.

He sighed contentedly. He could stay here forever.

"Ryker?"

That voice. That sweet, sweet voice. Even if he went centuries without hearing it, he'd recognize it immediately.

He opened his eyes, unsurprised to find Brynleigh stretched out beside him. After all, this was his dream, and he couldn't stop thinking about her. Even after everything that had happened between them, she still haunted him, waking and sleeping.

"Hey, sweetheart," he murmured, reaching for her.

They were in his apartment, his navy sheets covering their nakedness as they lay together. Golden waves tumbled over her shoulder, and her red lips were parted, showing off her fangs.

By the Black Sands, his wife was beautiful.

He'd never met anyone as stunning as her. She was a brilliant moon shining in the night sky after a month of darkness. A flower blooming amid frigid snow. She was everything he'd ever wanted without even knowing he was missing something.

Ryker brushed his knuckles down Brynleigh's cheek, delighting in the responding shiver that ran through her. His cock hardened, straining for her. Unable to help himself, he leaned in, cupped her cheek, and kissed her.

The moment their mouths fused, everything in his world righted itself. His mind cleared like he'd been living in a fog, but now it was gone.

This was where he belonged. With her. Always.

"More, Ry," Brynleigh moaned against his lips.

Had so sweet a sound ever been spoken before this moment?

He thought not.

Brynleigh's lips parted, and he slipped his tongue into her mouth. She let him in willingly, and he tasted her.

He groaned.

It wasn't enough. It would never be enough.

She moaned, rolling on top of him as their tongues battled for dominance. He was as hard as steel, pure need burning through him.

The sheet slipped, unveiling her beautiful body. Her pale skin glowed in the moonlight as she straddled him, the heat from her core pressing against his length.

"I want you," she pleaded against his lips. Her fingers trailed down his chest, every touch sending fire blazing through him. "I never stopped wanting you."

Those words were fucking everything.

He reared up, claiming her lips in a searing kiss. At the same time, he gripped her hips and lifted her.

Brynleigh gasped into his mouth, a moan running through her as he lowered her onto his hardened shaft. He tried to take his time, but he needed her so badly. Restraint tightened his muscles, and he groaned as she took him to the hilt.

Fuck. This was everything he ever wanted.

When they came together, nothing else mattered. Nothing that had happened in the past could ruin them; nothing could break them. He wouldn't allow it.

Brynleigh's movements were languid, as though she was desperate to stretch the moment out for as long as possible.

He reached for her, pulling her mouth to his. He needed to taste her again. She was like ambrosia of the gods, and he was a mortal eager for the smallest sample.

Each caress was deeper than the last. Their lips and tongues danced to a tune as old as time itself as their bodies moved together.

Ryker groaned, his fingers digging into Brynleigh's hips as he thrust into her warmth. He didn't have to worry about being rough with her—she could take everything he gave her.

She moaned, throwing her head back and digging her nails into his chest as she rode him, chasing her pleasure. Shadows slipped from her palms, covering them in a black mist.

She was an angel of darkness, and he would happily follow her into a starless night.

Ryker slid his hand between them, finding her clit, and rubbing that sensitive bundle of nerves. She gasped, her movements gaining a frantic edge as she climbed towards her release.

There was nothing sweeter in the world than watching the woman he loved find pleasure with him.

"Come for me," Ryker ordered on a groan.

Brynleigh obeyed beautifully, breaking apart with a cry he was certain could be heard for miles. Her mouth parted, her fangs glimmering in the pearly moonlight. Her walls clenched around him, pulling his release from him with a strangled groan.

"I love you," he panted as soon as he could form words once again, peppering her with kisses. "I promise I'll never stop loving you."

CHAPTER 21
The Couple that Slays Together

Brynleigh was pacing.

Fucking *pacing* like a nervous wreck who couldn't sit still. It was an odd feeling that was wholly unbecoming of a graceful vampire. Her Maker would surely frown upon this action, yet she couldn't seem to stop. Even the beautiful vampire-safe glass that allowed her to watch the sun didn't calm her nerves.

Ryker was returning home. He'd texted an hour ago that he was picking Marlowe up from the kennel and coming to the apartment.

She'd been sitting by the windows; her attention split between the book she'd stolen from Jelisette and the noon sun glowing so brilliantly in the sky when her phone buzzed. His message broke her concentration, and she hadn't been able to read a single word since then.

After her victory at Horizon and the subsequent meeting with Dimitri, Brynleigh had returned to the apartment and nursed her injuries. Several pints of blood later, both her wounds and the fight were just memories. Painful, but in the past.

Yesterday, Jelisette messaged that she'd have another job soon. She also hinted at another rebel meeting.

Thank all the gods, it seemed like Brynleigh's theft had gone unnoticed.

Brynleigh's socked feet padded silently along the hardwood floors of Ryker's apartment. Their apartment? She wasn't sure.

The blanket she'd used for the past few days was folded at the base of the couch, with her pillow on top. She wasn't returning his shirt, though. She'd claimed it as hers.

He could fight her for it. She'd probably win.

Last night, she'd dreamed of Ryker. That, in and of itself, wasn't strange. She'd dreamed of him every night since he'd left for Sandhaven. But last night had felt more... real, somehow. As if he'd really been there.

Brynleigh had dreamed of them coming together, and when she'd woken, she could have sworn she tasted him on her lips. It must've been their conversation. Talking to him on the phone and hearing him call her sweetheart had been the highlight of her week, if not her entire fucking month.

They were mending things. Every text they exchanged and every word they spoke closed the distance between them a little bit more.

That was why Brynleigh was so nervous. She didn't want to ruin all the work they had done. Not now, when things were finally improving.

So, she paced and paced and paced.

Every so often, she looked out the window. She briefly admired the sun's golden glow before continuing her path across the wooden floors.

Then she heard it.

The soft *ding* of the elevator, a sound she'd come to recognize over the past few days, was followed a minute later by a key turning in the lock.

They were here.

Brynleigh's heart caught in her throat, and butterflies exploded in her stomach. She closed her eyes, inhaling deeply in an attempt to calm her nerves.

It didn't work.

She had always thought vampires were cold, emotionless creatures, but maybe that was something her kind learned after several centuries of life. She was as far from emotionless as possible.

A *thump* came from the other side of the door, and a canine growl quickly followed. The doorknob twisted.

Brynleigh's stomach contorted, and her palms grew sweaty. She wiped them on her leggings, shifting her weight from one foot to the other. Would telling Ryker she'd dreamed about him last night be too forward? Should she hug him or just shake his hand? Or should she keep her distance and let him dictate the physical parameters of their relationship?

She probably should've devoted some time to these questions earlier. It would've been better than pacing. It was too late now, though. She was out of time.

The door swung open. Brynleigh's eyes widened as a big black ball of fur bolted across the room, clambered onto the couch, and leaped off the back.

Unlike their initial meeting, this time, she was prepared for Marlowe. The dog, more of a bear than a canine, sailed through the air. She widened her stance and braced for impact moments before Marlowe smashed into her.

The pup was massive. He stood on his hind legs, his front paws pressing against her chest, and he ran his enormous, wet, pink tongue up her face. His tail thrummed a rapid beat, moving so fast she was worried it would break something every time it slammed into the side of the nearby table.

"Hey, Marlowe. It's nice to see you." Brynleigh grinned, patting the dog's head.

She loved all animals, but dogs had always held a soft spot in her heart.

Even with Brynleigh's vampiric strength, Marlow was pushing her back. Good thing he was so adorable. He could probably eat her favorite shoes, and she'd still forgive him.

Probably.

She'd rather not test the theory, though.

A baritone chuckle came from the door.

"Down, Marlie. Let her breathe."

Marlowe listened immediately, dropping to the ground. His tongue lolled out of his mouth as he looked eagerly between Brynleigh and Ryker.

"Come here." Ryker pointed to the floor at his feet.

The dog obeyed instantly, running across the living room and sitting for his master.

Fuck, that demanding tone made Brynleigh's core twist. She had half a mind to cross the room and sit beside Marlowe.

Who knew hearing someone take charge could be so attractive?

Then Ryker whispered Brynleigh's name. The deep rumble of his voice was like silk caressing her skin. Talking on the phone had nothing compared to being in person.

She lifted her eyes, heart thundering as she met the fae captain's gaze. How was it possible that he was even more handsome now than before?

The corners of his eyes crinkled. "Hi."

A smile dug at her lips.

"Hey." She stepped towards him, but the couch still stood between them. "How are you?"

His chocolate gaze held hers. "I'm... happy to be home. I'm happy to be with you."

Did she imagine the way his voice deepened in the last few words? She hoped not. Gods, she hoped he was at least as fucking nervous as her, if not more.

"I'm glad you're here, too. I kept the apartment clean and didn't leave a mess. I wasn't sure where you wanted me, so I slept on the couch. I hope you don't mind, but I grabbed a pillow and blanket." Brynleigh was blabbing, but like the pacing earlier, she didn't know how to make it stop. "Was that alright? I did some laundry because there was some blood on my clothes, but I wasn't sure if you wanted..."

Her voice trailed off as Ryker crossed the room like a swift current, moving with a speed she didn't know he possessed.

Power rippled off him in waves, and darkness flickered through his eyes as they burned into hers.

"Why was there blood?"

Damn. Maybe she shouldn't have mentioned that so soon after he arrived. It just slipped out.

Judging by the pinch of Ryker's lips and the feathering in his jaw, he wasn't pleased about it. Probably not the best way to kick off their reunion.

Brynleigh swallowed. "I... uh..."

His hands landed on her shoulders.

"Who hurt you?" he growled.

Well, if she was being technical about it, two people had hurt her.

First, Jelisette had almost decapitated her. *That* had been a wholly unpleasant experience. But the fight against The Crimson Shade hadn't been much better.

However, Brynleigh didn't think that's what he wanted to hear.

She put her hands on his, reveling in the warmth that seeped into her.

"It doesn't matter," she half-whispered, half-pleaded. "I healed."

A fierce, primal growl rumbled through Ryker.

Seconds later, Marlowe echoed the sound. It would have been cute if the moment hadn't been drenched in tension.

"It fucking does matter," Ryker bit out through clenched teeth. "Who hurt you? Don't make me ask again."

Her tongue darted out and wet her lips. She had to tell him something.

Deciding to save the information about her fight at Horizon for later, she admitted, "Jelisette."

Had she thought Ryker was upset before?

No.

That was nothing compared to what happened next.

The temperature in the apartment plummeted. Frost crawled up the windows. Ice covered his hands, which remained on her shoulders.

Outside, thunder rumbled. The sky darkened, hiding the sun from view.

Ryker snarled, "That fanged ancient bitch. What *exactly* did she do?"

If Brynleigh had been a wiser vampire, she might have considered bending the truth. But she wasn't wise, and she didn't want to keep this from him.

Taking a deep breath, she wove her fingers through Ryker's freezing ones.

Bringing their joined hands between them, Brynleigh swept her thumb over the back of his hand and marveled at the ice crawling over his fingers. She probably should've been concerned about the way he was freezing everything, but she wasn't. All she knew was he needed her.

She stepped closer until the warmth of his breath danced across her forehead.

"What did she do?" Ryker repeated with a growl.

Even now, he was beautiful in a way that made thinking difficult.

"She... choked me."

If it was cold before, now it was as if they'd been transported to the Northern Region and dropped in the middle of a blizzard. Goosebumps peppered Brynleigh's arms, and she shivered.

A snarl ripped through the apartment. "She fucking *what*?"

The acidic tang of magic filled the air, and a feral look flashed through Ryker's eyes. Maybe he was closer to losing control than she'd originally thought. Having already survived one life-and-death situation with an unrestrained water fae, Brynleigh wasn't keen on dealing with that again.

The sky darkened further. Black clouds rolled towards the apartment building, covering the sun.

Brynleigh's heart seized. They were indoors, but she didn't know if the windows were storm-proof. Nothing had survived River's storm.

No.

She couldn't think about that right now. She had to focus on the situation at hand. She hadn't been able to control anything that happened with River, but this was different. She and Ryker had something. She could calm him down... right?

She had to try.

"It's fine, Ryker." She spoke to him slowly, like he was an injured animal, and ran her thumb down his frigid hand.

"No, it isn't."

Brynleigh was willing to concede that he might be right. 'Fine' was probably a slight exaggeration, but she had survived Jelisette's wrath.

That's what Brynleigh did best. She prevailed. She had survived River's tempest, the bombing at the Masked Ball, and the Pit.

It was fucking ironic that Zanri was the feline shifter because Brynleigh seemed to have nine lives.

"Maybe not, but I healed." Trying to add some levity to this tenuous situation, she quipped, "At least I got a book out of the deal."

Apparently, Ryker didn't appreciate her attempt at humor.

"I'm going to kill her." His grip tightened around Brynleigh's fingers. "Her death will be painful for touching what's mine."

Brynleigh raised a brow at his claim. At any other time, she would've contested his words.

Wife or not, she wasn't a fucking possession. She was her own person, and no one owned her, not even Ryker Waterborn with his too-handsome face, dimples, and alpha fae energy. This wasn't the time of the Four Kingdoms anymore—women had rights. The High Ladies of Life and Death had ensured that was the case.

Still, the roiling clouds outside and the frost covering the windows were a reminder that this wasn't the moment to contest her so-called ownership. They had bigger problems at hand.

Thunder boomed outside as if proving her point.

"Yes, well, you'll have to fight me for that honor, Captain." Brynleigh forced a smile on her face despite the racing of her heart. "I'm rather furious with Jelisette myself."

She wouldn't be the first vampire to kill her Maker. Long ago, the Last Vampire King had rid himself of his Maker in a famous battle for power. If he could do it, so could she.

"Maybe we'll kill her together," Ryker said gravely.

Brynleigh's jaw dropped.

It was one thing for him to be present when she killed the Earth Elf—one could argue he'd simply been doing his job—but she was pretty certain society as a whole frowned upon cold-blooded killing.

She probably should've been worried that Ryker was willing to commit murder for her, but she wasn't. Instead, something deep within her warmed at the thought that her fae captain was willing to break one of society's most stringent rules to defend her.

Fuck, something was seriously wrong with her.

Brynleigh chuckled, "You know what they say, the couple that slays together stays together."

Alas, the fae captain didn't even crack a smile at her joke. All she got in return was a stern look of warning.

Her core twisted at the sight, which was highly inappropriate considering their topic of conversation.

Brynleigh would have a chat with her body about that later. It was choosing wildly inappropriate moments to remind her that she desired Ryker. She didn't even know if they'd ever be together again. Not like that.

"You promise you've healed?" he asked.

"Mhmm. I'm good as new."

Brynleigh made the executive decision that this wasn't the right moment to mention that shock had set in after she had shadowed back here, nor did she mention the blood she'd cleaned off the wall.

That was over, and she just wanted to move on from that night.

Flicking her hair over her shoulder, she displayed her neck to him. "See?"

He pulled his hand from her grasp and trailed his fingers over her neck. They were still cold but no longer freezing.

"This doesn't hurt?"

Her skin pebbled as his fingers grazed her flesh. "No."

Neither of them pulled away as he traced her throat. His mouth parted, and his stormy scent deepened as he drew closer. His fingers pressed deeper into her skin, but the sensation wasn't painful.

Not. At. All.

"What about this?" Ryker wrapped his hand around the back of her neck and tilted up her head. "Does this hurt?"

Her heart was a drum in her ears. Could he hear it? "No, it doesn't."

He moved closer until mere inches separated them and slowly lowered his head. His gaze searched hers, and the promise in it had her core twisting.

Outside, the storm clouds lifted, but she barely noticed.

"I meant what I said on the phone," he breathed, his lips hovering over hers. "I'm so sorry."

Ryker had always been handsome, almost to a fault, but when apologizing, he looked like a god brought to life.

"I'm sorry, too," she whispered. "Not just for lying to you in the Choosing, but for everything. I want to try to be better. For us. Do you... do you think you can forgive me?"

He gazed into her eyes as if he could uncover the world's secrets if he looked at her long enough.

"There's nothing to forgive." Ryker leaned in and kissed the corner of her mouth.

By the gods, that was both far too little and too much at the same time. She wanted more.

He added, "I understand why you felt you needed to do it."

Brynleigh blinked. Of all the things she expected him to say, that wasn't one of them.

"You mean, when I planned on..." The thought was so horrible that she couldn't even form the words.

"Killing me?" A morose laugh escaped him. "Yeah. Though I will admit, I'm glad you decided not to follow through. I rather enjoy being alive."

Forming words was proving to be troublesome, so she nodded.

"I am sorry your family is gone," Ryker murmured. "I know apologies can't bring back the dead, but still, I'm sorry."

Her heart cracked.

"Me, too." A tear coasted down her cheek. "They would've liked you."

Several minutes passed in silence before Ryker drew her closer to him. The storm clouds were long gone, and the sun shone through the windows again.

"I'm the one who should be begging for your forgiveness," he said gruffly. "I never should've let them take you to The Pit. I'm so sorry for what was done to you."

Brynleigh hadn't realized how badly she needed to hear him say those words until that moment. They sank deep into her soul, the broken pieces of her heart coming together and forming a new creation. Her chest warmed, and hope blossomed like a flower within her.

This was why she had gone to Horizon, why she fought the Crimson Shade, and why she was ready to do whatever it took to stop the rebels.

Ryker was looking at her like she was his entire universe, and she couldn't imagine a world where they weren't together.

Her next words flowed like water from her lips.

"Forgiven. I just want you. The past is over. We both made mistakes.

I want to look forward and rebuild what we had." Brynleigh squeezed his hands. "Just us. Me and you."

And Marlowe, who had moved to the couch and was now snoring like he owned the place.

At least one of them was relaxed.

Had time dragged on before? It was nothing compared to how she felt now, waiting for his response. They were on the precipice of something massive, and his next words could either propel them forward or forever destroy them.

Eventually, he exhaled. His lips melted in a smile. For the first time since their wedding, his dimples appeared.

She bit the inside of her cheek.

"Thank fuck." Ryker lowered his head, his breath warming her lips once again. "I want to kiss you."

Those words were the sweetest symphony, and that flower of hope burst into an entire field.

"I want that more than anything else." Brynleigh's core twisted, and those butterflies made a reappearance.

It had taken her a long time to reach this point, but she loved him. She'd given him her heart and finally accepted that there was nothing wrong with that.

Ryker groaned, and his hand tightened around the back of her neck, reminding her of its presence. He lowered his lips, and her heart raced in her chest.

Every inch between them felt like a mile until finally—*fucking finally*—they kissed.

Oh gods.

His mouth captured hers, and it was everything she had ever wanted.

This wasn't the passionate embrace of their wedding, nor was it comparable to the feverish kisses they'd shared that night.

This was a gentle exploration, a mutual apology, and a promise never to break them again. It was a second chance, a flower blooming after a long winter, and a fresh start.

It was fucking beautiful.

Brynleigh wasn't sure whether angels were real—probably not, considering the shit she'd been through—but if they were, they would've been singing at that moment.

Unbidden, tears rushed to her eyes. She tried to keep them inside, but there were too many. They slipped past her eyelids, trailing hot tracks down her cheeks.

Ryker pulled away and frowned.

He noticed. Of course, he noticed.

Cupping her cheek, he collected her tears on his thumb. "What's wrong?"

Despite the tears running down her face, Brynleigh smiled. "I'm just... happy."

The warmth in her chest was a foreign, beautiful feeling.

She raised her chin, wanting to kiss him again.

Unfortunately, instead of obliging her, he tilted his head and creased his brows. "You're happy... so you're crying?"

She placed her hand on his heart, silently reveling in the fact that he didn't pull away.

"Yes. I can't explain it, but I promise, I'm happy."

It was more than that. Happiness was fleeting, but this feeling inside her was different. Permanent. Joy was latching onto Brynleigh's bones, making a home inside her just as her shadows lived in her veins.

Ryker was back, and he'd forgiven her. Who knew second chances could feel so incredible?

His gaze swept over her. "I'm happy, too, but can you stop crying? I'm... not sure what to do about it. It makes me want to hurt someone for hurting you."

Just when she thought Ryker couldn't get any sweeter, he said things like that.

Laughing through her tears, Brynleigh rested her head against his chest and drew in several deep breaths. "Yes, I can."

It took her a few minutes, but eventually, the tears dried up.

He tilted up her face and kissed her softly. "You're beautiful even when you cry."

It was difficult to remember they'd ever been broken when he said things like that. He made her feel whole despite the torture she'd endured.

They spent several minutes in each other's arms before Brynleigh remembered Jelisette's book.

Tugging Ryker over to where she'd been reading, she picked up the small tome and thumbed through the pages until she found the section from earlier. She showed it to him.

"What do you think about this?"

Ryker wrapped an arm around her and held her close as he read over her shoulder. "That's interesting."

"I think it's a code," she said. "But there's no key."

At least, not that she could find.

It would stand to reason that Jelisette would have a cipher for her coded book, but where was it? Brynleigh couldn't exactly ask her Maker, and searching the safe house from top to bottom was out of the question. There was no way to do that without drawing the older vampire's attention.

There had to be another way.

Ryker released her and raked a hand through his hair. Lines creased his forehead, and he rubbed his temples.

"If she has a key..." He cursed. "I have an idea, but I'm not sure it's good."

"What is it?"

"I think I might know someone who could help, but..." Groaning, Ryker shook his head. "It's dangerous."

Of course it was. That was the story of their lives. Nothing was easy or simple when it came to them. Still, it needed to be done.

Her stomach twisted into a knot. "Tell me."

Between the attack at Jade Academy, her visit to Horizon, and meeting Dimitri, it was clear that the rebels were a far bigger problem than she had initially thought.

Brynleigh wasn't a paragon of virtue, but the rebels had tried to kill *children*. That was the line, and they'd crossed it. The Republic of Balance was broken, but the rebels weren't a viable solution.

"The person we need to talk to is in prison," Ryker said.

That knot turned leaden in Brynleigh's stomach. Her mouth dried, and she trembled as memories of what had been done to her ran through her mind.

"In the..." She pushed past the growing lump in her throat. "In the Pit?"

She wasn't sure she could go back there. Not after everything. Not even with Ryker by her side.

"No, not there." He moved, taking her hands in his. His touch calmed her, but the tremors remained. "I promise I'll keep you safe. No one will ever take you from me again. You are under my protection."

Brynleigh's heart raced as Ryker's words settled upon her, his vow ringing with truth.

"Okay, thank you." She dipped her head. "So, if it's not The Pit, where are we going?"

As soon as he told her, she knew he was right.

This was a bad idea.

CHAPTER 22

The Tenth Rule is the Most Important

Ryker's fingers tightened around Brynleigh's as he led her up the concrete front steps of Moonwater Prison.

From the outside, the red-bricked, three-story building looked like a boarding school. A scary one that promised nightmarish headmasters, rods across the backs of legs, and agonizing punishments, but still, a school.

It was all a lie, though. The interior of this building was anything but scholarly.

Ryker hated that he was bringing Brynleigh here, but she'd insisted on coming with him. She was so strong, this wife of his, but sometimes she made him want to tear his hair out. It had taken two days for Ryker to receive the necessary permissions to come to Moonwater Prison, but they were finally here.

"This is where they're keeping Zanri?" she murmured as they climbed the last steps.

He nodded, squeezing her hand once in affirmation.

A week and a half ago, Zanri Olyt had been transferred here for continued interrogation. He would remain here until he was released... or he died.

The latter was far more likely than the former. Most of the Republic's prisoners were never released. Not after they entered the depths of the justice system.

"I've got you," Ryker reminded Brynleigh as their feet hit the landing. A ward crawled over his skin, buzzing like a bee. Not only would the ward protect the prison, but it would alert the wardens of their presence. "I promise."

"Thank you." Brynleigh tugged the sleeve of her oversized black sweater, her outfit looking more like she was going out for a night on the town than into a prison.

"Of course." He would protect her until his dying breath.

Placing his palm on the scanner embedded in the wall by the front door, he smiled reassuringly at her. A red light flashed as the scanner read his handprint, and locks tumbled.

The massive black door swung open on its own volition.

Ryker squeezed Brynleigh's hand, a silent reminder that he was here. She was strong, but even the strongest people felt afraid sometimes.

He walked slightly ahead of her as they entered the expansive lobby. Black marble tiles complemented dark walls stretching two stories high. Two tall, leafy green plants stood sentinel on either side of the door. The only other furnishing was the expansive desk in the middle of the space.

Green eyes were trained on them. An Earth Elf dressed in military gear sat behind the desk, his appearance incongruous with their faux-academic surroundings. His sleeves were rolled up, displaying the green Maturation mark running up his left arm like a vine. The soldier's black hair was cropped short, and he sat perfectly straight in his chair. Though Ryker couldn't see it, he was certain a gun was strapped to the man's belt.

For a long moment, no one spoke.

The air in this space was heavy, and Brynleigh's icy fingers twitched in Ryker's as she pressed against him. He wasn't sure she knew she was doing it, but his chest swelled with masculine pride. She was seeking safety in him, and by the Black Sands, it made him feel something he had thought was forever lost.

He wouldn't let her down.

"Captain Ryker Waterborn?" The elf behind the desk finally spoke.

"Yes," Ryker replied. "We're here to see Prisoner 07562."

The Earth Elf's gaze swung over to Brynleigh, and he frowned. "It's highly unusual to bring visitors here, Captain."

Disapproval dripped from the soldier's tone, and there was nothing kind about the way he looked at Ryker's wife. Obviously, the fae captain knew visitors didn't visit Moonwater often. After all, prisons weren't high on the Republic of Balance's list of tourist destinations.

"I'm aware, but the circumstances warrant it." Ryker canted his head.

He'd used a considerable amount of influence to get the clearance. Sometimes, there were benefits to being the son of a Representative. It wasn't the first time Ryker had pulled strings using the power of his name, and it probably wouldn't be the last. Being a Waterborn was fucking exhausting, but there were some advantages.

The Earth Elf furrowed his brows. "Still, some would say this is rather foolish—"

"I'm bringing her in," Ryker said, his tone brokering no room for discussion. "I have the clearance to be here, and so does my wife."

Inwardly, he acknowledged the Earth Elf might be right. It wasn't outside the realm of possibility that his actions bordered on being foolish. After all, he was taking the woman who had planned on killing him just over a month ago on a sensitive mission. However, there was a high likelihood this would provide them with the break they needed to learn more about the Black Night, so it was worth the potential risk.

Outwardly, Ryker showed no sign that he thought the Earth Elf's words had any value. He ranked higher than this soldier, and he was done with this conversation.

Several tense moments passed before the Earth Elf seemed to realize arguing wouldn't get him anywhere. He dipped his chin, stood, and strode to the door behind his desk. His movements were stiff as he punched a code into the keypad.

"Good luck," the guard said dryly, swinging open the door.

Grunting a reply that sounded somewhat like, "Thanks," Ryker placed his hand on Brynleigh's lower back and led her past the desk.

The door slammed shut when they crossed the threshold, leaving them in a frigid, dimly lit corridor. The stone walls and cement floor lacked the lobby's beauty, reflecting this place's true, depraved nature.

Ryker curled his fingers around his wife's.

"Welcome to Moonwater Prison," he said grimly.

THE ROOM they sought was located on the third floor. The scholarly atmosphere was long gone, leaving them surrounded by institutional, white-washed walls, locked doors, and windowless corridors. It was nighttime, but that didn't matter in here. Bright lights shone from the ceiling, chasing away even the hint of shadows.

Guards were strategically placed throughout the prison, stoically standing watch as Ryker and Brynleigh strode past. Unlike the Earth Elf at the entrance, none of them attempted to stop them.

The first two floors had been loud, filled with a symphony of pain. Endless screams and cries had come from the cells.

Ryker would take those dreadful melodies over the eerie silence of the third floor.

There were no more screams. No more pleas for mercy. Somehow, the quiet was even worse. Every beat of his heart was too loud, every breath too much.

He gripped Brynleigh's fingers. She hadn't spoken since they left the Earth Elf at the entrance.

Maybe he should've pushed back more on bringing her here, but it was too late. The cell they sought was right in front of them. Black numbers were etched onto the white door. A silver scanner was above the handle, like the one they'd encountered entering the prison.

Institutional. Secure. Cold. Heartless.

A dozen other prisons within the Republic fit the same description.

Brynleigh pressed herself against Ryker's side, and she shivered.

"This is where they're keeping him?"

Her voice was so quiet that he had to strain to hear her.

"Yes."

"Oh."

They stared at the door for a long minute but couldn't wait forever.

Raising his free hand, Ryker scrubbed it over his face. "Before we go in... You might not like what he has to say."

By all accounts, Zanri had been forthcoming with his answers. That wasn't entirely surprising. Most people talked after weeks of torture. Ryker had studied notes from the interrogations, and there was one common thread: the shifter was angry. Not that Ryker blamed him, but he didn't want the man directing that anger towards his vampire.

Brynleigh had enough to deal with already.

"I know, but... I need to do this. I thought he was my friend." She looked up at him, her black eyes wide and sorrowful. "Right up until those last moments, I thought... but I was wrong."

He tightened his grip around her hand, even as his heart cracked for Brynleigh.

Ryker's instincts had him wanting to hurt the shifter for betraying Brynleigh in such a manner. That wouldn't help anything, though.

Instead, he reiterated his promise from earlier, knowing he would say it a thousand times over if it made her feel better.

Brynleigh drew in a deep breath, and she dipped her head.

"Alright, I'm ready."

The captain didn't do her the disservice of questioning whether that was true. He didn't really think anyone could be ready for what awaited them, but his vampire was strong. If anyone could handle this, it was her. And if she couldn't, he'd be here for her. Just like he promised.

Ryker placed his hand on the keypad. Once the light turned green, he twisted the handle.

"Let me go first," he murmured, brushing the lightest kiss against her temple.

To her credit, Brynleigh didn't fight him.

Ryker pulled his hand from hers, instantly missing their connection, and stepped inside the cell.

Gods, it was tiny. The space was maybe ten feet long and four feet wide. A metal cot rested against the wall. The floor and walls were made of cement. The only light came from a flickering yellow bulb dangling from the ceiling. It barely lit the cell, casting it in shades of grey despair.

And the smell. The air was thick with sweat, blood, and sickness.

A ghost was huddled on the cot, the shifter was barely recognizable as the man who'd attacked Ryker a month ago.

Brynleigh whimpered as she entered.

"Isvana have mercy on us all," she breathed.

Ryker knew the prisoner was in bad shape, but this was worse than he'd expected.

Red hair coated in blood and grime hung limply around the shifter's face. Black and blue bruises covered his visible skin. Dried blood crusted his lip. Several deep cuts were scattered over his body. They weren't healing.

Zanri cradled his right arm to his chest, the bone jutting out oddly from the socket. Thick prohiberis manacles were attached to the shifter's feet, connected to a chain locking him to the bed. He had just enough leeway to get to the small toilet and sink in the corner, but that was it.

The shifter's name left Brynleigh's lips on a whisper, but the man didn't show any sign he'd heard it.

Brynleigh glanced up at Ryker, eyes wide with horror. Then, she darted around him to the sink before Ryker could stop her. She ripped off her sweater, leaving her in a black tank top, and turned on the tap.

The shifter was a statue on the cot.

Ryker's gaze darted between the prisoner and his wife. Fuck, taking Brynleigh here had been a bad idea. Why had he thought he could keep his wife under control? He'd stupidly assumed she would stay behind him at all times.

Clearly, he'd been mistaken.

"What are you doing?" he growled.

She dipped the sweater under the tap, soaking it. "I'm helping him."

Before Ryker could tell her what a dangerous idea that was—the man was in chains for a reason—she glanced over her shoulder. Her eyes flashed as if to say, *Just try to stop me.*

By all the gods, why had Ryker Chosen such a strong-willed wife? Most people never dared to talk back to him, and yet Brynleigh was challenging him in the middle of a fucking prison.

Damn it all, he was equally frustrated and turned on.

Ryker balled his fists and clenched his teeth as Brynleigh took her damp sweater and approached the shifter. His magic urged him to act, yet he trusted his wife. He'd seen her kill. Surely, she could handle a broken man in chains.

"Z?" Brynleigh whispered. "Can you hear me?"

The shifter's gaze was still trained on the floor.

Brynleigh inched closer.

"It's me," she murmured, standing in front of the cot.

Long, agonizing seconds passed before a chain creaked. The curtain of hair slowly parted as the feline shifter looked up.

His gaze sharpened before flickering with recognition and... fear.

"Fuck, no," the man rasped, his voice sounding like he'd been screaming for hours. "Get out of here, B. She'll kill you for this. The rules... you know the rules."

"I do." She crouched in front of him, her brows furrowed. "But I already broke them."

Her voice was gentle, as though she was afraid to speak too loudly lest she spook him.

The shifter shuddered. "The tenth rule is the most important. That's what I keep telling them. Rule number ten. I can't break it. But I did. You did."

"Zanri, it's okay," Brynleigh whispered.

"We all broke the rules and the game... the game... the game is over." He swayed back and forth, and his voice had an almost frantic tone.

By the gods, the man was shattered.

In the videos, the shifter had been in pain but still sane. His words had made sense. But now...

This kind of suffering could only be caused by Victor Orpheus.

Ryker already knew the fae was a sadist, but seeing the proof with his own eyes was another matter entirely. Thank all the gods, he'd gotten to Brynleigh when he did.

If Ryker had shown up later and found her like this...

Ryker would've killed them all. There was no question in his mind. Laws or not, he would burn the entire fucking world for his vampire.

"Don't worry about me." Brynleigh lifted the damp sweater. "Will you let me help you?"

Another long moment went by before the prisoner nodded.

Brynleigh's movements were slow and methodical as she ran the material down the shifter's face. She was gentle, but he still winced.

Despite the prisoner's current state, Ryker didn't trust him. He watched silently as Brynleigh cleaned the shifter's face and neck but touched her shoulder when she moved onto Zanri's right arm.

"We don't have long."

Even the Waterborn name and Ryker's position in the army couldn't buy them an endless amount of time in Moonwater Prison. They would have to leave soon, hopefully with the necessary information.

Brynleigh nodded, moving down the shifter's arm to his hand.

Three of his fingers were bent, and dried blood was crusted under his broken fingernails. Ryker didn't like the prisoner, but he couldn't help but feel bad for him. No one deserved to be treated like this.

"We need your help, Zanri," Brynleigh murmured. "That's why we're here. "

Silence.

Undeterred, she ran her cloth over his fingers. "It's about the Black Night."

The shifter bucked. He pulled his hand from hers, widened his eyes, and shook his head violently.

"I can't... I don't... Please." He gripped the mattress with white-knuckled hands, and his breaths were battered. "She'll make me wish I were dead if she knows I talked. I can't."

Terror leaked from the shifter, tasting bitter in the back of Ryker's mouth. The fae pulled on his magic, ready to use it in a heartbeat if necessary.

Brynleigh placed her hand on the shifter's leg.

"Breathe, Z," she commanded softly. "We won't tell anyone the information came from you. We just need some help."

The shifter's ragged breaths were the only sounds Ryker could hear, and his heart raced from the fear in the man's eyes.

Who was Jelisette that she inspired such emotion from a once-strong shifter?

The broken man raised his gaze.

He didn't look at Brynleigh but at Ryker. "Do you love her?"

Despite the strangeness of the question, the fae captain didn't hesitate to answer. "I haven't stopped."

Truth. Even when he hated her, he still loved her.

The prisoner's eyes sharpened. For a moment, he appeared lucid.

"Take care of your love," he instructed. "Don't let *her* get her claws into it. Don't let her infect what you have. Owen and me... she destroyed us. Twisted us into something... Don't allow her to do that to you."

Ryker dipped his head. "I understand."

Zanri's gaze was intense and piercing as he studied Ryker for a long moment before he nodded. He turned his attention back to Brynleigh, who'd begun washing his left arm. "What do you need?"

Without divulging the confidential information about Ryker's deal, Brynleigh told Zanri about the book she'd found and its coded letters.

"You're searching for the cipher?" Zanri's voice wavered, and he slumped. "I... I shouldn't. The rules..."

"Please, Z. The rebels attacked a *school*." Brynleigh squeezed his hand. "They need to be stopped. Do you know where we can find it?"

The shifter's chest heaved as though he'd just run a race. His gaze swung like a pendulum between the couple before landing on Ryker's.

"I think I know where it is, but you won't like this, Captain."

And as the shifter explained what he knew, a hole yawned in Ryker's stomach. By the Obsidian Sands, things were getting worse and worse.

Why couldn't anything ever be easy?

CHAPTER 23
Goodnight Kisses and Important Meetings

Several days had passed since Moonwater Prison, but Brynleigh couldn't stop thinking about it.

Her stomach had twisted into knots the moment they stepped foot inside that awful place, and it had yet to unravel. She'd barely eaten, barely slept.

She and Ryker were at the kitchen table in the apartment. The remnants of his late dinner sat on a plate before him, and she nursed her second glass of blood-wine.

"There has to be another way." Ryker dragged his hand through his hair, looking more exhausted than she'd ever seen him. "Maybe the shifter was wrong."

"Maybe." Swirling her wine, Brynleigh gazed into the crimson depths.

After a long moment, she released her wings. The black appendages draped over her back.

Yesterday, Ryker surprised her with new dining room chairs with room for her wings. Gods, he was considerate, this husband of hers.

"I don't think he is," she admitted with a sigh.

Why would Zanri lie? He was already in prison, already being tortured. He would gain nothing by sending them on a wild goose chase.

Leaving her friend in that horrible place had been one of the most difficult things Brynleigh had ever done. She hadn't fought to get Zanri out because she had no idea what the next steps would've been. Where could he go? He was destroyed.

This was all Jelisette's fault.

At first, when Brynleigh had been thrown into prison, she blamed both Zanri and her Maker for betraying her. But that wasn't true. Jelisette must have been forcing Zanri to do what he did because the way that he spoke about the rules...

Brynleigh knew what genuine fear looked like, and she'd seen it carved into her friend's broken face.

Guilt swirled in her stomach, souring the wine she'd already imbibed.

"Is there really nothing you can do for Zanri?" This wasn't the first time she'd asked Ryker, but she needed to be sure. "Maybe your mom can help?"

"I'm sorry, sweetheart." He reached over and placed his hand on hers. "If I was a Representative, then maybe I could, but I'm not. And Mom... she won't help."

Unfortunately, Brynleigh had expected that.

Tertia Waterborne was one of the coldest women she'd ever encountered, and that spoke fucking volumes. Thank all the gods, her mother-in-law was still on a work trip in the north.

"Alright." She sighed, glanced at the clock, and cursed. "I have to go. I have that... job I told you about."

She had yet to explain to Ryker that she was trying to infiltrate the Black Night.

Searching for the cipher was one thing, but pretending to join the rebels for further information was another. Hopefully, she would get some solid information tonight to share with him.

She wasn't leaving him alone at the apartment. Ryker had an important meeting at the base.

The fae in question frowned. "You're sure you have to go tonight?"

"I'm sure." Brynleigh had learned about the meeting from Dimitri after defeating the Crimson Shade, and something told her the rebels didn't do rain checks.

Besides, this wasn't like the Rosewood, where a veil of secrecy had protected Ryker. The rebels wouldn't hesitate to hurt or even execute Ryker just because he was the son of a powerful Representative.

No, she had to do this on her own. At least for now.

"I wish I was going with you." He cleared his plate.

She stood and followed him with her wine glass.

"I'll be fine," she assured him, wiggling her wings. "Who would dare fight me with these? I'll just smack them in the face with one, and they'll reconsider everything."

He snorted, but concern still filled his eyes. "You'll come straight home after?"

"Yes, I promise." Washing her glass, she placed it on the counter and brushed her lips over his cheek. "I wouldn't miss our goodnight kiss for the world."

They hadn't discussed the state of their relationship, but they would have to do it soon. The Reunion was coming.

It wasn't as though they were ignoring each other, though. On the contrary, every night since their return from Moonwater Prison, they'd shared a very steamy, definitely not platonic, goodnight kiss before going their separate ways. Brynleigh went to the couch, and Ryker went to his bedroom.

Without fail, she dreamed of him. She woke with an ache between her legs that was growing more insistent with each passing day. She wanted him. Needed him, even. Every kiss was a taste of what they'd had, and she cherished each one.

So no, she wouldn't be missing their kiss.

Ryker wrapped his hand around hers and pressed his chest against her wings. He kissed her neck, murmuring, "Don't do anything stupid. Don't be brave. Just stay in one piece. I don't trust Jelisette."

Neither did Brynleigh, but this was the best way to get the information for Ryker.

"I will." Tugging the sleeves of her cardigan, Brynleigh stepped back. "I'll see you in a few hours."

Chocolate eyes met hers. "I can't wait."

Releasing her shadows, she allowed them to embrace her. Even as the apartment slipped away and she stepped into the Void, she held Ryker's gaze.

THE WAREHOUSE HAD UNDERGONE a serious transformation since Brynleigh's last visit. The tables, bar, and stage were gone, as though they'd never existed. Dim lighting had replaced the spotlights. Several large crates were stacked in clusters.

Where too-loud music had once filled the industrial space, now every hushed whisper of feet on the cement floor felt out of place.

If Brynleigh hadn't seen the fight club or bled on the stage, she never would have believed this was the same place.

And yet, it was.

She'd shadowed to the same alley, walked across the same street, and spoken to the same burly guard at the door. The same wards had tickled her skin as she walked into the space, and now, she occupied a seat in the last of four rows of metal folding chairs. Her wings were draped over the back, fanned out behind her.

Crossing her arms, Brynleigh willed her shadows to stop throbbing in her veins. They didn't like her presence here, but they'd have to deal with it. She wasn't leaving until she got what she came for.

Instead of focusing on her shadows' unease, Brynleigh took in the space. All the other seats were occupied except the two on either side of her. She'd probably be insulted if she was in another mood, but as it was, she was grateful she wouldn't have to make small talk with anyone.

Not that anyone *was* talking. Furtive glances and furrowed brows were shot in Brynleigh's direction, but no one spoke to her or anyone else.

It was gods-damned awkward, and minutes dragged on.

It seemed as though every single species in the Republic of Balance was present tonight, save the merfolk. Several humans sat among shifters, werewolves, fae, elves, and witches. There were even a few other vampires, although Brynleigh didn't recognize them.

That wasn't entirely surprising. She had spent the past six years preparing for her revenge, so she hadn't spent much time in the vampiric community. Maybe once this was over, she could find some vampires to befriend. Ones that weren't insanely cruel, lying bitches like her Maker.

But one problem at a time.

First things first: staying under the radar in this meeting, getting information for Ryker, and then getting out of here in one piece.

Then, once this was over, she'd figure out the rest of her life.

Brynleigh wanted to mend things with Hallie, but no matter how many times she typed out an apology text, none of them seemed right. How did one ask for forgiveness for missing the most important day of someone's life? She couldn't seem to find the right words.

Footsteps echoed through the space, drawing Brynleigh out of her thoughts. She looked up, her eyes landing on two figures approaching the gathered group.

Those seemingly ever-present knots in Brynleigh's stomach tightened to the point of pain.

Jelisette strode beside Dimitri, the pair deep in conversation. The werewolf was handsome in his own way, but there was a definite mortality to his beauty.

A scar ran down his cheek that Brynleigh had been too distracted to notice the last time they met, and his face was covered in freckles. His forehead was wrinkled, and his nose was a little too crooked. He was still conventionally attractive, though. Beautiful in a way that most Mature creatures were.

But next to Jelisette, the Alpha looked average. Normal. Not quite... right.

Jelisette's deadly, too-beautiful-to-be-real appearance had always amazed Brynleigh. Darkness surrounded the older vampire. She had an aura of harshness, death, and danger. Yet, when one looked upon the vampire with her chestnut hair, smooth features, and black eyes, one couldn't help but be awed by her violent grace. The older vampire had seen over nine centuries, but she appeared no older than three human decades.

Except for her eyes.

Those eyes had been the first thing Brynleigh saw when she woke after the storm; sometimes, she still had nightmares about them.

Now, Jelisette's dark, lifeless orbs drilled into Brynleigh. Shivers crawled down the younger vampire's spine, and she shifted in her metal seat.

As much as Brynleigh thought she'd won some kind of favor in fighting and besting the Crimson Shade, she would never forget the sting of her Maker's betrayal. It was a sharp, endless burn in her heart that would keep her warm on the coldest of days.

She would never forget that it was Jelisette who'd sent her to kill Ryker even though River had been the one to destroy Chavin, just like she would never forget that Zanri had come to kill Ryker on Jelisette's command.

Brynleigh might be playing the part of the dutiful progeny out to destroy the Representatives, but she would always remember that her Maker had lied to her and left her in prison to rot.

Jelisette moved her gaze as she came to stand in front of the group, but Brynleigh didn't relax. She wouldn't until she was back home with Ryker.

"Welcome, brethren." Dimitri stood in front of the assembly, his stance relaxed and his hands tucked in the pockets of his jeans. "I'm glad so many of you could make it. Tonight, our time is short. I won't keep us waiting with pleasantries. We—"

A chair was shoved back in the second row.

A woman stood, her rounded ears and average stature speaking to her human heritage. "Seriously, Dimitri? You're not going to address the fucking elephant in the room?"

The werewolf canted his head in a predatory manner, and his orange eyes glowed. "What elephant are you referring to, Mercy?"

Mercy swung on her heel and pointed at Brynleigh. "That one. It's big, blonde, and has black batwings."

Fucking hell. So much for flying under the radar. How come Brynleigh kept attracting the attention of mean girls? First, Valentina Rose, the bitchy fire fae from the Choosing. Now, this human. She was over it.

"That's a vampire, not an elephant," Dimitri said calmly.

"Fuck off," Mercy snarled. "You know what I mean. She's married to a gods-damned *Waterborn*. I watched her wedding on the Choosing. What in the name of all the gods is she doing here?"

Mercy's voice had risen to a shrill shriek. It was like she broke the spell because the earlier quiet disappeared. Murmurs of agreement rose from the others, and Brynleigh shifted in her seat.

Had she miscalculated, coming here alone? It wasn't as though she'd forgotten that the Choosing had been broadcast to the entire Republic, but she had been a little too busy to consider all the potential ramifications.

Discontent rose, and her stomach twisted tighter and tighter. Her shadows' throb was incessant, as though they were saying, "I told you so."

Maybe they'd been right.

Faces painted in hatred turned and sneered at Brynleigh. More people stood—some humans, a fae, and an elf—and all of them shouted their discontent at her presence. No one seemed to care that she had been here before, but maybe the fight club was different.

Tension ratcheted up, up, up, until Brynleigh's skin felt too tight for her bones. The voices echoed off the steel walls like clanging cymbals. Her heart was a horse galloping in her chest. She kept her wings out and clenched her fists. Would she have to fight her way out of here?

Dimitri didn't say anything as the rebels spewed their venomous anger for several minutes.

"She's with me." Jelisette stepped forward, her quiet words steeped with power. Shadows hung lazily around her hands, and her black gaze met Brynleigh's. "My progeny harbors a hatred for the Representatives and their oppressive ways, just like the rest of you."

That was not true, but Brynleigh had enough preservation instincts to keep that to herself.

Most of the others sat back down, but Mercy remained on her feet.

"She might as well *be* a Representative," the human sneered. "Those fucking bastards killed my husband and children! Do you expect me to work with the likes of her?"

As if the rebels hadn't just blown up a school. Fucking hypocrites.

"Yes." An Alpha command was laced through Dimitri's voice, and even though Brynleigh wasn't a werewolf, she recognized the power in his words. "That's exactly what I expect. You may not trust her, but you know her Maker."

He gestured to Jelisette, who stood to his right.

The werewolf continued, "For decades, Jelisette de la Point has worked tirelessly for our cause. Because of her endless efforts, we have satellite groups in each of the five regions. Without her, we never would've been able to accomplish half the things we have."

Mercy gripped the back of the chair in front of her. "So, you speak for her? After what Representatives did to Eme—"

In a movement too quick for even Brynleigh to track, Jelisette crossed the room. Her hand circled Mercy's throat.

"Do. Not. Fucking. Say. His. Name."

Shadows flooded the warehouse, and Mercy clawed at the hand holding her in the air. It was a useless endeavor. What was a measly, weak human against an almost thousand-year-old enraged vampire?

Mercy squeaked like a terrified mouse, and tears ran down her cheeks.

A twinge of pity ran through Brynleigh. After all, she'd been in that position not long ago.

Snarling, Jelisette shook Mercy back and forth like a rag doll.

"If you ever say his name again, I will rip out your throat and feast on your blood so gods-damned fast you won't even know what hit you. You don't even think about *him*. Is that understood?"

If Brynleigh had any doubts about Emery Sylvain's existence or that the Representatives had killed him, this violent display would've rid her of them.

Mercy gasped something vaguely like, "Yes," and then Jelisette released her hold.

The human dropped to the floor, gulping in deep, echoing breaths.

"My progeny desires to see the Representatives taken down a few notches, just like the rest of us." Jelisette turned and addressed the crowd. "Does anyone else have any concerns?"

Silence was the only answer.

Jelisette nodded at Dimitri.

"Very well," the Alpha said calmly as if a woman hadn't almost been murdered a few feet away from him. "As I was saying, we have several ideas for how to make our cause known soon. First..."

As Dimitri continued speaking, Brynleigh's stomach turned to lead. Their plans would make the attack on Jade Academy seem like nothing.

By the time the meeting was over, Brynleigh knew one thing for certain: they had to stop the rebels, no matter the cost.

It was time to tell Ryker where she'd been.

CHAPTER 24
Ruination

Shadows pooled on the living room floor, and Ryker exhaled a sigh of relief.

Half an hour ago, he'd returned home from his meeting to an empty apartment. He took Marlowe for a quick run, hoping to distract himself, but it didn't work. His vampire was strong, but he didn't trust her Maker.

Even exchanging messages with River hadn't calmed Ryker's nerves. His sister and her best friend Ember were coming over tomorrow night to watch a game of laser, along with Nikhail and Atlas. Cyrus was doing well on his meds, and River felt confident going out for the night.

This would be an excellent first step for Ryker and Brynleigh to practice for the Reunion. It wasn't a public event, but they needed to get used to being around others again.

As soon as Brynleigh's form materialized by the couch, Ryker strode towards her.

"Are you okay?" he asked, even as his eyes swept over her and confirmed she had no visible injuries.

Brynleigh nodded, but her gaze was guarded. She wrapped her arms around herself and worried her bottom lip.

His gut pinched. Something was wrong.

"I'm fine," she answered. "But… I have to tell you something."

Ryker's chest tightened, and an alarm blared in his head. Immediately, his mind went to worst-case scenarios and ran through them one by one. Usually, doing this helped settle his mind and gave him strategies for moving forward. It was one of the reasons he was so good at chess and his job. Predictions and calculations were an integral part of strategy.

He'd never predicted that his wife would try to kill him, though, so maybe he was off his game.

Ryker was so tense that he might snap in half if she didn't put his mind at ease soon. Somehow, he kept his voice calm and asked, "What do you mean?"

"Promise not to yell?" she asked.

Nothing good ever started like that. He drew in a deep breath and nodded. "I'll do my best."

For her, he'd do anything.

"Okay. I… I wasn't at a job tonight," Brynleigh admitted.

His eyes widened, and anger surged, burning a path through his veins.

She'd lied to him again? He thought they were past that and trying to fix things. This felt awfully like the opposite of that.

It took every ounce of control he had, but he kept his promise not to yell. Somehow.

"What do you mean?"

She stepped towards him, moving slowly as if to give him time to back away. When he didn't, she put her hand on his. Her touch, always colder than his own, grounded him. She was here, and she was safe.

How bad could it be?

"I sort of… went to a rebel meeting."

Bad.

This was so gods-damned bad that he couldn't even wrap his mind around it.

Forgetting his promise, he snarled loudly, "Why the fuck would you do that?"

What in the name of all the gods had she been thinking? This was so far outside the realm of intelligent choices; he hadn't even considered that she might do something like this. Did she agree with the rebels? Did she want to work with them?

A growl rumbled through Ryker's chest, and Brynleigh's eyes widened.

"I... I thought it was a good idea. I mean, I still do." She swallowed and spoke quickly as if she was afraid he might cut her off if she didn't get it all out. "When Jelisette tried to kill me the night you went to Sandhaven, I told her I wasn't done. That's why she let me live. I convinced her I still wanted to take down the Representatives."

A rushing filled Ryker's ears, and his heart pounded so loudly, he could barely hear his own thoughts. He'd known Brynleigh had made some questionable choices in the past, but this...

He frowned. "So, she handed you an invitation to a rebel meeting? Just like that?"

People had been trying to infiltrate the Black Night for decades. It couldn't be that easy.

Brynleigh blanched, breathing in deeply through her nose. "Ah... no."

Unease churned Ryker's stomach, and he crossed his arms. "Explain."

To his wife's credit, she did exactly that. Pacing a path across the living room floor, she told him everything. Visiting a warehouse, drinking some blood wine, overhearing conversations, and fighting a Death Elf called the Crimson Shade.

By the time Brynleigh wrapped up her story, Ryker was half-inclined to throttle her.

What the hell had she been thinking? Who walked into a rebel meeting not once but twice without backup? It was incredibly foolish. Brave—so fucking brave that it warmed his heart—but also life-threateningly idiotic.

He could've lost her.

By the Black Sands, she could've died, and he never would have known what happened to her.

"They could've killed you," Ryker growled.

She raised a brow. "True, but they didn't. I'm alive and in one piece."

Unbidden, visions of his beautiful wife cut up into pieces and scattered across the Republic flashed through Ryker's mind. Red tinged his vision, and his nails dug into his flesh. She'd been in mortal danger tonight, and he'd been in a gods-damned bureaucratic meeting.

"Why?" he asked, unable to form but the simplest of words.

Why put herself in that kind of danger? Why not tell him? For that matter, why tell him now? He had so many questions he wasn't sure which one he was asking.

She seemed to understand, though, even if he didn't. "For you."

His brows knit together. "What?"

Apparently, anger greatly hampered his linguistic capabilities.

Brynleigh's dark eyes swept over his, and for a long moment, it seemed like she wouldn't answer.

"You need to know about the Black Night, right?" she asked.

"I... yes." In an ideal world, they'd get ahead of the rebels and put a permanent stop to them.

She took his hand again, her fingers frighteningly small against his. "I have an in, and honestly? It's the least I can do. I want to make amends, Ryker."

He shook his head. "Sweetheart, you don't need—"

She kissed him. Their mouths slanted together, and she swallowed the rest of his words. It was a soft, gentle embrace. Hardly anything at all.

And yet, desire coursed through him like bolts of lightning.

She didn't pull away, so he deepened their embrace. Every taste, every touch of her lips against his was heavenly. He needed her. He pressed his hardness against her stomach, and she moaned against his lips.

That lightning became a storm within him. He was tired of taking care of himself in the shower, tired of waking up hard and in need, tired of not having her in his arms. Yet, he didn't want to push her too fast. He wouldn't risk breaking them again.

"Let me do this for you, Ry," she murmured against his mouth. "I want to see this situation with the rebels through."

He was just a fae. How was he supposed to argue when a gorgeous female was pressed against him?

Raising his hand, he broke their kiss and ran his knuckles down her cheek. "What am I going to do with you, little vampire?"

Who knew having a wife would be so much work? Every moment of every day, he worried about her.

"I don't know," Brynleigh whispered, pressing her cheek into his palm.

He bent his head, his forehead brushing against hers.

"I worry about you endlessly," he whispered. "Every time the sun rises, I wonder if this will be our last day together before it all ends."

She fisted his shirt and held him close.

"I'm not going anywhere, Ry." She looked up at him, black eyes wide as she held his gaze and kissed the corner of his mouth. "I promise."

"And yet you put yourself in danger tonight," he reminded her. "You could've been killed. I would've lost you."

His voice cracked on the last word. He couldn't even imagine the heartache that would've haunted him if that had happened.

"It was for a good cause," she murmured, pressing a feather-light kiss against his lips. "Us."

How could such a small word sound so good?

"Say it again," he breathed, his heart pounding in his chest.

The corner of her mouth tugged up. "Us."

Despite the situation, despite her recklessness, despite everything else, warmth ran through him.

"I like hearing that almost as much as I like you."

Brynleigh chuckled. "You like me, Captain? Is that all you feel for me?"

Her tone was teasing, but desperation and need were buried beneath her words.

"No."

He stepped away from her and took her hand. Lacing their fingers together, he led her to the window. Stars peeked through the clouds, and the moon was a half-crescent hanging in the sky.

"It's beautiful," she murmured.

He hummed in approval. "It is, but you are far more beautiful than any night sky."

His vampire inhaled, but he didn't give her the chance to speak.

"Like the moon that rises every night and the stars that follow its lead, I am drawn to you." Even when they had been at their most broken, he'd been drawn to her. "You are mine in every way. My wife. My vampire."

"Ryker—"

He turned to look at her. "Sometimes, I think you could be my ruination."

Her hand twitched in his, but he wasn't done.

"If you're going to ruin me, do it by my side. Remain with me. Let us work this out, and whatever happens, happens." He traced her wedding ring. "There's no one I'd rather be ruined by than you."

For the longest moment, she was a statue, and then her lips tilted up.

Gods above, had there ever been as beautiful of a sight as his wife's perfect smile?

"You have a way with words, Ry." She squeezed his hand. "Has anyone ever told you that?"

"A few," he admitted, his gaze searching hers.

She stepped towards him and lifted her chin.

"I'm drawn to you, too, and I promise I'm not going anywhere," she murmured. "I don't think you could get rid of me now, even if you tried."

"I don't plan on it." He wrapped his arms around her and held her close.

He wasn't sure how much time had passed before Marlowe snorted in his sleep, the sound breaking them out of whatever spell had been cast over them.

Ryker kissed the top of Brynleigh's head. "So, this meeting..."

She stiffened. "Yeah, we should probably talk about that." Pulling out of his grasp, she headed to the kitchen and spoke over her shoulder. "Let me grab you a beer. I think you'll need it when you hear what happened tonight."

That did not bode well.

Ryker agreed, and Brynleigh returned in a vampiric flash, carrying drinks for them both.

She handed him the bottle. "Should we sit?"

"Good idea." He took her hand and led her to the couch, where Marlowe lounged like he owned the entire place. "Down, Marlie."

The pup hopped off immediately, curling up on the carpet by the front door instead.

Ryker sat, pulling Brynleigh down with him. Their legs brushed against each other, and neither of them pulled away. Thank all the gods.

"Okay." He slung an arm over her shoulder and twisted a lock of her blonde hair around his finger. "Tell me what happened."

Slowly, Brynleigh explained everything that she'd learned at the rebel meeting. She paused and answered his questions when they came up, not minding when he grabbed his phone and jotted down several pertinent pieces of information.

When Ryker dragged her closer so their sides lined up from their shoulders to their toes, she didn't pull away. Instead, she leaned against him and kept speaking.

This was so much better than a single goodnight kiss.

"So that's it." Brynleigh dragged her finger around the rim of her empty glass an hour later. "The next time Jelisette calls me to the safe house, I'll look for the cipher. That should help, too, right?"

Ryker nodded.

"Anything you can find will help. This is already far more than we've ever gotten on the Black Night." All because of his wife. Pride was a burning flame in his chest, and he squeezed her shoulder. He hated that she was endangering herself for this information, but he was so impressed by her actions and bravery. "Thank you."

The rebels had already proven they would do anything to get what they wanted. Maybe, with Brynleigh as the army's secret weapon, this would be the lead they needed to get ahead once and for all.

CHAPTER 25

This was Where He was Meant to Be

"Explain this game to me one more time?" Brynleigh fiddled with the zipper of her scarlet sweater.

She'd styled her hair in a slick golden ponytail that hung down her back, and every time she turned around, Ryker envisioned wrapping his fist around it and pulling her against him.

He discretely adjusted himself. This wasn't the moment for those types of thoughts. Their guests were a few minutes out.

Still, he had to touch her. He couldn't stop touching her. Not since their kiss and subsequent conversation last night. Catching her fingers in his, he held her hand and drew her close.

"It's simple, really. Two teams play in a large, enclosed arena. It's filled with obstacles and targets, and the team with the highest points at the end of the fourth quarter wins."

Brynleigh frowned. "They get points by shooting lasers at each other?"

Between her tone and raised brow, it was clear that she didn't understand the point of the game.

"Not each other, the targets," Ryker explained patiently.

There were offensive and defensive positions, and some targets were worth significantly more than others.

"But people *can* get shot." She seemed hung up on that, which was delightfully ironic considering her line of work.

Ryker smirked. "It's a sport, sweetheart. Sometimes, people get hurt, but the athletes are highly trained and get paid a lot of money to play. There are rules against intentionally hurting or blinding your opponents."

Not that those rules had always stopped the players. There were a few incidents over the years of laser athletes suffering career-ending injuries.

"Mhmm." She nibbled on her lip. "And this is... fun?"

"Very." Ryker squeezed her hands. "Players need to work together and implement various strategies to defeat the opposing team."

Her eyes lit up. "Like chess?"

"Yeah, exactly like that." Grinning, he glanced at the board on the coffee table. "Maybe we can play tomorrow?"

The responding smile that spread across Brynleigh's face made Ryker burn hotter than any fire ever had.

"I'd love that," she said.

He stepped towards her, unable to pull himself away from the magnetic draw of her stunning lips when a wet nose bumped into his leg.

Pausing, he looked down.

Marlowe stood with his leash in his mouth, his tail thumping eagerly as he looked between the fae and vampire.

"I'll take him," Brynleigh offered. "The sun's set. We'll walk around the block while you wait for River."

"Thank you." Ryker kissed her cheek before crouching. He hooked Marlowe's leash on his collar and looked the dog in the eye. "You listen to your mom, okay? Her word is just as good as mine."

Marlowe barked, saying what Ryker could only assume was a resounding, *Yes, sir.*

Straightening, Ryker handed Brynleigh the leash. "Don't let him pull you around. Show him who's boss."

"You got it, Captain."

Brynleigh gave him a mock salute and blew him a kiss as she headed out the door. Marlowe trotted eagerly behind her, happy to go outside.

Ryker watched them go, a grin on his face. His chest heated, and he rubbed a fist over his heart. It took him a moment to realize what he was feeling.

Happiness.

This was what he'd always wanted, ever since he'd made his Choice. Finally, it seemed like they would get the future he wanted. As long as everything worked out.

Ryker had just pulled a sweatshirt over his head when a knock came on the door. "Open up. Your favorite sister's here!"

He hurried through the apartment, moving a few pairs of shoes aside in the mud room before flinging open the door.

River beamed up at him. Like Brynleigh, his sister was wearing black leggings. Unlike the vampire, River wore a cropped navy blue and white jersey. A dragon flew across the front, the symbol of the Drahanian Dragons. The jersey was tied above River's belly button, showing off her newest piercing.

"Who says you're my favorite sister, Shortie?" Ryker teased, pulling her in for a hug.

She laughed, wrapped her arms around him, and squeezed. "I'm your only sister, so obviously, the title belongs to me."

Ryker chuckled as he pulled back and ruffled her hair. "I suppose that's true. How was training earlier?"

Two water fae Ryker trusted, Gabriel and Carson, were continuing with his sister's magical training while he dealt with the Black Night. Hopefully, he could get back to personally supervising her sessions once things died down.

"It went well. I told you, I've got my magic under control. Nothing bad will ever happen again." She jabbed him in the side. "Stop worrying about me."

"Never." Still, he released her. "What time is Ember coming?"

"The second quarter. She has a late class." River held up her phone, showing Ryker her text thread with the fire fae.

The background was a selfie of the two friends, Ember's glowing russet skin and midnight hair contrasting River's tan. The two fae were grinning, and there was an air of lightness about them that Ryker rarely saw around his sister.

"Wonderful." Ryker meant it.

He was pleased River had someone to confide in, especially since he knew how difficult life in Waterborne House could be.

River peered around him into the mud room. "Where's your wife?"

"She took Marlowe for a walk, but they'll be back soon." Ryker placed a hand on his sister's arm and waited until she looked at him before he continued, "Brynleigh's been through a lot over the past few weeks." Understatement of the century. "Try not to overwhelm her."

His sister's brown eyes widened, and she gasped. "Who, me? I would *never*."

Yet, Ryker knew firsthand that River could very easily do that. At school, she was the quiet academic type, but she could be unhinged when it came to sports.

"I'm serious, River. I don't want you to scare her off." Especially not now, after last night.

River must have picked up on the seriousness of the situation because she swallowed.

"Okay. I understand. I'll be good." She smiled, gesturing to her feet. "I stopped and picked up a few snacks on my way."

Ryker's eyes widened. "A few?" Five overflowing cloth tote bags surrounded her. "We're not hosting the entire army."

She smirked, handing him several bags. "I know, but I got hungry and couldn't decide, so I bought everything that looked good."

He laughed. That was just like River. He loved her, but she had no concept of money.

Picking up the remainder of the bags, Ryker led his sister inside. They unpacked the snacks, putting them out while River updated her brother on the state of her life. She was halfway through a tale about an incident in her senior chemistry class earlier this week when another knock came on the door.

"Hello, anyone home?" Atlas's deep tenor was audible through the door.

Ryker grabbed a stack of colorful bowls from the cabinet that had been a housewarming gift from a teenage River when he first moved into the apartment.

"Come on in," he hollered.

Moments later, the door opened. Atlas came in first, carrying a case of beer in each hand. The tall redheaded earth fae wore a T-shirt despite the cold weather, showing off his tattoos.

"I'll put these on the balcony." He lifted the cases in demonstration. "The temperature is dropping fast. The winter will be long—the land is preparing for a cold snap."

When Ryker first met Atlas, he found it strange that the earth fae often spoke for the land. Now, it was just one of his friend's amusing little quirks.

Despite looking like he should be part of a dangerous gang, Atlas had a gentle side that he hid from the world. Even his students would never guess their tattooed professor could be soft outside of the classroom.

Thanking Atlas, Ryker set the bowls down as Nikhail entered the kitchen. The air fae placed two wine bottles on the counter before leaning against the marble.

"Hey, River, nice to see you," Nikhail said.

She turned from the fridge, smiling shyly at the air fae dressed in his signature suit.

"Hey, Nik. How are you?"

Something in River's tone had Ryker narrowing his eyes. His gaze danced between the two, and he glowered.

Whatever *this* was, he wasn't pleased about it. Nikhail was a good man, but he wasn't suitable for River.

At. All.

She deserved someone perfect, and Nikhail, for all his good qualities, was not that.

Frowning, Ryker glared at his best friend. This had better not be what he thought it was. He already had enough going on without dealing with his sister and his...

No. He wouldn't even entertain the thought.

Nikhail didn't seem to notice Ryker's displeasure as he dipped his head.

"I'm good. Glad to have a night off."

River chewed on her lip, the ring glinting from the artificial light in the kitchen. "You deserve it. You army folk work too hard, which says a lot, coming from a medical student."

The air fae shrugged and smiled.

Smiled!

Nikhail never did that.

"Well, you know. Someone's got to do it."

The pair stared at each other as if both had forgotten Ryker was standing in the kitchen with them. It was... wrong. All of this was wrong.

Ryker wanted to punch something and tear his sister away from Nikhail, but he didn't want to ruin the evening.

Thank the Blessed Black Sands, Atlas chose that moment to come back inside.

"Want a beer, River?" the professor called out. "The game's about to start."

"Yes, please." River grabbed a couple of bowls of salty snacks and hurried into the living room.

Nikhail stared at her as she left, which was...

Upsetting.

Ryker cleared his throat and scrubbed a hand over his face.

"Hey, man. You're not... with River..."

He couldn't even say the words.

Nikhail's gaze shot back to him, and he shook his head. "Gods, no. She's your little sister. We're just friends."

Just friends.

If Nikhail had been staring at anyone else like that, Ryker would've pointed out that friends didn't lock eyes the way the two of them just had. However, seeing as how Ryker would never, ever approve of his best friend and his sister in any sort of relationship, he didn't.

"I see," Ryker grumbled, unconvinced.

He would let it drop. For now.

"So, how are things with Brynleigh?" Nikhail asked, clearly trying to change the subject.

The water fae leaned his hip against the counter. "We're... good. Or at least, we're getting there."

"Really?" Nikhail's brows rose, surprise evident in his tone.

Ryker supposed that was fair. After all, he'd been a mess after finding his wife in the Pit.

"Yeah. I love her, Nik." He stared at the front door as if he could summon her with his thoughts. "Even with everything that happened, I still love Brynleigh. And I... I need her."

More and more with every passing day. He needed her like he needed air to breathe or water to drink. She had woven herself into the very fabric of his soul, and he couldn't imagine living without her. Not anymore.

Nikhail's gaze swept over his for a long moment before he dipped his head. "Good for you, Ryker. I'll admit, I've had my doubts about her, but if you say you love her—"

"I do," he said gruffly. "She's my whole world."

Truth. He couldn't lie about this, even if he wanted to.

"Then you have my support." Nikhail clapped Ryker on the back. "No matter what. That's what friends do."

A few minutes later, Brynleigh and Marlowe came back.

Everyone was kind as they greeted her, and they settled on the couch as the game began.

A grin stretched across Ryker's lips as Brynleigh curled up next to him. River stretched out on the floor, pointing out her favorite players as they ran across the screen. Atlas and Nikhail claimed the armchairs, and Marlowe dozed by the door. Ember arrived, joining River on the floor, and together, they laughed and screamed every time the Dragons got a point.

By the time the game was over—the Dragons won—Ryker's cheeks hurt from grinning. Even the news that Jelisette had a job for Brynleigh tomorrow didn't shake him from his happiness.

This was where he was meant to be, the life he was meant to live, and it felt *right*.

CHAPTER 26
More than Just an Asset

Two days had passed since the laser game, and the relaxed air from that night was long gone.

Now, Brynleigh's stomach was twisted up once again. That had been happening frequently, but it was worse tonight, thanks to Ryker's pacing up and down the living room floor.

Brynleigh sat on the couch, her legs crossed beneath her, as he walked back and forth.

The laser game had been nice, although she still didn't understand the purpose of the supposedly recreational activity. A bunch of grown men chasing each other with bright beams across a field for hours seemed silly to her, but everyone else had enjoyed it. She'd been happy to spend time with Ryker and get to know his friends.

The normalcy of that night was a million miles away now.

"I don't like this," her fae captain growled for the tenth time that hour. "So many things could go wrong."

He'd made his displeasure clear. This discussion had been going on all day; now, the moon was high in the sky.

Last night, Brynleigh had gone on a job in the Western Region. In a show of growing trust, Ryker hadn't tagged along.

That had been for the best.

Her target had been one of the worst men she'd ever encountered, which said a lot. Josef Longrun was a prizewinning photographer who'd pivoted photos of landscapes to ones of youth in compromising positions. His actions were deplorable, and Brynleigh had found twisted pleasure in ending his life.

Without Ryker there, she'd been able to concentrate on her job. Josef Longrun hadn't deserved an easy death. He'd bled, whimpered, and screamed all night long before she finally killed him.

Usually, she hated the whiners, but she'd found Josef's sniveling weakness empowering. Every cry, every plea, and every time he begged for forgiveness had drawn a smile to her lips.

The peace she'd gotten from last night's kill was gone now.

Sighing, Brynleigh caught Ryker's hand in hers. She tugged him over to the couch.

"Sit with me?" she asked.

He gave her a look that made it clear he'd rather still pace, but to his credit, he complied. He was like a furnace next to her, and she leaned into his warmth.

"We've been over this," she said calmly. She appreciated his protectiveness, but this was the only way forward. "We need the cipher. Zanri told us where it is, and I'm going to get it. I'll go in, debrief Jelisette, then find the key. I'll be long gone before she realizes I took anything. If she even realizes I took it."

Brynleigh had already stolen one thing from Jelisette. How difficult could it be to take another?

Besides, she had to do this. It would be a disservice to Zanri if they didn't use the information he'd given them. She was still hopeful they'd be able to get him out of prison. Somehow.

Ryker grabbed a black hoodie off the back of the couch and yanked it over his head.

"Jelisette is unstable," he snarled. "She fed you lies for six gods-damned years, and she's fucking dangerous."

He didn't want her to get hurt. That was sweet of him.

"I'm well aware." Brynleigh fiddled with the hem of her dark pink and black sweater. It hugged her curves and gave her confidence, which she desperately needed before going to see her Maker.

Merely calling Jelisette unstable was a disservice to instability. The older vampire was certifiably insane.

It was the Binding.

This past week, Brynleigh had researched Bound Partners. While scholars debated the specific adverse effects that would strike a vampire if their Bound Partner died, they all agreed that losing half of a bond would be mentally and physically devastating.

Something had irrevocably shattered in Jelisette when Emery Sylvain died. From a factual perspective, it was incredible that she was still alive and functioning. Half her heart and soul had perished with her partner.

Brynleigh glanced at Ryker. They weren't Bound, but she couldn't even fathom his death. She didn't even want to think about the fact that while fae were long-lived, they weren't truly immortal like vampires. She loved him so deeply that there would be no life without him.

At least now, Brynleigh understood why her Maker was so set against Representatives. It made sense, in a twisted sort of way, that Jelisette wanted to inflict harm upon the upper class after what they'd done to her.

If only she hadn't used Brynleigh as an unwitting pawn in her game.

"I can handle my Maker," Brynleigh said with more confidence than she felt. "I'm strong."

Ryker frowned. "I know you are. But this..."

"It's too late. She's expecting me."

"But—"

"No." Brynleigh waved her left arm, her bracelet dangling over her wrist. "You signed me up for this, remember? This is my job as your asset."

The words tasted like ash, and she hated them.

His fingers tightened around hers, and with his free hand, he lifted her chin until she looked at him. Storms flashed through his gaze.

"You are far more than an asset," Ryker growled. "You know that."

"I do." She understood that doing this was the price of her freedom, just as she understood that her Maker was waiting for her. "But Jelisette doesn't. And besides, she... trusts me. I think."

At least, Jelisette hadn't killed her. *And* she'd introduced Brynleigh to Dimitri. That meant something. Right?

"She may trust *you*, but I don't fucking trust *her*." Ryker's grip was just on this side of pain. "By the Black Sands and all that is holy, promise me you'll do everything to stay safe tonight. In and out. No dilly-dallying."

Ryker's magic rippled off him in waves, a mighty tempest running through the room.

Brynleigh dipped her head. "I promise I won't do anything stupid."

She didn't want to linger anywhere near her Maker.

Ryker didn't release her. Instead, he pulled her close and cupped her cheek.

"Listen to me. You're my wife, and I need you to make it out of there alive. Jelisette might have Made you, but you aren't hers. You're *mine*."

Her heart raced at his words, but he wasn't done.

"This can't be the end. If she hurts you, I will make River's storm look like a trickle of water when I seek my retribution. Is that clear?"

The fae's possessive words should have probably turned Brynleigh off, but instead, her core twisted.

Brynleigh's fangs ached, and not for the first time, she wondered what Ryker would taste like. Would his blood be rich, deep, and full of the storms swirling in his gaze? Or perhaps smooth, with a touch of spice?

She'd never wanted to bite someone as much as she did right now.

She squeezed her thighs together. These were entirely inappropriate thoughts to have minutes before meeting her Maker.

What did it say about Brynleigh that her husband's show of possessive fae ownership turned her on? Probably nothing good.

A problem for another time.

"Yes, it's clear." She smiled. "Don't worry; I'll be quick."

He stared at her. "I'll always worry about you."

That was sweet. Unnecessary but sweet.

After all, Brynleigh was more than capable of keeping herself safe. She was a weapon, through and through.

Brynleigh smiled. "I'm capable of taking care of myself."

"I know you are, but it won't stop me from worrying," he said.

"Whether it's tonight, when you're at the safe house, in three days, when you're at the next rebel meeting, or just when you're sleeping. I cannot stop worrying about you any more than I can stop my lungs from drawing air."

Gods, he was good with words.

"I appreciate that," she murmured. "I want to get this over with. The sooner I can be done with Jelisette, the better."

Brynleigh's shadows were already jumpy.

"We are in agreement there." Ryker's brows furrowed, and he stood. "About that..."

His voice trailed off, and his gaze locked onto the chessboard in the corner.

He eventually said, "The Reunion."

Brynleigh frowned. "Excuse me?"

He helped her stand and drew her close, wrapping his arms around her.

She burrowed her face into his chest, inhaling his thunderstorm and bergamot scent.

"The rebels," Ryker spoke into her hair, his fingers gripping her tightly as if he were afraid she would disappear on him. "If they were going to attack again, they might choose the Reunion."

"Okay..." She wasn't entirely sure where he was going with this.

"If you planted seeds with Jelisette tonight, encouraging the rebels to attack during the live stream, we could entrap the Black Night." He kissed her forehead. "For once, we could be on the offensive."

Her eyes widened, understanding flooding through her. "I see."

It sounded incredibly dangerous, but she couldn't deny that the thought of getting ahead of the rebels was appealing.

Ryker's tone shifted into the analytical one he used when they played chess. "It'll be busy, and we could slip extra guards into the party without being noticed."

Nodding, Brynleigh wrapped her mind around his plan. "That... could work."

It was unsafe and potentially deadly, but it made sense.

As if he knew where her mind had gone, Ryker tightened his grip around her.

"I'll keep you safe, sweetheart. Nothing will happen to you under my watch. But if we can draw out the rebels..."

"This might be the leg up you need to defeat them." It was a good, solid strategy. If it worked, it would save lives.

He dipped his chin, clearly deep in thought. "I'll talk to some people about adding extra security. Maybe I'll see if—"

A resounding knock came from the front door, cutting him off.

Marlowe burst out of the kitchen where he'd been eating, his bark as loud as a drum.

"Ryker Elias Waterborn, open the door this instant!"

Brynleigh paled at the sound of her mother-in-law's voice.

"Fuck." Ryker glanced at the door. "Of all the times she could return from her trip, why now?"

Brynleigh wished she was surprised by the unfortunate timing, but she was a magnet for bad luck. Gods damn it all.

She had only had the displeasure of being in Tertia Waterborn's company twice—once at Waterborn House and once at the wedding—and quite frankly, that was enough for her.

She would rather step on a thousand tacks than deal with the water fae Representative tonight. Or ever again, if she was being completely honest.

Another knock. This one sounded like Tertia put her full force behind it.

"Let me in, son. The doorman confirmed you were here, and I won't leave until we speak."

Ryker rubbed his forehead and raised his voice. "Just a minute, Mother!"

Her response came less than a second later, her words as cold as ice as they swept through the apartment. "Don't you try to hide from me, Ryker. We will be speaking. Tonight."

Brynleigh had heard death threats that sounded warmer than her mother-in-law's voice.

Ryker looked simultaneously pained and exhausted as he kissed Brynleigh's cheek.

"You should probably go," he whispered. "I'll deal with her."

Thank all the gods.

"You don't mind?" Brynleigh asked, even as she drew shadows to her palms.

Ryker winced as his mother started banging on the door. "Not at all. Be safe. I'll be waiting for you."

Before he had gone to Sandhaven, those words would've sounded like a threat. Now, they warmed Brynleigh's heart.

Day by day, word by word, and action by action, the ocean that had once divided them was drying up.

Shrouded in shadows, she leaned over and brushed her lips over his. "Good luck, Ry."

Having previously been the recipient of Tertia Waterborn's ire, Brynleigh knew he needed it.

He smiled, but the expression didn't reach his eyes. "You, too, sweetheart."

Giving his hands one final squeeze, she let the shadows swallow her whole. The last thing she heard was Ryker saying, "Hello, Mother."

Once again, Brynleigh stood before her Maker.

The office seemed even creepier than before, the carpet redder, the walls tighter as she recounted the mission from the previous night, her hands clasped behind her back.

"Josef Longrun did not die with dignity," Brynleigh reported.

On the outside, she was calm and composed.

Inside, she was shivering. The air in the safe house was colder tonight than normal, and her shadows throbbed.

Brynleigh's stomach had twisted the moment she entered this place, and everything within her was screaming to leave. Her shadows throbbed, insisting danger was present.

She agreed with them. There was something wrong here. Something dangerous.

It was probably the ancient, deadly vampire sitting in front of her.

"That doesn't surprise me. Most men of his... caliber"—Jelisette's lip curled, revealing her sharp, deadly fangs—"do not walk into death's embrace with any form of honor."

For once, Brynleigh agreed with her Maker.

She'd been in this line of work long enough to know that evil people were often the most cowardly. They wept, moaned, and screamed when faced with the same horrors they inflicted upon their victims.

Isvana-damned bastards.

"Yes, ma'am." Brynleigh tucked a lock of hair behind her ear even though her stomach was cramping. "He lived a dishonorable life, and he died in the same manner."

"I see." Jelisette canted her head and studied her progeny.

She drummed her nails on the desk, the *tap, tap, tap* the only sound in the office.

Even though Brynleigh was used to her Maker's oddities, the knowledge that this behavior was somewhat normal didn't ease the tension coursing through her. Every part of her was on edge as minutes dragged on.

Brynleigh needed to leave. Quieting her instincts and forcing herself to remain in this place of death was becoming more difficult by the second.

Eventually, the drumming ceased.

Another long minute later, Jelisette placed her palms flat on the desk.

"Do you have anything else to report?" She studied her manicured nails.

Brynleigh's shadows thrummed, and she drew in a deep breath. "I had a thought. About the Representatives."

When Brynleigh had first arrived, her Maker had launched into a tirade about the ruling class. Jelisette's hatred of the Representatives seemed to be getting worse with each passing day.

Honestly, some of Jelisette's points made sense, but Brynleigh would never admit to that. She'd think about them later when she was safe.

Her Maker bristled, dragging up her gaze.

Darkness gleamed in Jelisette's eyes as she snarled, "What about them?"

Brynleigh's heart thundered. Her neck ached in remembrance of the last time she stood in this office, and tears rushed to her eyes as she recalled the sensation of death coming for her, but she forced those emotions away.

Even though she hated this place, she couldn't show that right now. Tears would be seen as weakness, and she couldn't break down in front of Jelisette.

"I'm sure many Representatives will be at the Reunion. I know there were several mentions of planning an attack for next month, but if we,"—Brynleigh fucking hated using that word and associating herself with the rebels—"attack the Reunion, it would be devastating."

"Oh? Do tell."

In the same monotone tone she'd used when describing Josef's death, Brynleigh laid out why this plan would work.

When she was done, she closed her mouth and waited. She ignored the creepy painting, ignored the sensation of death sweeping over her, ignored everything except her Maker.

Please let this work.

Brynleigh wanted to bring good news to her fae captain.

Ten excruciating minutes later, the older vampire nodded.

"That's... not a bad idea. I'd have to speak with Dimitri..." The drumming picked up, and a faraway look came over Jelisette's eyes. "Yes. I like this. Did you come up with this plan on your own?"

"Yes," Brynleigh lied.

A raised brow. "Good girl."

Shivers ran through Brynleigh at her Maker's praise, and her stomach churned. The need to leave was stronger than ever.

Jelisette waved her hand in the air. "You may go. I have an appointment. I trust you can see yourself out?"

"Of course." Thank Isvana, the first part of Brynleigh's plan was over. "Before I leave, could I grab a book from my room? I left it here before the Choosing."

"Go ahead." Her sire gathered shadows around herself. "I'll message you."

Maybe Brynleigh's luck was turning. Maybe the sensation of death was nothing but a cold breeze.

Maybe.

She didn't want to wait and find out. Brynleigh left, hurrying through the safe house before Jelisette could decide there was another task she needed her to do.

Brynleigh's room looked identical to the day she left for the Choosing, but even it had a sense of eeriness that had never been there before.

This space had never really felt like home, but now it was like it belonged to a stranger. The woman she had been before Ryker was gone.

Brynleigh shivered as she looked over the space, still holding those tears at bay.

She hadn't lied to Jelisette. There was a book she wanted to grab—two, in fact. One was a guide to the history of vampires from the Rose Empire up to modern times. Jelisette had gifted Brynleigh the book upon her Making.

The second was a history of the fae's Great Migration across the Indigo Ocean. They weren't riveting reads like *The Shadow and The Sparrow*, but she'd read them many times over the past six years.

Brynleigh grabbed both books off the desk and the small black case she kept in the drawer, stuffing all three items in a tote bag.

Slinging it over her shoulder, she went back the way she came. At the door, Brynleigh paused and took in the bedroom one last time. She didn't think she'd ever return.

This was her past, and Ryker was her future.

Part of her wished she could regret her time in this place. She certainly regretted that her Maker had used and betrayed her. She even regretted that she'd been planning to kill Ryker.

But Brynleigh couldn't find it in herself to wish that she'd never been Made. It was only because of her Making that she'd met her husband. She never would've been Selected to participate in the Choosing otherwise, nor would she and Ryker have fallen in love.

Now that they were together, she couldn't imagine a life without him.

No, she would never regret anything that had brought her to Ryker, except for Chavin's destruction. She would give anything to turn back the hands of time and save her family and all the others who perished that watery night.

But since that was impossible, Brynleigh would do the next best thing and focus on stopping the Black Night. Her family was beyond saving, but the rebels had shown that they didn't care about the cost of a few lives to get their point across. Every time they attacked, they put someone's mother or father, someone's brother or sister, or someone's loved one at risk.

Those nameless people, those families that were still intact, were the reason Brynleigh was still fighting.

Problematic as the Representatives were—and they were fucking problematic, she wasn't ignoring that—the rebels were worse. Their solutions relied on death and destruction.

Brynleigh might not have been a political scientist, but even she knew that wasn't the right way to encourage change.

No. The Black Night needed to be stopped. That's why she was here.

At the reminder of her purpose, Brynleigh straightened. She couldn't waste any more time. Jelisette could be back any second.

Slipping out the door to her old room, she paused in the hallway and extended her senses. If she were anywhere else, she'd cloak herself in shadows, but those wouldn't protect her from her Maker.

She didn't hear anything out of the ordinary, but her skin crawled all the same. The air was cold, and death waited around every corner.

She was alone... for now. Brynleigh had no way of knowing how long Jelisette's appointment would be.

Thanking Isvana for vampiric speed, Brynleigh blurred through the hallway, ending up at the door to Zanri's office in the blink of an eye. She jiggled the doorknob, testing it.

Locked.

She'd expected that, but part of her had hoped she'd be wrong. All the doors in the safe house were warded against shadows, so there was only one thing left to do.

Reaching into the tote bag, she withdrew the black lock-picking set Zanri had gifted her several years ago.

Brynleigh popped it open, thankful that the feline shifter had taught her this particular skill. Her first attempt at lock-picking had been laughably horrible, but she'd practiced tirelessly until she could open any lock in under a minute.

Holding her breath, Brynleigh quickly set to work. The goddess of the moon must have been smiling down on her because seconds later, the locks tumbled.

She rose to her feet, opening the door.

Zanri's woodsy scent slammed into her like a ton of bricks. It was strong from the hours he'd spent in here, but behind it were traces of something cold and off.

This space, more than any other in the safe house, made Brynleigh feel sick. Or maybe it was just the memories of Zanri's broken body in Moonwater Prison that made holding back her tears even harder.

Either way, Brynleigh couldn't shake the feeling of wrongness burrowing its way into her. It was in the air.

In the house.

In her soul.

Goosebumps pebbled on her arms, and she shuddered.

Wrong.

The hairs on the back of her neck prickled. The rest of the safe house had felt strange, but this...

This room felt like death warmed over.

Urgency pulsed through her veins, even as her entire body protested her presence here.

She had to move quickly.

Hoping Zanri hadn't lied, Brynleigh dropped her tools in her bag and entered the office. Ignoring her shadows' warnings, she slid the door shut, leaving it open just a crack so she could hear if anyone came.

It was time to find a cipher.

CHAPTER 27
Motherly Affection

Ryker's head was pounding mercilessly. This was no longer just a headache. That had come and gone an hour ago. Now, his brain was making a concerted effort to escape the confines of his skull through any means necessary.

Tertia had started yelling as soon as Ryker opened the door to greet her, and she hadn't stopped since. Her list of disappointments was longer than ever. Surprisingly—or perhaps not—she was upset about both his life choices and the fact that the rebels hadn't been stopped yet.

Apparently, Ryker was failing Tertia, the Representatives, and the Waterborn name all at once.

The only good thing was that a few minutes ago, Tertia had moved from the main apartment into the mud room.

Maybe she was planning on leaving soon.

Ryker leaned against the wall, rubbing his temples. He was fucking exhausted.

"Are you listening to me, son?" Tertia asked sharply.

"Yes, Mother," he said wearily. "You're not happy. I understand."

She hissed in a breath. The walls of the small mud room seemed to close in on them.

"No, I don't think you do. It was one thing for you to live in an apartment like a commoner with this *dog*." She glared disapprovingly at Marlowe, who sat obediently at Ryker's feet. "But it was another entirely for you to Choose a vampire who turned out to be a murderer. That was one step too far, even for you."

Ryker sighed but didn't respond. Arguing would only elongate Tertia's stay.

Reaching into her pocket, his mother withdrew a silk ivory scarf. She wrapped it around her neck, daintily tucking the edges into her black coat before she raised piercing brown eyes to Ryker.

"Of all the things I thought would happen after your Choosing, this wasn't one of them." Tertia's voice was as silky as her scarf, but there was nothing maternal about the way she spoke. "You will be a Representative one day, child."

As if he could ever forget about that. The mantle of his future position had hung on his shoulders from the moment of his birth.

"No one else knows what Brynleigh planned," Ryker ground out.

He'd worked hard to keep everything under wraps. Nikhail, Victor and his team, Myrrah, and a few other Representatives were the only ones who knew the truth.

Tertia's eyes narrowed. "For now. Do you think keeping things out of the press is easy? I've had enough trouble with your sister, and now you add *this* to my plate. Don't you love me at all?"

"I do, Mother." Somehow, Ryker spoke the truth.

It might not have been the same kind of love he had for his father, but he cared deeply for his mother, even with all her coldness.

"Then think of how this looks."

That's what it always came down to for Tertia. All she ever cared about was the public's perception of the illustrious Waterborn family.

When she had hidden River's involvement in the Incident and helped wipe all traces of Ryker online six years ago, it wasn't out of the kindness of her heart.

Ryker wasn't even sure his mother could express emotions like most people. She loved her family, but she showed it differently from Cyrus. Ryker's father had always been there for his children, always present, ready and willing to talk. Day in and day out, he'd been available to them.

Tertia was more of the "I will provide for you, but don't come talk to me about your feelings" type of parent.

Right now, Ryker didn't feel an ounce of affection from his mother, and he wanted her to leave.

Brynleigh would be back soon, and the last thing Ryker wanted was for Tertia to still be here when that happened. This already volatile situation would become ten times worse.

"I will, Mother." Pecking Tertia on her cold cheek, Ryker steered her towards the door. "Have a good night."

She frowned, and even though Ryker towered over her by a foot, she looked down her nose at him.

"That is an impossible task when one's children are such disappointments."

What a loving mother.

Unfortunately, Tertia wasn't done.

"Why did the Obsidian Sands not see fit to bless me with offspring who understand the value of their name and know how to act properly? Instead, I got you two." Her red lips curled into a hateful sneer. "The vampire-lover and the Cursed One."

Ryker bristled at his mother's term for River. It was one thing for River to call her power a curse, but it was another for their mother to use that term.

Staying silent was no longer an option.

"River trains every single day, Mother." Ryker gripped the door, wishing he could shove the Representative out of it and force her to leave. "You know she's worked tirelessly to keep things under control."

The temperature in the room plummeted as Tertia straightened her spine.

"Your sister trains because she knows I will not tolerate another blemish against the Waterborn name. Untamed, wild magic will not reside beneath my roof. Not when your father could be injured."

It took every ounce of restraint Ryker had accumulated in his entire life not to snarl at his mother.

"She's your *daughter*."

Did familial bonds mean nothing to her?

Sometimes, Ryker wished Cyrus wasn't the parent who had

contracted the Stillness. It was a horrible thought and would probably land Ryker in the pits of hell, but it was the truth.

Tertia narrowed her eyes, and the look in them would have made a lesser fae run for the hills.

"I'm well aware of that fact, Ryker, thank you. One does not simply *forget* they've given birth. It's a rather painful experience." She sniffed. "Some days, I wonder if procreating was even worth the effort of carrying on the Waterborn name."

Ryker growled.

"I'm sorry you feel that way, *Mother*." He nudged the door, hoping Tertia would get the hint. "I'll call you tomorrow."

Or not. He'd rather swim naked in the icy Black Sea for hours.

Thank all the gods, with a final huff and glare, Tertia left.

When the elevator doors closed, Ryker slumped against the wall. He ran his hand through his hair, shut his eyes, and groaned. That was, without a doubt, one of the most miserable conversations he'd ever had the displeasure of having with his mother.

He wasn't sure how long he remained there before a wet nose pressed against his hand.

Marlowe's black tail thumped enthusiastically, and he looked up at Ryker with wide, anticipation-filled eyes.

"Want to go outside, Marlie?" Ryker scratched the dog behind the ears.

Woof.

"You've got it."

A run was a good idea. Fresh air would clear his head, and hopefully, Brynleigh would be back by the time he returned.

He texted her to let her know he was taking out the dog and would be back soon. He ran his face under cold water, shook off the last remnants of his mother's visit, and changed into black running shorts and a pale blue T-shirt. It was cold outside, but he'd warm up quickly once he started moving.

Hooking Marlowe onto the leash, Ryker closed the door behind him. They jogged down the stairs, avoiding the elevator and the lobby in case Tertia was still lingering. He didn't even know why she had bothered to come to his apartment. He'd gotten her message loud and clear from the numerous emails, texts, and voicemails she'd left him over the last few weeks.

The only good thing about this was that, for once, River wasn't taking the brunt of their mother's anger.

Gray clouds hid the stars from view as Ryker and Marlowe slipped out the side door. The cool air pricked at his skin, and he shivered. A heavy mist hung in the air, warning of impending rain. His magic swirled as if it wanted to come out and play.

Another time.

The water fae slid wireless headphones into his ears, connected them to his phone, and dialed his sister's number.

As soon as it started ringing, he took off running down Center Street towards Eleyta Park. He and Marlowe always ran this familiar, comforting path. Three parks were within equal distance of Ryker's apartment, but he preferred this one. The trail was fenced, there was a small pond where dogs could swim, and pets were allowed off-leash.

He wasn't worried about waking up his sister—she was a night owl. Sure enough, she picked up on the third ring. "Hello?"

"Mom was here," Ryker informed her, his voice steady despite the pounding of his feet on the sidewalk.

"Ah." She sucked in a sharp breath. "I'm sure that was..."

"Delightful, as always." Ryker turned the corner, staying beneath the streetlights as Eleyta Park came into view at the end of the road. "But it's okay, she left. How are you?"

"I'm... alright."

It was evident by her tone that she wasn't telling him the whole story.

"You can tell me," he gently prodded. "Is it Dad?"

By the Black Sands, he hoped their father was alright. If the deities that ruled this continent cared about them, they would allow Cyrus to live. Their family couldn't handle another catastrophe right now.

"No, he's stable, and the meds are working." River exhaled. "I've just been... worried. I don't know. I have a bad feeling."

Ryker slowed. "What do you mean?"

"I can't explain it. It's not my magic," she hurried to say. "But I feel... uneasy. Like something is coming."

Ryker frowned. “Maybe it’s nothing.”

“Maybe.” But it didn’t sound like River agreed with him. “I’ll mention it in my prayers tomorrow. I think Dyna is helping Dad.”

River’s faith in the goddess of life and healing was sweet, but Ryker thought the medicine and round-the-clock care were the reasons their father was improving. He didn’t say that, though. He didn’t want to break his sister’s spirit, especially since he knew how much she cared for the fae religion.

“How’s school?” he asked instead.

“Good.” River made a sound of amusement. “I can’t wait to be done, though. It feels like I’ve been learning forever. I want to *help* people. I can’t wait to start my internship next year.”

He smiled and led Marlowe across the street. “I know you do, River. You’ll be an amazing doctor.”

She hitched a breath. “Do you think so?”

Even though Ryker couldn’t see his sister, he imagined she was drawing her lip ring through her teeth.

“I know it. You’ll be an incredible addition to any medical team. I’m so proud of you.”

If Tertia refused to say the words, Ryker would say them twice as often.

“I hope so. This week, we learned how to treat Alphas and Omegas...” River continued, telling Ryker all about the werewolf medicine they covered this week in her classes.

He listened intently and asked a few questions as he entered the park. He passed three more runners before reaching the enclosed dog run.

Unlocking the gate, he slipped inside with Marlowe. The dog bounded with excited energy. Ryker unhooked the leash, and Marlowe raced away, a series of joyful barks filling the air.

Ryker followed, chuckling at his dog’s enthusiasm. This was exactly what he needed.

He fell into a steady run, the ground absorbing the sound of his footfalls as he pumped his arms and legs. Running had always cleared Ryker’s mind, and the stress from his mother’s visit diminished with every passing minute.

"How was training this morning?" Ryker asked when River took a breath.

They never outright spoke of the Incident, and now that Ryker knew Brynleigh's family had died at his sister's hand...

Well, the situation was fucking complicated.

He knew one thing for certain: he would never tell River how Brynleigh had lost her family. She already felt enough guilt for what she'd done without having to put a face on the grief and devastation she'd caused.

"It went well. I've got my magic under control." River inhaled. "And actually..."

"Yes?" he prompted.

"I think I'm going to Mature soon." He could hear the smile in her voice. "I can feel it. My power is growing, but it doesn't seem as wild as before. It feels like I can control it better. Does that make sense?"

Hope sparked in Ryker's chest, and a grin spread across his face. "It does make sense, and that's fucking amazing news."

He felt lighter than ever as he ran down the trail.

Like most species that called the Republic of Balance their home, fae Matured in their twenties. Not only did Maturation extend lifetimes, but it also increased power and control. When River was fully Mature, managing her magic would be easier than ever. While Ryker would never stop worrying about his sister entirely, this was a boon they desperately needed.

After ensuring that she would tell him the moment she Matured, their conversation shifted toward the tattoos River wanted to get after graduation. She had an entire sleeve planned, and Ryker was pretty certain that, given enough time, his sister would cover every available inch of skin in ink.

Their mother hated tattoos, but Ryker was sure that was just a coincidence.

By the time River finished describing the floral design she planned on getting on her lower back, the mist had picked up and turned into a steady rain. Ryker bid his sister farewell, reminding her how much he loved her and how proud he was of her before hanging up.

Switching to the upbeat playlist he usually played while he ran, Ryker whistled for Marlowe.

Moments later, the dog bounded out of the forest, his black fur plastered to his sides and his tongue lolling out of his mouth. His front paws were brown and caked in dirt, and Ryker knew that somewhere in the park, a hole the size of Marlowe's head now existed.

"Gods above, you sure know how to make a mess, don't you?" He scratched the dog behind the ears.

Marlowe barked in agreement, his tail wagging. He looked delighted by the mess he'd made.

Chuckling, Ryker reached within himself and drew out some water. It flowed from his hands and ran over the pup in gentle streams, washing the mud away until black, silky fur was the only thing that remained.

"There, good as new." Ryker released his magic, attached the leash, and led Marlowe out of the park. "Come on, boy. Let's go see if your mom is home."

And if Brynleigh was hurt, Jelisette de la Point would pay.

CHAPTER 28

I'll Always be Here for You

By the time Ryker and Marlowe returned to the apartment building, the rain had become a full-blown thunderstorm. They were both soaked to the bone and despite the water magic running through Ryker's veins, he was freezing.

A hot shower was definitely in his future.

Thank the gods; his phone was waterproof. He could dump it in the Emerald Sea, and it would come out unscathed. It was one of the many technologies the fae had brought during the Great Migration.

Although it was almost midnight, Karson Yellowcrest, one of the concierges, sat bright-eyed and bushy-tailed at his post behind the front desk. The human was in his late forties or early fifties with salt-and-pepper hair, russet skin, and a kind smile.

"Hello, Captain," Karson said. "Got caught in the rain, did you?"

Ryker ran a hand through his hair, grimacing as it came away soaked. "We certainly did."

Marlowe shook his coat, spraying water droplets everywhere and accentuating Ryker's point. Some people might've been upset by the dog's actions, but the concierge merely chuckled.

"Any mail for me, Karson?" Ryker asked.

"Let me check." A line furrowed the concierge's brow as he ducked beneath his desk. A hum filled the air before he popped up. "Yep! This was delivered for you earlier today."

Ryker crossed the lobby and took the envelope. Golden paper was crisp beneath his fingers, the Republic's emblem was stamped on the back, and it was addressed to *Mr. and Mrs. Waterborn.*

"Thank you." He smiled.

"Any time, sir." The concierge leaned over his desk and raised a brow. "By the way, when will I get to meet that lovely wife of yours? My husband and I watched the Choosing religiously, and we were cheering for you both the whole time."

Ryker bit his lip. He didn't want to make any assumptions about whether he and Brynleigh were ready for public appearances. It was like they were pottery that had been smashed and glued back together. They were in one piece—or at least, getting there—but a single wrong move could shatter them if they weren't careful.

In the end, he told the concierge he would confer with Brynleigh and get back to him.

"Of course, I understand. Thank you, Captain. Either way, we'll be watching the Reunion. We can't wait to see all the couples together once again."

"It will be an event to remember," Ryker promised.

Especially if they could stop the Black Night before they hurt anyone else.

A few minutes later, Ryker and Marlowe exited the elevator and entered the apartment. Ryker kicked off his wet shoes and placed the letter on the stand he kept in the entryway for that purpose.

"Brynleigh?" He unhooked Marlowe's leash, pushing open the door to the main apartment. "Are you here?"

No response. The apartment was too quiet. The silence pressed up against him, constricting his lungs.

Shouldn't she be back by now?

Worry nibbled at his mind, and he grabbed a towel from the laundry basket sitting by the door. Running it through his hair, he debated pulling up the tracking app. He wasn't usually anxious, but as was normal when it came to Brynleigh, she turned his world on its head.

Thank all the fucking gods, by the time he finished toweling his hair, shadows pooled on the ground.

Brynleigh materialized a few feet in front of him.

Ryker scanned her for injuries. Golden strands were slipping out of her ponytail, and her eyes were heavy, but she appeared uninjured.

He exhaled a sigh of relief, satisfied that his vampire was healthy and in one piece.

"How did it go?"

"As expected." She shrugged. "Jelisette is never delightful, and tonight was no exception."

His gaze snagged on the bag slung over her shoulder. "Is that..."

She held the bag, twisting the handle through her fingers. "It is."

"Great." Except, it didn't seem great. An air of heaviness that hadn't been there before hung around his wife. "Where was it?"

Brynleigh chewed on her lip. "The cipher was in the safe, and I had to break into it. I hadn't expected it, but I should have. Why would something this important be kept out in the open? That's what took me so long."

And Jelisette could have found her at any time. Ryker's heart raced as he realized how close Brynleigh had been to death.

Relief flooded through Ryker, and he gripped the bag. Brynleigh was home, she was safe, and they had the cipher.

Now that she stood in front of him, he allowed himself to think about what this really meant. Between the book, the cipher, and setting a trap for the rebels at the Reunion, they were finally getting somewhere.

Maybe soon, they could put an end to all this madness. Close out the deal and just live their lives as they'd always intended.

"Thank you, Brynleigh." The words weren't enough to properly convey Ryker's feelings, but he needed to say them all the same. He sensed something was still wrong, though. "Are you okay?"

Her mouth pinched, and she shuddered.

"I'm just glad it's over. Zanri's office was... creepy." Shadows passed through her eyes. "The whole place was creepy."

"But you're safe," Ryker repeated, needing to hear her confirm it.

"Yes, I am." Brynleigh twisted the bracelet around her wrist, and her gaze dropped. "It was... I don't know if I can go back. I don't want to. Death lives in that place, and I'm... scared."

The last word was a whisper, and her eyes widened as it slipped out, as if she hadn't meant to say it.

The admission shook Ryker to his core. He'd never heard his fierce wife admit to being afraid before.

He hated that she had been forced to return to that place because of him. When he'd made the deal with Myrrah, he'd been so blinded by his grief that he hadn't stopped to consider what going back to her Maker would do to Brynleigh.

Ryker wished he could rip the tracking bracelet off Brynleigh's wrist and fling it into the depths of the ocean, but he couldn't. He couldn't even promise that she'd never have to return to the safe house. It wasn't up to him.

He'd made a deal to get her out of prison, and now they were both tied to it.

Tomorrow, Ryker would turn the book and the cipher over to the army's code breakers.

He and Brynleigh had done their part in finding the evidence. Hopefully, between the coded book and the inside information on the rebels, it would be enough.

Even though Ryker didn't have the power to end the arrangement, he refused to stand here and let his vampire suffer on her own. Placing the tote on a nearby table, he opened his arms.

"Come here, sweetheart."

He wasn't sure she would take him up on the offer, and every second stretched on until she launched herself towards him. He caught her, stumbling back a step as her weight settled against him.

For a very long moment, neither of them spoke.

She gripped him, and he held her, relishing the feeling of her body against his. Her scent of night-blooming roses washed over him, and he pressed his cheek against her head.

"I've got you, love," he murmured.

The endearment slipped out, but it felt *right*.

She burrowed her face against his neck, her fingers tightened in his shirt, and she trembled.

She was... crying.

Oh gods.

Each tear slipping from her eyes was a tiny dagger shoved beneath his skin. He hated that she was crying, hated that she was hurting.

Kissing the top of her head, Ryker whispered, "I'll always be here for you."

Those three weeks where he'd lived without her had been awful, and he would rather die than let them go through that again.

As he held his vampire close, letting her cry out her frustrations and fears, Ryker made a silent vow. No matter what obstacles came their way or who else they'd have to go up against, he would never let anyone tear them apart. Not the rebels, the Chancellor, Valentina Rose, or Tertia.

They would work through their problems, finish bridging their brokenness, and be stronger than ever when they reached the other side.

Their relationship had been a battlefield, but they would emerge victorious from this war.

Ryker lost track of time as he held his wife. He rubbed her back, murmuring quiet nonsense until her tears slowly gave way to deep, shuddering breaths.

Still, he held her. He would hold her as long as she needed. There was something incredibly powerful about the way this strong, fierce vampire was allowing him to comfort her. He wasn't sure he deserved the honor, but he would work for it.

Eventually, Brynleigh pulled back. She sniffled and plucked at his shirt, making a face.

"You're all wet." She glanced down at herself, where the center of her sweater was noticeably darker. "And I am, too."

Ryker had honestly forgotten all about it. "Yeah. Marlie and I went for a run."

She frowned, and her gaze swept over him. "Things didn't go well with your mother, did they? I'm sorry, I should've asked earlier."

"Don't worry about it. You were upset, and that was more important. Besides, Mother is... testy."

Brynleigh's lips tightened. "She's upset because of me."

It wasn't a question.

By the Obsidian Sands, Ryker wished he could lie. Just once, so he could shield his wife from this pain.

"Not just you," he hedged. "She also thinks I've failed her because I'm not the perfect son she expects me to be."

Tertia's standards were impossibly high.

Even if Ryker had Chosen Valentina Rose—which would've been a monumental blunder—he wouldn't have been able to live up to his mother's expectations. Sooner or later, he would've made a mistake.

"I see." The sigh that left Brynleigh's lips confirmed she understood. "And does she know the whole story of...?"

The rest of her sentence was unspoken, but he clearly heard it. *What I planned to do?*

"She does. She found out the day she called me when you were first released." His heart clenched, recalling the utter agony of those first few days. "I tried to keep it under wraps, but keeping things from her is practically impossible."

Ryker had learned that many times over when he was a teenager. The first time he snuck out of the house and went to a party, someone called Tertia in the middle of the night.

She'd shown up, eyes blazing and magic at her fingertips, and dragged him out of the gathering at three in the morning.

Brynleigh's eyes hardened, and she stiffened in Ryker's arms.

Did he say something wrong?

The air in the apartment shifted, and Brynleigh stepped out of his embrace.

"It's because she's a Representative. You can't hide things from them. This is *exactly* what Jelisette was talking about earlier."

Ryker stiffened. "Your Maker isn't sane. You know that."

That was the wrong thing to say. Instead of calming Brynleigh down, the words seemed to incense her.

"No, but even a broken clock is right twice a day." Brynleigh's voice was cool, and shadows slipped from her palms. "It always comes down to this."

"What does?"

"This. Us." She waved between them. "Every single fucking time I think I can forget about the things dividing us, something else comes up. There's the Representatives and everyone else."

Ryker frowned. "I know there's some division, but—"

"*Some*? No. 'Some' implies a relatively small amount. There's a canyon standing between the Representatives and the rest of the world."

He reached for her. "Brynleigh—"

She ducked away from him, her wings appearing and curling around her protectively. "No, don't. Not right now."

His heart ached. "What's wrong?"

"What's wrong?" She laughed bitterly, shaking her head. "This is what Jelisette was saying. The Representatives rule this land, and obviously, I don't agree with the rebels, but something needs to change."

On that, they were in agreement.

Ryker slowly nodded, picking his words with care. "So... what do you suggest?"

A drawn-out moment passed as Brynleigh studied Ryker. Her eyes softened, the anger shifting and her lips slanting into a frown.

"I don't know." Sad eyes met his. "I just know that everything is out of balance. Life isn't fair."

"I know that."

"Do you?" She canted her head, and a long moment stretched between them. "Then tell me, Ryker, what would've happened to River if she hadn't been your mother's daughter?"

A protective growl rumbled through him despite himself. "Don't bring my sister into this."

"She's already in it," Brynleigh said softly. "She's been in it since she destroyed my town six years ago."

Ryker stepped back. "Brynleigh, I don't want to—"

"Tell me," she insisted softly. "What would've happened to River if she had destroyed Chavin and hadn't been tied to a Representative?"

His hackles rose. Why was she pushing him like this? His fae instincts urged him to protect his family at all costs, and he balled his fists.

"Don't do this. Don't make me talk about this."

Of course, she didn't listen.

"It's a simple question," Brynleigh whispered sadly. "What would've happened to River if she hadn't been related to a Representative?"

"Why does it matter?"

"Because we need to discuss it." Her eyes met his. "We can't just ignore it forever. Otherwise, it'll just grow and fester between us."

Really? Because he'd done a pretty good job of not thinking about this over the past six years.

His gut churned, and he shook his head. He didn't want to go down this path, didn't want to think about these things. It wasn't that he was unaware of the consequences.

No, the problem was Ryker was all too aware of them. He didn't need any help conjuring this specific scenario because he wasn't some random citizen. He understood the inner workings of the Republic's judicial system.

"Tell me, Ryker," his wife whispered. "What would've happened?"

His heart beat was so loud that he could barely hear his thoughts. He knew what she wanted him to say. The truth was, he'd always known what would've happened to River had their mother not been able to help with the fallout from the Incident.

But to know something and to speak it into existence were two very different things.

The words rose in his throat. They were on the tip of his tongue but got stuck.

He didn't want to say them.

Six years ago, he had convinced himself that everything he did was for River's own good—and he still believed that. He had made reparations for the Incident as best he could. He spent hours and hours training River so nothing like this would ever happen again. He poured an indecent sum of money into flood relief and storm prevention.

He did his fucking best to help fix things.

But this?

He'd never gone down this path. Never allowed himself to think about the way things might have turned out had their mother not been a Representative.

Brynleigh was still silently staring at him, still waiting for him to answer.

His chest squeezed tighter and tighter. The walls in the apartment were closing in on him. His heart galloped in his chest. He raked his hand through his damp hair, but it did little to quell the unease that had taken up residence deep within him.

That onyx gaze, filled with darkness, shadows, and the night itself, held his as minutes dragged on.

Eventually, Ryker couldn't take the weight of her stare anymore.

"I know what would've happened to her," he said gruffly.

Brynleigh's gaze softened further. "Tell me."

He didn't want to. He didn't want to confront this truth. And yet, he couldn't stop the words from slipping from his lips.

"They would've fucking prosecuted her for her crimes," he half-whispered, half-hissed, his heart thundering. "Is that what you wanted me to say? Do you want me to admit that being related to a Representative is the only reason River isn't rotting in a gods-damned prohiberis-lined cell?"

His nostrils flared, and he balled his fists. "Do you want me to say that my baby sister, who was barely more than a fucking *child*, is only free because of our mother's influence?"

Every. Word. Hurt.

Every syllable made his chest ache.

Drawing breath was like breathing shards of glassy death.

He moved closer to Brynleigh, looming over her. Her wings spread behind her, flaring as he pressed her against the wall.

"You're upset," she whispered.

"Of course I am!"

She forced this out of him.

His water magic was a swirling storm churning in his veins, moments away from bursting like a geyser out of him. The temperature dropped, and he flexed his fingers.

Mere inches separated them.

His chest heaved, and his arms bracketed the wall above Brynleigh's head. He looked down at her.

Why wasn't she speaking? Why were her eyes searching his?

"Is that what you wanted?" he half-yelled, half-begged, needing her to speak. "Tell me!" He drew ragged breath after ragged fucking breath. "Is that the truth you wanted to hear?"

His heart hurt. His head hurt. All of him hurt.

Silver lined Brynleigh's eyes, and she dipped her head.

"Yes," she murmured. "I wanted you to admit that the Representatives are inherently above everyone else and that life in the Republic of Balance is unfair."

His nostrils flared, and his chest heaved.

"You married the son of a Representative. One day, I will take my mother's place," he reminded her, biting out the words. "Did you forget that?"

Slowly, her head moved left, then right. She could break his hold in a heartbeat, but she didn't.

"I didn't marry you *because* your mother is a Representative, Ry." A tear ran down Brynleigh's cheek, and her voice was so soft that he had to strain to hear the words. "I married you in spite of it. I Chose you for *you*. Not for her position. I love *you*."

A long, never-ending moment went by as they stared at each other. Chests heaving. Hearts pounding.

Universes were formed and destroyed during that time. Stars were birthed. The planets spun round and round. Babies were born, and the elderly Faded. Storms raged and calmed.

None of it carried even a drop of significance.

The only thing that mattered was the woman in front of him.

Ryker drew in a deep breath, and then, did he the first thing that came to mind.

He kissed her.

This wasn't a gentle meeting of their mouths or a slow, languid caress. This kiss was fire. It was passion, ardor, and anger all mixed in a burning embrace.

It was hurt and forgiveness, pain and passion, sorrow and joy.

It was fucking *everything*.

This was nothing like their first kiss or those stolen, timid touches during the Choosing.

Those people, that picture-perfect couple, no longer existed. Maybe they never had. Hurt and pain lay between them… but so did truth, honesty, and love.

Their mouths warred for attention.

Brynleigh nipped his lip.

He moaned.

Ryker ran his tongue across the seam of her mouth, and she opened for him. He tasted her, and gods above, he almost came right there.

This was the most passionate embrace of his entire gods-damned life. He desired this vampire unlike anyone else he'd ever met. His cock strained against his shorts, his blood pumped through his veins, and every part of him wanted her.

Needed her.

Keeping one arm on the wall above her head, he threaded his other hand behind her neck. He angled her head just so, tilting her so he could properly devour her.

And she let him.

A moan slipped from her lips, and he swallowed it with his mouth.

Her hands fisted in his damp shirt, and she tugged him even closer. The unspoken message was crystal clear.

More.

By the Sands, Ryker would give her what she was asking for. It wasn't a hardship. This was everything he'd wanted since he first heard her voice during the Choosing.

Every stitch of clothing was far too great of a barrier.

They kissed, becoming a tangle of lips, tongues, and teeth.

Brynleigh sucked on his bottom lip, and he groaned. He released her neck, cradled her bottom, and lifted her off the floor.

She wrapped her legs around him, rubbing her core against his hardened length.

"I want you, Ry," she moaned, retracting her wings. "I haven't stopped wanting you."

The words were permission, an unleashing, and a summoning. They were everything Ryker had ever wanted to hear.

A growl rumbled through his chest as he reclaimed her lips, turned from the wall, and strode to the bedroom.

CHAPTER 29

You're Going to Be the Death of Me

How in the world had they ended up here?

One moment, Brynleigh was pushing Ryker to accept the truth about Representatives, and the next, their mouths were fused in a passionate embrace. A fire had ignited in her core when his lips touched hers.

More.

Desire had her clinging to him, her legs hooked around his waist as he carried her to the bedroom.

She hadn't been in here since her first night in the apartment.

The moment Ryker crossed the threshold, his thunderstorm and bergamot scent slammed into her, increasing her desire tenfold.

She wanted this—she wanted him.

Brynleigh belonged here, with him. There was nowhere else in the world she'd rather be, no one else she'd rather spend time with.

Her shadows sang in her veins, and her entire body ached for him.

"I need you," she gasped against Ryker's mouth, grinding against his impressive length.

She'd never needed anyone so badly in her life.

Kicking the door shut, he carried her to the middle of the room.

From her peripheral vision, she made out the edges of the mattress behind her.

His chest heaved as he lifted his lips from hers, and he gruffly said, "Let go, sweetheart."

Once, she would've questioned whether she could trust this fae. Once, she would've berated herself for breaking all the rules to be with him.

No longer. She was free from her rules, and her heart belonged to him.

She trusted him.

Brynleigh gasped as that realization hit her just as strong as his scent had moments ago. The last bit of water that had divided them dried up, leaving nothing separating them.

As she unhooked her legs and released her grip on his shirt, she smiled. The mattress was a soft cloud when she landed on it.

The moon peeked through the clouds, lining Ryker's body in silver as he gazed upon her.

Fuck, he was stunning.

Reddish-brown damp hair framed his face. Beautiful chocolate eyes studied her. There was a new depth to his gaze that hadn't been there before, but if anything, it made him more alluring. Not that he needed any help. He was so gods-damned handsome, this husband of hers.

Her eyes traveled lower.

Ryker's shirt clung to him like a second skin, accentuating his muscles and the hard planes of his chest. Her gaze dipped lower still, past the waistband of his shorts. She paused on the evidence of his arousal, unable to stifle the small moan that rose through her.

Knowing he wanted her as much as she did him sent a rush of warmth through her. She pressed her thighs together, achingly empty.

Ryker noticed the direction of her gaze and smirked.

Those fucking dimples made another appearance. Without them, he was a handsome fae. Too handsome, if she was honest. But when those dimples showed up, she was rendered completely and utterly helpless. Add in the sight of his elongated canines, a marker of his fae descent, and a thrill raced through her.

Her fangs throbbed in her gums, echoing the desire pulsing through her.

Back in The Pit, she never thought she'd be with Ryker again, let alone experience another moment like the one they'd shared on their wedding night.

Somehow, this felt better than their first night tonight. They'd been through hell and back; now, nothing was between them.

No more lies. No betrayal. No revenge plots.

Just... them.

Husband and wife.

Fae and vampire.

Chosen partners.

It felt *good*. Brynleigh was able to be wholly and completely herself with Ryker. He knew everything about her, every dark secret, every fear she'd ever had. Nothing was keeping them apart.

Freedom was sweet on her tongue, and she wanted to drown in it. In him.

Reaching up, she tugged on the hem of his shirt. "Take this off."

She wanted to gaze upon every inch of him and commit him to memory.

Storms darkened his eyes, and he licked his lips. "Would you like that?"

"Yes," she breathed, not even caring that desperation leaked into her tone. "I need to see you."

She could have sworn thunder boomed outside as his hand slipped behind his neck, but she didn't dare look out the window. Her gaze was locked on him as he pulled his shirt over his head with one smooth tug. The fabric glided up, revealing the sculpted plains of his stomach.

Brynleigh pushed herself onto her elbows, not bothering to hide her intrigue as he dropped the garment on the ground.

Every inch of him was fucking perfection. It was as though the gods had sculpted him by hand.

Ryker was a gorgeous fae male... and he was hers. Her wedding band marked him as such, but she didn't need a piece of jewelry to know he belonged to her.

For as much as she was admiring him, he was studying her. His eyes trailed over every part of her like she was an exotic creature, and he was memorizing her for further study. That kind of stare would've made her want to kill anyone else, but coming from him, it made her feel loved.

The scent of their mutual desire filled the air as he stepped towards her. His hands landed on her hips, and he moved her to the middle of the bed. She didn't fight him as he leaned over her. His left hand hit the mattress, supporting his weight as his right one trailed over her still-clothed stomach.

That small touch was enough to send bolts of need racing through her.

Brynleigh gasped, her breaths coming in short bursts. Had she been on fire before? Now, she was an inferno, burning up from the inside out.

His teasing touch was far too light as it trailed down her stomach over her sweater to the waistband of her leggings. It took everything she had not to react as he hooked a finger in the elastic.

"Like what you see, little vampire?" Ryker raised a knowing brow, that smirk still dancing on his handsome lips.

"Very much so," she replied honestly.

She wasn't sure she could've lied now, even if she wanted to.

He flattened his hand on her stomach, his thumb achingly close to her clit.

His lips brushed hers, the kiss maddeningly brief. "Me, too."

She didn't have time to mourn the lack of Ryker's mouth on hers because he kneeled at the edge of the bed and tugged on her top.

He asked, "Do you like this sweater?"

Such an odd question to ask at a moment like this. She frowned. "I mean, as much as I like most of my clothes."

It was neither here nor there. She wasn't all that involved in fashion. Not like Sarai had been.

"Good to know." A twinkle entered his eyes. "Can I take it off?"

"Please." She lifted her arms above her head, but he chuckled darkly.

Taking hold of the neckline with both hands, he shifted his weight so his legs straddled her on either side. He leaned over and kissed her, his firmness resting in the apex of her still-clothed thighs. She gasped as he pressed against her.

A low chuckle rumbled against her mouth, and a loud *rip* filled the room. Startled, she made a sound of protest, but he swallowed the noise with his mouth. He slid the scraps of her sweater out from beneath her and tossed them aside. He pulled off her leggings and panties, and his shorts quickly followed.

She didn't have time to admire his naked moonlit figure before he returned to his position, his head dipping as he kissed her jaw. She gasped, pressing herself closer to him.

More. She needed more.

"I missed you." Ryker kissed her neck. "Every night, I wanted you." A trail of searing kisses went across her collarbone. "You haunted my dreams and my nightmares." Kiss, kiss, kiss. "I've never stopped needing you."

He covered her in kisses, tasting her as though he was starving and had never eaten in his life. Every time he lifted his lips from her flesh, he told her how much he wanted her. Needed her. Cared for her.

How he would take care of her from now until the end of their days. Again and again and again, he devoured her with kisses until she was a writhing mess beneath him.

When Brynleigh felt like she would die from the fire inside her, Ryker cupped her breasts. He rolled her nipples beneath her thumbs, his gaze dark as it met hers.

"You're mine," he told her before sucking a nipple into his mouth.

She arched her back, a strangled cry rising as he played with her other breast.

Oh gods.

When she didn't reply, he released her nipple and rested his chin on her chest. His eyes flashed with that same possessiveness she'd glimpsed on their wedding day. "Whose are you?"

"Yours," she gasped.

"Good girl." He rewarded her by taking her other nipple in his mouth.

She moaned as he licked and sucked as though his life depended on it. On and on and on he went, tasting her.

Every gasp, every moan, every movement seemed to spur him on. He didn't stop, though. Not until she was a desperate puddle beneath him, begging for more.

Ryker was playing with her. The audacity. She could sense his playfulness in every kiss, every nip, every time he ground his hips against hers, his cock just outside of where she desperately needed it.

He wasn't the only one capable of playing games. There was no doubt he wanted her—but would he let her take control?

She'd find out.

Ryker moved on from her breasts and was pressing languid kisses over her stomach, slowly moving towards her damp core when she reached for her shadows.

Those dark wisps that were her vampiric birthright flooded from her palms. In a smooth movement, Brynleigh hooked her legs around his waist and flipped them around. Shadows coated the bedroom floor as she straddled him.

His eyes widened, but his expression showed no fear or anger as he looked over her. "You released your wings again."

He reached out to touch them, but she quickly snapped them back. Touching wings was a delicate intimacy she'd never shared with anyone, and she wanted to remain in control.

For now.

"I did." Brynleigh bent and kissed him. "Do you like them?"

His gaze swept over them. "They're beautiful, just like you."

"If you're good, I'll take you flying one day," she said cheekily.

A smirk danced on those lips, and he thrust his hips upwards.

"Oh, sweetheart." Ryker's hands landed on her upper thighs. "You have no idea how good I can be. Let me show you."

The last words were barely more than a growl, and Brynleigh realized she was rapidly losing control of the situation. She'd flipped them for a reason, but she was having trouble remembering what that was.

"Maybe later. I have plans for you." She rolled her hips over his length experimentally.

His tip rubbed her clit, and she gasped, clinging to his shoulders before doing it again. Waves of pleasure shot through her.

Ryker groaned, his head falling back on the mattress and his hands leaving her thighs. "Fuck, little vampire. You're going to be the death of me."

Maybe it was the fact that Ryker looked like he was on the brink of losing control, or perhaps it was the way his hands grappled at the sheets as she rubbed wantonly against him, but Brynleigh felt like a powerful goddess of the night.

They were alone; the barriers between them were gone, and this was *right*.

Fanning out her wings behind her, she kissed him as her hands traveled over his bare flesh. She never lingered in one place too long, wanting to make him come undone.

Besides, she had a lot of missed time to make up for.

Eventually, he captured her wrists, stopping their tantalizing trail across his stomach.

"I need you," he groaned.

Hearing him confess his desire was doing wonders for her self-esteem.

She shifted her hips over his length, letting her wetness coat him. "How badly do you want me?"

"I would give anything to be inside you right now," he admitted.

More shadows flooded from her palms, and she spread her wings. Lifting her hips, she leaned forward and kissed him. He tasted like everything she'd ever desired, and she'd never get enough of this.

Reaching between them, Brynleigh took his cock in her hand.

A mangled groan rumbled through his chest. She drank in the sound, her fangs aching with need.

Isvana help her, but she loved that he was reacting like this because of *her*. She stroked him several times before lowering herself onto his length. The moment his tip entered her, she threw back her head and moaned.

This was even better than she'd remembered.

Pain and pleasure surged through her as she took him inch by inch, stretching around him. Her eyes fluttered shut, and the pain soon disappeared as she took him to the hilt.

"Oh, gods," she breathed, adjusting to his size.

Ryker reached up and brushed a hand down her cheek. "There are no gods here, love. Just me and you."

Once, she would've waited and let her body adjust to his size. Once, she would've been gentler. But after everything they'd been through, she couldn't wait.

Their eyes met, and through some unspoken command, they moved as one.

She gripped his shoulders.

His hands came to her hips, his thumbs stroking her flesh as she rode him.

"I love you," she whispered, her back arching as he thrust his hips upwards and met her movements. "So fucking much."

Love was a difficult thing, she'd learned. It was possible to fall in love without ever seeing the other person—the Choosing had made that perfectly clear. It was even possible to fall in love with the person you were supposed to kill.

But love without trust? It was dangerous. Deadly, even. It could destroy someone from the inside out. It was too close to hate and anger. She and Ryker had hovered there for far too long.

No longer.

Now, they were stronger than before. She hadn't even known that was possible. He'd proven to her that he would be there for her, that he would keep her safe, and that she was more than an asset to him.

He was hers as much as she was his.

His eyes darkened. "I love you, too."

The words were exactly what she needed to hear. Knowing he could take whatever she gave him, Brynleigh abandoned the last shreds of her control.

There was nothing gentle or slow about the way she moved. Her wings spread behind her, and darkness slipped from her palms. This wasn't a tryst meant to appease physical aches, nor was it the lovemaking of their wedding night.

This was a claiming, an apology, and forgiveness all wrapped up in one.

With every rise and fall of her hips, every gasp and moan and sound of pleasure that came from her, that trust strengthened.

She drew closer and closer to her release. She hovered on the precipice, her entire body coiled in eager anticipation.

"More," she gasped. "I need more."

Ryker's gaze swept over hers, and he nodded. In a matter of moments, he lifted her hips and was out from under her. She barely had time to mourn the emptiness inside her before he drew up behind her. He kissed the back of her neck, his hands trailing over her bottom.

"You might want to hold onto something, love." There was a dark promise in his voice that she desperately wanted to explore.

She grabbed the headboard seconds before his hands landed on her hips. Not even a heartbeat later, he lined his cock up at her entrance and thrust into her.

Stars exploded in her vision from the new angle.

This.

This was exactly what she needed.

He held her hip with one hand, his other trailing over her wings as he drove into her.

His cock hit that perfect spot, and she cried out. Everything else faded away except for the fae behind her.

She was his, and he was hers.

And when Ryker dragged his canines over her neck and growled, "Come for me," she did.

She fell over the cliff, pleasure running through her like a tsunami, and she screamed his name. His own release followed moments later, his groans of pleasure music to her ears.

He held her close through the waves of pleasure, murmuring sweet nothings as they came down from the high together.

Eventually, she released the headboard.

Ryker left the bedroom long enough to get a damp washcloth, and she retracted her wings while he was gone. She was tired, and her body was limp and sore in all the right places.

He returned, a soft smile dancing on his face. He crawled over to her, gently washing between her legs before placing the sweetest kiss on her lips.

"I love you so much," he whispered, throwing the washcloth into the laundry bin.

Brynleigh snuggled against him, letting his warmth seep into her. "Until the end of time?"

He chuckled, drawing the covers over them both.

"Forever," he promised.

A single word had never sounded so good.

He kissed her forehead. "Sleep, love."

She did.

CHAPTER 30
I Can't Lose You Again

A high-pitched, agonized cry pulled Ryker from his dreams. His eyes flung open, and he jolted upright with a gasp. His magic was a storm in his veins, and his heart hammered in his chest.

Instinct had his gaze swinging to his left to check on Brynleigh.

His heart nearly stopped.

She was sitting straight up, the sheet pooling at her naked waist. Her fists were clutched over her heart, her face was as pale as snow, and she was drawing in air as though she'd been drowning. Tears streamed down her cheeks, and sobs racked her body.

Ryker whispered her name, his voice low as though he were addressing a wounded animal, not the strong vampire he'd been losing himself in hours ago.

Her black eyes were unseeing, staring at the wall.

"It's okay," he murmured, reaching for her slowly so as not to scare her. "It was a nightmare." At least, he hoped it was just a nightmare. "I'm just going to hold you. Is that alright?"

Taking a vampire by surprise, especially one who seemed to be in a bad mental state, would never be a good idea.

Several seconds went by before she dipped her chin.

It was the slightest movement, but it was all he needed.

Wrapping his arms around Brynleigh, Ryker drew her against him. She seemed so much smaller than she had when they were together earlier. She trembled, tears dampening his chest as her cheek pressed over his heart.

"I've got you," he whispered, kissing her forehead. "I won't let you go."

And he didn't.

Her shaking, gasping breaths continued for what felt like forever but was probably just a few minutes.

Ryker held his wife and rubbed her back, murmuring about nothing in particular. He didn't care if he had to hold her all day; he would do it without question.

What had Brynleigh dreamed about that left her in such a state? She hadn't even been this broken when he got her from The Pit.

He leaned back, still holding her against his chest, and looked out the window.

The sun was high; the yellowed rays tinted slightly gray by the special windowpanes he'd had installed. They'd stayed up until the early hours of the dawn, so it wasn't surprising that they'd slept well into the day.

After several minutes had passed, Brynleigh's breathing slowed. She lifted her chin and sniffled. "I couldn't stop her."

Worry creased his brows. "Stop who?"

Brynleigh drew in another shuddering breath and laced her hand through his.

"Jelisette," she whispered, the word painfully quiet.

In the silence of their bedroom—because there was no doubt in his mind, this bedroom was theirs after last night—it was like she shouted her Maker's name.

He tensed despite his efforts to stay calm.

Of fucking course, this had something to do with Brynleigh's insane Maker.

It took everything he had not to growl as he asked, "What did she do?"

"She... oh, gods." Another shuddering sob ripped through his vampire, and fresh tears flowed down her cheeks. "She chased me through a forest, staked me, and killed me. I mean... I thought..."

Ryker couldn't take it anymore. Witnessing his wife's suffering was like watching someone rip his heart to shreds in front of him.

Keeping one arm wrapped around her, he put the other beneath her chin and tilted it up. "It was a nightmare."

Brynleigh nodded. "I know, but..."

He brushed his lips over her cheeks, kissing away her salty tears. "But what?"

"But it felt so fucking real." She rubbed her chest, drawing in deep breaths. "I thought that was it for us, Ryker. I really did. She was so angry."

"I hate her," he said vehemently.

He hated her more than anyone else in the entire world.

"Me too."

They sat in silence for several minutes before those eyes that he loved so dearly rose to meet his.

"Do you know what my last thought was before she staked me?"

He shook his head. "No."

"You." Brynleigh brushed her fingers down his cheek. "I was sorry that we didn't get more time. That hurt more than anything else. More than the stake she drove into my heart. More than the fear and pain of death. The knowledge that we had just found each other again and now were being torn apart was agonizing."

Ryker's heart broke at the pain in her voice."I'm so sorry, sweetheart."

Long minutes passed.

"Me too. It was a nightmare, but the fear... I can't lose you again, Ry." The vulnerability in her words shot straight to his heart. "I love you, and I need you like I need blood. When I first fell in love with you, I was frightened. I didn't understand what was happening. But now... now I know I was finding the other half of my soul."

Ryker's chest warmed. He'd never known love like this existed. He'd experienced familial love, but that was incomparable to the way he felt about Brynleigh. Even when the divide between them had felt insurmountable, his need for her remained.

"I love you, too," he murmured.

Her eyes locked onto his, and his breath caught in his throat.

Ryker wasn't sure who moved first, only that they both did. He bent his head, and she raised her chin. A heartbeat later, their mouths fused in a burning embrace. She shifted, clasping his arms, and he swept his tongue across her mouth.

Gods, he wanted her again.

"Don't ever leave me," Brynleigh gasped against his lips.

He shook his head, kissing her. "Not even death will separate us."

If that ever happened, he would bridge that divide, too.

"Promise?" she asked.

He flipped them and nudged her thighs open with his knee. Slipping a hand between them, he growled at the wetness that greeted him.

Removing his fingers, he fitted himself at her entrance.

"I swear it." He thrust inside her, letting her heat envelop his cock. She groaned, and he caught the sound with his lips. Gods, she was perfect. "You are mine. Forever."

And then he showed her exactly what it meant to belong to him.

SEVERAL HOURS LATER, they finally extricated themselves from the bedroom. Ryker and Marlowe ran to Eleyta Park while Brynleigh showered. Even though he knew it was ridiculous, part of him felt sad about being separated from her for that short time.

Every minute of his run, he thought about their relationship—where they'd started and how far they'd come—and his love for her. It shocked him how much he cared about her, yet he wouldn't have it any other way.

When he and Marlowe returned, Brynleigh was in a chair by the window. Her hair hung in blonde waves down her back, and she hugged her legs to herself as she sipped a mug of warm blood.

Ryker unhooked the dog's leash and walked towards her. Brushing away her hair, he kissed the back of her neck.

"What are you looking at?" he murmured.

She glanced over her shoulder and smiled. He'd never get enough of that.

"The sun," she replied.

"It is beautiful."

Not too hot, nor too cold. Today was a wonderful fall day.

She sighed contentedly, resting her head against him as he placed his hand on her shoulder. "I missed it so much."

"Now you can watch it every day."

They looked out the glass for several minutes in companionable silence before Brynleigh hummed.

"This was the moment I knew I was done for." She raised a brow and met his gaze. "Did I ever tell you that?"

Ryker shook his head. He would've remembered something like that.

She chuckled, trailing a finger down the windowpane.

"I walked in here expecting to hate you. Fucking *determined* to hate you. I tried so gods-damned hard, Ryker. I needed you to be evil. To be the one who hurt me. And you... you made it impossible."

"I was already in love with you," he admitted, staring at the afternoon sun. "I think I loved you the moment I went to look for you after the rebel attack."

Even then, he'd been ready to give her everything. His soul had known they were meant to be.

She put down her mug and stood, taking his hand in hers. Her thumb swept over the back of his palm, and she leaned against him.

"You were amazing, Ry. You were kind, considerate, funny, and competitive—nothing like what I expected. And I... I fell for you. When I saw the sun, I knew I was yours. And then later that night when River..." Her voice trailed off, and she winced.

"When she told you about the storm," he finished softly.

"Yeah." She nodded. "I knew it was over for me. I couldn't do it."

Ryker wrapped his arms around Brynleigh and held her close. What would've happened if River hadn't told her the truth about the Incident?

He didn't even want to think about it.

But it was over now. They were together, and their life was shaping up to be something beautiful.

Clearing his mind of the past, Ryker focused on the stunning woman in his arms. Together, they studied the city. Even Marlowe was quiet, his soft snores rising from his favorite spot on the couch.

Several minutes passed before Ryker remembered the envelope he'd gotten yesterday.

"Hold on." He kissed her forehead and stepped back, grabbing the letter from where he'd left it and returning to her side. "This came for us."

She ran her fingers over the front.

"Mr. and Mrs. Waterborn," she murmured, lifting her gaze to his. "I like the sound of that."

"Me too." He kissed her because he couldn't seem to help himself. "Want to open it?"

The smile Brynleigh shot in his direction could have warmed even the darkest souls.

She carefully opened the envelope, revealing a smaller gilded letter. The size of a postcard, it slipped into her palm with ease.

The invitation was almost identical to the one Ryker had first gotten to confirm his place in the Choosing. Mere months had passed since then, yet it felt like centuries ago.

On the front, scrawling black letters read, *You're Invited!*

Brynleigh hummed and turned it around. Written in the same cursive as the front was an invitation to the Reunion, set to take place a week from today.

"There you go. Seven days." She tapped her index finger on the edge of the envelope for a long moment before looking up at him.

"All the pieces are falling into place. You do your army thing,"—she spun a finger in the air like a little tornado, which he found ridiculously endearing—"and I'll work on the rebels. We'll trap them before they harm anyone else, putting a stop to this once and for all."

She sounded so sure. So confident.

Ryker admired and loved that about her, but unease crawled up the back of his neck. Would it truly be that simple? He hoped so.

He wanted nothing more than to put this entire portion of their lives behind them when the Reunion was over. He wanted to bring Brynleigh to his cabin and spend weeks enjoying life by the lake. He wanted long nights in front of the chess board, playing—and winning—against her.

He wanted laughter, joy, and peace, and he wouldn't stop until they'd achieved that.

It was so close that he could practically taste it.

CHAPTER 31

A Return to the Hall of Choice

"You look positively stunning," Hallie gushed from her seat in the limo beside Brynleigh.

Davis, Ryker's driver, had picked them up half an hour ago from the Fortune Elf's house. He had successfully navigated the traffic of downtown Golden City while the two women enjoyed a glass of Faerie Wine and chatted.

Brynleigh had been nervous about seeing her friend again, agonizing over asking Hallie if she wanted to ride with her to the Reunion. In the end, she'd messaged her friend, and the Fortune Elf had agreed to get together this afternoon.

Ryker and Therian, Hallie's husband, were busy with last-minute plans for tonight. They would meet their wives at the Reunion. Ryker had called an hour ago, letting Brynleigh know he was taking Marlowe for a run before coming to meet her at the Hall of Choice.

It had been a long but fruitful week. Brynleigh had attended yet another rebel meeting and deceived even more of them into thinking she was on their side. She'd gone with Ryker to deliver the cipher and book she'd stolen to the army's code-breakers. It looked promising, and Ryker seemed confident it would give them enough evidence to arrest and convict several suspected rebels.

She'd even braved Waterborn House and Tertia's wrath yesterday to visit Ryker's father. Tertia had been cold, which was expected, but Brynleigh had enjoyed seeing her father-in-law. He'd opened his eyes, and Ryker had been happy all night, even after Brynleigh beat him twice at chess.

None of that had been as scary as pulling up to Hallie and Therian's house had been earlier today. Their quaint neighborhood looked like it had been lifted from a storybook. Laughing children ran on emerald lawns. Parents sat on porches, watching their offspring play. Even the houses seemed to radiate happiness.

Brynleigh had felt out of place. There was a reason that vampires didn't go in the sun. With hearts as black as ink, they didn't deserve to experience the beauty of daylight.

She'd been so nervous that her friend would hate her, but it turned out Hallie was a far better person than Brynleigh. She'd forgiven her, and they'd hugged and spent the afternoon together.

Now, they were pulling up to the Hall of Choice, where four other limos were lined up in front of the entrance.

Brynleigh ran her fingers down the black shimmering silk of her floor-length gown. "You think so?"

She'd picked up the dress a few evenings ago. It had a high halter neck and long, fitted sleeves that came past her wrists. The back was practically non-existent, giving plenty of room for wings if she set them free. Although most of the other women would probably be wearing heels, Brynleigh had opted for a pair of flats. She wore her necklace and tracking bracelet, both pieces of jewelry hidden by the dress.

"I know so." Hallie took a generous gulp of her wine and swayed in her seat. "Ryker is going to lose his shit when he sees you."

Brynleigh snorted. She had never heard Hallie swear, but apparently, all it took was one glass of wine to loosen the Fortune Elf right up. "Thank you. You look beautiful, too."

Hallie's dress was a pale pink, glittery cloud. It was strapless, with a tight bodice before flaring out at the hips. Layers of tulle formed a full, fluffy skirt. The back was low, allowing room for the elf's wings. Her white hair was styled in loose waves over her shoulder, and diamond earrings studded her lobes.

"Thank you." Hallie swallowed the last of her wine as the car inched forward. There was only one limo in front of them now. "You know, I'm glad the Choosing is ending. It was nice, and obviously, I'm grateful for the experience, but it's been..."

"A lot," Brynleigh finished for her friend. "I couldn't agree more."

The experience has been exhausting, but she got Ryker out of it. Honestly, she couldn't be happier. Like fresh flowers blooming in the spring, the first rays of sunlight after a long, never-ending night, and the first flicker of warmth from a fire. Brynleigh's fae captain had breathed life into her cold, dark heart.

She looked out the window, taking in the crowds lining the steps of the Hall of Choice. Much like the first night of the Choosing, flashing cameras lit up the dark sky as the press tried to get the best shot of each participant.

In a mirror image of the first night, men and women were arriving separately, alone, or in groups like Brynleigh and Hallie. Usually, the couples came together, but there had been a last-minute change this year.

A tall fae with blue-black hair swept into a dazzling updo stepped out of the limo in front of them. Pointed ears were adorned with glittering tear-drop diamond earrings. An ivory handbag hung over one shoulder, and an aura of power surrounded the woman.

Brynleigh inhaled sharply.

Even from behind, she instantly recognized Valentina Rose.

The Chancellor's daughter wore a blood-red gown that was tight from her bosom to her thighs before flaring out. The mermaid-style gown was beautifully made and probably cost thousands.

On anyone else, it would've been stunning. But no amount of money could smooth over the hard, frigid edge of violence surrounding the bitchy fire fae.

Valentina strode up the steps of the Hall of Choice, her gown trailing behind her like a river of blood. Even from here, Brynleigh could make out the sharpened points of Valentina's heels as they clicked on the stairs.

"Well, she certainly knows how to make an entrance, doesn't she?" Hallie muttered.

"Yes, she certainly does." Brynleigh scowled.

Hallie leaned closer and loudly whispered, "Did I tell you that Therian and I watched her wedding on the livestream? It was *so* extravagant. They must've spent hundreds of thousands on it."

"Really?"

"Mhmm." The Fortune Elf hiccuped. "Most people are calling it the wedding of the century."

"Fascinating. I'm sure that's exactly what she was hoping for."

Valentina stopped on the last step and turned. A fake smile spread across the fae's face, and she waved to the press.

It was all an act. Of all the women Brynleigh had met during the Choosing, Valentina Rose was the worst.

Brynleigh had never truly been inclined to rip someone's throat out just for being an entitled, cruel bitch until she met the Chancellor's daughter. To be fair, Valentina seemed like she wanted to kill Brynleigh, too, so the hatred went both ways.

What had Ryker ever seen in her?

Hallie leaned close and looked out the window over Brynleigh's shoulder.

"I'm not usually one to judge others, but their wedding seemed like a lot. Too much, if I'm being honest."

Oh, she was definitely being honest. Faerie Wine had that effect on some people—it loosened tongues and made people lose their inhibitions.

"Her veil was purportedly an ancient relic from the Rose Empire, and her shoes were encrusted with diamonds. It was all rather opulent," Hallie continued, eyes wide. "Her flowers and Edward's tie were dusted in gold."

All the while, people were starving in the streets. Because, of course, the Chancellor's daughter would have a luxurious, absurdly elaborate, over-the-top wedding while others suffered.

That fucking tracked.

"That's... interesting."

Eventually, Valentina turned and entered the Hall of Choice.

"Mhmm. Oh, we're moving!" Hallie swayed, bumping into Brynleigh.

Chuckling, Brynleigh steadied her friend as she took in the scene outside.

Four soldiers guarded the entrance. They weren't in uniform, and their black suits were just as crisp as any partygoer's clothes, but no suit and tie could disguise their military strength or the power they oozed.

Even if Brynleigh hadn't known that there would be an increased military presence at the Reunion tonight, she would've known the men were soldiers.

Davis parked, cut the engine, and walked around the vehicle. He opened the door, a smile on his kind, older face.

"Ladies," he said in a baritone voice, extending a hand. "Welcome to the Reunion."

Brynleigh grabbed her black clutch containing her phone, Sarai's picture, and the invitation. Placing her fingers in the driver's, she exited the vehicle, the cold night air brushing against her.

"Thank you." She smiled and stepped aside, making room for Hallie to exit.

Cameras flashed, and Brynleigh glanced at the sky to avoid looking at them.

Then she saw it.

Crimson edged the moon like a splash of blood on an otherwise pristine piece of paper. It was incredibly out of place. A frown tugged at Brynleigh's lips, and her shadows throbbed at the sight.

Now that she'd noticed the odd sight, she couldn't look away. A heavy sense of foreboding filled her, and her stomach twisted.

Red moons were never a good sign. The last time a Blood Moon had appeared, a queen died, two battles took place, and the world was forever changed. Everyone knew about that turning point in the Four Kingdom's history.

So what did this one mean? Were the gods playing with them?

She stared at the moon until a hand landed on her arm.

"Brynleigh, what's wrong?" Hallie asked.

Hopefully, it didn't mean anything. But she couldn't shake the sick feeling. Shaking her head, she ripped her gaze away from the bloody moon.

"Oh, nothing."

It had to be nothing, right?

Tonight would be fine. Ryker and his team had spent days preparing for this. Everything was in position. They would ambush the rebels, stop them before anyone got hurt, and end the Black Night's madness once and for all.

And yet, that uneasy feeling remained.

Gods, she hoped Ryker would arrive soon. His presence grounded her like nothing else in this world.

Entering the Hall of Choice was a blur.

Arm in arm, Brynleigh and Hallie climbed the steps and posed for the press. They smiled and answered a few questions, but Brynleigh barely paid them any attention.

She kept looking back at the red moon.

No matter how often she told herself it didn't mean anything, she couldn't shake the feeling that something was wrong.

CRIMSON CRYSTALS HUNG from a dozen glistening chandeliers in the ballroom, casting shades of red over the massive space. Ruby tapestries embedded with hundreds of tiny gems hung on the walls, glittering like bloody skies. A red carpet lined the stage where the Reunion would take place, and all the couches were the same color.

Hallie had stepped away to use the restroom, leaving Brynleigh alone for a few minutes. She didn't mind. It gave her time to assess the gathered crowd.

The ballroom was already teeming with people. Crew members wearing black ran across the stage, talking into headsets. Audience members filled the nearly three dozen rows of seats, many wearing crimson to match the theme. Most were smiling and chatting with their neighbors, but several sat stoically, their gazes moving methodically through the space.

One of the audience members locked eyes with Brynleigh, and he dipped his chin. Nikhail wore a black suit and tie, looking just as distinguished as the first time Brynleigh met him.

She wasn't entirely sure what the air fae did for the army, but she knew that Ryker trusted the man, which was good enough for her.

"Excuse me, Mrs. Waterborn?" a pleasant voice came from behind Brynleigh.

It took a moment for Brynleigh to realize they were speaking to her. It would take time to get used to that name, and changing her name legally to Ryker's would be a legal pain, but it would be worth it to shed her Maker's hold on her.

It wasn't normal for vampires to stop using their sire's last names, but she didn't care about social norms when it came to Jelisette.

Brynleigh turned around and smiled. "Yes?"

A shifter with kind eyes, dark skin, and a clipboard in hand stood a few feet behind her.

"I'm supposed to set up your microphone and run over a few things with you. If you'd come with me, please."

"Sure thing."

She followed the man through the crowd. Her dress swished as she moved slowly, the material not conducive to essential activities such as walking. She preferred leggings, but unfortunately, the Reunion had a dress code.

They climbed the stairs, traversed through a door, and went behind the stage.

Here, the audience's excited chatter was nothing more than a murmur, replaced by the hustle and bustle of frantic crew members. They shouted orders at each other, moving like their feet were on fire.

Brynleigh had never considered how many people worked behind the scenes of the Choosing, but it had to be a significant amount. Live streaming an event couldn't be easy, and based on the strained expressions on several faces around her, she guessed that tonight would be more difficult than normal.

"Over here, please." The shifter led her to a table with just over a dozen microphones. He picked one up and gestured for Brynleigh to turn around. "I'm going to attach this to the back of your dress."

"Of course, go ahead."

There was a slight tug behind her as the shifter worked.

Brynleigh studied the thick black curtains hiding the backstage from sight when a muffled curse caught her ear.

She subtly shifted towards the sound.

"... none of them are here yet," said a low, bass voice.

"What the fuck do you mean?" This speaker was much louder than the first. "Where could they be?"

"Fuck if I know! But we'll have to delay if they don't arrive soon."

Something that sounded like a fist banged into a wall.

"Find them! Do you think I want a bunch of fucking Representatives breathing down my neck? This many men don't just disappear..."

The voice dropped, becoming too quiet even for Brynleigh to hear.

A snicker came from her right.

"Well, well, well. It looks like the bloodsucking leech finally showed up." Valentina sauntered up to Brynleigh, a ruby goblet clutched between her manicured fingers.

Her lips twisted into a reptilian sneer, and violence glimmered in her violet eyes. An enormous diamond that probably cost as much as Hallie's house sat on Valentina's ring finger.

Extravagant, indeed.

"Hello, Valentina," Brynleigh said stiffly, forcing a tight smile on her face. "Congratulations on your wedding. I heard it was... glittery."

That was about as nice as she could manage around Valentina.

The fire fae sniffed.

"It was amazing, but I'm not surprised that a commoner such as yourself is incapable of appreciating the effort it takes to throw a lavish, beautiful wedding." Valentina paused, her eyes narrowing. "Yours was... quaint. But I should have expected that since your husband made such an... *interesting* Choice."

Brynleigh's lips curled, and she clenched her fists. So much for being polite.

"First of all, my wedding was perfect."

She could've married Ryker in a back alley and wouldn't have cared. It wasn't about the clothes, decorations, or the location. It was about the man. Something Valentina clearly didn't understand.

The fire fae snarled, but Brynleigh continued over her, "Second of all, how dare you insult my husband's Choice, you fucking bit—"

"And that's enough socializing for tonight." Hallie appeared out of nowhere, tugging Brynleigh away. "Valentina, as always, it's... interesting to see you."

The fire fae's gaze turned to Hallie, her sneer deepening. "*You*. I can't believe you, a *Selected*, married a dragon shifter. The head of the Carinoc Division, no less. By all the gods. If you think—"

"Ladies! It's time." A human crew member hurried between the trio and ushered them towards the stage. "Come, come. You need to take your seats. The stream is scheduled to begin in ten minutes. The Chancellor has arrived, and her time is limited."

Several other women were already seated. A massive seventy-inch screen stood to their right, and an empty armchair for their interviewer was in the middle of the semi-circle.

Hallie sat on one of the ruby couches, and Valentina took another, but Brynleigh remained standing.

That unease from earlier returned, worse than ever. Her eyes darted around the stage. More women were filtering out, but...

Where was Ryker? Where were *any* of the men? They were supposed to be here. The rebels would be showing up halfway through, but...

Wrong, wrong, wrong.

Brynleigh extended her senses, listening for Ryker or any male voice she recognized.

None reached her ears.

And then, the television screen on the side of the stage crackled to life.

CHAPTER 32
None of this was Right

A man—or at least, Brynleigh assumed he was a man since he wore a black mask over his face, leaving only his eyes visible—stepped up to the camera.

No amount of cloth could hide the breadth of his shoulders or the bulk of his muscles. A menacing gleam filled his eyes, and the room behind him was pitch-black.

Something about him made Brynleigh's skin crawl. A few shadows slipped from her palms, and a cold sweat appeared on her forehead.

"What's happening?" someone in the audience yelled.

"Is this part of the Reunion?"

Brynleigh's sense of unease increased tenfold.

A pair of soldiers ran to the TV, yelling about turning it off.

"I wouldn't do that if I were you." The masked man's voice was edged with violence. He must have had a camera set up to watch the room.

"If you want to see any of your men again, you'll clear the room and find me someone in charge. No one try anything stupid. I don't want any press involved. If I catch a whiff of this on the news or if this stream is cut, we will kill them all."

One silent second passed before utter pandemonium exploded.

People screamed, each battling over the others to be heard. Shouts of alarm came from the audience. A few women erupted into tears. Someone fainted. The soldiers seemed just as confused and in shock as everyone else.

Cold, sickening, toe-curling, stomach-turning dread filled Brynleigh's stomach.

The masked man turned his head to the side, and Brynleigh caught sight of something on his neck.

Was that...

"Isvana help us all," she breathed.

Oh, this would not end well.

Etched among swirling tattoos of flowers and vines was a symbol she'd come to know all too well. A dagger stabbed a crescent moon, taking up a place of prominence on the rebel's neck.

Fuck.

The curse seemed to be the only thing Brynleigh could think of. Her brain wasn't functioning. She could barely breathe, let alone find words.

The Black Night was here early, and they'd gone off script. This was wrong. They were supposed to attack the Reunion, not take the men. No one was supposed to get hurt. Hostages had never been part of the plan.

Had they ever intended to attack tonight as Brynleigh had suggested?

She had *known* something was wrong when she saw the moon. Why hadn't she done something earlier? Instead of calling Ryker, she'd been busy fighting with Valentina.

Brynleigh couldn't help but feel that she'd brought this upon everyone here by suggesting that the rebels attack at the Reunion.

Was this her fault?

She didn't scream or cry because what good would tears do in a situation like this?

Oh gods, oh gods, oh gods.

Bile rose in her throat. Her vision swam, and a tremor ran through her.

Her stomach hollowed, and her attention returned to the TV.

The room behind the masked man was dark, but she could make

out flickers of movements. Her vampiric hearing picked up muffled cries and grunts.

Each sound caused the emptiness within her to grow until it felt like she was falling into a pit of nothingness.

Internally, she screamed Ryker's name. She wished they had a bond, a link, or even those gods-damned earrings that let him hear her. Anything would be better than this empty, silent, not-knowing state where she found herself.

That empty pit threatened to swallow Brynleigh whole. She needed to act, to move, but all her strength and bravado were so far away.

Someone cleared out the audience until only a few people remained.

Soldiers surrounded the women, herding them like sheep into a circle.

Nikhail made it on stage. He stood several feet from the others, furiously typing into his phone.

Sending for help, Brynleigh hoped.

"There now," the man on the screen said after a few minutes had passed. "It seems like I have your attention. Very good. Now that you're listening, I have some demands."

"Demands?" One of the soldiers standing near the screen scoffed. "You don't get to make demands. How do we know this isn't a hoax? You could just be playing a game with us."

Brynleigh didn't think interrupting the rebel was wise, but she wasn't a trained soldier.

"I get it. You want proof. That's fair." The rebel's eyes gleamed. He raised a gloved hand and motioned to a person off-camera. "Hit the lights."

A bulb flickered above the masked man, casting faint yellow rays over the space. It wasn't bright, but it was enough.

Isvana help them all, but it was fucking enough.

Screams rose once again. Esme, who had seemed so fierce the first night of the Choosing, fainted.

Even Valentina cried out in alarm.

Brynleigh's heart caught in her throat. Black spots filled her vision. Tighter, tighter, tighter, her lungs squeezed. Her fangs ached, and shadows slipped from her hands.

By all the gods, this was worse than her most terrifying nightmares.

"Here's your *proof.*" The rebel's eyes hardened, and he stepped to the side.

Hallie screamed, "Therian!"

Eleven men were huddled together, all on their knees. Their arms were tied behind their backs. Brown canvas sacks covered their faces. Prohiberis cuffs were locked around their hands and feet. Clothes were torn and dirty.

Several other masked men surrounded them, each holding impressive-looking guns that could probably kill someone in one shot.

It took Brynleigh two seconds to find Ryker.

He was in the middle of the group, hooded like the rest, but it didn't matter. She would recognize his form anywhere. Those hands that held her close. His arms. He was still wearing his running gear, for the gods' sake.

Momentary worry flashed through Brynleigh's head for Marlowe, but she'd have to deal with that later.

Her gaze snagged on the red trail of blood on Ryker's shirt. It wasn't enough to be a severe injury, especially with his fae healing, but still.

Someone had *hurt* him and made him bleed.

Her fangs burned, and she clenched her fists. She would kill them for this.

He was *hers.*

Brynleigh was so distracted by the bloody shirt that it took her a moment to realize the masked man had returned. His eyes were stony and filled with violence.

"You've gotten what you asked for," he snarled. "Now it's my turn. If you wish to see these men alive, Chancellor Ignatia Rose will announce tonight that she is dismantling the Representative government and stepping down from her position, effective immediately."

"I. Will. Not." The Chancellor spoke with confidence.

Brynleigh hadn't even realized the head of the Republic was on stage.

Four broad-shouldered bodyguards flanked the Chancellor as she strode towards the screen. Her emerald wide-legged pantsuit looked expertly tailored as it hugged her fae form. Black heels gave her several inches over most of the others, clicking as she walked.

"We do not negotiate with people like you," the Chancellor continued.

Her voice was like ice. She spoke in a measured, quiet tone, and power was woven through every word.

Brynleigh's stomach bottomed out.

"People like me? I know who you are, *Ignatia*." The rebel hissed her name as if there was something personal between them. "What you and your inner circle have done in the name of the Representatives. The people of this continent have suffered long enough beneath your 'care.' It's time for a change of pace."

The energy in the room shifted. The air thickened, and breathing was more difficult than ever.

Brynleigh's heart pounded, and the Chancellor bristled. Embers crackled at the fae's fingertips.

Long moments passed as the rebel and the Chancellor stared at each other before the fire fae shook her head.

"No," she said calmly. "Release them, and this will go easier on you."

The rebel laughed as if this was all a joke.

"Easier? Nothing is ever easy for those of us who aren't born into power."

"You—"

"No. Your reign of terror has gone on long enough." He canted his head, a dangerous glint in his eye. "Perhaps you need some additional motivation."

Brynleigh forced herself to breathe and analyze the situation despite the horror coursing through her veins.

The rebels couldn't be that far away—she'd spoken to Ryker only a few hours ago. Some of the men wore suits and ties, so they must've been taken on their way to the Reunion. How had the rebels pulled this off without the women realizing their husbands were missing?

Her fingers dug into the back of the couch, and she stared behind the rebel.

The dark room appeared windowless, and the walls and floors were made of cement. Maybe they were underground?

The Chancellor strode with authority to the TV. "I'm ordering you to let them go."

The man on the screen laughed. As if this was a joke to him. As if he knew something no one else did.

"That's funny, Chancellor. You still believe you're in charge. However, that is not the case." He gestured to one of his armed companions. "Pick one of them and bring them to me."

A cry of alarm erupted from the women on stage.

Even Valentina hissed, "Mother, put a stop to this."

But the Chancellor did not respond to any of them. Not even her daughter.

One of the masked gunmen strode into the group of captives.

The rebel in charge looked back to the camera.

"You see, Ignatia, this is not a negotiation. You will do as we say, or Representative blood will spill."

The one with the gun made a show of looking around the group. He bent, but a hand covered the camera before anyone could see who he'd picked.

They could still hear, though.

"That one."

A grunt. The sound of flesh against flesh. A moan.

It was the worst soundtrack Brynleigh had ever heard.

Someone on the stage was crying.

The shock in the Hall of Choice was palpable, and horror was a bitter tang in the air. Even the Chancellor's guards didn't seem to know what to do.

Suddenly, the camera was uncovered, and visibility was restored.

Now, the rebels were in a smaller space. A light dangled from the ceiling, casting dark shadows on the room. Kneeling between two masked men, hoodless, bound, gagged, and struggling against their iron grip was....

"No!" Valentina screamed.

The fire fae broke free of the guards circling the other women and ran to the screen. In a show of emotion that Brynleigh hadn't known the other woman possessed, Valentina grabbed the television.

"Edward!"

The fae's head reared up. He screamed against the gag. His words were garbled, but there was no mistaking the fear in his eyes.

"Release him!" For the first time that evening, the Chancellor's voice shook. "Let him go."

The masked man reappeared, and the look in his eyes was darker than ever.

"No, I don't think I will."

A red ribbon of magic slipped from his palm, slithering through the air like a deadly snake until it hit Edward and vanished into him.

For one long, drawn-out moment, nothing happened.

Then Edward groaned. An anguished, guttural sound came from his chest. Sweat beaded on his forehead, and his eyes widened.

"What did you do?" Valentina screamed, struggling against the guard who was pulling her back.

The masked man shrugged. "Did you know Death Elves can kill someone slowly by draining their life force from the inside out?"

"What?" Valentina screamed. "No!"

Red ribbons swirled around the man—the Death Elf.

"You have one hour before this man dies, Ignatia. Then, I'll pick another. And another." He sent another ribbon of magic towards the fae on his knees, and Edward screamed. "I could do this all night long. I'll even give you a few minutes to decide what to do. Talk to you soon."

The screen went black.

Three heartbeats passed in absolute silence before chaos descended on the stage. Shouts and screams and cries battled for attention. Valentina's sobs could be heard above them all.

It turned out the fae did have a heart, and it sounded like it was breaking.

People were yelling at the Chancellor, but Ignatia Rose was giving orders to her guards.

Brynleigh wouldn't sit still and do nothing. Not while Ryker was in danger. Releasing the couch, she strode towards Nikhail. The air fae seemed to have the same idea as her.

He gripped her arm. "Backstage. Now."

A dark-skinned woman walked beside him, the tailored jacket of her feminine suit flapping open and revealing the gun tucked in her waistband.

She didn't have the pointed ears of a fae or elf, and she didn't smell like a shifter. Maybe she was a witch or an especially skilled human.

As they walked backstage, Nikhail ripped off Brynleigh's microphone. He handed it to the other woman, who pressed a button before throwing it away.

"It's off," she said in a soft voice.

Brynleigh looked at Nikhail. "I need to find Ryker."

At the same time, the air fae said, "I know everything."

Something in his eyes made the predator deep within Brynleigh stand on end. He was dangerous like she was dangerous.

Her eyes widened as she carefully drew shadows into her palms. She wouldn't let anyone hurt her, not even one of her husband's friends. "I didn't do this. I would never hurt Ryker."

When she'd suggested to Jelisette that the rebels attack, this was never her plan. She never wanted anyone to get hurt. She just wanted to stop the Black Night.

How had everything gone so fucking wrong?

A long, long moment passed before Nikhail nodded. "I believe you. I've seen you and Ryker together. You love him."

Brynleigh exhaled, and she released her grip on her shadows. "With all my heart."

A high-pitched screech came from the stage as Valentina begged her mother to do something. Anything.

Brynleigh turned her attention back to Nikhail. "I've been to the rebels' meeting place. I don't think they're keeping them there, but we might find something useful." She drew shadows into her palms. "I'm going."

Nikhail's grip tightened on Brynleigh's arm. "Take us with you."

On one hand, Brynleigh liked to work alone. On the other, she'd do anything for Ryker.

Brynleigh frowned, glancing at Nikhail's companion. "Who is she?"

"This is Indira." Nikhail dipped his chin toward the mysterious woman. "She works with me and may be able to help."

At another time, Brynleigh would probably ask more questions, like what did Nikhail and Indira do, and what did they think was happening? But this wasn't the time for questions, so she bottled them up inside.

Every second they spent talking was one where Ryker was suffering. "Okay. I'll do it, but first..."

Her gaze snagged on a knife sitting nearby. She grabbed it and tore away the bottom third of her gown with a few quick slashes. Destroying such a beautiful dress didn't feel great, but there was no way she would've been able to walk, let alone run or fight, in the tight material.

Now, the dress fell to mid-thigh, and Brynleigh could move freely.

Dropping the blade back where she'd found it, she extended her hands to the other two.

"I'll shadow us out of here." She glanced back at the stage and frowned, remembering the others. "Should we—"

"Don't worry about them." Nikhail waved his phone in the air. "We need to stop this. I've already informed the officers that we're leaving."

"Understood," she said. "Let's go."

As soon as they put their hands in hers, Brynleigh pulled on her shadows and stepped into the Void. She prayed to Isvana that they wouldn't be too late.

CHAPTER 33
This was Wrong

Brynleigh's skin crawled without Ryker, and the urge to find him filled every part of her.

She needed him.

They stepped out of the darkness, her two companions releasing her hands as she kept shadows cloaked around them. The alley across from Horizon looked exactly as it had before, save for the crimson moon shining overhead.

But Brynleigh could feel in her bones that something was wrong.

It wasn't just from what they'd witnessed at the Hall of Choice, nor was it simply from having her husband stolen from her. The very air seemed to vibrate with... something.

Brynleigh raised her hand and gestured for her companions to be quiet and follow her. They complied, and the shadow-cloaked trio snuck around the building. A breeze tickled her cheek, and she glanced over to see Nikhail wielding wind. Even their footsteps were silent.

She sent him a small smile in thanks, her heart thundering as she led them around the corner. She curled her fists, expecting to encounter the burly guard at the door.

Except...

The back lot was empty. The guard wasn't there.

Brynleigh's brows furrowed, and she stopped in front of the door.

Nikhail glanced at her, then the building, before dropping his hands. "This is their meeting place?"

"Yes, but... something's off." Her skin crawled, and she shivered. "Where is everyone?"

Nikhail glanced at Indira. "Thoughts?"

"I don't sense anyone inside," she said.

Indira wasn't a human then. Maybe a witch?

"Neither do I," he replied.

But that didn't make sense. There had to be people here. If no one was here, how would they find Ryker?

Brynleigh wasn't stupid. If the rebels knew she'd deceived them—and obviously, they did to some extent because she hadn't known about this plan—they wouldn't keep the men in this location.

But she'd been banking on the fact that they'd find *something*. A clue. A lead. Even a fucking piece of paper would be better than nothing.

Now, though, she was beginning to doubt they'd even find that.

Nikhail moved towards the door, spinning a gust of wind above his outstretched left hand.

Brynleigh's brows furrowed.

"He's blocking us from the cameras," Indira whispered, answering Brynleigh's unasked question.

He strode to the door, put his hand on the knob, and turned.

And it...

Swung open.

Nikhail glanced over his shoulder and raised a brow. He tilted his head towards the interior, putting a finger on his lips.

"This doesn't bode well," Indira muttered, following the air fae.

Brynleigh's shadows writhed in agreement. She trailed the pair, keeping her footsteps silent as they entered the warehouse.

Only, they didn't have to worry about being quiet because—

"Fuck!" Brynleigh screamed, horror twisting her stomach into knots. "This isn't right."

Her words echoed through the empty warehouse, the walls singing them back to her as if laughing at her awful predicament.

"This is the right place," she said, mostly to herself. "I shadowed us directly here. This is where the fight club and all the meetings I attended took place. There should be a clue here. Something."

And yet, the warehouse was as empty as the Void.

Even the air had somehow been scrubbed of anyone's presence. The only scents were those of dirt, dust, and stale air.

"Let's walk around and see if we find something," Nikhail suggested.

Brynleigh didn't think that would help, but standing still wasn't an option.

Walking through the massive space was like entering an abandoned cave. Every footstep echoed; every whisper was like a shout.

Soon, it was clear they were the only living beings around.

Despair curled Brynleigh's stomach in knots, making her want to fall on the floor and collapse in defeat. "I don't... there's nothing here."

What were they going to do now? She didn't want to return to the Hall of Choice and sit by helplessly, waiting for someone else to act. Especially if the Chancellor continued refusing to negotiate. She could very well let all the men die.

On the one hand, Brynleigh hoped that even Ignatia Rose wasn't that cold-hearted. After all, her son-in-law was in the group. On the other hand, the fire fae was a Representative, and Brynleigh wouldn't put it past her to sacrifice a dozen lives to hold onto power.

And that just wouldn't be happening. Not if Brynleigh had anything to do with it.

She had been through too fucking much to lose Ryker now. They'd worked too hard and come too far. By the gods, she wasn't done with him. They had so much life left to live.

There had to be some way to get to her husband. Some way to find him without knowing where he was. Not after everything they'd been through.

If only they had a bond, a link—

Brynleigh's eyes widened, and her gaze shot to her left arm.

"Of course." She turned to Nikhail, who was running a hand through his hair and scowling at the empty warehouse. "I have an idea."

The air fae raised his brows. "What is it?"

She tugged up her sleeve, revealing the blue bracelet.

"Ryker gave me this. He said..." She swallowed, remembering the coldness in his voice on that day in the small bungalow. "He said there's a tracker in this. Could you... Is it possible to flip it around? Find him through that?"

She didn't know much about technology, but that seemed like something that should theoretically be possible.

Nikhail canted his head and glanced at Indira. "What do you think?"

The other woman drew her bottom lip through her teeth. "Can I see it?"

"Indira's a witch, but she's also a technical genius. If someone can make this happen, it's her," Nikhail explained.

"Okay." Brynleigh extended her wrist, and Indira stepped forward.

Her touch was gentle but firm as she twisted the bracelet around Brynleigh's wrist, studying it. "It's enchanted, but I think I'll be able to do it."

"Great," Nikhail said. "What do you need?"

Every single minute without Ryker felt like hours.

Even though only fifteen minutes had gone by since they left the warehouse, it seemed like an eternity had passed. Indira required a computer, so Brynleigh shadowed them back to Ryker's apartment.

She refused to return to the safe house lest Jelisette was there, and she could only shadow to locations where she'd previously been.

Brynleigh's heart hurt, and her body, mind, and soul ached. If someone had told her a few months ago she'd be desperate for Ryker's presence, she would've called them a liar.

Now, all she wanted was to look him in the eyes and know he was okay.

When they first arrived at the apartment, Indira had worked on her magic on the bracelet and released the magical lock. The bracelet fell away, and the witch took it to the computer to get to work.

Ryker's computer was password protected, but Indira bypassed it with a blue ribbon of magic and a few murmured spells.

A handy skill.

Brynleigh grabbed a few bags of blood from the fridge and downed them before chewing on her fingernails. Being here without Ryker and Marlowe didn't feel right.

Thank Isvana, Nikhail had contacted Atlas, who confirmed Marlowe had arrived at his house, leash dragging on the ground behind him.

That problem aside, nothing else was going well tonight.

The TV was on, and reporters on the nightly news were talking about the Reunion—or, more specifically, the lack thereof. The live stream had never started, and they speculated that it was because of technical issues.

Brynleigh and Nikhail watched the report in grim silence for a few minutes before the air fae's phone rang. He went into the hallway, where the faint, tense streams of his voice filtered through the crack in the door.

Brynleigh turned the sound off on the TV.

The steady clicking of keys filled the apartment as Indira typed away on the laptop. She cursed occasionally, but every time Brynleigh glanced over, the witch was hard at work.

So, Brynleigh resorted to what she always seemed to do in this apartment when she was nervous: she paced.

She'd never been good at waiting, even before her Making. Her fingers twitched at her sides, and she wished there was something for her to do. Being patient on a good day was hard, but it felt nearly impossible right now.

The door swung open.

Nikhail returned, scrubbing a hand over his face. His skin was paler than before, and when his gaze met Brynleigh's, her knees buckled.

She grabbed the back of the couch, and blood drained from her face. "Is Ryker… is he…"

She could barely get the words out, barely breathe. Her heart raced. Ryker had to survive this. She'd already grieved him once, and she wasn't sure she would be able to do it again.

Nikhail's mouth pinched in a line. "He's okay."

But the look in his eyes spoke volumes, and Brynleigh knew something had happened.

"Tell me," she said.

He swallowed, and for the first time since Brynleigh had met Nikhail, he looked shaken.

"They executed Edward Kingstar on camera five minutes ago." Valentina's husband. "His wife is... inconsolable."

Brynleigh's stomach cramped, bile rising in her throat. Pity for Valentina flooded through her. She didn't like the fire fae, but no one deserved to lose their husband, especially not like this.

"Gods, that's horrible." Brynleigh trembled. "If that... if he..."

"It won't happen to Ryker." The air fae strode over to Brynleigh. How he remained so composed in a moment like this was beyond her.

"How do you know?" She'd tried so hard to be strong, but this... if Ryker...

She couldn't live without him.

Nikhail clasped Brynleigh's shoulder. "Ryker is strong. He's been through worse than this, and he'll make it."

He sounded so sure. So calm.

Drawing strength from Nikhail's words, Brynleigh inhaled deeply. "Okay. You're right. I know Ryker is strong. He's going to be okay."

He had to be okay. Their story couldn't end here.

"Yeah, he will be." Nikhail's amber eyes glowed. "We'll find him."

"Thank you," Brynleigh said. "I know we don't know each other well yet, but thank you."

"Anything for Ryker. We will get to him in time."

But they hadn't gotten to them in time to save Edward.

Brynleigh said a small prayer for the fae's soul before asking, "Did they take someone else?"

The masked man had seemed so dangerous. So deadly.

"Yes." Nikhail's voice was pained.

The typing stopped, and even though Brynleigh didn't dare look away from Nikhail, she was certain Indira was listening closely.

"Who?" She barely dared ask.

"Horatio Montclair, one of the vampires. He isn't doing well."

The typing resumed, and Brynleigh closed her eyes for a long moment. Thank all the gods, it wasn't Ryker. She should feel happy about that.

And yet, all she felt was grief.

One man was already dead. Another was in harm's way.

She couldn't shake the feeling that, somehow, this was her fault.

"What did they do?" Brynleigh forced the words out of her dry throat.

"The rebels—"

"I've got it." Indira stood up so fast that her chair tumbled to the ground. "I know where they are."

CHAPTER 34

Dragonsbane and Desperate Measures

Ryker was losing track of time. Minutes felt like hours, and seconds dragged on.

He had never been this sore in his entire life.

His head throbbed like a mallet was beating against his skull. His eyes hurt. He was lightheaded, his limbs were aching and heavy, and a wrongness coursed through him.

He groaned, the sound muffled and wrong. His mouth was dry, and he was gagged.

Damn it all. Ryker should've been more careful.

He'd been out for a run with Marlowe when four masked men ambushed him coming out of Eleyta Park. They'd shouted something about freeing the Republic as they jumped him.

He immediately dropped the dog's leash and commanded him to run. The moment Marlowe bolted away, Ryker pulled on his magic.

He threw powerful waves at the men, forming ice daggers in his hands at the same time. Two of them fell, but the others managed to avoid his attack. They swarmed him, and one of them stabbed a needle into the back of his neck.

Ryker didn't stop fighting, sending out magic and throwing several ice daggers, but ultimately, he went down.

Abducted in plain fucking daylight.

If it weren't such a dire situation, he would've been embarrassed. He'd gotten complacent and started taking the same route for his run several months ago. He knew better, but he honestly never thought anything would happen to him.

As a child, his mother had drilled into them the importance of always staying alert, but over the years, he had relaxed and let down his guard.

He'd fucked up. He wasn't above admitting that.

A strange, bitter taste had been at the back of Ryker's mouth when he woke up. Between that and the trouble he was having thinking, he was sure he'd been drugged.

Rebel bastards.

At some point after they dragged the first man away, the captors removed the bags from their heads.

The drugs were wearing off, leaving Ryker with a pulsing headache.

At least now, he could think more clearly. He was level-headed enough to know that letting your hostages see was a bad fucking sign. Their captors didn't intend for them to leave in one piece.

Edward was gone.

Ryker wasn't sure where he'd been taken, but he hadn't returned. A few minutes ago, he'd heard a female voice calling out orders in the corridor, and then another man was dragged away.

Horatio.

The vampire had been kind to Ryker during the Choosing, and it was thanks to his suggestion that Ryker had installed the vampire-safe windows in his apartment.

The vampire had cried out, the gag muffling his protests as he struggled against the guards dragging him.

And the rebels? They'd fucking *laughed*, commenting amongst themselves that the silencing ward around the entire level meant no one could hear the vampire's screams anyways.

Bastards.

Ryker was kneeling, his arms and legs having long since turned numb. Uncomfortable prohiberis cuffs were clamped around his wrists, and the rope binding his arms behind his back was making matters worse. The temperature verged on freezing, and goosebumps peppered his flesh.

Four armed guards circled their group, and none of them looked friendly.

Therian kneeled a few feet away from Ryker. A massive purple bruise covered the left side of the dragon shifter's face, and his eye on that same side of his face was swollen shut.

The dragon shifter was unnaturally pale, and a cut several inches long ran down his right cheek. In addition to the prohiberis clamped around Therian's arms and legs, a metal collar that reeked of lemons and cedar was clamped around his neck.

A recessed memory worked its way to the front of Ryker's mind, a lesson from when he first joined the military.

Dragonsbane is one of the only substances known to halt a dragon shifter's magic. It's powerful. Historical examples include when the Crimson King used it against the High Lady of Life's mate. With its lemon and cedar scent, dragonsbane is instantly recognizable. It's dangerous, and prolonged exposure to the substance can permanently injure a dragon shifter, and even stop them from ever shifting again.

It was also incredibly rare.

Ryker had to give it to the rebels, they were prepared for this. Dragonsbane was even less accessible than prohiberis, yet the rebels had found enough to subdue Therian.

Ryker shifted slowly so as not to attract the rebels' attention. Not much, but enough to catch Therian's eye.

The shifter tilted his head, his blond hair dusted in grime and blood. They met each other's gazes, and Therian widened his eyes a fraction. Ryker dipped his chin.

A silent agreement: they were going to get out of here.

No matter the cost.

THE OPPORTUNITY TO escape arose a few minutes later. Or was it half an hour?

The door creaked open, and a tall man appeared at the entrance.

Light from the hallway beyond illuminated his broad frame. He radiated violence.

"Hey, the boss needs some help upstairs."

"What about them?" The guard closest to the door gestured to the group with his gun.

The newcomer scoffed. "They don't have any magic or weapons. Come on."

The guard snorted but followed his companion and another soldier into the hallway. They spoke too quietly for Ryker to hear, but if their tones were anything to go by, they were enjoying their roles as captors.

Ryker could've sworn he caught a flash of chestnut hair in the hallway before the door shut behind the men, but he wasn't sure.

The lock clicked back into place, leaving them alone once again.

If the guards thought they would be silent, willing captives, they were wrong. Taking on four guards at once while bound and lacking magic would've been suicide.

But two?

That was a manageable number.

Nine Choosing participants, including Ryker, remained in the room, and even with their bindings, they'd have a fighting chance.

Usually, he hoped for more than just a chance, but since neither Edward nor Horatio had returned, he'd take anything over whatever cruel, cold outcomes awaited them if they did nothing.

Less than a minute after the door had closed, Ryker met Therian's eye.

He spat out his gag, mouthing, *This is our chance.*

The corner of the dragon shifter's lips twitched, and he nodded subtly.

A few heartbeats later, Ryker witnessed first-hand why everyone in the army feared and respected the Head of the Carinoc Division.

The dragon shifter twisted his fingers behind his back. His arm muscles bulged, and then, as if the rope around his hands were nothing but floss, it snapped.

The moment the rope broke, several things happened at once.

Therian stood with a roar that shook the walls. Even with the dragonsbane blocking his beast, power rippled off the blond shifter in waves.

The two remaining guards swung their attention to Therian and raised their guns, pointing them at his chest.

"Get down, or we'll shoot," the taller one yelled.

Instead of doing that—because that was a fucking one-way ticket to death—Therian charged the rebel.

At the same time, Ryker pushed himself to his feet, throwing himself at the other guard. He slammed into him, his shoulder screaming in pain as they collided. Together, they smashed into the concrete wall.

Absolute chaos descended upon the small cell.

The others stood and fought. Guards shouted. A gun fired. Someone screamed. Something wet splattered across Ryker's bare arm. A grunt of pain came from behind him. Flesh smacked against flesh. A yell. A guttural scream. Another gunshot. A loud *snap*.

Then, silence blanketed the space so quickly that the quiet came as a shock.

Ryker's breath came in short bursts.

A grunt came from behind him. He tensed, balling his fists, when the rope binding his hands tightened.

"It's me," Therian said, having removed his gag, as he snapped the rope binding Ryker's hands. "Help me with the others."

Ryker's arms throbbed. With the prohiberis blocking his magic, he couldn't heal, but at least he could move.

Searing pain ran through his right shoulder as he attempted to shift his arm, and tears rushed to his eyes.

Turning, Ryker ignored his pain and untied Oliver. The witch thanked him with a grunt and went to help one of the others. When Oliver moved, Ryker got a good look at the guard Therian had rushed at.

The rebel was lying on the floor, a massive hole where his chest cavity used to be. Gods damn. There would be no coming back from that, even for a Mature being.

At least that accounted for the blood that had landed on Ryker's arm.

The other rebel was a few feet away, still hanging onto life. Jacques, the other vampire participant, had his knee pressed against the guard's neck, even though his own hands were still bound.

Ryker and Therian freed all the men from their rope bindings. They were unable to remove the prohiberis since the manacles required keys. They searched the guards for the keys but didn't find them.

Their injuries were numerous. Many of them had fought back when they were captured, and they were all bloody and bruised. In addition to Ryker's shoulder, three others had dislocated or broken arms. No one's legs were broken, though, which would make escaping easier.

A quick conversation confirmed they'd all been drugged, all their phones were missing, and no one knew where they were. The men stood, some in worse shape than others, and stared at the door.

"What now?" Philippe asked, wiping a hand across his bloody brow.

Ryker crouched in front of the unconscious guard. "Now we talk to our new friend and find out how to get out of here."

"Good plan." Therian knelt beside Ryker and gestured for Jacques to get off the rebel.

Once the vampire had moved, Therian slapped their prisoner.

The fae woke with a start. He snarled, but the sound quickly disappeared as he took in the situation.

"Fuck," the rebel breathed.

Ryker glared at the fae. "Where are we?"

The rebel clamped his mouth shut.

Of course, this wouldn't be a simple interrogation. Ryker rubbed his good hand over his face.

"Look. This has been an incredibly long night, and none of us want to hurt you." Growls rose from some of the others, disproving his point. "Just tell us."

A long moment passed as the fae's gaze swept over them all. His eyes hardened, and he clenched his jaw.

"Even if you manage to get off this level, you'll never escape. People like you are our biggest enemies. My comrades will take pride in being the ones to kill you."

"People like us?" one of the other men asked.

"Representatives," spat the guard. "You think you're so far above the rest of us that you don't even realize the trouble you cause. We're suffering while you live your lives of luxury."

Ryker recoiled at the hatred in the man's voice.

"We should just kill him and get out of here." This came from Lincoln, Death Elf and son of a Northern Representative. "He's not going to help us."

Time was ticking. Any minute now, the guards who'd left could return.

"He's right," the rebel said defiantly. "I won't help you."

Ryker exchanged a look with Therian. As the only two with military training, they'd easily slipped into leadership roles.

Therian raised a brow as if to say, *your call.*

Ryker was used to making tough decisions, but it didn't mean he enjoyed them. After a moment, he dipped his head.

"So be it." He grabbed the guard's gun and gripped it firmly. "I'm sorry."

The rebel's eyes flashed. "You're just proving me right. You—"

Ryker flipped the weapon around, slamming the butt into the rebel's temples.

The guard's eyes closed, and his body slumped to the side.

"Have a nice nap," Ryker muttered.

Maybe when the rebel woke up and discovered he was still alive, his perception of the Representatives would change. It was unlikely, but... maybe.

"Grab his left arm," Ryker directed Philippe as he grabbed the right with his good arm.

Together, they maneuvered the unconscious man across the room. His feet trailed behind him, leaving a red track when they got a little too close to the dead rebel. Ryker grunted and readjusted his grip. It was uncomfortable, but he got the rebel's hand on the biometric scanner.

The door unlocked and opened with a hiss, letting a sliver of light into the space.

They dropped the guard on the ground.

Ryker turned around, addressing the rag-tag group.

"We move as one." He met the dragon shifter's gaze. "Therian, you take the back."

The captain's mind was working overtime, mapping out the most efficient way out of this mess with the limited information they'd been given. Ryker felt a kinship with the other Choosing participants and wanted to keep them safe. They weren't born of the same blood, nor were they all related to Representatives, as the rebel had erroneously assumed. Even so, they'd built connections during the Choosing and deserved to live.

The dragon shifter grunted and moved to the rear.

Ryker adjusted his grip on the weapon and dipped his head. "On three, we run."

He waited for the others to agree before he counted them down. He hit three and swung open the door, revealing a hallway. Lights dotted the ceiling like a runway, illuminating a path.

Another door was at the end, and there was a glowing biometric lock.

Ryker cursed, and they paused to retrieve the unconscious guard.

Three times, they used the rebel to unlock a door, only to find themselves in yet another hallway.

"Is this a fucking labyrinth?" someone grumbled.

The fae captain was beginning to feel the same way, although he didn't say that. One of the first rules of leadership was looking confident, even if one didn't feel that way on the inside. And inside, he wasn't calm.

He needed to get out of here. A thousand-pound weight was pressing down on his chest, and he wouldn't be able to rest until he saw Brynleigh with his own eyes.

"You'll never get out of here," the rebel fae slurred. He'd woken up sometime between the second and third door. "They'll stop you. You have no magic and two guns. What do you think you'll do?"

"We'll fight," Ryker grunted, slapping the man's hand on the next biometric lock.

That was the only option.

The door hissed open, just like all the others, but this time...

The rebel chuckled. "Told you so."

CHAPTER 35

Death Threats and Late Arrivals

The fourth door didn't open into a hallway like the others. It revealed a large workspace that might have been an office at one point. Several long tables covered in papers and computers took up floor space. Warm lights hung from the ceiling. They must've still been underground because there were no windows.

It wasn't the change in scenery that had Ryker's heart racing and his stomach dropping. It wasn't even the dozen impressive guns trained on his group or the multiple strands of deadly Death and Earth Elf magic hovering threateningly in the air.

No.

That was caused by the too-beautiful-to-be-real vampire standing in the middle of the group of rebels.

Jelisette de la Point's cold, obsidian eyes drilled into Ryker's, and a malicious smile crept across her features. Dressed in black training leathers, she looked like a warrior vampire from the time of the Four Kingdoms.

"Greetings, Captain Waterborne." The violent vampire strode towards him and smirked. "Going somewhere?"

Hatred coiled in Ryker's gut, and keeping his stolen weapon trained on Jelisette, he snarled, "You bitch."

She did this, somehow. Set Brynleigh up. Ryker could sense it in his gut.

"Is that any way to speak to your mother-in-law?" Jelisette raised a brow.

"Fuck you. Brynleigh doesn't see you as a mother, and neither do I."

Both he and his wife were sorely lacking in the maternal department.

"I would have kept her as a daughter, you know," Jelisette said cruelly. "Once, I thought she'd be able to replace me. But now I see the truth. My progeny is nothing but a lying, backstabbing bitch."

He growled.

"I tried to offer her the world. I gave her immortality and rules to live by, and what did she do?" Jelisette's lips curled into a hateful sneer. "She threw it all away. She told you *everything*. How dare she think she can play me and the Black Night? Your wife is nothing but a fucking waste of blood. I should've let her die all those years ago."

Ryker wanted to rip Jelisette's heart out of her chest.

His finger found the trigger. The gun probably wouldn't kill the vampire, but shooting her would feel fucking incredible. "Don't speak about my wife like that."

Brynleigh deserved all the respect and care in the world, and he would ensure she knew exactly how amazing she was.

Once he survived this.

He glanced at the collection of weapons.

If he survived this, he amended.

His analytical mind had already surveyed the situation, confirming what he'd already suspected: they were probably fucked. Even with their stolen weapons, their tattered group wouldn't be much of a match against the rebels.

As if confirming his thoughts, his shoulder throbbed again, reminding him of his injury.

Jelisette bared her fangs.

"Did you really think I was so stupid?" She stepped towards him. "I know Brynleigh stole the cipher. What kind of idiot would I be if I didn't have my entire house under constant surveillance?"

Ryker swallowed. "What did you do?"

The vampire's smile widened, and for the first time, Ryker glimpsed the true predator living beneath Jelisette de la Point's skin. It was as though she was peeling off layers, letting the mask of the well-adjusted woman fall away from her features. Even the other rebels took a step back.

Promises of a painful, drawn-out death glowed in the vampire's ancient obsidian eyes. Rolling her sleeves to her elbows, Jelisette displayed her Binding Mark and curled her fingers into claws.

"Isn't it clear?" Jelisette answered. "I arranged all of this. I'm going to take great pleasure in destroying you. Then I'm going to find your wife and ruin her, too. She'll be begging for death by the time I'm done with her."

Ryker clenched his fists, and an animalistic snarl rumbled through him.

"Bring it on," he growled.

Madness glinted in Jelisette's eyes, and in Ryker's gut, he knew this was the end. Making it out of here alive had been statistically improbable before, but now it was clear it wouldn't happen.

His heart twisted. He wished he could return to this morning and give Brynleigh one last kiss. Tell her he loved her one last time.

But this was it. There was only so much a fae bound by prohiberis could do against a vengeful vampire, a dozen guns, and deadly Death and Earth Elves.

Jelisette moved so fast that he could barely track her.

One moment, she stood in front of him. The next, she stole Ryker's gun and threw it halfway across the room before he could react. It clattered against the ground, reminding him exactly how helpless he was against such a powerful vampire.

Ryker lunged, and Jelisette swung out of his reach.

He ran at her, and she blurred around him. He spun, but he wasn't fast enough.

The vampire wrapped her arms around his stomach, flinging Ryker through the air.

He roared, arms flailing as he landed on a table. Pain flashed through his back, and the wood beneath him splintered.

The other rebels circled the Choosing participants, training their guns on the captives.

Jelisette cackled.

Insane. She was truly insane.

Gasping, Ryker rolled off the broken table and stumbled to his feet. Before he could take a single step, Jelisette threw herself at him. She moved with a speed unlike anything he had ever seen. Even Brynleigh had never moved this fast.

Jelisette was a blur as shadows streamed from her hands like ribbons. She grinned and snapped her teeth at him like a feral animal. She formed a shield of pure night and threw it at him.

The impact slammed him into the wall, and he groaned.

Damn the prohiberis.

Damn the rebels.

Damn it all.

Jelisette was toying with him like a cat playing with a mouse.

He peeled himself away from the wall. Every single movement hurt more than the last. It took a lot to kill a Mature being, but this...

He wouldn't be able to do this for much longer.

Especially since Jelisette seemed amused more than anything. That was the worst part about this horrid game.

Jelisette threw another wall of shadows at him. He rolled to the left, but she blurred across the room, grabbed his bad wrist, and pulled.

The bone snapped, and Ryker roared as fire ran through him.

He would not welcome death with open arms. He struggled, ignoring the flashing, searing pain as he tried to wrench his hand away. He would fight with everything he had until he had nothing left to give.

Jelisette smiled, her hands circling the captain's neck. Her nails dug into his skin, and she squeezed.

Ryker roared and thrashed against the vampire, clawing at her arms.

His lungs tightened, and black spots filled his vision. He couldn't breathe.

Death drew nearer.

But then, the strangest thing happened.

The overhead lights flickered.

Somewhere in the distance, a scream rose.

An alarm blared.

For the briefest moment, fear flickered across Jelisette's face.

It was gone as quickly as it appeared, but Ryker had seen it.

Jelisette pulled her hands off Ryker's throat and threw him towards the others.

He landed in a heap, his body slamming into the ground. Gasping, he drew in deep gulps of air as fire ran through him.

"Well now, Captain," Jelisette said. "It seems I may have a better use for you after all."

Hands seized Ryker and roughly pulled him back. He didn't spare the rebels a glance, though. Instead, his gaze locked on the ground.

Tendrils of blessed black darkness snaked across the floor. Different from Jelisette's shadows, these were ones that Ryker recognized.

Hope sparked deep in his soul.

Another scream came from nearby, piercing through the silence of this place of death.

One of the Death Elf rebels stumbled back. "What the fuck? What's happening?"

A third cry rose through the air, this one even closer.

Ryker's chest warmed with pride, and despite the brokenness of his body, he felt lighter than before.

He knew that darkness like he knew his own soul. It called to him.

The scent of copper filled the air.

He met the Death Elf's gaze and smiled. "My wife has arrived."

CHAPTER 36
Bloodlust and Death

Brynleigh was death, and death was Brynleigh.

As soon as the trio arrived at the Black Night's hideout, a red-bricked three-story building in the middle of fucking nowhere, the rebels attacked.

Nikhail had called the base for backup, but Brynleigh wasn't willing to wait. Ryker was inside, having the gods only knew what done to him.

Between Brynleigh's vampiric nature, the fae's air magic, and the witch's blue ribbons, they dispatched the six guards out front quickly enough.

Before they charged inside, Indira wove blue threads of magic in the air. She sent them into Brynleigh, helping fortify the vampire against the Fledgling desires of her heart. The last thing they needed was for Brynleigh to lose control and turn on them.

Unlike Emilia's painful magic, this felt almost... warm.

And then they went in.

There was so much blood.

Even with Indira's barriers in place, Brynleigh could feel the monster deep within her digging its claws into her soul. Every death brought it closer and closer to the edge. It took everything she had to hold onto control as she fought her way through the rebels.

Her fangs ripped through necks as though they were made of paper. Every scream, every cry, every plea for mercy fed the darkness in her soul.

She couldn't focus on anything except her need for Ryker.

They traveled down, down, down.

More rebels died.

Ryker was still missing.

They paused twice so Indira could pour more magic into Brynleigh, staving off her Fledgling bloodlust, but Brynleigh didn't think it would work much longer.

Where was Ryker?

People stood in their way. Brynleigh got rid of them.

Blood. There was so much fucking blood.

Every time they entered a room and Ryker wasn't there, a part of Brynleigh died.

But she wouldn't stop. She couldn't.

Nikhail had cut off a dead rebel's hand when they first arrived, and he was using the severed limb to unlock doors. It probably should've disgusted Brynleigh, but she didn't have room for feelings.

Remaining in control took everything she had.

Shadows poured from her, darkening everything in sight.

Her heart raced. Her skin was tight.

Part of her screamed to pay attention, to stop before it was too late, and this deadly monster shoved the last bits of her humanity aside forever, but that voice was growing fainter by the minute.

She needed Ryker like she needed blood.

Someone darted in front of her, and they raised a weapon.

A *boom* echoed through the tight corridor.

Fire burst through Brynleigh's side, but just as quickly, she began to heal.

The fools.

Nothing short of a wooden stake would stop her now.

There were more doors, more corridors, more guns.

Until there weren't.

The moment Brynleigh barreled through the last door, she stumbled to a stop.

Armed rebels surrounded a group of familiar men.

A mangled scream crawled out of Brynleigh's throat at the sight of Ryker on his knees.

Hurt.

Her breath came faster and faster as her last defenses against the bloodlust threatened to crumble.

The creature of death within her roared and clawed at her soul. It screamed, begging for her to release it.

And she almost did.

But then, his eyes met hers. Love and trust filled his gaze, infusing her with strength.

She inhaled, and it was like breathing for the first time. She shoved the monster down.

For Ryker, she would remain in control.

She had to.

But she lost seconds—precious, precious seconds—pushing the bloodlust away. Footsteps echoed on the cold cement floor. Across the room, separated by a few tables and chairs, was Jelisette.

"Greetings, daughter of my blood." Jelisette's lyrical voice was discordant with the darkness radiating off her. "I see you've been busy."

Brynleigh snarled, surprised that her voice still functioned after so much killing, and she balled her fists.

"Let my husband go," she demanded.

Jelisette snorted. "I don't think you understand the severity of the situation. But you will." She waved a hand in the air. "Take the others."

The last words had barely left her mouth before rebels came out of nowhere and converged on Nikhail and Indira.

They yelled. Wind and blue magic burst from the two as they stood back to back in the middle of the room. Power cycloned around their hands, tornadoes of magic that threatened death.

But Jelisette raised a brow. "Put your magic away, or we shoot them all right now. You won't win. You can't."

Nikhail stared at Jelisette for a long moment, his amber gaze assessing. Then he dropped his hands.

"Do as she says, Indira," the fae ordered.

The witch cursed but complied.

A deadly smirk waltzed across Jelisette's face as rebels approached cautiously, slapping prohiberis on the fae and witch before adding them to their group of captives.

But the guns didn't lower.

Instead, one of the rebels shifted, moving the barrel of his weapon to the back of Ryker's head.

A feral growl ripped from Brynleigh's chest.

This would not be the end.

Ryker's beautiful eyes rose to meet hers. Her breath caught in her throat, and time, which had been playing games with her tonight, froze. His gaze sliced through the remnants of the crimson fog in her mind like a lantern shining in the darkness.

For one long, eternal, never-ending moment, she couldn't breathe.

Her shadows, which had been flooding from her, froze. Entire universes could have collided in the time that her gaze locked onto his.

He was *hers*.

Her Chosen partner.

Her husband.

Her *everything*.

They dared threaten his life?

Brynleigh tore her gaze away from her husband.

"You," she snarled at her Maker. "You did this. Why?"

"Isn't it obvious?" Jelisette stepped around a table, making her way toward Brynleigh. "You broke the rules. *Again*. Did you think you could betray and outwit me? I Made you. I own you. And I will fucking destroy you."

"Don't listen to her. You're stronger than she could ever be," Ryker yelled.

"Isn't that sweet?" Jelisette crooned as she reached behind her and pulled something out of her back pocket. "He thinks you can beat me."

Brynleigh's gaze darted between Jelisette and the captives. She needed to free them, yet her Maker was the most dangerous person here.

"Allow me to let you in on a little secret." The ancient vampire sneered. "No one can beat me because I have nothing left to lose. You think you know pain? You know *nothing*."

"I know pain." Brynleigh's hand went to the necklace at her throat. "I lost my family."

Those high winds and deadly waves would forever be seared in Brynleigh's memory. She'd never forget the screams of that night, the cries of death, and the horror of learning everyone she loved was dead. She would mourn them right up until she took her final breath.

"Your pain is nothing compared to mine. You lost your family, but I lost my *soul*!"

Jelisette screamed the last word, her eyes widening as she pulled her hand out from behind her back.

Somewhere outside of herself, Brynleigh heard Ryker roar, but she didn't dare move.

Her gaze was locked on the wooden stake in Jelisette's hand, and her heart seized.

"You have no idea what it's like." Jelisette twisted the stake through her fingers. "Emery did not deserve to die like that. They took him, broke him, and destroyed him. He was my love, and they *stole* him from me.

"He was *good*, my Emery. He never killed anyone who didn't deserve it. He spent his immortal life fighting those who hurt others. And in the end, did it matter? No. The Representatives fucking killed him. They took him, and now, I will destroy them all."

The stake was as sharp as any knife, mocking Brynleigh as Jelisette calmly walked around the last table.

Fear sluiced through Brynleigh's veins like streams of ice. She glanced around, searching for a weapon. A knife. A blade. Something. Fucking anything that she could use to defend herself.

Jelisette didn't even seem to notice the others in the room. All her focus was trained on Brynleigh, and nothing was more frightening than being the object of this dangerous vampire's attention.

"I'm so sorry he died." Brynleigh inched around the table, trying to keep space between them. "But you can't just kill everyone else because he's gone."

Brynleigh understood where her Maker was coming from. Really, she did.

In theory, revenge sounded marvelous. Spilling blood in the name of vengeance was addicting.

But what no one had ever told Brynleigh, and what she almost didn't learn until it was too late, was that revenge could never heal a broken heart. Revenge would never cross the divide between life and death.

Death was final, and nothing could be done to bring back those who had crossed that barrier.

There was something deeply heartbreaking about spending one's life seeking vengeance.

Hardening one's heart took a lot of work. It was a painful process, and even then, emotions could ruin everything. Brynleigh's relationship with Ryker was proof of that.

Her Maker smirked.

"That's where you're wrong, young one. I *can* kill everyone, and with the help of the Black Night, I will destroy this country from the top down."

She stepped closer.

Brynleigh mirrored her sire's movements, keeping distance between them. "That won't work."

"Oh, but it will." Jelisette's eyes twinkled with darkness and death. "First, I'm going to kill you. Then, I'll deal with the rest."

She turned towards the other rebels.

"Hold him. I want him to watch as I destroy her."

The rebel holding the gun to Ryker's head grabbed his arms and pinned them behind his back. Ryker roared.

"No!" Brynleigh screamed. She turned to her husband, desperation leaking into her tone. "I'll save you. I promise."

"Now, now, daughter of my blood. Didn't anyone ever teach you not to make promises you can't keep?" Jelisette smiled. "None of you will be leaving here alive."

CHAPTER 37
Destined to be Alone Forever

Jelisette de la Point cackled as shadows poured out of her, stealing the light.

Her fangs ached with the need to spill blood.

The shadows didn't prevent her from seeing in the dark. She was Made for the darkness.

Her Binding Mark burned, and she knew that somewhere far from here, Emery was watching her.

Avenge me, my love, he murmured.

Jelisette had heard her beloved's voice every Ithiar-damned day ever since that horrific night. Every time she closed her eyes, every time she dreamed, she went back to that moment when her life forever changed. She could still hear the echoes of her scream as she stumbled onto the ice and fell to her knees in front of his too-still gray body.

Too late, too late, too late.

That night, The Binding Mark had burned like a fucking fire. It blazed through her upon his death, and she'd *felt* her soul rip in two.

Emery had left this world, and he'd taken her half of her with him.

If only she'd been faster. If only she'd been able to get to him in time. Maybe they could've been happy. Maybe they could've lived in peace.

Instead, Representative Kyani had driven a stake into Emery's beautiful heart and murdered him.

In return, Jelisette had killed the Representative and his family. It hadn't brought Emery back, but it had momentarily made her feel better. In the Representative's mansion, with their gilded picture frames and golden candelabras, she'd sworn her life's mission: she would destroy the Representatives, no matter how long it took.

And then she went to work.

She wormed her way into the Black Night, and through the decades, she rose in their ranks. They weren't small, nor were they particularly trusting, but Jelisette had time.

She had so much gods-damned time.

It was the only thing she had since Emery died.

Alone, alone, alone.

Jelisette was always fucking alone.

Emery had been hers. They'd understood each other. He'd been a deadly man, but he loved her. The two of them had been happy. They'd Bound together after Emery almost died from a werewolf attack, and then, they hunted criminals together.

But then he was murdered. Gone. And Jelisette's progeny? *Twice,* she'd betrayed her.

It was time for Brynleigh to die.

Twisting the stake in her hand, Jelisette smiled. She knew Emery would approve of every single action she'd taken since his death. Ever since she'd seen him that night across Starless Lake, he'd been her biggest champion.

It was with his face in mind that she leaped across the table. His voice she heard as a war cry slipped from her lips.

Brynleigh scrambled out of the way as if that would save her from her Maker's wrath.

Jelisette wasn't too proud to admit that she'd made a mistake, letting her progeny live after she'd broken the rules the first time. That day, when Brynleigh showed up at her door, a ridiculously sentimental notion had entered Jelisette's mind. Maybe this was her chance to have the daughter she'd never have.

She let Brynleigh live, and look where it got her.

Never fucking again.

Jelisette was destined to be alone forever.

The others would keep the captives secured until she was done here, and then she'd kill each man who'd participated in the Choosing.

Then, Jelisette would hunt. She'd find their families. Their loved ones. Their friends.

Anyone with ties to the Representatives would die until the entire upper class was wiped away from the land like the scourge they were.

And it would be good.

Jelisette flung out her hand, a swarm of shadows flying in her progeny's direction. The girl screamed, and the sound was fucking music to Jelisette's ears.

Somewhere in the room, that awful fae captain roared. He would die next.

But first, Jelisette would finish her progeny, once and for all.

A spark of something deliciously cruel came to life within the vampire, and she retracted her shadows. She wanted the fae to watch as she killed his wife.

After all the pain Jelisette had endured, it would only be fitting for him to feel even a fraction of the agony that had been her daily torment ever since Emery's death.

Jelisette ran with the speed of her kind and collided with Brynleigh. The two women fell, and Jelisette straddled the younger vampire, pinning her to the floor. With a wave of her hand, she commanded her shadows to wrap around the younger vampire's wrists, pinning them above her head.

Brynleigh struggled, but she was no match for her Maker.

No one here was. Ancient power ran through Jelisette's veins.

She raised the stake in the air, and her progeny's eyes bulged.

"This won't bring him back," Brynleigh whispered desperately. "It won't help the pain."

As if this little bitch could comprehend Jelisette's daily agony.

Jelisette sneered. "No, but hearing your fae captain scream as you die will make me happy."

And happiness was fleeting these days. She had to grab it wherever she could.

"Don't do this," Brynleigh begged.

Begged!

That was the final straw.

Jelisette was done. Done with talking. Done with fighting. Done with this night. Done with it all.

Do it, love.

Jelisette raised the stake.

The fae captain screamed. His rage and fear spurned her forward.

Without a second thought, Jelisette plunged the weapon towards Brynleigh's heart.

CHAPTER 38
Is it Over?

"No!" Ryker roared.

The hands restraining him tightened, but it didn't matter. Nothing mattered at all except for Brynleigh.

He thrashed and kicked and pulled. His shoulder burned, the pain getting worse with every passing second, but he could be on fire right now, and he wouldn't care.

He had to get to her.

Brynleigh had fought her way to him. She couldn't die now. What kind of cruel fate was this?

Ryker had promised he'd always be by her side, and he was a fae of his words.

So, he fought.

He dug within himself, and despite the prohiberis blocking his magic, despite the pain and agony and exhaustion running through him, he pulled up every last ounce of strength in his possession.

As Jelisette lowered the stake, he funneled every bit of power he had into breaking free from his captors. He shoved his arms up, slamming his good fist into the rebel's nose. It broke, blood gushing, and Ryker used the commotion to push the armed rebel away.

Ryker barreled to his feet. His arm moved oddly, and he was pretty certain it was broken in several places, but he didn't care. He raced across the room towards his wife.

He was vaguely aware of the other men yelling and using his escape as a distraction to fight back against the rebels, but he couldn't focus on them.

A gun went off. Then, two more. Someone screamed.

None of it registered.

He moved as quickly as his fae feet would allow, throwing himself over the table.

The older vampire didn't seem to notice.

"No!" he yelled again.

Finally, Jelisette looked up. Her eyes sparked with alarm before hardening once again.

It was just a moment, but it was enough.

Ryker grabbed Jelisette, one arm wrapping around her neck and the other around her middle. He landed awkwardly behind her, the weight of his body enough to shift her back a few inches. It wasn't much, but it bought Brynleigh distance between her and the stake.

"Fight, love!" he yelled as the older vampire screamed and thrashed against his hold.

Jelisette was far stronger than any other vampire Ryker had ever encountered.

Brynleigh didn't hesitate. Hands still bound by shadows in a praying position, she grabbed the stake and ripped it from her Maker's hand.

Time slowed to a crawl.

With a warrior's cry, Brynleigh plunged the stake into Jelisette's heart.

Fighting continued behind them, but Ryker didn't pay any attention to it.

A long, undying howl like a bitter winter's wind came from Jelisette's lips. The sound sent shivers cascading down Ryker's spine.

Jelisette clawed at the stake buried deep in her heart, but Brynleigh's grip held firm.

Ryker reached around the ancient vampire with his good arm and clasped his hand over Brynleigh's. Her hand, cold beneath his, tightened around the stake. He grunted, flipping all three of them.

Jelisette was on the ground beneath them, and they kneeled on either side of the evil woman.

The howl went on and on and on.

Death had never taken so long to claim its prize.

Black lines spiderwebbed from the stake, covering Jelisette from head to toe. Skin that had been fair and smooth moments ago was now gray and sunken. Silky hair turned to straw. Life-filled eyes drained. She opened her mouth wider, the howl morphing into a never-ending scream. She slashed at them both, her movements brittle and unsteady.

And then, after what felt like a lifetime, Jelisette fell silent. Her hand froze, outstretched towards the heavens, and one last breath slipped from her cracked, ashen lips. The shadows binding Brynleigh's wrists together vanished.

In the sudden silence, Ryker's heart was a booming drum in his ears.

Brynleigh whimpered, "She's... dead."

Her white-knuckled fingers were still clasped over the stake, along with Ryker's.

He stared at the shriveled corpse of the woman who had made their lives a living hell. This was the kind of death there was no coming back from.

"Yes, she is."

A horrible death for a horrible woman.

A tear slid down Brynleigh's cheek.

"She'll be with him now," she murmured. "Emery. I think... I think she loved him. Or whatever kind of love she was capable of feeling."

Ryker grunted in agreement, and for several long minutes, neither of them moved.

Someone touched Ryker's shoulder. He looked up and met Nikhail's eyes. A line of blood streaked across the air fae's face, and a gash slashed across his left shoulder, but he appeared to be in one piece.

"It's time to go," Nikhail said.

Ryker closed his eyes. "Thanks for coming, Nik."

He didn't even want to think about what would've happened if they hadn't arrived.

"Thank your wife." The air fae gestured to Brynleigh. "She fought well."

A tremor ran through Brynleigh at Nikhail's words. She was still gripping the stake.

Ryker slowly peeled his wife's fingers off the weapon, wrapping them in his hand instead.

"Let's get out of here, love."

She didn't fight him as he rose and tugged her away from the dead woman.

It was only then that Ryker took in the scene around them.

Jelisette wasn't the only one Death had visited.

Of the nine captive men from the Choosing, seven were standing. All were injured. Only one member of the Black Night remained alive, a man Therian was pinning to the ground. The dragon shifter had a gun pointed at the rebel's head.

Therian met Ryker's eye, and the two men communicated silently.

The dragon shifter nodded. Hauling the rebel to his feet, he ordered, "Get us the fuck out of here, now."

Exhaustion had woven itself into the very fabric of Ryker's being. An entire day had passed since their rag-tag group had stumbled out of the rebels' compound, bloody, bruised, and broken...

But alive.

Thank the Blessed Black Sands for that.

Ryker hadn't released Brynleigh's hand. Not as they staggered out of the building, not while they debriefed with the backup Nikhail had called, who had just gotten to the scene, and not even when they were taken to the army base.

He wasn't sure he could ever let go of his wife again. He'd come so close to losing her.

As soon as they arrived on the base, soldiers cut off their prohiberis cuffs.

A witch came in and healed Ryker's shoulder and arm. The process was unpleasant, but the break was set and healing.

Then, the questioning began. Representatives, military personnel, and even the Chancellor filtered through the rooms where they were keeping the survivors.

There were so many questions—too many, even for Ryker.

What happened?

How were you taken?

Who was there?

And then the questions got increasingly personal.

Tell us about the Black Night.

You got your wife out of The Pit. Why?

Explain the deal you made with Myrrah Challard.

How did you come to be involved with the rebels?

Tell us about Horizon.

The questions were never-ending. Just when he thought they'd be done, someone else walked in. Ryker was over this.

It wasn't until they'd started directing questions at Brynleigh that Ryker snapped, though.

General Whitecliff, an Earth Elf who'd served in the army for decades, sat across from the couple. Her fiery hair was pulled back in a tight bun, and she looked every bit the fierce soldier Ryker had heard her to be. Perhaps at another time, he'd enjoy speaking with the elf, but seeing as how she was interrogating them—because that's what this had fucking become—he was in no mood for pleasantries.

"Mrs. Waterborn, I need you to detail your role in this for me again." General Whitecliff's voice brokered no room for discussion.

Brynleigh sighed. This was the third time she'd been asked this question. "As I've already told your colleagues, I don't have a role in this. I was helping you."

The Earth Elf tilted her head, and her emerald eyes gleamed. "Is that so?"

"Yes," Brynleigh said. "It is."

A long moment passed in terse silence before the general said, "Then I'm sure you wouldn't mind—"

"Enough!" Ryker slammed his free hand on the table. "My wife *saved* us all. If you have a fucking problem with that, you can take it up with me. *Later.*"

He stood, tugging Brynleigh with him.

"Captain Waterborn—" General Whitecliff started.

"No. We've been here long enough. I'm taking my wife home. She needs to shower and rest." They both did. "If you have further questions, call Representative Waterborn. I'm sure she'd be willing to set up an appointment."

At the mention of Ryker's mother, the general paled.

Ryker rarely enjoyed his mother's cold-hearted, difficult nature, but sometimes, it came in handy—not that he would ever tell her that.

Maybe it was the blood covering his wife, or maybe it was the look on Ryker's face, but either way, no one tried to stop them as they left the interrogation room.

Ryker led Brynleigh through the military buildings to the underground parking garage. He commandeered the keys of an emergency vehicle from a soldier who quaked when they saw Brynleigh's bloody face.

It wasn't until they were alone and standing in front of the sleek black vehicle with tinted windows that Brynleigh exhaled.

"Is it over?" She raised her black eyes to his, exhaustion etched into her face. "Are we done?"

After everything that had just happened, there was no way anyone could question Brynleigh's loyalties. She'd saved the family members of several Representatives and killed a high-ranking rebel within the Black Night.

Ryker dipped his chin, drew her into his arms, and confidently said, "Yes, love, we're done."

CHAPTER 39
Use Me

Brynleigh stretched her arms over her head, reveling in the warmth and comfort radiating from the fae resting beside her. Sunlight filtered through the window, casting beautiful yellow light onto the bed.

A smile crept across her face as she stared at the sun.

Three weeks had passed since the failed Reunion, yet she still couldn't believe it was over. Not really. She still had nightmares about Jelisette staking her, but every time she woke up, she saw Ryker and knew it had been a dream.

She glanced to her right, where Ryker slept on his back. The sheet had slipped to his waist, and they were both naked from their late-night activities. Marlowe's quiet snores came from the living room, where he slept on the couch, but Brynleigh couldn't pull her gaze from her fae.

Gods above, Ryker was beautiful. His muscles were defined, his chest was sculpted, and even in his sleep, his mouth was perfectly kissable.

Her fangs ached as she admired him. Every inch of him was delectable.

Ryker's lips twitched. His eyes were still closed as he drawled, "See something you like, little vampire?"

Heat rushed to her cheeks, but she refused to be embarrassed about admiring him. He was hers as much as she was his.

"I do." She leaned over and kissed him. "Good morning."

He rolled them over, pressing her back into the mattress as his eyes blinked open. "Morning, sweetheart. How'd you sleep?"

"Fine."

He studied her. "How many nightmares?"

He knew. He always knew.

"Only one."

They were getting better. Slowly. One day, she hoped to have none at all.

Ryker kissed the corner of her mouth.

"Good, I'm glad." His hand trailed over her hip. "Are you ready for today?"

She bit her lip. "This is the last one, right?"

He nodded.

"Then yes, I'm ready."

Two and a half weeks ago, Chancellor Rose convened an emergency meeting of the entire governing body of the Republic of Balance. Since then, Brynleigh and Ryker had been forced to attend three meetings. They each testified on record about the events leading up to the Reunion and provided their accounts of the night itself.

"You'll be amazing." Ryker lifted Brynleigh's left wrist and kissed the spot where the blue bracelet had been. "I have a surprise for you after."

She smiled and studied him, searching for a clue. "What is it?"

"You'll have to be patient." He booped her nose. "That's the point of a surprise."

Of course, she knew what surprises were, but it wasn't like Ryker to keep things from her.

"You really won't tell me?"

"No. There's nothing you can do to make me spill. It's a secret."

Brynleigh highly doubted that there was *nothing* she could do. She could think of several things that would make even the most battle-hardened fae talk. But she would be patient.

Honestly, she was just ready for all this to be over.

She wanted to live a quiet life with her captain, away from the spotlight of the Choosing and everything that had happened to them since then.

Brynleigh said as much to Ryker, and he smiled.

"A quiet life? Is that all you want?"

She waggled her brows. "Well, it's not the only thing I want."

"Oh? I endeavor to please your every whim." He kissed her slowly as if they had all the time in the world. "What else do you want? Tell me, and I'll do whatever it takes to make it happen."

He looked at her with so much love and devotion that, for a moment, she thought her heart would combust. She'd never known it was possible to be so loved and cared for. And yet, here they were. They'd picked up the pieces of their relationship and emerged stronger than ever on the other side.

Brynleigh arched her back, delighting in Ryker's ragged exhale as her nipples brushed his chest. Her hand slipped between them, and she trailed her fingers over his already-hard cock.

"This," she breathed. "You."

His eyes darkened above her. "You have me, love. I am yours, and you can do with me as you wish. Say the word, and I'll do it. I would do anything for you."

He'd proven that to her time and time again.

Her fangs ached, and before she could think twice about her request —or take it back—she breathed, "I want to bite you."

This was the one thing they'd yet to share, the one act reserved for only the most intimate of relationships. She'd never bitten anyone before. The fridge was stocked with blood, but it wasn't *his*.

A rumble rolled through Ryker's chest, and his length hardened against her stomach.

It pleased her to no end that the thought excited him as well.

"By the Obsidian Sands, yes." He practically growled the words as he arched his head, exposing the long column of his neck to her. "Of course, you can bite me. Go ahead, little vampire. I'm yours. Use me."

So, she did.

She laced one hand behind him, pulling him to her. Threading the other through his hair, she kissed his neck.

He groaned, and the sound was all the encouragement she needed.

Brynleigh drew back her lips, and without a moment's hesitation, she sank her fangs into his throat.

At the first taste of Ryker's blood, Brynleigh knew she was done for.

How had she lived without this before? He tasted like a storm. Crisp and dark and powerful. With each sip, she drowned in his essence. There was a depth to his blood that she'd never experienced.

This was heaven. It was little wonder that vampires of old had spent their lives defending their right to Sources and drinking from the vein. This was addicting.

Brynleigh had never done anything so enjoyable in her entire life.

And then Ryker *moaned*. The sound was pure pleasure as it slipped from his lips.

"I want you," he murmured.

In response, she parted her legs.

He sank into her heat with ease as she drank from him. She took him to the hilt, and both of them stilled. Pleasure, unlike anything she had ever known, ran through her. It was almost too much, drinking from him while he was sheathed within her.

Had she thought she was in heaven before?

She'd been mistaken.

Brynleigh had never known true pleasure. Not until that very moment. Nothing in the world could top this; nothing could make her feel better than she did right now.

A strangled groan came from above her. "Gods, you feel so fucking good."

Good was an understatement. This was *everything*.

Brynleigh couldn't respond, not with her fangs in his neck, but she lifted her hips in encouragement for him to move.

He did exactly that.

Ryker had already proven himself to be a skilled lover, not that she'd ever doubted his abilities, but this...

He didn't just make love to her.

He *ravished* her.

With his head thrown back and hands digging into the mattress on either side of her, he gave her everything he had. His cock slammed into her with each thrust.

More, more, more, until it was almost too much.

She pulled her fangs from his throat, licking the small trail of blood, as her head fell back on a gasp.

"Oh gods, oh gods, oh gods." She could barely breathe, barely think, barely do anything except feel.

His mouth fused to hers. This embrace was a searing claim as his tongue parted her lips. He didn't just kiss her.

He devoured her.

He matched each gasp, each moan, each nearly incoherent plea that slipped from her lips with one of his own.

Their sweat-slicked bodies moved as one as they drove each other nearer to the edge of oblivion.

"Ry, I'm so close," she moaned.

"Look at me," he ordered.

She did, her body tightening as the pleasure she so desperately sought remained just out of reach.

His lips descended on hers again, and he held her gaze as his hand slipped between them. His thumb found her clit, and in a gruff voice, he ordered, "Come for me, love."

That was all she needed.

Stars burst behind her eyes as her climax took her over like a storm. Wave after wave of pleasure ran through her, and then he came with a roar that she was sure could be heard through the entire building.

When they finally broke apart, Ryker brushed his thumb down Brynleigh's cheek.

"I love you," he whispered. "I will never let anything break us again."

Sealing his promise with a kiss, Ryker showed her exactly how much he loved her. Again. And again. And again.

CHAPTER 40
Important Matters and Surprises

Brynleigh adjusted the hem of her black knee-length dress, shifting her weight from one heeled foot to the other. The small office where they'd been directed to wait had black-out blinds covering the windows, and it felt too much like a tomb for her liking. The sooner they got out of here, the better.

A hand smoothed over her lower back.

"Relax," Ryker murmured in a low, soft voice. He wore a black suit and a crisp white shirt underneath, looking every bit of the Representative's son he was. "There's nothing to be afraid of. This will be different from the others."

Brynleigh wasn't scared, exactly. She just didn't enjoy spending time surrounded by Representatives. Unsurprisingly, not much had changed on that front over the past few weeks. Chancellor Rose was still in power, the Representatives were still in charge, and inequality still existed in the Republic of Balance.

Not all Representatives were bad, though.

That, perhaps, was one of the most surprising things Brynleigh had learned. They had met with Myrrah Challard again last week, and the witch had seemed amenable to working on removing the divide between the Representatives and the lower classes.

Not only that, but the code breakers had finally been able to crack the cipher. The book Brynleigh had retrieved from Jelisette's contained many things, including a list of rebel operatives within the Republic and overseas.

It provided several damning pieces of evidence that were being used to bring down half a dozen key members of the rebel organization. Finally, the government had solid proof against the Black Night.

"I'll relax when we get to leave." She elbowed Ryker in the side. "I still get my surprise, right?"

He grinned, and gods, it was a beautiful sight. Every time he directed a smile at her, she felt like the luckiest woman in the world.

"Absolutely." He squeezed her hand. "It's all set up. You'll get it as soon as we're done here."

A knock came on the door, and then it opened.

A human in her forties wearing a stylish maroon pantsuit smiled at them. "Mr. and Mrs. Waterborn, the Council is ready for you. Follow me, please."

Brynleigh drew in a deep breath and exchanged a look with Ryker. There was so much admiration and encouragement in his eyes that she knew she could do this. With him by her side, she could do anything.

What were a few Representatives when she'd defeated the Crimson Shade, survived the Black Night, and killed her Maker?

Holding her head up high, Brynleigh laced her fingers through Ryker's. Together, they trailed the woman down a short hallway and through an unmarked black door.

Bright lights illuminated the stage where they stood, but though the seated Representatives were hidden from view, Brynleigh still felt the weight of their gazes. She'd been to the Council Chamber before, but this was her first time on the stage, not in the testimonial box. Her stomach twisted as nerves threatened to erupt, but then, Ryker squeezed her hand.

The simple action grounded her, and she straightened her shoulders.

"Ah, the Waterborns are here." Chancellor Rose stood and strode onto the stage from the left, looking just as put together as she had the night of the Reunion.

Hallie had confided in Brynleigh that Valentina had broken down in the Hall of Choice after they'd left. She'd been inconsolable, and she'd since locked herself away to grieve for her husband.

Apparently, the Chancellor had only visited her daughter once.

Brynleigh hadn't thought someone could be as cold as Jelisette de la Point, but maybe in another life, the vampire and fire fae would've been bosom friends instead of mortal enemies.

"Come, come," Ignatia said. "We don't have all day, and there are more important matters to get to."

Like the rebels.

They were still a problem. They'd dealt with part of them, but Dimitri hadn't been in the building that night. The rebel organization was just so big. Brynleigh was certain this wasn't the last time they would cause problems in the Republic of Balance.

But at least for now, they'd been stopped.

An entire camera crew was present. Unlike the other times they'd been here, today would be televised.

Brynleigh had known the press would be here, but it didn't make standing in front of them any easier. After this, she hoped to never be on camera again in her entire life.

Hand in hand, she and Ryker strode to the middle of the stage.

"People of the Republic of Balance, it is my honor to come to you today with a story of bravery." Chancellor Rose reached out and placed a hand on Brynleigh's shoulder. Her touch was as cold as ice. "You may not know it, but several weeks ago, this courageous young vampire infiltrated a dangerous organization for the good of our country."

The Chancellor kept talking. She twisted the truth with impressive skill, making it seem like she had sanctioned and orchestrated Brynleigh's infiltration of the Black Night.

Brynleigh hated every second of this charade, but she didn't protest. This was the final price of her freedom. After this, they would be left alone for good. The Chancellor had promised to wipe the slate clean, and the legal documents were already drawn up and signed.

Knowing she was almost done, Brynleigh smiled, nodded, and shook the Chancellor's hand when the fire fae thanked her for helping her country.

And then, one last time, she turned to the camera and waved.

"THANK ISVANA, THAT'S FINISHED." Brynleigh leaned against Ryker as they exited the elevator in the underground parking garage. She couldn't wait to get in the vehicle and remove her shoes. These damned heels were horrible, and the dress wasn't much better.

Ryker kissed her forehead. "You were amazing, and now, it's over."

Over.

One word had never sounded so good.

She could scarcely believe it. When she'd first entered the Choosing with the desire to avenge her family, she never imagined this would be the outcome.

Jelisette was dead, Brynleigh had married her mark, and despite the betrayal and hurt they'd inflicted upon each other, they'd come out stronger on the other side. The rebels were no longer an imminent threat, and Ryker's father was responding well to treatment.

Not only that, but Ryker had petitioned the Chancellor to remove Victor, her torturer, and his sadistic friends from prison duty. He had assured Brynleigh that not only would they not hurt anyone else, but she'd never have to see them again. That meant more to her than any gift he could have ever given her.

Was this what it meant to be happy?

She must've said the last question out loud because Ryker chuckled as he opened the car door for her.

"Yes, love." He kissed her as she ducked inside the vehicle.

He walked to the other side and slid into the driver's seat. He turned on the car, expertly backed out of the space, and took her hand.

"This is exactly what happiness feels like."

Like warmth and sunlight and butterflies all mixed together.

Brynleigh had never known she'd been living in frigid darkness until Ryker cracked open her heart and showed her just how much she was missing.

She wouldn't have it any other way.

Buckling in, she pulled off her heels and beamed at her husband.

"So, my surprise." She wiggled her toes, grateful to be freed from the confines of horrible footwear. "Will you tell me what it is now? Another chess board?"

Since the rebels' attack, she and Ryker had played several chess matches together. She was currently winning by one game, but she wanted to extend her lead.

Ryker flashed her a grin as he navigated the car onto the highway.

"No, this is bigger than that."

He refused to say anything else, though. She tried to get information out of him, asking question after question, but he was skilled at evasiveness.

Eventually, Brynleigh gave up and stared out the windows. Like the apartment, the car had vampire-safe glass, and she admired the sun. The skyline slowly shifted, the industrial metropolis of Golden City giving way to sprawling golden fields and, eventually, sun-kissed forests. A companionable silence filled the vehicle, and Ryker's thumb stroked the back of her hand.

Peace as silent as a winter's night and as comforting as a heavy blanket settled between them.

This was right. This was where they were always meant to be. Just the two of them.

Eventually, Brynleigh's eyes grew heavy. She drifted off to sleep, anchored to reality by Ryker's fingers laced through hers.

She'd never let him go.

LIPS BRUSHED BRYNLEIGH'S FOREHEAD. "We're here, sweetheart."

She smiled as she woke, leaving a quiet, nightmare-free sleep. Her eyes fluttered open, meeting Ryker's.

"Where are we?"

They were parked in front of a single-story log cabin with a wooden wrap-around porch. In many ways, it reminded her of the small bungalow where he'd brought her after The Pit. Tall trees reached for the night sky, pine needles dusted the ground, and a still, blue lake was off in the distance.

"This is my cabin." The corner of Ryker's mouth tugged up as he reached over and unbuckled her seatbelt. "Well, *our* cabin."

"It's beautiful." She returned her gaze to him. "Is this my surprise?"

He shook his head. "No, your surprise is inside."

Intrigued, she followed him out of the car. She considered putting her shoes back on, but she took one look at the discarded heels and decided to leave them. The cold winter wind howled through the trees. There was no snow on the ground, but if the heavy clouds were any indication, a white blanket would cover the land come sunrise. She'd enjoy her bare feet while she could.

Ryker offered Brynleigh his hand and helped her up the steps. It was unnecessary but also ridiculously sweet, so she allowed him to assist her.

She thought he'd unlock the door, but instead, he knocked.

She shot him a quizzical look, but he just smiled and squeezed her hand. "Patience, love."

Footsteps came from inside, and then, the door swung open.

Brynleigh stared, blinking repeatedly. She opened and closed her mouth, but words were hard to find.

"I... This... Zanri?"

No matter how many times she closed and reopened her eyes, he remained standing in front of her. He looked... well, probably as good as she had when she'd first gotten out of prison. He was leaning on a cane, his skin was a collection of bruises, and he was far too thin.

But he was here.

Alive.

She turned to Ryker, her brows furrowed. "How?"

Her fae captain smiled and squeezed her hand. "After the Reunion, several teams searched Jelisette's safe house. They uncovered information about her nefarious dealings. She was blackmailing dozens of people, including Zanri. Once we had that, I petitioned the Chancellor to release him as an act of goodwill."

Silver lined Brynleigh's eyes, and she held a hand over her mouth. This was... it was... Unexpected. Generous. Considerate. She'd felt so horrible about leaving her friend in Moonwater Prison, especially after everything that had happened.

"Thank you, Ryker." Tears slipped down her cheeks. "Thank you so much."

She couldn't seem to think of any other words that would adequately convey the depth of her appreciation, but she'd show him later just how much this unexpected gesture meant to her.

Would this man never cease to surprise her?

He untangled their fingers and gently pushed her inside.

"Go ahead, catch up. I'll make some dinner and warm up some blood for you."

Ryker was so gods-damned considerate.

And he was hers.

Forever.

CHAPTER 41

He'd Chosen Well

T*hree months later*

Snow fell leisurely from the midnight, star-speckled sky, dancing towards the ground. Ryker inhaled deeply, the crisp air infiltrating his lungs. The Northern Region was always cold, but it was even more frigid than normal after the winter they'd just had.

It didn't bother him at all. No amount of cold could chase the warmth that had taken up residency in his heart since the Reunion.

Ryker hadn't known that happiness could be so consuming or that it could completely alter every aspect of one's life. Everything he did was made easier with Brynleigh by his side. She made him a better man; each day was better than the last.

"It's beautiful," she murmured from beside him.

Marlowe barked as if emphasizing her point. The dog sat patiently at Ryker's feet, waiting to be allowed to run around.

The fae wiggled his fingers in his gloves, the cold permeating every layer he wore. It was true that the Northern Region was especially stunning in the winter, not that there were many seasonal differences this far north.

In the land once known as Eleyta, winter reigned ten months out of the year. Snow-capped mountains speared the skies. Evergreen trees wearing white coats rose all around them. The Black Sea was in front of them, stretching as far as the eye could see. A massive hunting lodge was at their backs, and the vacation rental was exactly as pictured.

It was perfect.

Ryker looked to his left. Brynleigh was staring at the mountains, and Ryker unabashedly studied his beautiful wife. Her cheeks were tinged in pink, and golden tendrils escaped her braid. A black scarf and mittens only added to her vampiric beauty, accentuating her pale skin and goddess-touched features. Cast in the moon's silver light, she had an ethereal air that drew him to her.

"You are," he murmured.

He still couldn't believe she was his. From the first moment he'd seen her in the infirmary, he'd known they were meant to be.

It took a second for his words to settle, but he saw the moment they did because a shy smile spread across Brynleigh's face as she looked up at him.

"You're not so bad yourself, Captain."

Chuckling, he kissed her. He'd never get enough of this. Of her.

"Are you happy?" he asked.

She beamed. "More than I ever thought possible."

"Me too." Ryker wrapped his arms around her and held her against his chest. If someone had told him *this* would be where they ended up in those horrible days after their wedding, he never would've believed them.

And yet, they were on their second-chance honeymoon, waiting for their friends, and ready for whatever life would throw at them next. Even Tertia seemed to be slowly softening towards Brynleigh after the vampire had saved her son's life. Cyrus was healing, and River had finished Maturing a month ago.

Ryker tightened his grip around his wife.

They were together, and life was good.

Several minutes passed in companionable silence before a dark shadow covered the moon.

"Oh, I see them!" Brynleigh grinned, practically vibrating with excitement.

A streak of fire lit up the sky, and then, the shadow descended. It grew larger until a black dragon landed on the ice several dozen feet away from them.

A small, winged form slipped off the dragon's back, and then, Brynleigh ripped herself out of Ryker's grasp. The fae captain watched with amusement, petting Marlowe's head, as his wife darted across the ice with vampiric speed and hugged Hallie.

White flashed. Therian shifted and dressed, and then the group of four made their way inside.

Laughter filled the air, and hours passed with pleasant chatter. They'd grown closer than ever since the night of the Reunion, and Ryker was pleased to call Therian Firebreath a good friend. Violet flames danced in the hearth, Marlowe slept at their feet, and warmth filled Ryker's soul.

His heart was no longer aching, no longer broken. It had been made whole once again, repaired by the beautiful woman at his side. He wouldn't have it any other way.

That night, after staying up far too late, Ryker and Brynleigh made their way to the primary bedroom overlooking the obsidian ice. His heart was full as he stretched out on the enormous fur-covered bed, naked and entangled with his vampire, and showed her exactly how much he loved her.

Thank the Blessed Obsidian Sands, he'd Chosen well.

CHAPTER 42
Epilogue

E*ighteen months later*

Fiery tears streamed down River Waterborn's face as she sprinted through the streets of Lakewater.

Her running shoes pounded the sidewalk. Pink scrubs were plastered to her body like a second skin. Water poured from charcoal clouds, thunder roared above her, and lightning slashed through the night sky like the surgeon's blade she regularly wielded.

Her heart pounded in her chest; the *lub-dub* of that life-giving organ too fucking loud as it roared in her ears. Her skin was tight, and she clenched her hands as internally, she screamed and screamed and fucking screamed.

She had to keep going. Had to keep running. She couldn't let it out. Not now. Not while someone else could get hurt.

That all-too-familiar ache began in her chest as her curse whirled in her veins. Her magic throbbed, wanting to get out.

Needing to get out.

"No," she sobbed desperately. "Not yet. Not again."

Nearly a decade had passed since the last time this had happened, yet she could feel it bubbling up within her.

She should've known.

She should've seen this coming.

She was cursed. Nothing good ever happened to her.

Ever since River wielded her first drop of water magic, she knew something was wrong.

There was too much magic in her. Too much power.

And now...

A sob wrenched through her.

If she'd been in Golden City, she would've run for Ryker. Her brother could've helped her. But she'd been so stupid. So fucking cocky.

She'd assumed that between her training and Maturation, she'd gotten everything under control. She'd accepted the residency in Lakewater a year ago, and she'd been training in the local hospital since then.

But tonight...

Death had come to River's workplace. The curse had broken through the restraints she'd placed on it, bubbled up in her veins, and now...

It was all too much.

Thank all the gods, her destination came into view.

"Hold on," she told herself, taking the stairs to the townhouse two at a time.

Clenching her fists, she pounded on the door like the crazed fae she was. Seconds that felt like hours passed before the door opened.

Concerned amber eyes framed by rugged black hair met hers.

"River? What's wrong?"

Her heart throbbed, and that age-old desire that had plagued her for years rose within her. She shoved it down, that forbidden feeling not helping the situation at all.

River threw herself into his arms and sobbed, "I need your help, Nikhail."

The End

Thank you for coming along with Ryker and Brynleigh for the second half of their journey.

Reviews mean the world to indie authors like me. If you enjoyed this story, it would mean the world to me if you could leave one.

Want to talk about this ending? Come hang out with me and my readers on Facebook! Join Elayna R. Gallea's Reader Group

Not done with Ryker and Brynleigh? You can read Use Me from Ryker's POV here.

BE sure to return to the Republic of Balance for Nikhail and River's story in A Curse of Stars and Storms, coming 2025.

Acknowledgments

It seems that no matter how many books I write, I cannot believe it when I get to this point. Ryker and Brynleigh's story was so much fun to write, but it took so much out of me.

I cried so much, dear reader. I spent more writing days in tears than not, especially working on the first half of this story. My heart broke for these two as they dealt with their hurts and betrayals.

And yet, we made it. For all the pain and heartache, I hope you feel like it was worth it to see Ryker and Brynleigh get their happily ever after.

As I'm sure you noticed in the epilogue, this won't be the last time we find ourselves in the Republic of Balance. I can feel at least four more books (two couples) waiting to have their stories told, and there may be more. After all, as Brynleigh noted, the Black Night isn't going anywhere anytime soon.

It takes a lot of work to put a book together, and there are so many people working behind the scenes to make it happen.

I am eternally grateful to every single person who has come alongside me in writing this story.

First and foremost, to my husband, Aaron. He is my constant champion, my supporter, and the one who remembers to feed me when I get too deep into the story. None of my books would exist without him.

To my children. One day, you'll be able to read these and see why I was crying. I love you.

To my alpha and beta readers, thank you. Your feedback is invaluable and helps shape the story into what it is today. I couldn't do this without you.

To my writing group, I'm so grateful for your support ever since book 1.

And to you, dear reader.

Thank you so much for letting me stomp all over your heart before putting it back together again.

It's because of you that my dreams are coming true.

- Elayna

Also by Elayna R. Gallea

The Binding Chronicles (*A high fantasy arranged marriage vampire romance series in the Four Kingdoms*)

Tethered

Tormented

Treasured

Troubled

The Ithenmyr Chronicles (*An interconnected series that takes place in the Four Kingdoms at the same time as Tethered)*

Of Earth and Flame

Of Wings and Briars

Of Ash and Ivy

Of Thistles and Talons

Of Shale and Smoke

Legends of Love (New Adult Standalones)

A Court of Fire and Frost (a Romeo and Juliet Retelling)

A Court of Seas and Storms (a Little Mermaid Retelling)

A Court of Wind and Wings (a Hades and Persephone Retelling)

About the Author

Elayna R. Gallea lives in beautiful New Brunswick, Canada with her husband and two children. They live in the land of snow and forests in the Saint John River Valley.

When Elayna isn't living in her head, she can be found toiling around her house watching Food Network, listening to broadway, and planning her next meal.

Elayna enjoys copious amounts of chocolate, cheese, and wine.

Not in that order.

You can find her making a fool of herself on Tiktok and Instagram on a daily basis.

Made in the USA
Monee, IL
11 November 2024

69867471R10443